WILLIAM HAZLITT was born in Maidstone, Kent, on April 10, 1778. Educated at home by his scholarly father, a Unitarian minister, William displayed from his earliest years an alert mind, a keen social awareness, and a fiery temper that was to characterize him—for good or ill—throughout his life. His first newspaper article, an attack on a mob that had burned the home of scientist Joseph Priestly, appeared when William was a lad of thirteen; but it was to be many years before he settled upon a career as a professional essayist. At seventeen, he decided against becoming a Unitarian minister, as his father had wished for him, and for the next eight years immersed himself in erudite study at home. In 1802, he set out for Paris, determined to become a painter. However, after a decade of effort, during which he enjoyed moderate success, he abandoned painting and finally turned his full attention toward his literary pursuits. Within a short time, he had established himself as a radical thinker and prose stylist of the first order. His political essays, art criticism, sketches, and lectures enraged as many people as they endeared; but friends and foes alike recognized the beauty of his style and the literary influence he exerted upon his contemporaries. Unfortunately, this master essayist also achieved a reputation as a social scoundrel, an adulterer, and a drunk, and when death came to him on September 18, 1830, he was friendless, penniless, and living in a London slum.

*S E L E C T E D*

*W R I T I N G S   O F*

# William Hazlitt

---

E D I T E D

AND WITH AN INTRODUCTION BY

## CHRISTOPHER SALVESEN

---

A SIGNET CLASSIC from
## NEW AMERICAN LIBRARY
TIMES MIRROR
New York and Scarborough, Ontario
The New English Library Limited, London

CAREFULLY SELECTED, EDITED, AND PRINTED,
SIGNET CLASSICS PROVIDE A TREASURY OF THE WORLD'S
GREAT WRITINGS IN HANDSOMELY DESIGNED VOLUMES.

SIGNET TRADEMARK REG. U.S. PAT. OFF. AND FOREIGN COUNTRIES
REGISTERED TRADEMARK—MARCA REGISTRADA
HECHO EN CHICAGO, U.S.A.

SIGNET, SIGNET CLASSICS, SIGNETTE, MENTOR AND PLUME BOOKS
are published in the United States by
The New American Library, Inc.,
1301 Avenue of the Americas, New York, New York 10019,
in Canada by The New American Library of Canada Limited,
81 Mack Avenue, Scarborough, 704, Ontario,
in the United Kingdom by The New English Library Limited,
Barnard's Inn, Holborn, London, E.C. 1, England

First Printing, February, 1972

PRINTED IN THE UNITED STATES OF AMERICA

# Contents

## iv THE SPIRIT OF THE AGE

## v FINAL YEARS

# Chronology

[FOR DATES OF HAZLITT'S PRINCIPAL WORKS, SEE Bibliography]

1778    born Maidstone, Kent, April 10

1779    Hazlitt family move to Bandon, County Cork, Ireland

1781    [Yorktown: Cornwallis surrenders to Washington]

1783    Hazlitt family sail for America

1787    return to England: Wem, Shropshire

1789    [Fall of the Bastille]

1793    [England declares war on France]
Hazlitt enters Unitarian New College at Hackney, London

1796?    Hazlitt leaves College; returns home

1798    meets Coleridge (January); visits Coleridge, meets Wordsworth, reads *Lyrical Ballads* in manuscript (May–June)

1799    exhibition of Italian masters, London; Hazlitt becomes a painter

1802    [Peace of Amiens]
Hazlitt in Paris, especially the Louvre

1804    meets Charles Lamb

1805    *Essay on the Principles of Human Action,* Hazlitt's first book

1808    marries Sarah Stoddart

1811    birth of their son William

1812    lectures on English Philosophy; joins *Morning Chronicle* as reporter

1814   writes for the *Examiner* and becomes an *Edinburgh Reviewer*

1815   [Waterloo: Napoleon defeated]
Hazlitt "prostrated" (according to Haydon)

1815–17   intensely active in political and other journalism

1818–19   lectures on English Poetry, Comic Writers, Elizabethan Dramatists

1820   joins *London Magazine*: "Table Talk I," June; "Essays of Elia I," August (via Hazlitt's encouragement)

1821–22   infatuated with Sarah Walker

1822   divorce granted at Edinburgh

1824   marries Isabella Bridgwater, a widow

1824–25   tour of France and Italy

1826–27   returns to Paris, working on *Life of Napoleon*

1830   [July Revolution, Fall of the Bourbons]
dies at his lodgings, 6 Frith St., Soho, London, on Saturday, September 18, at about half-past four in the afternoon, aged fifty-two years

# Introduction

*A treatise on the Millennium is dull; but who was ever weary of reading the fables of the Golden Age?*  —ON THE PAST AND FUTURE

HAZLITT was a master of regret who by force of intellect and style became the best prose writer of his age. He was the second son of a Dissenting Minister active in "the cause of civil and religious liberty." In 1783, when Hazlitt was five, his father embarked for America, whose independence he had supported; official hostility to his protests for the better treatment of nearby American prisoners hastened his departure. Hazlitt's father failed to establish himself as a Unitarian preacher, and four years later the family returned to England, to the village of Wem in Shropshire. Independence, the idea of freedom, Hazlitt knew from childhood, and the Fall of the Bastille in 1789 confirmed this knowledge.

> For my part, I set out in life with the French Revolution, and that event had considerable influence on my early feelings, as on those of others. Youth was then doubly such. It was the dawn of a new era, a new impulse had been given to men's minds, and the sun of Liberty rose upon the sun of Life in the same day, and both were proud to run their race together. Little did I dream, while my first hopes and wishes went hand in hand with those of the human race, that long before my eyes should close, that dawn would be overcast, and set once more in the night of despotism—"total eclipse!"
> [ON THE FEELING OF IMMORTALITY IN YOUTH]

Hazlitt's response to his age was simple. He would never accept the disillusionment and the political reaction which followed the Revolution and the ambitions of Napoleon. He clung to his first ideals. He remained a radical, a Jacobin. Napoleon was his hero; Waterloo was a disaster. The restoration of the Bourbons and the Divine Right of Kings was an abomination. Hazlitt as a child had glimpsed the Millennium; as he advanced in life, it receded and took on the coloring of a Golden Age. But he revived the memory of it continuously, actively, in his writing.

Hazlitt's life is easily enough recorded. The year after the Bastille fell, provincial life at Wem was enlivened by a stay in Liverpool, where he heard sermons and went to the theater. He was a pious and intelligent child. At fourteen, the strains of adolescence and independent thinking made themselves felt. He went to the Unitarian College at Hackney near London, produced an outline of "a New Theory of Civil and Criminal Legislation" (which his tutor "good-naturedly accepted in lieu of the customary *themes*"), and resolved not to become a Dissenting Minister. He came home and spent two years reading: the English poets and novelists, Burke, Junius, Rousseau. Then occurred one of the most important events in Hazlitt's life. "Never, the longest day I have to live, shall I have such another walk as this cold, raw, comfortless one, in the winter of the year 1798." This January walk took Hazlitt to hear Coleridge preach. What this led to "My First Acquaintance with Poets" makes clear: ". . . that my understanding . . . did not remain dumb and brutish, or at length found a language to express itself, I owe to Coleridge." Throughout Hazlitt's writing he addresses Coleridge with a deep sense of intellectual and emotional debt—often mixed with a sense of betrayal in Coleridge's apostasy from Revolution to Reaction. He visited Coleridge in the spring, met Wordsworth and Dorothy, and "had free access" to the *Lyrical Ballads,* "which were still in manuscript."

Though a reader and a thinker, Hazlitt was by no means yet a writer. Following his elder brother, John, he decided to be a painter—unenthusiastically. Then about a year after Hazlitt met Coleridge came another revelation. He saw in London an exhibition of old Italian masters—Titians, Raphaels. "I was staggered when I saw the works there collected, and looked at them with wondering and with longing eyes. A mist passed away from my sight . . . A new sense came upon me." He applied himself intensely, he copied Rembrandts, he painted portraits. In 1802 he went to Paris, to the Louvre hung with the Italian spoils of Napoleon: another revelation to which he often recurs. "Here, for four months together, I strolled and studied, and daily heard the warning sound—'*Quatre heures passées, il faut fermer, Citoyens*' (Ah! why did they ever change their style?) muttered in coarse provincial French . . ." Gradually Hazlitt convinced himself he would never become a great painter; but his portrait of Charles Lamb (1804, in the National Portrait Gallery, London) is proof that he was a good one. Painfully, Hazlitt had written his first book, *An Essay on the Principles of Human Action* (1805); dry but firm about man's essential disinterested goodness, he opposes the mechanistic philosophies of his time.

For the next few years, Hazlitt's literary life is miscellaneous: a political pamphlet, an abridgement, a selection, a reply to Malthus, an English grammar, the editing and completion of a memoir. He is friendly with Charles and Mary Lamb; they introduce him to Sarah Stoddart; he marries her in 1808. She was three years older than Hazlitt, with short hair, with a small private income and a cottage in the village of Winterslow on the edge of Salisbury Plain which provided him with a working retreat.

In 1812 Hazlitt delivered his course of lectures on English Philosophy and began his career in journalism. He started as a parliamentary reporter for *The Morning Chronicle*, the leading Whig paper, the opposite of *The Times*. But he soon branched out; he contributed some short essays in the eighteenth-century style, a caustic note on Southey, and some dramatic criticism. He added political and art criticism and other pieces. Mary Russell Mitford records of the editor "the doleful visage with which Mr. Perry used to contemplate the long column of criticism, and how he used to execrate 'the d——d fellow's d——d stuff' for filling up so much of the paper in the very height of the advertisement season."[1] Perry then seems to have behaved rather badly and "turned him off." This directed Hazlitt to the columns of *The Examiner*, the lively and important radical weekly edited by John and Leigh Hunt. (They had already served their two-year prison sentences for remarking of the Prince Regent, amongst other things, that "This Adonis in loveliness was a corpulent man of fifty.") *The Examiner*, Bentham noted in 1812, "is the one that at present, especially among the high political men, is most in vogue. It sells already between 7,000 and 8,000." In 1814, in *The Examiner*, appeared Hazlitt's first masterpiece of criticism, his account of Wordsworth's *Excursion*. His growing reputation was confirmed when toward the end of the year he was invited to contribute to the *Edinburgh Review*.

For about the next four years Hazlitt's activity as a literary journalist is at its height. He is art and drama critic of a new paper, *The Champion;* he produces *The Round Table* ("A Collection of Essays on Literature, Men, and Manners") and

[1] *The Life of Mary Russell Mitford*, ed. A. G. L'Estrange, 3 vols., London, 1870, II, 47–8.

the *Characters of Shakespear's Plays;* he is a tireless political commentator and aligns himself even more resolutely on the Radical side, in his association with John Hunt and *The Examiner.* In 1818 he incurred the unwelcome attentions of the Tory *Quarterly Review* and of *Blackwood's.* The crudest demarcations of politics lie behind the meaningless abuse which these journals (especially the latter in the persons of John Wilson and J. G. Lockhart) launched at "the Cockney School"—Keats, Hazlitt, and (more understandably) Leigh Hunt. There was barely an inkling of literary criticism, but much irresponsible malice and invective. Hazlitt was able to take care of himself, as in his *Letter to William Gifford* ("Sir—You have an ugly trick of saying what is not true of anyone you do not like; and it will be the object of this letter to cure you of it."). As for *Blackwood's,* Hazlitt threatened a lawsuit which was settled out of court in his favor. But despite his resilience, he found the attacks deeply wounding in their blatant untruthfulness; while a hostile *Quarterly* review of the *Characters of Shakespear's Plays* put a complete stop—so his publishers told him—to its previously successful sale.

In January 1818 Hazlitt had embarked on his three series of lectures on English literature. The popularity of lectures was fairly recent; the lecture was a kind of democratic education especially for those who wanted to pursue "the career open to talent." Hazlitt contributes much to this new form. He had obviously thought about it: he varies the pace, knowing that no audience can concentrate solidly; his lectures, though full of thinking, do not have the close dialectic of the essays. He offers copious quotation, reading out in full, for example, "Tam o' Shanter" ("I shall give the beginning of it, but I am afraid I shall hardly know when to leave off") or "Hart-Leap Well" ("As Mr Wordsworth's poems have been little known to the public, or chiefly through garbled extracts from them, I will here give an entire poem . . ."). Hazlitt describes his basic approach to lecturing:

what I have undertaken to do . . . is merely to read over a set of authors with the audience, as I would do with a friend, to point out a favourite passage, to explain an objection; or if a remark or a theory occurs, to state it in illustration of the subject, but neither to tire him nor puzzle myself with pedantic rules and pragmatical *formulas* of criticism that can do no good to anybody . . . In a word, I have endeavoured to feel what was good, and to 'give a reason for the faith that was in me' . . .[2]

[2] *Lectures on the Age of Elizabeth* VI.

But they are not as informal as all that; they are deliberate, they have plenty of intellectual attack. Crabb Robinson complained of one set of lectures by Coleridge (who was a pioneer in the field) that each was an "immethodical rhapsody"—a danger Hazlitt avoided, partly by reading his lectures. Of his first one on philosophy, Robinson complained that Hazlitt had "no conception of the difference between a lecture and a book." But Hazlitt took advice, improved his manner, and in his later series engaged the active participation of his audience. The staid Crabb Robinson himself was provoked: "He was so contemptuous, speaking of [Wordsworth's] letter about Burns, that I lost my temper and hissed . . ." Thomas Noon Talfourd has left the most interesting account of the lectures. Hazlitt, he remarks, had but "an imperfect sympathy" with his hearers:

> They consisted chiefly of Dissenters, who agreed with him in his hatred of Lord Castlereagh, but who 'loved no plays'; of Quakers, who approved him as the opponent of Slavery and Capital Punishment, but who 'heard no music'; of citizens devoted to the main chance, who had a hankering after the 'improvement of the mind,' but to whom his favourite doctrine of its natural disinterestedness was a riddle; of a few enemies, who came to sneer; and a few friends, who were eager to learn and to admire.

Among these latter was Keats, whose greatest poetry echoes again and again, faintly but unmistakably, with signs of how attentively he listened. Talfourd continues:

> The comparative insensibility of the bulk of his audience to his finest passages, sometimes provoked him to awaken their attention by points which broke the train of his discourse, after which he could make himself amends by some abrupt paradox which might set their prejudices on edge, and make them fancy they were shocked. He startled many of them at the onset, by observing that, since Jacob's dream, 'the heavens have gone further off, and become astronomical'—a fine extravagance, which the ladies and gentlemen who had grown astronomical themselves under the preceding lecturer, felt called on to resent as an attack on their severer studies. When he had read a well-known extract from Cowper, comparing a poor cottager with Voltaire, and had pronounced the line, 'A truth the brilliant Frenchman never knew', they broke into a joyous shout of self-gratulation, that they were so much wiser than a wicked Frenchman. When he passed by Mrs. Hannah More with observing that 'she had written a great deal which he had never read,' a voice gave expression to the general commiseration and surprise, by calling out 'More pity for you!' They were confounded at his reading with more emphasis, perhaps, than discretion, Gay's epigrammatic lines on Sir Richard Blackmore, in which scriptural persons are freely hitched

into rhyme; but he went doggedly on to the end, and, by his perseverance, baffled those who, if he had acknowledged himself wrong by stopping, would have hissed him without mercy.

Talfourd concludes:

> He was not eloquent in the true sense of the term; for his thoughts were too weighty to be moved along by the shallow stream of feeling which an evening's excitement can arouse. He wrote all his lectures, and read them as they were written; but his deep voice and earnest manner suited his matter well.

With the publication of his collected *Political Essays* in 1819 Hazlitt signaled his retirement from political journalism. His engagement by John Scott of the *London Magazine* in 1820, first to write monthly surveys of the drama, and then to contribute "Table Talks," marks the beginning of Hazlitt's final, great decade. In August of this year Hazlitt began his involvement with Sarah Walker, the daughter of a tailor in whose house he lodged (he now lived apart from his wife). Sarah Walker was a dull girl—scrawny, intellectually inert—about whom Hazlitt worked himself into a romantic frenzy. She gave him neither rebuffs nor real encouragement. His infatuation has something willed in it, as well as intense suffering. He went to Edinburgh to make use of the easier Scottish divorce laws, but once fully separated from his wife, he found that Sarah Walker was unobtainable at any price. All that was left was to record the whole affair in the *Liber Amoris*. But nothing could stop him writing: he had written over fifty "Table Talks" in two years; the rest of his life was almost equally industrious, and comparatively uneventful. He married again in 1824, a widow who stayed with him three years. He toured France and Italy with her; he lived for some time in Paris collecting material for his *Life of Napoleon*. This gigantic compilation is fairly described as an apologia for his own life, if we remember that Hazlitt's Napoleon-worship was politically rather than psychologically inspired. In 1822 he had written:

> There are some persons of that reach of soul that they would like to live two hundred and fifty years hence, to see to what height of empire America will have grown up in that period, or whether the English constitution will last so long. These are points beyond me. But I confess I should like to live to see the downfall of the Bourbons. That is a vital question with me; and I shall like it the better, the sooner it happens!

He just lived to see it, to have his faith in freedom confirmed. As he put it in "Personal Politics," one of his last essays, "The

Revolution of the Three Days was like a resurrection from the dead, and showed plainly that liberty too has a spirit of life in it . . ." Hazlitt's last words, recorded by his son, were "Well, I've had a happy life." His writings confirm this: despite the years of inarticulateness, of hackwork, despite his precarious career, the malicious attacks and the quarrels, despite the disappointment of his ideals and longings.

The vitality, the mixture of application and spontaneity in all his writing, was not always immediately apparent in the man himself. But from Coleridge's impression of him in 1803— "brow-hanging, shoe-contemplative, *strange*"—our views of Hazlitt's demeanor and temperament are consistent enough, making allowance for whether friend or foe is talking, and for some increase in his self-confidence and reputation. Benjamin Haydon has an amusing account of his visit to the christening of Hazlitt's son in 1813. No dinner when he arrived:

At last came in a maid who laid a cloth and put down knives and forks in a heap. Then followed a dish of potatoes, cold, waxy and yellow. Then came a great bit of beef with a bone like a battering-ram, toppling on all its corners. Neither Hazlitt nor Lamb seemed at all disturbed, but set to work helping each other; while the boy, half-clean and obstinate, kept squalling to put his fingers into the gravy.—Even Lamb's wit and Hazlitt's disquisitions, in a large room, wainscotted and ancient, where Milton had meditated, could not reconcile me to such violation of all the decencies of life.

In this room of august literary memories, Hazlitt scribbled notes above the mantelpiece. Bryan Waller Procter recorded his first meeting:

At the time I refer to (it must, I think, have been in the year 1816) he was publishing, in the *Examiner,* some of his papers called "The Round Table." His name was not so extensively circulated then as it since has been; but he was, nevertheless, well known to be a first-rate critic in matters connected with art and the theatres; and by his associates (some of them not too ready to admit the claims of literary candidates) he was characterized as an acute and profound thinker. His countenance did not belie this opinion. His figure was indeed indifferent, and his movements shy and awkward; but there was something in his earnest irritable face, his restless eyes, his black hair, combed backwards and curling (not too resolutely) about a well-shaped head, that was very striking.[3]

[3] *New Monthly Magazine,* 1830, Pt. II, p. 469.

Procter comments elsewhere:

> At home, his style of dress (or undress) was perhaps slovenly, because there was no one to please; but he always presented a very clean and neat appearance when he went abroad. His mode of walking was loose, weak and unsteady; although his arms displayed strength, which he used to put forth when he played at racquets with Martin Burney and others. He played in the old Fives Court (now pulled down) in St. Martin's Street; and occasionally exhibited impatience when the game went against him.[4]

Diffident but irascible, a man of concealed nervous energy, committed to ideas and abstractions, caring little for bourgeois comforts, Hazlitt clung to his personality: "We had as lief *not be* as *not be ourselves*" ("On the Fear of Death," 1822). His happiness lay in the accumulated identity of his hard life.

After Wordsworth, Hazlitt draws more fully on the sense of the past than any other English Romantic. All the same, the prime quality of Hazlitt's imagination is an energetic delight in ideas and their working-out. Ideas have a life of their own; Hazlitt's great virtue is to make them personal without reducing their vitality. A nostalgic temperament combines with supremely incisive thinking. This is not a matter of contrast; Hazlitt works with ideas which he has made his own through years of rehearsal. He knows and loves the repetitions of the mind, "still occupied with something interesting, still recalling some old impression, still recurring to some difficult question and making progress in it, every step accompanied with a sense of power . . ." ("On the Past and Future"). He *owns* his speculations no less than his particular memories. For example, at the end of "A Farewell to Essay-Writing" (1828) he recalls a time when he used to walk out in the evenings with Charles and Mary Lamb,

> to look at the Claude Lorraine skies over our heads, melting from azure into purple and gold, and to gather mushrooms, that sprung up at our feet, to throw into our hashed mutton at supper . . . It is in looking back to such scenes that I draw my best consolation for the future. Later impressions come and go, and serve to fill up the intervals; but these are my standing resource, my true classics.

And he continues, still sounding the note of regret inseparable from such memories: "If I have had few real pleasures or advantages, my ideas, from their sinewy texture, have been to me in the nature of realities; and if I should not be able to

[4] *Autobiographical Fragment*, 1877, p. 179.

add to my stock, I can live by husbanding the interest." His ideas have become almost a physical part of him (". . . I have brooded over an idea till it has become a kind of substance in my brain").

For Hazlitt, ideas are emotions; often reflected on, they remain ideas, opinions deeply grounded, forcefully put; yet they also come across with the impact of feelings. This may remind us of what T. S. Eliot discovered in early seventeenth-century poetry, "a direct sensuous apprehension of thought or a recreation of thought into feeling." But in the essays not only are ideas emotions, but we feel how these ideas have *become* emotions, in the strictly Romantic mode of growing. And yet their immediate coming across in Hazlitt's prose is what counts; there is no "dissociation of sensibility." The gap is closed, thanks to another feeling Hazlitt imparts, that of ideas *still* developing, "every step accompanied with a sense of power"; more generally, it is due to his remarkable ability to make thought and feeling cohere in the total form of an essay. One of the pleasures of a Hazlitt essay is to feel the "sinewy texture" of ideas both intellectually and emotionally, to be aware of ideas in action and of Hazlitt "husbanding the interest" on them.

The sequence of a Hazlitt essay, like the syntax of the Metaphysicals, displays "fidelity to thought and feeling." It is an epitome of past and present; it works because Hazlitt is confidently grounded in what he calls "continuity of impression." After years of hard thinking and writing, Hazlitt need not always distinguish sharply between feelings and ideas. According to Eliot, "there are traces of a struggle toward unification of sensibility" in one or two passages of Shelley and Keats. But Wordsworth came nearest to solving the essentially new problem: how to combine thinking and feeling with the added Romantic dimension—and difficulty—of memory. Hazlitt applies this mode to himself and to more purely intellectual material. Wordsworth's poetry combines the "sensuous and intellectual" being[5]—subjectively. Hazlitt solves that closely connected Romantic problem, the proper relation of Sense and Sensibility.

Whether fusing them or, as he sometimes does, distinguishing carefully between them, he gets the proportions right. The backward look, so often an invitation to sensibility and nothing more, provides the main impulse of Hazlitt's continued intellectual activity. He refers throughout the essays of the last decade to his feeling for time. "As we advance in life, we acquire a keener sense of the value of time. Nothing

[5] *Prelude* XI, 169 (1805 text).

else, indeed, seems of any consequence; and we become misers in this respect" ("On the Feeling of Immortality in Youth," 1827). He celebrates the more philosophical applications too: "Time, like distance, spreads a haze and a glory round all things. Not to perceive this, is to want a sense, is to be without imagination" ("On Antiquity," 1821). Hazlitt makes full use of this sense, indulging it, controlling it.

Regret, for Hazlitt, is a matter of temperament, something inherent. It crops up, for example, in his early *Reply to Malthus* (1807) in a characteristic confessional interlude: "I never fell in love but once . . . it was like a vision, a dream, like thoughts of childhood, an everlasting hope, a distant joy, a heaven, a world that might be. The dream is still left, and sometimes comes confusedly over me in solitude and silence, and mingles with the softness of the sky, and veils my eyes from mortal grossness . . ." But it appears more in connection with the French Revolution and the disappointment of the hopes then aroused. Other private occasions may have compelled Hazlitt's backward look but it is first fully invoked by the large public events of his time. It appears strongly, for example, in a letter of 1814 to the *Morning Chronicle* where Hazlitt offers a definition of a "true Jacobin" as someone who "has seen the evening star set over a poor man's cottage, or has connected the feeling of hope with the heart of man, and who, though he may have lost the feeling, has never ceased to reverence it . . . " (he uses the image again in "On the Pleasure of Painting"). It appears at greater length in his review of *The Excursion,* where he laments "that spring-time of the world, in which the hopes and expectations of the human race seemed opening in the same gay career with our own . . ." It may have fled; but it "has left behind traces . . . To those hopes eternal regrets are due . . ." Pastoral regret seems inseparable from any imaginative response to contemporary politics—think of George Eliot or even of George Orwell. This kind of personal-political regret is Hazlitt's own version of the Romantic sense of onwardness and fading: like Wordsworth, he is left with "the memory of what has been and never more will be."

From 1820 onward Hazlitt the essayist claims the right to reverie. The tone may be relaxed, but the claim is serious. ". . . . I conceive that the past is as real and substantial a part of our being, that it is as much a *bona fide,* undeniable consideration in the estimate of human life, as the future can possibly be." The past may be gone:

but it *has had* a real existence, and we can still call up a vivid recollection of it as having once been . . . Let us not rashly quit

our hold upon the past, when perhaps there may be little else left
to bind us to existence. Is it nothing to have been, and to have
been happy or miserable? . . . Or, to use the language of a fine
poet (who is himself among my earliest and not least painful
recollections)—

> What though the radiance which was once so bright
> Be now for ever vanish'd from my sight,
> Though nothing can bring back the hour
> Of glory in the grass, of splendour in the flow'r—

yet am I mocked with a lie, when I venture to think of it?

These lines from the "Immortality Ode" are one of Hazlitt's
talismanic quotations; the examples of Wordsworth or of
Rousseau are frequently in his mind when he looks back. "It is
the past that gives me most delight and most assurance of
reality"; he continues,

> What to me constitutes the great charm of the Confessions of
> Rousseau is their turning so much upon this feeling. He seems
> to gather up the past moments of his being like drops of honey-
> dew to distil a precious liquor from them . . . was he not to live
> the first and best part of it over again, and once more be all that
> he then was?

His enthusiasm is partly based on literary-cum-temperamental
affinities. How far does he actually resemble him? He is, Irving
Babbitt notes,[6] one of Rousseau's "chief disciples in the art of
impassioned recollection." Rousseau obviously helped to form
Hazlitt's own use of his past; and, unlike Wordsworth, he was
one of Hazlitt's most pleasurable recollections. Of *The New
Eloise* and the *Confessions* Hazlitt recalled: "We spent two
whole years in reading these two works; and," he adds, ". . . in
shedding tears over them . . . They were the happiest years
of our life. We may well say of them, sweet is the dew of their
memory and pleasant the balm of their recollection!" He prefers the *Confessions*

> because it contains the fewest set paradoxes or general opinions.
> It relates entirely to himself; and no one was ever so much at
> home on this subject as he was. From the strong hold which they
> had taken of his mind, he makes us enter into his feelings as if
> they had been our own, and we seem to remember every incident
> and circumstance of his life as if it had happened to ourselves.

In his *Round Table* essay on Rousseau Hazlitt writes,

> The only quality which he possessed in an eminent degree, which
> alone raised him above ordinary men, and which gave to his writ-

[6] *Rousseau and Romanticism*, 1919; Ch. 6.

ings and opinions an influence greater, perhaps, than has been
exerted by any individual in modern times, was extreme sensibility, or an acute and even morbid feeling of all that related to
his own impressions, to the objects and events of his own life.
He had the most intense consciousness of his own existence. No
object that had once made an impression on him was ever after
effaced. Every feeling in his mind became a passion. His craving
after excitement was an appetite and a disease. His interest in his
own thoughts and feelings was always wound up to the highest
pitch; and hence the enthusiasm which he excited in others.

Like Rousseau, Hazlitt had an "intense consciousness of his
own existence." But he is much less of an exhibitionist: his one
foray in this direction, the *Liber Amoris*, is an aberration,
though interesting both psychologically and artistically as a
"documentary." He is also against the Wordsworthian "ego-
tistical sublime." He may impart an air of self-indulgence to
his more personal moments; his tone is quite different from
Wordsworth's philosophical meditations on his own being. He
does not use himself in the solemn "representative" manner
of Wordsworth; nor does he justify himself in Rousseau's spirit
of informative "confessional" self-revelation. At an appropriate
point in an essay, Hazlitt turns to his past in a short controlled
episode of intensified feeling. He is in many ways remarkably
reticent. He has little to say about his childhood; he records
only one memory of his years in America. "The taste of barberries which have hung out in the snow during the severity
of a North American winter, I have in my mouth still, after an
interval of thirty years; for I have met with no other taste,
in all that time, at all like it." Hazlitt presents it mainly as a
psychological curiosity. It is the complete opposite of Proust
tasting his madeleine: for Hazlitt nothing has been forgotten,
nothing revived. "It remains by itself, almost like the impression of a sixth sense." But in the same essay ("Why Distant
Objects Please") Hazlitt evokes a different kind of memory,
dating from immediately after his return from America, which
is rich, evocative, and especially Proustian in being so deeply
incorporated as to be involuntary. "When I was quite a boy,
my father used to take me to the Montpelier Tea-gardens at
Walworth. Do I go there now? No; the place is deserted, and
its borders and its beds o'erturned." But it lives in his memory.

A new sense comes upon me, as in a dream; a richer perfume,
brighter colours start out; my eyes dazzle; my heart heaves with
its new load of bliss, and I am a child again. My sensations are
all glossy, spruce, voluptuous, and fine: they wear a candied coat,
and are in holiday trim. I see the beds of larkspur with purple
eyes; tall holy-oaks, red and yellow; the broad sunflowers, caked

in gold, with bees buzzing round them; wildernesses of pinks, and hot-glowing pionies; poppies run to seed; the sugared lily, and faint mignionette, all ranged in order, as thick as they can grow; the box-tree borders; the gravel-walks, the painted alcove, the confectionary, the clotted cream—I think I see them now with sparkling looks; or have they vanished while I have been writing this description of them? No matter; they will return again when I least think of them.

The poetic Hazlitt takes his part with the psychologist who remembered the taste of barberries. But where Wordsworth remembered himself as a naked five-year-old,[7] or went back more mystically to infancy and birth, Hazlitt's sense of origin is fixed in adolescence and youth, in the period of intellectual excitement and growth.

The Romantic problem was how best to make use of an "intense consciousness of existence"—what sort of form to put it in. Rousseau's *Confessions*, Wordsworth's *Prelude*, Byron's *Childe Harold* are some of the answers; the Hazlitt essay is another. The expression of personality is the purpose and controlling factor of the essay. Egotism, therefore, cannot be avoided; but the personality is integrated with the chosen form. Montaigne, says Hazlitt, "whom I have proposed to consider as the father of this kind of personal authorship among the moderns . . . was a most magnanimous and undisguised egotist." Hazlitt values Montaigne's egotism. He recommends him "to anyone to read who has ever thought at all, or who would learn to think justly on any subject"; and he himself must have learnt much about the individual *tone* of thought. He celebrates him as "the first who had the courage to say as an author, what he felt as a man." His great virtue lay in "merely daring to tell us whatever passed through his mind, in its naked simplicity and force, that he thought any ways worth communicating." Montaigne claims: "I describe not the essence, but the passage . . . from day to day, from minute to minute . . ." Montaigne presents himself as an unpremeditated creature, a mind at work. Hazlitt likewise shows us a mind in action, but one which is backward-looking too, drawing on "standing resources" and "true classics"—that is the Romantic difference. Yet you could also claim for Hazlitt in his essays what Dr. Johnson claimed for Burke's conversation: "His stream of mind is perpetual." There is nothing random, no mere "stream of consciousness"—but the sense of momentum is important.

Hazlitt combines the force of mind and interest in self

[7] *Prelude* I, 291–2 (1805 text).

of Montaigne with something of the observant sensibility of
Addison and Steele. That is partly why, both as social and
literary critic, he understands the eighteenth century, why he
is so good on Fielding, Hogarth, Crabbe. He responds fully
to the demands of realism, to the world created by the novelists; at the same time, he maintains his absolute attachment to
"the ideal," that world "which exists only in conception and
in power, the universe of thought and sentiment, that surrounds and is raised above the ordinary world of reality . . ."
He is not an urbane writer; he is however urban, a Londoner,
and as he observes,

> In London there is a *public;* and each man is part of it . . . We
> have a sort of abstract existence; and a community of ideas and
> knowledge (rather than local proximity) is the bond of society
> and good-fellowship. This is one great cause of the tone of politi-
> cal feeling in large and populous cities. There is here a visible
> body-politic, a type and image of that huge Leviathan the State.
> We comprehend that vast denomination, the *People,* of which we
> see a tenth part daily moving before us . . .

This kind of insight gives a special quality to Hazlitt's role
(which he assigns to the essayist in general) of "moral historian." Hazlitt, commentator and censor, observes the political
behavior of his contemporaries with a new sort of intellectual
penetration. He introduces in one essay a story of Wordsworth
and some inconsistent behavior concerning candles[8] by saying that he will "give some instances of a change in sentiment
in individuals, which may serve for materials of a history of
opinion in the beginning of the 19th century." It is an original
concept, "a history of opinion"; in *The Spirit of the Age*

---

[8] A gentleman went to live, some years ago, in a remote part of
the country, and as he did not wish to affect singularity he used
to have two candles on his table of an evening. A romantic acquaintance of his in the neighbourhood, smit with the love of
simplicity and equality, used to come in, and without ceremony
snuff one of them out, saying, it was a shame to indulge in such
extravagance, while many a poor cottager had not even a rush-light
to see to do their evening's work by. This might be about the year
1802, and was passed over as among the ordinary occurrences of
the day. In 1816 (oh! fearful lapse of time, pregnant with strange
mutability), the same enthusiastic lover of economy, and hater of
luxury, asked his thoughtless friend to dine with him in company
with a certain lord, and to lend him his man servant to wait at
table; and just before they were sitting down to dinner, he heard
him say to the servant in a sonorous whisper—'and be sure you don't
forget to have six candles on the table!'

["On Consistency of Opinion"]

Hazlitt himself goes some way toward writing it. "The spirit of the age" is likewise a new concept (you can't imagine Dr. Johnson considering it a useful subject for discussion). What is significant about Hazlitt's rendering of something so cloudy and Teutonic is that he does it in terms of individuals; the dangers of "totalitarian" thinking are avoided. He refuses to offer any systematic definition; he is interested in the variety of human example. Yet his ability to attempt the "extensive view" is important. His comprehensive mixture of principle and his own personality gives his work a literary tone which does not exist in any previous age. Neither *philosophe* nor journalist, Hazlitt combines a little of each in his continual task of self-expression and the creation of lasting work.

The Hazlitt essay is one of the great formal achievements of English Romanticism. The form derives from Hazlitt's presence therein; he creates an authentic mode of shaping experience. "I have turned for consolation to the past, gathering up fragments of my early recollections, and putting them into a form that might live." We need not overemphasize the word "form" here; but Hazlitt pursues form unequivocally. It is sometimes remarked that he is at his best in small-scale works; but small is a relative term, and the Hazlitt essay (running to 7,000–8,000 words) is, by any standards applicable to the form in general, immense. At the same time it should be granted that the true scale of the essay is intimate; it is a personal colloquial mode. The essay is particularly interesting in being essentially discursive while at the same time being one of the most musical of prose forms. Its changes of mood and style (see, for example, "On the Feeling of Immortality in Youth") trace a rhythmic pattern which can be felt whole by the reader. Hazlitt once called his essays "these voluntaries of composition": one way of thinking of them formally, though used with some self-disparagement. He talked in similar terms of Coleridge's Watchman and Friend pieces; "whoever will be at pains to examine them closely, will find them to be *voluntaries*, fugues, solemn capriccios, not set compositions with any *malice prepense* in them, or much practical meaning." (Hazlitt's criticism of Coleridge often has this "symbolist" touch. Of "Kubla Khan" he writes: "It is not a poem, but a musical composition";[9] and he characterizes Coleridge as "the man of all others . . . to write marginal notes without a text"—which sounds like an adumbration of his alignment in Symbolist tradition, or the matter of a poem by Wallace Stevens.) The formal pattern of a Hazlitt essay is really a

---

[9] "Mr. Coleridge's Christabel," June 2, 1816 (*Examiner*).

question of what Hazlitt had heard Coleridge propound, "the metaphysical distinction between the grace of form, and the grace that arises from motion."[10]

Style—the manner in which Hazlitt gets on with his argument and brings forward his personality—further defines the structure. Hazlitt the stylist is characterized by the title of his last collection of essays—the Plain Speaker. He is a rhetorician, concerned with the different ways of using language and of combining them effectively. He is interested in the musical qualities of prose, in rhapsody and exclamatory flights. But what he aims at most often is plain-speaking—the frank expression of opinion in straightforward language. This, Hazlitt knows, is difficult. His ideal is a "pure conversational prose-style"; hard to achieve because the exact word must always be found—the approximations of actual talk will not do:

> There is a research in the choice of a plain, as well as of an ornamental or learned style; and, in fact, a great deal more. Among common English words, there may be ten expressing the same thing with different degrees of force and propriety, and only one that answers exactly with the idea we have in our minds. Each word in familiar use has a different set of associations and shades of meaning attached to it . . . it is in having the whole of these at our command, and in knowing which to choose . . . that the perfection of a pure conversational prose-style consists.

And Hazlitt adds: "But in writing a florid and artificial style, neither the same range of invention, nor the same quick sense of propriety—nothing but learning is required." Hazlitt admits to versions of the florid in his own prose; but he recognizes the problem of any style however simple—that, being the product of "research," the difficulty is to preserve plainness. A history of English style might be written by working out what at any given time was meant by "plain" speaking. It is a Shakespearean concern ("Honest plain words best pierce the ear of grief," after the euphuistic fun of *Love's Labour's Lost*). Hazlitt, a stylist with a taste for rhapsody, and a reverence for poetry, considered the problem deeply as it affected the prose writer.

> It has always appeared to me that the most perfect prose-style, the most powerful, the most dazzling, the most daring, that which went nearest to the verge of poetry, and yet never fell over, was Burke's . . . It differs from poetry . . . like the chamois from the eagle: it climbs to an almost equal height, touches upon a cloud, overlooks a precipice, is picturesque, sublime—but all the

[10] "The Drama" XI, December 1820 (*London Magazine*).

while, instead of soaring through the air, it stands upon a rocky cliff, clambers up by abrupt and intricate ways, and browzes on the roughest bark, or crops the tender flower.

Hazlitt here allows himself a "poetic" but appropriate illustration of Burke, metaphorical without being fanciful, a brisk feet-on-the-ground "flight" doing homage to Burke's prose by providing a useful reminder of it. He goes on: "The principle which guides his pen is truth, not beauty—not pleasure, but power." Hazlitt as an essayist was nothing like so constrained as Burke, who "had to treat of political questions, mixed modes, abstract ideas, and his fancy (or poetry, if you will) was ingrafted on these artificially . . ." But Hazlitt as prose writer is always committed to saying what is true, clearly. He is marked off from the poet, however powerfully he brings his "fancy or poetry" into play. Throughout the essays, he is intent on arguing a point, demonstrating a theory, maintaining a belief; "the professed object of prose is to impart conviction." The intellectual activity involved allows little room for merely decorative imagery: "Every word should be a blow: every thought should instantly grapple with its fellow." This interlocking ideal, with the texture of thought and the momentum of discovery, informs the Hazlitt essay. In discussing Milton he indicates clearly the connection between the meaning and music of language. He defends Milton from the charge that because his ideas "were in the highest degree musical" they were not also powerfully descriptive, especially in the main subjects of *Paradise Lost*, "the daring ambition and fierce passions of Satan" and "the paradisaical happiness, and the loss of it" (Hazlitt responds fully to these twin themes of Revolution and Regret). He fully recognizes the power of "the language of music" because of its immediacy. But that "force of style" which is "one of Milton's great excellences" contains other elements. Of the speeches and debates in Pandemonium he notes:

There is a decided manly tone in the arguments and sentiments, an eloquent dogmatism, as if each person spoke from thorough conviction; an excellence which Milton probably borrowed from his spirit of partisanship . . . That approximation to the severity of impassioned prose which has been made an objection to Milton's poetry, and which is chiefly to be met with in these bitter invectives, is one of its great excellences.

"The severity of impassioned prose," with its fusion of style and conviction, is a Hazlitt ideal. Milton's style is both "musical" and "manly"; Hazlitt, as prose writer and political partisan, naturally admires it. The essayist discovered his "answerable style" in a similar mixture of plain speaking and passion.

Milton's own prose style dissatisfied Hazlitt; it savored "too much of poetry . . . and of an imitation of the Latin." But for Hazlitt ideals of poetry and conversation do not necessarily conflict with regard to prose. He considered Leigh Hunt's prose writing had "the raciness, the sharpness, and sparkling effect of poetry"; if there was also some "relaxation and trifling . . . Still the genuine master-spirit of the prose-writer is there; the tone of lively sensible conversation." Hazlitt's own prose certainly displays this; it also has affinities with Coleridge's development of Cowper's poetry (which Hazlitt admired), the Conversation Poem. The movement from colloquial ease to impassioned meditation, Coleridge's special achievement, likewise informs the Hazlitt essay. Hazlitt of course usually begins with an abstract proposition, and he aims to pursue a course of reasoning—but through a range of mood, in controlled, plain-speaking intimacy.

Hazlitt often returns to the relation of writing and speaking. He cites the opinion of Horne Tooke, that "no one could write a good prose style, who was not accustomed to express himself *viva voce*, or to talk in company." To which Hazlitt responds:

> I certainly so far agree with the above theory as to conceive that no style is worth a farthing that is not calculated to be read out, or that is not allied to spirited conversation; but I at the same time think the process of modulation and inflection may be quite as complete, or more so, without the external enunciation: and that an author had better try the effect of his sentences on his stomach than on his ear. He may be deceived by the last, not by the first.

The ultimate test is an inward one, involving the whole physical being and yet all but silent. He repeats the idea in his essay "On the Conversation of Authors": ". . . there is a method of trying periods on the ear, or weighing them with the scales of the breath, without any articulate sound." And he adds, quoting from his friend J. S. Knowles, "Authors, as they write, may be said to 'hear a sound so fine, there's nothing lives 'twixt it and silence.' Even musicians generally compose in their heads." Hazlitt recognizes that all imaginative language, if it does not aspire to the condition of music, at least approaches musical composition. But he concludes by remarking "I agree that no style is good, that is not fit to be spoken or read aloud with effect. This holds true not only of emphasis and cadence, but also with regard to natural idiom and colloquial freedom. Sterne's was in this respect the best style that ever was written. You fancy that you hear the people talking." It is a rarer quality than you might think; but in Hazlitt's style too you hear the man talking, a clear energetic voice beautifully informed with common sense, with deep feeling, with conviction.

—CHRISTOPHER SALVESEN

# i

---

## LITERATURE AND POLITICS

# Observations on
# Mr. Wordsworth's Poem
## *The Excursion**

---

THE POEM OF *The Excursion* resembles that part of the country in which the scene is laid. It has the same vastness and magnificence, with the same nakedness and confusion. It has the same overwhelming, oppressive power. It excites or recalls the same sensations which those who have traversed that wonderful scenery must have felt. We are surrounded with the constant sense and superstitious awe of the collective power of matter, of the gigantic and eternal forms of nature, on which, from the beginning of time, the hand of man has made no impression. Here are no dotted lines, no hedge-row beauties, no box-tree borders, no gravel walks, no square mechanic enclosures; all is left loose and irregular in the rude chaos of aboriginal nature. The boundaries of hill and valley are the poet's only geography, where we wander with him incessantly over deep beds of moss and waving fern, amidst the troops of red-deer and wild animals. Such is the severe simplicity of Mr. Wordsworth's taste, that we doubt whether he would not reject a druidical temple, or time-hallowed ruin as too modern and artificial for his purpose. He only familiarises himself or his readers with a stone, covered with lichens, which has slept in the same spot of ground from the creation of the world, or with the rocky fissure between two mountains caused by thunder, or with a cavern scooped out by the sea. His mind is, as it were, coëval with the primary forms of things; his imagination holds immediately from nature, and 'owes no allegiance' but 'to the elements.'

*The Excursion* may be considered as a philosophical pastoral poem—as a scholastic romance. It is less a poem on the country,

* [*Round Table;* first published in more expansive form in *The Examiner*, Aug.–Oct. 1814.]

than on the love of the country. It is not so much a description of natural objects, as of the feelings associated with them; not an account of the manners of rural life, but the result of the poet's reflections on it. He does not present the reader with a lively succession of images or incidents, but paints the outgoings of his own heart, the shapings of his own fancy. He may be said to create his own materials; his thoughts are his real subject. His understanding broods over that which is 'without form and void,' and 'makes it pregnant.'[1] He sees all things in himself. He hardly ever avails himself of remarkable objects or situations, but, in general, rejects them as interfering with the workings of his own mind, as disturbing the smooth, deep, majestic current of his own feelings. Thus his descriptions of natural scenery are not brought home distinctly to the naked eye by forms and circumstances, but every object is seen through the medium of innumerable recollections, is clothed with the haze of imagination like a glittering vapour, is obscured with the excess of glory, has the shadowy brightness of a waking dream. The image is lost in the sentiment, as sound in the multiplication of echoes.

> And visions, as prophetic eyes avow,
> Hang on each leaf, and cling to every bough.[2]

In describing human nature, Mr. Wordsworth equally shuns the common 'vantage-grounds of popular story, of striking incident, or fatal catastrophe, as cheap and vulgar modes of producing an effect. He scans the human race as the naturalist measures the earth's zone, without attending to the picturesque points of view, the abrupt inequalities of surface. He contemplates the passions and habits of men, not in their extremes, but in their first elements; their follies and vices, not at their height, with all their embossed evils upon their heads, but as lurking in embryo—the seeds of the disorder inwoven with our very constitution. He only sympathises with those simple forms of feeling, which mingle at once with his own identity, or with the stream of general humanity. To him the great and the small are the same; the near and the remote; what appears, and what only is. The general and the permanent, like the Platonic ideas, are his only realities. All accidental varieties and individual contrasts are lost in an endless continuity of feeling, like drops of water in the ocean-stream! An intense intellectual egotism swallows up everything. Even the dialogues introduced in the present volume are soliloquies of the same character, taking different views of the subject. The recluse, the pastor, and the pedlar, are three persons in one poet. We ourselves disapprove of these 'interlocutions between Lucius and Caius'³ as impertinent babbling, where there is no dramatic distinction of character. But the evident scope and tendency of Mr. Wordsworth's mind is the reverse of dramatic. It resists all change of character, all variety of scenery, all the bustle, machinery, and pantomime of the stage, or of real life—whatever might relieve, or relax, or change the direction of its own activity, jealous of all competition. The power of his mind preys upon itself. It is as if there were nothing but himself and the universe. He lives in the busy solitude of his own heart; in the deep silence of thought. His imagination lends life and feeling only to 'the bare trees and mountains bare'; peoples the viewless tracts of air, and converses with the silent clouds!

We could have wished that our author had given to his work the form of a didactic poem altogether, with only occasional digressions or allusions to particular instances. But he has chosen to encumber himself with a load of narrative and description, which sometimes hinders the progress and effect of the general reasoning, and which, instead of being inwoven with the text, would have come in better in plain prose as notes at the end of the volume. Mr. Wordsworth, indeed, says finely, and perhaps as truly as finely:

> Exchange the shepherd's frock of native grey
> For robes with regal purple tinged; convert
> The crook into a sceptre; give the pomp
> Of circumstance; and here the tragic Muse
> Shall find apt subjects for her highest art.
> Amid the groves, beneath the shadowy hills,
> The generations are prepared; the pangs,
> The internal pangs, are ready; the dread strife
> Of poor humanity's afflicted will
> Struggling in vain with ruthless destiny.     [VI, 548–57]

But he immediately declines availing himself of these resources of the rustic moralist: for the priest, who officiates as 'the sad historian of the pensive plain'⁴ says in reply:

> Our system is not fashioned to preclude
> That sympathy which you for others ask:
> And I could tell, not travelling for my theme
> Beyond the limits of these humble graves,
> Of strange disasters; but I pass them by,
> Loth to disturb what Heaven hath hushed to peace.
> [567–72]

There is, in fact, in Mr. Wordsworth's mind an evident repugnance to admit anything that tells for itself, without the interpretation of the poet—a fastidious antipathy to immediate effect—a systematic unwillingness to share the palm with his subject. Where, however, he has a subject presented to him, 'such as the meeting soul may pierce,'[5] and to which he does not grudge to lend the aid of his fine genius, his powers of description and fancy seem to be little inferior to those of his classical predecessor, Akenside. Among several others which we might select we give the following passage, describing the religion of ancient Greece:

> In that fair clime, the lonely herdsman, stretch'd
> On the soft grass through half a summer's day,
> With music lulled his indolent repose:
> And in some fit of weariness, if he,
> When his own breath was silent, chanced to hear
> A distant strain, far sweeter than the sounds
> Which his poor skill could make, his fancy fetch'd,
> Even from the blazing chariot of the sun,
> A beardless youth, who touched a golden lute,
> And filled the illumined groves with ravishment.
> The nightly hunter, lifting up his eyes
> Towards the crescent moon, with grateful heart
> Called on the lovely wanderer, who bestowed
> That timely light, to share his joyous sport:
> And hence, a beaming Goddess with her Nymphs
> Across the lawn and through the darksome grove,
> (Nor unaccompanied with tuneful notes
> By echo multiplied from rock or cave),
> Swept in the storm of chase, as moon and stars
> Glance rapidly along the clouded heavens,
> When winds are blowing strong. The traveller slaked
> His thirst from rill, or gushing fount, and thanked
> The Naiad. Sun beams, upon distant hills
> Gliding apace, with shadows in their train,
> Might, with small help from fancy, be transformed
> Into fleet Oreads, sporting visibly.
> The zephyrs fanning as they passed their wings
> Lacked not for love fair objects, whom they wooed
> With gentle whisper. Withered boughs grotesque,
> Stripped of their leaves and twigs by hoary age,
> From depth of shaggy covert peeping forth
> In the low vale, or on steep mountain side:
> And sometimes intermixed with stirring horns
> Of the live deer, or goat's depending beard;
> These were the lurking satyrs, a wild brood
> Of gamesome Deities! or Pan himself,
> The simple shepherd's awe-inspiring God.   [IV, 851-87]

The foregoing is one of a succession of splendid passages equally enriched with philosophy and poetry, tracing the fictions of Eastern mythology to the immediate intercourse of the imagination with Nature, and to the habitual propensity of the human mind to endow the outward forms of being with life and conscious motion. With this expansive and animating principle, Mr. Wordsworth has forcibly, but somewhat severely, contrasted the cold, narrow, lifeless spirit of modern philosophy:

> How, shall our great discoverers obtain
> From sense and reason less than these obtained,
> Though far misled? Shall men for whom our age
> Unbaffled powers of vision hath prepared,
> To explore the world without and world within,
> Be joyless as the blind? Ambitious souls—
> Whom earth at this late season hath produced
> To regulate the moving spheres, and weigh
> The planets in the hollow of their hand;
> And they who rather dive than soar, whose pains
> Have solved the elements, or analysed
> The thinking principle—shall they in fact
> Prove a degraded race? And what avails
> Renown, if their presumption make them such?
> Inquire of ancient wisdom; go, demand
> Of mighty nature, if 'twas ever meant
> That we should pry far off, yet be unraised;
> That we should pore, and dwindle as we pore,
> Viewing all objects unremittingly
> In disconnection dead and spiritless;
> And still dividing and dividing still
> Break down all grandeur, still unsatisfied
> With the perverse attempt, while littleness
> May yet become more little; waging thus
> An impious warfare with the very life
> Of our own souls! And if indeed there be
> An all-pervading spirit, upon whom
> Our dark foundations rest, could he design,
> That this magnificent effect of power,
> The earth we tread, the sky which we behold
> By day, and all the pomp which night reveals,
> That these—and that superior mystery,
> Our vital frame, so fearfully devised,
> And the dread soul within it—should exist
> Only to be examined, pondered, searched,
> Probed, vexed, and criticised—to be prized
> No more than as a mirror that reflects
> To proud Self-love her own intelligence?          [IV, 941ff.]

From the chemists and metaphysicians our author turns to the laughing sage of France, Voltaire. 'Poor gentleman, it fares no better with him, for he's a wit.'[6] We cannot, however, agree with Mr. Wordsworth that *Candide* is *dull*.[7] It is, if our author

pleases, 'the production of a scoffer's pen,' or it is anything
but dull. It may not be proper in a grave, discreet, orthodox,
promising young divine, who studies his opinions in the con-
traction or distension of his patron's brow, to allow any merit
to a work like *Candide;* but we conceive that it would have
been more manly in Mr. Wordsworth, nor do we think it
would have hurt the cause he espouses, if he had blotted out
the epithet, after it had peevishly escaped him. Whatsoever
savours of a little, narrow, inquisitorial spirit, does not sit well
on a poet and a man of genius. The prejudices of a philosopher
are not natural. There is a frankness and sincerity of opinion,
which is a paramount obligation in all questions of intellect,
though it may not govern the decisions of the spiritual courts,
who may, however, be safely left to take care of their own
interests. There is a plain directness and simplicity of understanding, which is the only security against the evils of levity,
on the one hand, or of hypocrisy on the other. A speculative
bigot is a solecism in the intellectual world. We can assure
Mr. Wordsworth, that we should not have bestowed so much
serious consideration on a single voluntary perversion of language, but that our respect for his character makes us jealous
of his smallest faults!

With regard to his general philippic against the contracted-
ness and egotism of philosophical pursuits, we only object to
its not being carried further. We shall not affirm with Rousseau
(his authority would perhaps have little weight with Mr.
Wordsworth)—'*Tout homme reflechi est mechant*',[8] but we
conceive that the same reasoning which Mr. Wordsworth
applies so eloquently and justly to the natural philosopher and
metaphysician may be extended to the moralist, the divine,
the politician, the orator, the artist, and even the poet. And
why so? Because wherever an intense activity is given to any
one faculty, it necessarily prevents the due and natural exercise of others. Hence all those professions or pursuits, where
the mind is exclusively occupied with the ideas of things as
they exist in the imagination or understanding, as they call
for the exercise of intellectual activity, and not as they are
connected with practical good or evil, must check the genial
expansion of the moral sentiments and social affections; must
lead to a cold and dry abstraction, as they are found to suspend the animal functions, and relax the bodily frame. Hence
the complaint of the want of natural sensibility and constitutional warmth of attachment in those persons who have
been devoted to the pursuit of any art or science—of their
restless morbidity of temperament, and indifference to everything that does not furnish an occasion for the display of their

mental superiority and the gratification of their vanity. The philosophical poet himself, perhaps, owes some of his love of nature to the opportunity it affords him of analyzing his own feelings, and contemplating his own powers—of making every object about him a whole length mirror to reflect his favourite thoughts, and of looking down on the frailties of others in undisturbed leisure, and from a more dignified height.

One of the most interesting parts of this work is that in which the author treats of the French Revolution, and of the feelings connected with it, in ingenuous minds, in its commencement and its progress. The *solitary*,\* who, by do-mestic calamities and disappointments, had been cut off from society, and almost from himself, gives the following ac-count of the manner in which he was roused from his mel-ancholy:

From that abstraction I was roused—and how?
Even as a thoughtful shepherd by a flash
Of lightning, startled in a gloomy cave
Of these wild hills. For, lo! the dread Bastille,
With all the chambers in its horrid towers,
Fell to the ground: by violence o'erthrown
Of indignation; and with shouts that drowned
The crash it made in falling! From the wreck
A golden palace rose, or seemed to rise,
The appointed seat of equitable law
And mild paternal sway. The potent shock
I felt; the transformation I perceived,
As marvellously seized as in that moment,
When, from the blind mist issuing, I beheld
Glory—beyond all glory ever seen,
Dazzling the soul! Meanwhile prophetic harps
In every grove were ringing, "War shall cease:
Did ye not hear that conquest is abjured?
Bring garlands, bring forth choicest flowers, to deck
The tree of liberty!"—My heart rebounded:
My melancholy voice the chorus joined.
Thus was I reconverted to the world;
Society became my glittering bride,
And airy hopes my children. From the depths
Of natural passion seemingly escaped,
My soul diffused itself in wide embrace
Of institutions and the forms of things.
⸺If with noise
And acclamation, crowds in open air
Expressed the tumult of their minds, my voice
There mingled, heard or not. And in still groves,

\* This word is not English. [w. h.]

Where wild⁹ enthusiasts tuned a pensive lay
Of thanks and expectation, in accord
With their belief, I sang Saturnian rule
Returned—a progeny of golden years
Permitted to descend, and bless mankind.
   . . . . .
Scorn and contempt forbid me to proceed!
But history, time's slavish scribe, will tell
How rapidly the zealots of the cause
Disbanded—or in hostile ranks appeared:
Some, tired of honest service; these outdone,
Disgusted, therefore, or appalled by aims
Of fiercer zealots. So confusion reigned,
And the more faithful were compelled to exclaim,
As Brutus did to virtue, "Liberty,
I worshipped thee, and find thee but a shade!"
SUCH RECANTATION HAD FOR ME NO CHARM,
NOR WOULD I BEND TO IT.      [III, 706–79]

The subject is afterwards resumed, with the same magnanimity and philosophical firmness:

                  For that other loss,
The loss of confidence in social man,
By the unexpected transports of our age
Carried so high, that every thought which looked
Beyond the temporal destiny of the kind—
To many seemed superfluous; as no cause
For such exalted confidence could e'er
Exist; so, none is now for such despair.
The two extremes are equally remote
From truth and reason; do not, then, confound
One with the other, but reject them both;
And choose the middle point, whereon to build
Sound expectations. This doth he advise
Who shared at first the illusion. At this day,
When a Tartarian darkness overspreads
The groaning nations; when the impious rule,
By will or by established ordinance,
Their own dire agents, and constrain the good
To acts which they abhor; though I bewail
This triumph, yet the pity of my heart
Prevents me not from owning that the law,
By which mankind now suffers, is most just.
For by superior energies; more strict
Affiance in each other; faith more firm
In their unhallowed principles, the bad
Have fairly earned a victory o'er the weak,
The vacillating, inconsistent good.
               [IV, 260–73; 296–309]

In the application of these memorable lines, we should, perhaps, differ a little from Mr. Wordsworth; nor can we indulge with him in the fond conclusion afterwards hinted at, that one day *our* triumph, the triumph of humanity and liberty, may be complete. For this purpose, we think several things necessary which are impossible. It is a consummation which cannot happen till the nature of things is changed, till the many become as united as the *one*, till romantic generosity shall be as common as gross selfishness, till reason shall have acquired the obstinate blindness of prejudice, till the love of power and of change shall no longer goad man on to restless action, till passion and will, hope and fear, love and hatred, and the objects proper to excite them, that is, alternate good and evil, shall no longer sway the bosoms and businesses of men. All things move, not in progress, but in a ceaseless round; our strength lies in our weakness; our virtues are built on our vices; our faculties are as limited as our being; nor can we lift man above his nature more than above the earth he treads. But though we cannot weave over again the airy, unsubstantial dream, which reason and experience have dispelled,

> What though the radiance, which was once so bright,
> Be now for ever taken from our sight,
> Though nothing can bring back the hour
> Of glory in the grass, of splendour in the flower:[10]

yet we will never cease, nor be prevented from returning on the wings of imagination to that bright dream of our youth; that glad dawn of the day-star of liberty; that spring-time of the world, in which the hopes and expectations of the human race seemed opening in the same gay career with our own; when France called her children to partake her equal blessings beneath her laughing skies; when the stranger was met in all her villages with dance and festive songs, in celebration of a new and golden era; and when, to the retired and contemplative student, the prospects of human happiness and glory were seen ascending like the steps of Jacob's ladder, in bright and never-ending succession. The dawn of that day was suddenly overcast; that season of hope is past; it is fled with the other dreams of our youth, which we cannot recall, but has left behind it traces, which are not to be effaced by Birthday and Thanksgiving odes,[11] or the chaunting of *Te Deums* in all the churches of Christendom. To those hopes eternal regrets are due; to those who maliciously and wilfully blasted them, in the fear that they might be accom-

plished, we feel no less what we owe—hatred and scorn as
lasting!

### THE SAME SUBJECT CONTINUED

Mr. Wordsworth's writings exhibit all the internal power,
without the external form of poetry. He has scarcely any of
the pomp and decoration and scenic effect of poetry: no gorgeous palaces nor solemn temples awe the imagination; no
cities rise 'with glistering spires and pinnacles adorned';[12]
we meet with no knights pricked forth on airy steeds; no hair-
breadth 'scapes and perilous accidents by flood or field. Either
from the predominant habit of his mind not requiring the
stimulus of outward impressions, or from the want of an imagination teeming with various forms, he takes the common
every-day events and objects of nature, or rather seeks those
that are the most simple and barren of effect; but he adds to
them a weight of interest from the resources of his own mind,
which makes the most insignificant things serious and even
formidable. All other interests are absorbed in the deeper
interest of his own thoughts, and find the same level. His
mind magnifies the littleness of his subject, and raises its
meanness; lends it his strength, and clothes it with borrowed
grandeur. With him, a molehill, covered with wild thyme,
assumes the importance of 'the great vision of the guarded
mount':[13] a puddle is filled with preternatural faces, and agitated with the fiercest storms of passion.

The extreme simplicity which some persons have objected
to in Mr. Wordsworth's poetry, is to be found only in the subject and the style: the sentiments are subtle and profound.
In the latter respect, his poetry is as much above the common standard or capacity, as in the other it is below it. His
poems bear a distant resemblance to some of Rembrandt's
landscapes, who, more than any other painter, created the
medium through which he saw nature, and out of the stump
of an old tree, a break in the sky, and a bit of water, could
produce an effect almost miraculous.

Mr. Wordsworth's poems in general are the history of a
refined and contemplative mind, conversant only with itself
and nature. An intense feeling of the associations of this kind
is the peculiar and characteristic feature of all his productions. He has described the love of nature better than any
other poet. This sentiment, inly felt in all its force, and sometimes carried to an excess, is the source both of his strength
and of his weakness. However we may sympathise with Mr.
Wordsworth in his attachment to groves and fields, we cannot extend the same admiration to their inhabitants, or to the

manners of country life in general. We go along with him,
while he is the subject of his own narrative, but we take
leave of him when he makes pedlars and ploughmen his
heroes and the interpreters of his sentiments. It is, we think,
getting into low company, and company, besides, that we
do not like. We take Mr. Wordsworth himself for a great
poet, a fine moralist, and a deep philosopher; but if he insists
on introducing us to a friend of his, a parish clerk, or the barber of the village, who is as wise as himself, we must be
excused if we draw back with some little want of cordial
faith. We are satisfied with the friendship which subsisted
between Parson Adams and Joseph Andrews. The author
himself lets out occasional hints that all is not as it should be
amongst these northern Arcadians. Though, in general, he
professes to soften the harsher features of rustic vice, he has
given us one picture of depraved and inveterate selfishness,
which we apprehend could only be found among the inhabitants of these boasted mountain districts. The account of
one of his heroines concludes as follows:

> A sudden illness seiz'd her in the strength
> Of life's autumnal season. Shall I tell
> How on her bed of death the matron lay,
> To Providence submissive, so she thought;
> But fretted, vexed, and wrought upon—almost
> To anger, by the malady that griped
> Her prostrate frame with unrelaxing power,
> As the fierce eagle fastens on the lamb.
> She prayed, she moaned—her husband's sister watched
> Her dreary pillow, waited on her needs;
> And yet the very sound of that kind foot
> Was anguish to her ears! "And must she rule
> Sole mistress of this house when I am gone?
> Sit by my fire—possess what I possessed—
> Tend what I tended—calling it her own!"
> Enough;—I fear too much. Of nobler feeling
> Take this example:—One autumnal evening,
> While she was yet in prime of health and strength,
> I well remember, while I passed her door,
> Musing with loitering step, and upward eye
> Turned tow'rds the planet Jupiter, that hung
> Above the centre of the vale, a voice
> Roused me, her voice;—it said, "That glorious star
> In its untroubled element will shine
> As now it shines, when we are laid in earth,
> And safe from all our sorrows." She is safe,
> And her uncharitable acts, I trust,
> And harsh unkindnesses, are all forgiven;
> Though, in this vale, remembered with deep awe!

[vi, 741ff.]

We think it is pushing our love of the admiration of natural objects a good deal too far, to make it a set-off against a story like the preceding.

All country people hate each other. They have so little comfort, that they envy their neighbours the smallest pleasure or advantage, and nearly grudge themselves the necessaries of life. From not being accustomed to enjoyment, they become hardened and averse to it—stupid, for want of thought—selfish, for want of society. There is nothing good to be had in the country, or, if there is, they will not let you have it. They had rather injure themselves than oblige anyone else. Their common mode of life is a system of wretchedness and self-denial, like what we read of among barbarous tribes. You live out of the world. You cannot get your tea and sugar without sending to the next town for it: you pay double, and have it of the worst quality. The small-beer is sure to be sour—the milk skimmed—the meat bad, or spoiled in the cooking. You cannot do a single thing you like; you cannot walk out or sit at home, or write or read, or think or look as if you did, without being subject to impertinent curiosity. The apothecary annoys you with his complaisance; the parson with his superciliousness. If you are poor, you are despised; if you are rich, you are feared and hated. If you do anyone a favour, the whole neighbourhood is up in arms; the clamour is like that of a rookery; and the person himself, it is ten to one, laughs at you for your pains, and takes the first opportunity of showing you that he labours under no uneasy sense of obligation. There is a perpetual round of mischief-making and backbiting for want of any better amusement. There are no shops, no taverns, no theatres, no opera, no concerts, no pictures, no public-buildings, no crowded streets, no noise of coaches, or of courts of law—neither courtiers nor courtesans, no literary parties, no fashionable routs, no society, no books, or knowledge of books. Vanity and luxury are the civilisers of the world, and sweeteners of human life. Without objects either of pleasure or action, it grows harsh and crabbed: the mind becomes stagnant, the affections callous, and the eye dull. Man left to himself soon degenerates into a very disagreeable person. Ignorance is always bad enough; but rustic ignorance is intolerable. Aristotle has observed, that tragedy purifies the affections by terror and pity. If so, a company of tragedians should be established at the public expense, in every village or hundred,[14] as a better mode of education than either Bell's or Lancaster's.[15] The benefits of knowledge are never so well understood as from seeing the effects of ignorance, in their naked, undisguised state, upon the common country people. Their selfishness and insensibility are perhaps less owing to the hardships and privations, which make them, like people out at sea in a boat, ready to devour one another, than to their having no idea of anything beyond themselves and their immediate sphere of action. They have no knowledge of, and consequently can take no interest in, anything which is not an object of their senses, and of their daily pursuits. They hate all strangers, and have generally a nick-name for the inhabitants of the next village. The two young noblemen in *Guzman d'Alfarache*,[16] who went to visit their mistresses only a league out of Madrid, were set upon by the peasants, who came round them calling out, 'A wolf.' Those who have no enlarged or liberal ideas, can have no disinterested or generous sentiments. Persons who are in the habit of reading novels and romances, are compelled to take a deep interest in, and to have their affections strongly excited by, fictitious characters and imaginary situations; their thoughts and feelings are constantly carried out of themselves, to persons they never saw, and things that never existed: history enlarges the mind, by familiarising us with the great vicissitudes of human affairs, and the catastrophes of states and kingdoms; the study of morals accustoms us to refer our actions to a general standard of right and wrong; and abstract reasoning, in general, strengthens the love of truth, and produces an inflexibility of principle which cannot stoop to low trick and cunning. Books, in Lord Bacon's phrase, are 'a discipline of humanity.' Country people have none of these advantages, nor any others to supply the place of them. Having no circulating libraries to exhaust their love of the marvellous, they amuse themselves with fancying the disasters and disgraces of their particular acquaintance. Having no hump-backed Richard to excite their wonder and abhorrence, they make themselves a bug-bear of their own, out of the first obnoxious person they can lay their hands on. Not having the fictitious distresses and gigantic crimes of poetry to stimulate their imagination and their passions, they vent their whole stock of spleen, malice, and invention, on their friends and next-door neighbours. They get up a little pastoral drama at home, with fancied events, but real characters. All their spare time is spent in manufacturing and propagating the lie for the day, which does its office, and expires. The next day is spent in the same manner. It is thus that they embellish the simplicity of rural life! The common people in civilised countries are a kind of domesticated savages. They have not the wild imagination, the passions, the fierce energies, or dreadful vicissitudes of the savage tribes, nor have they the leisure, the indolent enjoyments and romantic superstitions, which belonged to the pastoral life in milder climates, and more remote periods of society. They are taken out of a state of nature, without being put in possession of the refinements of art. The customs and institutions of society cramp their imaginations without giving them knowledge. If the inhabitants of the mountainous districts described by Mr. Wordsworth are less gross and sensual than others, they are more selfish. Their egotism becomes more concentrated, as they are more insulated, and their purposes more inveterate, as they have less competition to struggle with. The weight of matter which surrounds them, crushes the finer sympathies. Their minds become hard and cold, like the rocks which they cultivate. The immensity of their mountains makes the human form appear little and insignificant. Men are seen crawling between Heaven and earth, like insects to their graves. Nor do they regard one another more than flies on a wall. Their physiognomy expresses the materialism of their character, which has only one principle—rigid self-will. They move on with their eyes and foreheads fixed, looking neither to the right nor to the left, with a heavy slouch in their gait, and seeming as if nothing would divert them from their path. We do not admire this plodding pertinacity, always directed to the main chance. There is nothing which excites so little sympathy in our minds, as exclusive selfishness. If our theory is wrong, at least it is taken from pretty close observation, and is, we think, confirmed by Mr. Wordsworth's own account.

Of the stories contained in the latter part of the volume, we like that of the Whig and Jacobite friends, and of the good knight, Sir Alfred Irthing, the best. The last reminded us of a fine sketch of a similar character in the beautiful poem of *Hart-Leap Well*. To conclude—if the skill with which the poet had chosen his materials had been equal to the power which he has undeniably exerted over them, if the objects (whether persons or things) which he makes use of as the vehicle of his sentiments, had been such as to convey them in all their depth and force, then the production before us might indeed 'have proved a monument,'[17] as he himself wishes it, worthy of the author, and of his country. Whether, as it is, this very original and powerful performance may not rather remain like one of those stupendous but half-finished structures, which have been suffered to moulder into decay, because the cost and labour attending them exceeded their use or beauty, we feel that it would be presumptuous in us to determine.

# A Modern Tory
# Delineated*

A TORY is a blind idolator of old times and long established customs; reveres the wisdom of former ages, and reprobates innovations and improvements; inculcates passive obedience and the divine right of kings in some countries, in others acknowledges the right of the people to dethrone an incompetent or tyrannical monarch and choose another. A Tory never objects to increasing the power of the Crown, or abridging the liberties of the people, or even calls in question the justice or wisdom of any of the measures of government. Ministers may act with impunity, and break their most solemn promises, and set public opinion at defiance. A Tory may with perfect consistency accept of a situation in administration to act with those whom he had formerly accused of ignorance, incapacity, gross neglect, and disregard of the public interest. A Tory exerts his eloquence to liberate negro slaves, yet constantly supports measures which tend to enslave his own countrymen; is averse from Parliamentary Reform, or retrenchment in the public expenditure; considers a large standing army as necessary in time of peace to support the dignity of the Crown, and preserve social order; approves of British troops being employed in the honourable service of bestowing the inexpressible blessings of a legitimate government on an ungrateful people; admires the 'great moral lesson' given to the French nation, in the faithful observance of the Treaty of Paris.[1] A Tory considers sinecure places and pensions as sacred and inviolable, to reduce, or abolish which, would be unjust and dangerous; is of opinion that war is productive of more good than evil, and never enquires into the justice or necessity of commencing hostilities; and accuses those who differ with him on political subjects of being Jacobins, Revolutionists, and enemies to their country. A Tory highly values a long pedigree and ancient families, and despises low-born

* [*The Examiner*, Oct. 6, 1816.]

45

persons (the newly created nobility excepted); adores coronets, stars, garters, ribbons, crosses, and titles of all sorts, bestowed on all sorts of persons (the estimable and philanthropic discoverer of the means of exterminating a fatal and contagious disease alone excepted!)[2] A Tory hates all dissenters from the Established Church, as fools or knaves and disaffected to government; venerates the beneficed clergy, for their zealous attention to their spiritual duties, their disinterestedness, and liberality, particularly to their curates; is averse to Catholic emancipation, or bettering the condition of the poor Irish, who would be contented and happy, existing in the lowest state of poverty and human degradation, if not instigated by Jacobins and Reformers; and deems martial law the best remedy for discontent. A Tory considers corporal punishment as necessary, mild, and salutary, notwithstanding soldiers and sailors frequently commit suicide to escape from it; asserts that the criminal laws are wise, humane, and just, and would never show mercy to any offender; sees nothing wrong in the conduct of the Police in the metropolis; considers thief-takers as most disinterested and deserving servants of the public; disapproves of the Insolvent Debtor's Bill, which prevents a vindictive creditor from imprisoning an unfortunate debtor for life; sees no hardship in a person's being confined for thirty years in the Fleet Prison, on an allowance of sixpence a day, for contempt of the Court of Chancery; considers the Libel Laws as not sufficiently severe, particularly when the conduct of Princes, Nobility, or Ministers, is called in question—the greater the truth the greater the libel. A Tory approves of Man-traps and Spring-guns, and killing a Poacher now and then, *in terrorem:*[3] considers breaking pheasants' eggs a most heinous crime, but mixing poison in a liquor that is only drank by the poor and vulgar, a trifling one, especially when committed by a gentleman conspicuous for his loyalty. A Tory thinks cruelty to and gross neglect of poor lunatics not a sufficient reason for dismissing eminent medical men from their appointments to public hospitals; condemns any improvement being made in the wretched interior of prisons, lest the poor should be induced to commit crimes in order to gain admittance; stigmatizes philanthropy, feeling, and sympathy for the sufferings of the indigent poor, as cant, affectation, and hypocrisy, and ridicules interfering about chimney sweepers, parish apprentices, etc. A Tory would rather withhold relief from ten deserving objects than give to one imposter; is averse to instructing the poor, lest they should be enabled to think and reason; is of opinion that the poor in general earn too much money, that a spare diet is best adapted to hard labour, and full living to ease and indolence; reprobates the absurdity of peasants and low mechanics becoming authors, and can discern no merit whatever in the works of a Bloomfield or a Burns; is against the diffusion of philosophical knowledge, by public lectures, as productive of self-conceit, scepticism, and opinions dangerous to social order; depreciates modern literature, and reads no poetry but birthday odes and verses in celebration of the battle of Waterloo. A Tory subscribes largely to German sufferers, while his own countrymen are starving at home, and lavishes immense sums on triumphal columns, etc., while the brave men who achieved the victories are pining in want. A Tory execrates the audacity of low-born fellows for presuming to form any opinions on political subjects, and harangue at public meetings to encourage the 'ignorant impatience of the people' at heavy taxation, low wages, and dear bread, and excite a spirit of discontent among the ignorant multitude. A Tory asserts that the present sufferings of the country are the usual and necessary consequence of the transition from war to peace, are merely temporary and trifling, though the gaols are filled with insolvent debtors, and criminals driven to theft by urgent want, the Gazette filled with bankruptcies, agriculture declining, commerce and manufactories nearly at a stand, while thousands are emigrating to foreign countries, whole parishes deserted, the burthen of the poor rates intolerable, and yet insufficient to maintain the increasing number of the poor, and hundreds of once respectable householders reduced to the sad necessity of soliciting admission into the receptacles for paupers and vagabonds, and thousands wandering about in search of that employment which it is no longer in the power of the gentleman or farmer to bestow! A Tory compares the situation of the country twenty-four years ago with the present period, and greatly prefers the latter, military glory being more than equivalent to all the distress experienced, which ought to silence all complaints. A Tory approves of the Alien Bill, and would never allow the unfortunate to find an asylum in this country. A Tory would never show mercy to a fallen foe, and is much dissatisfied that an Illustrious Character,[4] who trusted the generosity of the British Government in preference to any other, should have been so slightly punished as sending him a prisoner for life to the sterile rock of St. Helena. A Tory considers boundless extravagance in certain persons as noble munificence and public spirit, benefiting the nation, by causing a circulation of money among Court tradesmen and artists; and so deems a tailor's bill,[5] sometimes amounting to more than the annual pay of all the Admirals, Captains, and Lieutenants in the Navy—a jeweller's,[5] to more than the whole expense of the

Expedition to Algiers—and more money expended on useless furniture, pagodas, mandarins, Chinese lanterns, sphinxes, dragons, monsters, china vases, girandoles, clocks, snuff-boxes, and French frippery, than ten times the amount of the munificent subscription of all the Royal Family and Cabinet Ministers for the relief of the starving poor! A Tory execrated the cruelty of a few ignorant barbarians in putting to death two hundred unoffending Europeans, and approved of inflicting the severest punishment on the Infidels, but was averse from interfering when thousands of Protestants were tortured and massacred in an enlightened and Christian country![6] A Tory in former times hated the Bourbons as the most inveterate enemies of England, execrated their bad faith, ambition, and tyranny, and despised the French nation for submitting to so vile a Government: a Tory in these times hails their return to power with rapture, as ensuring good will and liberality towards England, and lasting peace to all the world! A Tory on one side of St. Stephen's[7] sees ignorance, incapacity, knavery, deception, selfishness, arrogance, emptiness, inconsistency, dullness, and folly: on the other side, transcendant talent, great integrity, pure patriotism, extensive information, perfect disinterestedness, extensive philanthropy, commanding eloquence, Attic salt, and fundamental wisdom—by whose wise counsel and unparalleled exertions, England has attained the summit of glory, restored the Pope, the Jesuits, and the Inquisition—re-established military, feudal, and ecclesiastical power—given to the Spanish Patriots their beloved Ferdinand, to the Italian States their adored Francis, to Genoa independence, to Prussia a free Government, to Norway a legitimate Monarch, to France Louis the desired, the just, the enlightened, the humane, the pattern of good faith and liberality, the enemy of oppression, bigotry and superstition, the chosen Sovereign of the French nation, and the friend of the human race!

GLOUCESTER, OCTOBER 1, 1816.

# Coriolanus[*]

SHAKESPEARE has in this play shown himself well versed in history and state-affairs. *Coriolanus* is a store-house of political commonplaces. Anyone who studies it may save himself the trouble of reading Burke's *Reflections*, or Paine's *Rights of Man*, or the Debates in both Houses of Parliament since the French Revolution or our own. The arguments for and against aristocracy or democracy, on the privileges of the few and the claims of the many, on liberty and slavery, power and the abuse of it, peace and war, are here very ably handled, with the spirit of a poet and the acuteness of a philosopher. Shakespeare himself seems to have had a leaning to the arbitrary side of the question, perhaps from some feeling of contempt for his own origin; and to have spared no occasion of baiting the rabble. What he says of them is very true: what he says of their betters is also very true, though he dwells less upon it.—The cause of the people is indeed but little calculated as a subject for poetry: it admits of rhetoric, which goes into argument and explanation, but it presents no immediate or distinct images to the mind, 'no jutting frieze, buttress, or coigne of vantage' for poetry 'to make its pendant bed and procreant cradle in.'[1] The language of poetry naturally falls in with the language of power. The imagination is an exaggerating and exclusive faculty: it takes from one thing to add to another: it accumulates circumstances together to give the greatest possible effect to a favourite object. The understanding is a dividing and measuring faculty, it judges of things not according to their immediate impression on the mind, but according to their relations to one another. The one is a monopolising faculty, which seeks the greatest quantity of present excitement by inequality and disproportion; the other is a distributive faculty, which seeks the greatest quantity of ultimate good, by justice and proportion. The one is an aristocratical, the other a republican faculty. The principle of

* [*Characters of Shakespear's Plays;* first appeared in *The Examiner*, Dec. 15, 1816.]

poetry is a very anti-levelling principle. It aims at effect, it exists by contrast. It admits of no medium. It is everything by excess. It rises above the ordinary standard of sufferings and crimes. It presents a dazzling appearance. It shows its head turretted, crowned, and crested. Its front is gilt and blood-stained. Before it 'it carries noise, and behind it leaves tears.'[2] It has its altars and its victims, sacrifices, human sacrifices. Kings, priests, nobles, are its train-bearers, tyrants and slaves its executioners.—'Carnage is its daughter.'[3]—Poetry is right-royal. It puts the individual for the species, the one above the infinite many, might before right. A lion hunting a flock of sheep or a herd of wild asses is a more poetical object than they; and we even take part with the lordly beast, because our vanity or some other feeling makes us disposed to place ourselves in the situation of the strongest party. So we feel some concern for the poor citizens of Rome when they meet together to compare their wants and grievances, till Coriolanus comes in and with blows and big words drives this set of 'poor rats,' this rascal scum, to their homes and beggary before him. There is nothing heroical in a multitude of miserable rogues not wishing to be starved, or complaining that they are like to be so; but when a single man comes forward to brave their cries and to make them submit to the last indignities, from mere pride and self-will, our admiration of his prowess is immediately converted into contempt for their pusillanimity. The insolence of power is stronger than the plea of necessity. The tame submission to usurped authority or even the natural resistance to it has nothing to excite or flatter the imagination: it is the assumption of a right to insult or oppress others that carries an imposing air of superiority with it. We had rather be the oppressor than the oppressed. The love of power in ourselves and the admiration of it in others are both natural to man: the one makes him a tyrant, the other a slave. Wrong dressed out in pride, pomp, and circumstance, has more attraction than abstract right.—Coriolanus complains of the fickleness of the people: yet, the instant he cannot gratify his pride and obstinacy at their expense, he turns his arms against his country. If his country was not worth defending, why did he build his pride on its defence? He is a conquerer and a hero; he conquers other countries, and makes this a plea for enslaving his own; and when he is prevented from doing so, he leagues with its enemies to destroy his country. He rates the people 'as if he were a God to punish, and not a man of their infirmity.'[4] He scoffs at one of their tribunes for maintaining their rights and franchises: 'Mark you his absolute *shall?*' not marking his own absolute *will* to take everything from them, his impatience of the

slightest opposition to his own pretensions being in proportion to their arrogance and absurdity. If the great and powerful had the beneficence and wisdom of Gods, then all this
would have been well: if with a greater knowledge of what
is good for the people, they had as great a care for their
interest as they have themselves, if they were seated above
the world, sympathising with the welfare, but not feeling
the passions of men, receiving neither good nor hurt from
them, but bestowing their benefits as free gifts on them, they
might then rule over them like another Providence. But this
is not the case. Coriolanus is unwilling that the senate should
show their 'cares' for the people, lest their 'cares' should be
construed into 'fears,' to the subversion of all due authority;
and he is no sooner disappointed in his schemes to deprive the
people not only of the cares of the state, but of all power to
redress themselves, than Volumnia is made madly to exclaim,

> Now the red pestilence strike all trades in Rome,
> And occupations perish.          [IV, i, 13–14]

This is but natural: it is but natural for a mother to have
more regard for her son than for a whole city; but then the
city should be left to take some care of itself. The care of the
state cannot, we here see, be safely entrusted to maternal
affection, or to the domestic charities of high life. The great
have private feelings of their own, to which the interests of
humanity and justice must courtesy. Their interests are so far
from being the same as those of the community, that they
are in direct and necessary opposition to them; their power
is at the expense of *our* weakness; their riches of *our* poverty;
their pride of *our* degradation; their splendour of *our* wretchedness; their tyranny of *our* servitude. If they had the superior
knowledge ascribed to them (which they have not) it would
only render them so much more formidable; and from Gods
would convert them into Devils. The whole dramatic moral
of *Coriolanus* is that those who have little shall have less, and
that those who have much shall take all that others have left.
The people are poor; therefore they ought to be starved. They
are slaves; therefore they ought to be beaten. They work
hard; therefore they ought to be treated like beasts of burden.
They are ignorant; therefore they ought not to be allowed
to feel that they want food, or clothing, or rest, that they are
enslaved, oppressed, and miserable. This is the logic of the
imagination and the passions; which seek to aggrandize what
excites admiration and to heap contempt on misery, to raise
power into tyranny, and to make tyranny absolute; to thrust
down that which is low still lower, and to make wretches

desperate: to exalt magistrates into kings, kings into gods; to degrade subjects to the rank of slaves, and slaves to the condition of brutes. The history of mankind is a romance, a mask, a tragedy, constructed upon the principles of *poetical justice;* it is a noble or royal hunt, in which what is sport to the few is death to the many, and in which the spectators halloo and encourage the strong to set upon the weak, and cry havoc in the chase though they do not share in the spoil. We may depend upon it that what men delight to read in books, they will put in practice in reality.

One of the most natural traits in this play is the difference of the interest taken in the success of Coriolanus by his wife and mother. The one is only anxious for his honour; the other is fearful for his life.

> *Volumnia.* Methinks I hither hear your husband's drum:
> I see him pluck Aufidius down by th' hair:
> Methinks I see him stamp thus—and call thus—
> Come on, ye cowards; ye were got in fear
> Though you were born in Rome; his bloody brow
> With his mail'd hand then wiping, forth he goes
> Like to a harvest man, that's task'd to mow
> Or all, or lose his hire.
> *Virgilia.* His bloody brow! Oh Jupiter, no blood.
> *Volumnia.* Away, you fool; it more becomes a man
> Than gilt his trophy. The breast of Hecuba,
> When she did suckle Hector, look'd not lovelier
> Than Hector's forehead, when it spit forth blood
> At Grecian swords contending.                    [I, iii, 29ff.]

When she hears the trumpets that proclaim her son's return, she says in the true spirit of a Roman matron,

> These are the ushers of Martius: before him
> He carries noise, and behind him he leaves tears.
> Death, that dark spirit, in 's nervy arm doth lie,
> Which being advanc'd, declines, and then men die.
>                                             [II, i, 149ff.]

Coriolanus himself is a complete character: his love of reputation, his contempt of popular opinion, his pride and modesty, are consequences of each other. His pride consists in the inflexible sternness of his will; his love of glory is a determined desire to bear down all opposition, and to extort the admiration both of friends and foes. His contempt for popular favour, his unwillingness to hear his own praises, spring from the same source. He cannot contradict the praises that are bestowed upon him; therefore he is impatient at hearing

them. He would enforce the good opinion of others by his
actions, but does not want their acknowledgments in words.

> Pray now, no more: my mother,
> Who has a charter to extol her blood,
> When she does praise me, grieves me.    [I, ix, 13–15]

His magnanimity is of the same kind. He admires in an
enemy that courage which he honours in himself; he places
himself on the hearth of Aufidius with the same confidence
that he would have met him in the field, and feels that by
putting himself in his power, he takes from him all temptation for using it against him. *[. . .]

* [Hazlitt concludes with two long quotations from Plutarch.]

# ii

## THE LECTURER

# On Poetry In General*

THE BEST GENERAL NOTION which I can give of poetry is, that it is the natural impression of any object or event, by its vividness exciting an involuntary movement of imagination and passion, and producing, by sympathy, a certain modulation of the voice, or sounds, expressing it.

In treating of poetry, I shall speak first of the subject-matter of it, next of the forms of expression to which it gives birth, and afterwards of its connection with harmony of sound.

Poetry is the language of the imagination and the passions. It relates to whatever gives immediate pleasure or pain to the human mind. It comes home to the bosoms and businesses of men;[1] for nothing but what so comes home to them in the most general and intelligible shape, can be a subject for poetry. Poetry is the universal language which the heart holds with nature and itself. He who has a contempt for poetry, cannot have much respect for himself, or for anything else. It is not a mere frivolous accomplishment (as some persons have been led to imagine), the trifling amusement of a few idle readers or leisure hours—it has been the study and delight of mankind in all ages. Many people suppose that poetry is something to be found only in books, contained in lines of ten syllables, with like endings: but wherever there is a sense of beauty, or power, or harmony, as in the motion of a wave of the sea, in the growth of a flower that 'spreads its sweet leaves to the air, and dedicates its beauty to the sun'[2]—there is poetry, in its birth. If history is a grave study, poetry may be said to be a graver; its materials lie deeper, and are spread wider. History treats, for the most part, of the cumbrous and unwieldy masses of things, the empty cases in which the affairs of the world are packed, under the heads of intrigue or war, in different states, and from cenutry to century: but there is no thought or feeling that can have entered into the mind of man, which he would be eager to communicate to others, or which they would listen to with delight, that is not a fit

* [Lectures on the English Poets I.]

subject for poetry. It is not a branch of authorship: it is 'the
stuff of which our life is made.' The rest is 'mere oblivion,' a
dead letter: for all that is worth remembering in life, is the
poetry of it. Fear is poetry, hope is poetry, love is poetry,
hatred is poetry; contempt, jealousy, remorse, admiration,
wonder, pity, despair, or madness, are all poetry. Poetry is
that fine particle within us, that expands, rarefies, refines,
raises our whole being: without it 'man's life is poor as
beast's.'³ Man is a poetical animal: and those of us who do
not study the principles of poetry, act upon them all our lives,
like Molière's *Bourgeois Gentilhomme*, who had always spoken
prose without knowing it. The child is a poet in fact, when
he first plays at hide-and-seek, or repeats the story of Jack
the Giant-killer; the shepherd-boy is a poet, when he first
crowns his mistress with a garland of flowers; the countryman,
when he stops to look at the rainbow; the city-apprentice,
when he gazes after the Lord Mayor's show; the miser, when
he hugs his gold; the courtier, who builds his hopes upon a
smile; the savage, who paints his idol with blood; the slave,
who worships a tyrant, or the tyrant, who fancies himself a
god—the vain, the ambitious, the proud, the choleric man,
the hero and the coward, the beggar and the king, the rich
and the poor, the young and the old, all live in a world of
their own making; and the poet does no more than describe
what all the others think and act. If his art is folly and madness, it is folly and madness at second hand. 'There is warrant
for it.' Poets alone have not 'such seething brains, such shaping
fantasies, that apprehend more than cooler reason' can.

> The lunatic, the lover, and the poet
> Are of imagination all compact.
> One sees more devils than vast hell can hold,
> The madman. While the lover, all as frantic,
> Sees Helen's beauty in a brow of Egypt.
> The poet's eye in a fine frenzy rolling,
> Doth glance from heav'n to earth, from earth to heav'n;
> And as imagination bodies forth
> The forms of things unknown, the poet's pen
> Turns them to shape, and gives to airy nothing
> A local habitation and a name.
> Such tricks hath strong imagination.⁴

If poetry is a dream, the business of life is much the same.
If it is a fiction, made up of what we wish things to be, and
fancy that they are, because we wish them so, there is no
other nor better reality. Ariosto has described the loves of
Angelica and Medoro: but was not Medoro, who carved the
name of his mistress on the barks of trees, as much enam-

oured of her charms as he? Homer has celebrated the anger of Achilles: but was not the hero as mad as the poet? Plato banished the poets from his Commonwealth,[5] lest their descriptions of the natural man should spoil his mathematical man, who was to be without passions and affections, who was neither to laugh nor weep, to feel sorrow nor anger, to be cast down nor elated by anything. This was a chimera, however, which never existed but in the brain of the inventor; and Homer's poetical world has outlived Plato's philosophical Republic.

Poetry then is an imitation of nature, but the imagination and the passions are a part of man's nature. We shape things according to our wishes and fancies, without poetry; but poetry is the most emphatical language that can be found for those creations of the mind 'which ecstasy is very cunning in.'[6] Neither a mere description of natural objects, nor a mere delineation of natural feelings, however distinct or forcible, constitutes the ultimate end and aim of poetry, without the heightenings of the imagination. The light of poetry is not only a direct but also a reflected light, that while it shows us the object, throws a sparkling radiance on all around it: the flame of the passions, communicated to the imagination, reveals to us, as with a flash of lightning, the inmost recesses of thought, and penetrates our whole being. Poetry represents forms chiefly as they suggest other forms; feelings, as they suggest forms or other feelings. Poetry puts a spirit of life and motion into the universe. It describes the flowing, not the fixed. It does not define the limits of sense, or analyse the distinctions of the understanding, but signifies the excess of the imagination beyond the actual or ordinary impression of any object or feeling. The poetical impression of any object is that uneasy, exquisite sense of beauty or power that cannot be contained within itself; that is impatient of all limit; that (as flame bends to flame) strives to link itself to some other image of kindred beauty or grandeur; to enshrine itself, as it were, in the highest forms of fancy, and to relieve the aching sense of pleasure by expressing it in the boldest manner, and by the most striking examples of the same quality in other instances. Poetry, according to Lord Bacon, for this reason, 'has something divine in it, because it raises the mind and hurries it into sublimity, by conforming the shows of things to the desires of the soul, instead of subjecting the soul to external things, as reason and history do.'[7] It is strictly the language of the imagination; and the imagination is that faculty which represents objects, not as they are in themselves, but as they are moulded by other thoughts and feelings, into an infinite variety of shapes and combinations of power. This language is not the less true to nature, because it is false in point of fact; but so much the more true and natural, if it conveys the impression which the object under the influence of passion makes on the mind. Let an object, for instance, be presented to the senses in a state of agitation or fear—and the imagination will distort or magnify the object, and convert it into the likeness of whatever is most proper to encourage the fear. 'Our eyes are made the fools' of our other faculties.[8] This is the universal law of the imagination,

> That if it would but apprehend some joy,
> It comprehends some bringer of that joy:
> Or in the night imagining some fear,
> How easy is each bush suppos'd a bear![9]

When Iachimo says of Imogen,

> The flame o' th' taper
> Bows toward her, and would under-peep her lids
> To see the enclosed lights—[10]

this passionate interpretation of the motion of the flame to accord with the speaker's own feelings, is true poetry. The lover, equally with the poet, speaks of the auburn tresses of his mistress as locks of shining gold, because the least tinge of yellow in the hair has, from novelty and a sense of personal beauty, a more lustrous effect to the imagination than the purest gold. We compare a man of gigantic stature to a tower: not that he is anything like so large, but because the excess of his size beyond what we are accustomed to expect, or the usual size of things of the same class, produces by contrast a greater feeling of magnitude and ponderous strength than another object of ten times the same dimensions. The intensity of the feeling makes up for the disproportion of the objects. Things are equal to the imagination, which have the power of affecting the mind with an equal degree of terror, admiration, delight, or love. When Lear calls upon the heavens to avenge his cause, 'for they are old like him,' there is nothing extravagant or impious in this sublime identification of his age with theirs; for there is no other image which could do justice to the agonising sense of his wrongs and his despair!

Poetry is the high-wrought enthusiasm of fancy and feeling. As in describing natural objects, it impregnates sensible impressions with the forms of fancy, so it describes the feelings of pleasure or pain, by blending them with the strongest movements of passion, and the most striking forms of nature. Tragic poetry, which is the most impassioned species of it, strives to carry on the feeling to the utmost point of sublimity or pathos, by all the force of comparison or contrast; loses the sense of present suffering in the imaginary exaggeration of it; exhausts the terror or pity by an unlimited indulgence of it; grapples with impossibilities in its desperate impatience of restraint; throws us back upon the past, forward into the future; brings every moment of our being or object of nature in startling review before us; and in the rapid whirl of events, lifts us from the depths of woe to the highest contemplations on human life. When Lear says of Edgar, 'Nothing but his unkind daughters could have brought him to this'; what a bewildered amazement, what a wrench of the imagination, that cannot be brought to conceive of any other cause of misery than that which has bowed it down, and absorbs all other sorrow in its own! His sorrow, like a flood, supplies the sources of all other sorrow. Again, when he exclaims in the mad scene, 'The little dogs and all, Tray, Blanche, and Sweetheart, see, they bark at me!' it is passion lending occasion to imagination to make every creature in league against him, conjuring up ingratitude and insult in their least looked-for and most galling shapes, searching every thread and fibre of his heart, and finding out the last remaining image of respect or attachment in the bottom of his breast, only to torture and kill it! In like manner, the 'So I am'[11] of Cordelia gushes from her heart like a torrent of tears, relieving it of a weight of love and of supposed ingratitude, which had pressed upon it for years. What a fine return of the passion upon itself is that in *Othello*—with what a mingled agony of regret and despair he clings to the last traces of departed happiness—when he exclaims

> Oh now, for ever
> Farewell the tranquil mind. Farewell content;
> Farewell the plumed troops and the big war,
> That make ambition virtue! Oh farewell!
> Farewell the neighing steed, and the shrill trump,
> The spirit-stirring drum, th' ear-piercing fife,
> The royal banner, and all quality,
> Pride, pomp, and circumstance of glorious war:
> And O you mortal engines, whose rude throats
> Th' immortal Jove's dread clamours counterfeit,
> Farewell! Othello's occupation's gone!

How his passion lashes itself up and swells and rages like a tide in its sounding course, when in answer to the doubts expressed of his returning love, he says,

> Never, Iago. Like to the Pontic sea,
> Whose icy current and compulsive course

Ne'er feels retiring ebb, but keeps due on
To the Propontic and the Hellespont:
Even so my bloody thoughts, with violent pace,
Shall ne'er look back, ne'er ebb to humble love,
Till that a capable and wide revenge
Swallow them up.

The climax of his expostulation afterwards with Desdemona
is at that line,

But there where I had garner'd up my heart,
To be discarded thence![12]

One mode in which the dramatic exhibition of passion
excites our sympathy without raising our disgust is, that in
proportion as it sharpens the edge of calamity and disappointment, it strengthens the desire of good. It enhances our
consciousness of the blessing, by making us sensible of the
magnitude of the loss. The storm of passion lays bare and
shows us the rich depths of the human soul: the whole of our
existence, the sum total of our passions and pursuits, of that
which we desire and that which we dread, is brought before
us by contrast; the action and re-action are equal; the keen-
ness of immediate suffering only gives us a more intense
aspiration after, and a more intimate participation with the
antagonist world of good; makes us drink deeper of the cup
of human life; tugs at the heart-strings; loosens the pressure
about them; and calls the springs of thought and feeling into
play with tenfold force.

Impassioned poetry is an emanation of the moral and intellectual part of our nature, as well as of the sensitive—of the
desire to know, the will to act, and the power to feel; and
ought to appeal to these different parts of our constitution, in
order to be perfect. The domestic or prose tragedy, which
is thought to be the most natural, is in this sense the least so,
because it appeals almost exclusively to one of these faculties,
our sensibility. The tragedies of Moore and Lillo,[13] for this
reason, however affecting at the time, oppress and lie like a
dead weight upon the mind, a load of misery which it is
unable to throw off: the tragedy of Shakespeare, which is true
poetry, stirs our inmost affections; abstracts evil from itself
by combining it with all the forms of imagination, and with
the deepest workings of the heart, and rouses the whole man
within us.

The pleasure, however, derived from tragic poetry, is not
anything peculiar to it as poetry, as a fictitious and fanciful
thing. It is not an anomaly of the imagination. It has its source

and groundwork in the common love of strong excitement.
As Mr. Burke observes,[14] people flock to see a tragedy; but if
there were a public execution in the next street, the theatre
would very soon be empty. It is not then the difference between fiction and reality that solves the difficulty. Children
are satisfied with the stories of ghosts and witches in plain
prose: nor do the hawkers of full, true, and particular accounts
of murders and executions about the streets, find it necessary
to have them turned into penny ballads, before they can dispose of these interesting and authentic documents. The grave
politician drives a thriving trade of abuse and calumnies
poured out against those whom he makes his enemies for no
other end than that he may live by them. The popular
preacher makes less frequent mention of heaven than of hell.
Oaths and nicknames are only a more vulgar sort of poetry or
rhetoric. We are as fond of indulging our violent passions
as of reading a description of those of others. We are as prone
to make a torment of our fears, as to luxuriate in our hopes of
good. If it be asked, Why we do so? the best answer will be,
Because we cannot help it. The sense of power is as strong
a principle in the mind as the love of pleasure. Objects of
terror and pity exercise the same despotic control over it as
those of love or beauty. It is as natural to hate as to love,
to despise as to admire, to express our hatred or contempt, as
our love or admiration.

> Masterless passion sways us to the mood
> Of what it likes or loathes.[15]

Not that we like what we loathe; but we like to indulge our
hatred and scorn of it; to dwell upon it, to exasperate our idea
of it by every refinement of ingenuity and extravagance of
illustration; to make it a bugbear to ourselves, to point it out
to others in all the splendour of deformity, to embody it to
the senses, to stigmatise it by name, to grapple with it in
thought, in action, to sharpen our intellect, to arm our will
against it, to know the worst we have to contend with, and
to contend with it to the utmost. Poetry is only the highest
eloquence of passion, the most vivid form of expression that
can be given to our conception of anything, whether pleasurable or painful, mean or dignified, delightful or distressing.
It is the perfect coincidence of the image and the words with
the feeling we have, and of which we cannot get rid in any
other way, that gives an instant 'satisfaction to the thought.'
This is equally the origin of wit and fancy, of comedy and

tragedy, of the sublime and pathetic. When Pope says of the Lord Mayor's show,

> Now night descending, the proud scene is o'er,
> But lives in Settle's numbers one day more![16]

—when Collins makes Danger, 'with limbs of giant mould,'

> Throw him on the steep
> Of some loose hanging rock asleep:[17]

when Lear calls out in extreme anguish,

> Ingratitude, thou marble-hearted fiend,
> How much more hideous show'st in a child
> Than the sea-monster![18]

—the passion of contempt in the one case, of terror in the other, and of indignation in the last, is perfectly satisfied. We see the thing ourselves, and show it to others as we feel it to exist, and as, in spite of ourselves, we are compelled to think of it. The imagination, by thus embodying and turning them to shape, gives an obvious relief to the indistinct and importunate cravings of the will.—We do not wish the thing to be so; but we wish it to appear such as it is. For knowledge is conscious power; and the mind is no longer, in this case, the dupe, though it may be the victim of vice or folly.

Poetry is in all its shapes the language of the imagination and the passions, of fancy and will. Nothing, therefore, can be more absurd than the outcry which has been sometimes raised by frigid and pedantic critics, for reducing the language of poetry to the standard of common sense and reason: for the end and use of poetry, 'both at the first and now, was and is to hold the mirror up to nature,'[19] seen through the medium of passion and imagination, not divested of that medium by means of literal truth or abstract reason. The painter of history might as well be required to represent the face of a person who has just trod upon a serpent with the still-life expression of a common portrait, as the poet to describe the most striking and vivid impressions which things can be supposed to make upon the mind, in the language of common conversation. Let who will strip nature of the colours and the shapes of fancy, the poet is not bound to do so; the impressions of common sense and strong imagination, that is, of passion and indifference, cannot be the same, and they must have a separate language to do justice to either. Objects must strike differently upon the mind, independently of what they are in themselves, as long as we have a different interest in them, as we see them in a different point of view, nearer or at a greater distance (morally or physically speaking) from novelty, from old acquaintance, from our ignorance of them, from our fear of their consequences, from contrast, from unexpected likeness. We can no more take away the faculty of the imagination, than we can see all objects without light or shade. Some things must dazzle us by their preternatural light; others must hold us in suspense, and tempt our curiosity to explore their obscurity. Those who would dispel these various illusions, to give us their drab-coloured creation in their stead, are not very wise. Let the naturalist, if he will, catch the glow-worm, carry it home with him in a box, and find it next morning nothing but a little grey worm; let the poet or the lover of poetry visit it at evening, when beneath the scented hawthorn and the crescent moon it has built itself a palace of emerald light. This is also one part of nature, one appearance which the glow-worm presents, and that not the least interesting; so poetry is one part of the history of the human mind, though it is neither science nor philosophy. It cannot be concealed, however, that the progress of knowledge and refinement has a tendency to circumscribe the limits of the imagination, and to clip the wings of poetry. The province of the imagination is principally visionary, the unknown and undefined: the understanding restores things to their natural boundaries, and strips them of their fanciful pretensions. Hence the history of religious and poetical enthusiasm is much the same; and both have received a sensible shock from the progress of experimental philosophy. It is the undefined and uncommon that gives birth and scope to the imagination; we can only fancy what we do not know. As in looking into the mazes of a tangled wood we fill them with what shapes we please, with ravenous beasts, with caverns vast, and drear enchantments, so in our ignorance of the world about us, we make gods or devils of the first object we see, and set no bounds to the wilful suggestions of our hopes and fears.

> And visions, as poetic eyes avow,
> Hang on each leaf and cling to every bough.[20]

There can never be another Jacob's dream. Since that time, the heavens have gone farther off, and grown astronomical. They have become averse to the imagination, nor will they return to us on the squares of the distances, or on Doctor Chalmers's *Discourses*.[21] Rembrandt's picture[22] brings the matter nearer to us.—It is not only the progress of mechanical knowledge, but the necessary advances of civilization that are unfavourable to the spirit of poetry. We not only stand in less awe of the preternatural world, but we can calculate more surely, and look with more indifference, upon the regular routine of this. The heroes of the fabulous ages rid the world of monsters and giants. At present we are less exposed to the vicissitudes of good or evil, to the incursions of wild beasts or 'bandit fierce,' or to the unmitigated fury of the elements. The time has been that 'our fell of hair would at a dismal treatise rouse and stir as life were in it.'[23] But the police spoils all; and we now hardly so much as dream of a midnight murder. *Macbeth* is only tolerated in this country for the sake of the music;[24] and in the United States of America, where the philosophical principles of government are carried still farther in theory and practice, we find that the *Beggar's Opera* is hooted from the stage.[25] Society, by degrees, is constructed into a machine that carries us safely and insipidly from one end of life to the other, in a very comfortable prose style.

> Obscurity her curtain round them drew,
> And siren Sloth a dull quietus sung.[26]

The remarks which have been here made, would, in some measure, lead to a solution of the question of the comparative merits of painting and poetry. I do not mean to give any preference, but it should seem that the argument which has been sometimes set up, that painting must affect the imagination more strongly, because it represents the image more distinctly, is not well founded. We may assume without much temerity, that poetry is more poetical than painting. When artists or connoisseurs talk on stilts about the poetry of painting, they show that they know little about poetry, and have little love for the art. Painting gives the object itself; poetry what it implies. Painting embodies what a thing contains in itself: poetry suggests what exists out of it, in any manner connected with it. But this last is the proper province of the imagination. Again, as it relates to passion, painting gives the event, but poetry the progress of events: but it is during the progress, in the interval of expectation and suspense, while our hopes and fears are strained to the highest pitch of breathless agony, that the pinch of the interest lies.

> Between the acting of a dreadful thing
> And the first motion, all the interim is
> Like a phantasma or a hideous dream.
> The mortal instruments are then in council;
> And the state of man, like to a little kingdom,
> Suffers then the nature of an insurrection.[27]

But by the time that the picture is painted, all is over. Faces are the best part of a picture; but even faces are not what we chiefly remember in what interests us most.—But it may be asked then, Is there anything better than Claude Lorraine's landscapes, than Titian's portraits, than Raphael's Cartoons, or the Greek statues? Of the two first I shall say nothing, as they are evidently picturesque, rather than imaginative. Raphael's cartoons[28] are certainly the finest comments that ever were made on the Scriptures. Would their effect be the same, if we were not acquainted with the text? But the New Testament existed before the cartoons. There is one subject of which there is no cartoon, Christ washing the feet of the disciples the night before his death. But that chapter does not need a commentary! It is for want of some such resting place for the imagination that the Greek statues[29] are little else than specious forms. They are marble to the touch and to the heart. They have not an informing principle within them. In their faultless excellence they appear sufficient to themselves. By their beauty they are raised above the frailties of passion or suffering. By their beauty they are deified. But they are not objects of religious faith to us, and their forms are a reproach to common humanity. They seem to have no sympathy with us, and not to want our admiration.

Poetry in its matter and form is natural imagery or feeling, combined with passion and fancy. In its mode of conveyance, it combines the ordinary use of language with musical expression. There is a question of long standing, in what the essence of poetry consists; or what it is that determines why one set of ideas should be expressed in prose, another in verse. Milton has told us his idea of poetry in a single line—

> Thoughts that voluntary move
> Harmonious numbers[30]

As there are certain sounds that excite certain movements, and the song and dance go together, so there are, no doubt, certain thoughts that lead to certain tones of voice, or modulations of sound, and change 'the words of Mercury into the songs of Apollo.'[31] There is a striking instance of this adaptation of the movement of sound and rhythm to the subject, in Spenser's description of the Satyrs accompanying Una to the cave of Sylvanus.

> So from the ground she fearless doth arise
>     And walketh forth without suspect of crime.
> They, all as glad as birds of joyous prime,
>     Thence lead her forth, about her dancing round,

Shouting and singing all a shepherd's rhyme;
   And with green branches strewing all the ground,
Do worship her as queen with olive garland crown'd.

And all the way their merry pipes they sound,
   That all the woods and doubled echoes ring;
And with their horned feet do wear the ground,
   Leaping like wanton kids in pleasant spring;
So towards old Sylvanus they her bring,
   Who with the noise awaked, cometh out.
                *Faery Queene*, I, vi, [13, 14]

On the contrary, there is nothing either musical or natural in
the ordinary construction of language. It is a thing altogether
arbitrary and conventional. Neither in the sounds themselves,
which are the voluntary signs of certain ideas, nor in their
grammatical arrangements in common speech, is there any principle of natural imitation, or correspondence to the individual
ideas, or to the tone of feeling with which they are conveyed to
others. The jerks, the breaks, the inequalities, and harshnesses
of prose, are fatal to the flow of a poetical imagination, as a jolt-
ing road or a stumbling horse disturbs the reverie of an absent
man. But poetry makes these odds all even. It is the music of
language, answering to the music of the mind, untying as it
were 'the secret soul of harmony.'[32] Wherever any object takes
such a hold of the mind as to make us dwell upon it, and
brood over it, melting the heart in tenderness, or kindling
it to a sentiment of enthusiasm—wherever a movement of
imagination or passion is impressed on the mind, by which
it seeks to prolong and repeat the emotion, to bring all other
objects into accord with it, and to give the same movement
of harmony, sustained and continuous, or gradually varied
according to the occasion, to the sounds that express it—this
is poetry. The musical in sound is the sustained and continuous;
the musical in thought is the sustained and continuous also.
There is a near connection between music and deep-rooted
passion. Mad people sing. As often as articulation passes
naturally into intonation, there poetry begins. Where one idea
gives a tone and colour to others, where one feeling melts
others into it, there can be no reason why the same principle
should not be extended to the sounds by which the voice
utters these emotions of the soul, and blends syllables and
lines into each other. It is to supply the inherent defect of
harmony in the customary mechanism of language, to make
the sound an echo to the sense, when the sense becomes a sort
of echo to itself—to mingle the tide of verse, 'the golden
cadences of poetry,'[33] with the tide of feeling, flowing and
murmuring as it flows—in short, to take the language of the

imagination from off the ground, and enable it to spread its wings where it may indulge its own impulses—

> Sailing with supreme dominion
> Through the azure deep of air—[34]

without being stopped, or fretted, or diverted with the abruptnesses and petty obstacles, and discordant flats and sharps of prose, that poetry was invented. It is to common language, what springs are to a carriage, or wings to feet. In ordinary speech we arrive at a certain harmony by the modulations of the voice: in poetry the same thing is done systematically by a regular collocation of syllables. It has been well observed, that everyone who declaims warmly, or grows intent upon a subject, rises into a sort of blank verse or measured prose. The merchant, as described in Chaucer, went on his way 'sounding always the increase of his winning.' Every prose-writer has more or less of rhythmical adaptation, except poets, who, when deprived of the regular mechanism of verse, seem to have no principle of modulation left in their writings.

An excuse might be made for rhyme in the same manner. It is but fair that the ear should linger on the sounds that delight it, or avail itself of the same brilliant coincidence and unexpected recurrence of syllables, that have been displayed in the invention and collocation of images. It is allowed that rhyme assists the memory; and a man of wit and shrewdness has been heard to say, that the only four good lines of poetry are the well-known ones which tell the number of days in the months of the year.

> Thirty days hath September, etc.

But if the jingle of names assists the memory, may it not also quicken the fancy? and there are other things worth having at our fingers' ends, besides the contents of the almanac.— Pope's versification is tiresome, from its excessive sweetness and uniformity. Shakespeare's blank verse is the perfection of dramatic dialogue.

All is not poetry that passes for such: nor does verse make the whole difference between poetry and prose. The *Iliad* does not cease to be poetry in a literal translation; and Addison's *Campaign*[35] has been very properly denominated a Gazette in rhyme.[36] Common prose differs from poetry, as treating for the most part either of such trite, familiar, and irksome matters of fact, as convey no extraordinary impulse to the imagination, or else of such difficult and laborious processes of the understanding, as do not admit of the wayward or violent movements either of the imagination or the passions.

I will mention three works which come as near to poetry as possible without absolutely being so, namely, the *Pilgrim's Progress, Robinson Crusoe,* and the Tales of Boccaccio. Chaucer and Dryden have translated some of the last into English rhyme, but the essence and the power of poetry was there before. That which lifts the spirit above the earth, which draws the soul out of itself with indescribable longings, is poetry in kind, and generally fit to become so in name, by being 'married to immortal verse.'[37] If it is of the essence of poetry to strike and fix the imagination, whether we will or no, to make the eye of childhood glisten with the starting tear, to be never thought of afterwards with indifference, John Bunyan and Daniel Defoe may be permitted to pass for poets in their way. The mixture of fancy and reality in the *Pilgrim's Progress* was never equalled in any allegory. His pilgrims walk above the earth, and yet are on it. What zeal, what beauty, what truth of fiction! What deep feeling in the description of Christian's swimming across the water at last, and in the picture of the Shining Ones within the gates, with wings at their backs and garlands on their heads, who are to wipe all tears from his eyes! The writer's genius, though not 'dipped in dews of Castilie,'[38] was baptised with the Holy Spirit and with fire. The prints in this book are no small part of it. If the confinement of Philoctetes in the island of Lemnos was a subject for the most beautiful of all the Greek tragedies,[39] what shall we say to Robinson Crusoe in his? Take the speech of the Greek hero on leaving his cave, beautiful as it is, and compare it with the reflections of the English adventurer in his solitary place of confinement. The thoughts of home, and of all from which he is for ever cut off, swell and press against his bosom, as the heaving ocean rolls its ceaseless tide against the rocky shore, and the very beatings of his heart become audible in the eternal silence that surrounds him. Thus he says,

As I walked about, either in my hunting, or for viewing the country, the anguish of my soul at my condition would break out upon me on a sudden, and my very heart would die within me to think of the woods, the mountains, the deserts I was in; and how I was a prisoner, locked up with the eternal bars and bolts of the ocean, in an uninhabited wilderness, without redemption. In the midst of the greatest composures of my mind, this would break out upon me like a storm, and make me wring my hands, and weep like a child. Sometimes it would take me in the middle of my work, and I would immediately sit down and sigh, and look upon the ground for an hour or two together, and this was still worse to me, for if I could burst into tears or vent myself in words, it would go off, and the grief having exhausted itself would abate.

The story of his adventures would not make a poem like the *Odyssey*, it is true; but the relator had the true genius of a poet. It has been made a question whether Richardson's romances are poetry; and the answer perhaps is, that they are not poetry, because they are not romance. The interest is worked up to an inconceivable height; but it is by an infinite number of little things, by incessant labour and calls upon the attention, by a repetition of blows that have no rebound in them. The sympathy excited is not a voluntary contribution, but a tax. Nothing is unforced and spontaneous. There is a want of elasticity and motion. The story does not 'give an echo to the seat where love is throned.'[40] The heart does not answer of itself like a chord in music. The fancy does not run on before the writer with breathless expectation, but is dragged along with an infinite number of pins and wheels, like those with which the Lilliputians dragged Gulliver pinioned to the royal palace.—Sir Charles Grandison is a coxcomb. What sort of a figure would he cut, translated into an epic poem, by the side of Achilles? Clarissa, the divine Clarissa, is too interesting by half. She is interesting in her ruffles, in her gloves, her samplers, her aunts and uncles—she is interesting in all that is uninteresting. Such things, however intensely they may be brought home to us, are not conductors to the imagination. There is infinite truth and feeling in Richardson; but it is extracted from a *caput mortuum*[41] of circumstances: it does not evaporate of itself. His poetical genius is like Ariel confined in a pine-tree, and requires an artificial process to let it out. Shakespeare says—

> Our poesy is as a gum
> Which issues whence 'tis nourished, our gentle flame
> Provokes itself, and like the current flies
> Each bound it chafes.*[42]

* Burke's writings are not poetry, notwithstanding the vividness of the fancy, because the subject matter is abstruse and dry, not natural, but artificial. The difference between poetry and eloquence is, that the one is the eloquence of the imagination, and the other of the understanding. Eloquence tries to persuade the will, and convince the reason: poetry produces its effect by instantaneous sympathy. Nothing is a subject for poetry that admits of a dispute. Poets are in general bad prose-writers, because their images, though fine in themselves, are not to the purpose, and do not carry on the argument. The French poetry wants the forms of the imagination. It is didactic more than dramatic. And some of our own poetry which has been most admired, is only poetry in the rhyme, and in the studied use of poetic diction. [W. H.]

I shall conclude this general account with some remarks on four of the principal works of poetry in the world, at different periods of history—Homer, the Bible, Dante, and let me add, Ossian.[43] In Homer, the principle of action or life is predominant; in the Bible, the principle of faith and the idea of Providence; Dante is a personification of blind will; and in Ossian we see the decay of life, and the lag end of the world. Homer's poetry is the heroic: it is full of life and action: it is bright as the day, strong as a river. In the vigour of his intellect, he grapples with all the objects of nature, and enters into all the relations of social life. He saw many countries, and the manners of many men; and he has brought them all together in his poem. He describes his heroes going to battle with a prodigality of life, arising from an exuberance of animal spirits: we see them before us, their number, and their order of battle, poured out upon the plain 'all plumed like estriches, like eagles newly bathed, wanton as goats, wild as young bulls, youthful as May, and gorgeous as the sun at midsummer,'[44] covered with glittering armour, with dust and blood; while the Gods quaff their nectar in golden cups, or mingle in the fray; and the old men assembled on the walls of Troy rise up with reverence as Helen passes by them. The multitude of things in Homer is wonderful; their splendour, their truth, their force, and variety. His poetry is, like his religion, the poetry of number and form: he describes the bodies as well as the souls of men.

The poetry of the Bible is that of imagination and of faith: it is abstract and disembodied: it is not the poetry of form, but of power; not of multitude, but of immensity. It does not divide into many, but aggrandizes into one. Its ideas of nature are like its ideas of God. It is not the poetry of social life, but of solitude: each man seems alone in the world, with the original forms of nature, the rocks, the earth, and the sky. It is not the poetry of action or heroic enterprise, but of faith in a supreme Providence, and resignation to the power that governs the universe. As the idea of God was removed farther from humanity, and a scattered polytheism, it became more profound and intense, as it became more universal, for the Infinite is present to everything: 'If we fly into the uttermost parts of the earth, it is there also; if we turn to the east or the west, we cannot escape from it.'[45] Man is thus aggrandized in the image of his Maker. The history of the patriarchs is of this kind; they are founders of a chosen race of people, the inheritors of the earth; they exist in the generations which are to come after them. Their poetry, like their religious creed, is vast, unformed, obscure, and infinite; a vision is upon it—an invisible hand is suspended over it. The spirit of the Christian religion consists in the glory hereafter to be revealed; but in the Hebrew dispensation, Providence took an immediate share in the affairs of this life. Jacob's dream arose out of this intimate communion between heaven and earth: it was this that let down, in the sight of the youthful patriarch, a golden ladder from the sky to the earth, with angels ascending and descending upon it, and shed a light upon the lonely place, which can never pass away. The story of Ruth, again, is as if all the depth of natural affection in the human race was involved in her breast. There are descriptions in the book of Job more prodigal of imagery, more intense in passion, than anything in Homer, as that of the state of his prosperity, and of the vision that came upon him by night. The metaphors in the Old Testament are more boldly figurative. Things were collected more into masses, and gave a greater *momentum* to the imagination.

Dante was the father of modern poetry, and he may therefore claim a place in this connection. His poem is the first great step from Gothic darkness and barbarism; and the struggle of thought in it to burst the thraldom in which the human mind had been so long held, is felt in every page. He stood bewildered, not appalled, on that dark shore which separates the ancient and the modern world; and saw the glories of antiquity dawning through the abyss of time, while revelation opened its passage to the other world. He was lost in wonder at what had been done before him, and he dared to emulate it. Dante seems to have been indebted to the Bible for the gloomy tone of his mind, as well as for the prophetic fury which exalts and kindles his poetry; but he is utterly unlike Homer. His genius is not a sparkling flame, but the sullen heat of a furnace. He is power, passion, self-will personified. In all that relates to the descriptive or fanciful part of poetry, he bears no comparison to many who had gone before, or who have come after him; but there is a gloomy abstraction in his conceptions, which lies like a dead weight upon the mind; a benumbing stupor, a breathless awe, from the intensity of the impression; a terrible obscurity, like that which oppresses us in dreams; an identity of interest, which moulds every object to its own purposes, and clothes all things with the passions and imaginations of the human soul—that make amends for all other deficiencies. The immediate objects he presents to the mind are not much in themselves, they want grandeur, beauty, and order; but they become everything by the force of the character he impresses upon them. His mind lends its own power to the objects which it contem-

plates, instead of borrowing it from them. He takes advantage
even of the nakedness and dreary vacuity of his subject. His
imagination peoples the shades of death, and broods over the
silent air. He is the severest of all writers, the most hard and
impenetrable, the most opposite to the flowery and glittering;
who relies most on his own power, and the sense of it in
others, and who leaves most room to the imagination of his
readers. Dante's only endeavour is to interest; and he interests
by exciting our sympathy with the emotion by which he is
himself possessed. He does not place before us the objects
by which that emotion has been created; but he seizes on the
attention, by showing us the effect they produce on his feelings; and his poetry accordingly gives the same thrilling and
overwhelming sensation, which is caught by gazing on the
face of a person who has seen some object of horror. The
improbability of the events, the abruptness and monotony in
the Inferno, are excessive: but the interest never flags, from
the continued earnestness of the author's mind. Dante's great
power is in combining internal feelings with external objects.
Thus the gate of hell, on which that withering inscription is
written,[46] seems to be endowed with speech and consciousness, and to utter its dread warning, not without a sense of
mortal woes. This author habitually unites the absolutely
local and individual with the greatest wildness and mysticism.
In the midst of the obscure and shadowy regions of the
lower world, a tomb suddenly rises up with the inscription, 'I
am the tomb of Pope Anastasius the Sixth':[47] and half the
personages whom he has crowded into the Inferno are his own
acquaintance. All this, perhaps, tends to heighten the effect
by the bold intermixture of realities, and by an appeal, as it
were, to the individual knowledge and experience of the
reader. He affords few subjects for picture. There is, indeed,
one gigantic one, that of Count Ugolino,[48] of which Michael
Angelo made a bas-relief, and which Sir Joshua Reynolds
ought not to have painted.[49]

Another writer whom I shall mention last, and whom I
cannot persuade myself to think a mere modern in the groundwork, is Ossian. He is a feeling and a name that can never be
destroyed in the minds of his readers. As Homer is the first
vigour and lustihed, Ossian is the decay and old age of poetry.
He lives only in the recollection and regret of the past. There
is one impression which he conveys more entirely than all
other poets, namely, the sense of privation, the loss of all
things, of friends, of good name, of country—he is even without God in the world. He converses only with the spirits of
the departed; with the motionless and silent clouds. The cold
moonlight sheds its faint lustre on his head; the fox peeps out

of the ruined tower; the thistle waves its beard to the wandering gale; and the strings of his harp seem, as the hand of age, as the tale of other times, passes over them, to sigh and rustle like the dry reeds in the winter's wind! The feeling of cheerless desolation, of the loss of the pith and sap of existence, of the annihilation of the substance, and the clinging to the shadow of all things as in a mock-embrace, is here perfect. In this way, the lamentation of Selma for the loss of Salgar is the finest of all.[50] If it were indeed possible to show that this writer was nothing, it would only be another instance of mutability, another blank made, another void left in the heart, another confirmation of that feeling which makes him so often complain, 'Roll on, ye dark brown years, ye bring no joy on your wing to Ossian!'

# Sir Joshua Reynolds*

[. . .] IN OUR OPINION, Sir Joshua did not possess either that
high imagination, or those strong feelings, without which no
painter can become a poet in his art. His larger historical compositions have been generally allowed to be most liable to
objection, considered in a critical point of view. We shall not
attempt to judge them by scientific or technical rules, but
make one or two observations on the character and feeling
displayed in them. The highest subject which Sir Joshua has
attempted was the "Count Ugolino," and it was, as might be
expected from the circumstances, a total failure. He had, it
seems, painted a study of an old beggarman's head; and some
person, who must have known as little of painting as of poetry,
persuaded the unsuspecting artist, that it was the exact expression of Dante's Count Ugolino, one of the most grand, terrific,
and appalling characters in modern fiction. Reynolds, who
knew nothing of the matter but what he was told, took his
good fortune for granted, and only extended his canvas to
admit the rest of the figures, who look very much like apprentices hired to sit for the occasion from some neighbouring
workshop. There is one pleasing and natural figure of a little
boy kneeling at his father's feet, but it has no relation to the
supposed story. The attitude and expression of Count Ugolino
himself are what the artist intended them to be till they were
pampered into something else by the officious vanity of
friends—those of a common mendicant at the corner of a street,
waiting patiently for some charitable donation. There is all
the difference between what the picture is and what it ought
to be, that there is between Crabbe and Dante. The imagination of the painter took refuge in a parish work-house, instead of ascending the steps of the Tower of Famine. The hero
of Dante is a lofty, high-minded, and unprincipled Italian
nobleman, who had betrayed his country to the enemy, and
who, as a punishment for his crime, is shut up with his four
sons in the dungeon of the citadel, where he shortly finds the

* [From *The Champion*, Oct.–Nov. 1814.]

doors barred against him, and food withheld. He in vain
watches with eager feverish eye the opening of the door at
the accustomed hour, and his looks turn to stone; his children
one by one drop down dead at his feet; he is seized with
blindness, and, in the agony of his despair, he gropes on his
knees after them,

> Calling each by name
> For three days after they were dead.

Even in the other world he is represented with the same
fierce, dauntless, unrelenting character, 'gnawing the skull of
his adversary, his fell repast.' The subject of the Laocoon[1]
is scarcely equal to that described by Dante. The horror *there*
is physical and momentary; in the other, the imagination fills
up the long, obscure, dreary void of despair, and joins its
unutterable pangs to the loud cries of nature. What is there
in the picture to convey the ghastly horrors of the scene, or
the mighty energy of soul with which they are borne?*
Nothing! Yet Dr. Warton, who has related this story so well;[2]
Burke, who wrote that fine description of the effects of
famine;[3] Goldsmith, and all his other friends, were satisfied
with his success. Why then should not Sir Joshua be so too?—
Because he was bound to understand the language which he
used, as well as that which was given him to translate. [. . .]

* Why does not the British Institution, instead of patronising pictures of the battle of Waterloo, of red coats, foolish faces, and labels
of victory, offer a prize for a picture of the subject of Ugolino that
shall be equal to the group of the Laocoon? *That* would be the way
to do something, if there is anything to be done by such patronage.
[w. h.]

# Milton*

[. . .] SHAKESPEARE discovers in his writings little religious enthusiasm, and an indifference to personal reputation; he had none of the bigotry of his age, and his political prejudices were not very strong. In these respects, as well as in every other, he formed a direct contrast to Milton. Milton's works are a perpetual invocation to the Muses; a hymn to Fame. He had his thoughts constantly fixed on the contemplation of the Hebrew theocracy, and of a perfect commonwealth; and he seized the pen with a hand just warm from the touch of the ark of faith. His religious zeal infused its character into his imagination; so that he devotes himself with the same sense of duty to the cultivation of his genius, as he did to the exercise of virtue, or the good of his country. The spirit of the poet, the patriot, and the prophet, vied with each other in his breast. His mind appears to have held equal communion with the inspired writers, and with the bards and sages of ancient Greece and Rome;

> Blind Thamyris, and blind Mæonides,
> And Tiresias, and Phineus, prophets old.[1]

He had a high standard, with which he was always comparing himself, nothing short of which could satisfy his jealous ambition. He thought of nobler forms and nobler things than those he found about him. He lived apart, in the solitude of his own thoughts, carefully excluding from his mind whatever might distract its purposes or alloy its purity, or damp its zeal. 'With darkness and with dangers compassed round,'[2] he had the mighty models of antiquity always present to his thoughts, and determined to raise a monument of equal height and glory, 'piling up every stone of lustre from the brook,'[3] for the delight and wonder of posterity. He had girded himself up, and as it were, sanctified his genius to

* [From *Lectures on the English Poets* III, "On Shakespeare and Milton."]

this service from his youth. 'For after,' he says, 'I had from my first years, by the ceaseless diligence and care of my father, been exercised to the tongues, and some sciences as my age could suffer, by sundry masters and teachers, it was found that whether aught was imposed upon me by them, or betaken to of my own choice, the style by certain vital signs it had, was likely to live; but much latelier, in the private academies of Italy, perceiving that some trifles which I had in memory, composed at under twenty or thereabout, met with acceptance above what was looked for; I began thus far to assent both to them and divers of my friends here at home, and not less to an inward prompting which now grew daily upon me, that by labour and intense study (which I take to be my portion in this life), joined with the strong propensity of nature, I might perhaps leave something so written to after-times as they should not willingly let it die. The accomplishment of these intentions, which have lived within me ever since I could conceive myself anything worth to my country, lies not but in a power above man's to promise; but that none hath by more studious ways endeavoured, and with more unwearied spirit that none shall, that I dare almost aver of myself, as far as life and free leisure will extend. Neither do I think it shame to covenant with any knowing reader, that for some few years yet, I may go on trust with him toward the payment of what I am now indebted, as being a work not to be raised from the heat of youth or the vapours of wine; like that which flows at waste from the pen of some vulgar amourist, or the trencher fury of a rhyming parasite, nor to be obtained by the invocation of Dame Memory and her Siren daughters, but by devout prayer to that eternal spirit who can enrich with all utterance and knowledge, and sends out his Seraphim with the hallowed fire of his altar, to touch and purify the lips of whom he pleases: to this must be added industrious and select reading, steady observation, and insight into all seemly and generous arts and affairs. Although it nothing content me to have disclosed thus much beforehand; but that I trust hereby to make it manifest with what small willingness I endure to interrupt the pursuit of no less hopes than these, and leave a calm and pleasing solitariness, fed with cheerful and confident thoughts, to embark in a troubled sea of noises and hoarse disputes, from beholding the bright countenance of truth in the quiet and still air of delightful studies.'[4]

So that of Spenser:

> The noble heart that harbours virtuous thought,
> And is with child of glorious great intent,

Can never rest until it forth have brought
The eternal brood of glory excellent.[5]

Milton, therefore, did not write from casual impulse, but
after a severe examination of his own strength, and with a
resolution to leave nothing undone which it was in his power
to do. He always labours, and almost always succeeds. He
strives hard to say the finest things in the world, and he does
say them. He adorns and dignifies his subject to the utmost:
he surrounds it with every possible association of beauty or
grandeur, whether moral, intellectual, or physical. He refines
on his descriptions of beauty; loading sweets on sweets, till
the sense aches at them; and raises his images of terror to a
gigantic elevation, that 'makes Ossa like a wart.'[6] In Milton,
there is always an appearance of effort: in Shakespeare,
scarcely any.

Milton has borrowed more than any other writer, and exhausted every source of imitation, sacred or profane; yet he is
perfectly distinct from every other writer. He is a writer of
centos,[7] and yet in originality scarcely inferior to Homer. The
power of his mind is stamped on every line. The fervour of
his imagination melts down and renders malleable, as in a
furnace, the most contradictory materials. In reading his
works, we feel ourselves under the influence of a mighty
intellect, that the nearer it approaches to others, becomes
more distinct from them. The quantity of art in him shows the
strength of his genius: the weight of his intellectual obligations would have oppressed any other writer. Milton's learning has the effect of intuition. He describes objects, of which
he could only have read in books, with the vividness of actual
observation. His imagination has the force of nature. He
makes words tell as pictures.

> Him followed Rimmon, whose delightful seat
> Was fair Damascus, on the fertile banks
> Of Abbana and Pharphar, lucid streams.
>                    [*Paradise Lost* I, 467–9]

The word *lucid* here gives to the idea all the sparkling effect
of the most perfect landscape.
And again:

> As when a vulture on Imaus bred,
> Whose snowy ridge the roving Tartar bounds,
> Dislodging from a region scarce of prey,
> To gorge the flesh of lambs and yeanling kids
> On hills where flocks are fed, flies towards the springs
> Of Ganges or Hydaspes, Indian streams;

> But in his way lights on the barren plains
> Of Sericana, where Chineses drive
> With sails and wind their cany waggons light.
>
> [*PL* III, 431–9]

If Milton had taken a journey for the express purpose, he could not have described this scenery and mode of life better. Such passages are like demonstrations of natural history. Instances might be multiplied without end.

We might be tempted to suppose that the vividness with which he describes visible objects, was owing to their having acquired an unusual degree of strength in his mind, after the privation of his sight; but we find the same palpableness and truth in the descriptions which occur in his early poems. In *Lycidas* he speaks of 'the great vision of the guarded mount,' with that preternatural weight of impression with which it would present itself suddenly to 'the pilot of some small night-foundered skiff':[8] and the lines in the *Penseroso*, describing 'the wandering moon,'

> Riding near her highest noon,
> Like one that had been led astray
> Through the heaven's wide pathless way,

are as if he had gazed himself blind in looking at her. There is also the same depth of impression in his descriptions of the objects of all the different senses, whether colours, or sounds, or smells—the same absorption of his mind in whatever engaged his attention at the time. It has been indeed objected to Milton, by a common perversity of criticism, that his ideas were musical rather than picturesque, as if because they were in the highest degree musical, they must be (to keep the sage critical balance even, and to allow no one man to possess two qualities at the same time) proportionably deficient in other respects. But Milton's poetry is not cast in any such narrow, common-place mould; it is not so barren of resources. His worship of the Muse was not so simple or confined. A sound arises 'like a steam of rich distilled perfumes';[9] we hear the pealing organ, but the incense on the altars is also there, and the statues of the gods are ranged around! The ear indeed predominates over the eye, because it is more immediately affected, and because the language of music blends more immediately with, and forms a more natural accompaniment to, the variable and indefinite associations of ideas conveyed by words. But where the associations of the imagination are not the principal thing, the individual object is given by Milton with equal force and beauty. The strongest and best proof of this, as a characteristic power of his mind, is, that the persons of Adam and Eve, of Satan, etc. are always accompanied, in our imagination, with the grandeur of the naked figure; they convey to us the ideas of sculpture. As an instance, take the following:

> He soon
> Saw within ken a glorious Angel stand,
> The same whom John saw also in the sun:
> His back was turned, but not his brightness hid;
> Of beaming sunny rays a golden tiar
> Circled his head, nor less his locks behind
> Illustrious on his shoulders fledge with wings
> Lay waving round; on some great charge employ'd
> He seem'd, or fix'd in cogitation deep.
> Glad was the spirit impure, as now in hope
> To find who might direct his wand'ring flight
> To Paradise, the happy seat of man,
> His journey's end, and our beginning woe.
> But first he casts to change his proper shape,
> Which else might work him danger or delay
> And now a stripling cherub he appears,
> Not of the prime, yet such as in his face
> Youth smiled celestial, and to every limb
> Suitable grace diffus'd, so well he feign'd:
> Under a coronet his flowing hair
> In curls on either cheek play'd; wings he wore
> Of many a colour'd plume sprinkled with gold,
> His habit fit for speed succinct, and held
> Before his decent steps a silver wand.    [PL III, 621-44]

The figures introduced here have all the elegance and precision of a Greek statue; glossy and impurpled, tinged with golden light, and musical as the strings of Memnon's harp![10]

Again, nothing can be more magnificent than the portrait of Beelzebub:

> With Atlantean shoulders fit to bear
> The weight of mightiest monarchies.    [PL II, 306-7]

Or the comparison of Satan, as he 'lay floating many a rood,' to 'that sea beast,'

> Leviathan, which God of all his works
> Created hugest that swim the ocean-stream!    [PL I, 196ff.]

What a force of imagination is there in this last expression! What an idea it conveys of the size of that hugest of created beings, as if it shrunk up the ocean to a stream, and took up the sea in its nostrils as a very little thing? Force of style is one of Milton's greatest excellences. Hence, perhaps, he stimulates us more in the reading, and less afterwards. The way to defend Milton against all impugners, is to take down the book and read it.

Milton's blank verse is the only blank verse in the language (except Shakespeare's) that deserves the name of verse. Dr. Johnson, who had modelled his ideas of versification on the regular sing-song of Pope, condemns the *Paradise Lost* as harsh and unequal. I shall not pretend to say that this is not sometimes the case; for where a degree of excellence beyond the mechanical rules of art is attempted, the poet must sometimes fail. But I imagine that there are more perfect examples in Milton of musical expression, or of an adaptation of the sound and movement of the verse to the meaning of the passage, than in all our other writers, whether of rhyme or blank verse, put together (with the exception already mentioned). Spenser is the most harmonious of our stanza writers, as Dryden is the most sounding and varied of our rhymists. But in neither is there anything like the same ear for music, the same power of approximating the varieties of poetical to those of musical rhythm, as there is in our great epic poet. The sound of his lines is moulded into the expression of the sentiment, almost of the very image. They rise or fall, pause or hurry rapidly on, with exquisite art, but without the least trick or affectation, as the occasion seems to require.

The following are some of the finest instances:

> His hand was known
> In Heaven by many a tower'd structure high . . .
> Nor was his name unheard or unador'd
> In ancient Greece: and in the Ausonian land
> Men called him Mulciber: and how he fell
> From Heaven, they fabled, thrown by angry Jove
> Sheer o'er the chrystal battlements; from morn
> To noon he fell, from noon to dewy eve,
> A summer's day; and with the setting sun
> Dropt from the zenith like a falling star
> On Lemnos, the Ægean isle: thus they relate,
> Erring.                                    [*PL* 1, 732ff.]

> But chief the spacious hall . . .
> Thick swarm'd, both on the ground and in the air,
> Brush'd with the hiss of rustling wings. As bees
> In spring time, when the sun with Taurus rides,
> Pour forth their populous youth about the hive
> In clusters; they among fresh dews and flow'rs
> Fly to and fro: or on the smoothed plank,

The suburb of their straw-built citadel,
New rubb'd with balm, expatiate and confer
Their state affairs. So thick the airy crowd
Swarm'd and were straiten'd; till the signal giv'n,
Behold a wonder! They but now who seem'd
In bigness to surpass earth's giant sons,
Now less than smallest dwarfs, in narrow room
Throng numberless, like that Pygmean race
Beyond the Indian mount, or fairy elves,
Whose midnight revels by a forest side
Or fountain, some belated peasant sees,
Or dreams he sees, while over-head the moon
Sits arbitress, and nearer to the earth
Wheels her pale course: they on their mirth and dance
Intent, with jocund music charm his ear;
At once with joy and fear his heart rebounds.

[*PL* I, 762ff.]

I can only give another instance, though I have some difficulty in leaving off.

Round he surveys (and well might, where he stood
So high above the circling canopy
Of night's extended shade) from th' eastern point
Of Libra to the fleecy star that bears
Andromeda far off Atlantic seas
Beyond the horizon: then from pole to pole
He views in breadth, and without longer pause
Down right into the world's first region throws
His flight precipitant, and winds with ease
Through the pure marble air his oblique way
Amongst innumerable stars that shone
Stars distant, but nigh hand seem'd other worlds;
Or other worlds they seem'd or happy isles, etc.

[*PL* III, 555–67]

The verse, in this exquisitely modulated passage, floats up and down as if it had itself wings. Milton has himself given us the theory of his versification—

Such as the meeting soul may pierce
In notes with many a winding bout
Of linked sweetness long drawn out.[11]

Dr. Johnson and Pope would have converted his vaulting Pegasus into a rocking-horse. Read any other blank verse but Milton's—Thomson's, Young's, Cowper's, Wordsworth's— and it will be found, from the want of the same insight into 'the hidden soul of harmony,' to be mere lumbering prose.

To proceed to a consideration of the merits of *Paradise Lost*, in the most essential point of view, I mean as to the poetry of character and passion. I shall say nothing of the fable,[12] or of other technical objections or excellences; but I shall try to explain at once the foundation of the interest belonging to the poem. I am ready to give up the dialogues in Heaven, where, as Pope justly observes, 'God the Father turns a school-divine';[13] nor do I consider the battle of the angels as the climax of sublimity, or the most successful effort of Milton's pen. In a word, the interest of the poem arises from the daring ambition and fierce passions of Satan, and from the account of the paradisaical happiness, and the loss of it by our first parents. Three-fourths of the work are taken up with these characters, and nearly all that relates to them is unmixed sublimity and beauty. The two first books alone are like two massy pillars of solid gold.

Satan is the most heroic subject that ever was chosen for a poem; and the execution is as perfect as the design is lofty. He was the first of created beings, who, for endeavouring to be equal with the highest, and to divide the empire of heaven with the Almighty, was hurled down to hell. His aim was no less than the throne of the universe; his means, myriads of angelic armies bright, the third part of the heavens, whom he lured after him with his countenance, and who durst defy the Omnipotent in arms. His ambition was the greatest, and his punishment was the greatest; but not so his despair, for his fortitude was as great as his sufferings. His strength of mind was matchless as his strength of body; the vastness of his designs did not surpass the firm, inflexible determination with which he submitted to his irreversible doom, and final loss of all good. His power of action and of suffering was equal. He was the greatest power that was ever overthrown, with the strongest will left to resist or to endure. He was baffled, not confounded. He stood like a tower; or

> As when Heaven's fire
> Hath scathed the forest oaks or mountain pines.
> [*PL* I, 612–3]

He was still surrounded with hosts of rebel angels, armed warriors, who own him as their sovereign leader, and with whose fate he sympathises as he views them round, far as the eye can reach; though he keeps aloof from them in his own mind, and holds supreme counsel only with his own breast. An outcast from Heaven, Hell trembles beneath his feet, Sin and Death are at his heels, and mankind are his easy prey.

> All is not lost; th' unconquerable will,
> And study of revenge, immortal hate,
> And courage never to submit or yield,
> And what else is not to be overcome,[14]
>
> [PL I, 106–9]

are still his. The sense of his punishment seems lost in the magnitude of it; the fierceness of tormenting flames is qualified and made innoxious by the greater fierceness of his pride; the loss of infinite happiness to himself is compensated in thought, by the power of inflicting infinite misery on others. Yet Satan is not the principle of malignity, or of the abstract love of evil—but of the abstract love of power, of pride, of self-will personified, to which last principle all other good and evil, and even his own, are subordinate. From this principle he never once flinches. His love of power and contempt for suffering are never once relaxed from the highest pitch of intensity. His thoughts burn like a hell within him; but the power of thought holds dominion in his mind over every other consideration. The consciousness of a determined purpose, of 'that intellectual being, those thoughts that wander through eternity,' though accompanied with endless pain, he prefers to nonentity, to 'being swallowed up and lost in the wide womb of uncreated night.'[15] He expresses the sum and substance of all ambition in one line. 'Fallen cherub, to be weak is miserable, doing or suffering!'[16] After such a conflict as his, and such a defeat, to retreat in order, to rally, to make terms, to exist at all, is something; but he does more than this—he founds a new empire in hell, and from it conquers this new world, whither he bends his undaunted flight, forcing his way through nether and surrounding fires. The poet has not in all this given us a mere shadowy outline; the strength is equal to the magnitude of the conception. The Achilles of Homer is not more distinct; the Titans were not more vast; Prometheus chained to his rock was not a more terrific example of suffering and of crime. Wherever the figure of Satan is introduced, whether he walks or flies, 'rising aloft incumbent on the dusky air,'[17] it is illustrated with the most striking and appropriate images: so that we see it always before us, gigantic, irregular, portentous, uneasy, and disturbed—but dazzling in its faded splendour, the clouded ruins of a god. The deformity of Satan is only in the depravity of his will; he has no bodily deformity to excite our loathing or disgust. The horns and tail are not there, poor emblems of the unbending, unconquered spirit, of the writhing agonies within. Milton was too magnanimous and open an antagonist to support his argument by the bye-tricks of a hump and

cloven foot; to bring into the fair field of controversy the good
old catholic prejudices of which Tasso and Dante have availed
themselves, and which the mystic German critics would restore. He relied on the justice of his cause, and did not scruple
to give the devil his due. Some persons may think that he
has carried his liberality too far, and injured the cause he
professed to espouse by making him the chief person in his
poem. Considering the nature of his subject, he would be
equally in danger of running into this fault, from his faith in
religion, and his love of rebellion; and perhaps each of these
motives had its full share in determining the choice of his
subject.

Not only the figure of Satan, but his speeches in council,
his soliloquies, his address to Eve, his share in the war in
heaven, or in the fall of man, show the same decided superiority of character. To give only one instance, almost the
first speech he makes:

> Is this the region, this the soil, the clime,
> Said then the lost archangel, this the seat
> That we must change for Heaven; this mournful gloom
> For that celestial light? Be it so, since he
> Who now is sov'rain can dispose and bid
> What shall be right: farthest from him is best,
> Whom reason hath equal'd, force hath made supreme
> Above his equals. Farewell happy fields,
> Where joy for ever dwells: Hail horrors, hail
> Infernal world, and thou profoundest Hell,
> Receive thy new possessor: one who brings
> A mind not to be chang'd by place or time.
> The mind is its own place, and in itself
> Can make a Heav'n of Hell, a Hell of Heav'n.
> What matter where, if I be still the same,
> And what I should be, all but less than he
> Whom thunder hath made greater? Here at least
> We shall be free; th' Almighty hath not built
> Here for his envy, will not drive us hence:
> Here we may reign secure, and in my choice
> To reign is worth ambition, though in Hell:
> Better to reign in Hell, than serve in Heaven.
>
> [PL I, 242–63]

The whole of the speeches and debates in Pandemonium
are well worthy of the place and the occasion—with Gods for
speakers, and angels and archangels for hearers. There is a
decided manly tone in the arguments and sentiments, an eloquent dogmatism, as if each person spoke from thorough conviction; an excellence which Milton probably borrowed from

his spirit of partisanship, or else his spirit of partisanship from the natural firmness and vigour of his mind. In this respect Milton resembles Dante (the only modern writer with whom he has anything in common), and it is remarkable that Dante, as well as Milton, was a political partisan. That approximation to the severity of impassioned prose which has been made an objection to Milton's poetry, and which is chiefly to be met with in these bitter invectives, is one of its great excellences. The author might here turn his philippics against Salmasius[18] to good account. The rout in Heaven is like the fall of some mighty structure, nodding to its base, 'with hideous ruin and combustion down.'[19] But, perhaps, of all the passages in *Paradise Lost,* the description of the employments of the angels during the absence of Satan, some of whom 'retreated in a silent valley, sing with notes angelical to many a harp their own heroic deeds and hapless fall by doom of battle,'[20] is the most perfect example of mingled pathos and sublimity.—What proves the truth of this noble picture in every part, and that the frequent complaint of want of interest in it is the fault of the reader, not of the poet, is that when any interest of a practical kind takes a shape that can be at all turned into this (and there is little doubt that Milton had some such in his eye in writing it), each party converts it to its own purposes, feels the absolute identity of these abstracted and high speculations; and that, in fact, a noted political writer of the present day[21] has exhausted nearly the whole account of Satan in the *Paradise Lost,* by applying it to a character whom he considered as after the devil (though I do not know whether he would make even that exception), the greatest enemy of the human race.[22] This may serve to show that Milton's Satan is not a very insipid personage.

Of Adam and Eve it has been said, that the ordinary reader can feel little interest in them, because they have none of the passions, pursuits, or even relations of human life, except that of man and wife, the least interesting of all others, if not to the parties concerned, at least to the by-standers. The preference has on this account been given to Homer, who, it is said, has left very vivid and infinitely diversified pictures of all the passions and affections, public and private, incident to human nature—the relations of son, of brother, parent, friend, citizen, and many others. Longinus preferred the *Iliad* to the *Odyssey,* on account of the greater number of battles it contains; but I can neither agree to his criticism, or assent to the present objection. It is true, there is little action in this part of Milton's poem; but there is much repose, and more enjoyment. There are none of the every-day occurrences, contentions, disputes, wars, fightings, feuds, jealousies, trades, professions, liveries, and common handicrafts of life; 'no kind of traffic; letters are not known; no use of service, of riches, poverty, contract, succession, bourne, bound of land, tilth, vineyard none; no occupation, no treason, felony, sword, pike, knife, gun, nor need of any engine.'[23] So much the better; thank Heaven, all these were yet to come. But still the die was cast, and in them our doom was sealed. In them

> The generations were prepared; the pangs,
> The internal pangs, were ready, the dread strife
> Of poor humanity's afflicted will,
> Struggling in vain with ruthless destiny.[24]

In their first false step we trace all our future woe, with loss of Eden. But there was a short and precious interval between, like the first blush of morning before the day is overcast with tempest, the dawn of the world, the birth of nature from 'the unapparent deep,'[25] with its first dews and freshness on its cheek, breathing odours. Theirs was the first delicious taste of life, and on them depended all that was to come of it. In them hung trembling all our hopes and fears. They were as yet alone in the world, in the eye of nature, wondering at their new being, full of enjoyment and enraptured with one another, with the voice of their Maker walking in the garden, and ministering angels attendant on their steps, winged messengers from heaven like rosy clouds descending in their sight. Nature played around them her virgin fancies wild; and spread for them a repast where no crude surfeit reigned. Was there nothing in this scene, which God and nature alone witnessed, to interest a modern critic? What need was there of action, where the heart was full of bliss and innocence without it! They had nothing to do but feel their own happiness, and 'know to know no more.'[26] 'They toiled not, neither did they spin; yet Solomon in all his glory was not arrayed like one of these.'[27] All things seem to acquire fresh sweetness, and to be clothed with fresh beauty in their sight. They tasted as it were for themselves and us, of all that there ever was pure in human bliss. 'In them the burthen of the mystery, the heavy and the weary weight of all this unintelligible world, is lightened.'[28] They stood awhile perfect, but they afterwards fell, and were driven out of Paradise, tasting the first fruits of bitterness as they had done of bliss. But their pangs were such as a pure spirit might feel at the sight—their tears 'such as angels weep.'[29] The pathos is of that mild contemplative kind which arises from regret for the loss of unspeakable happiness, and resignation to inevitable fate.

There is none of the fierceness of intemperate passion, none of the agony of mind and turbulence of action, which is the result of the habitual struggles of the will with circumstances, irritated by repeated disappointment, and constantly setting its desires most eagerly on that which there is an impossibility of attaining. This would have destroyed the beauty of the whole picture. They had received their unlooked-for happiness as a free gift from their Creator's hands, and they submitted to its loss, not without sorrow, but without impious and stubborn repining.

> In either hand the hast'ning angel caught
> Our ling'ring parents, and to th' eastern gate
> Led them direct, and down the cliff as fast
> To the subjected plain; then disappear'd.
> They looking back, all th' eastern side beheld
> Of Paradise, so late their happy seat,
> Wav'd over by that flaming brand, the gate
> With dreadful faces throng'd, and fiery arms:
> Some natural tears they dropt, but wip'd them soon;
> The world was all before them, where to choose
> Their place of rest, and Providence their guide.

# On the Periodical Essayists*

## 'THE PROPER STUDY OF MANKIND IS MAN'[1]

I NOW COME to speak of that sort of writing which has been so successfully cultivated in this country by our periodical Essayists, and which consists in applying the talents and resources of the mind to all that mixed mass of human affairs, which, though not included under the head of any regular art, science, or profession, falls under the cognizance of the writer, and 'comes home to the business and bosoms of men.'[2] *Quicquid agunt homines nostri farrago libelli*,[3] is the general motto of this department of literature. It does not treat of minerals or fossils, of the virtues of plants, or the influence of planets; it does not meddle with forms of belief, or systems of philosophy, nor launch into the world of spiritual existences; but it makes familiar with the world of men and women, records their actions, assigns their motives, exhibits their whims, characterises their pursuits in all their singular and endless variety, ridicules their absurdities, exposes their inconsistencies, 'holds the mirror up to nature, and shows the very age and body of the time its form and pressure;'[4] takes minutes of our dress, air, looks, words, thoughts, and actions; shows us what we are, and what we are not; plays the whole game of human life over before us, and by making us enlightened spectators of its many-coloured scenes, enables us (if possible) to become tolerably reasonable agents in the one in which we have to perform a part. 'The act and practic part of life is thus made the mistress of our theorique.'[5] It is the best and most natural course of study. It is in morals and manners what the experimental is in natural philosophy, as opposed to the dogmatical method. It does not deal in sweeping clauses of proscription and anathema, but in nice distinc-

* [*Lectures on the English Comic Writers* V.]

tions and liberal constructions. It makes up its general accounts from details, its few theories from many facts. It does not try to prove all black or all white as it wishes, but lays on the intermediate colours (and most of them not unpleasing ones), as it finds them blended with 'the web of our life, which is of a mingled yarn, good and ill together.'[6] It inquires what human life is and has been, to show what it ought to be. It follows it into courts and camps, into town and country, into rustic sports or learned disputations, into the various shades of prejudice or ignorance, of refinement or barbarism, into its private haunts or public pageants, into its weaknesses and littlenesses, its professions and its practices —before it pretends to distinguish right from wrong, or one thing from another. How, indeed, should it do so otherwise?

> Quid sit pulchrum, quid turpe, quid utile, quid non,
> Plenius et melius Chrysippo et Crantore dicit.[7]

The writers I speak of are, if not moral philosophers, moral historians, and that's better: or if they are both, they found the one character upon the other; their premises precede their conclusions; and we put faith in their testimony, for we know that it is true.

Montaigne was the first person who in his Essays led the way to this kind of writing among the moderns.[8] The great merit of Montaigne then was, that he may be said to have been the first who had the courage to say as an author what he felt as a man. And as courage is generally the effect of conscious strength, he was probably led to do so by the richness, truth, and force of his own observations on books and men. He was, in the truest sense, a man of original mind, that is, he had the power of looking at things for himself, or as they really were, instead of blindly trusting to, and fondly repeating what others told him that they were. He got rid of the go-cart of prejudice and affectation, with the learned lumber that follows at their heels, because he could do without them. In taking up his pen he did not set up for a philosopher, wit, orator, or moralist, but he became all these by merely daring to tell us whatever passed through his mind, in its naked simplicity and force, that he thought any ways worth communicating. He did not, in the abstract character of an author, undertake to say all that could be said upon a subject, but what in his capacity as an inquirer after truth he happened to know about it. He was neither a pedant nor a bigot. He neither supposed that he was bound to know all things, nor that all things were bound to conform to what he had fancied or would have them to be. In treating of men and manners, he spoke of them as he found them, not according to preconceived notions and abstract dogmas; and he began by teaching us what he himself was. In criticising books he did not compare them with rules and systems, but told us what he saw to like or dislike in them. He did not take his standard of excellence 'according to an exact scale' of Aristotle, or fall out with a work that was good for anything, because 'not one of the angles at the four corners was a right one.'[9] He was, in a word, the first author who was not a book-maker, and who wrote not to make converts of others to established creeds and prejudices, but to satisfy his own mind of the truth of things. In this respect we know not which to be most charmed with, the author or the man. There is an inexpressible frankness and sincerity, as well as power, in what he writes. There is no attempt at imposition or concealment, no juggling tricks or solemn mouthing, no laboured attempts at proving himself always in the right, and everybody else in the wrong; he says what is uppermost, lays open what floats at the top or the bottom of his mind, and deserves Pope's character of him, where he professes to

> pour out all as plain
> As downright Shippen, or as old Montaigne.* [10]

He does not converse with us like a pedagogue with his pupil, whom he wishes to make as great a blockhead as himself, but like a philosopher and friend who has passed through life with thought and observation, and is willing to enable others to pass through it with pleasure and profit. A writer of this stamp, I confess, appears to me as much superior to a common bookworm, as a library of real books is superior to a mere book-case, painted and lettered on the outside with the names of celebrated works. As he was the first to attempt this new way of writing, so the same strong natural impulse which prompted the undertaking, carried him to the end of his career. The same force and honesty of mind which urged him to throw off the shackles of custom and prejudice, would enable him to complete his triumph over them. He has left little for his successors to achieve in the way of just and original speculation on human life. Nearly all the thinking of the two last centuries of that kind which the French denominate *morale observatrice*,[11] is to be found in Montaigne's *Essays:* there is the germ, at least, and generally much more.

* Why Pope should say in reference to him, 'Or *more wise* Charron,'[12] is not easy to determine. [w. h.]

He sowed the seed and cleared away the rubbish, even where others have reaped the fruit, or cultivated and decorated the soil to a greater degree of nicety and perfection. There is no one to whom the old Latin adage is more applicable than to Montaigne, 'Pereant isti qui ante nos nostra dixerunt.'[13] There has been no new impulse given to thought since his time. Among the specimens of criticisms on authors which he has left us, are those on Virgil, Ovid, and Boccaccio, in the account of books which he thinks worth reading, or (which is the same thing) which he finds he can read in his old age, and which may be reckoned among the few criticisms which are worth reading at any age.*

Montaigne's *Essays* were translated into English by Charles Cotton, who was one of the wits and poets of the age of Charles II; and Lord Halifax, one of the noble critics of that day, declared it to be 'the book in the world he was the best pleased with.' This mode of familiar Essay-writing, free from the trammels of the schools, and the airs of professed authorship, was successfully imitated, about the same time, by Cowley and Sir William Temple, in their miscellaneous Es-

---

* As an instance of his general power of reasoning, I shall give his chapter entitled *One Man's Profit is another's Loss*, in which he has nearly anticipated Mandeville's celebrated paradox of private vices being public benefits:

'Demades, the Athenian, condemned a fellow-citizen, who furnished out funerals, for demanding too great a price for his goods: and if he got an estate, it must be by the death of a great many people: but I think it a sentence ill grounded, forasmuch as no profit can be made, but at the expense of some other person, and that every kind of gain is by that rule liable to be condemned. The tradesman thrives by the debauchery of youth, and the farmer by the dearness of corn; the architect by the ruin of buildings, the officers of justice by quarrels and law-suits; nay, even the honour and function of divines is owing to our mortality and vices. No physician takes pleasure in the health even of his best friends, said the ancient Greek comedian, nor soldier in the peace of his country; and so of the rest. And, what is yet worse, let every one but examine his own heart, and he will find that his private wishes spring and grow up at the expense of some other person. Upon which consideration this thought came into my head, that nature does not hereby deviate from her general policy; for the naturalists hold, that the birth, nourishment, and increase of any one thing is the decay and corruption of another:

> *Nam quodcunque suis mutatum finibus exit,*
> *Continuo hoc mors est illius, quod fuit ante.*[14]i.e.

For what from its own confines chang'd doth pass,
Is straight the death of what before it was.'

*Vol.* i, *Chap.* xxi. [w. h.]

says, which are very agreeable and learned talking upon paper. Lord Shaftesbury,[15] on the contrary, who aimed at the same easy, *dégagé*[16] mode of communicating his thoughts to the world, has quite spoiled his matter, which is sometimes valuable, by his manner, in which he carries a certain flaunting, flowery, figurative, flirting style of amicable condescension to the reader, to an excess more tantalising than the most starched and ridiculous formality of the age of James I. There is nothing so tormenting as the affectation of ease and freedom from affectation.

The ice being thus thawed, and the barrier that kept authors at a distance from common sense and feeling broken through, the transition was not difficult from Montaigne and his imitators, to our Periodical Essayists. These last applied the same unrestrained expression of their thoughts to the more immediate and passing scenes of life, to temporary and local matters; and in order to discharge the invidious office of *Censor Morum*[17] more freely, and with less responsibility, assumed some fictitious and humorous disguise, which, however, in a great degree corresponded to their own peculiar habits and character. By thus concealing their own name and person under the title of the Tatler, Spectator, etc. they were enabled to inform us more fully of what was passing in the world, while the dramatic contrast and ironical point of view to which the whole is subjected, added a greater liveliness and *piquancy* to the descriptions. The philosopher and wit here commences newsmonger, makes himself master of 'the perfect spy o' th' time,'[18] and from his various walks and turns through life, brings home little curious specimens of the humours, opinions, and manners of his contemporaries, as the botanist brings home different plants and weeds, or the mineralogist different shells and fossils, to illustrate their several theories, and be useful to mankind.

The first of these papers that was attempted in this country was set up by Steele in the beginning of the last century;[19] and of all our periodical Essayists, the *Tatler* (for that was the name he assumed) has always appeared to me the most amusing and agreeable. Montaigne, whom I have proposed to consider as the father of this kind of personal authorship among the moderns, in which the reader is admitted behind the curtain, and sits down with the writer in his gown and slippers, was a most magnanimous and undisguised egotist; but Isaac Bickerstaff Esq.[20] was the more disinterested gossip of the two. The French author is contented to describe the peculiarities of his own mind and constitution, which he does with a copious and unsparing hand. The English journalist good-naturedly lets you into the secret both of his own

affairs and those of others. A young lady, on the other side
Temple Bar, cannot be seen at her glass for half a day together, but Mr. Bickerstaff takes due notice of it; and he has
the first intelligence of the symptoms of the *belle* passion
appearing in any young gentleman at the West-end of the
town. The departures and arrivals of widows with handsome
jointures, either to bury their grief in the country, or to procure a second husband in town, are punctually recorded in
his pages. He is well acquainted with the celebrated beauties
of the preceding age at the court of Charles II; and the old
gentleman (as he feigns himself) often grows romantic in
recounting 'the disastrous strokes which his youth suffered'
from the glances of their bright eyes, and their unaccountable
caprices. In particular, he dwells with a secret satisfaction on
the recollection of one of his mistresses, who left him for a
richer rival, and whose constant reproach to her husband, on
occasion of any quarrel between them, was 'I, that might
have married the famous Mr. Bickerstaff, to be treated in this
manner!'[21] The club at the Trumpet[22] consists of a set of persons almost as well worth knowing as himself. The cavalcade
of the justice of the peace, the knight of the shire, the country
squire, and the young gentleman, his nephew, who came to
wait on him at his chambers, in such form and ceremony,[23]
seem not to have settled the order of their precedence to this
hour; and I should hope that the upholsterer and his companions,[24] who used to sun themselves in the Green Park, and
who broke their rest and fortunes to maintain the balance of
power in Europe, stand as fair a chance for immortality as some
modern politicians. Mr. Bickerstaff himself is a gentleman
and a scholar, a humourist, and a man of the world; with a
great deal of nice easy *naïveté* about him. If he walks out and
is caught in a shower of rain, he makes amends for this unlucky accident by a criticism on the shower in Virgil, and
concludes with a burlesque copy of verses on a city-shower.[25]
He entertains us, when he dates from his own apartment,
with a quotation from Plutarch, or a moral reflection; from the
Grecian coffee-house with politics; and from Wills', or the
Temple, with the poets and players, the beaux and men of wit
and pleasure about town. In reading the pages of the *Tatler*,
we seem as if suddenly carried back to the age of Queen
Anne, of toupees and full-bottomed periwigs. The whole appearance of our dress and manners undergoes a delightful
metamorphosis. The beaux and the belles are of a quite different species from what they are at present; we distinguish
the dappers, the smarts, and the pretty fellows, as they pass
by Mr. Lilly's shop-windows in the Strand;[26] we are intro-

duced to Betterton[27] and Mrs. Oldfield behind the scenes; are made familiar with the persons and performances of Will Estcourt or Tom Durfey; we listen to a dispute at a tavern, on the merits of the Duke of Marlborough, or Marshal Turenne; or are present at the first rehearsal of a play by Vanbrugh, or the reading of a new poem by Mr. Pope. The privilege of thus virtually transporting ourselves to past times, is even greater than that of visiting distant places in reality. London, a hundred years ago, would be much better worth seeing than Paris at the present moment.

It will be said, that all this is to be found, in the same or a greater degree, in the *Spectator*.[28] For myself, I do not think so; or at least, there is in the last work a much greater proportion of commonplace matter. I have, on this account, always preferred the *Tatler* to the *Spectator*. Whether it is owing to my having been earlier or better acquainted with the one than the other, my pleasure in reading these two admirable works is not in proportion to their comparative reputation. The *Tatler* contains only half the number of volumes, and, I will venture to say, nearly an equal quantity of sterling wit and sense. 'The first sprightly runnings'[29] are there; it has more of the original spirit, more of the freshness and stamp of nature. The indications of character and strokes of humour are more true and frequent; the reflections that suggest themselves arise more from the occasion, and are less spun out into regular dissertations. They are more like the remarks which occur in sensible conversation, and less like a lecture. Something is left to the understanding of the reader. Steele seems to have gone into his closet chiefly to set down what he observed out of doors. Addison seems to have spent most of his time in his study, and to have spun out and wire-drawn the hints, which he borrowed from Steele, or took from nature, to the utmost. I am far from wishing to depreciate Addison's talents, but I am anxious to do justice to Steele, who was, I think, upon the whole, a less artificial and more original writer. The humorous descriptions of Steele resemble loose sketches, or fragments of a comedy; those of Addison are rather comments or ingenious paraphrases on the genuine text. The characters of the club not only in the *Tatler*, but in the *Spectator*, were drawn by Steele. That of Sir Roger de Coverley[30] is among the number. Addison has, however, gained himself immortal honour by his manner of filling up this last character. Who is there that can forget, or be insensible to, the inimitable nameless graces and varied traits of nature and of old English character in it—to his unpretending virtues and amiable weaknesses—to his modesty, generosity, hospitality, and eccentric

whims—to the respect of his neighbours, and the affection of
his domestics—to his wayward, hopeless, secret passion for his
fair enemy, the widow, in which there is more of real romance
and true delicacy, than in a thousand tales of knight-errantry—
(we perceive the hectic flush of his cheek, the faltering of his
tongue in speaking of her bewitching airs and 'the whiteness
of her hand')[31]—to the havoc he makes among the game in his
neighbourhood[32]—to his speech from the bench, to show the
Spectator what is thought of him in the country[33]—to his unwillingness to be put up as a sign-post, and his having his own
likeness turned into the Saracen's head[34]—to his gentle reproof
of the baggage of a gipsy that tells him 'he has a widow in his
line of life'[35]—to his doubts as to the existence of witch-craft,
and protection of reputed witches[36]—to his account of the
family pictures,[37] and his choice of a chaplain[38]—to his falling
asleep at church, and his reproof of John Williams, as soon
as he recovered from his nap, for talking in sermon-time.[39]
The characters of Will Wimble,[40] and Will Honeycomb[41] are
not a whit behind their friend, Sir Roger, in delicacy and
felicity. The delightful simplicity and good-humoured offi-
ciousness in the one, are set off by the graceful affectation and
courtly pretension in the other. How long since I first became
acquainted with these two characters in the *Spectator!* What
old-fashioned friends they seem, and yet I am not tired of
them, like so many other friends, nor they of me! How airy
these abstractions of the poet's pen stream over the dawn of
our acquaintance with human life! how they glance their fairest colours on the prospect before us! how pure they remain
in it to the last, like the rainbow in the evening-cloud, which
the rude hand of time and experience can neither soil nor
dissipate! What a pity that we cannot find the reality, and yet
if we did, the dream would be over. I once thought I knew a
Will Wimble, and Will Honeycomb, but they turned out but
indifferently; the originals in the *Spectator* still read, word
for word, the same that they always did. We have only to turn
to the page, and find them where we left them!—Many of the
most exquisite pieces in the *Tatler*, it is to be observed, are
Addison's, as the Court of Honour,[42] and the Personification
of Musical Instruments,[43] with almost all those papers that
form regular sets or series. I do not know whether the picture
of the family of an old college acquaintance, in the *Tatler*,
where the children run to let Mr. Bickerstaff in at the door,
and where the one that loses the race that way, turns back to
tell the father that he is come; with the nice gradation of
incredulity in the little boy, who is got into Guy of War-
wick, and the Seven Champions, and who shakes his head at

the improbability of Æsop's *Fables,* is Steele's or Addison's, though I believe it belongs to the former.[44] The account of the two sisters, one of whom held up her head higher than ordinary, from having on a pair of flowered garters,[45] and that of the married lady who complained to the *Tatler* of the neglect of her husband, with her answers to some *home* questions that were put to her,[46] are unquestionably Steele's.—If the *Tatler* is not inferior to the *Spectator* as a record of manners and character, it is superior to it in the interest of many of the stories. Several of the incidents related there by Steele have never been surpassed in the heart-rending pathos of private distress. I might refer to those of the lover and his mistress, when the theatre, in which they were, caught fire;[47] of the bridegroom, who by accident kills his bride on the day of their marriage;[48] the story of Mr. Eustace and his wife;[49] and the fine dream about his own mistress when a youth.[50] What has given its superior reputation to the *Spectator,* is the greater gravity of its pretensions, its moral dissertations and critical reasonings, by which I confess myself less edified than by other things, which are thought more lightly of. Systems and opinions change, but nature is always true. It is the moral and didactic tone of the Spectator which makes us apt to think of Addison (according to Mandeville's sarcasm) as 'a parson in a tie-wig.'[51] Many of his moral Essays are, however, exquisitely beautiful and quite happy. Such are the reflections on cheerfulness, those in Westminster Abbey, on the Royal Exchange, and particularly some very affecting ones on the death of a young lady in the fourth volume. These, it must be allowed, are the perfection of elegant sermonising. His critical Essays are not so good. I prefer Steele's occasional selection of beautiful poetical passages, without any affectation of analysing their beauties, to Addison's finer-spun theories. The best criticism in the *Spectator,* that on the Cartoons of Raphael,[52] of which Mr. Fuseli has availed himself with great spirit in his Lectures,[53] is by Steele.* I owed this acknowledgment to a writer who has so often put me in good humour with myself, and everything about me, when few things else could, and when the tomes of casuistry and ecclesiastical history, with which the little duodecimo volumes of the *Tatler* were overwhelmed and surrounded, in the only library to which I had access when a boy, had tried their tranquillising effects

---

* The antithetical style and verbal paradoxes which Burke was so fond of, in which the epithet is a seeming contradiction to the substantive, such as 'proud submission and dignified obedience,' are, I think, first to be found in the *Tatler.* [w. h.]

upon me in vain. I had not long ago in my hands, by favour
of a friend, an original copy of the quarto edition of the *Tatler*,
with a list of the subscribers. It is curious to see some names
there which we should hardly think of (that of Sir Issac
Newton is among them), and also to observe the degree of
interest excited by those of the different persons, which is not
determined according to the rules of the Herald's College. One
literary name lasts as long as a whole race of heroes and their
descendants! The *Guardian*,[54] which followed the *Spectator*,
was, as may be supposed, inferior to it.

The dramatic and conversational turn which forms the distinguishing feature and greatest charm of the *Spectator* and
*Tatler*, is quite lost in the *Rambler*[55] by Dr. Johnson. There
is no reflected light thrown on human life from an assumed
character, nor any direct one from a display of the author's
own. The *Tatler* and *Spectator* are, as it were, made up of
notes and memorandums of the events and incidents of the
day, with finished studies after nature, and characters fresh
from the life, which the writer moralises upon, and turns to
account as they come before him: the *Rambler* is a collection
of moral Essays, or scholastic theses, written on set subjects,
and of which the individual characters and incidents are
merely artificial illustrations, brought in to give a pretended
relief to the dryness of didactic discussion. The *Rambler* is a
splendid and imposing common place book of general topics,
and rhetorical declamation on the conduct and business of
human life. In this sense, there is hardly a reflection that had
been suggested on such subjects which is not to be found in
this celebrated work, and there is, perhaps, hardly a reflection
to be found in it which had not been already suggested and
developed by some other author, or in the common course of
conversation. The mass of intellectual wealth here heaped
together is immense, but it is rather the result of gradual
accumulation, the produce of the general intellect, labouring
in the mine of knowledge and reflection, than dug out of the
quarry, and dragged into the light by the industry and sagacity
of a single mind. I am not here saying that Dr. Johnson was
a man without originality, compared with the ordinary run of
men's minds, but he was not a man of original thought or
genius, in the sense in which Montaigne or Lord Bacon was.
He opened no new vein of precious ore, nor did he light upon
any single pebbles of uncommon size and unrivalled lustre.
We seldom meet with anything to 'give us pause;' he does not
set us thinking for the first time. His reflections present themselves like reminiscences; do not disturb the ordinary march
of our thoughts; arrest our attention by the stateliness of their

appearance, and the costliness of their garb, but pass on and mingle with the throng of our impressions. After closing the volumes of the *Rambler*, there is nothing that we remember as a new truth gained to the mind, nothing indelibly stamped upon the memory; nor is there any passage that we wish to turn to as embodying any known principle or observation, with such force and beauty that justice can only be done to the idea in the author's own words. Such, for instance, are many of the passages to be found in Burke, which shine by their own light, belong to no class, have neither equal nor counterpart, and of which we say that no one but the author could have written them! There is neither the same boldness of design, nor mastery of execution in Johnson. In the one, the spark of genius seems to have met with its congenial matter: the shaft is sped; the forked lightning dresses up the face of nature in ghastly smiles, and the loud thunder rolls far away from the ruin that is made. Dr. Johnson's style, on the contrary, resembles rather the rumbling of mimic thunder at one of our theatres; and the light he throws upon a subject is like the dazzling effect of phosphorus, or an *ignis fatuus*[56] of words. There is a wide difference, however, between perfect originality and perfect commonplace: neither ideas nor expressions are trite or vulgar because they are not quite new. They are valuable, and ought to be repeated, if they have not become quite common; and Johnson's style both of reasoning and imagery holds the middle rank between startling novelty and vapid commonplace. Johnson has as much originality of thinking as Addison; but then he wants his familiarity of illustration, knowledge of character, and delightful humour.—What most distinguishes Dr. Johnson from other writers is the pomp and uniformity of his style. All his periods are cast in the same mould, are of the same size and shape, and consequently have little fitness to the variety of things he professes to treat of. His subjects are familiar, but the author is always upon stilts. He has neither ease nor simplicity, and his efforts at playfulness, in part, remind one of the lines in Milton:

> The elephant
> To make them sport wreath'd his proboscis lithe.[57]

His Letters from Correspondents, in particular, are more pompous and unwieldy than what he writes in his own person. This want of relaxation and variety of manner has, I think, after the first effects of novelty and surprise were over, been prejudicial to the matter. It takes from the general power, not only to please, but to instruct. The monotony of style produces an apparent monotony of ideas. What is really striking and valuable, is lost in the vain ostentation and circumlocution of the expression; for when we find the same pains and pomp of diction bestowed upon the most trifling as upon the most important parts of a sentence or discourse, we grow tired of distinguishing between pretension and reality, and are disposed to confound the tinsel and bombast of the phraseology with want of weight in the thoughts. Thus, from the imposing and oracular nature of the style, people are tempted at first to imagine that our author's speculations are all wisdom and profundity: till having found out their mistake in some instances, they suppose that there is nothing but common-place in them, concealed under verbiage and pedantry; and in both they are wrong. The fault of Dr. Johnson's style is, that it reduces all things to the same artificial and unmeaning level. It destroys all shades of difference, the association between words and things. It is a perpetual paradox and innovation. He condescends to the familiar till we are ashamed of our interest in it: he expands the little till it looks big. 'If he were to write a fable of little fishes,' as Goldsmith said of him, 'he would make them speak like great whales.'[58] We can no more distinguish the most familiar objects in his descriptions of them, than we can a well-known face under a huge painted mask. The structure of his sentences, which was his own invention, and which has been generally imitated since his time, is a species of rhyming in prose, where one clause answers to another in measure and quantity, like the tagging of syllables at the end of a verse; the close of the period follows as mechanically as the oscillation of a pendulum, the sense is balanced with the sound; each sentence, revolving round its centre of gravity, is contained with itself like a couplet, and each paragraph forms itself into a stanza. Dr. Johnson is also a complete balance-master in the topics of morality. He never encourages hope, but he counteracts it by fear; he never elicits a truth, but he suggests some objection in answer to it. He seizes and alternately quits the clue of reason, lest it should involve him in the labyrinths of endless error: he wants confidence in himself and his fellows. He dares not trust himself with the immediate impressions of things, for fear of compromising his dignity; or follow them into their consequences, for fear of committing his prejudices. His timidity is the result, not of ignorance, but of morbid apprehension. 'He runs the great circle, and is still at home.'[59] No advance is made by his writings in any sentiment, or mode of reasoning. Out of the pale of established authority and received dogmas, all is sceptical, loose, and desultory: he seems in imagination to strengthen the dominion of prejudice, as he weakens and dissipates that of reason; and round the rock of faith and power, on the edge of which he slumbers blindfold and uneasy, the waves and billows of uncertain and dangerous opinion roar and heave for evermore. His *Rasselas* is the most melancholy and debilitating moral speculation that ever was put forth. Doubtful of the faculties of his mind, as of his organs of vision, Johnson trusted only to his feelings and his fears. He cultivated a belief in witches as an out-guard to the evidences of religion; and abused Milton, and patronised Lauder,[60] in spite of his aversion to his countrymen, as a step to secure the existing establishment in church and state. This was neither right feeling nor sound logic.

The most triumphant record of the talents and character of Johnson is to be found in Boswell's Life of him. The man was superior to the author. When he threw aside his pen, which he regarded as an incumbrance, he became not only learned and thoughtful, but acute, witty, humorous, natural, honest; hearty and determined, 'the king of good fellows and wale of old men.'[61] There are as many smart repartees, profound remarks, and keen invectives to be found in Boswell's 'inventory of all he said,' as are recorded of any celebrated man. The life and dramatic play of his conversation forms a contrast to his written works. His natural powers and undisguised opinions were called out in convivial intercourse. In public, he practised with the foils on: in private, he unsheathed the sword of controversy, and it was 'the Ebro's temper.' The eagerness of opposition roused him from his natural sluggishness and acquired timidity; he returned blow for blow; and whether the trial were of argument or wit, none of his rivals could boast much of the encounter. Burke seems to have been the only person who had a chance with him: and it is the unpardonable sin of Boswell's work, that he has purposely omitted their combats of strength and skill. Goldsmith asked, 'Does he wind into a subject like a serpent, as Burke does?'[62] And when exhausted with sickness, he himself said, 'If that fellow Burke were here now, he would kill me.'[63] It is to be observed, that Johnson's colloquial style was as blunt, direct, and downright, as his style of studied composition was involved and circuitous. As when Topham Beauclerc and Langton knocked him up at his chambers, at three in the morning, and he came to the door with the poker in his hand, but seeing them, exclaimed, 'What, is it you, my lads? then I'll have a frisk with you!' and he afterwards reproaches Langton, who was a literary milksop, for leaving them to go to an engagement 'with some *un-idead* girls.'[64] What words to come from the mouth of the great moralist and lexicographer! His good deeds were as many as his good sayings. His domestic habits, his tenderness to servants, and readiness to oblige his friends; the quantity of strong tea that he drank to keep down sad thoughts; his many labours reluctantly begun, and irresolutely laid aside; his honest acknowledgement of his own, and indulgence to the weaknesses of others; his throwing himself back in the post-chaise with Boswell, and saying, 'Now I think I am a good-humoured fellow,'[65] though nobody thought him so, and yet he was; his quitting the society of Garrick and his actresses, and his reason for it;[66] his dining with Wilkes, and his kindness to Goldsmith; his sitting with the young ladies on his knee at the Mitre, to give them good advice,[67] in which situation, if not explained, he might be taken for Falstaff; and last and noblest, his carrying the unfortunate victim of disease and dissipation on his back up through Fleet Street[68] (an act which realises the parable of the good Samaritan)—all these, and innumerable others, endear him to the reader, and must be remembered to his lasting honour. He had faults, but they lie buried with him. He had his prejudices and his intolerant feelings; but he suffered enough in the conflict of his own mind with them. For if no man can be happy in the free exercise of his reason, no wise man can be happy without it. His were not time-serving, heartless, hypocritical prejudices; but deep, inwoven, not to be rooted out but with life and hope, which he found from old habit necessary to his own peace of mind, and thought so to the peace of mankind. I do not hate, but love him for them. They were between himself and his conscience; and should be left to that higher tribunal, 'where they in trembling hope repose, the bosom of his Father and his God.'[69] In a word, he has left behind him few wiser or better men.

The herd of his imitators showed what he was by their disproportionate effects. The Periodical Essayists, that succeeded the *Rambler*, are, and deserve to be, little read at present. The *Adventurer*,[70] by Hawksworth, is completely trite and vapid, aping all the faults of Johnson's style, without anything to atone for them. The sentences are often absolutely unmeaning; and one half of each might regularly be left blank. The *World*, and *Connoisseur*,[71] which followed, are a little better; and in the last of these there is one good idea,[72] that of a man in indifferent health, who judges of everyone's title to respect from their possession of this blessing, and bows to a sturdy beggar with sound limbs and a florid complexion, while he turns his back upon a lord who is a valetudinarian.

Goldsmith's *Citizen of the World*,[73] like all his works, bears the stamp of the author's mind. It does not 'go about to cozen reputation without the stamp of merit.'[74] He is more observing, more original, more natural and picturesque than Johnson. His work is written on the model of the *Persian Letters*;[75] and contrives to give an abstracted and somewhat perplexing view of things, by opposing foreign prepossessions to our own, and thus stripping objects of their customary disguises. Whether truth is elicited in this collision of contrary absurdities, I do not know; but I confess the process is too ambiguous and full of intricacy to be very amusing to my plain understanding. For light summer reading, it is like walking in a garden full of traps and pitfalls. It necessarily gives rise to paradoxes, and there are some very bold ones in the Essays, which would subject an author less established to no very agreeable sort of *censura literaria*.[76] Thus the Chinese philosopher exclaims very unadvisedly, 'The bonzes and priests of all religions keep up superstition and imposture: all reformations begin with the laity.'[77] Goldsmith, however, was staunch in his practical creed, and might bolt speculative extravagances with impunity. There is a striking difference in this respect between him and Addison, who, if he attacked authority, took care to have common sense on his side, and never hazarded anything offensive to the feelings of others, or on the strength of his own discretional opinion. There is another inconvenience in this assumption of an exotic character and tone of sentiment, that it produces an inconsistency between the knowledge which the individual has time to acquire, and which the author is bound to communicate. Thus the Chinese has not been in England three days before he is acquainted with the characters of the three countries which compose this kingdom, and describes them to his friend at Canton, by extracts from the newspapers of each metropolis. The nationality of Scotchmen is thus ridiculed: '*Edinburgh*. We are positive when we say, that Sanders Macgregor, lately executed for horse-stealing, is not a native of Scotland, but born at Carrickfergus.' Now this is very good; but how should our Chinese philosopher find it out by instinct? Beau Tibbs, a prominent character in this little work, is the best comic sketch since the time of Addison; unrivalled in his finery, his vanity, and his poverty.

I have only to mention the names of the *Lounger* and the *Mirror*,[78] which are ranked by the author's admirers with Sterne for sentiment, and with Addison for humour. I shall not enter into that: but I know that the story of La Roche[79] is not like the story of Le Fevre,[80] nor one hundredth part so good. Do I say this from prejudice to the author? No: for I have read his novels. Of *The Man of the World*[81] I cannot think so favourably as some others; nor shall I here dwell on the picturesque and romantic beauties of *Julia de Roubigné*,[82] the early favourite of the author of Rosamond Gray,[83] but of

*The Man of Feeling*[84] I would speak with grateful recollections: nor is it possible to forget the sensitive, irresolute, interesting Harley: and that lone figure of Miss Walton in it, that floats in the horizon, dim and ethereal, the day-dream of her lover's youthful fancy—better, far better than all the realities of life!

# On the English
# Novelists *

THERE IS an exclamation in one of Gray's Letters[1]—'Be mine
to read eternal new romances of Marivaux and Crebillon!'—
If I did not utter a similar aspiration at the conclusion of the
last new novel which I read (I would not give offence by
being more particular as to the name) it was not from any
want of affection for the class of writing to which it belongs:
for, without going so far as the celebrated French philosopher,
who thought that more was to be learnt from good novels and
romances than from the gravest treatises on history and morality, yet there are few works to which I am oftener tempted to
turn for profit or delight, than to the standard productions
in this species of composition. We find there a close imitation
of men and manners; we see the very web and texture of
society as it really exists, and as we meet with it when we
come into the world. If poetry has 'something more divine in
it,' this savours more of humanity. We are brought acquainted
with the motives and characters of mankind, imbibe our
notions of virtue and vice from practical examples, and are
taught a knowledge of the world through the airy medium
of romance. As a record of past manners and opinions, too,
such writings afford the best and fullest information. For
example, I should be at a loss where to find in any authentic
documents of the same period so satisfactory an account of
the general state of society, and of moral, political, and religious feeling in the reign of George II[2] as we meet with in the
*Adventures of Joseph Andrews and his friend Mr. Abraham
Adams.* This work, indeed, I take to be a perfect piece of
statistics in its kind. In looking into any regular history of that
period, into a learned and eloquent charge to a grand jury or
the clergy of a diocese, or into a tract on controversial divinity,
we should hear only of the ascendancy of the Protestant suc-

* [*Lectures on the English Comic Writers* VI; based on an article
written for *The Edinburgh Review*, Feb. 1815.]

cession, the horrors of Popery, the triumph of civil and religious liberty, the wisdom and moderation of the sovereign, the happiness of the subject, and the flourishing state of manufactures and commerce. But if we really wish to know what all these fine-sounding names come to, we cannot do better than turn to the works of those, who having no other object than to imitate nature, could only hope for success from the fidelity of their pictures; and were bound (in self-defence) to reduce the boasts of vague theorists and the exaggerations of angry disputants to the mortifying standard of reality. Extremes are said to meet: and the works of imagination, as they are called, sometimes come the nearest to truth and nature. Fielding in speaking on this subject,[3] and vindicating the use and dignity of the style of writing in which he excelled against the loftier pretensions of professed historians, says, that in their productions nothing is true but the names and dates, whereas in his everything is true but the names and dates. If so, he has the advantage on his side.

I will here confess, however, that I am a little prejudiced on the point in question; and that the effect of many fine speculations has been lost upon me, from an early familiarity with the most striking passages in the work to which I have just alluded. Thus nothing can be more captivating than the description somewhere given by Mr. Burke of the indissoluble connection between learning and nobility; and of the respect universally paid by wealth to piety and morals. But the effect of this ideal representation has always been spoiled by my recollection of Parson Adams sitting over his cup of ale in Sir Thomas Booby's kitchen. Echard[4] 'On the Contempt of the Clergy' is, in like manner, a very good book, and 'worthy of all acceptation:' but, somehow, an unlucky impression of the reality of Parson Trulliber involuntarily checks the emotions of respect, to which it might otherwise give rise: while, on the other hand, the lecture which Lady Booby reads to Lawyer Scout on the immediate expulsion of Joseph and Fanny from the parish, casts no very favourable light on the flattering accounts of our practical jurisprudence which are to be found in Blackstone or De Lolme. The most moral writers, after all, are those who do not pretend to inculcate any moral. The professed moralist almost unavoidably degenerates into the partisan of a system; and the philosopher is too apt to warp the evidence to his own purpose. But the painter of manners gives the facts of human nature, and leaves us to draw the inference: if we are not able to do this, or do it ill, at least it is our own fault.

The first-rate writers in this class, of course, are few; but those few we may reckon among the greatest ornaments and best benefactors of our kind. There is a certain set of them who, as it were, take their rank by the side of reality, and are appealed to as evidence on all questions concerning human nature. The principal of these are Cervantes and Le Sage, who may be considered as having been naturalised among ourselves; and, of native English growth, Fielding, Smollett, Richardson, and Sterne.* As this is a department of criticism which deserves more attention than has been usually bestowed upon it, I shall here venture to recur (not from choice, but necessity) to what I have said upon it in a well known periodical publication; and endeavour to contribute my mite towards settling the standard of excellence, both as to degree and kind, in these several writers.

I shall begin with the history of the renowned Don Quixote de la Mancha; who presents something more stately, more romantic, and at the same time more real to the imagination than any other hero upon record. His lineaments, his accoutrements, his pasteboard vizor, are familiar to us; and Mambrino's helmet still glitters in the sun! We not only feel the greatest veneration and love for the knight himself, but a certain respect for all those connected with him, the curate and Master Nicolas the barber, Sancho and Dapple, and even for Rosinante's leanness and his errors.—Perhaps there is no work which combines so much whimsical invention with such an air of truth. Its popularity is almost unequalled; and yet its merits have not been sufficiently understood. The story is the least part of them; though the blunders of Sancho, and the unlucky adventures of his master, are what naturally catch the attention of the majority of readers. The pathos and dignity of the sentiments are often disguised under the ludicrousness of the subject; and provoke laughter when they might well draw tears. The character of Don Quixote himself is one of the most perfect disinterestedness. He is an enthusiast of the most amiable kind; of a nature equally open, gentle, and generous; a lover of truth and justice; and one who had brooded over the fine dreams of chivalry and romance, till they had robbed him of himself, and cheated his brain into a belief of their reality. There cannot be a greater mistake than to consider *Don Quixote* as a merely satirical work, or as a vulgar attempt to explode 'the long-forgotten order of chivalry.' There could be no need to explode what no longer existed. Besides, Cervantes himself was a man of the most sanguine and enthusiastic temperament; and even through the crazed and battered figure

* It is not to be forgotten that the author of *Robinson Crusoe* was also an Englishman. His other works, such as the *Life of Colonel Jack,* etc., are of the same cast, and leave an impression on the mind more like that of things than words. [w. h.]

of the knight, the spirit of chivalry shines out with undiminished lustre; as if the author had half-designed to revive the example of past ages, and once more 'witch the world with noble horsemanship.' Oh! if ever the mouldering flame of Spanish liberty is destined to break forth, wrapping the tyrant and the tyranny in one consuming blaze, that the spark of generous sentiment and romantic enterprise, from which it must be kindled, has not been quite extinguished, will perhaps be owing to thee, Cervantes, and to thy Don Quixote!

The character of Sancho is not more admirable in itself, than as a relief to that of the knight. The contrast is as picturesque and striking as that between the figures of Rosinante and Dapple. Never was there so complete a *partie quarrée*[5]: they answer to one another at all points. Nothing need surpass the truth of physiognomy in the description of the master and man, both as to body and mind; the one lean and tall, the other round and short; the one heroical and courteous, the other selfish and servile; the one full of high-flown fancies, the other a bag of proverbs; the one always starting some romantic scheme, the other trying to keep to the safe side of custom and tradition. The gradual ascendancy, however, obtained by Don Quixote over Sancho, is as finely managed as it is characteristic. Credulity and a love of the marvellous are as natural to ignorance, as selfishness and cunning. Sancho by degrees becomes a kind of lay-brother of the order; acquires a taste for adventures in his own way, and is made all but an entire convert, by the discovery of the hundred crowns in one of his most comfortless journeys. Towards the end, his regret at being forced to give up the pursuit of knight-errantry, almost equals his master's; and he seizes the proposal of Don Quixote for them to turn shepherds with the greatest avidity—still applying it in his own fashion; for while the Don is ingeniously torturing the names of his humble acquaintance into classical terminations, and contriving scenes of gallantry and song, Sancho exclaims, 'Oh, what delicate wooden spoons shall I carve! what crumbs and cream shall I devour!'—forgetting, in his milk and fruits, the pullets and geese at Camacho's wedding.

This intuitive perception of the hidden analogies of things, or, as it may be called, this *instinct of the imagination,* is, perhaps, what stamps the character of genius on the productions of art more than any other circumstance: for it works unconsciously, like nature, and receives its impressions from a kind of inspiration. There is as much of this indistinct keeping and involuntary unity of purpose in Cervantes, as in any author whatever. Something of the same unsettled, rambling humour extends itself to all the subordinate parts and characters of the work. Thus we find the curate confidentially informing Don Quixote, that if he could get the ear of the government, he has something of considerable importance to propose for the good of the state; and our adventurer afterwards (in the course of his peregrinations) meets with a young gentleman who is a candidate for poetical honours, with a mad lover, a forsaken damsel, a Mahometan lady converted to the Christian faith, etc.—all delineated with the same truth, wildness, and delicacy of fancy. The whole work breathes that air of romance, that aspiration after imaginary good, that indescribable longing after something more than we possess, that in all places and in all conditions of life,

> still prompts the eternal sigh,
> For which we wish to live, or dare to die!⁶

The leading characters in *Don Quixote* are strictly individuals; that is, they do not so much belong to, as form a class by themselves. In other words, the actions and manners of the chief *dramatis personæ* do not arise out of the actions and manners of those around them, or the situation of life in which they are placed, but out of the peculiar dispositions of the persons themselves, operated upon by certain impulses of caprice and accident. Yet these impulses are so true to nature, and their operation so exactly described, that we not only recognise the fidelity of the representation, but recognise it with all the advantages of novelty superadded. They are in the best sense *originals*, namely, in the sense in which nature has her originals. They are unlike anything we have seen before—may be said to be purely ideal; and yet identify themselves more readily with our imagination, and are retained more strongly in memory, than perhaps any others: they are never lost in the crowd. One test of the truth of this ideal painting, is the number of allusions which *Don Quixote* has furnished to the whole of civilised Europe; that is to say, of appropriate cases and striking illustrations of the universal principles of our nature. The detached incidents and occasional descriptions of human life are more familiar and obvious; so that we have nearly the same insight here given us into the characters of innkeepers, barmaids, ostlers, and puppet-show men, that we have in Fielding. There is much greater mixture, however, of the pathetic and sentimental with the quaint and humorous, than there ever is in Fielding. I might instance the story of the countryman whom Don Quixote and Sancho met in their doubtful search after Dulcinea, driving his mules to plough at break of day, and 'singing the ancient ballad of Ronscevalles!' The episodes, which are frequently introduced, are excellent, but have, upon the whole, been overrated. They derive their interest from their connexion with the main story. We are so pleased with that, that we are disposed to receive pleasure from everything else. Compared, for instance, with the serious tales in Boccaccio, they are slight and somewhat superficial. That of Marcella, the fair shepherdess, is, I think, the best. I shall only add, that *Don Quixote* was, at the time it was published,⁷ an entirely original work in its kind, and that the author claims the highest honour which can belong to one, that of being the inventor of a new style of writing. I have never read his *Galatea,* nor his *Loves of Persiles and Sigismunda,* though I have often meant to do it, and I hope to do so yet. Perhaps there is a reason lurking at the bottom of this dilatoriness: I am quite sure the reading of these works could not make me think higher of the author of *Don Quixote,* and it might, for a moment or two, make me think less.

There is another Spanish novel, *Gusman D'Alfarache,*⁸ nearly of the same age as *Don Quixote,* and of great genius, though it can hardly be ranked as a novel or a work of imagination. It is a series of strange, unconnected adventures, rather drily told, but accompanied by the most severe and sarcastic commentary. The satire, the wit, the eloquence and reasoning, are of the most potent kind: but they are didactic rather than dramatic. They would suit a homily or a pasquinade as well or better than a romance. Still there are in this extraordinary book occasional sketches of character and humorous descriptions, to which it would be difficult to produce anything superior. This work, which is hardly known in this country except by name, has the credit, without any reason, of being the original of *Gil Blas.* There is one incident the same, that of the unsavoury ragout, which is served up for supper at the inn. In all other respects these two works are the very reverse of each other, both in their excellences and defects.—*Lazarillo de Tormes*⁹ has been more read than the Spanish *Rogue,*¹⁰ and is a work more readable, on this account among others, that it is contained in a duodecimo instead of a folio volume. This, however, is long enough, considering that it treats of only one subject, that of eating, or rather the possibility of living without eating. Famine is here framed into an art, and feasting is banished far hence. The hero's time and thoughts are taken up in a thousand shifts to procure a dinner; and that failing, in tampering with his stomach till supper time, when being forced to go supperless to bed, he comforts himself with the hopes of a breakfast the next morning, of which being again disappointed, he reserves his appetite for a luncheon, and then has to stave it off again by some meagre excuse or other till dinner; and so on, by a perpetual adjournment of this necessary process, through the four and twenty hours round. The quantity of food proper to keep body and soul together is reduced to a *minimum*; and the most uninviting morsels with which Lazarillo meets once a week as a God's-send, are pampered into the most sumptuous fare by a long course of inanition. The scene of this novel could be laid nowhere so properly as in Spain, that land of priestcraft and poverty, where hunger seems to be the ruling passion, and starving the order of the day.

*Gil Blas*[11] has, next to *Don Quixote*, been more generally read and admired than any other novel; and in one sense, deservedly so: for it is at the head of its class, though that class is very different from, and I should say inferior to the other. There is little individual character in *Gil Blas*. The author is a describer of manners, and not of character. He does not take the elements of human nature, and work them up into new combinations (which is the excellence of *Don Quixote*); nor trace the peculiar and shifting shades of folly and knavery as they are to be found in real life (like Fielding): but he takes off, as it were, the general, habitual impression which circumstances make on certain conditions of life, and moulds all his characters accordingly. All the persons whom he introduces, carry about with them the badge of their profession; and you see little more of them than their costume. He describes men as belonging to distinct classes in society; not as they are in themselves, or with the individual differences which are always to be discovered in nature. His hero, in particular, has no character but that of the successive circumstances in which he is placed. His priests are only described as priests: his valets, his players, his women, his courtiers and his sharpers, are all alike. Nothing can well exceed the monotony of the work in this respect—at the same time that nothing can exceed the truth and precision with which the general manners of these different characters are preserved, nor the felicity of the particular traits by which their common foibles are brought out. Thus the Archbishop of Grenada will remain an everlasting memento of the weakness of human vanity; and the account of Gil Blas' legacy, of the uncertainty of human expectations. This novel is also deficient in the fable as well as in the characters. It is not a regularly constructed story; but a series of amusing adventures told with equal gaiety and good sense, and in the most graceful style imaginable.

It has been usual to class our own great novelists as imitators of one or other of these two writers. Fielding, no doubt, is more like *Don Quixote* than *Gil Blas;* Smollett is more like *Gil Blas* than *Don Quixote;* but there is not much resemblance in either case. Sterne's *Tristram Shandy* is a more direct instance of imitation. Richardson can scarcely be called an imitator of anyone; or if he is, it is of the sentimental refinement of Marivaux, or of the verbose gallantry of the writers of the seventeenth century.

There is very little to warrant the common idea that Fielding was an imitator of Cervantes, except his own declaration of such an intention in the title-page of *Joseph Andrews,* the romantic turn of the character of Parson Adams (the only romantic character in his works), and the proverbial humour of Partridge, which is kept up only for a few pages. Fielding's novels are, in general, thoroughly his own; and they are thoroughly English. What they are most remarkable for, is neither sentiment, nor imagination, nor wit, nor even humour, though there is an immense deal of this last quality; but profound knowledge of human nature, at least of English nature; and masterly pictures of the characters of men as he saw them existing. This quality distinguishes all his works, and is shown almost equally in all of them. As a painter of real life, he was equal to Hogarth; as a mere observer of human nature, he was little inferior to Shakespeare, though without any of the genius and poetical qualities of his mind. His humour is less rich and laughable than Smollett's; his wit as often misses as hits; he has none of the fine pathos of Richardson or Sterne; but he has brought together a greater variety of characters in common life, marked with more distinct peculiarities, and without an atom of caricature, than any other novel writer whatever. The extreme subtlety of observation on the springs of human conduct in ordinary characters, is only equalled by the ingenuity of contrivance in bringing those springs into play, in such a manner as to lay open their smallest irregularity. The detection is always complete, and made with the certainty and skill of a philosophical experiment, and the obviousness and familiarity of a casual observation. The truth of the imitation is indeed so great, that it has been argued that Fielding must have had his materials ready-made to his hands, and was merely a transcriber of local manners and individual habits. For this conjecture, however, there seems to be no foundation. His representations, it is true, are local and individual; but they are not the less profound and conclusive. The feeling of the general principles of human nature operating in particular circumstances, is always intense, and uppermost in his mind; and he makes use of incident and situation only to bring out character.

It is scarcely necessary to give any illustrations. *Tom Jones* is full of them. There is the account, for example, of the gratitude of the elder Blifil to his brother, for assisting him to obtain the fortune of Miss Bridget Allworthy by marriage; and of the gratitude of the poor in his neighbourhood to Allworthy himself, who had done so much good in the country that he had made everyone in it his enemy. There is the account of the Latin dialogues between Partridge and his maid, of the assault made on him during one of these by Mrs. Partridge, and the severe bruises he patiently received on that occasion, after which the parish of Little Baddington rung with the story, that the school-master had killed his wife. There is the exquisite keeping in the character of Blifil, and the want of it in that of Jones. There is the gradation in the lovers of Molly Seagrim; the philosopher Square succeeding to Tom Jones, who again finds that he himself had succeeded to the accomplished Will Barnes, who had the first possession of her person, and had still possession of her heart, Jones being only the instrument of her vanity, as Square was of her interest. Then there is the discreet honesty of Black George, the learning of Thwackum and Square, and the profundity of Squire Western, who considered it as a physical impossibility that his daughter should fall in love with Tom Jones. We have also that gentleman's disputes with his sister, and the inimitable appeal of that lady to her niece.—'I was never so handsome as you, Sophy: yet I had something of you formerly. I was called the cruel Parthenissa. Kingdoms and states, as Tully Cicero says, undergo alteration, and so must the human form!' The adventure of the same lady with the highwayman, who robbed her of her jewels, while he complimented her beauty, ought not to be passed over, nor that of Sophia and her muff, nor the reserved coquetry of her cousin Fitzpatrick, nor the description of Lady Bellaston, nor the modest overtures of the pretty widow Hunt, nor the indiscreet babblings of Mrs. Honour. The moral of this book has been objected to, without much reason; but a more serious objection has been made to the want of refinement and elegance in two principal characters. We never feel this objection, indeed, while we are reading the book: but at other times, we have something like a lurking suspicion that Jones was but an awkward fellow, and Sophia a pretty simpleton. I do not know how to account for this effect, unless it is that Fielding's constantly assuring us of the beauty of his hero, and the good sense of his heroine, at last produces a distrust of both. The story of Tom Jones is allowed to be unrivalled: and it is this circumstance, together with the vast variety of characters, that has given the history of a Foundling so decided a preference over Fielding's other novels. The characters themselves, both in *Amelia* and *Joseph Andrews,* are quite equal to any of those in *Tom Jones.* The account of Miss Matthews and Ensign Hibbert, in the former of these; the way in which that lady reconciles herself to the

death of her father; the inflexible Colonel Bath; the insipid
Mrs. James, the complaisant Colonel Trent, the demure, sly,
intriguing, equivocal Mrs. Bennet, the lord who is her seducer, and who attempts afterwards to seduce Amelia by the
same mechanical process of a concert-ticket, a book, and the
disguise of a great coat; his little, fat- short-nosed, red-faced,
good-humoured accomplice, the keeper of the lodging-house,
who, having no pretensions to gallantry herself, has a disinterested delight in forwarding the intrigues and pleasures of
others (to say nothing of honest Atkinson, the story of the
miniature-picture of Amelia, and the hashed mutton, which are
in a different style), are masterpieces of description. The whole
scene at the lodging-house, the masquerade, etc. in *Amelia*,
are equal in interest to the parallel scenes in *Tom Jones*, and
even more refined in the knowledge of character. For instance,
Mrs. Bennet is superior to Mrs. Fitzpatrick in her own way.
The uncertainty, in which the event of her interview with her
former seducer is left, is admirable. Fielding was a master of
what may be called the *double entendre* of character, and
surprises you no less by what he leaves in the dark (hardly
known to the persons themselves), than by the unexpected
discoveries he makes of the real traits and circumstances in a
character with which, till then, you find you were unac-
quainted. There is nothing at all heroic, however, in the usual
style of his delineations. He does not draw lofty characters or
strong passions; all his persons are of the ordinary stature as
to intellect; and possess little elevation of fancy, or energy of
purpose. Perhaps, after all, Parson Adams is his finest character. It is equally true to nature, and more ideal than any of the
others. Its unsuspecting simplicity makes it not only more
amiable, but doubly amusing, by gratifying the sense of superior sagacity in the reader. Our laughing at him does not once
lessen our respect for him. His declaring that he would willingly walk ten miles to fetch his sermon on vanity, merely to
convince Wilson of his thorough contempt of this vice, and his
consoling himself for the loss of his Aeschylus, by suddenly
recollecting that he could not read it if he had it, because it is
dark, are among the finest touches of *naïveté*. The night-
adventures at Lady Booby's with Beau Didapper, and the
amiable Slipslop, are the most ludicrous; and that with the
huntsman, who draws off the hounds from the poor Parson,
because they would be spoiled by following *vermin*, the most
profound. Fielding did not often repeat himself; but Dr. Har-
rison, in *Amelia*, may be considered as a variation of the character of Adams: so also is Goldsmith's *Vicar of Wakefield;* and
the latter part of that work, which sets out so delightfully, an

almost entire plagiarism from Wilson's account of himself, and Adams's domestic history.

Smollett's first novel, *Roderick Random,* which is also his best, appeared[12] about the same time as Fielding's *Tom Jones;* and yet it has a much more modern air with it: but this may be accounted for, from the circumstance that Smollett was quite a young man at the time, whereas Fielding's manner must have been formed long before. The style of *Roderick Random* is more easy and flowing than that of *Tom Jones;* the incidents follow one another more rapidly (though, it must be confessed, they never come in such a throng, or are brought out with the same dramatic effect); the humour is broader, and as effectual; and there is very nearly, if not quite, an equal interest excited by the story. What then is it that gives the superiority to Fielding? It is the superior insight into the springs of human character, and the constant development of that character through every change of circumstance. Smollett's humour often arises from the situation of the persons, or the peculiarity of their external appearance; as, from Roderick Random's carrotty locks, which hung down over his shoulders like a pound of candles, or Strap's ignorance of London, and the blunders that follow from it. There is a tone of vulgarity about all his productions. The incidents frequently resemble detached anecdotes taken from a newspaper or magazine; and, like those in *Gil Blas,* might happen to a hundred other characters. He exhibits the ridiculous accidents and reverses to which human life is liable, not 'the stuff' of which it is composed. He seldom probes to the quick, or penetrates beyond the surface; and, therefore, he leaves no stings in the minds of his readers, and in this respect is far less interesting than Fielding. His novels always enliven, and never tire us: we take them up with pleasure, and lay them down without any strong feeling of regret. We look on and laugh, as spectators of a highly amusing scene, without closing in with the combatants, or being made parties in the event. We read *Roderick Random* as an entertaining story; for the particular accidents and modes of life which it describes have ceased to exist: but we regard *Tom Jones* as a real history; because the author never stops short of those essential principles which lie at the bottom of all our actions, and in which we feel an immediate interest —*intus et in cute.*[13] Smollett excels most as the lively caricaturist: Fielding as the exact painter and profound metaphysician. I am far from maintaining that this account applies uniformly to the productions of these two writers; but I think that, as far as they essentially differ, what I have stated is the general distinction between them. *Roderick Random* is the purest of Smollett's novels: I mean in point of style and description. Most of the incidents and characters are supposed to have been taken from the events of his own life; and are, therefore, truer to nature. There is a rude conception of generosity in some of his characters, of which Fielding seems to have been incapable, his amiable persons being merely good-natured. It is owing to this that Strap is superior to Partridge; as there is a heartiness and warmth of feeling in some of the scenes between Lieutenant Bowling and his nephew, which is beyond Fielding's power of impassioned writing. The whole of the scene on ship-board is a most admirable and striking picture, and, I imagine, very little if at all exaggerated, though the interest it excites is of a very unpleasant kind, because the irritation and resistance to petty oppression can be of no avail. The picture of the little profligate French friar, who was Roderick's travelling companion, and of whom he always kept to the windward, is one of Smollett's most masterly sketches. *Peregrine Pickle* is no great favourite of mine, and *Launcelot Greaves* was not worthy of the genius of the author.

*Humphry Clinker* and *Count Fathom* are both equally admirable in their way. Perhaps the former is the most pleasant gossiping novel that ever was written; that which gives the most pleasure with the least effort to the reader. It is quite as amusing as going the journey could have been; and we have just as good an idea of what happened on the road, as if we had been of the party. Humphry Clinker himself is exquisite; and his sweetheart, Winifred Jenkins, not much behind him. Matthew Bramble, though not altogether original, is excellently supported, and seems to have been the prototype of Sir Anthony Absolute in *The Rivals*.[14] But Lismahago is the flower of the flock. His tenaciousness in argument is not so delightful as the relaxation of his logical severity, when he finds his fortune mellowing in the wintry smiles of Mrs. Tabitha Bramble. This is the best preserved, and most severe of all Smollett's characters. The resemblance to *Don Quixote* is only just enough to make it interesting to the critical reader, without giving offence to anybody else. The indecency and filth in this novel, are what must be allowed to all Smollett's writings.— The subject and characters in *Count Fathom* are, in general, exceedingly disgusting: the story is also spun out to a degree of tediousness in the serious and sentimental parts; but there is more power of writing occasionally shown in it than in any of his works. I need only to refer to the fine and bitter irony of the Count's address to the country of his ancestors on his landing in England; to the robber scene in the forest, which has never been surpassed; to the Parisian swindler who personates a raw English country squire (Western is tame in the comparison); and to the story of the seduction in the west of England. It would be difficult to point out, in any author, passages written with more force and mastery than these.

It is not a very difficult undertaking to class Fielding or Smollett;—the one as an observer of the characters of human life, the other as a describer of its various eccentricities. But it is by no means so easy to dispose of Richardson, who was neither an observer of the one, nor a describer of the other; but who seemed to spin his materials entirely out of his own brain, as if there had been nothing existing in the world beyond the little room in which he sat writing. There is an artificial reality about his works, which is nowhere else to be met with. They have the romantic air of a pure fiction, with the literal minuteness of a common diary. The author had the strongest matter-of-fact imagination that ever existed, and wrote the oddest mixture of poetry and prose. He does not appear to have taken advantage of any thing in actual nature, from one end of his works to the other; and yet, throughout all his works, voluminous as they are—(and this, to be sure, is one reason why they are so)—he sets about describing every object and transaction, as if the whole had been given in on evidence by an eye-witness. This kind of high finishing from imagination is an anomaly in the history of human genius; and, certainly, nothing so fine was ever produced by the same accumulation of minute parts. There is not the least distraction, the least forgetfulness of the end: every circumstance is made to tell. I cannot agree that this exactness of detail produces heaviness; on the contrary, it gives an appearance of truth, and a positive interest to the story; and we listen with the same attention as we should to the particulars of a confidential communication. I at one time used to think some parts of *Sir Charles Grandison* rather trifling and tedious, especially the long description of Miss Harriet Byron's wedding clothes, till I was told of two young ladies who had severally copied out the whole of that very description for their own private gratification. After that, I could not blame the author.

The effect of reading this work is like an increase of kindred. You find yourself all of a sudden introduced into the midst of a large family, with aunts and cousins to the third and fourth generation, and grandmothers both by the father's and mother's side;—and a very odd set of people they are, but people whose real existence and personal identity you can no more dispute than your own senses, for you see and hear all that they do or say. What is still more extraordinary, all this extreme elaborateness in working out the story, seems to have cost the author nothing; for it is said, that the published works are mere abridgments. I have heard (though this I suspect must be a pleasant exaggeration) that *Sir Charles Grandison* was originally written in eight and twenty volumes.

*Pamela* is the first of Richardson's productions, and the very child of his brain. Taking the general idea of the character of a modest and beautiful country girl, and of the ordinary situation in which she is placed, he makes out all the rest, even to the smallest circumstance, by the mere force of a reasoning imagination. It would seem as if a step lost, would be as fatal here as in a mathematical demonstration. The development of the character is the most simple, and comes the nearest to nature that it can do, without being the same thing. The interest of the story increases with the dawn of understanding and reflection in the heroine: her sentiments gradually expand themselves, like opening flowers. She writes better every time, and acquires a confidence in herself, just as a girl would do, writing such letters in such circumstances; and yet it is certain *that no girl would write such letters in such circumstances.* What I mean is this: Richardson's nature is always the nature of sentiment and reflection, not of impulse or situation. He furnishes his characters, on every occasion, with the presence of mind of the author. He makes them act, not as they would from the impulse of the moment, but as they might upon reflection, and upon a careful review of every motive and circumstance in their situation. They regularly sit down to write letters: and if the business of life consisted in letter-writing, and was carried on by the post (like a Spanish game at chess), human nature would be what Richardson represents it. All actual objects and feelings are blunted and deadened by being presented through a medium which may be true to reason, but is false in nature. He confounds his own point of view with that of the immediate actors in the scene; and hence presents you with a conventional and factitious nature, instead of that which is real. Dr. Johnson seems to have preferred this truth of reflection to the truth of nature, when he said that there was more knowledge of the human heart in a page of Richardson, than in all Fielding.[15] Fielding, however, saw more of the practical results, and understood the principles as well; but he had not the same power of speculating upon their possible results, and combining them in certain ideal forms of passion and imagination, which was Richardson's real excellence.

It must be observed, however, that it is this mutual good understanding, and comparing of notes between the author and the persons he describes; his infinite circumspection, his exact process of ratiocination and calculation, which gives such an appearance of coldness and formality to most of his characters—which makes prudes of his women, and coxcombs of his men. Everything is too conscious in his works. Everything is distinctly brought home to the mind of the actors in the scene, which is a fault undoubtedly: but then it must be confessed, everything is brought home in its full force to the mind of the reader also; and we feel the same interest in the story as if it were our own. Can anything be more beautiful or more affecting than Pamela's reproaches to her 'lumpish heart,' when she is sent away from her master's at her own request; its lightness, when she is sent for back; the joy which the conviction of the sincerity of his love diffuses in her heart, like the coming on of spring; the artifice of the stuff gown; the meeting with Lady Davers after her marriage; and the trial-scene with her husband? Who ever remained insensible to the passion of Lady Clementina, except Sir Charles Grandison himself, who was the object of it? Clarissa is, however, his masterpiece, if we except Lovelace. If she is fine in herself, she is still finer in his account of her. With that foil, her purity is dazzling indeed: and she who could triumph by her virtue, and the force of her love, over the regality of Lovelace's mind, his wit, his person, his accomplishments, and his spirit, conquers all hearts. I should suppose that never sympathy more deep or sincere was excited than by the heroine of Richardson's romance, except by the calamities of real life. The links in this wonderful chain of interest are not more finely wrought, than their whole weight is overwhelming and irresistible. Who can forget the exquisite gradations of her long dying-scene, or the closing of the coffin-lid, when Miss Howe comes to take her last leave of her friend; or the heart-breaking reflection that Clarissa makes on what was to have been her wedding-day? Well does a certain writer exclaim—

> Books are a real world, both pure and good,
> Round which, with tendrils strong as flesh and blood,
> Our pastime and our happiness may grow![16]

Richardson's wit was unlike that of any other writer—his humour was so too. Both were the effect of intense activity of mind—laboured, and yet completely effectual. I might refer to Lovelace's reception and description of Hickman, when he calls out Death in his ear, as the name of the person with whom Clarissa had fallen in love; and to the scene at the glove-shop. What can be more magnificent than his enumeration of his companions—'Belton, so pert and so pimply—Tourville, so fair and so foppish!' etc. In casuistry this author is quite at home; and, with a boldness greater even than his puritanical severity, has exhausted every topic on virtue and vice. There is another peculiarity in Richardson, not perhaps so uncommon, which is, his systematically preferring his most insipid characters to his finest, though both were equally his own invention, and he must be supposed to have understood something of their qualities. Thus he preferred the little, selfish, affected, insignificant Miss Byron to the divine Clementina; and again, Sir Charles Grandison to the nobler Lovelace. I have nothing to say in favour of Lovelace's morality; but Sir Charles is the prince of coxcombs—whose eye was never once taken from his own person, and his own virtues; and there is nothing which excites so little sympathy as this excessive egotism.

It remains to speak of Sterne; and I shall do it in few words. There is more of *mannerism* and affectation in him, and a more immediate reference to preceding authors; but his excellences, where he is excellent, are of the first order. His characters are intellectual and inventive, like Richardson's; but totally opposite in the execution. The one are made out by continuity, and patient repetition of touches: the others, by glancing transitions and graceful apposition. His style is equally different from Richardson's: it is at times the most rapid, the most happy, the most idiomatic of any that is to be found. It is the pure essence of English conversational style. His works consist only of *morceaux*—of brilliant passages. I wonder that Goldsmith, who ought to have known better, should call him 'a dull fellow.'[17] His wit is poignant, though artificial; and his characters (though the groundwork of some of them had been laid before) have yet invaluable original differences; and the spirit of the execution, the master-strokes constantly thrown into them, are not to be surpassed. It is sufficient to name them—Yorick, Dr. Slop, Mr. Shandy, My Uncle Toby, Trim, Susanna, and the Widow Wadman. In these he has contrived to oppose, with equal felicity and originality, two characters, one of pure intellect, and the other of pure good nature, in My Father and My Uncle Toby. There appears to have been in Sterne a vein of dry, sarcastic humour, and of extreme tenderness of feeling; the latter sometimes carried to affectation, as in the tale of Maria, and the apostrophe to the recording angel: but at other times pure, and without blemish. The story of Le Fevre is perhaps the finest in the English language. My Father's restlessness, both of body and mind, is inimitable. It is the model from which all those despicable performances against modern philosophy ought to have been copied, if their authors had known anything of the subject they were writing about. My Uncle Toby is one of the finest compliments ever paid to human nature. He is the most unoffending of God's creatures; or, as the French express it, *un tel petit bon homme!*[18] Of his bowling-green, his sieges, and his amours, who would say or think anything amiss!

It is remarkable that our four best novel-writers belong nearly to the same age. We also owe to the same period (the reign of George II) the inimitable Hogarth, and some of our best writers of the middle style of comedy. If I were called upon to account for this coincidence, I should waive the consideration of more general causes, and ascribe it at once to the establishment of the Protestant ascendancy, and the succession of the House of Hanover.[19] These great events appear to have given a more popular turn to our literature and genius, as well as to our government. It was found high time that the people should be represented in books as well as in Parliament. They wished to see some account of themselves in what they read; and not to be confined always to the vices, the miseries, and frivolities of the great. Our domestic tragedy, and our earliest periodical works, appeared a little before the same period. In despotic countries, human nature is not of sufficient importance to be studied or described. The *canaille* are objects rather of disgust than curiosity; and there are no middle classes. The works of Racine and Molière are either imitations of the verbiage of the court, before which they were represented, or fanciful caricatures of the manners of the lowest of the people. But in the period of our history in question, a security of person and property, and a freedom of opinion had been established, which made every man feel of some consequence to himself, and appear an object of some curiosity to his neighbours: our manners became more domesticated; there was a general spirit of sturdiness and independence, which made the English character more truly English than perhaps at any other period—that is, more tenacious of its own opinions and purposes. The whole surface of society appeared cut out into square enclosures and sharp angles, which extended to the dresses of the time, their gravel-walks, and clipped hedges. Each individual had a certain ground-plot of his own to cultivate his particular humours in, and let them shoot out at pleasure; and a most plentiful crop they have produced accordingly. The reign of George II was, in a word, the age of *hobby-horses:* but, since that period, things have taken a different turn.

His present Majesty[20] (God save the mark!) during almost the whole of his reign, has been constantly mounted on a great war-horse; and has fairly driven all competitors out of the field. Instead of minding our own affairs, or laughing at each other, the eyes of all his faithful subjects have been fixed on the career of the sovereign, and all hearts anxious for the safety of his person and government. Our pens and our swords have been alike drawn in their defence; and the returns of killed and wounded, the manufacture of newspapers and parliamentary speeches, have exceeded all former example. If we have had little of the blessings of peace, we have had enough of the glories and calamities of war. His Majesty has indeed contrived to keep alive the greatest public interest ever known, by his determined manner of riding his hobby for half a century together, with the aristocracy, the democracy, the clergy, the landed and monied interest, and the rabble, in full cry after him;—and at the end of his career, most happily and unexpectedly succeeded, amidst empires lost and won, kingdoms overturned and created, and the destruction of an incredible number of lives, in restoring *the divine right of kings*, and thus preventing any future abuse of the example which seated his family on the throne!* [. . .]

* [Hazlitt continues by discussing Fanny Burney, Mrs. Radcliffe, Godwin, and Scott.]

# On the Works
# of Hogarth.
# On the Grand
# And Familiar Style
# of Painting*

---

IF THE QUANTITY of amusement, or of matter for more serious reflection which their works have afforded, is that by which we are to judge of precedence among the intellectual benefactors of mankind, there are, perhaps, few persons who can put in a stronger claim to our gratitude than Hogarth. It is not hazarding too much to assert, that he was one of the greatest comic geniuses that ever lived, and he was certainly one of the most extraordinary men this country has produced. The wonderful knowledge which he possessed of human life and manners, is only to be surpassed (if it can be) by the power of invention with which he has combined and contrasted his materials in the most ludicrous and varied points of view, and by the mastery of execution with which he has embodied and made tangible the very thoughts and passing movements of the mind. Critics sometimes object to the style of Hogarth's pictures, or to the class to which they belong. First, he belongs to no class, or if he does, it is to the same class as Fielding, Smollett, Vanbrugh, and Molière. Besides, the merit of his pictures does not depend on the nature of the subject, but on the knowledge displayed of it, on the number of ideas they excite, on the fund of thought and observation contained in them. They are to be studied as works of science as well as of amusement; they satisfy our love of truth; they fill up the void in the mind; they form a series of plates in natural history, and of that most interesting part of natural history, the history of our own species. Make what deductions

* [*Lectures on the English Comic Writers* VII.]

you please for the vulgarity of the subject, yet in the research, the profundity, the absolute truth and precision of the delineation of character; in the invention of incident, in wit and humour; in the life with which they are 'instinct in every part'; in everlasting variety and originality; they never have, and probably never will be surpassed. They stimulate the faculties as well as soothe them. 'Other pictures we see, Hogarth's we read.'[1]

The public had not long ago an opportunity of viewing most of Hogarth's pictures, in the collection made of them at the British Gallery. The superiority of the original paintings to the common prints, is in a great measure confined to the "Marriage-à-la-Mode," with which I shall begin my remarks.

Boccaccio, the most refined and sentimental of all the novel-writers, has been stigmatised as a mere inventor of licentious tales, because readers in general have only seized on those things in his works which were suited to their own taste, and have thus reflected their own grossness back upon the writer. So it has happened, that the majority of critics having been most struck with the strong and decided expression in Hogarth, the extreme delicacy and subtle gradations of character in his pictures have almost entirely escaped them. In the first picture of the "Marriage-à-la-Mode," the three figures of the young Nobleman, his intended Bride, and her Inamorato, the Lawyer, show how much Hogarth excelled in the power of giving soft and effeminate expression. They have, however, been less noticed than the other figures, which tell a plainer story, and convey a more palpable moral. Nothing can be more finely managed than the differences of character in these delicate personages. The beau sits smiling at the looking-glass with a reflected simper of self-admiration, and a languishing inclination of the head, while the rest of his body is perked up on his high heels with a certain air of tip-toe elevation. He is the Narcissus of the reign of George II; whose powdered peruke, ruffles, gold-lace, and patches, divide his self-love unequally with his own person—the true *Sir Plume* of his day;

Of amber-lidded snuff box justly vain,
And the nice conduct of a clouded cane.[2]

Again we find the same felicity in the figure and attitude of the Bride, courted by the Lawyer. There is the utmost flexibility, and yielding softness in her whole person, a listless languor and tremulous suspense in the expression of her face. It is the precise look and air which Pope has given to his favourite Belinda, just at the moment of the Rape of the Lock. The heightened glow, the forward intelligence, and loosened soul of love in the same face, in the Assignation scene before the masquerade, form a fine and instructive contrast to the delicacy, timidity, and coy reluctance expressed in the first. The Lawyer in both pictures is much the same, perhaps too much so; though even this unmoved, unaltered appearance may be designed as characteristic. In both cases he has 'a person, and a smooth dispose, framed to make women false.'[3] He is full of that easy good-humour, and easy good opinion of himself, with which the sex are often delighted. There is not a sharp angle in his face to obstruct his success, or give a hint of doubt or difficulty. His whole aspect is round and rosy, lively and unmeaning, happy without the least expense of thought, careless and inviting; and conveys a perfect idea of the uninterrupted glide and pleasing murmur of the soft periods that flow from his tongue.

The expression of the Bride in the "Morning Scene" is the most highly seasoned, and at the same time the most vulgar in the series. The figure, face, and attitude of the husband, are inimitable. Hogarth has with great skill contrasted the pale countenance of the husband with the yellow whitish colour of the marble chimney-piece behind him, in such a manner as to preserve the fleshy tone of the former. The airy splendour of the view of the inner-room in this picture is probably not exceeded by any of the productions of the Flemish school.

The young girl in the third picture, who is represented as the victim of fashionable profligacy, is unquestionably one of the artist's *chef-d'œuvres*. The exquisite delicacy of the painting is only surpassed by the felicity and subtlety of the conception. Nothing can be more striking than the contrast between the extreme softness of her person, and the hardened indifference of her character. The vacant stillness, the docility to vice, the premature suppression of youthful sensibility, the doll-like mechanism of the whole figure, which seems to have no other feeling but a sickly sense of pain—show the deepest insight into human nature, and into the effects of those refinements in depravity, by which it has been good-naturedly asserted, that 'vice loses half its evil in losing all its grossness.'[4] The story of this picture is in some parts very obscure and enigmatical. It is certain that the nobleman is not looking straight forward to the quack, whom he seems to have been threatening with his cane; but that his eyes are turned up with an ironical leer of triumph to the procuress. The commanding attitude and size of this woman, the swelling circumference of her dress, spread out like a turkey-cock's feathers, the fierce, ungovernable, inveterate malignity of her countenance, which hardly needs the comment of the clasp-knife to explain her purpose, all are admirable in themselves, and still

more so, as they are opposed to the mute insensibility, the
elegant negligence of dress, and the childish figure of the girl
who is supposed to be her *protegée*.—As for the Quack, there
can be no doubt entertained about him. His face seems as if it
were composed of salve, and his features exhibit all the chaos
or confusion of the most gross, ignorant, and impudent em-
piricism. The gradations of ridiculous affectation in the Music
scene are finely imagined and preserved. The preposterous,
overstrained admiration of the lady of quality; the sentimental,
insipid, patient delight of the man, with his hair in papers, and
sipping his tea: the pert, smirking, conceited, half-distorted
approbation of the figure next to him; the transition to the total
insensibility of the round face in profile; and then to the wonder of the negro-boy at the rapture of his mistress, form a
perfect whole. The sanguine complexion and flame-coloured
hair of the female virtuoso throw an additional light on the
character. This is lost in the print. The continuing the red
colour of the hair into the back of the chair, has been pointed
out as one of those instances of what may be termed allitera-
tion in colouring, of which these pictures are everywhere full.
The gross bloated appearance of the Italian singer is well relieved by the hard features of the instrumental performer
behind him, which might be carved of wood. The negro-boy
holding the chocolate, both in expression, colour, and execution, is a masterpiece. The gay, lively derision of the other
negro-boy playing with the Acteon, is an ingenious contrast
to the profound amazement of the first. Some account has
already been given of the two lovers in this picture. It is curious to observe the infinite activity of mind which the artist displays on every occasion. An instance occurs in the present
picture. He has so contrived the papers in the hair of the
bride, as to make them look almost like a wreath of half-
blown flowers; while those which he has placed on the head
of the musical amateur, very much resemble a *chevaux-de-
frise*[5] of horns, which adorn and fortify the lacklustre expression, and mild resignation of the face beneath.

The "Night Scene" is inferior to the rest of the series. The
attitude of the husband, who is just killed, is one in which it
would be impossible for him to stand or even to fall. It resembles the loose pasteboard figures they make for children.
The characters in the last picture, in which the wife dies, are
all masterly. I would particularly refer to the captious, petu-
lant, self-sufficiency of the Apothecary, whose face and figure
are constructed on exact physiognomical principles; and to
the fine example of passive obedience and non-resistance in
the servant, whom he is taking to task, and whose coat, of
green and yellow livery, is as long and as melancholy as his

face. The disconsolate look and haggard eyes, the open mouth, the comb sticking in the hair, the broken gapped teeth, which, as it were, hitch in an answer, everything about him denotes the utmost perplexity and dismay. The harmony and gradations of colour in this picture are uniformly preserved with the greatest nicety, and are well worthy the attention of the artist.—I have so far attempted to point out the fund of observation, physical and moral, contained in one set of these pictures, the "Marriage-à-la-Mode." The rest would furnish as many topics to descant upon, were the patience of the reader as inexhaustible as the painter's invention. But as this is not the case, I shall content myself with barely referring to some of those figures in the other pictures, which appear to me the most striking, and which we see not only while we are looking at them, but which we have before us at all other times. For instance, who, having seen, can easily forget that exquisite frost-piece of religion and morality, the antiquated Prude[6] in the "Morning Scene"; or that striking commentary on the *good old times,* the little wretched appendage of a Foot-boy, who crawls, half famished and half frozen, behind her? The French man and woman in the Noon, are the perfection of flighty affectation and studied grimace; the amiable *fraternization* of the two old women saluting each other, is not enough to be admired; and in the little Master, in the same national group, we see the early promise and personification of that eternal principle of wondrous self-complacency, proof against all circumstances, and which makes the French the only people who are vain even of being cuckolded and being conquered! Or shall we prefer to this the outraged distress and unmitigated terrors of the Boy who has dropped his dish of meat, and who seems red all over with shame and vexation, and bursting with the noise he makes? Or what can be better than the good housewifery of the Girl underneath, who is devouring the lucky fragments; or than the plump, ripe, florid, luscious look of the Servant-wench near her, embraced by a greasy rascal of an Othello, with her pie-dish tottering like her virtue, and with the most precious part of its contents running over? Just—no, not quite—as good is the joke of the Woman overhead, who, having quarrelled with her Husband, is throwing their Sunday's dinner out of the window, to complete this chapter of accidents of baked-dishes. The Husband in the "Evening Scene" is certainly as meek as any recorded in history; but I cannot say that I admire this picture, or the "Night Scene" after it. But then, in the "Taste in High-Life," there is that inimitable pair, differing only in sex, congratulating and delighting one another by 'all the mutually reflected charities' of folly and affectation, with the

young Lady, coloured like a rose, dandling her little, black,
pug-faced, white-teethed, chuckling favourite; and with the
portrait of Monsieur Des Noyers in the back-ground, dancing
in a grand ballet, surrounded by butterflies. And again, in the
"Election Dinner," is the immortal Cobbler, surrounded by
his Peers, who

> frequent and full,
> In *loud* recess and *brawling* conclave sit—[7]

the Jew in the second picture, a very Jew in grain; innumerable fine sketches of heads in the "Polling for Votes," of which
the Nobleman overlooking the Caricaturist is the second best,
and the Blind-man going up to vote, the best; and then the
irresistible, tumultuous display of broad humour in the "Chair-
ing the Member," which is, perhaps, of all Hogarth's pictures,
the most full of laughable incidents and situations; the yellow,
rusty-faced Thresher, with his swinging flail breaking the
head of one of the chairmen; and his redoubted antagonist,
the Sailor, with his oak-stick, and stumping wooden-leg, a
supplemental cudgel; the persevering ecstasy of the hobbling
Blind Fiddler, who, in the fray, appears to have been trod
upon by the artificial excrescence of the honest tar; Monsieur,
the monkey, with piteous aspect, speculating the impending
disaster of the triumphant Candidate, and his brother Bruin,
appropriating the paunch; the precipitous flight of the Pigs,
souse[8] over head into the water; the fine Lady fainting, with
vermilion lips; and the two Chimney Sweepers, satirical young
rogues!—I had almost forgot the Politician, who is burning a hole through his hat with a candle in reading a newspaper; and the Chickens, in the "March to Finchley," wandering in search of their lost dam, who is found in the pocket
of the Serjeant. Of the pictures in the "Rake's Progress," exhibited in this collection, I shall not here say anything, because I think them on the whole inferior to the prints, and
because they have already been criticised by a writer, to whom
I could add nothing, in a paper which ought to be read by
every lover of Hogarth and of English genius—I mean, Mr.
Lamb's Essay on the works of Hogarth. I shall at present proceed to form some estimate of the style of art in which this
painter excelled.

What distinguishes his compositions from all others of the
same general kind, is, that they are equally remote from caricature, and from mere still life. It of course happens in subjects taken from common life, that the painter can procure
real models, and he can get them to sit as long as he pleases.
Hence, in general, those attitudes and expressions have been

chosen which could be assumed the longest; and in imitating which, the artist by taking pains and time might produce almost as complete *fac-similes* as he could of a flower or a flower-pot, of a damask curtain or a china-vase. The copy was as perfect and as uninteresting in the one case as in the other. On the contrary, subjects of drollery and ridicule affording frequent examples of strange deformity and peculiarity of features, these have been eagerly seized by another class of artists, who, without subjecting themselves to the laborious drudgery of the Dutch school and their imitators, have produced our popular caricatures, by rudely copying or exaggerating the casual irregularities of the human countenance. Hogarth has equally avoided the faults of both these styles: the insipid tameness of the one, and the gross extravagance of the other, so as to give to the productions of his pencil equal solidity and effect. For his faces go to the very verge of caricature, and yet never (I believe in any single instance) go beyond it: they take the very widest latitude, and yet we always see the links which bind them to nature: they bear all the marks, and carry all the conviction of reality with them, as if we had seen the actual faces for the first time, from the precision, consistency, and good sense with which the whole and every part is made out. They exhibit the most uncommon features, with the most uncommon expressions: but which yet are as familiar and intelligible as possible, because with all the boldness, they have all the truth of nature. Hogarth has left behind him as many of these memorable faces, in their memorable moments, as, perhaps, most of us remember in the course of our lives, and has thus doubled the quantity of our experience.

It will assist us in forming a more determinate idea of the peculiar genius of Hogarth, to compare him with a deservedly admired artist in our own times. The highest authority on art in this country,[9] I understand, has pronounced that Mr. Wilkie[10] united the excellences of Hogarth to those of Teniers.[11] I demur to this decision in both its branches; but in demurring to authority, it is necessary to give our reasons. I conceive that this ingenious and attentive observer of nature has certain essential, real, and indisputable excellences of his own; and I think it, therefore, the less important to clothe him with any vicarious merits which do not belong to him. Mr. Wilkie's pictures, generally speaking, derive almost their whole value from their *reality,* or the truth of the representation. They are works of pure imitative art; and the test of this style of composition is to represent nature faithfully and happily in its simplest combinations. It may be said of an artist like Mr. Wilkie, that *nothing human is indifferent to* *him.* His mind takes an interest in, and it gives an interest to, the most familiar scenes and transactions of life. He professedly gives character, thought, and passion, in their lowest degrees, and in their every-day forms. He selects the commonest events and appearances of nature for his subjects; and trusts to their very commonness for the interest and amusement he is to excite. Mr. Wilkie is a serious, prosaic, literal narrator of facts; and his pictures may be considered as diaries, or minutes of what is passing constantly about us. Hogarth, on the contrary, is essentially a comic painter; his pictures are not indifferent, unimpassioned descriptions of human nature, but rich, exuberant satires upon it. He is carried away by a passion for the *ridiculous.* His object is 'to show vice her own feature, scorn her own image.' He is so far from contenting himself with still-life, that he is always on the verge of caricature, though without ever falling into it. He does not represent folly or vice in its incipient, or dormant, or *grub* state; but full grown, with wings, pampered into all sorts of affectation, airy, ostentatious, and extravagant. Folly is there seen at the height—the moon is at the full; it is 'the very error of the time.' There is a perpetual collision of eccentricities—a tilt and tournament of absurdities; the prejudices and caprices of mankind are let loose, and set together by the ears, as in a bear-garden. Hogarth paints nothing but comedy, or tragi-comedy. Wilkie paints neither one nor the other. Hogarth never looks at any object but to find out a moral or a ludicrous effect. Wilkie never looks at any object but to see that it is there. Hogarth's pictures are a perfect jest-book, from one end to the other. I do not remember a single joke in Wilkie's, except one very bad one of the boy in the "Blind Fiddler," scraping the gridiron, or fire-shovel, I forget which it is.* In looking at Hogarth, you are ready to burst your sides with laughing at the unaccountable jumble of odd things which are brought together; you look at Wilkie's pictures with a mingled feeling of curiosity, and admiration at the accuracy of the representation. For instance, there is a most admirable head of a man coughing in the "Rent-day"; the action, the keeping, the choked sensation, are inimitable: but there is nothing to laugh at in a man coughing. What strikes the mind is the difficulty of a man's being painted coughing, which here certainly is a masterpiece of art. But turn to the blackguard Cobbler in the "Election Dinner," who has been smutting his neighbour's face over, and who is lolling out his tongue at the joke, with a most surprising obliquity of vision; and immediately 'your lungs begin to crow like chanticleer.'

* The Waiter drawing the cork, in the "Rent-day," is another exception, and quite Hogarthian. [w. h.]

Again, there is the little boy crying in the "Cut Finger," who only gives you the idea of a cross, disagreeable, obstinate child in pain: whereas the same face in Hogarth's "Noon," from the ridiculous perplexity it is in, and its extravagant, noisy, unfelt distress, at the accident of having let fall the pie-dish, is quite irresistible. Mr. Wilkie, in his picture of the "Ale-house Door," I believe, painted Mr. Liston[12] as one of the figures, without any great effect. Hogarth would have given any price for such a subject, and would have made it worth any money. I have never seen anything, in the expression of comic humour, equal to Hogarth's pictures, but Liston's face!

Mr. Wilkie paints interiors: but still you generally connect them with the country. Hogarth, even when he paints people in the open air, represents them either as coming from London, as in the polling for votes at Brentford, or as returning to it, as the dyer and his wife at Bagnigge Wells. In this last picture,[13] he has contrived to convert a common rural image into a type and emblem of city honours. In fact, I know no one who had a less pastoral imagination than Hogarth. He delights in the thick of St. Giles's or St. James's. His pictures breathe a certain close, greasy, tavern air. The fare he serves up to us consists of high-seasoned dishes, ragouts and olla podridas, like the supper in *Gil Blas*, which it requires a strong stomach to digest. Mr. Wilkie presents us with a sort of lenten fare, very good and wholesome, but rather insipid than overpowering! Mr. Wilkie's pictures are, in general, much better painted than Hogarth's; but the "Marriage-à-la-Mode" is superior both in colour and execution to any of Wilkie's. I may add, here, without any disparagement, that, as an artist, Mr. Wilkie is hardly to be mentioned with Teniers. Neither in truth and brilliant clearness of colouring, nor in facility of execution, is there any comparison. Teniers was a perfect master in all these respects; and our own countryman is positively defective, notwithstanding the very laudable care with which he finishes every part of his pictures. There is an evident smear and dragging of the paint, which is also of a bad purple, or puttyish tone, and which never appears in the pictures of the Flemish artist, any more than in a looking-glass. Teniers, probably from his facility of execution, succeeded in giving a more local and momentary expression to his figures. They seem each going on with his particular amusement or occupation; Wilkie's have, in general, more a look of sitting for their pictures. Their compositions are very different also: and in this respect, I believe, Mr. Wilkie has the advantage. Teniers's boors are usually amusing themselves at skittles, or dancing, or drinking, or smoking, or doing what they like, in a careless, desultory way; and so the composition is loose and irregular. Wilkie's figures are all drawn up in a regular order, and engaged in one principal action, with occasional episodes. The story of the "Blind Fiddler" is the most interesting, and the best told. The two children standing before the musician are delightful. The "Card-players" is the best coloured of his pictures, if I am not mistaken. "The Village Politicians," though excellent as to character and composition, is inferior as a picture to those which Mr. Wilkie has since painted. His latest pictures, however, do not appear to me to be his best. There is something of manner and affectation in the grouping of the figures, and a pink and rosy colour spread over them, which is out of place. The hues of Rubens and Sir Joshua do not agree with Mr. Wilkie's subjects. One of his last pictures, that of Duncan Gray, is equally remarkable for sweetness and simplicity in colour, composition, and expression. I must here conclude this very general account; for to point out the particular beauties of every one of his pictures in detail, would require an Essay by itself.

I have promised to say something in this Lecture on the difference between the grand and familiar style of painting; and I shall throw out what imperfect hints I have been able to collect on this subject, so often attempted, and never yet succeeded in, taking the examples and illustrations from Hogarth, that is, from what he possessed or wanted in each kind.

And first, the difference is not that between imitation and invention: for there is as much of this last quality in Hogarth, as in any painter or poet whatever. As, for example, to take two of his pictures only, I mean the "Enraged Musician" and the "Gin Lane"; in one of which every conceivable variety of disagreeable and discordant sound—the razor-grinder turning his wheel; the boy with his drum, and the girl with her rattle momentarily suspended; the pursuivant blowing his horn,[14] the shrill milkwoman; the inexorable ballad-singer, with her squalling infant; the pewterer's shop close by; the fishwomen; the chimney-sweepers at the top of a chimney, and the two cats in melodious concert on the ridge of the tiles; with the bells ringing in the distance, as we see by the flags flying: and in the other, the complicated forms and signs of death and ruinous decay—the woman on the stairs of the bridge asleep, letting her child fall over; her ghastly companion opposite, next to death's door, with hollow, famished cheeks and staring ribs; the dog fighting with the man for the bare shin-bone; the man hanging himself in a garret; the female corpse put into a coffin by the parish beadle; the men marching after a funeral, seen through a broken wall in the background; and the very houses reeling as if drunk and tumbling about the ears of the infatuated victims below, the pawn-broker's being the only one that stands firm and unimpaired—enforce the moral meant to be conveyed by each of these pieces with a richness and research of combination and artful contrast not easily paralleled in any production of the pencil or the pen. The clock pointing to four in the morning, in "Modern Midnight Conversation," just as the immoveable Parson Ford[15] is filling out another glass from a brimming punch-bowl, while most of his companions, with the exception of the sly Lawyer, are falling around him 'like leaves in October'; and again, the extraordinary mistake of the man leaning against the post, in the "Lord Mayor's Procession"—show a mind capable of seizing the most rare and transient coincidences of things, of imagining what either never happened at all, or of instantly fixing on and applying to its purpose what never happened but once. So far, the invention shown in the great style of painting is poor in the comparison. Indeed, grandeur is supposed (whether rightly or not, I shall not here inquire) to imply a simplicity inconsistent with this inexhaustible variety of incident and circumstantial detail.

Secondly, the difference between the ideal and familiar style is not to be explained by the difference between the genteel and vulgar; for it is evident that Hogarth was almost as much at home in the genteel comedy, as in the broad farce of his pictures. He excelled not only in exhibiting the coarse humours and disgusting incidents of low life, but in exhibiting the vices, follies, and frivolity of the fashionable manners of his time: his fine ladies hardly yield the palm to his waiting-maids, and his lords and his footmen are on a respectable footing of equality. There is no want, for example, in the "Marriage-à-la-Mode," or in "Taste in High Life," of affectation verging into idiotism, or of languid sensibility, that might

Die of a rose in aromatic pain.[16]

In short, Hogarth was a painter, not of low but of actual life; and the ridiculous and prominent features of high or low life, of the great vulgar or the small, lay equally open to him. The Country Girl, in the first plate of the "Harlot's Progress," coming out of the wagon, is not more simple and ungainly, than the same figure, in the second, is thoroughly initiated into the mysteries of her art, and suddenly accomplished in all the airs and graces of affectation, ease, and impudence. The affected languor and imbecility of the same girl afterwards, when put to beat hemp in Bridewell, is exactly in keeping with the character she has been taught to assume. Sir Joshua could do nothing like it in his line of portrait, which differed chiefly in the background. The fine gentleman at his levee, in the "Rake's Progress," is also a complete model of a person of rank and fortune, surrounded by needy and worthless adventurers, fiddlers, poetasters and virtuosi, as was the custom in those days. Lord Chesterfield himself would not have been disgraced by sitting for it. I might multiply examples to show that Hogarth was not characteristically deficient in that kind of elegance which arises from an habitual attention to external appearance and deportment. I will only add as instances, among his women, the two *elégantes* in the Bedlam scene, which are dressed (allowing for the difference of not quite a century) in the manner of Ackerman's dresses for May[17]; and among the men, the Lawyer in "Modern Midnight Conversation," whose gracious significant leer and sleek lubricated countenance exhibit all the happy finesse of his profession, when a silk gown has been added, or is likely to be added to it; and several figures in the "Cockpit," who are evidently, at the first glance, gentlemen of the old school, and where the mixture of the blacklegs with the higher character is a still further test of the discriminating skill of the painter.

Again, Hogarth had not only a perception of fashion, but a sense of natural beauty. There are as many pleasing faces in his pictures as in Sir Joshua. Witness the girl picking the Rake's pocket in the Bagnio scene, whom we might suppose to be 'the Charming Betsy Careless';[18] the Poet's wife, handsomer than falls to the lot of most poets, who are generally more intent upon the idea in their own minds than on the image before them, and are glad to take up with Dulcineas of their own creating; the theatrical heroine in the "Southwark Fair," who would be an accession to either of our playhouses; the girl asleep, ogled by the clerk in church time, and the sweetheart of the "Good Apprentice" in the reading desk in the second of that series, almost an ideal face and expression; the girl in her cap selected for a partner by the footman in the print of "Morning," very handsome; and many others equally so, scattered like 'stray-gifts of love and beauty'[19] through these pictures. Hogarth was not then exclusively the painter of deformity. He painted beauty or ugliness indifferently, as they came in his way; and was not by nature confined to those faces which are painful and disgusting, as many would have us believe.

Again, neither are we to look for the solution of the difficulty in the difference between the comic and the tragic, between loose laughter and deep passion. For Mr. Lamb has shown unanswerably that Hogarth is quite at home in scenes of the deepest distress, in the heart-rending calamities of com-

mon life, in the expression of ungovernable rage, silent despair, or moody madness, enhanced by the tenderest sympathy, or aggravated by the frightful contrast of the most
impenetrable and obdurate insensibility, as we see strikingly
exemplified in the latter prints of the "Rake's Progress." To
the unbeliever in Hogarth's power over the passions and the
feelings of the heart, the characters there speak like 'the
hand-writing on the wall.' If Mr. Lamb has gone too far in
paralleling some of these appalling representations with Shakespeare, he was excusable in being led to set off what may be
considered as a staggering paradox against a rooted prejudice. At any rate, the inferiority of Hogarth (be it what it
may) did not arise from a want of passion and intense feeling; and in this respect he had the advantage over Fielding,
for instance, and others of our comic writers, who excelled
only in the light and ludicrous. There is in general a distinction, almost an impassable one, between the power of
embodying the serious and ludicrous; but these contradictory
faculties were reconciled in Hogarth, as they were in Shakespeare, in Chaucer; and as it is said that they were in another
extraordinary and later instance, Garrick's acting.

None of these then will do: neither will the most masterly
and entire keeping of character lead us to an explanation of
the grand and ideal style; for Hogarth possessed the most
complete and absolute mastery over the truth and identity
of expression and features in his subjects. Every stroke of
his pencil tells according to a preconception in his mind. If
the eye squints, the mouth is distorted; every feature acts,
and is acted upon by the rest of the face; even the dress and
attitude are such as could be proper to no other figure: the
whole is under the influence of one impulse, that of truth and
nature. Look at the heads in the "Cockpit," already mentioned, one of the most masterly of his productions in this
way, where the workings of the mind are seen in every
muscle of the face; and the same expression, more intense
or relaxed, of hope or of fear, is stamped on each of the
characters, so that you could no more transpose any part of
one countenance to another, than you could change a profile to a front face. Hogarth was, in one sense, strictly an historical painter: that is, he represented the manners and humours of mankind in action, and their characters by varied
expression. Everything in his pictures has life and motion in
it. Not only does the business of the scene never stand still,
but every feature is put into full play; the exact feeling of
the moment is brought out, and carried to its utmost height,
and then instantly seized and stamped on the canvas for ever.
The expression is always taken *en passant*, in a state of prog-

ress or change, and, as it were, at the salient point. Besides
the excellence of each individual face, the reflection of the
expression from face to face, the contrast and struggle of
particular motives and feelings in the different actors in the
scene, as of anger, contempt, laughter, compassion, are conveyed in the happiest and most lively manner. His figures
are not like the background on which they are painted: even
the pictures on the wall have a peculiar look of their own.
All this is effected by a few decisive and rapid touches of the
pencil, careless in appearance, but infallible in their results;
so that one great criterion of the grand style insisted on by
Sir Joshua Reynolds, that of leaving out the details, and attending to general character and outline, belonged to Hogarth.
He did not indeed arrive at middle forms or neutral expression, which Sir Joshua makes another test of the ideal; for
Hogarth was not insipid. That was the last fault with which
he could be charged. But he had breadth and boldness of
manner, as well as any of them; so that neither does that
constitute the *ideal*.

What then does? We have reduced this to something like
the last remaining quantity in an equation, where all the
others have been ascertained. Hogarth had all the other parts
of an original and accomplished genius except this, but this
he had not. He had an intense feeling and command over
the impressions of sense, of habit, of character, and passion,
the serious and the comic, in a word, of nature, as it fell
within his own observation, or came within the sphere of his
actual experience; but he had little power beyond that sphere,
or sympathy with that which existed only *in idea*. He was
'conformed to this world, not transformed.'[20] If he attempted
to paint Pharaoh's daughter, and Paul before Felix, he lost
himself. His mind had feet and hands, but not wings to fly
with. There is a mighty world of sense, of custom, of every-
day action, of accidents and objects coming home to us, and
interesting because they do so; the gross, material, stirring,
noisy world of common life and selfish passion, of which
Hogarth was absolute lord and master: there is another
mightier world, that which exists only in conception and in
power, the universe of thought and sentiment, that surrounds
and is raised above the ordinary world of reality, as the
empyrean surrounds this nether globe, into which few are
privileged to soar with mighty wings outspread, and in
which, as power is given them to embody their aspiring
fancies, to 'give to airy nothing a local habitation and a
name,'[21] to fill with imaginary shapes of beauty or sublimity,
and make the dark abyss pregnant, bringing that which is
remote home to us, raising themselves to the lofty, sustaining

themselves on the refined and abstracted, making all things like not what we know and feel in ourselves, in this 'ignorant present' time, but like what they must be in themselves, or in our noblest idea of them, and stamping that idea with reality, (but chiefly clothing the best and the highest with grace and grandeur): this is the ideal in art, in poetry, and in painting. There are things which are cognisable only to sense, which interest only our more immediate instincts and passions; the want of food, the loss of a limb, or a sum of money: there are others that appeal to different and nobler faculties; the wants of the mind, the hunger and thirst after truth and beauty; that is, to faculties commensurate with objects greater and of greater refinement, which to be grand must extend beyond ourselves to others, and our interests in which must be refined in proportion as they do so.* The interest in these subjects is in proportion to the power of conceiving them and the power of conceiving them is in proportion to the interest and affection for them, to the innate bias of the mind to elevate itself above everything low, and purify itself from everything gross. Hogarth only transcribes or transposes what was tangible and visible, not the abstracted and intelligible. You see in his pictures only the faces which you yourself have seen, or others like them; none of his characters are thinking of any person or thing out of the picture: you are only interested in the objects of their contention or pursuit, because they themselves are interested in them. There is nothing remote in thought, or comprehensive in feeling. The whole is intensely personal and local: but the interest of the ideal and poetical style of art, relates to more permanent and universal objects; and the characters and forms must be such as to correspond with and sustain that interest, and give external grace and dignity to it. Such were the subjects which Raphael chose; faces imbued with unalterable sentiment, and figures, that stand in the eternal silence of thought. He places before you objects of everlasting interest, events of greatest magnitude, and persons in them fit for the scene and action —warriors and kings, princes and nobles, and, greater yet, poets and philosophers; and mightier than these, patriarchs and apostles, prophets and founders of religion, saints and martyrs, angels and the Son of God. We know their impor-

* When Meg Merrilies says in her dying moments[22]—'Nay, nay, lay my head to the East,' what was the East to her? Not a reality but an idea of distant time and the land of her forefathers; the last, the strongest, and the best that occurred to her in this world. Her gipsy slang and dress were quaint and grotesque; her attachment to the Kaim of Derncleugh and the wood of Warrock was romantic; her worship of the East was *ideal*. [w. h.]

tance and their high calling, and we feel that they do not belie it. We see them as they were painted, with the eye of faith. The light which they have kindled in the world, is reflected back upon their faces: the awe and homage which has been paid to them, is seated upon their brow, and encircles them like a glory. All those who come before them, are conscious of a superior presence. For example, the beggars, in the "Gate Beautiful,"[23] are impressed with this ideal borrowed character. Would not the cripple and the halt feel a difference of sensation, and express it outwardly in such circumstances? And was the painter wrong to transfer this sense of preternatural power and the confidence of a saving faith to his canvas? Hogarth's "Pool of Bethesda," on the contrary, is only a collection of common beggars receiving an alms. The waters may be stirred, but the mind is not stirred with them. The fowls, again, in the "Miraculous Draught of Fishes,"[23] exult and clap their wings, and seem lifted up with some unusual cause of joy. There is not the same expansive, elevated principle in Hogarth. He has amiable and praiseworthy characters, indeed, among his bad ones. The Master of the Industrious and Idle Apprentice is a good citizen and a virtuous man; but his benevolence is mechanical and confined: it extends only to his shop, or, at most, to his ward. His face is not ruffled by passion, nor is it inspired by thought. To give another instance, the face of the faithful Female, fainting in the prison-scene in the "Rake's Progress," is more one of effeminate softness than of distinguished tenderness, or heroic constancy. But in the pictures of the Mother and Child, by Raphael and Leonard da Vinci, we see all the tenderness purified from all the weakness of maternal affection, and exalted by the prospects of religious faith; so that the piety and devotion of future generations seems to add its weight to the expression of feminine sweetness and parental love, to press upon the heart, and breathe in the countenance. This is the *ideal*, passion blended with thought and pointing to distant objects, not debased by grossness, not thwarted by accident, nor weakened by familiarity, but connected with forms and circumstances that give the utmost possible expansion and refinement to the general sentiment. With all my admiration of Hogarth, I cannot think him equal to Raphael. I do not know whether, if the portfolio were opened, I would not as soon look over the prints of Hogarth as those of Raphael; but, assuredly, if the question were put to me, I would sooner never have seen the prints of Hogarth than never have seen those of Raphael. It is many years ago since I first saw the prints of the Cartoons hanging round the old-fashioned parlour of a little inn in a remote part of the country. I was then young: I had heard of the fame of the Cartoons, but this was the first time I had ever been admitted face to face into the presence of those divine guests. 'How was I then uplifted!' Prophets and Apostles stood before me as in a dream, and the Saviour of the Christian world, with his attributes of faith and power; miracles were working on the walls; the hand of Raphael was there; and as his pencil traced the lines, I saw godlike spirits and lofty shapes descend and walk visibly the earth, but as if their thoughts still lifted them above the earth. There I saw the figure of St. Paul, pointing with noble fervour to 'temples not made with hands, eternal in the heavens;'[24] and that finer one of Christ in the boat, whose whole figure seems sustained by meekness and love; and that of the same person surrounded by his disciples, like a flock of sheep listening to the music of some divine shepherd. I knew not how enough to admire them.—Later in life, I saw other works of this great painter (with more like them) collected in the Louvre: where Art, at that time, lifted up her head, and was seated on her throne, and said, 'All eyes shall see me, and all knees shall bow to me!' Honour was done to her and all hers. There was her treasure, and there the inventory of all she had. There she had gathered together her pomp, and there was her shrine, and there her votaries came and worshipped as in a temple. The crown she wore was brighter than that of kings. Where the struggles for human liberty had been, there were the triumphs of human genius. For there, in the Louvre, were the precious monuments of art.—There 'stood the statue that enchants the world;'[25] there was Apollo, the Laocoon, the Dying Gladiator, the head of the Antinous, Diana with her Fawn, the Muses and the Graces in a ring, and all the glories of the antique world:

> There was old Proteus coming from the sea,
> And wreathed Triton blew his winding horn.[26]

There, too, were the two "St. Jeromes," Correggio's, and Domenichino's; there was Raphael's "Transfiguration"; the "St. Mark" of Tintoret; Paul Veronese's "Marriage of Cana"; the "Deluge" of Poussin; and Titian's "St. Peter Martyr." It was there that I learned to become an enthusiast of the lasting works of the great painters, and of their names no less magnificent; grateful to the heart as the sound of celestial harmony from other spheres, waking around us (whether heard or not) from youth to age; the stay, the guide, and anchor of our purest thoughts;[27] whom, having once seen, we always remember, and who teach us to see all things through them; without whom life would be to begin again,

and the earth barren; of Raphael, who lifted the human form
half way to heaven; of Titian, who painted the mind in the
face, and unfolded the soul of things to the eye; of Rubens,
around whose pencil gorgeous shapes thronged numberless,
startling us by the novel accidents of form and colour, putting
the spirit of motion into the universe, and weaving a gay
fantastic round and Bacchanalian dance with nature; of Rembrandt, too, who 'smoothed the raven down of darkness till
it smiled,'[28] and tinged it with a light like streaks of burning
ore: of these, and more than these, of whom the world was
scarce worthy, and for the loss of whom nothing could console me—not even the works of Hogarth!

# The Age of Elizabeth:
## A General View *

THE AGE OF ELIZABETH was distinguished, beyond, perhaps, any other in our history, by a number of great men, famous in different ways, and whose names have come down to us with unblemished honours; statesmen, warriors, divines, scholars, poets, and philosophers, Raleigh, Drake, Coke, Hooker, and higher and more sounding still, and still more frequent in our mouths, Shakespeare, Spenser, Sidney, Bacon, Jonson, Beaumont and Fletcher, men whom fame has eternised in her long and lasting scroll, and who, by their words and acts, were benefactors of their country, and ornaments of human nature. Their attainments of different kinds bore the same general stamp, and it was sterling: what they did, had the mark of their age and country upon it. Perhaps the genius of Great Britain (if I may so speak without offence or flattery), never shone out fuller or brighter, or looked more like itself, than at this period. Our writers and great men had something in them that savoured of the soil from which they grew: they were not French, they were not Dutch, or German, or Greek, or Latin; they were truly English. They did not look out of themselves to see what they should be; they sought for truth and nature, and found it in themselves. There was no tinsel, and but little art; they were not the spoiled children of affectation and refinement, but a bold, vigorous, independent race of thinkers, with prodigious strength and energy, but none but natural grace, and heartfelt unobtrusive delicacy. They were not at all sophisticated. The mind of their country was great in them, and it prevailed. With their learning and unexampled acquirement, they did not forget that they were men: with all their endeavours after excellence, they did not lay aside the strong original bent and character of their minds. What they performed was chiefly nature's handiwork; and time has

* [*Lectures on the Dramatic Literature of the Age of Elizabeth* I.]

claimed it for his own.—To these, however, might be added others not less learned, nor with a scarce less happy vein, but less fortunate in the event, who, though as renowned in their day, have sunk into 'mere oblivion,' and of whom the only record (but that the noblest) is to be found in their works. Their works and their names, 'poor, dumb names,' are all that remains of such men as Webster, Dekker, Marston, Marlowe, Chapman, Heywood, Middleton, and Rowley! 'How lov'd, how honour'd once, avails them not:' though they were the friends and fellow-labourers of Shakespeare, sharing his fame and fortunes with him, the rivals of Jonson, and the masters of Beaumont and Fletcher's well-sung woes! They went out one by one unnoticed, like evening lights; or were swallowed up in the headlong torrent of puritanic zeal which succeeded, and swept away everything in its unsparing course, throwing up the wrecks of taste and genius at random, and at long fitful intervals, amidst the painted gewgaws and foreign frippery of the reign of Charles II and from which we are only now recovering the scattered fragments and broken images to erect a temple to true Fame! How long, before it will be completed?

If I can do anything to rescue some of these writers from hopeless obscurity, and to do them right, without prejudice to well-deserved reputation, I shall have succeeded in what I chiefly propose. I shall not attempt, indeed, to adjust the spelling, or restore the pointing, as if the genius of poetry lay hid in errors of the press, but leaving these weightier matters of criticism to those who are more able and willing to bear the burden, try to bring out their real beauties to the eager sight, 'draw the curtain of Time, and show the picture of Genius,' restraining my own admiration within reasonable bounds!

There is not a lower ambition, a poorer way of thought, than that which would confine all excellence, or arrogate its final accomplishment to the present, or modern times. We ordinarily speak and think of those who had the misfortune to write or live before us, as labouring under very singular privations and disadvantages in not having the benefit of those improvements which we have made, as buried in the grossest ignorance, or the slaves 'of poring pedantry'; and we make a cheap and infallible estimate of their progress in civilization upon a graduated scale of perfectibility, calculated from the meridian of our own times. If we have pretty well got rid of the narrow bigotry that would limit all sense or virtue to our own country, and have fraternized, like true cosmopolites, with our neighbours and contemporaries, we have made our self-love amends by letting the generation we live in engross nearly all our admiration and by pronouncing a sweeping sentence of barbarism and ignorance on our ancestry backwards, from the commencement (as near as can be) of the nineteenth, or the latter end of the eighteenth century. From thence we date a new era, the dawn of our own intellect and that of the world, like 'the sacred influence of light'[1] glimmering on the confines of Chaos and old night; new manners rise, and all the cumbrous 'pomp of elder days' vanishes, and is lost in worse than Gothic darkness. Pavilioned in the glittering pride of our superficial accomplishments and upstart pretensions, we fancy that everything beyond that magic circle is prejudice and error; and all, before the present enlightened period, but a dull and useless blank in the great map of time. We are so dazzled with the gloss and novelty of modern discoveries, that we cannot take into our mind's eye the vast expanse, the lengthened perspective of human intellect, and a cloud hangs over and conceals its loftiest monuments, if they are removed to a little distance from us—the cloud of our own vanity and shortsightedness. The modern sciolist *stultifies* all understanding but his own, and that which he conceives like his own. We think, in this age of reason and consummation of philosophy, because we knew nothing twenty or thirty years ago, and began to think then for the first time in our lives, that the rest of mankind were in the same predicament, and never knew anything till we did; that the world had grown old in sloth and ignorance, had dreamt out its long minority of five thousand years in a dozing state, and that it first began to wake out of sleep, to rouse itself, and look about it, startled by the light of our unexpected discoveries, and the noise we made about them. Strange error of our infatuated self-love! Because the clothes we remember to have seen worn when we were children, are now out of fashion, and our grandmothers were then old women, we conceive with magnanimous continuity of reasoning, that it must have been much worse three hundred years before, and that grace, youth, and beauty are things of modern date—as if nature had ever been old, or the sun had first shone on our folly and presumption. Because, in a word, the last generation, when tottering off the stage, were not so active, so sprightly, and so promising as we were, we begin to imagine, that people formerly must have crawled about in a feeble, torpid state, like flies in winter, in a sort of dim twilight of the understanding; 'nor can we think what thoughts they could conceive,' in the absence of all those topics that so agreeably enliven and diversify our conversation and literature, mistaking the imperfection of our knowledge for the defect of their organs, as if it was necessary for us to have a register and certificate of their thoughts, or as if, because they did not see with our eyes, hear with our ears, and understand with our understandings, they could hear, see, and understand nothing. A falser inference could not be drawn, nor one more contrary to the maxims and cautions of a wise humanity. 'Think,' says Shakespeare, the prompter of good and true feelings, 'there's livers out of Britain.'[2] So there have been thinkers, and great and sound ones, before our time. They had the same capacities that we have, sometimes greater motives for their exertion, and, for the most part, the same subject-matter to work upon. What we learn from nature, we may hope to do as well as they; what we learn from them, we may in general expect to do worse.—What is, I think, as likely as anything to cure us of this overweening admiration of the present, and unmingled contempt for past times, is the looking at the finest old pictures; at Raphael's heads, at Titian's faces, at Claude's landscapes. We have there the evidence of the senses, without the alterations of opinion or disguise of language. We there see the blood circulate through the veins (long before it was known that it did so), the same red and white 'by nature's own sweet and cunning hand laid on,' the same thoughts passing through the mind and seated on the lips, the same blue sky, and glittering sunny vales, 'where Pan, knit with the Graces and the Hours in dance, leads on the eternal spring.'[3] And we begin to feel, that nature and the mind of man are not a thing of yesterday, as we had been led to suppose; and that 'there are more things between heaven and earth, than were ever dreamt of in our philosophy.'[4] Or grant that we improve, in some respects, in a uniformly progressive ratio, and build, Babel-high, on the foundation of other men's knowledge, as in matters of science and speculative inquiry, where by going often over the same general ground, certain general conclusions have been arrived at, and in the number of persons reasoning on a given subject, truth has at last been hit upon, and long-established error exploded; yet this does not apply to cases of individual power and knowledge, to a million of things beside, in which we are still to seek as much as ever, and in which we can only hope to find, by going to the fountain-head of thought and experience. We are quite wrong in supposing (as we are apt to do), that we can plead an exclusive title to wit and wisdom, to taste and genius, as the net produce and clear reversion of the age we live in, and that all we have to do to be great, is to despise those who have gone before us as nothing.

Or even if we admit a saving clause in this sweeping proscription, and do not make the rule absolute, the very nature of the exceptions shows the spirit in which they are made. We single out one or two striking instances, say Shakespeare or Lord Bacon, which we would fain treat as prodigies, and as a marked contrast to the rudeness and barbarism that surrounded them. These we delight to dwell upon and magnify; the praise and wonder we heap upon their shrines, are at the expense of the time in which they lived, and would leave it poor indeed. We make them out something more than human, 'matchless, divine, what we will,'[5] so to make them no rule for their age, and no infringement of the abstract claim to superiority which we set up. Instead of letting them reflect any lustre, or add any credit to the period of history to which they rightfully belong, we only make use of their example to insult and degrade it still more beneath our own level.

It is the present fashion to speak with veneration of old English literature; but the homage we pay to it is more akin to the rites of superstition, than the worship of true religion. Our faith is doubtful; our love cold; our knowledge little or none. We now and then repeat the names of some of the old writers by rote; but we are shy of looking into their works. Though we seem disposed to think highly of them, and to give them every credit for a masculine and original vein of thought, as a matter of literary courtesy and enlargement of taste, we are afraid of coming to the proof, as too great a trial of our candour and patience. We regard the enthusiastic admiration of these obsolete authors, or a desire to make proselytes to a belief in their extraordinary merits, as an amiable weakness, a pleasing delusion; and prepare to listen to some favourite passage, that may be referred to in support of this singular taste, with an incredulous smile; and are in no small pain for the result of the hazardous experiment; feeling much the same awkward condescending disposition to patronise these first crude attempts at poetry and lispings of the Muse, as when a fond parent brings forward a bashful child to make a display of its wit or learning. We hope the best, put a good face on the matter, but are sadly afraid the thing cannot answer.—Dr. Johnson said of these writers generally, that 'they were sought after because they were scarce, and would not have been much esteemed, had they been much esteemed.' His decision is neither true history nor sound criticism. They were esteemed, and they deserved to be so.

One cause that might be pointed out here, as having contributed to the long-continued neglect of our earlier writers, lies in the very nature of our academic institutions, which unavoidably neutralizes a taste for the productions of native genius, estranges the mind from the history of our own literature, and makes it in each successive age like a book sealed. The Greek and Roman classics are a sort of privileged text-books, the standing order of the day, in a University education, and leave little leisure for a competent acquaintance with, or due admiration of, a whole host of able writers of our own, who are suffered to moulder in obscurity on the shelves of our libraries, with a decent reservation of one or two top-names, that are cried up for form's sake, and to save the national character. Thus we keep a few of these always ready in capitals, and strike off the rest, to prevent the tendency to a superfluous population in the republic of letters; in other words, to prevent the writers from becoming more numerous than the readers. The ancients are become effete in this respect, they no longer increase and multiply; or if they have imitators among us, no one is expected to read, and still less to admire them. It is not possible that the learned professors and the reading public should clash in this way, or necessary for them to use any precautions against each other. But it is not the same with the living languages, where there is danger of being overwhelmed by the crowd of competitors; and pedantry has combined with ignorance to cancel their unsatisfied claims.

We affect to wonder at Shakespeare, and one or two more of that period, as solitary instances upon record; whereas it is our own dearth of information that makes the waste; for there is no time more populous of intellect, or more prolific of intellectual wealth, than the one we are speaking of. Shakespeare did not look upon himself in this light, as a sort of monster of poetical genius, or on his contemporaries as 'less than smallest dwarfs,'[6] when he speaks with true, not false modesty, of himself and them, and of his wayward thoughts, 'desiring this man's art, and that man's scope.'[7] We fancy that there were no such men, that could either add to or take anything away from him, but such there were. He indeed overlooks and commands the admiration of posterity, but he does it from the *tableland* of the age in which he lived. He towered above his fellows, 'in shape and gesture proudly eminent';[8] but he was one of a race of giants, the tallest, the strongest, the most graceful, and beautiful of them; but it was a common and a noble brood. He was not something sacred and aloof from the vulgar herd of men, but shook hands with nature and the circumstances of the time, and is distinguished from his immediate contemporaries, not in kind, but in degree and greater variety of excellence. He did not form a class or species by himself, but belonged to a class or species. His age was necessary to him; nor could he have been wrenched from his place in the edifice of which he was so conspicuous a part, without equal injury to himself and it. Mr. Wordsworth says of Milton, 'that his soul was like a star, and dwelt apart.'[9] This cannot be said with any propriety of Shakespeare, who certainly moved in a constellation of bright luminaries, and 'drew after him a third part of the heavens.'[10] If we allow, for argument's sake (or for truth's, which is better), that he was in himself equal to all his competitors put together; yet there was more dramatic excellence in that age than in the whole of the period that has elapsed since. If his contemporaries, with their united strength, would hardly make one Shakespeare, certain it is that all his successors would not make half a one. With the exception of a single writer, Otway, and of a single play of his (*Venice Preserved*),[11] there is nobody in tragedy and dramatic poetry (I do not here speak of comedy) to be compared to the great men of the age of Shakespeare, and immediately after. They are a mighty phalanx of kindred spirits closing him round, moving in the same orbit, and impelled by the same causes in their whirling and eccentric career. They had the same faults and the same excellences; the same strength and depth and richness, the same truth of character, passion, imagination, thought and language, thrown, heaped, massed together without careful polishing or exact method, but poured out in unconcerned profusion from the lap of nature and genius in boundless and unrivalled magnificence. The sweetness of Dekker, the thought of Marston, the gravity of Chapman, the grace of Fletcher and his young-eyed wit, Jonson's learned sock,[12] the flowing vein of Middleton, Heywood's ease, the pathos of Webster, and Marlowe's deep designs, add a double lustre to the sweetness, thought, gravity, grace, wit, artless nature, copiousness, ease, pathos, and sublime conceptions of Shakespeare's Muse. They are indeed the scale by which we can best ascend to the true knowledge and love of him. Our admiration of them does not lessen our relish for him: but, on the contrary, increases and confirms it.—For such an extraordinary combination and development of fancy and genius many causes may be assigned; and we may seek for the chief of them in religion, in politics, in the circumstances of the time, the recent diffusion of letters, in local situation, and in the character of the men who adorned that period, and availed themselves so nobly of the advantages placed within their reach.

I shall here attempt to give a general sketch of these causes, and of the manner in which they operated to mould and stamp the poetry of the country at the period of which I have to treat; independently of incidental and fortuitous causes, for which there is no accounting, but which, after all, have often the greatest share in determining the most important results.

The first cause I shall mention, as contributing to this general effect, was the Reformation, which had just then taken place. This event gave a mighty impulse and increased activity to thought and inquiry, and agitated the inert mass of accumulated prejudices throughout Europe. The effect of the concussion was general; but the shock was greatest in this country. It toppled down the full-grown, intolerable abuses of centuries at a blow; heaved the ground from under the feet of bigotted faith and slavish obedience; and the roar and dashing of opinions, loosened from their accustomed hold, might be heard like the noise of an angry sea, and has never yet subsided. Germany first broke the spell of misbegotten fear, and gave the watch-word; but England joined the shout, and echoed it back with her island voice, from her thousand cliffs and craggy shores, in a longer and a louder strain. With that cry, the genius of Great Britain rose, and threw down the gauntlet to the nations. There was a mighty fermentation: the waters were out; public opinion was in a state of projection. Liberty was held out to all to think and speak the truth. Men's brains were busy; their spirits stirring; their hearts full; and their hands not idle. Their eyes were opened to expect the greatest things, and their ears burned with curiosity and zeal to know the truth, that the truth might make them free. The death-blow which had been struck at scarlet vice and bloated hypocrisy, loosened their tongues, and made the talismans and love-tokens of Popish superstition, with which she had beguiled her followers and committed abominations with the people, fall harmless from their necks.

The translation of the Bible was the chief engine in the great work. It threw open, by a secret spring, the rich treasures of religion and morality, which had been there locked up as in a shrine. It revealed the visions of the prophets, and conveyed the lessons of inspired teachers (such they were thought) to the meanest of the people. It gave them a common interest in the common cause. Their hearts burnt within them as they read. It gave a *mind* to the people, by giving them common subjects of thought and feeling. It cemented their union of character and sentiment: it created endless diversity and collision of opinion. They found objects to employ their faculties, and a motive in the magnitude of the consequences attached to them, to exert the utmost eagerness in the pursuit of truth, and the most daring intrepidity in maintaining it. Religious controversy sharpens the understanding by the subtlety and remoteness of the topics it discusses, and braces the will by their infinite importance. We perceive in the history of this period a nervous masculine intellect. No levity, no feebleness, no indifference; or if there were, it is a relaxation from the intense activity which gives a tone to its general character. But there is a gravity approaching to piety; a seriousness of impression, a conscientious severity of argument, an habitual

fervour and enthusiasm in their mode of handling almost every
subject. The debates of the schoolmen were sharp and subtle
enough; but they wanted interest and grandeur, and were
besides confined to a few: they did not affect the general mass
of the community. But the Bible was thrown open to all ranks
and conditions 'to run and read,'[13] with its wonderful table
of contents from Genesis to the Revelations. Every village in
England would present the scene so well described in Burns's
"Cotter's Saturday Night." I cannot think that all this variety
and weight of knowledge could be thrown in all at once upon
the mind of a people, and not make some impressions upon it,
the traces of which might be discerned in the manners and
literature of the age. For to leave more disputable points, and
take only the historical parts of the Old Testament, or the
moral sentiments of the New, there is nothing like them in the
power of exciting awe and admiration, or of rivetting sympathy. We see what Milton has made of the account of the
Creation, from the manner in which he has treated it, imbued
and impregnated with the spirit of the time of which we
speak. Or what is there equal (in that romantic interest and
patriarchal simplicity which goes to the heart of a country,
and rouses it, as it were, from its lair in wastes and wildernesses) equal to the story of Joseph and his Brethren, of
Rachel and Laban, of Jacob's Dream, of Ruth and Boaz, the
descriptions in the book of Job, the deliverance of the Jews
out of Egypt, or the account of their captivity and return from
Babylon? There is in all these parts of the Scripture, and
numberless more of the same kind, to pass over the Orphic
hymns of David, the prophetic denunciations of Isaiah, or the
gorgeous visions of Ezekiel, an originality, a vastness of conception, a depth and tenderness of feeling, and a touching simplicity in the mode of narration, which he who does not feel,
need be made of no 'penetrable stuff.' There is something in the
character of Christ too (leaving religious faith quite out of the
question) of more sweetness and majesty, and more likely to
work a change in the mind of man, by the contemplation of
its idea alone, than any to be found in history, whether actual
or feigned. This character is that of a sublime humanity, such
as was never seen on earth before, nor since. This shone mani-
festly both in his words and actions. We see it in his washing
the Disciples' feet the night before his death, that unspeakable
instance of humility and love, above all art, all meanness, and
all pride, and in the leave he took of them on that occasion,
'My peace I give unto you, that peace which the world cannot
give, give I unto you'; and in his last commandment, that 'they
should love one another.'[14] Who can read the account of his

behaviour on the cross, when turning to his mother he said, 'Woman, behold thy son,' and to the Disciple John, 'Behold thy mother,' and 'from that hour that Disciple took her to his own home,'[15] without having his heart smote within him! We see it in his treatment of the woman taken in adultery, and in his excuse for the woman who poured precious ointment on his garment as an offering of devotion and love, which is here all in all. His religion was the religion of the heart. We see it in his discourse with the Disciples as they walked together towards Emmaus, when their hearts burned within them; in his sermon from the Mount, in his parable of the good Samaritan, and in that of the Prodigal Son—in every act and word of his life, a grace, a mildness, a dignity and love, a patience and wisdom worthy of the Son of God. His whole life and being were imbued, steeped in this word, *charity*; it was the spring, the well-head from which every thought and feeling gushed into act; and it was this that breathed a mild glory from his face in that last agony upon the cross, 'when the meek Saviour bowed his head and died,' praying for his enemies. He was the first true teacher of morality; for he alone conceived the idea of a pure humanity. He redeemed man from the worship of that idol, self, and instructed him by precept and example to love his neighbour as himself, to forgive our enemies, to do good to those that curse us and despitefully use us. He taught the love of good for the sake of good, without regard to personal or sinister views, and made the affections of the heart the sole seat of morality, instead of the pride of the understanding or the sternness of the will. In answering the question, 'who is our neighbour?' as one who stands in need of our assistance, and whose wounds we can bind up, he has done more to humanize the thoughts and tame the unruly passions, than all who have tried to reform and benefit mankind. The very idea of abstract benevolence, of the desire to do good because another wants our services, and of regarding the human race as one family, the offspring of one common parent, is hardly to be found in any other code or system. It was 'to the Jews a stumbling block, and to the Greeks foolishness.'[16] The Greeks and Romans never thought of considering others, but as they were Greeks or Romans, as they were bound to them by certain positive ties, or, on the other hand, as separated from them by fiercer antipathies. Their virtues were the virtues of political machines, their vices were the vices of demons, ready to inflict or to endure pain with obdurate and remorseless inflexibility of purpose. But in the Christian religion, 'we perceive a softness coming over the heart of a nation, and the iron scales that fence and harden it,

melt and drop off.'[17] It becomes malleable, capable of pity, of
forgiveness, of relaxing in its claims, and remitting its power.
We strike it, and it does not hurt us: it is not steel or marble,
but flesh and blood, clay tempered with tears, and 'soft as
sinews of the new-born babe.'[18] The gospel was first preached
to the poor, for it consulted their wants and interests, not its
own pride and arrogance. It first promulgated the equality of
mankind in the community of duties and benefits. It de-
nounced the iniquities of the chief Priests and Pharisees, and
declared itself at variance with principalities and powers, for
it sympathizes not with the oppressor, but the oppressed. It
first abolished slavery, for it did not consider the power of the
will to inflict injury, as clothing it with a right to do so. Its law
is good, not power. It at the same time tended to wean the
mind from the grossness of sense, and a particle of its divine
flame was lent to brighten and purify the lamp of love!

There have been persons who, being sceptics as to the
divine mission of Christ, have taken an unaccountable prejudice to his doctrines, and have been disposed to deny the
merit of his character; but this was not the feeling of the great
men in the age of Elizabeth (whatever might be their belief)
one of whom says of him, with a boldness equal to its piety:

> The best of men
> That e'er wore earth about him, was a sufferer;
> A soft, meek, patient, humble, tranquil spirit;
> The first true gentleman that ever breathed.[19]

This was old honest Dekker, and the lines ought to embalm
his memory to everyone who has a sense either of religion, or
philosophy, or humanity, or true genius. Nor can I help thinking, that we may discern the traces of the influence exerted by
religious faith in the spirit of the poetry of the age of Elizabeth, in the means of exciting terror and pity, in the delineation of the passions of grief, remorse, love, sympathy, the
sense of shame, in the fond desires, the longings after immortality, in the heaven of hope, and the abyss of despair it
lays open to us.*

The literature of this age then, I would say, was strongly
influenced (among other causes), first by the spirit of Christianity, and secondly by the spirit of Protestantism.

The effects of the Reformation on politics and philosophy
may be seen in the writings and history of the next and of the

---

* In some Roman Catholic countries, pictures in part supplied the
place of the translation of the Bible: and this dumb art arose in
the silence of the written oracles. [W. H.]

following ages. They are still at work, and will continue to be so. The effects on the poetry of the time were chiefly confined to the moulding of the character, and giving a powerful impulse to the intellect of the country. The immediate use or application that was made of religion to subjects of imagination and fiction was not (from an obvious ground of separation) so direct or frequent, as that which was made of the classical and romantic literature.

For much about the same time, the rich and fascinating stores of the Greek and Roman mythology, and those of the romantic poetry of Spain and Italy, were eagerly explored by the curious, and thrown open in translations to the admiring gaze of the vulgar. This last circumstance could hardly have afforded so much advantage to the poets of that day, who were themselves, in fact, the translators, as it shows the general curiosity and increasing interest in such subjects, as a prevailing feature of the times. There were translations of Tasso by Fairfax, and of Ariosto by Harington, of Homer and Hesiod by Chapman, and of Virgil long before, and Ovid soon after; there was Sir Thomas North's translation of Plutarch, of which Shakespeare has made such admirable use in his *Coriolanus* and *Julius Cæsar:* and Ben Jonson's tragedies of *Catiline* and *Sejanus* may themselves be considered as almost literal translations into verse, of Tacitus, Sallust, and Cicero's Orations in his consulship. Boccaccio, the divine Boccaccio, Petrarch, Dante, the satirist Aretine, Machiavel, Castiglione, and others, were familiar to our writers, and they make occasional mention of some few French authors, as Ronsard and Du Bartas; for the French literature had not at this stage arrived at its Augustan period, and it was the imitation of their literature a century afterwards, when it had arrived at its greatest height (itself copied from the Greek and Latin), that enfeebled and impoverished our own. But of the time that we are considering, it might be said, without much extravagance, that every breath that blew, that every wave that rolled to our shores, brought with it some accession to our knowledge, which was engrafted on the national genius. In fact, all the disposeable materials that had been accumulating for a long period of time, either in our own, or in foreign countries, were now brought together, and required nothing more than to be wrought up, polished, or arranged in striking forms, for ornament and use. To this every inducement prompted, the novelty of the acquisition of knowledge in many cases, the emulation of foreign wits, and of immortal works, the want and the expectation of such works among ourselves, the opportunity and encouragement afforded for their production by leisure and affluence; and, above all, the insatiable desire of the mind to beget its own image, and to construct out of itself, and for the delight and admiration of the world and posterity, that excellence of which the idea exists hitherto only in its own breast, and the impression of which it would make as universal as the eye of heaven, the benefit as common as the air we breathe. The first impulse of genius is to create what never existed before: the contemplation of that, which is so created, is sufficient to satisfy the demands of taste; and it is the habitual study and imitation of the original models that takes away the power, and even wish to do the like. Taste limps after genius, and from copying the artificial models, we lose sight of the living principle of nature. It is the effort we make, and the impulse we acquire, in overcoming the first obstacles, that projects us forward; it is the necessity for exertion that makes us conscious of our strength; but this necessity and this impulse once removed, the tide of fancy and enthusiasm, which is at first a running stream, soon settles and crusts into the standing pool of dulness, criticism, and *virtù*.[20]

What also gave an unusual *impetus* to the mind of man at this period, was the discovery of the New World, and the reading of voyages and travels. Green islands and golden sands seemed to arise, as by enchantment, out of the bosom of the watery waste, and invite the cupidity, or wing the imagination of the dreaming speculator. Fairy land was realised in new and unknown worlds. 'Fortunate fields and groves and flowery vales, thrice happy isles,' were found floating 'like those Hesperian gardens famed of old,'[21] beyond Atlantic seas, as dropt from the zenith. The people, the soil, the clime, everything gave unlimited scope to the curiosity of the traveller and reader. Other manners might be said to enlarge the bounds of knowledge, and new mines of wealth were tumbled at our feet. It is from a voyage to the Straits of Magellan that Shakespeare has taken the hint of Prospero's Enchanted Island, and of the savage Caliban with his god Setebos.* Spenser seems to have had the same feeling in his mind in the production of his *Faery Queen*, and vindicates his poetic fiction on this very ground of analogy.

> Right well I wote, most mighty sovereign,
> That all this famous antique history
> Of some the abundance of an idle brain
> Will judged be, and painted forgery,
> Rather than matter of just memory:
> Since none that breatheth living air, doth know
> Where is that happy land of faery

---

* See a "Voyage to the Straits of Magellan," 1594. [w. h.]

Which I so much do vaunt, but no where show,
But vouch antiquities, which nobody can know.

But let that man with better sense avise,
That of the world least part to us is read:
And daily how through hardy enterprize
Many great regions are discovered,
Which to late age were never mentioned.
Who ever heard of th' Indian Peru?
Or who in venturous vessel measured
The Amazons' huge river, now found true?
Or fruitfullest Virginia who did ever view?

Yet all these were when no man did them know,
Yet have from wisest ages hidden been:
And later times things more unknown shall show.
Why then should witless man so much misween
That nothing is but that which he hath seen?
What if within the moon's fair shining sphere,
What if in every other star unseen,
Of other worlds he happily should hear,
He wonder would much more; yet such to some appear.[22]

Fancy's air-drawn pictures after history's waking dream
showed like clouds over mountains; and from the romance of
real life to the idlest fiction, the transition seemed easy.—
Shakespeare, as well as others of his time, availed himself of
the old Chronicles, and of the traditions or fabulous inventions
contained in them in such ample measure, and which had not
yet been appropriated to the purposes of poetry or the drama.
The stage was a new thing; and those who had to supply its
demands laid their hands upon whatever came within their
reach: they were not particular as to the means, so that they
gained the end. Lear is founded upon an old ballad; Othello
on an Italian novel; Hamlet on a Danish, and Macbeth on a
Scotch tradition: one of which is to be found in Saxo-Gram-
maticus, and the last in Hollingshed. The Ghost-scenes and
the Witches in each, are authenticated in the old Gothic history. There was also this connecting link between the poetry
of this age and the supernatural traditions of a former one,
that the belief in them was still extant, and in full force and
visible operation among the vulgar (to say no more) in the
time of our authors. The appalling and wild chimeras of
superstition and ignorance, 'those bodiless creations that
ecstasy is very cunning in,'[23] were inwoven with existing manners and opinions, and all their effects on the passions of terror
or pity might be gathered from common and actual observation—might be discerned in the workings of the face, the expressions of the tongue, the writhings of a troubled conscience.
'Your face, my Thane, is as a book where men may read

strange matters.' Midnight and secret murders too, from the imperfect state of the police, were more common; and the ferocious and brutal manners that would stamp the brow of the hardened ruffian or hired assassin, more incorrigible and undisguised. The portraits of Tyrrel and Forrest were, no doubt, done from the life. We find that the ravages of the plague, the destructive rage of fire, the poisoned chalice, lean famine, the serpent's mortal sting, and the fury of wild beasts, were the common topics of their poetry, as they were common occurrences in more remote periods of history. They were the strong ingredients thrown into the cauldron of tragedy, to make it 'thick and slab.' Man's life was (as it appears to me) more full of traps and pit-falls; of hair-breadth accidents by flood and field; more way-laid by sudden and startling evils; it trod on the brink of hope and fear; stumbled upon fate unawares; while the imagination, close behind it, caught at and clung to the shape of danger, or 'snatched a wild and fearful joy' from its escape. The accidents of nature were less provided against; the excesses of the passions and of lawless power were less regulated, and produced more strange and desperate catastrophes. The tales of Boccaccio are founded on the great pestilence of Florence, Fletcher the poet died of the plague, and Marlowe was stabbed in a tavern quarrel. The strict authority of parents, the inequality of ranks, or the hereditary feuds between different families, made more unhappy loves or matches.

> The course of true love never did run even.[24]

Again, the heroic and martial spirit which breathes in our elder writers, was yet in considerable activity in the reign of Elizabeth. 'The age of chivalry was not then quite gone, nor the glory of Europe extinguished for ever.'[25] Jousts and tournaments were still common with the nobility in England and in foreign countries: Sir Philip Sidney[26] was particularly distinguished for his proficiency in these exercises (and indeed fell a martyr to his ambition as a soldier)—and gentle Surrey[27] was still more famous, on the same account, just before him. It is true, the general use of firearms gradually superseded the necessity of skill in the sword, or bravery in the person: and as a symptom of the rapid degeneracy in this respect, we find Sir John Suckling soon after boasting of himself as one—

> Who prized black eyes, and a lucky hit
> At bowls, above all the trophies of wit.[28]

It was comparatively an age of peace,

> Like strength reposing on his own right arm;[29]

but the sound of civil combat might still be heard in the distance, the spear glittered to the eye of memory, or the clashing of armour struck on the imagination of the ardent and the young. They were borderers on the savage state, on the times of war and bigotry, though in the lap of arts, of luxury, and knowledge. They stood on the shore and saw the billows rolling after the storm: 'they heard the tumult, and were still.' The manners and out-of-door amusements were more tinctured with a spirit of adventure and romance. The war with wild beasts, etc. was more strenuously kept up in country sports. I do not think we could get from sedentary poets, who had never mingled in the vicissitudes, the dangers, or excitements of the chase, such descriptions of hunting and other athletic games, as are to be found in Shakespeare's *Midsummer Night's Dream,* or Fletcher's *Noble Kinsmen.*

With respect to the good cheer and hospitable living of those times, I cannot agree with an ingenious and agreeable writer of the present day, that it was general or frequent. The very stress laid upon certain holidays and festivals, shows that they did not keep up the same Saturnalian licence and open house all the year round. They reserved themselves for great occasions, and made the best amends they could, for a year of abstinence and toil by a week of merriment and convivial indulgence. Persons in middle life at this day, who can afford a good dinner every day, do not look forward to it as any particular subject of exultation: the poor peasant, who can only contrive to treat himself to a joint of meat on a Sunday, considers it as an event in the week. So, in the old Cambridge comedy of *The Returne from Parnassus,* we find this indignant description of the progress of luxury in those days, put into the mouth of one of the speakers.

> Why is 't not strange to see a ragged clerke,
> Some stammell weaver, or some butcher's sonne,
> That scrubb'd a late within a sleeveless gowne,
> When the commencement, like a morrice dance,
> Hath put a bell or two about his legges,
> Created him a sweet cleane gentleman:
> How then he 'gins to follow fashions.
> He whose thin sire dwelt in a smokye roofe,
> Must take tobacco, and must wear a locke.
> His thirsty dad drinkes in a wooden bowle,
> But his sweet self is served in silver plate.
> His hungry sire will scrape you twenty legges
> For one good Christmas meal on new year's day,
> But his mawe must be capon cramm'd each day.    *III, ii*

This does not look as if in those days 'it snowed of meat and drink'[30] as a matter of course throughout the year!—The distinctions of dress, the badges of different professions, the very signs of the shops, which we have set aside for written inscriptions over the doors, were, as Mr. Lamb observes, a sort of visible language to the imagination, and hints for thought. Like the costume of different foreign nations, they had an immediate striking and picturesque effect, giving scope to the fancy. The surface of society was embossed with hieroglyphics, and poetry existed 'in act and complement extern.' The poetry of former times might be directly taken from real life, as our poetry is taken from the poetry of former times. Finally, the face of nature, which was the same glorious object then that it is now, was open to them; and coming first, they gathered her fairest flowers to live for ever in their verse —the movements of the human heart were not hid from them, for they had the same passions as we, only less disguised, and less subject to control. Dekker has given an admirable descrip-tion of a mad-house in one of his plays.[31] But it might be per-haps objected, that it was only a literal account taken from Bedlam at that time: and it might be answered, that the old poets took the same method of describing the passions and fancies of men whom they met at large, which forms the point of communion between us: for the title of the old play, "A Mad World, my Masters,"[32] is hardly yet obsolete; and we are pretty much the same Bedlam still, perhaps a little better managed, like the real one, and with more care and humanity shown to the patients!

Lastly, to conclude this account; what gave a unity and common direction to all these causes, was the natural genius of the country, which was strong in these writers in propor-tion to their strength. We are a nation of islanders, and we cannot help it; nor mend ourselves if we would. We are some-thing in ourselves, nothing when we try to ape others. Music and painting are not our *forte:* for what we have done in that way has been little, and that borrowed from others with great difficulty. But we may boast of our poets and philosophers. That's something. We have strong heads and sound hearts among us. Thrown on one side of the world, and left to bustle for ourselves, we have fought out many a battle for truth and freedom. That is our natural style; and it were to be wished we had in no instance departed from it. Our situation has given us a certain cast of thought and character; and our liberty has enabled us to make the most of it. We are of a stiff clay, not moulded into every fashion, with stubborn joints not easily bent. We are slow to think, and therefore

impressions do not work upon us till they act in masses. We
are not forward to express our feelings, and therefore they do
not come from us till they force their way in the most impetuous eloquence. Our language is, as it were, to begin anew,
and we make use of the most singular and boldest combinations to explain ourselves. Our wit comes from us, 'like bird-
lime, brains and all.'[33] We pay too little attention to form and
method, leave our works in an unfinished state, but still the
materials we work in are solid and of nature's mint; we do not
deal in counterfeits. We both under and over-do, but we keep
an eye to the prominent features, the main chance. We are
more for weight than show; care only about what interests
ourselves, instead of trying to impose upon others by plausible
appearances, and are obstinate and intractable in not conforming to common rules, by which many arrive at their ends with
half the real waste of thought and trouble. We neglect all but
the principal object, gather our force to make a great blow,
bring it down, and relapse into sluggishness and indifference
again. *Materiam superabat opus*,[34] cannot be said of us. We
may be accused of grossness, but not of flimsiness; of extravagance, but not of affectation; of want of art and refinement,
but not of a want of truth and nature. Our literature, in a
word, is Gothic and grotesque; unequal and irregular; not cast
in a previous mould, nor of one uniform texture, but of great
weight in the whole, and of incomparable value in the best
parts. It aims at an excess of beauty or power, hits or misses,
and is either very good indeed, or absolutely good for nothing.
This character applies in particular to our literature in the age
of Elizabeth, which is its best period, before the introduction
of a rage for French rules and French models; for whatever
may be the value of our own original style of composition,
there can be neither offence nor presumption in saying, that it
is at least better than our second-hand imitations of others.
Our understanding (such as it is, and must remain to be good
for anything) is not a thoroughfare for commonplaces, smooth
as the palm of one's hand, but full of knotty points and jutting
excrescences, rough, uneven, overgrown with brambles; and
I like this aspect of the mind (as some one said of the country), where nature keeps a good deal of the soil in her own
hands. Perhaps the genius of our poetry has more of Pan than
of Apollo; 'but Pan is a God, Apollo is no more!'[35]

# iii

---

## ESSAYIST AND CRITIC

# The Manager*

[ . . . ] IT IS no insignificant epoch in one's life the first time
that odd-looking thing, a play-bill, is left at our door in a little
market-town in the country (say W[e]m in S[hrop]shire). The
Manager, somewhat fatter and more erect, 'as Manager be-
seems,' than the rest of his Company, with more of the man
of business, and not less of the coxcomb, in his strut and manner, knocks at the door with the end of a walking cane (a
badge of office!) and a bundle of papers under his arm; presents one of them printed in large capitals, with a respectful
bow and a familiar shrug; hopes to give satisfaction in the
town; hints at the liberal encouragement they received at
W[hitchur]ch, the last place they stopped at; had every possible facility afforded by the Magistrates; supped one evening
with the Rev. Mr. J[enkin]s, a dissenting clergyman, and
really a very well-informed, agreeable, sensible man, full of
anecdote—no illiberal prejudices against the profession: then
talks of the strength of his company, with a careless mention
of his own favourite line—his benefit fixed for an early day,
but would do himself the honour to leave farther particulars
at a future opportunity—speaks of the stage as an elegant
amusement, that most agreeably enlivened a spare evening or
two in the week, and, under proper management (to which
he himself paid the most assiduous attention), might be made
of the greatest assistance to the cause of virtue and humanity
—had seen Mr. Garrick act the last night but one before his
retiring from the stage—had himself had offers from the London boards, and indeed could not say he had given up all
thoughts of one day surprising them—as it was, had no reason
to repine—Mrs. F—— tolerably advanced in life—his eldest
son a prodigious turn for the higher walks of tragedy—had said
perhaps too much of himself—had given universal satisfaction
—hoped that the young gentleman and lady, at least, would
attend on the following evening, when the *West-Indian* would
be performed at the market-hall, with the farce of *No Song*

* [*The London Magazine*, March 1820: "The Drama," No. III.]

*No Supper*—and so having played his part, withdraws in the full persuasion of having made a favourable impression, and of meeting with every encouragement the place affords! Thus he passes from house to house, and goes through the routine of topic after topic, with that sort of modest assurance, which is indispensable in the manager of a country theatre. This fellow, who floats over the troubles of life as the froth above the idle wave, with all his little expedients and disappointments, with pawned paste-buckles, mortgaged scenery, empty exchequer, and rebellious orchestra, is not of all men the most miserable—he is little less happy than a king, though not much better off than a beggar. He has little to think of, much to do, more to say; and is accompanied, in his incessant daily round of trifling occupations, with a never-failing sense of authority and self-importance, the one thing needful (above all others) to the heart of man. This however is their man of business in the company; he is a sort of fixture in their little state; like Nebuchadnezzar's image,[1] but half of earth and half of finer metal: he is not 'of imagination all compact:' he is not, like the rest of his aspiring crew, a feeder upon air, a drinker of applause, tricked out in vanity and in nothing else; he is not quite mad, nor quite happy. The whining Romeo, who goes supperless to bed, and on his pallet of straw dreams of a crown of laurel, of waving handkerchiefs, of bright eyes, and billets-doux breathing boundless love: the ranting Richard, whose infuriate execrations are drowned in the shouts of the all-ruling pit; he who, without a coat to his back, or a groat in his purse, snatches at Cato's robe, and binds the diadem of Cæsar on his brow—these are the men that Fancy has chosen for herself, and placed above the reach of fortune, and almost of fate. They take no thought for the morrow. What is it to them what they shall eat, or what they shall drink, or how they shall be clothed? 'Their mind to them a kingdom is.'— It is not a poor ten shillings a week, their share in the profits of the theatre, with which they have to pay for bed, board, and lodging, that bounds their wealth. They share (and not unequally) in all the wealth, the pomp, and pleasures of the world. They wield sceptres, conquer kingdoms, court princesses, are clothed in purple, and fare sumptuously every night. They taste, in imagination, 'of all earth's bliss, both living and loving:' whatever has been most the admiration or most the envy of mankind, they, for a moment, in their own eyes, and in the eyes of others, become. The poet fancies others to be this or that; the player fancies himself to be all that the poet but describes. A little rouge makes him a lover, a plume of feathers a hero, a brazen crown an emperor. Where will you buy rank, office, supreme delights, so cheap as at his shop of fancy? Is it nothing to dream whenever we please, and *seem* whatever we desire? Is real greatness, is real prosperity, more than what it seems? Where shall we find, or where shall the votary of the stage find, Fortunatus's[2] Wishing Cap, but in the wardrobe which we laugh at: or borrow the philosopher's stone but from the *property-man* of the theatre? He has discovered the true Elixir of Life, which is freedom from care: he quaffs the pure *aurum potabile*,[3] which is popular applause. He who is smit with the love of this *ideal* existence, cannot be weaned from it. Hoot him from the stage, and he will stay to sweep the lobbies or shift the scenes. Offer him twice the salary to go into a counting-house, or stand behind a counter, and he will return to poverty, steeped in contempt, but eked out with fancy, at the end of a week. Make a laughing-stock of an actress, lower her salary, tell her she is too tall, awkward, stupid, and ugly; try to get rid of her all you can—she will remain, only to hear herself courted, to listen to the echo of her borrowed name, to live but one short minute in the lap of vanity and tinsel show. Will you give a man an additional ten shillings a week, and ask him to resign the fancied wealth of the world, which he 'by his so potent art'[4] can conjure up, and glad his eyes, and fill his heart with it? When a little change of dress, and the muttering a few talismanic words, make all the difference between the vagabond and the hero, what signifies the interval so easily passed? Would you not yourself consent to be alternately a beggar and a king, but that you have not the secret skill to be so? The player has that 'happy alchemy of mind': why then would you reduce him to an equality with yourself?—The moral of this reasoning is known and felt, though it may be gainsaid. Wherever the players come, they send a welcome before them, and leave an air in the place behind them.* They shed a light upon the day, that does not very soon pass off. See how they glitter along the street, wandering, not where business but the bent of pleasure takes them, like mealy-coated butterflies, or insects flitting in the sun. They seem another, happier, idler race of mortals, prolonging the carelessness of childhood to old age, floating down the stream of life, or wafted by the wanton breeze to their final place of rest. We remember one (we must make the reader acquainted with him) who once overtook us loitering by 'Severn's sedgy side,' on a fine May morning, with a score of play-bills streaming from his pockets, for the use of the neighbouring villages, and a music-score in his hand,

---

\* So the old song joyously celebrates their arrival:
  The beggars are coming to town,
  Some in rags, and some in jags, and some in velvet gowns.

                                              [w. h.]

which he sung blithe and clear, advancing with light step and a loud voice! With a sprightly *bon jour*, he passed on, carolling to the echo of the babbling stream, brisk as a bird, gay as a mote, swift as an arrow from a twanging bow, heart-whole, and with shining face that shot back the sun's broad rays!— What is become of this favourite of mirth and song? Has care touched him? Has death tripped up his heels? Has an indigestion imprisoned him, and all his gaiety, in a living dungeon? Or is he himself lost and buried amidst the rubbish of one of our larger, or else of one of our Minor Theatres?

> Alas! how changed from him,
> That life of pleasure, and that soul of whim![5]

But as this was no doubt the height of his ambition, why should we wish to debar him of it? [ . . .]

# On the Pleasure
# of Painting*

'THERE is a pleasure in painting which none but painters know.' In writing, you have to contend with the world; in painting, you have only to carry on a friendly strife with Nature. You sit down to your task, and are happy. From the moment that you take up the pencil, and look Nature in the face, you are at peace with your own heart. No angry passions rise to disturb the silent progress of the work, to shake the hand, or dim the brow: no irritable humours are set afloat: you have no absurd opinions to combat, no point to strain, no adversary to crush, no fool to annoy—you are actuated by fear or favour to no man. There is 'no juggling here,' no sophistry, no intrigue, no tampering with the evidence, no attempt to make black white, or white black: but you resign yourself into the hands of a greater power, that of Nature, with the simplicity of a child, and the devotion of an enthusiast—'study with joy her manner, and with rapture taste her style.'[1] The mind is calm, and full at the same time. The hand and eye are equally employed. In tracing the commonest object, a plant or the stump of a tree, you learn something every moment. You perceive unexpected differences, and discover likenesses where you looked for no such thing. You try to set down what you see—find out your error, and correct it. You need not play tricks, or purposely mistake: with all your pains, you are still far short of the mark. Patience grows out of the endless pursuit, and turns it into a luxury. A streak in a flower, a wrinkle in a leaf, a tinge in a cloud, a stain in an old wall or ruin grey, are seized with avidity as the *spolia opima*[2] of this sort of mental warfare, and furnish out labour for another half day. The hours pass away untold, without chagrin, and without weariness; nor would you ever wish to pass them otherwise.

* [*Table-Talk; The London Magazine*, Dec. 1820; divided in two on reprinting; the first half is given here.]

Innocence is joined with industry, pleasure with business; and the mind is satisfied, though it is not engaged in thinking or in doing harm.*

I have not much pleasure in writing these Essays, or in reading them afterwards; though I own I now and then meet with a phrase that I like, or a thought that strikes me as a true one. But after I begin them, I am only anxious to get to the end of them, which I am not sure I shall do, for I seldom see my way a page or even a sentence beforehand; and when I have as by a miracle escaped, I trouble myself little more about them. I sometimes have to write them twice over: then it is necessary to read the *proof*, to prevent mistakes by the printer; so that by the time they appear in a tangible shape, and one can con them over with a conscious, sidelong glance to the public approbation, they have lost their gloss and relish, and become 'more tedious than a twice-told tale.' For a person to read his own works over with any great delight, he ought first to forget that he ever wrote them. Familiarity naturally breeds contempt. It is, in fact, like poring fondly over a piece of blank paper: from repetition, the words convey no distinct meaning to the mind, are mere idle sounds, except that our

---

* There is a passage in Werter which contains a very pleasing illustration of this doctrine, and is as follows.[3]

About a league from the town is a place called Walheim. It is very agreeably situated on the side of a hill: from one of the paths which leads out of the village, you have a view of the whole country; and there is a good old woman who sells wine, coffee, and tea there: but better than all this are two lime-trees before the church, which spread their branches over a little green, surrounded by barns and cottages. I have seen few places more retired and peaceful. I send for a chair and table from the old woman's, and there I drink my coffee and read Homer. It was by accident that I discovered this place one fine afternoon: all was perfect stillness; everybody was in the fields, except a little boy about four years old, who was sitting on the ground, and holding between his knees a child of about six months; he pressed it to his bosom with his little arms, which made a sort of great chair for it, and notwithstanding the vivacity which sparkled in his eyes, he sat perfectly still. Quite delighted with the scene, I sat down on a plough opposite, and had great pleasure in drawing this little picture of brotherly tenderness. I added a bit of the hedge, the barn-door, and some broken cart-wheels, without any order, just as they happened to lie; and in about an hour I found I had made a drawing of great expression and very correct design, without having put in anything of my own. This confirmed me in the resolution I had made before, only to copy nature for the future. Nature is inexhaustible, and alone forms the greatest masters. Say what you will of rules, they alter the true features, and the natural expression. [w. h.]

vanity claims an interest and property in them. I have more satisfaction in my own thoughts than in dictating them to others: words are necessary to explain the impression of certain things upon me to the reader, but they rather weaken and draw a veil over than strengthen it to myself. However, I might say with the poet, 'My mind to me a kingdom is,'[4] yet I have little ambition 'to set a throne or chair of state in the understandings of other men.'[5] The ideas we cherish most, exist best in a kind of shadowy abstraction,

Pure in the last recesses of the mind;[6]

and derive neither force nor interest from being exposed to public view. They are old established acquaintance, and any change in them, arising from the adventitious ornaments of style or dress, is hardly to their advantage. After I have once written on a subject, it goes out of my mind: my feelings about it have been melted down into words, and *them* I forget. I have, as it were, discharged my memory of its old habitual reckoning, and rubbed out the score of real sentiment. In future, it exists only for the sake of others.—But I cannot say, from my own experience, that the same process takes place in transferring our ideas to canvas; they gain more than they lose in the mechanical transformation. One is never tired of painting, because you have to set down not what you knew already, but what you have just discovered. In the former case, you translate feelings into words; in the latter, names into things. There is a continual creation out of nothing going on. With every stroke of the brush, a new field of inquiry is laid open; new difficulties arise, and new triumphs are prepared over them. By comparing the imitation with the original, you see what you have done, and how much you have still to do. The test of the senses is severer than that of fancy, and an overmatch even for the delusions of our self-love. One part of a picture shames another, and you determine to paint up to yourself, if you cannot come up to nature. Every object becomes lustrous from the light thrown back upon it by the mirror of art: and by the aid of the pencil we may be said to touch and handle the objects of sight. The air-wove visions that hover on the verge of existence have a bodily presence given them on the canvas: the form of beauty is changed into a substance: the dream and the glory of the universe is made 'palpable to feeling as to sight.'—And see! a rainbow starts from the canvas, with all its humid train of glory, as if it were drawn from its cloudy arch in heaven. The spangled landscape glitters with drops of dew after the shower. The 'fleecy fools' show their coats in the gleams of the setting sun. The shepherds pipe their farewell notes in the fresh evening air. And is this bright vision made from a dead dull blank, like a bubble reflecting the mighty fabric of the universe? Who would think this miracle of Rubens' pencil possible to be performed? Who, having seen it, would not spend his life to do the like? See how the rich fallows, the bare stubble-field, the scanty harvest-home, drag[7] in Rembrandt's landscapes! How often have I looked at them and nature, and tried to do the same, till the very 'light thickened,' and there was an earthiness in the feeling of the air! There is no end of the refinements of art and nature in this respect. One may look at the misty glimmering horizon till the eye dazzles and the imagination is lost, in hopes to transfer the whole interminable expanse at one blow upon the canvas. Wilson[8] said, he endeavoured to paint the effect of the motes dancing in the setting sun. At another time, a friend coming into his painting-room, when he was sitting on the ground in a melancholy posture, observed that his picture looked like a landscape after a shower: he started up with the greatest delight, and said, 'That is the effect I intended to represent, but thought I had failed.' Wilson was neglected; and, by degrees, neglected his art to apply himself to brandy. His hand became unsteady, so that it was only by repeated attempts that he could reach the place, or produce the effect he aimed at; and when he had done a little to a picture, he would say to any acquaintance who chanced to drop in, 'I have painted enough for one day: come, let us go somewhere.' It was not so Claude[9] left his pictures, or his studies on the banks of the Tiber, to go in search of other enjoyments, or ceased to gaze upon the glittering sunny vales and distant hills; and while his eye drank in the clear sparkling hues and lovely forms of nature, his hand stamped them on the lucid canvas to remain there for ever!—One of the most delightful parts of my life was one fine summer, when I used to walk out of an evening to catch the last light of the sun, gemming the green slopes or russet lawns, and gilding tower or tree, while the blue sky gradually turning to purple and gold, or skirted with dusky grey, hung its broad marble pavement over all, as we see it in the great master of Italian landscape. But to come to a more particular explanation of the subject.

The first head I ever tried to paint was an old woman with the upper part of the face shaded by her bonnet, and I certainly laboured it with great perseverance. It took me numberless sittings to do it. I have it by me still, and sometimes look at it with surprise, to think how much pains were thrown away to little purpose—yet not altogether in vain, if it taught me to see good in everything, and to know that there is nothing vulgar in nature seen with the eye of science or of true art. Refinement creates beauty everywhere: it is the grossness of the spectator that discovers nothing but grossness in the object. Be this as it may, I spared no pains to do my best. If art was long, I thought that life was so too at that moment. I got in the general effect the first day; and pleased and surprised enough I was at my success. The rest was a work of time—of weeks and months (if need were) of patient toil and careful finishing. I had seen an old head by Rembrandt at Burleigh-House, and if I could produce a head at all like Rembrandt in a year, in my life-time, it would be glory and felicity and wealth and fame enough for me! The head I had seen at Burleigh was an exact and wonderful fac-simile of nature, and I resolved to make mine (as nearly as I could) an exact fac-simile of nature. I did not then, nor do I now believe with Sir Joshua, that the perfection of art consists in giving general appearances without individual details, but in giving general appearances with individual details. Otherwise, I had done my work the first day. But I saw something more in nature than general effect, and I thought it worth my while to give it in the picture. There was a gorgeous effect of light and shade: but there was a delicacy as well as depth in the *chiaro-scuro*,[10] which I was bound to follow into all its dim and scarce perceptible variety of tone and shadow. Then I had to make the transition from a strong light to as dark a shade, preserving the masses, but gradually softening off the intermediate parts. It was so in nature: the difficulty was to make it so in the copy. I tried, and failed again and again; I strove harder, and succeeded, as I thought. The wrinkles in Rembrandt were not hard lines; but broken and irregular. I saw the same appearance in nature, and strained every nerve to give it. If I could hit off this crumbling appearance, and insert the reflected light in the furrows of old age in half a morning, I did not think I had lost a day. Beneath the shrivelled yellow parchment look of the skin, there was here and there a streak of blood-colour tinging the face; this I made a point of conveying, and did not cease to compare what I saw with what I did (with jealous, lynx-eyed watchfulness) till I succeeded to the best of my ability and judgment. How many revisions were there! How many attempts to catch an expression which I had seen the day before! How often did we strive to get the old position, and wait for the return of the same light! There was a puckering up of the lips, a cautious introversion of the eye under the shadow of the bonnet, indicative of the feebleness and suspicion of old age, which at last we managed, after many trials and some quarrels, to a tolerable nicety. The picture was never finished, and I might have gone on with it to the present hour.* I used to set it on the ground when my day's work was done, and saw revealed to me with swimming eyes the birth of new hopes, and of a new world of objects.— The painter thus learns to look at nature with different eyes. He before saw her 'as in a glass darkly, but now face to face.'[11] He understands the texture and meaning of the visible universe, and 'sees into the life of things,'[12] not by the help of mechanical instruments, but of the improved exercise of his faculties, and an intimate sympathy with nature. The meanest thing is not lost upon him, for he looks at it with an eye to itself, not merely to his own vanity or interest, or the opinion of the world. Even where there is neither beauty nor use—if that ever were—still there is truth, and a sufficient source of gratification in the indulgence of curiosity and activity of mind. The humblest painter is a true scholar; and the best of scholars—the scholar of nature. For myself, and for the real comfort and satisfaction of the thing, I had rather have been Jan Steen, or Gerard Dow,[13] than the greatest casuist or philologer that ever lived. The painter does not view things in clouds or 'mist, the common gloss of theologians,'[14] but applies the same standard of truth and disinterested spirit of inquiry, that influence his daily practice, to other subjects. He perceives form; he distinguishes character. He reads men and books with an intuitive glance. He is a critic as well as a connoisseur. The conclusions he draws are clear and convincing, because they are taken from actual experience. He is not a fanatic, a dupe, or a slave: for the habit of seeing for himself also disposes him to judge for himself. The most sensible men I know (taken as a class) are painters; that is, they are the most lively observers of what passes in the world about them, and the closest observers of what passes in their own minds. From their profession they in general mix more with the world than authors; and if they have not the same fund of acquired knowledge, are obliged to rely more on individual sagacity. I might mention the names of Opie, Fuseli, Northcote,[15] as persons distinguished for striking description and acquaintance with the subtle traits of character.† Painters in ordinary

* It is at present covered with a thick slough of oil and varnish (the perishable vehicle of the English school) like an envelope of gold-beaters' skin, so as to be hardly visible. [w. h.]

† Men in business, who are answerable with their fortunes for the consequences of their opinions, and are therefore accustomed to ascertain pretty accurately the grounds on which they act, before they commit themselves on the event, are often men of remarkably quick and sound judgments. Artists in like manner must know tolerably well what they are about, before they can bring the result of their observations to the test of ocular demonstration. [w. h.]

society, or in obscure situations where their value is not known, and they are treated with neglect and indifference, have sometimes a forward self-sufficiency of manner: but this is not so much their fault as that of others. Perhaps their want of regular education may also be in fault in such cases. Richardson,[16] who is very tenacious of the respect in which the profession ought to be held, tells a story of Michael Angelo, that after a quarrel between him and Pope Julius II 'upon account of a slight the artist conceived the pontiff had put upon him, Michael Angelo was introduced by a bishop, who, thinking to serve the artist by it, made it an argument that the Pope should be reconciled to him, because men of his profession were commonly ignorant, and of no consequence otherwise: his holiness, enraged at the bishop, struck him with his staff, and told him, it was he that was the blockhead, and affronted the man himself would not offend; the prelate was driven out of the chamber, and Michael Angelo had the Pope's benediction accompanied with presents. This bishop had fallen into the vulgar error, and was rebuked accordingly.'

Besides the employment of the mind, painting exercises the body. It is a mechanical as well as a liberal art. To do anything, to dig a hole in the ground, to plant a cabbage, to hit a mark, to move a shuttle, to work a pattern—in a word, to attempt to produce any effect, and to *succeed,* has something in it that gratifies the love of power, and carries off the restless activity of the mind of man. Indolence is a delightful but distressing state: we must be doing something to be happy. Action is no less necessary than thought to the instinctive tendencies of the human frame; and painting combines them both incessantly.* The hand furnishes a practical test of the correctness of the eye; and the eye, thus admonished, imposes fresh tasks of skill and industry upon the hand. Every stroke tells, as the verifying of a new truth; and every new observation, the instant it is made, passes into an act and emanation of the will. Every step is nearer what we wish, and yet there is always more to do. In spite of the facility, the fluttering grace, the evanescent hues, that play round the pencil of Rubens and Vandyke, however I may admire, I do not envy them this power so much as I do the slow, patient, laborious execution of Correggio, Leonardo da Vinci, and Andrea del Sarto, where every touch appears conscious of its charge, emulous of truth, and where the painful artist has so distinctly wrought,

That you might almost say his picture thought![17]

* The famous Schiller used to say, that he found the great happiness of life, after all, to consist in the discharge of some mechanical duty. [w. h.]

In the one case, the colours seem breathed on the canvas as by magic, the work and the wonder of a moment: in the other, they seem inlaid in the body of the work, and as if it took the artist years of unremitting labour, and of delightful never-ending progress to perfection.* Who would wish ever to come to the close of such works—not to dwell on them, to return to them, to be wedded to them to the last? Rubens, with his florid, rapid style, complained that when he had just learned his art, he should be forced to die. Leonardo, in the slow advances of his, had lived long enough!

Painting is not, like writing, what is properly understood by a sedentary employment. It requires not indeed a strong, but a continued and steady exertion of muscular power. The precision and delicacy of the manual operation makes up for the want of vehemence—as to balance himself for any time in the same position the rope-dancer must strain every nerve. Painting for a whole morning gives one as excellent an appetite for one's dinner, as old Abraham Tucker[18] acquired for his by riding over Banstead Downs. It is related of Sir Joshua Reynolds, that 'he took no other exercise than what he used in his painting-room'—the writer means, in walking backwards and forwards to look at his picture; but the act of painting itself, of laying on the colours in the proper place and proper quantity, was a much harder exercise than this alternate receding from and returning to the picture. The last would be rather a relaxation and relief than an effort. It is not to be wondered at, that an artist like Sir Joshua, who delighted so much in the sensual and practical part of his art, should have found himself at a considerable loss when the decay of his sight precluded him, for the last year or two of his life, from the following up of his profession—'the source,' according to his own remark, 'of thirty years uninterrupted enjoyment and prosperity to him.' It is only those who never think at all, or else who have accustomed themselves to brood invariably on abstract ideas, that never feel *ennui*.

To give one instance more, and then I will have done with this rambling discourse. One of my first attempts was a picture of my father, who was then in a green old age, with strong-marked features, and scarred with the small-pox. I drew it with a broad light crossing the face, looking down, with spectacles on, reading. The book was Shaftesbury's *Characteristics*, in a fine old binding, with Gribelin's etchings. My father would

---

* The rich *impasting* of Titian and Giorgione combines something of the advantages of both these styles, the felicity of the one with the carefulness of the other, and is perhaps to be preferred to either. [w. h.]

as lieve it had been any other book; but for him to read was to be content, was 'riches fineless.' The sketch promised well; and I set to work to finish it, determined to spare no time nor pains. My father was willing to sit as long as I pleased; for there is a natural desire in the mind of man to sit for one's picture, to be the object of continued attention, to have one's likeness multiplied; and besides his satisfaction in the picture, he had some pride in the artist, though he would rather I should have written a sermon than painted like Rembrandt or like Raphael! Those winter days, with the gleams of sunshine coming through the chapel-windows, and cheered by the notes of the robin-redbreast in our garden (that 'ever in the haunch of winter sings')[19]—as my afternoon's work drew to a close— were among the happiest of my life. When I gave the effect I intended to any part of the picture for which I had prepared my colours, when I imitated the roughness of the skin by a lucky stroke of the pencil, when I hit the clear pearly tone of a vein, when I gave the ruddy complexion of health, the blood circulating under the broad shadows of one side of the face, I thought my fortune made; or rather it was already more than made, in my fancying that I might one day be able to say with Correggio, '*I also am a painter!*' It was an idle thought, a boy's conceit; but it did not make me less happy at the time. I used regularly to set my work in the chair to look at it through the long evenings; and many a time did I return to take leave of it, before I could go to bed at night. I remember sending it with a throbbing heart to the Exhibition, and seeing it hung up there by the side of one of the Honourable Mr. Skeffington (now Sir George). There was nothing in common between them, but that they were the portraits of two very good-natured men. I think, but am not sure, that I finished this portrait (or another afterwards) on the same day that the news of the battle of Austerlitz[20] came; I walked out in the afternoon, and, as I returned, saw the evening star set over a poor man's cottage with other thoughts and feelings than I shall ever have again. Oh for the revolution of the great Platonic year, that those times might come over again! I could sleep out the three hundred and sixty-five thousand intervening years very contentedly!—The picture is left: the table, the chair, the window where I learned to construe Livy, the chapel where my father preached, remain where they were; but he himself is gone to rest, full of years, of faith, of hope, and charity!

# The Indian Jugglers*

COMING forward and seating himself on the ground in his white dress and tightened turban, the chief of the Indian Jugglers begins with tossing up two brass balls, which is what any of us could do, and concludes with keeping up four at the same time, which is what none of us could do to save our lives, nor if we were to take our whole lives to do it in. Is it then a trifling power we see at work, or is it not something next to miraculous? It is the utmost stretch of human ingenuity, which nothing but the bending the faculties of body and mind to it from the tenderest infancy with incessant, ever-anxious application up to manhood, can accomplish or make even a slight approach to. Man, thou art a wonderful animal, and thy ways past finding out! Thou canst do strange things, but thou turnest them to little account!—To conceive of this effort of extraordinary dexterity distracts the imagination and makes admiration breathless. Yet it costs nothing to the performer, any more than if it were a mere mechanical deception with which he had nothing to do but to watch and laugh at the astonishment of the spectators. A single error of a hair's-breadth, of the smallest conceivable portion of time, would be fatal: the precision of the movements must be like a mathematical truth, their rapidity is like lightning. To catch four balls in succession in less than a second of time, and deliver them back so as to return with seeming consciousness to the hand again, to make them revolve round him at certain intervals, like the planets in their spheres, to make them chase one another like sparkles of fire, or shoot up like flowers or meteors, to throw them behind his back and twine them round his neck like ribbons or like serpents, to do what appears an impossibility, and to do it with all the ease, the grace, the carelessness imaginable, to laugh at, to play with the glittering mockeries, to follow them with his eye as if he could fascinate them with its lambent fire, or as if he had only to see that they kept time

* [First published in *Table-Talk* vol. I, 1821.]

with the music on the stage—there is something in all this which he who does not admire may be quite sure he never really admired anything in the whole course of his life. It is skill surmounting difficulty, and beauty triumphing over skill. It seems as if the difficulty once mastered naturally resolved itself into ease and grace, and as if to be overcome at all, it must be overcome without an effort. The smallest awkwardness or want of pliancy or self-possession would stop the whole process. It is the work of witchcraft, and yet sport for children. Some of the other feats are quite as curious and wonderful, such as the balancing the artificial tree and shooting a bird from each branch through a quill; though none of them have the elegance or facility of the keeping up of the brass balls. You are in pain for the result, and glad when the experiment is over; they are not accompanied with the same unmixed, unchecked delight as the former; and I would not give much to be merely astonished without being pleased at the same time. As to the swallowing of the sword, the police ought to interfere to prevent it. When I saw the Indian Juggler do the same things before, his feet were bare, and he had large rings on the toes, which kept turning round all the time of the performance, as if they moved of themselves.—The hearing a speech in Parliament, drawled or stammered out by the Honourable Member or the Noble Lord, the ringing the changes on their common-places, which anyone could repeat after them as well as they, stirs me not a jot, shakes not my good opinion of myself: but the seeing the Indian Jugglers does. It makes me ashamed of myself. I ask what there is that I can do as well as this? Nothing. What have I been doing all my life? Have I been idle, or have I nothing to show for all my labour and pains? Or have I passed my time in pouring words like water into empty sieves, rolling a stone up a hill and then down again, trying to prove an argument in the teeth of facts, and looking for causes in the dark, and not finding them? Is there no one thing in which I can challenge competition, that I can bring as an instance of exact perfection, in which others cannot find a flaw? The utmost I can pretend to is to write a description of what this fellow can do. I can write a book: so can many others who have not even learned to spell. What abortions are these Essays! What errors, what ill-pieced transitions, what crooked reasons, what lame conclusions! How little is made out, and that little how ill! Yet they are the best I can do. I endeavour to recollect all I have ever observed or thought upon a subject, and to express it as nearly as I can. Instead of writing on four subjects at a time, it is as much as I can manage to keep the thread of one discourse clear and unentangled. I have also time on my hands to correct my opinions, and polish my periods: but the one I cannot, and the other I will not do. I am fond of arguing: yet with a good deal of pains and practice it is often as much as I can do to beat my man; though he may be a very indifferent hand. A common fencer would disarm his adversary in the twinkling of an eye, unless he were a professor like himself. A stroke of wit will sometimes produce this effect, but there is no such power or superiority in sense or reasoning. There is no complete mastery of execution to be shown there: and you hardly know the professor from the impudent pretender or the mere clown.*

I have always had this feeling of the inefficacy and slow progress of intellectual compared to mechanical excellence, and it has always made me somewhat dissatisfied. It is a great many years since I saw Richer, the famous rope-dancer, perform at Sadler's Wells. He was matchless in his art, and added to his extraordinary skill exquisite ease, and unaffected natural grace. I was at that time employed in copying a half-length picture of Sir Joshua Reynolds's; and it put me out of conceit with it. How ill this part was made out in the drawing! How heavy, how slovenly this other was painted! I could not help saying to myself, 'If the rope-dancer had performed his task in this manner, leaving so many gaps and botches in his work, he would have broke his neck long ago; I should never have seen that vigorous elasticity of nerve and precision of movement!'—Is it then so easy an undertaking (comparatively) to dance on a tight-rope? Let anyone, who thinks so, get up and try.[2] There is the thing. It is that which at first we cannot do at all, which in the end is done to such perfection. To account for this in some degree, I might observe that mechanical dexterity is confined to doing some one particular thing, which you can repeat as often as you please, in which you know whether you succeed or fail, and where the point of perfection consists in succeeding in a given undertaking.—In mechanical efforts, you improve by perpetual practice, and you do so infal-

---

* The celebrated Peter Pindar (Dr. Wolcot)[1] first discovered and brought out the talents of the late Mr. Opie, the painter. He was a poor Cornish boy, and was out at work in the fields, when the poet went in search of him. 'Well, my lad, can you go and bring me your very best picture?' The other flew like lightning, and soon came back with what he considered as his master-piece. The stranger looked at it, and the young artist, after waiting for some time without his giving any opinion, at length exclaimed eagerly, 'Well, what do you think of it?'—'Think of it?' said Wolcot, 'why I think you ought to be ashamed of it—that you who might do so well, do no better!' The same answer would have applied to this artist's latest performances, that had been suggested by one of his earliest efforts. [W. H.]

libly, because the object to be attained is not a matter of taste or fancy or opinion, but of actual experiment, in which you must either do the thing or not do it. If a man is put to aim at a mark with a bow and arrow, he must hit it or miss it, that's certain. He cannot deceive himself, and go on shooting wide or falling short, and still fancy that he is making progress. The distinction between right and wrong, between true and false, is here palpable; and he must either correct his aim or persevere in his error with his eyes open, for which there is neither excuse nor temptation. If a man is learning to dance on a rope, if he does not mind what he is about, he will break his neck. After that, it will be in vain for him to argue that he did not make a false step. His situation is not like that of Goldsmith's pedagogue.

> In argument they own'd his wondrous skill,
> And e'en though vanquish'd, he could argue still.[3]

Danger is a good teacher, and makes apt scholars. So are disgrace, defeat, exposure to immediate scorn and laughter. There is no opportunity in such cases for self-delusion, no idling time away, no being off your guard (or you must take the consequences)—neither is there any room for humour or caprice or prejudice. If the Indian Juggler were to play tricks in throwing up the three case-knives, which keep their positions like the leaves of a crocus in the air, he would cut his fingers. I can make a very bad antithesis without cutting my fingers. The tact of style is more ambiguous than that of double-edged instruments. If the Juggler were told that by flinging himself under the wheels of the Jaggernaut,[4] when the idol issues forth on a gaudy-day, he would immediately be transported into Paradise, he might believe it, and nobody could disprove it. So the Brahmins may say what they please on that subject, may build up dogmas and mysteries without end, and not be detected: but their ingenious countryman cannot persuade the frequenters of the Olympic Theatre that he performs a number of astonishing feats without actually giving proofs of what he says.—There is then in this sort of manual dexterity, first a gradual aptitude acquired to a given exertion of muscular power, from constant repetition, and in the next place, an exact knowledge how much is still wanting and necessary to be supplied. The obvious test is to increase the effort or nicety of the operation, and still to find it come true. The muscles ply instinctively to the dictates of habit. Certain movements and impressions of the hand and eye, having been repeated together an infinite number of times, are unconsciously but unavoidably cemented into closer and closer union; the limbs require little more than to be put in motion for them to follow a regular track with ease and certainty; so that the mere intention of the will acts mathematically, like touching the spring of a machine, and you come with Locksley in *Ivanhoe*, in shooting at a mark, 'to allow for the wind.'

Farther, what is meant by perfection in mechanical exercises is the performing certain feats to a uniform nicety, that is, in fact, undertaking no more than you can perform. You task yourself, the limit you fix is optional, and no more than human industry and skill can attain to: but you have no abstract, independent standard of difficulty or excellence (other than the extent of your own powers). Thus he who can keep up four brass balls does this *to perfection;* but he cannot keep up five at the same instant, and would fail every time he attempted it. That is, the mechanical performer undertakes to emulate himself, not to equal another. * But the artist undertakes to imitate another, or to do what nature has done, and this it appears is more difficult, *viz.* to copy what she has set before us in the face of nature or 'human face divine,' entire and without a blemish, than to keep up four brass balls at the same instant; for the one is done by the power of human skill and industry, and the other never was nor will be. Upon the whole, therefore, I have more respect for Reynolds, than I have for Richter: for, happen how it will, there have been more people in the world who could dance on a rope like the one than who could paint like Sir Joshua. The latter was but a bungler in his profession to the other, it is true; but then he had a harder task-master to obey, whose will was more wayward and obscure, and whose instructions it was more difficult to practise. You can put a child apprentice to a tumbler or rope-dancer with a comfortable prospect of success, if they are but sound of wind and limb: but you cannot do the same thing in painting. The odds are a million to one. You may make indeed as many H——s and H——s,[5] as you put into that sort of machine, but not one Reynolds amongst them all, with his grace, his grandeur, his blandness of *gusto,* 'in tones and gestures hit,' unless you could make the man over again. To snatch this grace beyond the reach of art is then the height of art—where fine art begins, and where mechanical skill ends. The soft suffusion of the soul, the speechless breathing eloquence, the looks 'commercing with the skies,' the ever-shifting forms of an eternal principle, that which is seen but for a moment, but dwells in the heart always, and is only seized as it passes by strong and secret sympathy, must be taught

---

* If two persons play against each other at any game, one of them necessarily fails. [W. H.]

by nature and genius, not by rules or study. It is suggested by feeling, not by laborious microscopic inspection: in seeking for it without, we lose the harmonious clue to it within: and in aiming to grasp the substance, we let the very spirit of art evaporate. In a word, the objects of fine art are not the objects of sight but as these last are the objects of taste and imagination, that is, as they appeal to the sense of beauty, of pleasure, and of power in the human breast, and are explained by that finer sense, and revealed in their inner structure to the eye in return. Nature is also a language. Objects, like words, have a meaning; and the true artist is the interpreter of this language, which he can only do by knowing its application to a thousand other objects in a thousand other situations. Thus the eye is too blind a guide of itself to distinguish between the warm or cold tone of a deep blue sky, but another sense acts as a monitor to it, and does not err. The colour of the leaves in autumn would be nothing without the feeling that accompanies it; but it is that feeling that stamps them on the canvas, faded, seared, blighted, shrinking from the winter's flaw, and makes the sight as true as touch—

> And visions, as poetic eyes avow,
> Cling to each leaf and hang on every bough.[6]

The more ethereal, evanescent, more refined and sublime part of art is the seeing nature through the medium of sentiment and passion, as each object is a symbol of the affections and a link in the chain of our endless being. But the unravelling this mysterious web of thought and feeling is alone in the Muse's gift, namely, in the power of that trembling sensibility which is awake to every change and every modification of its ever-varying impressions, that,

> Thrills in each nerve, and lives along the line.[7]

This power is indifferently called genius, imagination, feeling, taste; but the manner in which it acts upon the mind can neither be defined by abstract rules, as is the case in science, nor verified by continual unvarying experiments, as is the case in mechanical performances. The mechanical excellence of the Dutch painters in colouring and handling is that which comes the nearest in fine art to the perfection of certain manual exhibitions of skill. The truth of the effect and the facility with which it is produced are equally admirable. Up to a certain point, everything is faultless. The hand and eye have done their part. There is only a want of taste and genius. It is after we enter upon that enchanted ground that the human mind begins to droop and flag as in a strange road, or in a thick mist, benighted and making little way with many attempts and many failures, and that the best of us only escape with half a triumph. The undefined and the imaginary are the regions that we must pass like Satan, difficult and doubtful, 'half flying, half on foot.' The object in sense is a positive thing, and execution comes with practice.

Cleverness is a certain *knack* or aptitude at doing certain things, which depend more on a particular adroitness and off-hand readiness than on force or perseverance, such as making puns, making epigrams, making extempore verses, mimicking the company, mimicking a style, etc. Cleverness is either liveliness and smartness, or something answering to *sleight of hand,* like letting a glass fall sideways off a table, or else a trick, like knowing the secret spring of a watch. Accomplishments are certain external graces, which are to be learnt from others, and which are easily displayed to the admiration of the beholder, *viz.* dancing, riding, fencing, music, and so on. These ornamental acquirements are only proper to those who are at ease in mind and fortune. I know an individual[8] who if he had been born to an estate of five thousand a year, would have been the most accomplished gentleman of the age. He would have been the delight and envy of the circle in which he moved—would have graced by his manners the liberality flowing from the openness of his heart, would have laughed with the women, have argued with the men, have said good things and written agreeable ones, have taken a hand at piquet or the lead at the harpsichord, and have set and sung his own verses—*nugæ canoræ*[9]—with tenderness and spirit; a Rochester without the vice, a modern Surrey! As it is, all these capabilities of excellence stand in his way. He is too versatile for a professional man, not dull enough for a political drudge, too gay to be happy, too thoughtless to be rich. He wants the enthusiasm of the poet, the severity of the prose-writer, and the application of the man of business.—Talent is the capacity of doing anything that depends on application and industry, such as writing a criticism, making a speech, studying the law. Talent differs from genius, as voluntary differs from involuntary power. Ingenuity is genius in trifles, greatness is genius in undertakings of much pith and moment. A clever or ingenious man is one who can do anything well, whether it is worth doing or not: a great man is one who can do that which when done is of the highest importance. Themistocles said he could not play on the flute, but that he could make of a small city a great one. This gives one a pretty good idea of the distinction in question.

Greatness is great power, producing great effects. It is not enough that a man has great power in himself, he must show it to all the world in a way that cannot be hid or gainsaid. He must fill up a certain idea in the public mind. I have no other notion of greatness than this two-fold definition, great results springing from great inherent energy. The great in visible objects has relation to that which extends over space: the great in mental ones has to do with space and time. No man is truly great, who is great only in his life-time. The test of greatness is the page of history. Nothing can be said to be great that has a distinct limit, or that borders on something evidently greater than itself. Besides, what is short-lived and pampered into mere notoriety, is of a gross and vulgar quality in itself. A Lord Mayor is hardly a great man. A city orator or patriot of the day only show, by reaching the height of their wishes, the distance they are at from any true ambition. Popularity is neither fame nor greatness. A king (as such) is not a great man. He has great power, but it is not his own. He merely wields the lever of the state, which a child, an idiot, or a madman can do. It is the office, not the man we gaze at. Anyone else in the same situation would be just as much an object of abject curiosity. We laugh at the country girl who having seen a king expressed her disappointment by saying, 'Why, he is only a man!' Yet, knowing this, we run to see a king as if he was something more than a man.—To display the greatest powers, unless they are applied to great purposes, makes nothing for the character of greatness. To throw a barleycorn through the eye of a needle, to multiply nine figures by nine in the memory, argues infinite dexterity of body and capacity of mind, but nothing comes of either. There is a surprising power at work, but the effects are not proportionate, or such as take hold of the imagination. To impress the idea of power on others, they must be made in some way to feel it. It must be communicated to their understandings in the shape of an increase of knowledge, or it must subdue and overawe them by subjecting their wills. Admiration, to be solid and lasting, must be founded on proofs from which we have no means of escaping; it is neither a slight nor a voluntary gift. A mathematician who solves a profound problem, a poet who creates an image of beauty in the mind that was not there before, imparts knowledge and power to others, in which his greatness and his fame consists, and on which it reposes. Jedediah Buxton[10] will be forgotten; but Napier's bones[11] will live. Lawgivers, philosophers, founders of religion, conquerors and heroes, inventors and great geniuses in arts and sciences, are great men; for they are great public benefactors, or formidable scourges to mankind. Among ourselves, Shakespeare, Newton, Bacon, Milton, Cromwell, were great men; for they showed great power by acts and thoughts, which have not yet been consigned to oblivion. They must needs be men of lofty stature, whose shadows lengthen out to remote posterity. A great farce-writer may be a great man; for Molière was but a great farce-writer. In my mind, the author of *Don Quixote* was a great man. So have there been many others. A great chess-player is not a great man, for he leaves the world as he found it. No act terminating in itself constitutes greatness. This will apply to all displays of power or trials of skill, which are confined to the momentary, individual effort, and construct no permanent image or trophy of themselves without them. Is not an actor then a great man, because 'he dies and leaves the world no copy?' I must make an exception for Mrs. Siddons, or else give up my definition of greatness for her sake. A man at the top of his profession is not therefore a great man. He is great in his way, but that is all, unless he shows the marks of a great moving intellect, so that we trace the master-mind, and can sympathise with the springs that urge him on. The rest is but a craft or *mystery*. John Hunter[12] was a great man—*that* anyone might see without the smallest skill in surgery. His style and manner showed the man. He would set about cutting up the carcase of a whale with the same greatness of *gusto* that Michael Angelo would have hewn a block of marble. Lord Nelson was a great naval commander; but for myself, I have not much opinion of a sea-faring life. Sir Humphry Davy is a great chemist, but I am not sure that he is a great man. I am not a bit the wiser for any of his discoveries, nor I never met with anyone that was. But it is in the nature of greatness to propagate an idea of itself, as wave impels wave, circle without circle. It is a contradiction in terms for a coxcomb to be a great man. A really great man has always an idea of something greater than himself. I have observed that certain sectaries and polemical writers have no higher compliment to pay their most shining lights than to say that 'Such a one was a considerable man in his day.' Some new elucidation of a text sets aside the authority of the old interpretation, and a 'great scholar's memory outlives him half a century,' at the utmost. A rich man is not a great man, except to his dependants and his steward. A lord is a great man in the idea we have of his ancestry, and probably of himself, if we know nothing of him but his title. I have heard a story of two bishops, one of whom said (speaking of St. Peter's at Rome) that when he first entered it, he was rather awe-struck, but that as he walked up it, his mind seemed to swell and dilate with it, and at last to fill the whole building—the other said that as he saw more of it, he appeared to himself to grow less and less every step he took, and in the end to dwindle into nothing. This was in some respects a striking picture of a great and little mind—for greatness sympathises with greatness, and littleness shrinks into itself. The one might have become a Wolsey; the other was only fit to become a Mendicant Friar—or there might have been court-reasons for making him a bishop. The French have to me a character of littleness in all about them; but they have produced three great men that belong to every country, Molière, Rabelais, and Montaigne.

To return from this disgression, and conclude the Essay. A singular instance of manual dexterity was shown in the person of the late John Cavanagh, whom I have several times seen. His death was celebrated at the time in an article in the *Examiner* newspaper (Feb. 7, 1819), written apparently between jest and earnest:[13] but as it is *pat* to our purpose, and falls in with my own way of considering such subjects, I shall here take leave to quote it.

'Died at his house in Burbage-street, St. Giles's, John Cavanagh, the famous hand fives-player.[14] When a person dies, who does any one thing better than any one else in the world, which so many others are trying to do well, it leaves a gap in society. It is not likely that anyone will now see the game of fives played in its perfection for many years to come—for Cavanagh is dead, and has not left his peer behind him. It may be said that there are things of more importance than striking a ball against a wall—there are things indeed which make more noise and do as little good, such as making war and peace, making speeches and answering them, making verses and blotting them; making money and throwing it away. But the game of fives is what no one despises who has ever played at it. It is the finest exercise for the body, and the best relaxation for the mind. The Roman poet said that "Care mounted behind the horse-man and stuck to his skirts."[15] But this remark would not have applied to the fives-player. He who takes to playing at fives is twice young. He feels neither the past nor future "in the instant." Debts, taxes, "domestic treason, foreign levy, nothing can touch him further." He has no other wish, no other thought, from the moment the game begins, but that of striking the ball, of placing it, of *making* it! This Cavanagh was sure to do. Whenever he touched the ball, there was an end of the chase. His eye was certain, his hand fatal, his presence of mind complete. He could do what he pleased, and he always knew exactly what to do. He saw the whole game, and played it; took instant advantage of his adversary's weakness, and recovered balls, as

if by a miracle and from sudden thought, that everyone gave
for lost. He had equal power and skill, quickness, and judgment. He could either outwit his antagonist by finesse, or beat
him by main strength. Sometimes, when he seemed preparing
to send the ball with the full swing of his arm, he would by
a slight turn of his wrist drop it within an inch of the line.
In general, the ball came from his hand, as if from a racket,
in a straight horizontal line; so that it was in vain to attempt to
overtake or stop it. As it was said of a great orator that he
never was at a loss for a word, and for the properest word,
so Cavanagh always could tell the degree of force necessary
to be given to a ball, and the precise direction in which it
should be sent. He did his work with the greatest ease; never
took more pains than was necessary; and while others were
fagging themselves to death, was as cool and collected as if he
had just entered the court. His style of play was as remarkable
as his power of execution. He had no affectation, no trifling.
He did not throw away the game to show off an attitude, or
try an experiment. He was a fine, sensible, manly player, who
did what he could, but that was more than anyone else could
even affect to do. His blows were not undecided and ineffectual—lumbering like Mr. Wordsworth's epic poetry, nor wavering like Mr. Coleridge's lyric prose, nor short of the mark like
Mr. Brougham's speeches, nor wide of it like Mr. Canning's
wit, nor foul like the *Quarterly,* not *let* balls like the *Edinburgh
Review.* Cobbett and Junius together would have made a
Cavanagh. He was the best *up-hill* player in the world; even
when his adversary was fourteen, he would play on the same
or better, and as he never flung away the game through carelessness and conceit, he never gave it up through laziness or
want of heart. The only peculiarity of his play was that he
never *volleyed,* but let the balls hop; but if they rose an inch
from the ground, he never missed having them. There was
not only nobody equal, but nobody second to him. It is supposed that he could give any other player half the game, or
beat him with his left hand. His service was tremendous. He
once played Woodward and Meredith together (two of the
best players in England) in the Fives-court, St. Martin's-street,
and made seven and twenty aces[16] following by services alone
—a thing unheard of. He another time played Peru, who was
considered a first-rate fives-player, a match of the best out of
five games, and in the three first games, which of course
decided the match, Peru got only one ace. Cavanagh was an
Irishman by birth, and a house-painter by profession. He had
once laid aside his working-dress, and walked up, in his smart-
est clothes, to the Rosemary Branch to have an afternoon's

pleasure. A person accosted him, and asked him if he would have a game. So they agreed to play for half-a-crown a game, and a bottle of cider. The first game began—it was seven, eight, ten, thirteen, fourteen, all. Cavanagh won it. The next was the same. They played on, and each game was hardly contested. "There," said the unconscious fives-player, "there was a stroke that Cavanagh could not take: I never played better in my life, and yet I can't win a game. I don't know how it is." However, they played on, Cavanagh winning every game, and the by-standers drinking the cider, and laughing all the time. In the twelfth game, when Cavanagh was only four, and the stranger thirteen, a person came in, and said, "What! are you here, Cavanagh?" The words were no sooner pronounced than the astonished player let the ball drop from his hand, and saying, "What! have I been breaking my heart all this time to beat Cavanagh?" refused to make another effort. "And yet, I give you my word," said Cavanagh, telling the story with some triumph, "I played all the while with my clenched fist."—He used frequently to play matches at Copenhagen-house for wagers and dinners. The wall against which they play is the same that supports the kitchen-chimney, and when the wall resounded louder than usual, the cooks exclaimed, "Those are the Irishman's balls," and the joints trembled on the spit!—Goldsmith consoled himself that there were places where he too was admired:[17] and Cavanagh was the admiration of all the fives-courts where he ever played. Mr. Powell, when he played matches in the Court in St. Martin's-street, used to fill his gallery at half a crown a head, with amateurs and admirers of talent in whatever department it is shown. He could not have shown himself in any ground in England, but he would have been immediately surrounded with inquisitive gazers, trying to find out in what part of his frame his unrivalled skill lay, as politicians wonder to see the balance of Europe suspended in Lord Castlereagh's face, and admire the trophies of the British Navy lurking under Mr. Croker's hanging brow. Now Cavanagh was as good-looking a man as the Noble Lord, and much better looking than the Right Hon. Secretary. He had a clear, open countenance, and did not look sideways or down, like Mr. Murray the bookseller. He was a young fellow of sense, humour, and courage. He once had a quarrel with a water-man at Hungerford-stairs, and, they say, served him out in great style. In a word, there are hundreds at this day, who cannot mention his name without admiration, as the best fives-player that perhaps ever lived (the greatest excellence of which they have any notion)—and the noisy shout of the ring happily stood him in stead of the unheard voice of posterity!—The only person who seems to have excelled as much in another way as Cavanagh did in his, was the late John Davies, the racket-player. It was remarked of him that he did not seem to follow the ball, but the ball seemed to follow him. Give him a foot of wall, and he was sure to make the ball. The four best racket-players of that day were Jack Spines, Jem Harding, Armitage, and Church. Davies could give any one of these two hands a time, that is, half the game, and each of these, at their best, could give the best player now in London the same odds. Such are the gradations in all exertions of human skill and art. He once played four capital players together, and beat them. He was also a first-rate tennis-player, and an excellent fives-player. In the Fleet of King's Bench, he would have stood against Powell, who was reckoned the best open-ground player of his time. This last-mentioned player is at present the keeper of the Fives-court, and we might recommend to him for a motto over his door—"Who enters here, forgets himself, his country, and his friends." And the best of it is, that by the calculation of the odds, none of the three are worth remembering!—Cavanagh died from the bursting of a blood-vessel, which prevented him from playing for the last two or three years. This, he was often heard to say, he thought hard upon him. He was fast recovering, however, when he was suddenly carried off, to the regret of all who knew him. As Mr. Peel made it a qualification of the present Speaker, Mr. Manners Sutton, that he was an excellent moral character, so Jack Cavanagh was a zealous Catholic, and could not be persuaded to eat meat on a Friday, the day on which he died. We have paid this willing tribute to his memory.

> Let no rude hand deface it,
> And his forlorn "*Hic Jacet*." [18]

# On Antiquity*

THERE IS no such thing as Antiquity in the ordinary acceptation we affix to the term. Whatever is or has been, while it is passing, must be modern. The early ages may have been barbarous in themselves; but they have become *ancient* with the slow and silent lapse of successive generations. The 'olden times' are only such in reference to us. The past is rendered strange, mysterious, visionary, awful, from the great gap in time that parts us from it, and the long perspective of waning years. Things gone by and almost forgotten, look dim and dull, uncouth and quaint, from our ignorance of them, and the mutability of customs. But in their day—they were fresh, unimpaired, in full vigour, familiar, and glossy. The Children in the Wood, and Percy's Relics, were once recent productions; and Auld Robin Gray[1] was, in his time, a very commonplace old fellow! The wars of York and Lancaster, while they lasted, were, 'lively, audible, and full of vent,' as fresh and lusty as the white and red roses that distinguished their different banners, though they have since became a bye-word and a solecism in history.

The sun shone in Julius Cæsar's time just as it does now. On the road-side between Winchester and Salisbury are some remains of old Roman encampments, with their double lines of circumvallation (now turned into pasturage for sheep), which answer exactly to the descriptions of this kind in Cæsar's Commentaries. In a dull and cloudy atmosphere, I can conceive that this is the identical spot that the first Cæsar trod; and figure to myself the deliberate movements and scarce perceptible march of close-embodied legions. But if the sun breaks out, making its way through dazzling, fleecy clouds, lights up the blue serene, and gilds the sombre earth, I can no longer persuade myself that it is the same scene as formerly, or transfer the actual image before me so far back. The brightness of nature is not easily reduced to the low, twilight tone of history; and the impressions of sense defeat and

* [*Plain Speaker; London Magazine*, May 1821.]

dissipate the faint traces of learning and tradition. It is only by an effort of reason, to which fancy is averse, that I bring myself to believe that the sun shone as bright, that the sky was as blue, and the earth as green, two thousand years ago as it is at present. How ridiculous this seems; yet so it is!

The *dark* or middle ages, when everything was hid in the fog and haze of confusion and ignorance, seem, to the same involuntary kind of prejudice, older and farther off, and more inaccessible to the imagination, than the brilliant and well-defined periods of Greece and Rome. A Gothic ruin appears buried in a greater depth of obscurity, to be weighed down and rendered venerable with the hoar of more distant ages, to have been longer mouldering into neglect and oblivion, to be a record and memento of events more wild and alien to our own times, than a Grecian temple,* Amadis de Gaul,[3] and the seven Champions of Christendom,[4] with me (honestly speaking) rank as contemporaries with Theseus, Pirithous, and the heroes of the fabulous ages. My imagination will stretch no farther back into the commencement of time than the first traces and rude dawn of civilization and mighty enterprise, in either case; and in attempting to force it upwards by the scale of chronology, it only recoils upon itself, and dwindles from a lofty survey of 'the dark rearward and abyss of time,'[5] into a poor and puny calculation of insignificant cyphers. In like manner, I cannot go back to any time more remote and dreary than that recorded in Stow's and Holingshed's *Chronicles,*[6] unless I turn to 'the wars of old Assaracus and Inachus divine,'[7] and the gorgeous events of Eastern history, where the distance of place may be said to add to the length of time and weight of thought. That is old (in sentiment and poetry) which is decayed, shadowy, imperfect, out of date, and changed from what it was. That of which we have a distinct idea, which comes before us entire and made out in all its parts, will have a novel appearance, however old in reality; nor can it be impressed with the romantic and superstitious character of antiquity. Those times that we can parallel with our own in civilization and knowledge, seem advanced into

---

* 'The Gothic architecture, though not so ancient as the Grecian, is more so to our imagination, with which the artist is more concerned than with absolute truth.'—*Sir Joshua Reynolds's Discourses,* vol. ii. p. 138.

Till I met with this remark in so circumspect and guarded a writer as Sir Joshua, I was afraid of being charged with extravagance in some of the above assertions. *Pereant isti qui ante nos nostra dixerunt.*[2] It is thus that our favourite speculations are often accounted paradoxes by the ignorant—while by the learned reader they are set down as plagiarisms. [W.H.]

the same line with our own in the order of progression. The perfection of art does not look like the infancy of things. Or those times are prominent, and, as it were, confront the present age, that are raised high in the scale of polished society, and the trophies of which stand out above the low, obscure, grovelling level of barbarism and rusticity. Thus, Rome and Athens were two cities set on a hill, that could not be hid, and that everywhere meet the retrospective eye of history. It is not the full-grown, articulated, thoroughly accomplished periods of the world, that we regard with the pity or reverence due to age; so much as those imperfect, unformed, uncertain periods, which seem to totter on the verge of non-existence, to shrink from the grasp of our feeble imaginations, as they crawl out of, or retire into, the womb of time, and of which our utmost assurance is to doubt whether they ever were or not!

To give some other instances of this feeling, taken at random. Whittington and his Cat, the first and favourite studies of my childhood, are, to my way of thinking, as old and reverend personages as any recorded in more authentic history. It must have been long before the invention of triple bob-majors, that Bow-bells rung out their welcome never-to-be-forgotten peal, hailing him Thrice Lord Mayor of London. Does not all we know relating to the site of old London-wall, and the first stones that were laid of this mighty metropolis, seem of a far older date (hid in the lap of 'chaos and old night') than the splendid and imposing details of the decline and fall of the Roman Empire?—Again, the early Italian pictures of Cimabue, Giotto, and Ghirlandaio[8] are covered with the marks of unquestionable antiquity; while the Greek statues, done a thousand years before them, shine in glossy, undiminished splendour, and flourish in immortal youth and beauty. The latter Grecian Gods, as we find them there represented, are to all appearance a race of modern fine gentlemen, who *led the life of honour* with their favourite mistresses of mortal or immortal mould—were gallant, graceful, well-dressed, and well-spoken; whereas the Gothic deities long after, carved in horrid wood or misshapen stone, and worshipped in dreary waste or tangled forest, belong, in the mind's heraldry, to almost as ancient a date as those elder and discarded Gods of the Pagan mythology, Ops, and Rhea, and old Saturn—those strange anomalies of earth and cloudy spirit, born of the elements and conscious will, and clothing themselves and all things with shape and formal being. The "Chronicle of Brute," in Spenser's *Faery Queene*,[9] has a tolerable air of antiquity in it; so in the dramatic line, the Ghost of one of the old kings of Ormus, introduced as Prologue to Fulke Greville's play of Mustapha,[10] is reasonably far-fetched, and palpably obscure. A monk in the Popish Calendar, or even in the *Canterbury Tales*, is a more questionable and out-of-the-way personage than the Chiron of Achilles, or the high-priest in Homer. When Chaucer, in his *Troilus and Cressida*, makes the Trojan hero invoke the absence of light, in these two lines—

> Why proffer'st thou light me for to sell?
> Go sell it them that smallè seles grave!—11

he is guilty of an anachronism; or at least I much doubt whether there was such a profession as that of seal-engraver in the Trojan war. But the dimness of the objects and the quaintness of the allusion throw us farther back into the night of time, than the golden, glittering images of the *Iliad*. The *Travels* of Anacharsis[12] are less obsolete at this time of day, than Coryate's *Crudities*,[13] or Fuller's *Worthies*.[14] 'Here is some of the ancient city,' said a Roman, taking up a handful of dust from beneath his feet. The ground we tread on is as old as the creation, though it does not seem so, except when collected into gigantic masses, or separated by gloomy solitudes from modern uses and the purposes of common life. The lone Helvellyn and the silent Andes are in thought coeval with the globe itself, and can only perish with it. The Pyramids of Egypt are vast, sublime, old, eternal; but Stonehenge, built no doubt in a later day, satisfies my capacity for the sense of antiquity; it seems as if as much rain had drizzled on its grey, withered head, and it had watched out as many winter-nights; the hand of time is upon it, and it has sustained the burden of years upon its back, a wonder and a ponderous riddle, time out of mind, without known origin or use, baffling fable or conjecture, the credulity of the ignorant, or wise men's search.

> Thou noblest monument of Albion's isle,
> Whether by Merlin's aid, from Scythia's shore
> To Amber's fatal plain Pendragon bore,
> Huge frame of giant hands, the mighty pile,
> T'entomb his Britons slain by Hengist's guile:
> Or Druid priests, sprinkled with human gore,
> Taught mid thy massy maze their mystic lore:
> Or Danish chiefs, enrich'd with savage spoil,
> To victory's idol vast, an unhewn shrine,
> Rear'd the rude heap, or in thy hallow'd ground
> Repose the kings of Brutus' genuine line;
> Or here those kings in solemn state were crown'd;
> Studious to trace thy wondrous origin,
> We muse on many an ancient tale renown'd.

*Warton*.[15]

So it is with respect to ourselves also; it is the sense of change or decay that marks the difference between the real and apparent progress of time, both in the events of our own lives and the history of the world we live in.

Impressions of a peculiar and accidental nature, of which few traces are left, and which return seldom or never, fade in the distance, and are consigned to obscurity—while those that belong to a given and definite class are kept up, and assume a constant and tangible form, from familiarity and habit. That which was personal to myself merely, is lost and confounded with other things, like a drop in the ocean; it was but a point at first, which by its nearness affected me, and by its removal becomes nothing; while circumstances of a general interest and abstract importance present the same distinct, well-known aspect as ever, and are durable in proportion to the extent of their influence. Our own idle feelings and foolish fancies we get tired or grow ashamed of, as their novelty wears out; 'when we become men, we put away childish things'; but the impressions we derive from the exercise of our higher faculties last as long as the faculties themselves. They have nothing to do with time, place, and circumstance; and are of universal applicability and recurrence. An incident in my own history, that delighted or tormented me very much at the time, I may have long since blotted from my memory, or have great difficulty in calling to mind after a certain period; but I can never forget the first time of my seeing Mrs. Siddons act, which appears as if it happened yesterday; and the reason is because it has been something for me to think of ever since.[16] The petty and the personal, that which appeals to our senses and our appetites, passes away with the occasion that gives it birth. The grand and the ideal, that which appeals to the imagination, can only perish with it, and remains with us, unimpaired in its lofty abstraction, from youth to age; as wherever we go, we still see the same heavenly bodies shining over our heads! An old familiar face, the house that we were brought up in, sometimes the scenes and places that we formerly knew and loved, may be changed, so that we hardly know them again; the characters in books, the faces in old pictures, the propositions in Euclid, remain the same as when they were first pointed out to us. There is a continual alternation of generation and decay in individual forms and feelings, that marks the progress of existence, and the ceaseless current of our lives, borne along with it; but this does not extend to our love of art or knowledge of nature. It seems a long time ago since some of the first events of the French Revolution; the prominent characters that figured then have been swept away and succeeded by others; yet I cannot say that this circumstance has in any way abated my hatred of tyranny, or reconciled my understanding to the fashionable doctrine of Divine Right. The sight of an old newspaper of that date would give one a fit of the spleen for half an hour; on the other hand, it must be confessed, Mr. Burke's Reflections on this subject are as fresh and dazzling as in the year 1791; and his "Letter to a Noble Lord" is even now as interesting as Lord John Russell's "Letter to Mr. Wilberforce," which appeared only a few weeks back. Ephemeral politics and still-born productions are speedily consigned to oblivion; great principles and original works are a match even for time itself!

We may, by following up this train of ideas, give some account why time runs faster as our years increase. We gain by habit and experience a more determinate and settled, that is, a more uniform notion of things. We refer each particular to a given standard. Our impressions acquire the character of identical propositions. Our most striking thoughts are turned into truisms. One observation is like another, that I made formerly. The idea I have of a certain character or subject is just the same as I had ten years ago. I have learnt nothing since. There is no alteration perceptible, no advance made; so that the two points of time seem to touch and coincide. I get from the one to the other immediately by the familiarity of habit, by the undistinguishing process of abstraction. What I can recall so easily and mechanically does not seem far off; it is completely within my reach, and consequently close to me in apprehension. I have no intricate web of curious speculation to wind or unwind, to pass from one state of feeling and opinion to the other; no complicated train of associations, which place an immeasurable barrier between my knowledge or my ignorance at different epochs. There is no contrast, no repugnance to widen the interval; no new sentiment infused, like another atmosphere, to lengthen the perspective. I am but where I was. I see the object before me just as I have been accustomed to do. The ideas are written down in the brain as in the page of a book—*totidem verbis et literis.*[17] The mind becomes *stereotyped.* By not going forward to explore new regions, or break up new grounds, we are thrown back more and more upon our past acquisitions; and this habitual recurrence increases the facility and indifference with which we make the imaginary transition. By thinking of what has been, we change places with ourselves, and transpose our personal identity at will; so as to fix the slider of our improgressive continuance at whatever point we please. This is an advantage or a disadvantage, which we have not in youth. After a certain period, we neither lose nor gain, neither add to, nor diminish our stock; up to that period we do nothing else but lose our former notions and being, and gain a new one every instant. Our life is like the birth of a new day; the dawn breaks apace, and the clouds clear away. A new world of thought and observation is opened to our search. A year makes the difference of an age. A total alteration takes place in our ideas, feelings, habits, looks. We outgrow ourselves. A separate set of objects, of the existence of which we had not a suspicion, engages and occupies our whole souls. Shapes and colours of all varieties, and of gorgeous tint, intercept our view of what we were. Life thickens. Time glows on its axle. Every revolution of the wheel gives an unsettled aspect to things. The world and its inhabitants turn round, and we forget one change of scene in another. Art woos us; science tempts us into her intricate labyrinths; each step presents unlooked-for vistas, and closes upon us our backward path. Our onward road is strange, obscure, and infinite. We are bewildered in a shadow, lost in a dream. Our perceptions have the brightness and the indistinctness of a trance. Our continuity of consciousness is broken, crumbles, and falls in pieces. We go on, learning and forgetting every hour. Our feelings are chaotic, confused, strange to each other and to ourselves. Our life does not hang together—but straggling, disjointed, winds its slow length along, stretching out to the endless future—unmindful of the ignorant past. We seem many beings in one, and cast the slough of our existence daily. The birth of knowledge is the generation of time. The unfolding of our experience is long and voluminous; nor do we all at once recover from our surprise at the number of objects that distract our attention. Every new study is a separate, arduous, and insurmountable undertaking. We are lost in wonder at the magnitude, the difficulty, and the interminable prospect. We spell out the first years of our existence, like learning a lesson for the first time, where every advance is slow, doubtful, interesting; afterwards we rehearse our parts by rote, and are hardly conscious of the meaning. A very short period (from fifteen to twenty-five or thirty) includes the whole map and table of contents of human life. From that time we may be said to live our lives over again, to repeat ourselves—the same thoughts return at stated intervals, like the tunes of a barrel-organ; and the volume of the universe is no more than a form of words and book of reference.

Time in general is supposed to move faster or slower, as we attend more or less to the succession of our ideas, in the same manner as distance is increased or lessened by the greater or less variety of intervening objects. There is, however, a difference in this respect. Suspense, where the mind is engrossed with one idea, and kept from amusing itself with any other, is not only the most uncomfortable, but the most tiresome of all things. The fixing our attention on a single point makes us more sensible of the delay, and hangs an additional weight of fretful impatience on every moment of expectation. People in country-places, without employment or artificial resources, complain that time lies heavy on their hands. Its leaden pace is not occasioned by the quantity of thought, but by vacancy, and the continual languid craving after excitement. It wants spirit and vivacity to give it motion. We are on the watch to see how time goes; and it appears to lag behind, because, in the absence of objects to arrest our immediate attention, we are always getting on before it. We do not see its divisions, but we feel the galling pressure of each creeping sand that measures out our hours. Again, a rapid succession of external objects and amusements, which leave no room for reflection, and where one gratification is forgotten in the next, makes time pass quickly, as well as delightfully. We do not perceive an extent of surface, but only a succession of points. We are whirled swiftly along by the hand of dissipation, but cannot stay to look behind us. On the contrary, change of scene, travelling through a foreign country, or the meeting with a variety of striking adventures that lay hold of the imagination, and continue to haunt it in a waking dream, will make days seem weeks. From the crowd of events, the number of distinct points of view, brought into a small compass, we seem to have passed through a great length of time, when it is no such thing. In traversing a flat, barren country, the monotony of our ideas fatigues, and makes the way longer; whereas, if the prospect is diversified and picturesque, we get over the miles without counting them. In painting or writing, hours are melted almost into minutes: the mind, absorbed in the eagerness of its pursuit, forgets the time necessary to accomplish it; and, indeed, the clock often finds us employed on the same thought or part of a picture that occupied us when it struck last. It seems, then, there are several other circumstances besides the number and distinctness of our ideas, to be taken into the account in the measure of time, or in considering 'whom time ambles withal, whom time gallops withal, and whom he stands still withal.'[18] Time wears away slowly with a man in solitary confinement; not from the number or variety of his ideas, but from their weary sameness, fretting like drops of water. The imagination may distinguish the lapse of time by the brilliant variety of its tints, and the many striking shapes it assumes; the heart feels it by the weight of sadness, and 'grim-visaged, comfortless despair!'

I will conclude this subject with remarking, that the fancied shortness of life is aided by the apprehension of a future state.

The constantly directing our hopes and fears to a higher state of being beyond the present, necessarily brings death habitually before us, and defines the narrow limits within which we hold our frail existence, as mountains bound the horizon, and unavoidably draw our attention to it. This may be one reason among others why the fear of death was a less prominent feature in ancient times than it is at present; because the thoughts of it, and of a future state, were less frequently impressed on the mind by religion and morality. The greater progress of civilization and security in modern times has also considerably to do with our practical effeminacy; for though the old Pagans were not bound to think of death as a religious duty, they never could foresee when they should be compelled to submit to it, as a natural necessity, or accident of war, etc. They viewed death, therefore, with an eye of speculative indifference and practical resolution. That the idea of annihilation did not impress them with the same horror and repugnance as it does the modern believer, or even infidel, is easily accounted for (though a writer in the *Edinburgh Review* thinks the question insoluble)[19] from this plain reason, *viz.* that not being taught from childhood a belief in a future state of existence as a part of the creed of their country, the having this belief called into question or struck from under their feet did not cause the same uneasiness or confusion of mind in them as it does in us. He who has never been led to expect the reversion of an estate, does not severely feel the loss of it: for it is the indulgence of hope that embitters disappointment.

# On A Landscape
## of Nicolas Poussin*

*And blind Orion hungry for the morn.'*
KEATS. [*Endymion* II, 198]

ORION, the subject of this landscape,[1] was the classical Nimrod;
and is called by Homer, 'a hunter of shadows, himself a shade.'
He was the son of Neptune; and having lost an eye in some
affray between the Gods and men, was told that if he would
go to meet the rising sun, he would recover his sight. He is
represented setting out on his journey, with men on his
shoulders to guide him, a bow in his hand, and Diana in the
clouds greeting him. He stalks along, a giant upon earth, and
reels and falters in his gait, as if just awaked out of sleep, or
uncertain of his way; you see his blindness, though his back
is turned. Mists rise around him, and veil the sides of the green
forests; earth is dank and fresh with dews, the 'grey dawn and
the Pleiades before him dance,'[2] and in the distance are seen
the blue hills and sullen ocean. Nothing was ever more finely
conceived or done. It breathes the spirit of the morning; its
moisture, its repose, its obscurity, waiting the miracle of light
to kindle it into smiles: the whole is, like the principal figure
in it, 'a forerunner of the dawn.' The same atmosphere tinges
and imbues every object, the same dull light 'shadowy sets off'
the face of nature: one feeling of vastness, of strangeness, and
of primeval forms pervades the painter's canvas, and we are
thrown back upon the first integrity of things. This great and
learned man might be said to see nature through the glass of
time: he alone has a right to be considered as the painter of
classical antiquity. Sir Joshua has done him justice in this
respect. He could give to the scenery of his heroic fables that
unimpaired look of original nature, full, solid, large, luxuriant,
teeming with life and power; or deck it with all the pomp of
art, with temples and towers, and mythologic groves. His pic-

* [*Table-Talk; London Magazine*, Aug., 1821.]

tures 'denote a foregone conclusion.'[3] He applies nature to his
purposes, works out her images according to the standard of
his thoughts, embodies high fictions; and the first conception
being given, all the rest seems to grow out of, and be assimil-
ated to it, by the unfailing process of a studious imagination.
Like his own Orion, he overlooks the surrounding scene, appears to 'take up the isles as a very little thing, and to lay the
earth in a balance.'[4] With a laborious and mighty grasp, he
put nature into the mould of the ideal and antique; and was
among painters (more than anyone else) what Milton was
among poets. There is in both something of the same pedantry,
the same stiffness, the same elevation, the same grandeur, the
same mixture of art and nature, the same richness of borrowed
materials, the same unity of character. Neither the poet nor
the painter lowered the subjects they treated, but filled up
the outline in the fancy, and added strength and prominence
to it: and thus not only satisfied, but surpassed the expectations of the spectator and the reader. This is held for the
triumph and the perfection of works of art. To give us nature,
such as we see it, is well and deserving of praise; to give us
nature, such as we have never seen, but have often wished
to see it, is better, and deserving of higher praise. He who can
show the world in its first naked glory, with the hues of fancy
spread over it, or in its high and palmy state, with the gravity
of history stamped on the proud monuments of vanished empire—who, by his 'so potent art,' can recall time past, transport
us to distant places, and join the regions of imagination (a
new conquest) to those of reality—who teaches us not only
what nature is, but what she has been, and is capable of being
—he who does this, and does it with simplicity, with truth,
and grandeur, is lord of nature and her powers; and his mind
is universal, and his art the master-art!

There is nothing in this 'more than natural,' if criticism
could be persuaded to think so. The historic painter does not
neglect or contravene nature, but follows her more closely up
into her fantastic heights, or hidden recesses. He demonstrates
what she would be in conceivable circumstances, and under
implied conditions. He 'gives to airy nothing a local habitation,' not 'a name.'[5] At his touch, words start up into images,
thoughts become things. He clothes a dream, a phantom with
form and colour and the wholesome attributes of reality. *His*
art is a second nature; not a different one. There are those,
indeed, who think that *not to copy nature*, is the rule for
attaining perfection. Because they cannot paint the objects
which they have seen, they fancy themselves qualified to paint
the ideas which they have not seen. But it is possible to fail
in this latter and more difficult style of imitation, as well as in

the former humbler one. The detection, it is true, is not so easy, because the objects are not so nigh at hand to compare, and therefore there is more room both for false pretension and for self-deceit. They take an epic motto or subject, and conclude that the spirit is implied as a thing of course. They paint inferior portraits, maudlin lifeless faces, without ordinary expression, or one look, feature, or particle of nature in them, and think that this is to rise to the truth of history. They vulgarise and degrade whatever is interesting or sacred to the mind, and suppose that they thus add to the dignity of their profession. They represent a face that seems as if no thought or feeling of any kind had ever passed through it, and would have you believe that this is the very sublime of expression, such as it would appear in heroes, or demi-gods of old, when rapture or agony was raised to its height. They show you a landscape that looks as if the sun never shone upon it, and tell you that it is not modern—that so earth looked when Titan first kissed it with his rays. This is not the true *ideal*. It is not to fill the moulds of the imagination, but to deface and injure them: it is not to come up to, but to fall short of the poorest conception in the public mind. Such pictures should not be hung in the same room with that of Orion.*

---

* Everything tends to show the manner in which a great artist is formed. If any person could claim an exemption from the careful imitation of individual objects, it was Nicolas Poussin. He studied the antique, but he also studied nature. 'I have often admired,' says Vignuel de Marville, who knew him at a late period of his life, 'the love he had for his art. Old as he was, I frequently saw him among the ruins of ancient Rome, out in the Campagna, or along the banks of the Tiber, sketching a scene that had pleased him; and I often met him with his handkerchief full of stones, moss, or flowers, which he carried home, that he might copy them exactly from nature. One day I asked him how he had attained to such a degree of perfection, as to have gained so high a rank among the great painters of Italy?' He answered, 'I HAVE NEGLECTED NOTHING.'—*See his Life lately published.*[6] It appears from this account that he had not fallen into a recent error, that Nature puts the man of genius out. As a contrast to the foregoing description, I might mention, that I remember an old gentleman once asking Mr. West[7] in the British Gallery, if he had ever been at Athens? To which the President made answer, No; nor did he feel any great desire to go; for that he thought he had as good an idea of the place from the Catalogue, as he could get by living there for any number of years. What would he have said, if anyone had told him, he could get as good an idea of the subject of one of his great works from reading the Catalogue of it, as from seeing the picture itself! Yet the answer was characteristic of the genius of the painter. [W. H.]

Poussin was, of all painters, the most poetical. He was the painter of ideas. No one ever told a story half so well; nor so well knew what was capable of being told by the pencil. He seized on, and struck off with grace and precision, just that point of view which would be likely to catch the reader's fancy. There is a significance, a consciousness in whatever he does (sometimes a vice, but oftener a virtue) beyond any other painter. His Giants sitting on the tops of craggy mountains, as huge themselves, and playing idly on their Pan's-pipes, seem to have been seated there these three thousand years, and to know the beginning and the end of their own story. An infant Bacchus or Jupiter is big with his future destiny. Even inanimate and dumb things speak a language of their own. His snakes, the messengers of fate, are inspired with human intellect. His trees grow and expand their leaves in the air, glad of the rain, proud of the sun, awake to the winds of heaven. In his Plague of Athens,[8] the very buildings seem stiff with horror. His picture of the Deluge[9] is, perhaps, the finest historical landscape in the world. You see a waste of waters, wide, interminable: the sun is labouring, wan and weary, up in the sky; the clouds, dull and leaden, lie like a load upon the eye, and heaven and earth seem commingling into one confused mass! His human figures are sometimes 'o'er-informed' with this kind of feeling. Their actions have too much gesticulation, and the set expression of the features borders too much on the mechanical and caricatured style. In this respect, they form a contrast to Raphael's whose figures never appear to be sitting for their pictures, or to be conscious of a spectator, or to have come from the painter's hand. In Nicolas Poussin, on the contrary, everything seems to have a distinct understanding with the artist: 'the very stones prate of their whereabout:' each object has its part and place assigned, and is in a sort of compact with the rest of the picture. It is this conscious keeping, and, as it were, *internal* design, that gives their peculiar character to the works of our artist. There was a picture of Aurora[10] in the British Gallery a year or two ago. It was a suffusion of golden light. The Goddess wore her saffron-coloured robes, and appeared just risen from the gloomy bed of old Tithonus. Her very steeds, milk-white, were tinged with the yellow dawn. It was a personification of the morning.—Poussin succeeded better in classic than in sacred subjects. The latter are comparatively heavy, forced, full of violent contrasts of colour, of red, blue, and black, and without the true prophetic inspiration of the characters. But in his Pagan allegories and fables he was quite at home. The native gravity and native levity of the Frenchman were com-

bined with Italian scenery and an antique gusto, and gave
even to his colouring an air of learned indifference. He wants,
in one respect, grace, form, expression; but he has everywhere
sense and meaning, perfect costume and propriety. His personages always belong to the class and time represented, and
are strictly versed in the business in hand. His grotesque
compositions in particular, his Nymphs and Fauns, are superior (at least, as far as style is concerned) even to those of
Rubens. They are taken more immediately out of fabulous
history. Rubens's Satyrs and Bacchantes have a more jovial
and voluptuous aspect, are more drunk with pleasure, more
full of animal spirits and riotous impulses; they laugh and
bound along—

> Leaping like wanton kids in pleasant spring:[11]

but those of Poussin have more of the intellectual part of the
character, and seem vicious on reflection, and of set purpose.
Rubens's are noble specimens of a class; Poussin's are allegori-
cal abstractions of the same class, with bodies less pampered,
but with minds more secretly depraved. The Bacchanalian
groups of the Flemish painter were, however, his masterpieces in composition. Witness those prodigies of colour,
character, and expression, at Blenheim. In the more chaste
and refined delineation of classic fable, Poussin was without
a rival. Rubens, who was a match for him in the wild and
picturesque, could not pretend to vie with the elegance and
purity of thought in his picture of Apollo giving a poet a cup
of water to drink, nor with the gracefulness of design in the
figure of a nymph squeezing the juice of a bunch of grapes
from her fingers (a rosy wine-press) which falls into the
mouth of a chubby infant below. But, above all, who shall
celebrate, in terms of fit praise, his picture of the shepherds in
the Vale of Tempe going out in a fine morning of the spring,
and coming to a tomb with this inscription: ET EGO IN AR-
CADIA VIXI![12] The eager curiosity of some, the expression of
others who start back with fear and surprise, the clear breeze
playing with the branches of the shadowy trees, 'the valleys
low, where the mild zephyrs use,'[13] the distant, uninterrupted,
sunny prospect speak (and for ever will speak on) of ages
past to ages yet to come!*

Pictures are a set of chosen images, a stream of pleasant
thoughts passing through the mind. It is a luxury to have the
walls of our rooms hung round with them; and no less so to

---

* Poussin has repeated this subject more than once, and appears
to have revelled in its witcheries. I have before alluded to it. [W. H.]

have such a gallery in the mind, to con over the relics of
ancient art bound up 'within the book and volume of the
brain, unmixed (if it were possible) with baser matter!'[14] A
life spent among pictures, in the study and the love of art, is
a happy noiseless dream: or rather, it is to dream and to be
awake at the same time; for it has all 'the sober certainty of
waking bliss.'[15] with the romantic voluptuousness of a visionary and abstracted being. They are the bright consummate
essences of things, and we may say that he 'who of these delights can judge and knows to interpose them oft, is not un-
wise.'[16]

The Orion, which I have here taken occasion to descant
upon, is one of a collection of excellent pictures, as this collection is itself one of a series from the old masters, which
have for some years back embrowned the walls of the British
Gallery, and enriched the public eye. What hues (those of
nature mellowed by time) breathe around, as we enter! What
forms are there, woven into the memory! What looks, which
only the answering looks of the spectator can express! What
intellectual stores have been yearly poured forth from the
shrine of ancient art! The works are various, but the names
the same—heaps of Rembrandts frowning from the darkened
walls, Rubens's glad gorgeous groups, Titians more rich and
rare, Claudes always exquisite, sometimes beyond compare,
Guido's endless cloying sweetness, the learning of Poussin and
the Caracci, and Raphael's princely magnificence, crowning
all. We read certain letters and syllables in the catalogue, and
at the well-known magic sound, a miracle of skill and beauty
starts to view. It might be thought that one year's prodigal
display of such perfection would exhaust the labours of one
man's life; but the next year, and the next to that, we find
another harvest reaped and gathered in to the great garner of
art, by the same immortal hands—

> Old Genius the porter of them was;
> He letteth in, he letteth out to wend.[17]

Their works seem endless as their reputation—to be many as
they are complete—to multiply with the desire of the mind
to see more and more of them; as if there were a living power
in the breath of Fame, and in the very names of the great
heirs of glory 'there were propagation too!' It is something to
have a collection of this sort to count upon once a year; to
have one last, lingering look yet to come. Pictures are scattered
'like stray gifts through the world;' and while they remain,
earth has yet a little gilding left, not quite rubbed off, dis-
honoured, and defaced. There are plenty of standard works

still to be found in this country in the collections at Blenheim, at Burleigh, and in those belonging to Mr. Angerstein, Lord Grosvenor, the Marquis of Stafford, and others, to keep up this treat to the lovers of art for many years: and it is the more desirable to reserve a privileged sanctuary of this sort, where the eye may dote, and the heart take its fill of such pictures as Poussin's Orion, since the Louvre is stripped of its triumphant spoils,[18] and since he, who collected it, and wore it as a rich jewel in his Iron Crown, the hunter of greatness and of glory, is himself a shade!

# On Going A Journey*

ONE OF THE pleasantest things in the world is going a journey; but I like to go by myself. I can enjoy society in a room; but out of doors, nature is company enough for me. I am then never less alone than when alone.

> The fields his study, nature was his book.[1]

I cannot see the wit of walking and talking at the same time. When I am in the country, I wish to vegetate like the country. I am not for criticising hedge-rows and black cattle.[2] I go out of town in order to forget the town and all that is in it. There are those who for this purpose go to watering-places, and carry the metropolis with them. I like more elbow-room, and fewer incumbrances. I like solitude, when I give myself up to it, for the sake of solitude; nor do I ask for

> a friend in my retreat,
> Whom I may whisper solitude is sweet.[3]

The soul of a journey is liberty, perfect liberty, to think, feel, do just as one pleases. We go a journey chiefly to be free of all impediments and of all inconveniences; to leave ourselves behind, much more to get rid of others. It is because I want a little breathing-space to muse on indifferent matters, where Contemplation

> May plume her feathers and let grow her wings,
> That in the various bustle of resort
> Were all too ruffled, and sometimes impair'd,[4]

that I absent myself from the town for a while, without feeling at a loss the moment I am left by myself. Instead of a friend in a post-chaise or in a tilbury, to exchange good things with, and vary the same stale topics over again, for once let me have a truce with impertinence. Give me the clear blue sky

* [Table-Talk; New Monthly Magazine, Jan. 1822.]

over my head, and the green turf beneath my feet, a winding road before me, and a three hours' march to dinner—and then to thinking! It is hard if I cannot start some game on these lone heaths. I laugh, I run, I leap, I sing for joy. From the point of yonder rolling cloud, I plunge into my past being, and revel there, as the sun-burnt Indian plunges headlong into the wave that wafts him to his native shore. Then long-forgotten things, like 'sunken wrack and sumless treasuries,' burst upon my eager sight, and I begin to feel, think, and be myself again. Instead of an awkward silence, broken by attempts at wit or dull common-places, mine is that undisturbed silence of the heart which alone is perfect eloquence. No one likes puns, alliterations, antitheses, argument, and analysis better than I do; but I sometimes had rather be without them. 'Leave, oh, leave me to my repose!' I have just now other business in hand, which would seem idle to you, but is with me 'the very stuff of the conscience.' Is not this wild rose sweet without a comment? Does not this daisy leap to my heart, set in its coat of emerald? Yet if I were to explain to you the circumstance that has so endeared it to me, you would only smile. Had I not better then keep it to myself, and let it serve me to brood over, from here to yonder craggy point, and from thence onward to the far-distant horizon? I should be but bad company all that way, and therefore prefer being alone. I have heard it said that you may, when the moody fit comes on, walk or ride on by yourself, and indulge your reveries. But this looks like a breach of manners, a neglect of others, and you are thinking all the time that you ought to rejoin your party. 'Out upon such half-faced fellowship,' say I. I like to be either entirely to myself, or entirely at the disposal of others; to talk or be silent, to walk or sit still, to be sociable or solitary. I was pleased with an observation of Mr. Cobbett's, that 'he thought it a bad French custom to drink our wine with our meals, and that an Englishman ought to do only one thing at a time.' So I cannot talk and think, or indulge in melancholy musing and lively conversation by fits and starts. 'Let me have a companion of my way,' says Sterne, 'were it but to remark how the shadows lengthen as the sun goes down.' It is beautifully said: but in my opinion, this continual comparing of notes interferes with the involuntary impression of things upon the mind, and hurts the sentiment. If you only hint what you feel in a kind of dumb show, it is insipid: if you have to explain it, it is making a toil of a pleasure. You cannot read the book of nature, without being perpetually put to the trouble of translating it for the benefit of others. I am for the synthetical method on a journey, in preference to the analytical. I am content to lay in a stock of ideas then, and to examine and anatomise them afterwards. I want to see my vague notions float like the down of the thistle before the breeze, and not to have them entangled in the briars and thorns of controversy. For once, I like to have it all my own way; and this is impossible unless you are alone, or in such company as I do not covet. I have no objection to argue a point with anyone for twenty miles of measured road, but not for pleasure. If you remark the scent of a beanfield crossing the road, perhaps your fellow-traveller has no smell. If you point to a distant object, perhaps he is short-sighted, and has to take out his glass to look at it. There is a feeling in the air, a tone in the colour of a cloud which hits your fancy, but the effect of which you are unprepared to account for. There is then no sympathy, but an uneasy craving after it, and a dissatisfaction which pursues you on the way, and in the end probably produces ill humour. Now I never quarrel with myself, and take all my own conclusions for granted till I find it necessary to defend them against objections. It is not merely that you may not be of accord on the objects and circumstances that present themselves before you—they may recall a number of ideas, and lead to associations too delicate and refined to be possibly communicated to others. Yet these I love to cherish, and sometimes still fondly clutch them, when I can escape from the throng to do so. To give way to our feelings before company, seems extravagance or affectation; on the other hand, to have to unravel this mystery of our being at every turn, and to make others take an equal interest in it (otherwise the end is not answered) is a task to which few are competent. We must 'give it an understanding, but no tongue.' My old friend C[oleridge], however, could do both. He could go on in the most delightful explanatory way over hill and dale, a summer's day, and convert a landscape into a didactic poem or a Pindaric ode. 'He talked far above singing.'[5] If I could so clothe my ideas in sounding and flowing words, I might perhaps wish to have someone with me to admire the swelling theme; or I could be more content, were it possible for me still to hear his echoing voice in the woods of All-Foxden.[6] They had 'that fine madness in them which our first poets had;' and if they could have been caught by some rare instrument, would have breathed such strains as the following.

> Here be woods as green
> As any, air likewise as fresh and sweet
> As when smooth Zephyrus plays on the fleet
> Face of the curled stream, with flow'rs as many
> As the young spring gives, and as choice as any;

Here be all new delights, cool streams and wells,
Arbours o'ergrown with woodbine, caves and dells:
Choose where thou wilt, while I sit by and sing,
Or gather rushes to make many a ring
For thy long fingers; tell thee tales of love,
How the pale Phœbe, hunting in a grove,
First saw the boy Endymion, from whose eyes
She took eternal fire that never dies;
How she convey'd him softly in a sleep,
His temples bound with poppy, to the steep
Head of old Latmos, where she stoops each night,
Gilding the mountain with her brother's light,
To kiss her sweetest.

FAITHFUL SHEPHERDESS[7]

Had I words and images at command like these, I would attempt to wake the thoughts that lie slumbering on golden
ridges in the evening clouds: but at the sight of nature my
fancy, poor as it is, droops and closes up its leaves, like flowers
at sunset. I can make nothing out on the spot: I must have
time to collect myself.

In general, a good thing spoils out-of-door prospects: it
should be reserved for Table-talk. L[amb] is for this reason,
I take it, the worst company in the world out of doors; because
he is the best within. I grant, there is one subject on which it
is pleasant to talk on a journey; and that is, what one shall
have for supper when we get to our inn at night. The open
air improves this sort of conversation or friendly altercation,
by setting a keener edge on appetite. Every mile of the road
heightens the flavour of the viands we expect at the end of it.
How fine it is to enter some old town, walled and turreted,
just at the approach of night-fall, or to come to some straggling village, with the lights streaming through the surrounding gloom; and then after inquiring for the best entertainment
that the place affords, to 'take one's ease at one's inn!' These
eventful moments in our lives are in fact too precious, too full
of solid, heart-felt happiness to be frittered and dribbled away
in imperfect sympathy. I would have them all to myself, and
drain them to the last drop: they will do to talk of or to write
about afterwards. What a delicate speculation it is, after
drinking whole goblets of tea,

The cups that cheer, but not inebriate,[8]

and letting the fumes ascend into the brain, to sit considering
what we shall have for supper—eggs and a rasher, a rabbit
smothered in onions, or an excellent veal-cutlet! Sancho in
such a situation once fixed upon cow-heel; and his choice,

though he could not help it, is not to be disparaged. Then in the intervals of pictured scenery and Shandean contemplation, to catch the preparation and the stir in the kitchen— *Procul, O procul este profani!*[9] These hours are sacred to silence and to musing, to be treasured up in the memory, and to feed the source of smiling thoughts hereafter. I would not waste them in idle talk; or if I must have the integrity of fancy broken in upon, I would rather it were by a stranger than a friend. A stranger takes his hue and character from the time and place; he is a part of the furniture and costume of an inn. If he is a Quaker, or from the West Riding of Yorkshire, so much the better. I do not even try to sympathise with him, and he *breaks no squares*.[10] I associate nothing with my travelling companion but present objects and passing events. In his ignorance of me and my affairs, I in a manner forget myself. But a friend reminds one of other things, rips up old grievances, and destroys the abstraction of the scene. He comes in ungraciously between us and our imaginary character. Something is dropped in the course of conversation that gives a hint of your profession and pursuits; or from having someone with you that knows the less sublime portions of your history, it seems that other people do. You are no longer a citizen of the world: but your 'unhoused free condition is put into circumscription and confine.'[11] The *incognito* of an inn is one of its striking privileges—'lord of one's-self, uncumber'd with a name.'[12] Oh! it is great to shake off the trammels of the world and of public opinion—to lose our importunate, tormenting, everlasting personal identity in the elements of nature, and become the creature of the moment, clear of all ties—to hold to the universe only by a dish of sweetbreads, and to owe nothing but the score of the evening—and no longer seeking for applause and meeting with contempt, to be known by no other title than *the Gentleman in the parlour!* One may take one's choice of all characters in this romantic state of uncertainty as to one's real pretensions, and become indefinitely respectable and negatively right-worshipful. We baffle prejudice and disappoint conjecture; and from being so to others, begin to be objects of curiosity and wonder even to ourselves. We are no more those hackneyed commonplaces that we appear in the world: an inn restores us to the level of nature, and quits scores with society! I have certainly spent some enviable hours at inns—sometimes when I have been left entirely to myself, and have tried to solve some metaphysical problem, as once at Witham-common, where I found out the proof that likeness is not a case of the association of ideas— at other times, when there have been pictures in the room, as at St. Neot's (I think it was), where I first met with Gribelin's engravings of the Cartoons,[13] into which I entered at once; and at a little inn on the borders of Wales, where there happened to be hanging some of Westall's drawings, which I compared triumphantly (for a theory that I had, not for the admired artist) with the figure of a girl who had ferried me over the Severn, standing up in the boat between me and the fading twilight—at other times I might mention luxuriating in books, with a peculiar interest in this way, as I remember sitting up half the night to read *Paul and Virginia,* which I picked up at an inn at Bridgewater, after being drenched in the rain all day; and at the same place I got through two volumes of Madame D'Arblay's *Camilla.* It was on the tenth of April, 1798, that I sat down to a volume of the *New Eloise,* at the inn at Llangollen, over a bottle of sherry and a cold chicken. The letter I chose was that in which St. Preux describes his feelings as he first caught a glimpse from the heights of the Jura of the Pays de Vaud, which I had brought with me as a *bonne bouche* to crown the evening with.[14] It was my birthday, and I had for the first time come from a place in the neighbourhood to visit this delightful spot. The road to Llangollen turns off between Chirk and Wrexham; and on passing a certain point, you come all at once upon the valley, which opens like an amphitheatre, broad, barren hills rising in majestic state on either side, with 'green upland swells that echo to the bleat of flocks' below, and the river Dee babbling over its stony bed in the midst of them. The valley at this time 'glittered green with sunny showers,' and a budding ash-tree dipped its tender branches in the chiding stream. How proud, how glad I was to walk along the high road that commanded the delicious prospect, repeating the lines which I have just quoted from Mr. Coleridge's poems![15] But besides the prospect which opened beneath my feet, another also opened to my inward sight, a heavenly vision, on which were written, in letters large as Hope could make them, these four words, LIBERTY, GENIUS, LOVE, VIRTUE; which have since faded into the light of common day, or mock my idle gaze.

> The beautiful is vanished, and returns not.[16]

Still I would return some time or other to this enchanted spot; but I would return to it alone. What other self could I find to share that influx of thoughts, of regret, and delight, the traces of which I could hardly conjure up to myself, so much have they been broken and defaced! I could stand on some tall rock, and overlook the precipice of years that separates me from what I then was. I was at that time going shortly to

visit the poet whom I have above named. Where is he now?
Not only I myself have changed; the world, which was then
new to me, has become old and incorrigible. Yet will I turn
to thee in thought, O sylvan Dee,[17] as then thou wert, in joy,
in youth and gladness; and thou shalt always be to me the
river of Paradise, where I will drink of the waters of life freely!

There is hardly anything that shows the short-sightedness
or capriciousness of the imagination more than travelling does.
With change of place we change our ideas; nay, our opinions
and feelings. We can by an effort indeed transport ourselves
to old and long-forgotten scenes, and then the picture of the
mind revives again;[18] but we forget those that we have just
left. It seems that we can think but of one place at a time.
The canvas of the fancy has only a certain extent, and if we
paint one set of objects upon it, they immediately efface every
other. We cannot enlarge our conceptions; we only shift our
point of view. The landscape bares its bosom to the enraptured eye; we take our fill of it; and seem as if we could form
no other image of beauty or grandeur. We pass on, and think
no more of it: the horizon that shuts it from our sight also
blots it from our memory like a dream. In travelling through
a wild barren country, I can form no idea of a woody and
cultivated one. It appears to me that all the world must be
barren, like what I see of it. In the country we forget the
town, and in town we despise the country. 'Beyond Hyde
Park,' says Sir Fopling Flutter, 'all is a desert.'[19] All that part
of the map that we do not see before us is a blank. The world
in our conceit of it is not much bigger than a nutshell. It is
not one prospect expanded into another, county joined to
county, kingdom to kingdom, lands to seas, making an image
voluminous and vast; the mind can form no larger idea of
space than the eye can take in at a single glance. The rest is
a name written on a map, a calculation of arithmetic. For instance, what is the true signification of that immense mass of
territory and population, known by the name of China to us?
An inch of paste-board on a wooden globe, of no more account
than a China orange! Things near us are seen of the size of
life: things at a distance are diminished to the size of the
understanding. We measure the universe by ourselves, and
even comprehend the texture of our own being only piecemeal. In this way, however, we remember an infinity of things
and places. The mind is like a mechanical instrument that
plays a great variety of tunes, but it must play them in succession. One idea recalls another, but it at the same time ex-
cludes all others. In trying to renew old recollections, we
cannot as it were unfold the whole web of our existence; we
must pick out the single threads. So in coming to a place

where we have formerly lived and with which we have intimate associations, everyone must have found that the feeling
grows more vivid the nearer we approach the spot, from the
mere anticipation of the actual impression: we remember
circumstances, feelings, persons, faces, names, that we had not
thought of for years; but for the time all the rest of the world
is forgotten!—To return to the question I have quitted above.

I have no objection to go to see ruins, aqueducts, pictures,
in company with a friend or a party, but rather the contrary,
for the former reason reversed. They are intelligible matters,
and will bear talking about. The sentiment here is not tacit,
but communicable and overt. Salisbury Plain is barren of
criticism, but Stonehenge will bear a discussion antiquarian,
picturesque, and philosophical. In setting out on a party of
pleasure, the first consideration always is where we shall go:
in taking a solitary ramble, the question is what we shall meet
with by the way. The mind then is 'its own place'; nor are we
anxious to arrive at the end of our journey. I can myself do
the honours indifferently well to works of art and curiosity.
I once took a party to Oxford with no mean *éclat*—showed
them the seat of the Muses at a distance,

With glistering spires and pinnacles adorn'd—[20]

descanted on the learned air that breathes from the grassy
quadrangles and stone walls of halls and colleges—was at home
in the Bodleian; and at Blenheim quite superseded the powdered Cicerone that attended us, and that pointed in vain
with his wand to commonplace beauties in matchless pictures.
—As another exception to the above reasoning, I should not
feel confident in venturing on a journey in a foreign country
without a companion. I should want at intervals to hear the
sound of my own language. There is an involuntary antipathy
in the mind of an Englishman to foreign manners and notions
that requires the assistance of social sympathy to carry it off.
As the distance from home increases, this relief, which was at
first a luxury, becomes a passion and an appetite. A person
would almost feel stifled to find himself in the deserts of
Arabia without friends and countrymen: there must be allowed to be something in the view of Athens or old Rome that
claims the utterance of speech; and I own that the Pyramids
are too mighty for any single contemplation. In such situations, so opposite to all one's ordinary train of ideas, one seems
a species by one's-self, a limb torn off from society, unless one
can meet with instant fellowship and support.—Yet I did not
feel this want or craving very pressing once, when I first set
my foot on the laughing shores of France. Calais was peopled

with novelty and delight. The confused, busy murmur of the place was like oil and wine poured into my ears; nor did the mariners' hymn, which was sung from the top of an old crazy vessel in the harbour, as the sun went down, send an alien sound into my soul. I breathed the air of general humanity. I walked over 'the vine-covered hills and gay regions of France,'[21] erect and satisfied; for the image of man was not cast down and chained to the foot of arbitrary thrones. I was at no loss for language, for that of all the great schools of painting was open to me. The whole is vanished like a shade. Pictures, heroes, glory, freedom, all are fled: nothing remains but the Bourbons and the French people!—There is undoubtedly a sensation in travelling into foreign parts that is to be had nowhere else: but it is more pleasing at the time than lasting. It is too remote from our habitual associations to be a common topic of discourse or reference, and, like a dream or another state of existence, does not piece into our daily modes of life. It is an animated but a momentary hallucination. It demands an effort to exchange our actual for our ideal identity; and to feel the pulse of our old transports revive very keenly, we must 'jump' all our present comforts and connexions. Our romantic and itinerant character is not to be domesticated. Dr. Johnson remarked how little foreign travel added to the facilities of conversation in those who had been abroad.[22] In fact, the time we have spent there is both delightful and in one sense instructive; but it appears to be cut out of our substantial, downright existence, and never to join kindly on to it. We are not the same, but another, and perhaps more enviable individual, all the time we are out of our own country. We are lost to ourselves, as well as to our friends. So the poet somewhat quaintly sings,

> Out of my country and myself I go.

Those who wish to forget painful thoughts, do well to absent themselves for a while from the ties and objects that recall them: but we can be said only to fulfil our destiny in the place that gave us birth. I should on this account like well enough to spend the whole of my life in travelling abroad, if I could anywhere borrow another life to spend afterwards at home!

# The Fight*

> The *fight*, the *fight's* the thing,
> Wherein I'll catch the conscience of the king.

*Where there's a will, there's a way.* I said so to myself, as I walked down Chancery-lane, about half-past six o'clock on Monday the 10th of December, to inquire at Jack Randall's where the fight the next day was to be; and I found 'the proverb' nothing 'musty' in the present instance. I was determined to see this fight, come what would, and see it I did, in great style. It was my *first fight*, yet it more than answered my expectations. Ladies! it is to you I dedicate this description; nor let it seem out of character for the fair to notice the exploits of the brave. Courage and modesty are the old English virtues; and may they never look cold and askance on one another! Think, ye fairest of the fair, loveliest of the lovely kind, ye practisers of soft enchantment, how many more ye kill with poisoned baits than ever fell in the ring; and listen with subdued air and without shuddering, to a tale tragic only in appearance, and sacred to the FANCY![1]

I was going down Chancery-lane, thinking to ask at Jack Randall's where the fight was to be, when looking through the glass-door of the *Hole in the Wall*, I heard a gentleman asking the same question *at* Mrs. Randall, as the author of Waverley would express it. Now Mrs. Randall stood answering the gentleman's question, with the authenticity of the lady of the Champion of the Light Weights. Thinks I, I'll wait till this person comes out, and learn from him how it is. For to say a truth, I was not fond of going into this house of call for heroes and philosophers, ever since the owner of it (for Jack is no gentleman) threatened once upon a time to kick me out of doors for wanting a mutton-chop at his hospitable board, when the conqueror in thirteen battles was more full of *blue ruin*[2] than of good manners. I was the more mortified at this repulse, inasmuch as I had heard Mr. James Simpkins, hosier

* [*New Monthly Magazine;* Feb. 1822.]

in the Strand, one day when the character of the *Hole in the Wall* was brought in question, observe—'The house is a very good house, and the company quite genteel: I have been there myself!' Remembering this unkind treatment of mine host, to which mine hostess was also a party, and not wishing to put her in unquiet thoughts at a time jubilant like the present, I waited at the door, when, who should issue forth but my friend Joe Toms,[3] and turning suddenly up Chancery-lane with that quick jerk and impatient stride which distinguishes a lover of the FANCY, I said, 'I'll be hanged if that fellow is not going to the fight, and is on his way to get me to go with him.' So it proved in effect, and we agreed to adjourn to my lodgings to discuss measures with that cordiality which makes old friends like new, and new friends like old, on great occasions. We are cold to others only when we are dull in ourselves, and have neither thoughts nor feelings to impart to them. Give a man a topic in his head, a throb of pleasure in his heart, and he will be glad to share it with the first person he meets. Toms and I, though we seldom meet, were an *alter idem*[4] on this memorable occasion, and had not an idea that we did not candidly impart; and 'so carelessly did we fleet the time,' that I wish no better, when there is another fight, than to have him for a companion on my journey down, and to return with my friend Jack Pigott,[5] talking of what was to happen or of what did happen, with a noble subject always at hand, and liberty to digress to others whenever they offered. Indeed, on my repeating the lines from Spenser in an involuntary fit of enthusiasm,

> What more felicity can fall to creature,
> Than to enjoy delight with liberty?[6]

my last-named ingenious friend stopped me by saying that this, translated into the vulgate, meant '*Going to see a fight.*'

Joe Toms and I could not settle about the method of going down. He said there was a caravan, he understood, to start from Tom Belcher's[7] at two, which would go there *right out* and back again the next day. Now I never travel all night, and said I should get a cast to Newbury by one of the mails. Joe swore the thing was impossible, and I could only answer that I had made up my mind to it. In short, he seemed to me to waver, said he only came to see if I was going, had letters to write, a cause coming on the day after, and faintly said at parting (for I was bent on setting out that moment)—'Well, we meet at Philippi!'[8] I made the best of my way to Piccadilly. The mail coach stand was bare. 'They are all gone,' said I— 'this is always the way with me—in the instant I lose the

future—if I had not stayed to pour out that last cup of tea,
I should have been just in time—and cursing my folly and ill-
luck together, without inquiring at the coach-office whether
the mails were gone or not, I walked on in despite, and to
punish my own dilatoriness and want of determination. At any
rate, I would not turn back: I might get to Hounslow, or perhaps farther, to be on my road the next morning. I passed
Hyde Park Corner (my Rubicon), and trusted to fortune. Suddenly I heard the clattering of a Brentford stage, and the fight
rushed full upon my fancy. I argued (not unwisely) that even
a Brentford coachman was better company than my own
thoughts (such as they were just then), and at his invitation
mounted the box with him. I immediately stated my case to
him—namely, my quarrel with myself for missing the Bath or
Bristol mail, and my determination to get on in consequence
as well as I could, without any disparagement or insulting
comparison between longer or shorter stages. It is a maxim
with me that stage-coaches, and consequently stage-coachmen,
are respectable in proportion to the distance they have to
travel: so I said nothing on that subject to my Brentford
friend. Any incipient tendency to an abstract proposition, or
(as he might have construed it) to a personal reflection of this
kind, was however nipped in the bud; for I had no sooner
declared indignantly that I had missed the mails, than he
flatly denied that they were gone along, and lo! at the instant
three of them drove by in rapid, provoking, orderly succession,
as if they would devour the ground before them. Here again
I seemed in the contradictory situation of the man in Dryden
who exclaims,

> I follow Fate, which does too hard pursue![9]

If I had stopped to inquire at the White Horse Cellar, which
would not have taken me a minute, I should now have been
driving down the road in all the dignified unconcern and *ideal*
perfection of mechanical conveyance. The Bath mail I had set
my mind upon, and I had missed it, as I missed everything
else, by my own absurdity, in putting the will for the deed,
and aiming at ends without employing means. 'Sir,' said he
of the Brentford, 'the Bath mail will be up presently, my
brother-in-law drives it, and I will engage to stop him if there
is a place empty.' I almost doubted my good genius; but, sure
enough, up it drove like lightning, and stopped directly at the
call of the Brentford Jehu. I would not have believed this
possible, but the brother-in-law of a mail-coach driver is himself no mean man. I was transferred without loss of time from
the top of one coach to that of the other, desired the guard to

pay my fare to the Brentford coachman for me as I had no change, was accommodated with a great coat, put up my umbrella to keep off a drizzling mist, and we began to cut through the air like an arrow. The mile-stones disappeared one after another, the rain kept off; Tom Turtle,[10] the trainer, sat before me on the coach-box, with whom I exchanged civilities as a gentleman going to the fight; the passion that had transported me an hour before was subdued to pensive regret and conjectural musing on the next day's battle; I was promised a place inside at Reading, and upon the whole, I thought myself a lucky fellow. Such is the force of imagination! On the outside of any other coach on the 10th of December, with a Scotch mist drizzling through the cloudy moonlight air, I should have been cold, comfortless, impatient, and, no doubt, wet through; but seated on the Royal mail, I felt warm and comfortable, the air did me good, the ride did me good, I was pleased with the progress we had made, and confident that all would go well through the journey. When I got inside at Reading, I found Turtle and a stout valetudinarian, whose costume bespoke him one of the FANCY, and who had risen from a three months' sick bed to get into the mail to see the fight. They were intimate, and we fell into a lively discourse. My friend the trainer was confined in his topics to fighting dogs and men, to bears and badgers; beyond this he was 'quite chap-fallen,' had not a word to throw at a dog, or indeed very wisely fell asleep, when any other game was started. The whole art of training (I, however, learnt from him) consists in two things, exercise and abstinence, abstinence and exercise, repeated alternately and without end. A yolk of an egg with a spoonful of rum in it is the first thing in a morning, and then a walk of six miles till breakfast. This meal consists of a plentiful supply of tea and toast and beefsteaks. Then another six or seven miles till dinner-time, and another supply of solid beef or mutton with a pint of porter, and perhaps, at the utmost, a couple of glasses of sherry. Martin trains on water, but this increases his infirmity on another very dangerous side. The Gas-man[11] takes now and then a chirping glass[12] (under the rose) to console him, during a six weeks' probation, for the absence of Mrs. Hickman—an agreeable woman, with (I understand) a pretty fortune of two hundred pounds. How matter presses on me! What stubborn things are facts! How inexhaustible is nature and art! 'It is well,' as I once heard Mr. Richmond[13] observe, 'to see a variety.' He was speaking of cock-fighting as an edifying spectacle. I cannot deny but that one learns more of what *is* (I do not say of what *ought to be*) in this desultory mode of practical study, than from reading the same book twice over, even

though it should be a moral treatise. Where was I? I was sitting at dinner with the candidate for the honours of the ring,
'where good digestion waits on appetite, and health on both.'[14]
Then follows an hour of social chat and native glee; and afterwards, to another breathing over heathy hill or dale. Back to
supper, and then to bed, and up by six again—our hero

> Follows so the ever-running sun
> With profitable *ardour*—[15]

to the day that brings him victory or defeat in the green fairy
circle. Is not this life more sweet than mine? I was going to
say; but I will not libel any life by comparing it to mine, which
is (at the date of these presents) bitter as coloquintida[16] and
the dregs of aconitum![16]

The invalid in the Bath mail soared a pitch above the
trainer, and did not sleep so sound, because he had 'more
figures and more fantasies.' We talked the hours away merrily.
He had faith in surgery, for he had had three ribs set right,
that had been broken in a *turn-up* at Belcher's, but thought
physicians old women, for they had no antidote in their catalogue for brandy. An indigestion is an excellent common-place
for two people that never met before. By way of ingratiating
myself, I told him the story of my doctor, who, on my earnestly representing to him that I thought his regimen had done
me harm, assured me that the whole pharmacopeia contained
nothing comparable to the prescription he had given me; and,
as a proof of its undoubted efficacy, said that, 'he had had one
gentleman with my complaint under his hands for the last
fifteen years.' This anecdote made my companion shake the
rough sides of his three great coats with boisterous laughter;
and Turtle, starting out of his sleep, swore he knew how the
fight would go, for he had had a dream about it. Sure enough
the rascal told us how the three first rounds went off, but 'his
dream,' like others, 'denoted a foregone conclusion.' He knew
his men. The moon now rose in silver state, and I ventured,
with some hesitation, to point out this object of placid beauty,
with the blue serene beyond, to the man of science, to which
his ear he 'seriously inclined,' the more as it gave promise
*d'un beau jour*[17] for the morrow, and showed the ring un-
drenched by envious showers, arrayed in sunny smiles. Just
then, all going on well, I thought on my friend Toms, whom
I had left behind, and said innocently, 'There was a blockhead
of a fellow I left in town, who said there was no possibility of
getting down by the mail, and talked of going by a caravan
from Belcher's at two in the morning, after he had written
some letters.' 'Why,' said he of the lapels, 'I should not wonder

if that was the very person we saw running about like mad from one coach-door to another, and asking if anyone had seen a friend of his, a gentleman going to the fight, whom he had missed stupidly enough by staying to write a note.' 'Pray, Sir,' said my fellow-traveller, 'had he a plaid-cloak on?'—'Why, no,' said I, 'not at the time I left him, but he very well might afterwards, for he offered to lend me one.' The plaid-cloak and the letter decided the thing. Joe, sure enough, was in the Bristol mail, which preceded us by about fifty yards. This was droll enough. We had now but a few miles to our place of destination, and the first thing I did on alighting at Newbury, both coaches stopping at the same time, was to call out, 'Pray, is there a gentleman in that mail of the name of Toms?' 'No,' said Joe, borrowing something of the vein of Gilpin,[18] 'for I have just got out.' 'Well!' says he, 'this is lucky; but you don't know how vexed I was to miss you; for,' added he, lowering his voice, 'do you know when I left you I went to Belcher's to ask about the caravan, and Mrs. Belcher said very obligingly she couldn't tell about that, but there were two gentlemen who had taken places by the mail and were gone on in a landau, and she could frank us. It's a pity I didn't meet with you; we could then have got down for nothing. But *mum's the word*.' It's the devil for anyone to tell me a secret, for it's sure to come out in print. I do not care so much to gratify a friend, but the public ear is too great a temptation to me.

Our present business was to get beds and a supper at an inn; but this was no easy task. The public-houses were full, and where you saw a light at a private house, and people poking their heads out of the casement to see what was going on, they instantly put them in and shut the window, the moment you seemed advancing with a suspicious overture for accommodation. Our guard and coachman thundered away at the outer gate of the Crown for some time without effect—such was the greater noise within; and when the doors were unbarred, and we got admittance, we found a party assembled in the kitchen round a good hospitable fire, some sleeping, others drinking, others talking on politics and on the fight. A tall English yeoman (something like Matthews[19] in the face, and quite as great a wag)—

A lusty man to ben an abbot able,—[20]

was making such a prodigious noise about rent and taxes, and the price of corn now and formerly, that he had prevented us from being heard at the gate. The first thing I heard him say was to a shuffling fellow who wanted to be off a bet for a shilling glass of brandy and water—'Confound it, man, don't

be *insipid!*' Thinks I, that is a good phrase. It was a good
omen. He kept it up so all night, nor flinched with the approach of morning. He was a fine fellow, with sense, wit, and
spirit, a hearty body and a joyous mind, free-spoken, frank,
convivial—one of that true English breed that went with Harry
the Fifth to the siege of Harfleur—'standing like greyhounds
in the slips,' etc. We ordered tea and eggs (beds were soon
found to be out of the question) and this fellow's conversation
was *sauce piquante.* It did one's heart good to see him brandish
his oaken towel[21] and to hear him talk. He made mince-meat of
a drunken, stupid, red-faced, quarrelsome, *frowsy*[22] farmer,
whose nose 'he moralised into a thousand similes,' making it
out a firebrand like Bardolph's.[23] 'I'll tell you what, my friend,'
says he, 'the landlady has only to keep you here to save fire
and candle. If one was to touch your nose, it would go off like
a piece of charcoal.' At this the other only grinned like an
idiot, the sole variety in his purple face being his little peering
grey eyes and yellow teeth; called for another glass, swore he
would not stand it; and after many attempts to provoke his
humorous antagonist to single combat, which the other turned
off (after working him up to a ludicrous pitch of choler) with
great adroitness, he fell quietly asleep with a glass of liquor in
his hand, which he could not lift to his head. His laughing
persecutor made a speech over him, and turning to the opposite side of the room, where they were all sleeping in the
midst of this 'loud and furious fun,' said, 'There's a scene,
by G—d, for Hogarth to paint. I think he and Shakespeare
were our two best men at copying life.' This confirmed me
in my good opinion of him. Hogarth, Shakespeare, and Nature, were just enough for him (indeed for any man) to
know. I said, 'You read Cobbett, don't you? At least,' says I,
'you talk just as well as he writes.' He seemed to doubt this.
But I said, 'We have an hour to spare: if you'll get pen, ink,
and paper, and keep on talking, I'll write down what you say;
and if it doesn't make a capital Political Register,[24] I'll forfeit
my head. You have kept me alive to-night, however. I don't
know what I should have done without you.' He did not dislike this view of the thing, nor my asking if he was not about
the size of Jem Belcher; and told me soon afterwards, in the
confidence of friendship, that 'the circumstance which had
given him nearly the greatest concern in his life, was Cribb's
beating Jem after he had lost his eye by racket-playing.'[25]—
The morning dawns; that dim but yet clear light appears,
which weighs like solid bars of metal on the sleepless eyelids;
the guests drop down from their chambers one by one—but it
was too late to think of going to bed now (the clock was on
the stroke of seven), we had nothing for it but to find a

barber's (the pole that glittered in the morning sun lighted us to his shop), and then a nine miles' march to Hungerford. The day was fine, the sky was blue, the mists were retiring from the marshy ground, the path was tolerably dry, the sitting-up all night had not done us much harm—at least the cause was good; we talked of this and that with amicable difference, roving and sipping of many subjects, but still invariably we returned to the fight. At length, a mile to the left of Hungerford, on a gentle eminence, we saw the ring surrounded by covered carts, gigs, and carriages, of which hundreds had passed us on the road; Toms gave a youthful shout, and we hastened down a narrow lane to the scene of action.

Reader, have you ever seen a fight? If not, you have a pleasure to come, at least if it is a fight like that between the Gas-man and Bill Neate. The crowd was very great when we arrived on the spot; open carriages were coming up, with streamers flying and music playing, and the country-people were pouring in over hedge and ditch in all directions, to see their hero beat or be beaten. The odds were still on Gas, but only about five to four. Gully[26] had been down to try Neate, and had backed him considerably, which was a damper to the sanguine confidence of the adverse party. About two hundred thousand pounds were pending. The Gas says, he has lost £3000 which were promised him by different gentlemen if he had won. He had presumed too much on himself, which had made others presume on him. This spirited and formidable young fellow seems to have taken for his motto the old maxim, that 'there are three things necessary to success in life—Impudence! Impudence! Impudence!' It is so in matters of opinion, but not in the FANCY, which is the most practical of all things, though even here confidence is half the battle, but only half. Our friend had vapoured and swaggered too much, as if he wanted to grin and bully his adversary out of the fight. 'Alas! the Bristol man was not so tamed!'—'This is *the grave-digger*' (would Tom Hickman exclaim in the moments of intoxication from gin and success, showing his tremendous right hand), 'this will send many of them to their long homes; I haven't done with them yet!' Why should he—though he had licked four of the best men within the hour, yet why should he threaten to inflict dishonourable chastisement on my old master Richmond, a veteran going off the stage, and who has borne his sable honours meekly? Magnanimity, my dear Tom, and bravery, should be inseparable. Or why should he go up to his antagonist, the first time he ever saw him at the Fives-court, and measuring him from head to foot with a glance of contempt, as Achilles surveyed

Hector, say to him, 'What, are you Bill Neate? I'll knock more blood out of that great carcase of thine, this day fortnight, than you ever knock'd out of a bullock's!' It was not manly, 'twas not fighter-like. If he was sure of the victory (as he was not), the less said about it the better. Modesty should accompany the FANCY as its shadow. The best men were always the best behaved. Jem Belcher, the Game Chicken[27] (before whom the Gas-man could not have lived) were civil, silent men. So is Cribb, so is Tom Belcher, the most elegant of sparrers, and not a man for everyone to take by the nose. I enlarged on this topic in the mail (while Turtle was asleep), and said very wisely (as I thought) that impertinence was a part of no profession. A boxer was bound to beat his man, but not to thrust his fist, either actually or by implication, in everyone's face. Even a highwayman, in the way of trade, may blow out your brains, but if he uses foul language at the same time, I should say he was no gentleman. A boxer, I would infer, need not be a blackguard or a coxcomb, more than another. Perhaps I press this point too much on a fallen man—Mr. Thomas Hickman has by this time learnt that first of all lessons, 'That man was made to mourn.' He has lost nothing by the late fight but his presumption; and that every man may do as well without! By an over-display of this quality, however, the public had been prejudiced against him, and the *knowing-ones* were taken in. Few but those who had bet on him wished Gas to win. With my own prepossessions on the subject, the result of the 11th of December appeared to me as fine a piece of poetical justice as I had ever witnessed. The difference of weight between the two combatants (14 stone to 12) was nothing to the sporting men. Great, heavy, clumsy, long-armed Bill Neate kicked the beam in the scale of the Gas-man's vanity. The amateurs were frightened at his big words, and thought that they would make up for the difference of six feet and five feet nine. Truly, the FANCY are not men of imagination. They judge of what has been, and cannot conceive of anything that is to be. The Gas-man had won hitherto; therefore he must beat a man half as big again as himself—and that to a certainty. Besides, there are as many feuds, factions, prejudices, pedantic notions in the FANCY as in the state or in the schools. Mr. Gully is almost the only cool, sensible man among them, who exercises an unbiassed discretion, and is not a slave to his passions in these matters. But enough of reflections, and to our tale. The day, as I have said, was fine for a December morning. The grass was wet, and the ground miry, and ploughed up with multitudinous feet, except that, within the ring itself, there was a spot of virgin-green closed in and unprofaned by vulgar tread, that shone with dazzling brightness in the mid-day sun. For it was now noon, and we had an hour to wait. This is the trying time. It is then the heart sickens, as you think what the two champions are about, and how short a time will determine their fate. After the first blow is struck, there is no opportunity for nervous apprehensions; you are swallowed up in the immediate interest of the scene—but

> Between the acting of a dreadful thing
> And the first motion, all the interim is
> Like a phantasma, or a hideous dream.[28]

I found it so as I felt the sun's rays clinging to my back, and saw the white wintry clouds sink below the verge of the horizon. 'So,' I thought, 'my fairest hopes have faded from my sight!—so will the Gas-man's glory, or that of his adversary, vanish in an hour.' The *swells* were parading in their white box-coats,[29] the outer ring was cleared with some bruises on the heads and shins of the rustic assembly (for the *cockneys* had been distanced by the sixty-six miles); the time drew near, I had got a good stand; a bustle, a buzz, ran through the crowd, and from the opposite side entered Neate, between his second and bottle-holder. He rolled along, swathed in his loose great-coat, his knock-knees bending under his huge bulk; and, with a modest cheerful air, threw his hat into the ring. He then just looked round, and began quietly to undress; when from the other side there was a similar rush and an opening made, and the Gas-man came forward with a conscious air of anticipated triumph, too much like the cock-of-the-walk. He strutted about more than became a hero, sucked oranges with a supercilious air, and threw away the skin with a toss of his head, and went up and looked at Neate, which was an act of supererogation. The only sensible thing he did was, as he strode away from the modern Ajax, to fling out his arms, as if he wanted to try whether they would do their work that day. By this time they had stripped, and presented a strong contrast in appearance. If Neate was like Ajax, 'with Atlantean shoulders, fit to bear' the pugilistic reputation of all Bristol, Hickman might be compared to Diomed, light, vigorous, elastic, and his back glistened in the sun, as he moved about, like a panther's hide. There was now a dead pause—attention was awe-struck. Who at that moment, big with a great event, did not draw his breath short—did not feel his heart throb? All was ready. They tossed up for the sun, and the Gas-man won. They were led up to the *scratch*[30]—shook hands, and went at it.

In the first round everyone thought it was all over. After

making play a short time, the Gas-man flew at his adversary
like a tiger, struck five blows in as many seconds, three first,
and then following him as he staggered back, two more,
right and left, and down he fell, a mighty ruin. There was
a shout, and I said, 'There is no standing this.' Neate seemed
like a lifeless lump of flesh and bone, round which the Gas-
man's blows played with the rapidity of electricity or lightning, and you imagined he would only be lifted up to be
knocked down again. It was as if Hickman held a sword or
a fire in that right hand of his, and directed it against an un-
armed body. They met again, and Neate seemed, not cowed,
but particularly cautious. I saw his teeth clenched together
and his brows knit close against the sun. He held out both
his arms at full length straight before him, like two sledge-
hammers, and raised his left an inch or two higher. The Gas-
man could not get over this guard—they struck mutually and
fell, but without advantage on either side. It was the same in
the next round; but the balance of power was thus restored—
the fate of the battle was suspended. No one could tell how
it would end. This was the only moment in which opinion was
divided; for, in the next, the Gas-man aiming a mortal blow
at his adversary's neck, with his right hand, and failing from
the length he had to reach, the other returned it with his left
at full swing, planted a tremendous blow on his cheek-bone
and eyebrow, and made a red ruin of that side of his face.
The Gas-man went down, and there was another shout—a roar
of triumph as the waves of fortune rolled tumultuously from
side to side. This was a settler. Hickman got up, and 'grinned
horrible a ghastly smile,' yet he was evidently dashed in his
opinion of himself; it was the first time he had ever been so
punished; all one side of his face was perfect scarlet, and his
right eye was closed in dingy blackness, as he advanced to
the fight, less confident, but still determined. After one or two
rounds, not receiving another such remembrancer, he rallied
and went at it with his former impetuosity. But in vain. His
strength had been weakened—his blows could not tell at such
a distance—he was obliged to fling himself at his adversary,
and could not strike from his feet; and almost as regularly as
he flew at him with his right hand, Neate warded the blow, or
drew back out of its reach, and felled him with the return of
his left. There was little cautious sparring—no half-hits—no tap
ping and trifling, none of the *petit maîtreship* of the art—they
were almost all knock-down blows: the fight was a good stand
up fight. The wonder was the half-minute time. If there had
been a minute or more allowed between each round, it would
have been intelligible how they should by degrees recover
strength and resolution; but to see two men smashed to the

ground, smeared with gore, stunned, senseless, the breath
beaten out of their bodies; and then, before you recover from
the shock, to see them rise up with new strength and courage,
stand steady to inflict or receive mortal offence, and rush upon
each other 'like two clouds over the Caspian'[31]—this is the
most astonishing thing of all: this is the high and heroic state
of man! From this time forward the event became more certain
every round; and about the twelfth it seemed as if it must
have been over. Hickman generally stood with his back to me;
but in the scuffle, he had changed positions, and Neate just
then made a tremendous lunge at him, and hit him full in the
face. It was doubtful whether he would fall backwards or forwards; he hung suspended for a second or two, and then fell
back, throwing his hands in the air, and with his face lifted
up to the sky. I never saw anything more terrific than his
aspect just before he fell. All traces of life, of natural expression, were gone from him. His face was like a human skull,
a death's head, spouting blood. The eyes were filled with
blood, the nose streamed with blood, the mouth gaped blood.
He was not like an actual man, but like a preternatural, spectral appearance, or like one of the figures in Dante's *Inferno*.
Yet he fought on after this for several rounds, still striking the
first desperate blow, and Neate standing on the defensive, and
using the same cautious guard to the last, as if he had still all
his work to do; and it was not till the Gas-man was so stunned
in the seventeenth or eighteenth round, that his senses forsook
him, and he could not come to time, that the battle was declared over.* Ye who despise the FANCY, do something to
show as much *pluck*, or as much self-possession as this, before
you assume a superiority which you have never given a single
proof of by any one action in the whole course of your lives!—
When the Gas-man came to himself, the first words he uttered
were, 'Where am I? What is the matter?' 'Nothing is the matter, Tom—you have lost the battle, but you are the bravest
man alive.' And Jackson[32] whispered to him, 'I am collecting
a purse for you, Tom.'—Vain sounds, and unheard at that
moment! Neate instantly went up and shook him cordially by
the hand, and seeing some old acquaintance, began to flourish
with his fists, calling out, 'Ah, you always said I couldn't fight
—what do you think now?' But all in good humour, and with-

* Scroggins[33] said of the Gas-man, that he thought he was a man
of that courage, that if his hands were cut off, he would still fight on
with the stumps—like that of Widrington—[34]

> In doleful dumps,
> Who, when his legs were smitten off
> Still fought upon his stumps. [w. h.]

out any appearance of arrogance; only it was evident Bill Neate was pleased that he had won the fight. When it was over, I asked Cribb if he did not think it was a good one? He said, *'Pretty well!'* The carrier-pigeons now mounted into the air, and one of them flew with the news of her husband's victory to the bosom of Mrs. Neate. Alas, for Mrs. Hickman!

*Mais au revoir,* as Sir Fopling Flutter says. I went down with Toms; I returned with Jack Pigott, whom I met on the ground. Toms is a rattle-brain; Pigott is a sentimentalist. Now, under favour, I am a sentimentalist too—therefore I say nothing, but that the interest of the excursion did not flag as I came back. Pigott and I marched along the causeway leading from Hungerford to Newbury, now observing the effect of a brilliant sun on the tawny meads or moss-coloured cottages, now exulting in the fight, now digressing to some topic of general and elegant literature. My friend was dressed in character for the occasion, or like one of the FANCY; that is, with a double portion of great coats, clogs, and overhauls: and just as we had agreed with a couple of country-lads to carry his superfluous wearing-apparel to the next town, we were overtaken by a return post-chaise, into which I got, Pigott preferring a seat on the bar. There were two strangers already in the chaise, and on their observing they supposed I had been to the fight, I said I had, and concluded they had done the same. They appeared, however, a little shy and sore on the subject; and it was not till after several hints dropped, and questions put, that it turned out that they had missed it. One of these friends had undertaken to drive the other there in his gig: they had set out, to make sure work, the day before at three in the afternoon. The owner of the one-horse vehicle scorned to ask his way, and drove right on to Bagshot, instead of turning off at Hounslow: there they stopped all night, and set off the next day across the country to Reading, from whence they took coach, and got down within a mile or two of Hungerford, just half an hour after the fight was over. This might be safely set down as one of the miseries of human life. We parted with these two gentlemen who had been to see the fight, but had returned as they went, at Wolhampton, where we were promised beds (an irresistible temptation, for Pigott had passed the preceding night at Hungerford as we had done at Newbury), and we turned into an old bow-windowed parlour with a carpet and a snug fire; and after devouring a quantity of tea, toast, and eggs, sat down to consider, during an hour of philosophic leisure, what we should have for supper. In the midst of an Epicurean deliberation between a roasted fowl and mutton chops with mashed potatoes, we were interrupted by an inroad of Goths and Vandals—

*O procul este profani*[35]—not real flash-men,[36] but interlopers,
noisy pretenders, butchers from Tothill-fields, brokers from
Whitechapel, who called immediately for pipes and tobacco,
hoping it would not be disagreeable to the gentlemen, and
began to insist that it was *a cross*. Pigott withdrew from the
smoke and noise into another room, and left me to dispute
the point with them for a couple of hours *sans intermission*
by the dial. The next morning we rose refreshed; and on
observing that Jack had a pocket volume in his hand, in which
he read in the intervals of our discourse, I inquired what it
was, and learned to my particular satisfaction that it was a
volume of the *New Eloise*.[37] Ladies, after this, will you contend that a love for the FANCY is incompatible with the
cultivation of sentiment?—We jogged on as before, my friend
setting me up in a genteel drab great coat and green silk handkerchief (which I must say became me exceedingly), and
after stretching our legs for a few miles, and seeing Jack Randall, Ned Turner,[38] and Scroggins, pass on the top of one of
the Bath coaches, we engaged with the driver of the second
to take us to London for the usual fee. I got inside, and found
three other passengers. One of them was an old gentleman
with an aquiline nose, powdered hair, and a pigtail, and who
looked as if he had played many a rubber at the Bath rooms.
I said to myself, he is very like Mr. Windham; I wish he would
enter into conversation, that I might hear what fine observations would come from those finely-turned features. However,
nothing passed, till, stopping to dine at Reading, some inquiry
was made by the company about the fight, and I gave (as the
reader may believe) an eloquent and animated description
of it. When we got into the coach again, the old gentleman,
after a graceful exordium, said, he had, when a boy, been to
a fight between the famous Broughton and George Stevenson,
who was called the *Fighting Coachman*, in the year 1770,[39]
with the late Mr. Windham. This beginning flattered the spirit
of prophecy within me and rivetted my attention. He went
on—'George Stevenson was coachman to a friend of my father's. He was an old man when I saw him some years afterwards. He took hold of his own arm and said, "there was
muscle here once, but now it is no more than this young
gentleman's." He added, "Well, no matter; I have been here
long, I am willing to go hence, and I hope I have done no
more harm than another man." Once,' said my unknown companion, 'I asked him if he had ever beat Broughton? He said
Yes; that he had fought with him three times, and the last
time he fairly beat him, though the world did not allow it.
"I'll tell you how it was, master. When the seconds lifted us
up in the last round, we were so exhausted that neither of

us could stand, and we fell upon one another, and as Master Broughton fell uppermost, the mob gave it in his favour, and he was said to have won the battle. But," says he, "the fact was, that as his second (John Cuthbert) lifted him up, he said to him, 'I'll fight no more, I've had enough,' which," says Stevenson, "you know gave me the victory. And to prove to you that this was the case, when John Cuthbert was on his death-bed, and they asked him if there was anything on his mind which he wished to confess, he answered, 'Yes, that there was one thing he wished to set right, for that certainly Master Stevenson won that last fight with Master Broughton; for he whispered him as he lifted him up in the last round of all, that he had had enough.'" ' 'This,' said the Bath gentleman, 'was a bit of human nature;' and I have written this account of the fight on purpose that it might not be lost to the world. He also stated as a proof of the candour of mind in this class of men, that Stevenson acknowledged that Broughton could have beat him in his best day; but that he (Broughton) was getting old in their last rencounter. When we stopped in Piccadilly, I wanted to ask the gentleman some questions about the late Mr. Windham, but had not courage. I got out, resigned my coat and green silk handkerchief to Pigott (loth to part with these ornaments of life), and walked home in high spirits.

P.S. Toms called upon me the next day, to ask me if I did not think the fight was a complete thing? I said I thought it was. I hope he will relish my account of it.

# On the Prose-Style
# of Poets*

*Do you read or sing? If you sing, you sing
very ill!*[1]

I HAVE but an indifferent opinion of the prose-style of poets: not that it is not sometimes good, nay, excellent; but it is never the better, and generally the worse from the habit of writing verse. Poets are winged animals, and can cleave the air, like birds, with ease to themselves and delight to the beholders; but like those 'feathered, two-legged things,' when they light upon the ground of prose and matter-of-fact, they seem not to have the same use of their feet.

What is a little extraordinary, there is a want of *rhythmus* and cadence in what they write without the help of metrical rules. Like persons who have been accustomed to sing to music, they are at a loss in the absence of the habitual accompaniment and guide to their judgment. Their style halts, totters, is loose, disjointed, and without expressive pauses or rapid movements. The measured cadence and regular *sing-song* of rhyme or blank verse have destroyed, as it were, their natural ear for the mere characteristic harmony which ought to subsist between the sound and the sense. I should almost guess the Author of Waverley to be a writer of ambling verses from the desultory vacillation and want of firmness in the march of his style. There is neither *momentum* nor elasticity in it; I mean as to the *score*, or effect upon the ear. He has improved since in his other works: to be sure, he has had practice enough.† Poets either get into this incoherent, undetermined, shuffling style, made up of 'unpleasing flats and

---

* [*Plain Speaker;* written Aug. 1822.]

† Is it not a collateral proof that Sir Walter Scott is the Author of Waverley, that ever since these Novels began to appear, his Muse has been silent, till the publication of Halidon-Hill? [W. H.]

sharps,' of unaccountable starts and pauses, of doubtful odds
and ends, flirted about like straws in a gust of wind; or, to
avoid it and steady themselves, mount into a sustained and
measured prose (like the translation of Ossian's Poems, or
some parts of Shaftesbury's *Characteristics*) which is more
odious still, and as bad as being at sea in a calm. Dr. Johnson's style (particularly in his *Rambler*) is not free from the
last objection. There is a tune in it, a mechanical recurrence
of the same rise and fall in the clauses of his sentences, independent of any reference to the meaning of the text, or progress or inflection of the sense. There is the alternate roll of his
cumbrous cargo of words; his periods complete their revolutions at certain stated intervals, let the matter be longer or
shorter, rough or smooth, round or square, different or the
same. This monotonous and balanced mode of composition
may be compared to that species of portrait-painting which
prevailed about a century ago, in which each face was cast
in a regular and preconceived mould. The eye-brows were
arched mathematically as if with a pair of compasses, and the
distances between the nose and mouth, the forehead and chin,
determined according to a 'foregone conclusion,' and the features of the identical individual were afterwards accommodated to them, how they could!*

Horne Tooke[2] used to maintain that no one could write a
good prose style, who was not accustomed to express himself
*viva voce,* or to talk in company. He argued that this was the
fault of Addison's prose, and that its smooth, equable uniformity, and want of sharpness and spirit, arose from his not
having familiarised his ear to the sound of his own voice, or
at least only among friends and admirers, where there was
but little collision, dramatic fluctuation, or sudden contrariety
of opinion to provoke animated discussion, and give birth to
different intonations and lively transitions of speech. His style
(in this view of it) was not indented, nor did it project from
the surface. There was no stress laid on one word more than
another—it did not hurry on or stop short, or sink or swell with
the occasion: it was throughout equally insipid, flowing, and
harmonious, and had the effect of a studied recitation rather
than of a natural discourse. This would not have happened
(so the Member for Old Sarum contended) had Addison laid
himself out to argue at his club, or to speak in public; for then
his ear would have caught the necessary modulations of sound
arising out of the feeling of the moment, and he would have

---

* See the Portraits of Kneller, Richardson, and others. [w. h.]

transferred them unconsciously to paper. Much might be said on both sides of this quesion:* but Mr. Tooke was himself an unintentional confirmation of his own argument; for the tone of his written compositions is as flat and unraised as his manner of speaking was hard and dry. Of the poet it is said by someone, that

> He murmurs by the running brooks
> A music sweeter than their own.[3]

On the contrary, the celebrated person just alluded to might be said to grind the sentences between his teeth, which he afterwards committed to paper, and threw out crusts to the critics, or *bon-mots* to the Electors of Westminster (as we throw bones to the dogs), without altering a muscle, and without the smallest tremulousness of voice or eye!† I certainly so far agree with the above theory as to conceive that no style is worth a farthing that is not calculated to be read out, or that is not allied to spirited conversation: but I at the same time think the process of modulation and inflection may be quite as complete, or more so, without the external enunciation; and that an author had better try the effect of his sentences on his stomach than on his ear. He may be deceived by the last, not by the first. No person, I imagine, can dictate a good style; or spout his own compositions with impunity. In the former case, he will flounder on before the sense or words are ready, sooner than suspend his voice in air; and in the latter, he can supply what intonation he pleases, without consulting his readers. Parliamentary speeches sometimes read well aloud; but we do not find, when such persons sit down to write, that the prose-style of public speakers and great orators is the best, most natural, or varied of all others. It has almost always either a professional twang, a mechanical rounding off, or else is stunted and unequal. Charles Fox[4] was the most rapid and even *hurried* of speakers; but his written

---

* Goldsmith was not a talker, though he blurted out his good things now and then: yet his style is gay and voluble enough. Pope was also a silent man; and his prose is timid and constrained, and his verse inclining to the monotonous. [W. H.]

† As a singular example of steadiness of nerves, Mr. Tooke on one occasion had got upon the table at a public dinner to return thanks for his health having been drank. He held a bumper of wine in his hand, but he was received with considerable opposition by one party, and at the end of the disturbance, which lasted for a quarter of an hour, he found the wine glass still full to the brim. [W. H.]

style halts and creeps slowly along the ground.\*—A speaker is necessarily kept within bounds in expressing certain things, or in pronouncing a certain number of words, by the limits of the breath or power of respiration; certain sounds are observed to join in harmoniously or happily with others: an emphatic phrase must not be placed where the power of utterance is enfeebled or exhausted, etc. All this must be attended to in writing (and will be so unconsciously by a practised hand) or there will be *hiatus in manuscriptis*.[5] The words must be so arranged, in order to make an efficient readable style, as 'to come trippingly off the tongue.' Hence it seems that there is a natural measure of prose in the feeling of the subject and the power of expression in the voice, as there is an artificial one of verse in the number and co-ordination of the syllables; and I conceive that the trammels of the last do not (where they have been long worn) greatly assist the freedom or the exactness of the first.

Again, in poetry, from the restraints in many respects, a greater number of inversions, or a latitude in the transposition of words is allowed, which is not conformable to the strict laws of prose. Consequently, a poet will be at a loss, and flounder about for the common or (as we understand it) *natural* order of words in prose-composition. Dr. Johnson endeavoured to give an air of dignity and novelty to his diction by affecting the order of words usual in poetry. Milton's prose has not only this drawback, but it has also the disadvantage of being formed on a classic model. It is like a fine translation from the Latin; and indeed, he wrote originally in Latin. The frequency of epithets and ornaments, too, is a resource for which the poet finds it difficult to obtain an equivalent. A direct, or simple prose-style seems to him bald and

---

\* I have been told, that when Sheridan was first introduced to Mr. Fox, what cemented an immediate intimacy between them was the following circumstance. Mr. Sheridan had been the night before to the House of Commons; and being asked what his impression was, said he had been principally struck with the difference of manner between Mr. Fox and Lord Stormont. The latter began by declaring in a slow, solemn, drawling, nasal tone that 'when he considered the enormity and the unconstitutional tendency of the measures just proposed, he was hurried away in a torrent of passion and a whirlwind of impetuosity,' pausing between every word and syllable; while the first said (speaking with the rapidity of lightning, and with breathless anxiety and impatience), that 'such was the magnitude, such the importance, such the vital interest of this question, that he could not help imploring, he could not help adjuring the House to come to it with the utmost calmness, the utmost coolness, the utmost deliberation.' This trait of discrimination instantly won Mr. Fox's heart. [w. h.]

flat; and, instead of forcing an interest in the subject by severity of description and reasoning, he is repelled from it altogether by the absence of those obvious and meretricious allurements, by which his senses and his imagination have been hitherto stimulated and dazzled. Thus there is often at the same time a want of splendour and a want of energy in what he writes, without the invocation of the Muse—*invita Minerva*.[6] It is like setting a rope-dancer to perform a tumbler's tricks—the hardness of the ground jars his nerves; or it is the same thing as a painter's attempting to carve a block of marble for the first time—the coldness chills him, the colourless uniformity distracts him, the precision of form demanded disheartens him. So in prose-writing, the severity of composition required damps the enthusiasm, and cuts off the resources of the poet. He is looking for beauty, when he should be seeking for truth; and aims at pleasure, which he can only communicate by increasing the sense of power in the reader. The poet spreads the colours of fancy, the illusions of his own mind, round every object, *ad libitum*;[7] the prose-writer is compelled to extract his materials patiently and bit by bit, from his subject. What he adds of ornament, what he borrows from the pencil, must be sparing, and judiciously inserted. The first pretends to nothing but the immediate indulgence of his feelings: the last has a remote practical purpose. The one strolls out into the adjoining fields or groves to gather flowers: the other has a journey to go, sometimes through dirty roads, and at others through untrodden and difficult ways. It is this effeminacy, this immersion in sensual ideas, or craving after continual excitement, that spoils the poet for his prose-task. He cannot wait till the effect comes of itself, or arises out of the occasion: he must force it upon all occasions, or his spirit droops and flags under a supposed imputation of dulness. He can never drift with the current, but is always hoisting sail, and has his streamers flying. He has got a striking simile on hand; he *lugs* it in with the first opportunity, and with little connexion, and so defeats his object. He has a story to tell: he tells it in the first page, and where it would come in well, has nothing to say; like Goldsmith, who having to wait upon a Noble Lord, was so full of himself and of the figure he should make, that he addressed a set speech, which he had studied for the occasion, to his Lordship's butler, and had just ended as the nobleman made his appearance. The prose ornaments of the poet are frequently beautiful in themselves, but do not assist the subject. They are pleasing excrescences—hindrances, not helps in an argument. The reason is, his embellishments in his own walk grow out of the subject by natural association; that is, beauty gives birth to kindred beauty, grandeur leads the mind on to greater grandeur. But in treating a common subject, the link is truth, force of illustration, weight of argument, not a graceful harmony in the immediate ideas; and hence the obvious and habitual clue which before guided him is gone, and he hangs on his patch-work, tinsel finery at random, in despair, without propriety, and without effect. The poetical prose-writer stops to describe an object, if he admires it, or thinks it will bear to be dwelt on: the genuine prose-writer only alludes to or characterises it in passing, and with reference to his subject. The prose-writer is master of his materials: the poet is the slave of his style. Everything showy, everything extraneous tempts him, and he reposes idly on it: he is bent on pleasure, not on business. He aims at effect, at captivating the reader, and yet is contented with commonplace ornaments, rather than none. Indeed, this last result must necessarily follow, where there is an ambition to shine, without the effort to dig for jewels in the mine of truth. The habits of a poet's mind are not those of industry or research: his images come to him, he does not go to them; and in prose-subjects, and dry matters of fact and close reasoning, the natural stimulus that at other times warms and rouses, deserts him altogether. He sees no unhallowed visions, he is inspired by no day-dreams. All is tame, literal, and barren, without the Nine. Nor does he collect his strength to strike fire from the flint by the sharpness of collision, by the eagerness of his blows. He gathers roses, he steals colours from the rainbow. He lives on nectar and ambrosia. He 'treads the primrose path of dalliance,' or ascends 'the highest heaven of invention,' or falls flat to the ground. *He is nothing, if not fanciful!*

I shall proceed to explain these remarks, as well as I can, by a few instances in point.

It has always appeared to me that the most perfect prose-style, the most powerful, the most dazzling, the most daring, that which went the nearest to the verge of poetry, and yet never fell over, was Burke's. It has the solidity, and sparkling effect of the diamond: all other *fine writing* is like French paste or Bristol-stones[8] in the comparison. Burke's style is airy, flighty, adventurous, but it never loses sight of the subject; nay, is always in contact with, and derives its increased or varying impulse from it. It may be said to pass yawning gulfs 'on the unstedfast footing of a spear:' still it has an actual resting place and tangible support under it—it is not suspended on nothing. It differs from poetry, as I conceive, like the chamois from the eagle: it climbs to an almost equal height, touches upon a cloud, overlooks a precipice, is picturesque, sublime—but all the while, instead of soaring through the air, it stands upon a rocky cliff, clambers up by abrupt and intricate ways, and browses on the roughest bark, or crops the tender flower. The principle which guides his pen is truth, not beauty—not pleasure, but power. He has no choice, no selection of subject to flatter the reader's idle taste, or assist his own fancy: he must take what comes, and make the most of it. He works the most striking effects out of the most unpromising materials, by the mere activity of his mind. He rises with the lofty, descends with the mean, luxuriates in beauty, gloats over deformity. It is all the same to him, so that he loses no particle of the exact, characteristic, extreme impression of the thing he writes about, and that he communicates this to the reader, after exhausting every possible mode of illustration, plain or abstracted, figurative or literal. Whatever stamps the original image more distinctly on the mind, is welcome. The nature of his task precludes continual beauty; but it does not preclude continual ingenuity, force, originality. He had to treat of political questions, mixed modes, abstract ideas, and his fancy (or poetry, if you will) was ingrafted on these artificially, and as it might sometimes be thought, violently, instead of growing naturally out of them, as it would spring of its own accord from individual objects and feelings. There is a resistance in the *matter* to the illustration applied to it—the concrete and abstract are hardly co-ordinate; and therefore it is that, when the first difficulty is overcome, they must agree more closely in the essential qualities, in order that the coincidence may be complete. Otherwise, it is good for nothing; and you justly charge the author's style with being loose, vague, flaccid and imbecile. The poet has been said

> To make us heirs
> Of truth and pure delight in endless lays.[9]

Not so the prose-writer, who always mingles clay with his gold, and often separates truth from mere pleasure. He can only arrive at the last through the first. In poetry, one pleasing or striking image obviously suggests another: the increasing the sense of beauty or grandeur is the principle of composition: in prose, the professed object is to impart conviction, and nothing can be admitted by way of ornament or relief, that does not add new force or clearness to the original conception. The two classes of ideas brought together by the orator or impassioned prose-writer, to wit, the general subject and the particular image, are so far incompatible, and the identity must be more strict, more marked, more determinate, to make them coalesce to any practical purpose. Every word should be a blow: every thought should instantly grapple with its fellow. There must be a weight, a precision, a conformity from association in the tropes and figures of animated prose to fit them to their place in the argument, and make them *tell*, which may be dispensed with in poetry, where there is something much more congenial between the subject-matter and the illustration—

Like beauty making beautiful old rime![10]

What can be more remote, for instance, and at the same time more apposite, more *the same*, than the following comparison of the English Constitution to 'the proud Keep of Windsor,' in the celebrated Letter to a Noble Lord?[11]

'Such are *their* ideas, such *their* religion, and such *their* law. But as to *our* country and *our* race, as long as the well-compacted structure of our church and state, the sanctuary, the holy of holies of that ancient law, defended by reverence, defended by power—a fortress at once and a temple*—shall stand inviolate on the brow of the British Sion; as long as the British Monarchy—not more limited than fenced by the orders of the State—shall, like the proud Keep of Windsor, rising in the majesty of proportion, and girt with the double belt of its kindred and coeval towers; as long as this awful structure shall oversee and guard the subjected land, so long the mounds and dykes of the low, fat, Bedford level will have nothing to fear from all the pickaxes of all the levellers of France. As long as our Sovereign Lord the King, and his faithful subjects, the Lords and Commons of this realm—the triple cord which no man can break; the solemn, sworn, constitutional frank-pledge of this nation; the firm guarantees of each other's being, and each other's rights; the joint and several securities, each in its place and order, for every kind and every quality of property and of dignity—As long as these endure, so long the Duke of Bedford is safe: and we are all safe together—the high from the blights of envy and the spoliations of rapacity; the low from the iron hand of oppression and the insolent spurn of contempt. Amen! and so be it: and so it will be,

> *Dum domus Æneæ Capitoli immobile saxum*
> *Accolet; imperiumque pater Romanus habebit.'[12]*

Nothing can well be more impracticable to a simile than the vague and complicated idea which is here embodied in

---

* *Templum in modum arcis.*
                    TACITUS of the Temple of Jerusalem. [Burke's note]

one; yet how finely, how nobly it stands out, in natural grandeur, in royal state, with double barriers round it to answer for its identity, with 'buttress, frieze, and coigne of 'vantage' for the imagination to 'make its pendant bed and procreant cradle,' till the idea is confounded with the object representing it—the wonder of a kingdom; and then how striking, how determined the descent, 'at one fell swoop,' to the 'low, fat, Bedford level!' Poetry would have been bound to maintain a certain decorum, a regular balance between these two ideas; sterling prose throws aside all such idle respect to appearances, and with its pen, like a sword, 'sharp and sweet,' lays open the naked truth! The poet's Muse is like a mistress, whom we keep only while she is young and beautiful, *durante bene placito;*[13] the Muse of prose is like a wife, whom we take during life, *for better for worse*. Burke's execution, like that of all good prose, savours of the texture of what he describes, and his pen slides or drags over the ground of his subject, like the painter's pencil. The most rigid fidelity and the most fanciful extravagance meet, and are reconciled in his pages. I never pass Windsor but I think of this passage in Burke, and hardly know to which I am indebted most for enriching my moral sense, that or the fine picturesque stanza, in Gray,

> From Windsor's heights the expanse below
> Of mead, of lawn, of wood survey, etc.[14]

I might mention that the so much admired description in one of the India speeches,[15] of Hyder Ally's army (I think it is) which 'now hung like a cloud upon the mountain, and now burst upon the plain like a thunder bolt,' would do equally well for poetry or prose. It is a bold and striking illustration of a naturally impressive object. This is not the case with the Abbé Siéyès's far-famed 'pigeon-holes,' nor with the comparison of the Duke of Bedford to 'the Leviathan, tumbling about his unwieldy bulk in the ocean of royal bounty.'[16] Nothing here saves the description but the force of the invective; the startling truth, the vehemence, the remoteness, the aptitude, the perfect peculiarity and coincidence of the allusion. No writer would ever have thought of it but himself; no reader can ever forget it. What is there in common, one might say, between a Peer of the Realm, and 'that seabeast,' of those

> Created hugest that swim the ocean-stream?[17]

Yet Burke has knit the two ideas together, and no man can put them asunder. No matter how slight and precarious the

connection, the length of line it is necessary for the fancy to
give out in keeping hold of the object on which it has fastened, he seems to have 'put his hook in the nostrils'[18] of this
enormous creature of the crown, that empurples all its track
through the glittering expanse of a profound and restless
imagination!

In looking into the IRIS[19] of last week, I find the following
passages, in an article on the death of Lord Castlereagh.[20]

'The splendour of Majesty leaving the British metropolis,
careering along the ocean, and landing in the capital of the
North, is distinguished only by glimpses through the dense
array of clouds in which Death hid himself, while he struck
down to the dust the stateliest courtier near the throne, and
the broken train of which pursues and crosses the Royal
progress wherever its glories are presented to the eye of
imagination. . . . . .

'The same indefatigable mind—a mind of all work—which
thus ruled the Continent with a rod of iron, the sword—within
the walls of the House of Commons ruled a more distracted
region with a more subtle and finely-tempered weapon, the
tongue; and truly, if this *was* the only weapon his Lordship
wielded there, where he had daily to encounter, and frequently almost alone, enemies more formidable than Buonaparte, it must be acknowledged that he achieved greater victories than Demosthenes or Cicero ever gained in far more
easy fields of strife; nay, he wrought miracles of speech, out-
vying those miracles of song, which Orpheus is said to have
performed, when not only men and brutes, but rocks, woods,
and mountains, followed the sound of his voice and lyre. . . . . .

'But there was a worm at the root of the gourd that flour-
ished over his head in the brightest sunshine of a court; both
perished in a night, and in the morning, that which had been
his glory and his shadow, covered him like a shroud; while the
corpse, notwithstanding all his honours, and titles, and offices,
lay unmoved in the place where it fell, till a judgment had
been passed upon him, which the poorest peasant escapes
when he dies in the ordinary course of nature.'

*Sheffield Advertiser*, Aug. 20, 1822.

This, it must be confessed, is very unlike Burke: yet Mr.
Montgomery is a very pleasing poet, and a strenuous politician. The whole is *travelling out of the record*, and to no sort
of purpose. The author is constantly getting away from the
impression of his subject, to envelop himself in a cloud of
images, which weaken and perplex, instead of adding force
and clearness to it. Provided he is figurative, he does not care
how commonplace or irrelevant the figures are, and he wan-

ders on, delighted in a labyrinth of words, like a truant schoolboy, who is only glad to have escaped from his task. He has
a very slight hold of his subject, and is tempted to let it go
for any fallacious ornament of style. How obscure and circuitous is the allusion to 'the clouds in which Death hid himself, to strike down the stateliest courtier near the throne!'
How hackneyed is the reference to Demosthenes and Cicero,
and how utterly quaint and unmeaning is the ringing the
changes upon Orpheus and his train of men, beasts, woods,
rocks, and mountains in connection with Lord Castlereagh!
But he is better pleased with this classical fable than with the
death of the Noble Peer, and delights to dwell upon it, to
however little use. So he is glad to take advantage of the
scriptural idea of a gourd; not to enforce, but as a relief to his
reflections; and points his conclusion with a puling sort of
commonplace, that a peasant, who dies a natural death, has
no Coroner's Inquest to sit upon him. All these are the faults
of the ordinary poetical style. Poets think they are bound,
by the tenor of their indentures to the Muses, to 'elevate and
surprise' in every line; and not having the usual resources at
hand in common or abstracted subjects, aspire to the end without the means. They make, or pretend, an extraordinary interest where there is none. They are ambitious, vain, and
indolent—more busy in preparing idle ornaments, which they
take their chance of bringing in somehow or other, than
intent on eliciting truths by fair and honest inquiry. It should
seem as if they considered prose as a sort of waiting-maid to
poetry, that could only be expected to wear her mistress's
cast-off finery. Poets have been said to succeed best in fiction;
and the account here given may in part explain the reason.
That is to say, they must choose their own subject, in such a
manner as to afford them continual opportunities of appealing
to the senses and exciting the fancy. Dry details, abstruse
speculations, do not give scope to vividness of description;
and, as they cannot bear to be considered dull, they become
too often affected, extravagant, and insipid.

I am indebted to Mr. Coleridge for the comparison of
poetic prose to the second-hand finery of a lady's maid (just
made use of). He himself is an instance of his own observation, and (what is even worse) of the opposite fault—an affectation of quaintness and originality. With bits of tarnished
lace and worthless frippery, he assumes a sweeping oriental
costume, or borrows the stiff dresses of our ancestors, or starts
an eccentric fashion of his own. He is swelling and turgid—
everlastingly aiming to be greater than his subject; filling his
fancy with fumes and vapours in the pangs and throes of

miraculous parturition, and bringing forth only *still births*. He has an incessant craving, as it were, to exalt every idea into a metaphor, to expand every sentiment into a lengthened mystery, voluminous and vast, confused and cloudy. His style is not succinct, but incumbered with a train of words and images that have no practical, and only a possible relation to one another—that add to its stateliness, but impede its march. One of his sentences winds its 'forlorn way obscure' over the page like a patriarchal procession with camels laden, wreathed turbans, household wealth, the whole riches of the author's mind poured out upon the barren waste of his subject. The palm-tree spreads its sterile branches overhead, and the land of promise is seen in the distance. All this is owing to his wishing to overdo everything—to make something more out of everything than it is, or than it is worth. The simple truth does not satisfy him—no direct proposition fills up the moulds of his understanding. All is foreign, far-fetched, irrelevant, laboured, unproductive. To read one of his disquisitions is like hearing the variations to a piece of music without the score. Or, to vary the simile, he is not like a man going a journey by the stage-coach along the high-road, but is always getting into a balloon, and mounting into the air, above the plain ground of prose. Whether he soars to the empyrean, or dives to the centre (as he sometimes does), it is equally to get away from the question before him, and to prove that he owes everything to his own mind. His object is to invent; he scorns to imitate. The business of prose is the contrary. But Mr. Coleridge is a poet, and his thoughts are free.

I think the poet-laureate is a much better prose-writer. His style has an antique quaintness, with a modern familiarity. He has just a sufficient sprinkling of *archaisms*, of allusions to old Fuller, and Burton, and Latimer, to set off or qualify the the smart flippant tone of his apologies for existing abuses, or the ready, galling virulence of his personal invectives. Mr. Southey is a faithful historian, and no inefficient partisan. In the former character, his mind is tenacious of facts; and in the latter, his spleen and jealousy prevent the 'extravagant and erring spirit' of the poet from losing itself in Fancy's endless maze. He 'stoops to *earth*,'[21] at least, and prostitutes his pen to some purpose (not at the same time losing his own soul, and gaining nothing by it)—and he vilifies Reform, and praises the reign of George III in good set terms, in a straight-forward, intelligible, practical, pointed way. He is not buoyed up by conscious power out of the reach of common apprehensions, but makes the most of the obvious advantages he possesses. You may complain of a pettiness and petulance of

manner, but certainly there is no want of spirit or facility of
execution. He does not waste powder and shot in the air, but
loads his piece, takes a level aim, and hits his mark. One
would say (though his Muse is ambidexter) that he wrote
prose with his right hand; there is nothing awkward, circuitous, or feeble in it. 'The words of Mercury are harsh after
the songs of Apollo':[22] but this would not apply to him. His
prose-lucubrations are pleasanter reading than his poetry.
Indeed, he is equally practised and voluminous in both; and
it is no improbable conjecture, that Mr. Southey may have
had some idea of rivalling the reputation of Voltaire in the
extent, the spirit, and the versatility of his productions in
prose and verse, except that he has written no tragedies but
*Wat Tyler!*[23]

To my taste, the Author of *Rimini*, and Editor of the
*Examiner*,[24] is among the best and least corrupted of our
poetical prose-writers. In his light but well supported columns
we find the raciness, the sharpness, and sparkling effect of
poetry, with little that is extravagant or farfetched, and no
turgidity or pompous pretension. Perhaps there is too much
the appearance of relaxation and trifling (as if he had escaped
the shackles of rhyme), a caprice, a levity, and a disposition
to innovate in words and ideas. Still the genuine master-spirit
of the prose-writer is there; the tone of lively, sensible conversation; and this may in part arise from the author's being
himself an animated talker. Mr. Hunt wants something of the
heat and earnestness of the political partisan; but his familiar
and miscellaneous papers have all the ease, grace, and point
of the best style of Essay-writing. Many of his effusions in
the *Indicator*[25] show, that if he had devoted himself exclusively to that mode of writing, he inherits more of the spirit
of Steele than any man since his time.

Lord Byron's prose is bad; that is to say, heavy, laboured,
and coarse: he tries to knock someone down with the butt-
end of every line, which defeats his object—and the style of
the Author of Waverley (if he comes fairly into this discussion) as mere style, is villainous. It is pretty plain he is a poet;
for the sound of names runs mechanically in his ears, and he
rings the changes unconsciously on the same words in a sentence, like the same rhymes in a couplet.

Not to spin out this discussion too much, I would conclude
by observing, that some of the old English prose-writers (who
were not poets) are the best, and, at the same time, the most
*poetical* in the favourable sense. Among these we may reckon
some of the old divines, and Jeremy Taylor[26] at the head of
them. There is a flush like the dawn over his writings; the
sweetness of the rose, the freshness of the morning-dew.

There is a softness in his style, proceeding from the tenderness of his heart: but his head is firm, and his hand is free. His materials are as finely wrought up as they are original and attractive in themselves. Milton's prose-style savours too much of poetry, and, as I have already hinted, of an imitation of the Latin. Dryden's is perfectly unexceptionable, and a model, in simplicity, strength, and perspicuity, for the subjects he treated of.

# My First Acquaintance
# with Poets*

MY FATHER was a Dissenting Minister at W[e]m in Shropshire; and in the year 1798 (the figures that compose that date are to me like the 'dreaded name of Demogorgon').[1] Mr. Coleridge came to Shrewsbury, to succeed Mr. Rowe in the spiritual charge of a Unitarian Congregation there. He did not come till late on the Saturday afternoon before he was to preach; and Mr. Rowe, who himself went down to the coach in a state of anxiety and expectation, to look for the arrival of his successor, could find no one at all answering the description but a round-faced man in a short black coat (like a shooting jacket) which hardly seemed to have been made for him, but who seemed to be talking at a great rate to his fellow-passengers. Mr. Rowe had scarce returned to give an account of his disappointment, when the round-faced man in black entered, and dissipated all doubts on the subject, by beginning to talk. He did not cease while he stayed; nor has he since, that I know of. He held the good town of Shrewsbury in delightful suspense for three weeks that he remained there, 'fluttering the *proud Salopians* like an eagle in a dove-cote;'[2] and the Welsh mountains that skirt the horizon with their tempestuous confusion, agree to have heard no such mystic sounds since the days of

High-born Hoel's harp or soft Llewellyn's lay![3]

As we passed along between W[e]m and Shrewsbury, and I eyed their blue tops seen through the wintry branches, or the red rustling leaves of the sturdy oak-trees by the road-side, a sound was in my ears as of a Siren's song; I was stunned, startled with it, as from deep sleep; but I had no notion then that I should ever be able to express my admiration to others

* [*The Liberal*, III; April 1823.]

in motley imagery or quaint allusion, till the light of his
genius shone into my soul, like the sun's rays glittering in the
puddles of the road. I was at that time dumb, inarticulate,
helpless, like a worm by the way-side, crushed, bleeding, lifeless; but now, bursting from the deadly bands that 'bound
them,

> With Styx nine times round them,'[4]

my ideas float on winged words, and as they expand their
plumes, catch the golden light of other years. My soul has
indeed remained in its original bondage, dark, obscure, with
longings infinite and unsatisfied; my heart, shut up in the
prison-house of this rude clay, has never found, nor will it
ever find, a heart to speak to; but that my understanding also
did not remain dumb and brutish, or at length found a language to express itself, I owe to Coleridge. But this is not
to my purpose.

My father lived ten miles from Shrewsbury, and was in
the habit of exchanging visits with Mr. Rowe, and with Mr.
Jenkins of Whitchurch (nine miles farther on) according to
the custom of Dissenting Ministers in each other's neighbourhood. A line of communication is thus established, by
which the flame of civil and religious liberty is kept alive, and
nourishes its smouldering fire unquenchable, like the fires in
the Agamemnon of Æschylus, placed at different stations,
that waited for ten long years to announce with their blazing pyramids the destruction of Troy. Coleridge had agreed
to come over to see my father, according to the courtesy of
the country, as Mr. Rowe's probable successor; but in the
meantime I had gone to hear him preach the Sunday after
his arrival. A poet and a philosopher getting up into a Unitarian pulpit to preach the Gospel, was a romance in these
degenerate days, a sort of revival of the primitive spirit of
Christianity, which was not to be resisted.

It was in January, 1798, that I rose one morning before
daylight, to walk ten miles in the mud, and went to hear
this celebrated person preach. Never, the longest day I have
to live, shall I have such another walk as this cold, raw, comfortless one, in the winter of the year 1798. *Il y a des impressions que ni le tems ni les circonstances peuvent effacer.
Dusse-je vivre des siècles entiers, le doux tems de ma jeunesse
ne peut renaître pour moi, ni s'effacer jamais dans ma mém-
oire.*[5] When I got there, the organ was playing the 100th
psalm, and, when it was done, Mr. Coleridge rose and gave
out his text, 'And he went up into the mountain to pray,

HIMSELF, ALONE.'[6] As he gave out his text, his voice 'rose like a steam of rich distilled perfumes,'[7] and when he came to the last two words, which he pronounced loud, deep, and distinct, it seemed to me, who was then young, as if the sounds had echoed from the bottom of the human heart, and as if that prayer might have floated in solemn silence through the universe. The idea of St. John came into mind, 'of one crying in the wilderness, who had his loins girt about, and whose food was locusts and wild honey.'[8] The preacher then launched into his subject, like an eagle dallying with the wind. The sermon was upon peace and war; upon church and state—not their alliance, but their separation—on the spirit of the world and the spirit of Christianity, not as the same, but as opposed to one another. He talked of those who had 'inscribed the cross of Christ on banners dripping with human gore.' He made a poetical and pastoral excursion—and to show the fatal effects of war, drew a striking contrast between the simple shepherd boy, driving his team afield, or sitting under the hawthorn, piping to his flock, 'as though he should never be old,' and the same poor country-lad, crimped, kidnapped, brought into town, made drunk at an alehouse, turned into a wretched drummer-boy, with his hair sticking on end with powder and pomatum, a long cue at his back, and tricked out in the loathsome finery of the profession of blood.

Such were the notes our once-lov'd poet sung.[9]

And for myself, I could not have been more delighted if I had heard the music of the spheres. Poetry and Philosophy had met together. Truth and Genius had embraced, under the eye and with the sanction of Religion. This was even beyond my hopes. I returned home well satisfied. The sun that was still labouring pale and wan through the sky, obscured by thick mists, seemed an emblem of the *good cause;* and the cold dank drops of dew that hung half melted on the beard of the thistle, had something genial and refreshing in them; for there was a spirit of hope and youth in all nature, that turned everything into good. The face of nature had not then the brand of JUS DIVINUM[10] on it:

Like to that sanguine flower inscrib'd with woe.[11]

On the Tuesday following, the half-inspired speaker came. I was called down into the room where he was, and went half-hoping, half-afraid. He received me very graciously, and

I listened for a long time without uttering a word. I did not suffer in his opinion by my silence. 'For those two hours,' he afterwards was pleased to say, 'he was conversing with W. H.'s forehead!' His appearance was different from what I had anticipated from seeing him before. At a distance, and in the dim light of the chapel, there was to me a strange wildness in his aspect, a dusky obscurity, and I thought him pitted with the small-pox. His complexion was at that time clear, and even bright—

As are the children of yon azure sheen.[12]

His forehead was broad and high, light as if built of ivory, with large projecting eyebrows, and his eyes rolling beneath them like a sea with darkened lustre. 'A certain tender bloom his face o'erspread,' a purple tinge as we see it in the pale thoughtful complexions of the Spanish portrait-painters, Murillo and Velasquez. His mouth was gross, voluptuous, open, eloquent; his chin good-humoured and round; but his nose, the rudder of the face, the index of the will, was small, feeble, nothing—like what he has done. It might seem that the genius of his face as from a height surveyed and projected him (with sufficient capacity and huge aspiration) into the world unknown of thought and imagination, with nothing to support or guide his veering purpose, as if Columbus had launched his adventurous course for the New World in a scallop, without oars or compass. So at least I comment on it after the event. Coleridge in his person was rather above the common size, inclining to the corpulent, or like Lord Hamlet, 'somewhat fat and pursy.' His hair (now, alas! grey) was then black and glossy as the raven's, and fell in smooth masses over his forehead. This long pendulous hair is peculiar to enthusiasts, to those whose minds tend heavenward; and is traditionally inseparable (though a different colour) from the pictures of Christ. It ought to belong, as a character, to all who preach *Christ crucified*, and Coleridge was at that time one of those!

It was curious to observe the contrast between him and my father, who was a veteran in the cause, and then declining into the vale of years. He had been a poor Irish lad, carefully brought up by his parents, and sent to the University of Glasgow (where he studied under Adam Smith) to prepare him for his future destination. It was his mother's proudest wish to see her son a Dissenting Minister. So if we look back to past generations (as far as eye can reach) we see the same hopes, fears, wishes, followed by the same disappointments, throbbing in the human heart; and so we may see them (if we look forward) rising up for ever, and disappearing, like vapourish bubbles, in the human breast! After being tossed about from congregation to congregation in the heats of the Unitarian controversy, and squabbles about the American war, he had been relegated to an obscure village, where he was to spend the last thirty years of his life, far from the only converse that he loved, the talk about disputed texts of Scripture and the cause of civil and religious liberty. Here he passed his days, repining but resigned, in the study of the Bible, and the perusal of the Commentators—huge folios, not easily got through, one of which would outlast a winter! Why did he pore on these from morn to night (with the exception of a walk in the fields or a turn in the garden to gather broc-coli-plants or kidney-beans of his own rearing, with no small degree of pride and pleasure)?—Here were 'no figures nor no fantasies'—neither poetry nor philosophy—nothing to dazzle, nothing to excite modern curiosity; but to his lack-lustre eyes there appeared, within the pages of the ponderous, unwieldy, neglected tomes, the sacred name of JEHOVAH in Hebrew capitals; pressed down by the weight of the style, worn to the last fading thinness of the understanding, there were glimpses, glimmering notions of the patriarchal wanderings, with palm-trees hovering in the horizon, and processions of camels at the distance of three thousand years; there was Moses with the Burning Bush, the number of the Twelve Tribes, types, shadows, glosses on the law and the prophets; there were discussions (dull enough) on the age of Methuse-lah, a mighty speculation! there were outlines, rude guesses at the shape of Noah's Ark and of the riches of Solomon's Temple; questions as to the date of the creation, predictions of the end of all things; the great lapses of time, the strange mutations of the globe were unfolded with the voluminous leaf, as it turned over; and though the soul might slumber with an hieroglyphic veil of inscrutable mysteries drawn over it, yet it was in a slumber ill-exchanged for all the sharpened realities of sense, wit, fancy, or reason. My father's life was comparatively a dream; but it was a dream of infinity and eternity, of death, the resurrection, and a judgment to come!

No two individuals were ever more unlike than were the host and his guest. A poet was to my father a sort of non-descript: yet whatever added grace to the Unitarian cause was to him welcome. He could hardly have been more surprised or pleased, if our visitor had worn wings. Indeed, his thoughts had wings; and as the silken sounds rustled round our little wainscoted parlour, my father threw back his spectacles over

his forehead, his white hairs mixing with its sanguine hue;
and a smile of delight beamed across his rugged cordial face,
to think that Truth had found a new ally in Fancy!* Besides,
Coleridge seemed to take considerable notice of me, and that
of itself was enough. He talked very familiarly, but agreeably,
and glanced over a variety of subjects. At dinner-time he grew
more animated, and dilated in a very edifying manner on
Mary Wolstonecraft[13] and Mackintosh.[13] The last, he said,
he considered (on my father's speaking of his *Vindiciæ Gal-
licæ* as a capital performance) as a clever scholastic man—
a master of the topics—or as the ready warehouseman of letters, who knew exactly where to lay his hand on what he
wanted, though the goods were not his own. He thought him
no match for Burke, either in style or matter. Burke was a
metaphysician, Mackintosh a mere logician. Burke was an
orator (almost a poet) who reasoned in figures, because he had
an eye for nature: Mackintosh, on the other hand, was a
rhetorician, who had only an eye to commonplaces. On this
I ventured to say that I had always entertained a great opinion of Burke, and that (as far as I could find) the speaking
of him with contempt might be made the test of a vulgar
democratical mind. This was the first observation I ever made
to Coleridge, and he said it was a very just and striking one.
I remember the leg of Welsh mutton and the turnips on the
table that day had the finest flavour imaginable. Coleridge
added that Mackintosh and Tom Wedgwood[14] (of whom
however, he spoke highly) had expressed a very indifferent
opinion of his friend Mr. Wordsworth, on which he remarked
to them—'He strides on so far before you, that he dwindles
in the distance!' Godwin had once boasted to him of having
carried on an argument with Mackintosh for three hours
with dubious success; Coleridge told him—'If there had been
a man of genius in the room, he would have settled the question in five minutes.' He asked me if I had ever seen Mary
Wolstonecraft, and I said, I had once for a few moments, and
that she seemed to me to turn off Godwin's objections to something she advanced with quite a playful, easy air. He replied,
that 'this was only one instance of the ascendancy which people of imagination exercised over those of mere intellect.' He

* My father was one of those who mistook his talent after all. He
used to be very much dissatisfied that I preferred his Letters to his
Sermons. The last were forced and dry; the first came naturally from
him. For ease, half-plays on words, and a supine, monkish, indolent
pleasantry, I have never seen them equalled. [w. h.]

did not rate Godwin very high* (this was caprice or prejudice, real or affected) but he had a great idea of Mrs. Wolstone-craft's powers of conversation, none at all of her talent for book-making. We talked a little about Holcroft.[15] He had been asked if he was not much struck *with* him, and he said, he thought himself in more danger of being struck *by* him. I complained that he would not let me get on at all, for he required a definition of every the commonest word, exclaiming, 'What do you mean by a *sensation,* Sir? What do you mean by an *idea?*' This, Coleridge said, was barricadoing the road to truth: it was setting up a turnpike-gate at every step we took. I forget a great number of things, many more than I remember; but the day passed off pleasantly, and the next morning Mr. Coleridge was to return to Shrewsbury. When I came down to breakfast, I found that he had just received a letter from his friend T. Wedgwood, making him an offer of £150 a-year if he chose to waive his present pursuit, and devote himself entirely to the study of poetry and philosophy. Coleridge seemed to make up his mind to close with this proposal in the act of tying on one of his shoes. It threw an additional damp on his departure. It took the wayward enthusiast quite from us to cast him into Deva's[16] winding vales, or by the shores of old romance. Instead of living at ten miles distance, of being the pastor of a Dissenting congregation at Shrewsbury, he was henceforth to inhabit the Hill of Parnassus, to be a shepherd on the Delectable Mountains. Alas! I knew not the way thither, and felt very little gratitude for Mr. Wedgwood's bounty. I was presently relieved from this dilemma; for Mr. Coleridge, asking for a pen and ink, and going to a table to write something on a bit of card, advanced towards me with undulating step, and giving me the precious document, said that that was his address, *Mr. Cole-ridge, Nether-Stowey, Somersetshire;* and that he should be glad to see me there in a few weeks' time, and, if I chose, would come half-way to meet me. I was not less surprised than the shepherd-boy (this simile is to be found in *Cassandra*)[17] when he sees a thunder-bolt fall close at his feet. I stammered out my acknowledgments and acceptance of this offer (I thought Mr. Wedgwood's annuity a trifle to it) as well as I could; and this mighty business being settled, the poet-preacher took leave, and I accompanied him six miles on the

---

* He complained in particular of the presumption of attempting to establish the future immortality of man 'without' (as he said) 'knowing what Death was or what Life was'—and the tone in which he pronounced these two words seemed to convey a complete image of both. [w. h.]

road. It was a fine morning in the middle of winter, and he talked the whole way. The scholar in Chaucer is described as going

Sounding on his way.

So Coleridge went on his. In digressing, in dilating, in passing from subject to subject, he appeared to me to float in air, to slide on ice. He told me in confidence (going along) that he should have preached two sermons before he accepted the situation at Shrewsbury, one on Infant Baptism, the other on the Lord's Supper, showing that he could not administer either, which would have effectually disqualified him for the object in view. I observed that he continually crossed me on the way by shifting from one side of the foot-path to the other. This struck me as an odd movement; but I did not at that time connect it with any instability of purpose or involuntary change of principle, as I have done since. He seemed unable to keep on in a straight line. He spoke slightingly of Hume (whose Essay on Miracles he said was stolen from an objection started in one of South's sermons—*Credat Judæus Apella!*).[18] I was not very much pleased at this account of Hume, for I had just been reading, with infinite relish, that completest of all metaphysical *choke-pears,* his *Treatise on Human Nature,* to which the *Essays,* in point of scholastic subtlety and close reasoning, are mere elegant trifling, light summer-reading. Coleridge even denied the excellence of Hume's general style, which I think betrayed a want of taste or candour. He however made me amends by the manner in which he spoke of Berkeley. He dwelt particularly on his *Essay on Vision* as a masterpiece of analytical reasoning. So it undoubtedly is. He was exceedingly angry with Dr. Johnson for striking the stone with his foot, in allusion to this author's Theory of Matter and Spirit, and saying, 'Thus I confute him, Sir.'[19] Coleridge drew a parallel (I don't know how he brought about the connection) between Bishop Berkeley and Tom Paine. He said the one was an instance of a subtle, the other of an acute mind, than which no two things could be more distinct. The one was a shop-boy's quality, the other the characteristic of a philosopher. He considered Bishop Butler as a true philosopher, a profound and conscientious thinker, a genuine reader of nature and of his own mind. He did not speak of his *Analogy,* but of his *Sermons at the Rolls' Chapel,* of which I had never heard. Coleridge somehow always contrived to prefer the *unknown* to the *known.* In this instance he was right. The *Analogy* is a tissue of sophistry, of wire-drawn, theological special-pleading; the *Sermons* (with the Preface to them) are in a fine vein of deep, matured reflection, a candid appeal to our observation of human nature, without pedantry and without bias. I told Coleridge I had written a few remarks, and was sometimes foolish enough to believe that I had made a discovery on the same subject (the *Natural Disinterestedness of the Human Mind*)—and I tried to explain my view of it to Coleridge, who listened with great willingness, but I did not succeed in making myself understood. I sat down to the task shortly afterwards for the twentieth time, got new pens and paper, determined to make clear work of it, wrote a few meagre sentences in the skeleton-style of a mathematical demonstration, stopped half-way down the second page; and, after trying in vain to pump up any words, images, notions, apprehensions, facts, or observations, from that gulph of abstraction in which I had plunged myself for four or five years preceding, gave up the attempt as labour in vain, and shed tears of helpless despondency on the blank unfinished paper.[20] I can write fast enough now. Am I better than I was then? Oh no! One truth discovered, one pang of regret at not being able to express it, is better than all the fluency and flippancy in the world. Would that I could go back to what I then was! Why can we not revive past times as we can revisit old places? If I had the quaint Muse of Sir Philip Sidney to assist me, I would write a *Sonnet to the Road between W[e]m and Shrewsbury*, and immortalise every step of it by some fond enigmatical conceit. I would swear that the very milestones had ears, and that Harmer-hill stooped with all its pines, to listen to a poet, as he passed! I remember but one other topic of discourse in this walk. He mentioned Paley,[21] praised the naturalness and clearness of his style, but condemned his sentiments, thought him a mere time-serving casuist, and said that 'the fact of his work on Moral and Political Philosophy being made a text-book in our Universities was a disgrace to the national character.' We parted at the six-mile stone; and I returned homeward pensive but much pleased. I had met with unexpected notice from a person, whom I believed to have been prejudiced against me. 'Kind and affable to me had been his condescension, and should be honoured ever with suitable regard.'[22] He was the first poet I had known, and he certainly answered to that inspired name. I had heard a great deal of his powers of conversation, and was not disappointed. In fact, I never met with anything at all like them, either before or since. I could easily credit the accounts which were circulated of his holding forth to a large party of ladies and gentlemen, an evening or two before, on the Berkeleian Theory, when he made the whole material universe look like a transparency of fine words; and another story (which I believe he has somewhere told himself)[23] of his being asked to a party at Birmingham, of his smoking tobacco and going to sleep after dinner on a sofa, where the company found him to their no small surprise, which was increased to wonder when he started up of a sudden, and rubbing his eyes, looked about him, and launched into a three-hours' description of the third heaven, of which he had had a dream, very different from Mr. Southey's "Vision of Judgment," and also from that other Vision of Judgment,[24] which Mr. Murray,[25] the Secretary of the Bridge-street Junto, has taken into his especial keeping!

On my way back, I had a sound in my ears, it was the voice of Fancy: I had a light before me, it was the face of Poetry. The one still lingers there, the other has not quitted my side! Coleridge in truth met me half-way on the ground of philosophy, or I should not have been won over to his imaginative creed. I had an uneasy, pleasurable sensation all the time, till I was to visit him. During those months the chill breath of winter gave me a welcoming; the vernal air was balm and inspiration to me. The golden sunsets, the silver star of evening, lighted me on my way to new hopes and prospects. *I was to visit Coleridge in the spring.* This circumstance was never absent from my thoughts, and mingled with all my feelings. I wrote to him at the time proposed, and received an answer postponing my intended visit for a week or two, but very cordially urging me to complete my promise then. This delay did not damp, but rather increased my ardour. In the meantime, I went to Llangollen Vale, by way of initiating myself in the mysteries of natural scenery; and I must say I was enchanted with it. I had been reading Coleridge's description of England in his fine *Ode on the Departing Year*, and I applied it, *con amore*, to the objects before me. That valley was to me (in a manner) the cradle of a new existence: in the river that winds through it, my spirit was baptised in the waters of Helicon!

I returned home, and soon after set out on my journey with unworn heart and untried feet. My way lay through Worcester and Gloucester, and by Upton, where I thought of Tom Jones and the adventure of the muff. I remember getting completely wet through one day, and stopping at an inn (I think it was at Tewkesbury) where I sat up all night to read *Paul and Virginia*.[26] Sweet were the showers in early youth that drenched my body, and sweet the drops of pity that fell upon the books I read! I recollect a remark of Coleridge's upon this very book, that nothing could show the gross indelicacy of French manners and the entire corruption of their imagination more strongly than the behaviour of the heroine in the last fatal scene, who turns away from a person on board the sinking vessel, that offers to save her life, because he has thrown off his clothes to assist him in swimming. Was this a time to think of such a circumstance? I once hinted to Wordsworth, as we were sailing in his boat on Grasmere lake, that I thought he had borrowed the idea of his *Poems on the Naming of Places* from the local inscriptions of the same kind in *Paul and Virginia*. He did not own the obligation, and stated some distinction without a difference, in defence of his claim to originality. Any the slightest variation would be sufficient for this purpose in his mind; for whatever *he* added or omitted would inevitably be worth all that anyone else had done, and contain the marrow of the sentiment. I was still two days before the time fixed for my arrival, for I had taken care to set out early enough. I stopped these two days at Bridgewater, and when I was tired of sauntering on the banks of its muddy river, returned to the inn, and read *Camilla*.[27] So have I loitered my life away, reading books, looking at pictures, going to plays, hearing, thinking, writing on what pleased me best. I have wanted only one thing to make me happy; but wanting that, have wanted everything!

I arrived, and was well received. The country about Nether Stowey is beautiful, green and hilly, and near the sea-shore. I saw it but the other day, after an interval of twenty years, from a hill near Taunton. How was the map of my life spread out before me, as the map of the country lay at my feet! In the afternoon, Coleridge took me over to All-Foxden, a romantic old family-mansion of the St. Aubins, where Wordsworth lived. It was then in the possession of a friend of the poet's who gave him the free use of it.[28] Somehow that period (the time just after the French Revolution) was not a time when *nothing was given for nothing*. The mind opened, and a softness might be perceived coming over the heart of individuals, beneath 'the scales that fence' our self-interest. Wordsworth himself was from home, but his sister kept house, and set before us a frugal repast; and we had free access to her brother's poems, the *Lyrical Ballads*, which were still in manuscript, or in the form of *Sybilline Leaves*. I dipped into a few of these with great satisfaction, and with the faith of a novice. I slept that night in an old room with blue hangings, and covered with the round-faced family-portraits of the age of George I and II, and from the wooded declivity of the adjoining park that overlooked my window, at the dawn of day, could

hear the loud stag speak.[29]

In the outset of life (and particularly at this time I felt it so) our imagination has a body to it. We are in a state between sleeping and waking, and have indistinct but glorious glimpses of strange shapes, and there is always something to come better than what we see. As in our dreams the fulness of the blood gives warmth and reality to the coinage of the brain, so in youth our ideas are clothed, and fed, and pampered with our good spirits; we breathe thick with thoughtless happiness, the weight of future years presses on the strong pulses of the heart, and we repose with undisturbed faith in truth and good. As we advance, we exhaust our fund of enjoyment and of hope. We are no longer wrapped in *lamb's-wool*, lulled in Elysium. As we taste the pleasures of life, their spirit evaporates, the sense palls; and nothing is left but the phantoms, the lifeless shadows of what *has been!*

That morning, as soon as breakfast was over, we strolled out into the park, and seating ourselves on the trunk of an old ash-tree that stretched along the ground, Coleridge read aloud with a sonorous and musical voice, the ballad of Betty Foy.[30] I was not critically or sceptically inclined. I saw touches of truth and nature, and took the rest for granted. But in "The Thorn," "The Mad Mother," and "The Complaint of a Poor Indian Woman," I felt that deeper power and pathos which have been since acknowledged,

> In spite of pride, in erring reason's spite,[31]

as the characteristics of this author; and the sense of a new style and a new spirit in poetry came over me. It had to me something of the effect that arises from the turning up of the fresh soil, or of the first welcome breath of Spring,

> While yet the trembling year is unconfirmed.[32]

Coleridge and myself walked back to Stowey that evening, and his voice sounded high

> Of Providence, foreknowledge, will, and fate,
> Fix'd fate, free-will, foreknowledge absolute,[33]

as we passed through echoing grove, by fairy stream or water-fall, gleaming in the summer moonlight! He lamented that Wordsworth was not prone enough to believe in the traditional superstitions of the place, and that there was a something corporeal, a *matter-of-fact-ness*, a clinging to the palpable, or often to the petty, in his poetry, in consequence. His genius was not a spirit that descended to him through the air; it sprung out of the ground like a flower, or unfolded itself from a green spray, on which the gold-finch sang. He said, however (if I remember right), that this objection must be confined to his descriptive pieces, that his philosophic poetry had a grand and comprehensive spirit in it, so that his soul seemed to inhabit the universe like a palace, and to discover truth by intuition, rather than by deduction. The next day Wordsworth arrived from Bristol at Coleridge's cottage. I think I see him now. He answered in some degree to his friend's description of him, but was more gaunt and Don Quixote-like. He was quaintly dressed (according to the *costume* of that unconstrained period) in a brown fustian jacket and striped pantaloons. There was something of a roll, a lounge in his gait, not unlike his own Peter Bell. There was a severe, worn pressure of thought about his temples, a fire in his eye (as if he saw something in objects more than the outward appearance), an intense high narrow forehead, a Roman nose, cheeks furrowed by strong purpose and feeling, and a convulsive inclination to laughter about the mouth, a good deal at variance with the solemn, stately expression of the rest of his face. Chantry's[34] bust wants the marking traits; but he was teased into making it regular and heavy: Haydon's[35] head of him, introduced into the "Entrance of Christ into Jerusalem," is the most like his drooping weight of thought and expression. He sat down and talked very naturally and freely, with a mixture of clear gushing accents in his voice, a deep guttural intonation, and a strong tincture of the northern *burr*, like the crust on wine. He instantly began to make havoc of the half of a Cheshire cheese on the table, and said triumphantly that 'his marriage with experience had not been so unproductive as Mr. Southey's in teaching him a knowledge of the good things of this life.' He had been to see the *Castle Spectre* by Monk Lewis, while at Bristol, and described it very well. He said 'it fitted the taste of the audience like a glove.' This *ad captandum*[36] merit was however by no means a recommendation of it, according to the severe principles of the new school, which reject rather than court popular effect. Wordsworth, looking out of the low, latticed window, said, 'How beautifully the sun sets on that yellow bank!' I thought within myself, 'With what eyes these poets see nature!' and ever after, when I saw the sun-set stream upon the objects facing it, conceived I had made a discovery, or thanked Mr. Wordsworth for having made one for me! We went over to All-Foxden again the day following, and Wordsworth read us the story of Peter Bell[37] in the open air; and the comment made upon it by his face and voice was very different from that of some later critics! Whatever might be thought of the poem, 'his

face was as a book where men might read strange matters,'
and he announced the fate of his hero in prophetic tones.
There is a *chaunt* in the recitation both of Coleridge and
Wordsworth, which acts as a spell upon the hearer, and dis-
arms the judgment. Perhaps they have deceived themselves
by making habitual use of this ambiguous accompaniment.
Coleridge's manner is more full, animated, and varied; Wordsworth's more equable, sustained, and internal. The one might
be termed more *dramatic*, the other more *lyrical*. Coleridge
has told me that he himself liked to compose in walking over
uneven ground, or breaking through the straggling branches
of a copse-wood; whereas Wordsworth always wrote (if he
could) walking up and down a straight gravel-walk, or in
some spot where the continuity of his verse met with no collateral interruption. Returning that same evening, I got into
a metaphysical argument with Wordsworth, while Coleridge
was explaining the different notes of the nightingale to his
sister, in which we neither of us succeeded in making ourselves perfectly clear and intelligible. Thus I passed three
weeks at Nether Stowey and in the neighbourhood, generally
devoting the afternoons to a delightful chat in an arbour made
of bark by the poet's friend Tom Poole, sitting under two fine
elm-trees, and listening to the bees humming round us, while
we quaffed our *flip*.[38] It was agreed, among other things, that
we should make a jaunt down the Bristol Channel, as far as
Linton. We set off together on foot, Coleridge, John Chester,
and I. This Chester was a native of Nether Stowey, one of
those who were attracted to Coleridge's discourse as flies are
to honey, or bees in swarming-time to the sound of a brass
pan. He 'followed in the chase, like a dog who hunts, not like
one that made up the cry.' He had on a brown cloth coat,
boots, and corduroy breeches, was low in stature, bow-legged,
had a drag in his walk like a drover, which he assisted by a
hazel switch, and kept on a sort of trot by the side of Coleridge, like a running footman by a state coach, that he might
not lose a syllable or sound that fell from Coleridge's lips. He
told me his private opinion, that Coleridge was a wonderful
man. He scarcely opened his lips, much less offered an opinion
the whole way: yet of the three, had I to choose during that
journey, I would be John Chester. He afterwards followed
Coleridge into Germany, where the Kantean philosophers
were puzzled how to bring him under any of their categories.
When he sat down at table with his idol, John's felicity was
complete; Sir Walter Scott's, or Mr. Blackwood's, when they
sat down at the same table with the King,[39] was not more so.
We passed Dunster on our right, a small town between the
brow of a hill and the sea. I remember eyeing it wistfully as

it lay below us: contrasted with the woody scene around, it looked as clear, as pure, as *embrowned* and ideal as any landscape I have seen since, of Gaspar Poussin's or Domenichino's. We had a long day's march—(our feet kept time to the echoes of Coleridge's tongue)— through Minehead and by the Blue Anchor, and on to Linton, which we did not reach till near midnight, and where we had some difficulty in making a lodgment. We however knocked the people of the house up at last, and we were repaid for our apprehensions and fatigue by some excellent rashers of fried bacon and eggs. The view in coming along had been splendid. We walked for miles and miles on dark brown heaths overlooking the Channel, with the Welsh hills beyond, and at times descended into little sheltered valleys close by the sea-side, with a smuggler's face scowling by us, and then had to ascend conical hills with a path winding up through a coppice to a barren top, like a monk's shaven crown, from one of which I pointed out to Coleridge's notice the bare masts of a vessel on the very edge of the horizon and within the red-orbed disk of the setting sun, like his own spectre-ship in the *Ancient Mariner*. At Linton the character of the sea-coast becomes more marked and rugged. There is a place called the *Valley of Rocks* (I suspect this was only the poetical name for it) bedded among precipices overhanging the sea, with rocky caverns beneath, into which the waves dash, and where the sea-gull for ever wheels its screaming flight. On the tops of these are huge stones thrown transverse, as if an earthquake had tossed them there, and behind these is a fretwork of perpendicular rocks, something like the *Giant's Causeway*. A thunder-storm came on while we were at the inn, and Coleridge was running out bareheaded to enjoy the commotion of the elements in the *Valley of Rocks*, but as if in spite, the clouds only muttered a few angry sounds, and let fall a few refreshing drops. Coleridge told me that he and Wordsworth were to have made this place the scene of a prose-tale,[40] which was to have been in the manner of, but far superior to, the *Death of Abel*,[41] but they had relinquished the design. In the morning of the second day, we breakfasted luxuriously in an old-fashioned parlour, on tea, toast, eggs, and honey, in the very sight of the beehives from which it had been taken, and a garden full of thyme and wild flowers that had produced it. On this occasion Coleridge spoke of Virgil's Georgics, but not well. I do not think he had much feeling for the classical or elegant. It was in this room that we found a little worn-out copy of the *Seasons*, lying in a window-seat, on which Coleridge exclaimed, 'That is true fame!' He said Thomson was a great poet, rather than a good one; his style was as meretricious as his thoughts were natural. He spoke of Cowper as the best modern poet. He said the *Lyrical Ballads* were an experiment about to be tried by him and Wordsworth, to see how far the public taste would endure poetry written in a more natural and simple style than had hitherto been attempted; totally discarding the artifices of poetical diction, and making use only of such words as had probably been common in the most ordinary language since the days of Henry II. Some comparison was introduced between Shakespeare and Milton. He said 'he hardly knew which to prefer. Shakespeare appeared to him a mere stripling in the art; he was as tall and as strong, with infinitely more activity than Milton, but he never appeared to have come to man's estate; or if he had, he would not have been a man, but a monster.' He spoke with contempt of Gray, and with intolerance of Pope. He did not like the versification of the latter. He observed that 'the ears of these couplet-writers might be charged with having short memories, that could not retain the harmony of whole passages.' He thought little of Junius as a writer; he had a dislike of Dr. Johnson; and a much higher opinion of Burke as an orator and politician, than of Fox or Pitt. He however thought him very inferior in richness of style and imagery to some of our elder prose-writers, particularly Jeremy Taylor. He liked Richardson, but not Fielding; nor could I get him to enter into the merits of *Caleb Williams*.* 42 In short, he was profound and discriminating with respect to those authors whom he liked, and where he gave his judgment fair play; capricious, perverse, and prejudiced in his antipathies and distastes. We loitered on the 'ribbed sea-sands'43 in such talk as this, a whole morning, and I recollect met with a curious sea-weed, of which John Chester told us the country name! A fisherman gave Coleridge an account of a boy that had been drowned the day before, and that they had tried to save him at the risk of their own lives. He said 'he did not know how it was that they ventured, but, Sir, we have a *nature* towards one another.' This expression, Coleridge remarked to me, was a fine illustration of that theory of disinterestedness which I (in common with Butler) had adopted. I broached to him an argument of mine to prove that *likeness* was not mere association of ideas.

---

* He had no idea of pictures, of Claude or Raphael, and at this time I had as little as he. He sometimes gives a striking account at present of the Cartoons at Pisa, by Buffamalco and others; of one in particular, where Death is seen in the air brandishing his scythe, and the great and mighty of the earth shudder at his approach, while the beggars and the wretched kneel to him as their deliverer. He would of course understand so broad and fine a moral as this at any time. [w. h.]

I said that the mark in the sand put one in mind of a man's foot, not because it was part of a former impression of a man's foot (for it was quite new) but because it was like the shape of a man's foot. He assented to the justness of this distinction (which I have explained at length elsewhere,[44] for the benefit of the curious) and John Chester listened; not from any interest in the subject, but because he was astonished that I should be able to suggest anything to Coleridge that he did not already know. We returned on the third morning, and Coleridge remarked the silent cottage-smoke curling up the valleys where, a few evenings before, we had seen the lights gleaming through the dark.

In a day or two after we arrived at Stowey, we set out, I on my return home, and he for Germany. It was a Sunday morning, and he was to preach that day for Dr. Toulmin of Taunton. I asked him if he had prepared anything for the occasion? He said he had not even thought of the text, but should as soon as we parted. I did not go to hear him—this was a fault—but we met in the evening at Bridgewater. The next day we had a long day's walk to Bristol, and sat down, I recollect, by a well-side on the road, to cool ourselves and satisfy our thirst, when Coleridge repeated to me some descriptive lines from his tragedy of Remorse; which I must say became his mouth and that occasion better than they, some years after, did Mr. Elliston's and the Drury-lane boards—[45]

> Oh memory! shield me from the world's poor strife,
> And give those scenes thine everlasting life.[46]

I saw no more of him for a year or two, during which period he had been wandering in the Hartz Forest in Germany; and his return was cometary, meteorous, unlike his setting out. It was not till some time after that I knew his friends Lamb and Southey. The last always appears to me (as I first saw him) with a commonplace book under his arm, and the first with a *bon mot* in his mouth. It was at Godwin's that I met him with Holcroft and Coleridge, where they were disputing fiercely which was the best—*Man as he was, or man as he is to be*. 'Give me,' says Lamb, 'man as he is *not* to be.' This saying was the beginning of a friendship between us, which I believe still continues.—Enough of this for the present.

> But there is matter for another rhyme,
> And I to this may add a second tale.[47]

# On Londoners
# and Country People*

I DO not agree with Mr. Blackwood in his definition of the word "Cockney." He means by it a person who has happened at any time to live in London, and who is not a Tory—I mean by it a person who has never lived out of London, and who has got all his ideas from it.

The true Cockney has never travelled beyond the purlieus of the Metropolis, either in the body or the spirit. Primrose-hill is the Ultima Thule of his most romantic desires; Greenwich Park stands him in stead of the Vales of Arcady. Time and space are lost to him. He is confined to one spot, and to the present moment. He sees everything near, superficial, little, in hasty succession. The world turns round, and his head with it, like a roundabout at a fair, till he becomes stunned and giddy with the motion. Figures glide by as in a *camera obscura*.[1] There is a glare, a perpetual hubbub, a noise, a crowd about him; he sees and hears a vast number of things, and knows nothing. He is pert, raw, ignorant, conceited, ridiculous, shallow, contemptible. His senses keep him alive; and he knows, inquires, and cares for nothing farther. He meets the Lord Mayor's coach, and without ceremony treats himself to an imaginary ride in it. He notices the people going to court or to a city-feast, and is quite satisfied with the show. He takes the wall of a Lord,[2] and fancies himself as good as he. He sees an infinite quantity of people pass along the street, and thinks there is no such thing as life or a knowledge of character to be found out of London. 'Beyond Hyde Park all is a desart to him.' He despises the country, because he is ignorant of it, and the town, because he is familiar with it. He is as well acquainted with St. Paul's as if he had built it, and talks of Westminster Abbey and Poets' Corner with great indifference. The King, the House of Lords and Commons are his very

* [*Plain Speaker; New Monthly Magazine*, Aug. 1823.]

good friends. He knows the members for Westminster or the City by sight, and bows to the Sheriffs or the Sheriffs' men. He is hand and glove with the Chairman of some Committee. He is, in short, a great man by proxy, and comes so often in contact with fine persons and things, that he rubs off a little of the gilding, and is surcharged with a sort of second-hand, rapid, tingling, troublesome self-importance. His personal vanity is thus continually flattered and perked up into ridiculous self-complacency, while his imagination is jaded and impaired by daily misuse. Everything is vulgarised in his mind. Nothing dwells long enough on it to produce an interest; nothing is contemplated sufficiently at a distance to excite curiosity or wonder. *Your true Cockney is your only true leveller*. Let him be as low as he will, he fancies he is as good as anybody else. He has no respect for himself, and still less (if possible) for you. He cares little about his own advantages, if he can only make a jest at yours. Every feeling comes to him through a medium of levity and impertinence; nor does he like to have his habit of mind disturbed by being brought into collision with anything serious or respectable. He despairs (in such a crowd of competitors) of distinguishing himself, but laughs heartily at the idea of being able to trip up the heels of other people's pretensions. A Cockney feels no gratitude. This is a first principle with him. He regards any obligation you confer upon him as a species of imposition, a ludicrous assumption of fancied superiority. He talks about everything, for he has heard something about it; and understanding nothing of the matter, concludes he has as good a right as you. He is a politician; for he has seen the Parliament House: he is a critic; because he knows the principal actors by sight—has a taste for music, because he belongs to a glee-club at the West End, and is gallant, in virtue of sometimes frequenting the lobbies[3] at half-price. A mere Londoner, in fact, from the opportunities he has of knowing something of a number of objects (and those striking ones) fancies himself a sort of privileged person; remains satisfied with the assumption of merits, so much the more unquestionable as they are not his own; and from being dazzled with noise, show, and appearances, is less capable of giving a real opinion, or entering into any subject than the meanest peasant. There are greater lawyers, orators, painters, philosophers, poets, players in London, than in any other part of the United Kingdom: he is a Londoner, and therefore it would be strange if he did not know more of law, eloquence, art, philosophy, poetry, acting, than any one without his local advantages, and who is merely from the country. This is a *non sequitur;* and it constantly appears so when put to the test.

A real Cockney is the poorest creature in the world, the most literal, the most mechanical, and yet he too lives in a world of romance—a fairy-land of his own. He is a citizen of London; and this abstraction leads his imagination the finest dance in the world. London is the first city on the habitable globe; and therefore he must be superior to everyone who lives out of it. There are more people in London than anywhere else; and though a dwarf in stature, his person swells out and expands into *ideal* importance and borrowed magnitude. He resides in a garret or in a two pair of stairs' back room; yet he talks of the magnificence of London, and gives himself airs of consequence upon it, as if all the houses in Portman or in Grosvenor Square were his by right or in reversion. 'He is owner of all he surveys.' The Monument, the Tower of London, St. James's Palace, the Mansion House, White-Hall, are part and parcel of his being. Let us suppose him to be a lawyer's clerk at half-a-guinea a week: but he knows the Inns of Court, the Temple Gardens, and Gray's-Inn Passage, sees the lawyers in their wigs walking up and down Chancery Lane, and has advanced within half-a-dozen yards of the Chancellor's chair: who can doubt that he understands (by implication) every point of law (however intricate) better than the most expert country practitioner? He is a shopman, and nailed all day behind the counter: but he sees hundreds and thousands of gay, well-dressed people pass—an endless phantasmagoria—and enjoys their liberty and gaudy fluttering pride. He is a footman—but he rides behind beauty, through a crowd of carriages, and visits a thousand shops. Is he a tailor—that last infirmity of human nature? The stigma on his profession is lost in the elegance of the patterns he provides, and of the persons he adorns; and he is something very different from a mere country botcher. Nay, the very scavenger and nightman thinks the dirt in the street has something precious in it, and his employment is solemn, silent, sacred, peculiar to London! A *barker*[4] in Monmouth Street, a slop-seller[5] in Radcliffe Highway, a tapster at a night-cellar, a beggar in St. Giles's, a drab in Fleet-Ditch, live in the eyes of millions, and eke out a dreary, wretched, scanty, or loathsome existence from the gorgeous busy, glowing scene around them. It is a common saying among such persons that 'they had rather be hanged in London than die a natural death out of it anywhere else'—such is the force of habit and imagination. Even the eye of childhood is dazzled and delighted with the polished splendour of the jewellers' shops, the neatness of the turnery ware,[6] the festoons of artificial flowers, the confectionery, the chemists' shops, the lamps, the horses, the carriages, the sedanchairs: to this was formerly added a set of traditional associations—Whittington[7] and his Cat, Guy Faux and the Gunpowder Treason, the Fire and the Plague of London, and the Heads of the Scotch Rebels that were stuck on Temple Bar in 1745. These have vanished, and in their stead the curious and romantic eye must be content to pore in Pennant[8] for the site of old London-Wall, or to peruse the sentimental mile-stone that marks the distance to the place 'where Hickes's Hall formerly stood!'[9]

The *Cockney* lives in a go-cart of local prejudices and positive illusions; and when he is turned out of it, he hardly knows how to stand or move. He ventures through Hyde Park Corner, as a cat crosses a gutter. The trees pass by the coach very oddly. The country has a strange blank appearance. It is not lined with houses all the way, like London. He comes to places he never saw or heard of. He finds the world is bigger than he thought for. He might have dropped from the moon, for anything he knows of the matter. He is mightily disposed to laugh, but is half afraid of making some blunder. Between sheepishness and conceit, he is in a very ludicrous situation. He finds that the people walk on two legs, and wonders to hear them talk a dialect so different from his own. He perceives London fashions have got down into the country before him, and that some of the better sort are dressed as well as he is. A drove of pigs or cattle stopping the road is a very troublesome interruption. A crow in a field, a magpie in a hedge, are to him very odd animals—he can't tell what to make of them, or how they live. He does not altogether like the accommodations at the inns—it is not what he has been used to in town. He begins to be communicative—says he was 'born within the sound of Bow-bell,' and attempts some jokes, at which nobody laughs. He asks the coachman a question, to which he receives no answer. All this is to him very unaccountable and unexpected. He arrives at his journey's end; and instead of being the great man he anticipated among his friends and country relations, finds that they are barely civil to him, or make a butt of him; have topics of their own which he is as completely ignorant of as they are indifferent to what he says, so that he is glad to get back to London again, where he meets with his favourite indulgences and associates, and fancies the whole world is occupied with what he hears and sees.

A Cockney loves a tea-garden in summer, as he loves the play or the Cider-Cellar in winter—where he sweetens the air with the fumes of tobacco, and makes it echo to the sound of his own voice. This kind of suburban retreat is a most agreeable relief to the close and confined air of a city life. The imagination, long pent up behind a counter or between brick walls, with noisome smells, and dingy objects, cannot bear at once to launch into the boundless expanse of the country, but 'shorter excursions tries,' coveting something between the two, and finding it at White-conduit House, or the Rosemary Branch, or Bagnigge Wells. The landlady is seen at a bow-window in near perspective, with punch-bowls and lemons disposed orderly around—the lime-trees or poplars wave overhead to 'catch the breezy air,' through which, typical of the huge dense cloud that hangs over the metropolis, curls up the thin, blue, odoriferous vapour of Virginia or Oronooko—the benches are ranged in rows, the fields and hedge-rows spread out their verdure; Hampstead and Highgate are seen in the background, and contain the imagination within gentle limits —here the holiday people are playing ball; here they are playing bowls—here they are quaffing ale, there sipping tea—here the loud wager is heard, there the political debate. In a sequestered nook a slender youth with purple face and drooping head, nodding over a glass of gin toddy, breathes in tender accents—'There's nought so sweet on earth as Love's young dream'; while 'Rosy Ann' takes its turn, and 'Scots wha hae wi' Wallace bled' is thundered forth in accents that might wake the dead. In another part sit carpers and critics, who dispute the score of the reckoning or the game, or cavil at the taste and execution of the *would-be* Brahams and Durusets.[10] Of this latter class was Dr. Goodman, a man of other times— I mean of those of Smollett and Defoe—who was curious in opinion, obstinate in the wrong, great in little things, and inveterate in petty warfare. I vow he held me an argument once 'an hour by St. Dunstan's clock,' while I held an umbrella over his head (the friendly protection of which he was unwilling to quit to walk in the rain to Camberwell) to prove to me that Richard Pinch was neither a fives-player nor a pleasing singer. 'Sir,' said he, 'I deny that Mr. Pinch plays the game. He is a cunning player, but not a good one. I grant his tricks, his little mean dirty ways, but he is not a manly antagonist. He has no hit, and no left-hand. How then can he set up for a superior player? And then as to his always striking the ball against the side-wings at Copenhagen-house, Cavanagh, sir, used to say, "The wall was made to hit at!" I have no patience with such pitiful shifts and advantages. They are an insult upon so fine and athletic a game! And as to his setting up for a singer, it's quite ridiculous. You know, Mr. H——, that to be a really excellent singer, a man must lay claim to one of two things; in the first place, sir, he must have a naturally fine ear for music, or secondly, an early education, exclusively devoted to that study. But no one ever suspected Mr. Pinch of refined sensibility; and his education, as we all know, has been a little at large. Then again, why should he of all other things be always singing "Rosy Ann," and "Scots wha hae wi' Wallace bled," till one is sick of hearing them? It's preposterous, and I mean to tell him so. You know, I'm sure, without my hinting it, that in the first of these admired songs, the sentiment is voluptuous and tender, and in the last patriotic. Now Pinch's romance never wandered from behind his counter, and his patriotism lies in his breeches' pocket. Sir, the utmost he should aspire to would be to play upon the Jews' harp!' This story of the Jews' harp tickled some of Pinch's friends, who gave him various hints of it, which nearly drove him mad, till he discovered what it was; for though no jest or sarcasm ever had the least effect upon him, yet he cannot bear to think that there should be any joke of this kind about him, and he not in the secret: it makes against that *knowing* character which he so much affects. Pinch is in one respect a complete specimen of a "Cockney." He never has anything to say, and yet is never at a loss for an answer. That is, his pertness keeps exact pace with his dulness. His friend, the Doctor, used to complain of this in good set terms.—'You can never make anything of Mr. Pinch,' he would say. 'Apply the most cutting remark to him, and his only answer is, *"The same to you, sir."* If Shakespeare were to rise from the dead to confute him, I firmly believe it would be to no purpose. I assure you, I have found it so. I once thought indeed I had him at a disadvantage, but I was mistaken. You shall hear, sir. I had been reading the following sentiment in a modern play—"The Road to Ruin," by the late Mr. Holcroft—"For how should the soul of Socrates inhabit the body of a stocking-weaver?" This was pat to the point (you know our friend is a hosier and haberdasher). I came full with it to keep an appointment I had with Pinch, began a game, quarrelled with him in the middle of it on purpose, went up stairs to dress, and as I was washing my hands in the slop-basin (watching my opportunity) turned coolly round and said, "It's impossible there should be any sympathy between you and me, Mr. Pinch: for as the poet says, how should the soul of Socrates inhabit the body of a stocking-weaver?" "Ay," says he, "does the poet say so? *then the same to you, sir!*" I was confounded, I gave up the attempt to conquer him in wit or argument. He would pose the Devil, sir, by his *"The same to you, sir."* ' We had another joke against Richard Pinch, to which the Doctor was not a party, which was, that being asked after the respectability of the Hole in the Wall, at the time that Randall[11] took it, he answered quite unconsciously, 'Oh! it's a very genteel place, I go there myself sometimes!' Dr. Goodman was descended by the mother's side from the poet Jago, was a private gentleman in town, and a medical dilettante in the country, dividing his time equally between business and pleasure; had an inexhaustible flow of words, and an imperturbable vanity, and held 'stout notions on the metaphysical score.' He maintained the free agency of man, with the spirit of a martyr and the gaiety of a man of wit and pleasure about town—told me he had a curious tract on that subject by A. C. (Anthony Collins)[12] which he carefully locked up in his box, lest anyone should see it but himself, to the detriment of their character and morals, and put it to me whether it was not hard, on the principles of *philosophical necessity*, for a man to come to be hanged? To which I replied, 'I thought it hard on any terms!' A knavish *marker*, who had listened to the dispute, laughed at this retort, and seemed to assent to the truth of it, supposing it might one day be his own case.

Mr. Smith and the Brangtons, in *Evelina*, are the finest possible examples of the spirit of 'Cockneyism.' I once knew a linen-draper in the City, who owned to me he did not quite like this part of Miss Burney's novel. He said, 'I myself lodge in a first floor, where there are young ladies in the house: they sometimes have company, and if I am out, they ask me to lend them the use of my apartment, which I readily do out of politeness, or if it is an agreeable party, I perhaps join them. All this is so like what passes in the novel, that I fancy myself a sort of second Mr. Smith, and am not quite easy at it!' This was mentioned to the fair Authoress, and she was delighted to find that her characters were so true, that an actual person fancied himself to be one of them. The resemblance, however, was only in the externals; and the real modesty of the individual stumbled on the likeness to a city coxcomb!

It is curious to what a degree persons, brought up in certain occupations in a great city, are shut up from a knowledge of the world, and carry their simplicity to a pitch of unheard-of extravagance. London is the only place in which the child grows completely up into the man. I have known characters of this kind, which, in the way of childish ignorance and self-pleasing delusion, exceeded anything to be met with in Shakespeare or Ben Jonson, or the old comedy. For instance, the following may be taken as a true sketch. Imagine a person with a florid, shining complexion like a plough-boy, large staring teeth, a merry eye, his hair stuck into the fashion with curling-irons and pomatum, a slender figure, and a decent suit of black —add to which the thoughtlessness of the school-boy, the forwardness of the thriving tradesman, and the plenary consciousness of the citizen of London—and you have Mr. Dunster before you, the fishmonger in the Poultry. You shall hear how he chirps over his cups, and exults in his private opinions. 'I'll play no more with you,' I said, 'Mr. Dunster—you are five points in the game better than I am.' I had just lost three half-crown rubbers at cribbage to him, which loss of mine he presently thrust into a canvas pouch (not a silk purse) out of which he had produced just before, first a few halfpence, then half a dozen pieces of silver, then a handful of guineas, and lastly, lying *perdu* at the bottom, a fifty pound Bank-Note. 'I'll tell you what,' I said, 'I should like to play you a game at marbles'— this was at a sort of Christmas party or Twelfth Night merry-making. 'Marbles!' said Dunster, catching up the sound, and his eye brightening with childish glee, 'What! you mean *ring-taw?*' 'Yes.' 'I should beat you at it, to a certainty. I was one of the best in our school (it was at Clapham, sir, the Rev. Mr. Denman's at Clapham, was the place where I was brought up) though there were two others there better than me. They were the best that ever were. I'll tell you, sir, I'll give you an idea. There was a water-butt or cistern, sir, at our school, that turned with a cock. Now suppose that brass-ring that the window-curtain is fastened to, to be the cock, and that these boys were standing where we are, about twenty feet off—well, sir, I'll tell you what I have seen them do. One of them had a favourite taw (or *alley* we used to call them) he'd take aim at the cock of the cistern with this marble, as I may do now. Well, sir, will you believe it? such was his strength of knuckle and certainty of aim, he'd hit it, turn it, let the water out, and then, sir, when the water had run out as much as it was wanted, the other boy (he'd just the same strength of knuckle, and the same certainty of eye) he'd aim at it too, be sure to hit it, turn it round, and stop the water from running out. Yes, what I tell you is very remarkable, but it's true. One of these boys was named Cock, and t' other Butler.' 'They might have been named Spigot and Fawcett, my dear sir, from your account of them.' 'I should not mind playing you at fives neither, though I'm out of practice. I think I should beat you in a week: I was a real good one at that. A pretty game, sir! I had the finest ball, that I suppose ever was seen. Made it myself, I'll tell you how, sir. You see, I put a piece of cork at the bottom, then I wound some fine worsted yarn round it, then I had to bind it round with some pack-thread, and then sew the case on. You'd hardly believe it, but I was the envy of the whole school for that ball. They all wanted to get it from me, but lord, sir, I would let none of them come near it. I kept it in my waistcoat pocket all day, and at night I used to take it to bed with me and put it under my pillow. I couldn't sleep easy without it.'

The same idle vein might be found in the country, but I doubt whether it would find a tongue to give it utterance.

Cockneyism is a ground of native shallowness mounted with pertness and conceit. Yet with all this simplicity and extravagance in dilating on his favourite topics, Dunster is a man of spirit, of attention to business, knows how to make out and get in his bills, and is far from being hen-pecked. One thing is certain, that such a man must be a true Englishman and a loyal subject. He has a slight tinge of letters, with shame I confess it—has in his possession a volume of the *European Magazine* for the year 1761, and is an humble admirer of *Tristram Shandy* (particularly the story of the King of Bohemia and his Seven Castles, which is something in his own endless manner) and of *Gil Blas* of Santillane. Over these (the last thing before he goes to bed at night) he smokes a pipe, and meditates for an hour. After all, what is there in these harmless half-lies, these fantastic exaggerations, but a literal, prosaic, "Cockney" translation of the admired lines in Gray's "Ode to Eton College":

> What idle progeny succeed
> To chase the rolling circle's speed
> Or urge the flying ball?

A man shut up all his life in his shop, without anything to interest him from one year's end to another but the cares and details of business, with scarcely any intercourse with books or opportunities for society, distracted with the buzz and glare and noise about him, turns for relief to the retrospect of his childish years; and there, through the long vista, at one bright loop-hole, leading out of the thorny mazes of the world into the clear morning light, he sees the idle fancies and gay amusements of his boyhood dancing like motes in the sunshine. Shall we blame or should we laugh at him, if his eye glistens, and his tongue grows wanton in their praise?

None but a Scotchman would—that pragmatical sort of personage, who thinks it a folly ever to have been young, and who instead of dallying with the frail past, bends his brows upon the future, and looks only to the *main-chance*. Forgive me, dear Dunster, if I have drawn a sketch of some of thy venial foibles, and delivered thee into the hands of these Cockneys of the North, who will fall upon thee and devour thee, like so many cannibals, without a grain of salt!

If familiarity in cities breeds contempt, ignorance in the country breeds aversion and dislike. People come too much in contact in town: in other places they live too much apart, to unite cordially and easily. Our feelings, in the former case, are dissipated and exhausted by being called into constant and vain activity; in the latter they rust and grow dead for want of use. If there is an air of levity and indifference in London manners, there is a harshness, a moroseness, and disagreeable restraint in those of the country. We have little disposition to sympathy, when we have few persons to sympathise with: we lose the relish and capacity for social enjoyment, the seldomer we meet. A habit of sullenness, coldness, and misanthropy grows upon us. If we look for hospitality and a cheerful welcome in country places, it must be in those where the arrival of a stranger is an event, the recurrence of which need not be greatly apprehended, or it must be on rare occasions, on 'some high festival of once a year.' Then indeed the stream of hospitality, so long dammed up, may flow without stint for a short season; or a stranger may be expected with the same sort of eager impatience as a caravan of wild beasts, or any other natural curiosity, that excites our wonder and fills up the craving of the mind after novelty. By degrees, however, even this last principle loses its effect: books, newspapers, whatever carries us out of ourselves into a world of which we see and know nothing, becomes distasteful, repulsive; and we turn away with indifference or disgust from everything that disturbs our lethargic animal existence, or takes off our attention from our petty, local interests and pursuits. Man, left long to himself, is no better than a mere clod; or his activity, for want of some other vent, preys upon himself, or is directed to splenetic, peevish dislikes, or vexatious, harassing persecution of others. I once drew a picture of a country-life: it was a portrait of a particular place, a caricature if you will, but with certain allowances, I fear it was too like in the individual instance, and that it would hold too generally true. *See Round Table,* vol. ii. p. 116.[13]

If these then are the faults and vices of the inhabitants of town or of the country, where should a man go to live, so as to escape from them? I answer, that in the country we have the society of the groves, the fields, the brooks, and in London a man may keep to himself, or choose his company as he pleases.

It appears to me that there is an amiable mixture of these two opposite characters in a person who chances to have past his youth in London, and who has retired into the country for the rest of his life. We may find in such a one a social polish, a pastoral simplicity. He rusticates agreeably, and vegetates with a degree of sentiment. He comes to the next post-town to see for letters, watches the coaches as they pass, and eyes the passengers with a look of familiar curiosity, thinking that he too was a gay fellow in his time. He turns his horse's head down the narrow lane that leads homewards, puts on an old coat to save his wardrobe, and fills his glass nearer to the brim.

As he lifts the purple juice to his lips and to his eye, and in the dim solitude that hems him round, thinks of the glowing line—

This bottle's the sun of our table—[14]

another sun rises upon his imagination; the sun of his youth, the blaze of vanity, the glitter of the metropolis, 'glares round his soul, and mocks his closing eye-lids.' The distant roar of coaches in his ears—the pit stare upon him with a thousand eyes—Mrs. Siddons, Bannister, King, are before him—he starts as from a dream, and swears he will to London; but the expense, the length of way deters him, and he rises the next morning to trace the footsteps of the hare that has brushed the dew-drops from the lawn, or to attend a meeting of Magistrates! Mr. Justice Shallow answered in some sort to this description of a retired Cockney and indigenous country-gentlemen. He 'knew the Inns of Court, where they would talk of mad Shallow yet, and where the bona robas were, and had them at commandment: aye, and had heard the chimes at midnight!'[15]

It is a strange state of society (such as that in London) where a man does not know his next-door neighbour, and where the feelings (one would think) must recoil upon themselves, and either fester or become obtuse. Mr. Wordsworth, in the preface to his poem of *The Excursion,* represents men in cities as so many wild beasts or evil spirits, shut up in cells of ignorance, without natural affections, and barricadoed down in sensuality and selfishness. The nerve of humanity is bound up, according to him, the circulation of the blood stagnates. And it would be so, if men were merely cut off from intercourse with their immediate neighbours, and did not meet together generally and more at large. But man in London becomes, as Mr. Burke has it, a sort of 'public creature.' He lives in the eye of the world, and the world in his. If he witnesses less of the details of private life, he has better opportunities of observing its larger masses and varied movements. He sees the stream of human life pouring along the streets— its comforts and embellishments piled up in the shops—the houses are proofs of the industry, the public buildings of the art and magnificence of man; while the public amusements and places of resort are a centre and support for social feeling. A playhouse alone is a school of humanity, where all eyes are fixed on the same gay or solemn scene, where smiles or tears are spread from face to face, and where a thousand hearts beat in unison! Look at the company in a country-theatre (in comparison) and see the coldness, the sullenness, the want of sympathy, and the way in which they turn round to scan and scrutinise one another. In London there is a *public;* and each man is part of it. We are gregarious, and affect the kind. We have a sort of abstract existence; and a community of ideas and knowledge (rather than local proximity) is the bond of society and good-fellowship. This is one great cause of the tone of political feeling in large and populous cities. There is here a visible body-politic, a type and image of that huge Leviathan the State. We comprehend that vast denomination, the *People,* of which we see a tenth part daily moving before us; and by having our imaginations emancipated from petty interests and personal dependence, we learn to venerate ourselves as men, and to respect the rights of human nature. Therefore it is that the citizens and free-men of London and Westminster are patriots by prescription, philosophers and politicians by the right of their birth-place. In the country, men are no better than a herd of cattle or scattered deer. They have no idea but of individuals, none of rights or principles— and a king, as the greatest individual, is the highest idea they can form. He is 'a species alone,' and as superior to any single peasant as the latter is to the peasant's dog, or to a crow flying over his head. In London the king is but as one to a million (numerically speaking), is seldom seen, and then distinguished only from others by the superior graces of his person. A country squire or a lord of the manor is a greater man in his village or hundred!

# Whether Genius Is
# Conscious of Its
# Powers?*

NO REALLY great man ever thought himself so. The idea of
greatness in the mind answers but ill to our knowledge—or to
our ignorance of ourselves. What living prose-writer, for instance, would think of comparing himself with Burke? Yet
would it not have been equal presumption or egotism in him
to fancy himself equal to those who had gone before him—
Bolingbroke or Johnson or Sir William Temple? Because his
rank in letters is become a settled point with us, we conclude
that it must have been quite as self-evident to him, and that
he must have been perfectly conscious of his vast superiority
to the rest of the world. Alas! not so. No man is truly himself,
but in the idea which others entertain of him. The mind, as
well as the eye, 'sees not itself, but by reflection from some
other thing.'[1] What parity can there be between the effect of
habitual composition on the mind of the individual, and the
surprise occasioned by first reading a fine passage in an admired author; between what we do with ease, and what we
thought it next to impossible ever to be done; between the
reverential awe we have for years encouraged, without seeing
reason to alter it, for distinguished genius, and the slow,
reluctant, unwelcome conviction that after infinite toil and
repeated disappointments, and when it is too late and to little
purpose, we have ourselves at length accomplished what we
at first proposed; between the insignificance of our petty, personal pretensions, and the vastness and splendour which the
atmosphere of imagination lends to an illustrious name? He
who comes up to his own idea of greatness, must always have
had a very low standard of it in his mind. 'What a pity,' said
someone, 'that Milton had not the pleasure of reading *Paradise*

* [*Plain Speaker;* written autumn 1823.]

.ost!' He could not read it, as we do, with the weight of
npression that a hundred years of admiration have added to
—'a phœnix gazed by all'[2]—with the sense of the number
f editions it has passed through with still increasing reputa-
on, with the tone of solidity, time-proof, which it has
eceived from the breath of cold, envious maligners, with the
und which the voice of Fame has lent to every line of it!
he writer of an ephemeral production may be as much
azzled with it as the public: it may sparkle in his own eyes
r a moment, and be soon forgotten by everyone else. But
o one can anticipate the suffrages of posterity. Every man,
a judging of himself, is his own contemporary. He may feel
ne gale of popularity, but he cannot tell how long it will last.
[Iis opinion of himself wants distance, wants time, wants num-
ers, to set it off and confirm it. He must be indifferent to his
wn merits, before he can feel a confidence in them. Besides,
veryone must be sensible of a thousand weaknesses and defi-
iencies in himself; whereas Genius only leaves behind it the
nonuments of its strength. A great name is an abstraction of
ome one excellence: but whoever fancies himself an abstrac-
on of excellence, so far from being great, may be sure that
e is a blockhead, equally ignorant of excellence or defect, of
imself or others. Mr. Burke, besides being the author of the
*eflections,* and the *Letter to a Noble Lord,* had a wife and
on; and had to think as much about them as we do about
im. The imagination gains nothing by the minute details of
ersonal knowledge.

On the other hand, it may be said that no man knows so
ell as the author of any performance what it has cost him,
nd the length of time and study devoted to it. This is one,
mong other reasons, why no man can pronounce an opinion
pon himself. The happiness of the result bears no proportion
o the difficulties overcome or the pains taken. *Materiam
uperabat opus,*[3] is an old and fatal complaint. The definition
f genius is that it acts unconsciously; and those who have
roduced immortal works, have done so without knowing how
r why. The greatest power operates unseen, and executes its
ppointed task with as little ostentation as difficulty. Whatever
s done best, is done from the natural bent and disposition of
he mind. It is only where our incapacity begins, that we begin
o feel the obstacles, and to set an undue value on our triumph
ver them. Correggio, Michael Angelo, Rembrandt, did what
hey did without premeditation or effort—their works came
rom their minds as a natural birth—if you had asked them
vhy they adopted this or that style, they would have an-
wered, *because they could not help it,* and because they
new of no other. So Shakespeare says:

> Our poesy is as a gum which issues
> From whence 'tis nourish'd. The fire i' th' flint
> Shows not till it be struck: our gentle flame
> Provokes itself; and, like the current, flies
> Each bound it chafes.[4]

Shakespeare himself was an example of his own rule, and
appears to have owed almost everything to chance, scarce
anything to industry or design. His poetry flashes from him
like the lightning from the summer-cloud, or the stroke from
the sun-flower. When we look at the admirable comic design
of Hogarth, they seem, from the unfinished state in which
they are left, and from the freedom of the pencilling, to have
cost him little trouble; whereas the *Sigismunda* is a very
laboured and comparatively feeble performance, and he accordingly set great store by it. He also thought highly of his
portraits, and boasted that 'he could paint equal to Vandyke,
give him his time and let him choose his subject.' This was
the very reason why he could not. Vandyke's excellence consisted in this, that he could paint a fine portrait of anyone at
sight: let him take ever so much pains or choose ever so bad
a subject, he could not help making something of it. His eye,
his mind, his hand was cast in the mould of grace and delicacy. Milton again is understood to have preferred *Paradise
Regained* to his other works. This, if so, was either because
he himself was conscious of having failed in it; or because
others thought he had. We are willing to think well of that
which we know wants our favourable opinion, and to prop
the ricketty bantling. Every step taken, *invita Minerva*[5] costs
us something, and is set down to account; whereas we are
borne on the full tide of genius and success into the very
haven of our desires, almost imperceptibly. The strength of
the impulse by which we are carried along prevents the sense
of difficulty or resistance: the true inspiration of the Muse is
soft and balmy as the air we breathe; and indeed, leaves us
little to boast of, for the effect hardly seems to be our own.

There are two persons who always appear to me to have
worked under this involuntary, silent impulse more than any
others; I mean Rembrandt and Correggio. It is not known
that Correggio ever saw a picture of any great master. He
lived and died obscurely in an obscure village. We have few
of his works, but they are all perfect. What truth, what grace,
what angelic sweetness are there! Not one line or tone that is
not divinely soft or exquisitely fair; the painter's mind reject-
ing, by a natural process, all that is discordant, coarse, or
unpleasing. The whole is an emanation of pure thought. The
work grew under his hand as if of itself, and came out with-

ut a flaw, like the diamond from the rock. He knew not what e did; and looked at each modest grace as it stole from the anvas with anxious delight and wonder. Ah! gracious God! ot he alone; how many more in all time have looked at their orks with the same feelings, not knowing but they too may ave done something divine, immortal, and finding in that le doubt ample amends for pining solitude, for want, neglect, nd an untimely fate. Oh! for one hour of that uneasy rapture, hen the mind first thinks it has struck out something that ay last for ever; when the germ of excellence bursts from othing on the startled sight! Take, take away the gaudy iumphs of the world, the long deathless shout of fame, and ive back that heart-felt sigh with which the youthful enthu-iast first weds immortality as his secret bride! And thou too, embrandt! who wert a man of genius, if ever painter was man of genius, did this dream hang over you as you painted hat strange picture of *Jacob's Ladder*?[6] Did your eye strain ver those gradual dusky clouds into futurity, or did those hite-vested, beaked figures babble to you of fame as they pproached? Did you know what you were about, or did you ot paint much as it happened? Oh! if you had thought once bout yourself, or anything but the subject, it would have een all over with 'the glory, the intuition, the amenity,'[7] the ream had fled, the spell had been broken. The hills would ot have looked like those we see in sleep—that tatterdemalion igure of Jacob, thrown on one side, would not have slept as f the breath was fairly taken out of his body. So much do embrandt's pictures savour of the soul and body of reality, hat the thoughts seem identical with the objects—if there had een the least question what he should have done, or how he hould do it, or how far he had succeeded, it would have poiled everything. Lumps of light hung upon his pencil and ell upon his canvas like dew-drops: the shadowy veil was lrawn over his back-grounds by the dull, obtuse finger of ight, making darkness visible by still greater darkness that ould only be felt!

Cervantes is another instance of a man of genius, whose vork may be said to have sprung from his mind, like Minerva rom the head of Jupiter. Don Quixote and Sancho were a ind of twins; and the jests of the latter, as he says, fell from im like drops of rain when he least thought of it. Shake-speare's creations were more multiform, but equally natural nd unstudied. Raphael and Milton seem partial exceptions to this rule. Their productions were of the *composite order;* nd those of the latter sometimes even amount to centos. Accordingly, we find Milton quoted among those authors, who have left proofs of their entertaining a high opinion of

themselves, and of cherishing a strong aspiration after fame
Some of Shakespeare's Sonnets have been also cited to the
same purpose; but they seem rather to convey wayward and
dissatisfied complaints of his untoward fortune than anything
like a triumphant and confident reliance on his future renown
He appears to have stood more alone and to have thought less
about himself than any living being. One reason for this indif
ference may have been, that as a writer he was tolerably
successful in his life-time, and no doubt produced his work
with very great facility.

I hardly know whether to class Claude Lorraine as among
those who succeeded most 'through happiness or pains.' It is
certain that he imitated no one, and has had no successful
imitator. The perfection of his landscapes seems to have been
owing to an inherent quality of harmony, to an exquisite sense
of delicacy in his mind. His monotony has been complained of
which is apparently produced from a preconceived idea in his
mind; and not long ago I heard a person, not more distin
guished for the subtlety than the *naïveté* of his sarcasms,
remark, 'Oh! I never look at Claude: if one has seen one of
his pictures, one has seen them all; they are every one alike
there is the same sky, the same climate, the same time of day
the same tree, and that tree is like a cabbage. To be sure, they
say he did pretty well; but when a man is always doing one
thing, he ought to do it pretty well.' There is no occasion to
write the name under this criticism, and the best answer to it is
that it is true—his pictures always are the same, but we never
wish them to be otherwise. Perfection is one thing. I confess
I think that Claude knew this, and felt that his were the finest
landscapes in the world—that ever had been, or would ever be

I am not in the humour to pursue this argument any farther
at present, but to write a digression. If the reader is not al
ready apprised of it, he will please to take notice that I write
this at Winterslow. My style there is apt to be redundant and
excursive. At other times it may be cramped, dry, abrupt; but
here it flows like a river, and overspreads its banks. I have
not to seek for thoughts or hunt for images: they come of
themselves, I inhale them with the breeze, and the silent
groves are vocal with a thousand recollections—

> And visions, as poetic eyes avow,
> Hang on each leaf, and cling to ev'ry bough.[8]

Here I came fifteen years ago, a willing exile; and as I trod
the lengthened greensward by the low wood-side, repeated
the old line,

> My mind to me a kingdom is.[9]

found it so then, before, and since; and shall I faint, now
at I have poured out the spirit of that mind to the world,
d treated many subjects with truth, with freedom, and
ower, because I have been followed with one cry of abuse
ver since *for not being a government-tool?* Here I returned
few years after to finish some works I had undertaken, doubt-
l of the event, but determined to do my best; and wrote that
haracter of Millamant[10] which was once transcribed by fingers
irer than Aurora's, but no notice was taken of it, because
was not a government-tool, and must be supposed devoid
f taste and elegance by all who aspired to these qualities in
eir own persons. Here I sketched my account of that old
onest Signior Orlando Friscobaldo,[11] which with its fine,
icy, acrid tone that old crab-apple, G*ff***d,[12] would have
elished or pretended to relish, had I been a government-tool!
ere too I have written "Table-Talks" without number, and
s yet without a falling-off, till now that they are nearly done,
r I should not make this boast. I could swear (were they not
ine) the thoughts in many of them are founded as the rock,
ee as air, the tone like an Italian picture. What then? Had
e style been like polished steel, as firm and as bright, it
ould have availed me nothing, for I am not a government-
oll I had endeavoured to guide the taste of the English
eople to the best old English writers; but I had said that
nglish kings did not reign by right divine, and that his
resent majesty was descended from an elector of Hanover
a a right line; and no loyal subject would after this look into
Vebster or Dekker because I had pointed them out. I had
one something (more than anyone except Schlegel) to vindi-
ate the *Characters of Shakespear's Plays* from the stigma of
rench criticism; but our Anti-Jacobin and Anti-Gallican
riters soon found out that I had said and written that French-
ien, Englishmen, men were not slaves by birth-right. This
as enough to *damn* the work. Such has been the head and
ont of my offending. While my friend Leigh Hunt was writ-
ig the *Descent of Liberty*, and strewing the march of the
llied Sovereigns with flowers, I sat by the waters of Babylon
nd hung my harp upon the willows. I knew all along there
as but one alternative—the cause of kings or of mankind.
his I foresaw, this I feared; the world see it now, when it is
o late. Therefore I lamented, and would take no comfort
hen the Mighty[13] fell, because we, all men, fell with him,
ke lightning from heaven, to grovel in the grave of Liberty,
i the stye of Legitimacy! There is but one question in the
earts of monarchs, whether mankind are their property or
ot. There was but this one question in mine. I had made an
bstract, metaphysical principle of this question. I was not the

dupe of the voice of the charmers. By my hatred of tyrant
I knew what their hatred of the free-born spirit of man mus
be, of the semblance, of the very name of Liberty and Hu
manity. And while others bowed their heads to the image o
the BEAST,[14] I spit upon it and buffetted it, and made mouth
at it, and pointed at it, and drew aside the veil that then hal
concealed it, but has been since thrown off, and named it by
its right name; and it is not to be supposed that my having
penetrated their mystery would go unrequited by those whose
darling and whose delight the idol, half-brute, half-demon
was, and who were ashamed to acknowledge the image and
superscription as their own! Two half-friends of mine, who
would not make a whole one between them, agreed the other
day that the indiscriminate, incessant abuse of what I write
was mere prejudice and party-spirit, and that what I do in
periodicals and without a name does well, pays well, and is
'cried out upon in the top of the compass.' It is this indeed
that has saved my shallow skiff from quite foundering on Tory
spite and rancour; for when people have been reading and
approving an article in a miscellaneous journal, it does not
do to say when they discover the author afterwards (whatever
might have been the case before) it is written by a blockhead;
and even Mr. Jerdan[15] recommends the volume of *Characteristics* as an excellent little work, because it has no cabalistic
name in the title-page, and swears 'there is a first-rate article
of forty pages in the last number of the Edinburgh from
Jeffrey's own hand,' though when he learns against his will
that it is mine, he devotes three successive numbers of the *Literary Gazette* to abuse 'that *strange* article in the last number
of the *Edinburgh Review*.' Others who had not this advantage
have fallen a sacrifice to the obloquy attached to the suspicion
of doubting, or of being acquainted with anyone who is known
to doubt, the divinity of kings. Poor Keats paid the forfeit of
this *lèse-majesté*[16] with his health and life. What, though his
Verses were like the breath of spring, and many of his
thoughts like flowers—would this, with the circle of critics that
beset a throne, lessen the crime of their having been praised
in the *Examiner?* The lively and most agreeable Editors[17] of
that paper has in like manner been driven from his country
and his friends who delighted in him, for no other reason than
having written *The Story of Rimini*, and asserted ten years
ago, 'that the most accomplished prince in Europe was an
Adonis of fifty!'

> Return, Alpheus, the dread voice is past,
> That shrunk thy streams; return, Sicilian Muse![18]

look out of my window and see that a shower has just fallen:
the fields look green after it, and a rosy cloud hangs over the
brow of the hill; a lily expands its petals in the moisture,
dressed in its lovely green and white; a shepherd-boy has just
brought some pieces of turf with daisies and grass for his
young mistress to make a bed for her sky-lark, not doomed
to dip his wings in the dappled dawn—my cloudy thoughts
draw off, the storm of angry politics has blown over—Mr.
Blackwood,[19] I am yours—Mr. Croker, my service to you—
Mr. T. Moore, I am alive and well—Really, it is wonderful
how little the worse I am for fifteen years' wear and tear, how
I come upon my legs again on the ground of truth and nature,
and 'look abroad into universality,' forgetting that there is any
such person as myself in the world!

I have let this passage stand (however critical) because it
may serve as a practical illustration to show what authors
really think of themselves when put upon the defensive—
I confess, the subject has nothing to do with the title at the
head of the Essay!)—and as a warning to those who may
reckon upon their fair portion of popularity as the reward of
the exercise of an independent spirit and such talents as they
possess. It sometimes seems at first sight as if the low scur-
rility and jargon of abuse by which it is attempted to overlay
all common sense and decency by a tissue of lies and nicknames, everlastingly repeated and applied indiscriminately to
all those who are not of the regular government-party, was
peculiar to the present time, and the anomalous growth of
modern criticism; but if we look back, we shall find the same
system acted upon, as often as power, prejudice, dulness, and
spite found their account in playing the game into one another's hands—in decrying popular efforts, and in giving cur-
rency to every species of base metal that had their own
conventional stamp upon it. The names of Pope and Dryden
were assailed with daily and unsparing abuse—the epithet
A. P. E. was levelled at the sacred head of the former—and if
even men like these, having to deal with the consciousness
of their own infirmities and the insolence and spurns of wanton
enmity, must have found it hard to possess their souls in patience, any living writer amidst such contradictory evidence
can scarcely expect to retain much calm, steady conviction of
his own merits, or build himself a secure reversion in immortality.

However one may in a fit of spleen and impatience turn
round and assert one's claims in the face of low-bred, hireling
malice, I will here repeat what I set out with saying, that there
never yet was a man of sense and proper spirit, who would

not decline rather than court a comparison with any of those names, whose reputation he really emulates—who would not be sorry to suppose that any of the great heirs of memory had as many foibles as he knows himself to possess—and who would not shrink from including himself or being included by others in the same praise, that was offered to long-established and universally acknowledged merit, as a kind of profanation. Those who are ready to fancy themselves Raphaels and Homers are very inferior men indeed—they have not even an idea of the mighty names that 'they take in vain.' They are as deficient in pride as in modesty, and have not so much as served an apprenticeship to a true and honourable ambition. They mistake a momentary popularity for lasting renown, and a sanguine temperament for the inspirations of genius. The love of fame is too high and delicate a feeling in the mind to be mixed up with realities—it is a solitary abstraction, the secret sigh of the soul—

> It is all one as we should love
> A bright particular star, and think to wed it.[20]

A name 'fast-anchored in the deep abyss of time' is like a star twinkling in the firmament, cold, silent, distant, but eternal and sublime; and our transmitting one to posterity is as if we should contemplate our translation to the skies. If we are not contented with this feeling on the subject, we shall never sit in Cassiopeia's chair, nor will our names, studding Ariadne's crown or streaming with Berenice's locks, ever make

> the face of heaven so bright,
> That birds shall sing, and think it were not night.[21]

Those who are in love only with noise and show, instead of devoting themselves to a life of study, had better hire a booth at Bartlemy-Fair, or march at the head of a recruiting regiment with drums beating and colours flying!

It has been urged, that however little we may be disposed to indulge the reflection at other times or out of mere self-complacency, yet the mind cannot help being conscious of the effort required for any great work while it is about it, of

> The high endeavour and the glad success.[22]

I grant that there is a sense of power in such cases, with the exception before stated; but then this very effort and state of excitement engrosses the mind at the time, and leaves it listless and exhausted afterwards. The energy we exert, or the high state of enjoyment we feel, puts us out of conceit with ourselves at other times: compared to what we are in the act of composition, we seem dull, commonplace people, generally speaking; and what we have been able to perform is rather matter of wonder than of self-congratulation to us. The stimulus of writing is like the stimulus of intoxication, with which we can hardly sympathise in our sober moments, when we are no longer under the inspiration of the demon, or when the virtue is gone out of us. While we are engaged in any work, we are thinking of the subject, and cannot stop to admire ourselves; and when it is done, we look at it with comparative indifference. I will venture to say, that no one but a pedant ever read his own works regularly through. They are not *his*—they are become mere words, waste-paper, and have none of the glow, the creative enthusiasm, the vehemence, and natural spirit with which he wrote them. When we have once committed our thoughts to paper, written them fairly out, and seen that they are right in the printing, if we are in our right wits, we have done with them for ever. I sometimes try to read an article I have written in some magazine or review—(for when they are bound up in a volume, I dread the very sight of them)—but stop after a sentence or two, and never recur to the task. I know pretty well what I have to say on the subject, and do not want to go to school to myself. It is the worst instance of the *bis repetita crambe*[23] in the world. I do not think that even painters have much delight in looking at their works after they are done. While they are in progress, there is a great degree of satisfaction in considering what has been done, or what is still to do—but this is hope, is reverie, and ceases with the completion of our efforts. I should not imagine Raphael or Correggio would have much pleasure in looking at their former works, though they might recollect the pleasure they had had in painting them; they might spy defects in them (for the idea of unattainable perfection still keeps pace with our actual approaches to it), and fancy that they were not worthy of immortality. The greatest portrait-painter the world ever saw used to write under his pictures, *'Titianus faciebat,'*[24] signifying that they were imperfect; and in his letter to Charles V accompanying one of his most admired works, he only spoke of the time he had been about it. Annibal Caracci boasted that he could do like Titian and Correggio, and, like most boasters, was wrong. (*See his spirited Letter to his cousin Ludovico, on seeing the pictures at Parma.*)

The greatest pleasure in life is that of reading, while we are young. I have had as much of this pleasure as perhaps anyone. As I grow older, it fades; or else, the stronger stimulus of writing takes off the edge of it. At present, I have neither time nor inclination for it: yet I should like to devote a year's entire leisure to a course of the English Novelists; and perhaps clap on that old sly knave, Sir Walter, to the end of the list. It is astonishing how I used formerly to relish the style of certain authors, at a time when I myself despaired of ever writing a single line. Probably this was the reason. It is not in mental as in natural ascent—intellectual objects seem higher when we survey them from below, than when we look down from any given elevation above the common level. My three favourite writers about the time I speak of were Burke, Junius,[25] and Rousseau. I was never weary of admiring and wondering at the felicities of the style, the turns of expression, the refinements of thought and sentiment: I laid the book down to find out the secret of so much strength and beauty, and took it up again in despair, to read on and admire. So I passed whole days, months, and I may add, years; and have only this to say now, that as my life began, so I could wish that it may end. The last time I tasted this luxury in its full perfection was one day after a sultry day's walk in summer between Farnham and Alton. I was fairly tired out; I walked into an inn-yard (I think at the latter place); I was shown by the waiter to what looked at first like common out-houses at the other end of it, but they turned out to be a suite of rooms, probably a hundred years old—the one I entered opened into an old-fashioned garden, embellished with beds of larkspur and a leaden Mercury; it was wainscoted, and there was a grave-looking, dark-coloured portrait of Charles II hanging up over the tiled chimney-piece. I had *Love for Love* in my pocket, and began to read; coffee was brought in in a silver coffee-pot; the cream, the bread and butter, everything was excellent, and the flavour of Congreve's style prevailed over all. I prolonged the entertainment till a late hour, and relished this divine comedy better even than when I used to see it played by Miss Mellon, as *Miss Prue;* Bob Palmer, as *Tattle;* and Bannister, as honest *Ben.* This circumstance happened just five years ago, and it seems like yesterday. If I count my life so by lustres, it will soon glide away; yet I shall not have to repine, if, while it lasts, it is enriched with a few such recollections!

# The Dulwich Gallery[*]

IT WAS on the 5th of November that we went to see this Gallery. The morning was mild, calm, pleasant: it was a day to ruminate on the object we had in view. It was the time of year

> When yellow leaves, or few or none, do hang
> Upon the branches;[1]

their scattered gold was strongly contrasted with the dark green spiral shoots of the cedar trees that skirt the road; the sun shone faint and watery, as if smiling his last; Winter gently let go the hand of Summer, and the green fields, wet with the mist, anticipated the return of Spring. At the end of a beautiful little village, Dulwich College appeared in view, with modest state, yet mindful of the olden time; and the name of Allen[2] and his compeers rushed full upon the memory! How many races of schoolboys have played within its walls, or stammered out a lesson, or sauntered away their vacant hours in its shade: yet, not one Shakespeare is there to be found among them all! The boy is clothed and fed and gets through his accidence:[3] but no trace of his youthful learning, any more than of his saffron livery, is to be met with in the man. Genius is not to be 'constrained by mastery.'—Nothing comes of these endowments and foundations for learning—you might as well make dirt-pies, or build houses with cards. Yet something *does* come of them too—a retreat for age, a dream in youth—a feeling in the air around them, the memory of the past, the hope of what will never be. Sweet are the studies of the schoolboy, delicious his idle hours! Fresh and gladsome is his waking, balmy are his slumbers, book-pillowed! He wears a green and yellow livery perhaps; but 'green and yellow melancholy'[4] comes not near him, or if it does, is tempered with youth and innocence! To thumb his Eutropius,[5] or to knuckle down at taw,[6] are to him equally delightful; for whatever stirs

* [Sketches of the Principal Picture-Galleries in England; London Magazine, Jan. 1823.]

the blood, or inspires thought in him, quickens the pulse of life and joy. He has only to feel, in order to be happy; pain turns smiling from him, and sorrow is only a softer kind of pleasure. Each sensation is but an unfolding of his new being; care, age, sickness, are idle words; the musty records of antiquity look glossy in his sparkling eye, and he clasps immortality as his future bride! The coming years hurt him not—he hears their sound afar off, and is glad. See him there, the urchin, seated in the sun, with a book in his hand, and the wall at his back. He has a thicker wall before him—the wall that parts him from the future. He sees not the archers taking aim at his peace; he knows not the hands that are to mangle his bosom. He stirs not, he still pores upon his book, and, as he reads, a slight hectic flush passes over his cheek, for he sees the letters that compose the word FAME glitter on the page, and his eyes swim, and he thinks that he will one day write a book, and have his name repeated by thousands of readers, and assume a certain signature, and write Essays and Criticisms in a LONDON MAGAZINE, as a consummation of felicity scarcely to be believed. Come hither, thou poor little fellow, and let us change places with thee if thou wilt; here, take the pen and finish this article, and sign what name you please to it; so that we may but change our dress for yours, and sit shivering in the sun, and con over our little task, and feed poor, and lie hard, and be contented and happy, and think what a fine thing it is to be an author, and dream of immortality, and sleep o'nights!

There is something affecting and monastic in the sight of this little nursery of learning, simple and retired as it stands, just on the verge of the metropolis, and in the midst of modern improvements. There is a chapel, containing a copy of Raphael's "Transfiguration," by Julio Romano: but the great attraction to curiosity at present is the Collection of pictures left to the College by the late Sir Francis Bourgeois,[7] who is buried in a mausoleum close by. He once (it is said) spent an agreeable day here in company with the Masters of the College and some other friends; and he determined, in consequence, upon this singular mode of testifying his gratitude and his respect. Perhaps, also, some such idle thoughts as we have here recorded might have mingled with this resolution. The contemplation and the approach of death might have been softened to his mind by being associated with the hopes of childhood; and he might wish that his remains should repose, in monumental state, amidst 'the innocence and simplicity of poor "Charity Boys"!' Might it not have been so?

The pictures are 356 in number, and are hung on the walls of a large gallery, built for the purpose, and divided into five compartments. They certainly looked better in their old places, at the house of Mr. Desenfans[8] (the original collector), where they were distributed into a number of small rooms, and seen separately and close to the eye. They are mostly cabinet-pictures; and not only does the height, at which many of them are necessarily hung to cover a large space, lessen the effect, but the number distracts and deadens the attention. Besides, the skylights are so contrived as to 'shed a dim,' though not a 'religious light'[9] upon them. At our entrance, we were first struck by our old friends the Cuyps;[10] and just beyond, caught a glimpse of that fine female head by Carlo Maratti, giving us a welcome with cordial glances. May we not exclaim—

> What a delicious breath *painting* sends forth!
> The violet-bed's not sweeter.[11]

A fine gallery of pictures is a sort of illustration of Berkeley's Theory of Matter and Spirit. It is like a palace of thought —another universe, built of air, of shadows, of colours. Everything seems 'palpable to feeling as to sight.' Substances turn to shadows by the painter's arch-chemic touch; shadows harden into substances. 'The eye is made the fool of the other senses, or else worth all the rest.'[12] The material is in some sense embodied in the immaterial, or, at least, we see all things in a sort of intellectual mirror. The world of art is an enchanting deception. We discover distance in a glazed surface; a province is contained in a foot of canvas; a thin evanescent tint gives the form and pressure of rocks and trees; an inert shape has life and motion in it. Time stands still, and the dead reappear, by means of this 'so potent art!' Look at the Cuyp next the door (No. 3). It is woven of etherial hues. A soft mist is on it, a veil of subtle air. The tender green of the vallies beyond the gleaming lake, the purple light of the hills, have an effect like the down on an unripe nectarine. You may lay your finger on the canvas; but miles of dewy vapour and sunshine are between you and the objects you survey. It is almost needless to point out that the cattle and figures in the foreground, like dark, transparent spots, give an immense relief to the perspective. This is, we think, the finest Cuyp, perhaps, in the world. [. . .]

# The Marquis
# of Stafford's Gallery*

[. . .] A COMPLAINT has been made of the short-lived duration
of works of art, and particularly of pictures; and poets more
especially are apt to lament and to indulge in an elegiac strain
over the fragile beauties of the sister-art. The complaint is
inconsiderate, if not invidious. *They will last our time.* Nay,
they have lasted centuries before us, and will last centuries
after us; and even when they are no more, will leave a shadow
and a cloud of glory behind them, through all time. Lord
Bacon exclaims triumphantly, 'Have not the poems of Homer
lasted five-and-twenty hundred years, and not a syllable of
them is lost?'[1] But it might be asked in return, 'Have not
many of the Greek statues now lasted almost as long, without
losing a particle of their splendour or their meaning, while the
*Iliad* (except to a very few) has become almost a dead letter?'
Has not the Venus of Medicis[2] had almost as many partisans
and admirers as the Helen of the old blind bard? Besides,
what has Phidias gained in reputation even by the discovery
of the Elgin Marbles?[3] Or is not Michael Angelo's the greatest
name in modern art, whose works we only know from description and by report? Surely, there is something in a name, in
wide-spread reputation, in endless renown, to satisfy the ambition of the mind of man. Who in his works would vie immortality with nature? An epitaph, an everlasting monument
in the dim remembrance of ages, is enough below the skies.
Moreover, the sense of final inevitable decay *humanises*, and
gives an affecting character to the triumphs of exalted art.
Imperishable works executed by perishable hands are a sort
of insult to our nature, and almost a contradiction in terms.
They are ungrateful children, and mock the makers. Neither
is the noble idea of antiquity legibly made out without the
marks of the progress and lapse of time. That which is as

* [*Sketches of the Principal Picture Galleries in England; London
Magazine*, Feb. 1823.]

good now as ever it was, seems a thing of yesterday. Nothing is old to the imagination that does not appear to grow old. Ruins are grander and more venerable than any modern structure can be, or than the oldest could be if kept in the most entire preservation. They convey the perspective of time. So the Elgin Marbles are more impressive from their mouldering, imperfect state. They transport us to the Parthenon, and old Greece. The Theseus is of the age of Theseus: while the Apollo Belvedere[4] is a modern fine gentleman; and we think of this last figure only as an ornament to the room where it happens to be placed.—We conceive that those are persons of narrow minds who cannot relish an author's style that smacks of time, that has a crust of antiquity over it, like that which gathers upon old wine. These sprinklings of *archaisms* and obsolete turns of expression (so abhorrent to the fashionable reader) are intellectual links that connect the generations together, and enlarge our knowledge of language and of nature. Of the two, we prefer *black-letter* to hot-pressed paper. Does not every language change and wear out? Do not the most popular writers become quaint and old-fashioned every fifty or every hundred years? Is there not a constant conflict of taste and opinion between those who adhere to the established and triter modes of expression, and those who affect glossy innovations, in advance of the age? It is pride enough for the best authors *to have been read*. This applies to their own country; and to all others, they are 'a book sealed.' But Rubens is as good in Holland as he is in Flanders, where he was born, in Italy or in Spain, in England, or in Scotland—no, there alone he is *not* understood. The Scotch understand nothing but what is Scotch. What has the dry, husky, economic eye of Scotland to do with the florid hues and luxuriant extravagance of Rubens? Nothing. They like Wilkie's[5] *pauper* style better. It may be said that translations remedy the want of universality of language: but prints give (at least) as good an idea of pictures as translations do of poems, or of any productions of the press that employ the colouring of style and imagination. *Gil Blas* is translatable; Racine and Rousseau are not. The mere English student knows more of the character and spirit of Raphael's pictures in the Vatican, than he does of Ariosto or Tasso from Hoole's[6] Version. There is, however, one exception to the catholic language of painting, which is in French pictures. They are national fixtures, and ought never to be removed from the soil in which they grow. They will not answer anywhere else, nor are they worth Custom-House Duties. Flemish, Dutch, Spanish, Italian, are all good and intelligible in their several ways—we know what they mean—they require no interpreter: but the French painters see nature with organs and with minds peculiarly their own. One must be born in France to understand their painting, or their poetry. Their productions in art are either literal, or extravagant—dry, frigid *facsimiles*, in which they seem to take up nature by pin-points, or else vapid distorted caricatures, out of all rule and compass. They are, in fact, at home only in the light and elegant; and whenever they attempt to add force or solidity (as they must do in the severer productions of the pencil) they are compelled to substitute an excess of minute industry for a comprehension of the whole, or make a desperate mechanical effort at extreme expression, instead of giving the true, natural, and powerful workings of passion. Their representations of nature are meagre skeletons, that bear the same relation to the originals that botanical specimens, enclosed in a portfolio, flat, dry, hard, and pithless, do to flourishing plants and shrubs. Their historical figures are painful outlines, or graduated elevations of the common statues, spiritless, colourless, motionless, which have the form, but none of the power of the *antique*. What an abortive attempt is the "Coronation of Napoleon," by the celebrated David, lately exhibited in this country! It looks like a finished sign-post painting—a sea of frozen outlines.—Could the artist make nothing of 'the foremost man in all this world,'[7] but a stiff upright figure? The figure and attitude of the Empress are, however, pretty and graceful; and we recollect one face in profile, of an ecclesiastic, to the right, with a sanguine look of health in the complexion, and a large benevolence of soul. It is not Monsieur Talleyrand, whom the late Lord Castlereagh characterised as a worthy man and his friend. His Lordship was not a physiognomist! The whole of the shadowed part of the picture seems to be enveloped in a shower of blue powder.—But to make amends for all that there is or that there is not in the work, David has introduced his wife and his two daughters; and in the Catalogue has given us the places of abode, and the names of the husbands of the latter. This is a little out of place: yet these are the people who laugh at our blunders. We do not mean to extend the above sweeping censure to Claude, or Poussin: of course they are excepted: but even in them the national character lurked amidst unrivalled excellence. If Claude has a fault, it is that he is finical; and Poussin's figures might be said by a satirist to be antique puppets. [. . .] The story and figures [of Caracci's "Diana and Nymphs Bathing"] are more classical and better managed than those of the "Diana and Calisto" by Titian; but there is a charm in that picture and the fellow to it,[8] the "Diana and Actæon," (there is no other fellow to it in the world!) which no words can convey. It is the charm thrown over each by the greatest genius for colouring that the world ever saw. It is difficult, nay, impossible to say which is the finest in this respect: but either one or the other (whichever we turn to, and we can never be satisfied with looking at either—so rich a scene do they unfold, so serene a harmony do they infuse into the soul) is like a divine piece of music, or rises 'like an exhalation of rich distilled perfumes.' In the figures, in the landscape, in the water, in the sky, there are tones, colours, scattered with a profuse and unerring hand, gorgeous, but most true, dazzling with their force, but blended, softened, woven together into a woof like that of Iris—tints of flesh colour, as if you saw the blood circling beneath the pearly skin; clouds empurpled with setting suns; hills steeped in azure skies; trees turning to a mellow brown; the cold grey rocks, and the water so translucent, that you see the shadows and the snowy feet of the naked nymphs in it. With all this prodigality of genius, there is the greatest severity and discipline of art. The figures seem grouped for the effect of colour —the most striking contrasts are struck out, and then a third object, a piece of drapery, an uplifted arm, a bow and arrows, a straggling weed, is introduced to make an intermediate tint, or carry on the harmony. Every colour is melted, *impasted* into every other, with fine keeping and bold diversity. Look at that indignant, queen-like figure of Diana (more perhaps like an offended mortal princess, than an immortal Goddess, though the immortals could frown and give themselves strange airs), and see the snowy, ermine-like skin; the pale clear shadows of the delicately formed back; then the brown colour of the slender trees behind to set off the shaded flesh; and last, the dark figure of the Ethiopian girl behind, completing the gradation. Then the bright scarf suspended in the air connects itself with the glowing clouds, and deepens the solemn azure of the sky: Actæon's bow and arrows fallen on the ground are also red; and there is a little flower on the brink of the Bath which catches and pleases the eye, saturated with this colour. The yellowish grey of the earth purifies the low tone of the figures where they are in half-shadow; and this again is enlivened by the leaden-coloured fountain of the Bath, which is set off (or kept down in its proper place) by the blue vestments strewn near it. The figure of Actæon is spirited and natural; it is that of a bold rough hunter in the early ages, struck with surprise, abashed with beauty. The forms of some of the female figures are elegant enough, particularly that of Diana in the story of Calisto; and there is a very pretty-faced girl mischievously dragging the culprit forward; but it is the texture of the flesh that is throughout delicious, unrivalled, surpassingly fair. The landscape canopies the living scene with a sort of proud, disdainful consciousness. The trees nod to it, and the hills roll at a distance in a sea of colour. Everywhere tone, not form, pre-dominates—there is not a distinct line in the picture—but a gusto, a rich taste of colour is left upon the eye as if it were the palate, and the diapason of picturesque harmony is full to overflowing. 'Oh Titian and Nature! which of you copied the other?' [. . .]

# iv

---

## THE SPIRIT OF
## THE AGE

*(Selections)*

# Jeremy Bentham *

MR. BENTHAM is one of those persons who verify the old adage, that 'A prophet has most honour out of his own country.'[1] His reputation lies at the circumference; and the lights of his understanding are reflected, with increasing lustre, on the other side of the globe. His name is little known in England, better in Europe, best of all in the plains of Chili and the mines of Mexico.[2] He has offered constitutions for the New World, and legislated for future times. The people of Westminster, where he lives, hardly dream of such a person; but the Siberian savage has received cold comfort from his lunar aspect, and may say to him with Caliban—'I know thee, and thy dog and thy bush!' The tawny Indian may hold out the hand of fellowship to him across the GREAT PACIFIC. We believe that the Empress Catherine corresponded with him; and we know that the Emperor Alexander[3] called upon him, and presented him with his miniature in a gold snuff-box, which the philosopher, to his eternal honour, returned. Mr. Hobhouse[4] is a greater man at the hustings, Lord Rolle[5] at Plymouth Dock; but Mr. Bentham would carry it hollow, on the score of popularity, at Paris or Pegu. The reason is, that our author's influence is purely intellectual. He has devoted his life to the pursuit of abstract and general truths, and to those studies—

That waft a *thought* from Indus to the Pole—[6]

and has never mixed himself up with personal intrigues or party politics. He once, indeed, stuck up a hand-bill to say that he (Jeremy Bentham) being of sound mind, was of opinion that Sir Samuel Romilly[7] was the most proper person to represent Westminster; but this was the whim of the moment. Otherwise, his reasonings, if true at all, are true everywhere alike: his speculations concern humanity at large, and are not confined to the hundred or the bills of mortality.[8] It is in moral as in physical magnitude. The little is seen best near:

* [*New Monthly Magazine*, Jan. 1824.]

the great appears in its proper dimensions, only from a more commanding point of view, and gains strength with time, and elevation from distance!

Mr. Bentham is very much among philosophers what La Fontaine was among poets: in general habits and in all but his professional pursuits, he is a mere child. He has lived for the last forty years in a house in Westminster, overlooking the Park, like an anchorite in his cell, reducing law to a system, and the mind of man to a machine. He scarcely ever goes out, and sees very little company. The favoured few, who have the privilege of the *entrée*, are always admitted one by one. He does not like to have witnesses to his conversation. He talks a great deal, and listens to nothing but facts. When any-one calls upon him, he invites them to take a turn round his garden with him (Mr. Bentham is an economist of his time, and sets apart this portion of it to air and exercise)—and there you may see the lively old man, his mind still buoyant with thought and with the prospect of futurity, in eager conversation with some Opposition Member, some expatriated Patriot, or Transatlantic Adventurer, urging the extinction of Close Boroughs,[9] or planning a code of laws for some 'lone island in the watery waste,' his walk almost amounting to a run, his tongue keeping pace with it in shrill, cluttering accents, negligent of his person, his dress, and his manner, intent only on his grand theme of UTILITY—or pausing, perhaps, for want of breath and with lack-lustre eye to point out to the stranger a stone in the wall[10] at the end of his garden (overarched by two beautiful cotton-trees) *Inscribed to the Prince of Poets,* which marks the house where Milton formerly lived. To show how little the refinements of taste or fancy enter into our author's system, he proposed at one time to cut down these beautiful trees, to convert the garden where he had breathed the air of Truth and Heaven for near half a century into a paltry *Chrestomathic School,*[11] and to make Milton's house (the cradle of *Paradise Lost*) a thoroughfare, like a three-stalled stable, for the idle rabble of Westminster to pass back-wards and forwards to it with their cloven hoofs. Let us not, however, be getting on too fast—Milton himself taught school! There is something not altogether dissimilar between Mr. Bentham's appearance, and the portraits of Milton, the same silvery tone, a few dishevelled hairs, a peevish, yet puritanical expression, an irritable temperament corrected by habit and discipline. Or in modern times, he is something between Franklin[12] and Charles Fox,[13] with the comfortable double-chin and sleek thriving look of the one, and the quivering lip, the restless eye, and animated acuteness of the other. His eye is quick and lively; but it glances not from object to object, but from thought to thought. He is evidently a man occupied with some train of fine and inward association. He regards the people about him no more than the flies of a summer. He meditates the coming age. He hears and sees only what suits his purpose, or some 'foregone conclusion'; and looks out for facts and passing occurrences in order to put them into his logical machinery and grind them into the dust and powder of some subtle theory, as the miller looks out for grist to his mill! Add to this physiognomical sketch the minor points of costume, the open shirt-collar, the single-breasted coat, the old fashioned half-boots and ribbed stockings; and you will find in Mr. Bentham's general appearance a singular mixture of boyish simplicity and of the venerableness of age. In a word, our celebrated jurist presents a striking illustration of the difference between the *philosophical* and the *regal* look; that is, between the merely abstracted and the merely personal. There is a lackadaisical *bonhomie* about his whole aspect, none of the fierceness of pride or power; an unconscious neglect of his own person, instead of a stately assumption of superiority; a good-humoured, placid intelligence, instead of a lynx-eyed watchfulness, as if it wished to make others its prey, or was afraid they might turn and rend him; he is a beneficent spirit, prying into the universe, not lording it over it; a thoughtful spectator of the scenes of life, or ruminator on the fate of mankind, not a painted pageant, a stupid idol set up on its pedestal of pride for men to fall down and worship with idiot fear and wonder at the thing themselves have made, and which, without that fear and wonder, would in itself be nothing!

Mr. Bentham, perhaps, over-rates the importance of his own theories. He has been heard to say (without any appearance of pride or affectation) that 'he should like to live the remaining years of his life, a year at a time at the end of the next six or eight centuries, to see the effect which his writings would by that time have had upon the world.' Alas! his name will hardly live so long! Nor do we think, in point of fact, that Mr. Bentham has given any new or decided impulse to the human mind. He cannot be looked upon in the light of a discoverer in legislation or morals. He has not struck out any great leading principle or parent-truth, from which a number of others might be deduced; nor has he enriched the common and established stock of intelligence with original observations, like pearls thrown into wine. One truth discovered is immortal, and entitles its author to be so: for, like a new substance in nature, it cannot be destroyed. But Mr. Bentham's forte is arrangement; and the form of truth, though not its essence, varies with time and circumstance. He has methodised, collated, and condensed all the materials prepared to his hand on the subjects of which he treats, in a masterly and scientific manner; but we should find a difficulty in adducing from his different works (however elaborate or closely reasoned) any new element of thought, or even a new fact or illustration. His writings are, therefore, chiefly valuable as *books of reference,* as bringing down the account of intellectual inquiry to the present period, and disposing the results in a compendious, connected, and tangible shape; but books of reference are chiefly serviceable for facilitating the acquisition of knowledge, and are constantly liable to be superseded and to grow out of fashion with its progress, as the scaffolding is thrown down as soon as the building is completed. Mr. Bentham is not the first writer (by a great many) who has assumed the principle of UTILITY as the foundation of just laws, and of all moral and political reasoning; his merit is, that he has applied this principle more closely and literally; that he has brought all the objections and arguments, more distinctly labelled and ticketed, under this one head, and made a more constant and explicit reference to it at every step of his progress, than any other writer. Perhaps the weak side of his conclusions also is, that he has carried this single view of his subject too far, and not made sufficient allowance for the varieties of human nature, and the caprices and irregularities of the human will. 'He has not allowed for the *wind.*' It is not that you can be said to see his favourite doctrine of Utility glittering everywhere through his system, like a vein of rich, shining ore (that is not the nature of the material)— but it might be plausibly objected that he had struck the whole mass of fancy, prejudice, passion, sense, whim, with his petrific, leaden mace, that he had 'bound volatile Hermes,'[14] and reduced the theory and practice of human life to a *caput mortuum*[15] of reason, and dull, plodding, technical calculation. The gentleman is himself a capital logician; and he has been led by this circumstance to consider man as a logical animal. We fear this view of the matter will hardly hold water. If we attend to the *moral* man, the constitution of his mind will scarcely be found to be built up of pure reason and a regard to consequences: if we consider the *criminal* man (with whom the legislator has chiefly to do) it will be found to be still less so.

Every pleasure, says Mr. Bentham, is equally a good, and is to be taken into account as such in a moral estimate, whether it be the pleasure of sense or of conscience, whether it arise from the exercise of virtue or the perpetration of crime. We are afraid the human mind does not readily come into this doctrine, this *ultima ratio philosophorum*,[16] interpreted according to the letter. Our moral sentiments are made up of sympathies and antipathies, of sense and imagination, of understanding and prejudice. The soul, by reason of its weakness, is an aggregating and an exclusive principle; it clings obstinately to some things, and violently rejects others. And it must do so, in a great measure, or it would act contrary to its own nature. It needs helps and stages in its progress, and 'all appliances and means to boot,' which can raise it to a partial conformity to truth and good (the utmost it is capable of) and bring it into a tolerable harmony with the universe. By aiming at too much, by dismissing collateral aids, by extending itself to the farthest verge of the conceivable and possible, it loses its elasticity and vigour, its impulse and its direction. The moralist can no more do without the intermediate use of rules and principles, without the vantage ground of habit, without the levers of the understanding, than the mechanist can discard the use of wheels and pulleys, and perform everything by simple motion. If the mind of man were competent to comprehend the whole of truth and good, and act upon it at once, and independently of all other considerations, Mr. Bentham's plan would be a feasible one, and *the truth, the whole truth, and nothing but the truth,* would be the best possible ground to place morality upon. But it is not so. In ascertaining the rules of moral conduct, we must have regard not merely to the nature of the object, but to the capacity of the agent, and to his fitness for apprehending or attaining it. Pleasure is that which is so in itself: good is that which approves itself as such on reflection, or the idea of which is a source of satisfaction. All pleasure is not, therefore (morally speaking) equally a good; for all pleasure does not equally bear reflecting on. There are some tastes that are sweet in the mouth and bitter in the belly; and there is a similar contradiction and anomaly in the mind and heart of man.

Again, what would become of the *Posthæc meminisse juvabit*[17] of the poet, if a principle of fluctuation and reaction is not inherent in the very constitution of our nature, or if all moral truth is a mere literal truism? We are not, then, so much to inquire what certain things are abstractedly or in themselves, as how they affect the mind, and to approve or condemn them accordingly. The same object seen near strikes us more powerfully than at a distance: things thrown into masses give a greater blow to the imagination than when scattered and divided into their component parts. A number of mole-hills do not make a mountain, though a mountain is

actually made up of atoms: so moral truth must present itself
under a certain aspect and from a certain point of view, in
order to produce its full and proper effect upon the mind. The
laws of the affections are as necessary as those of optics. A
calculation of consequences is no more equivalent to a sentiment, than a seriatim enumeration of square yards or feet
touches the fancy like the sight of the Alps or Andes.

To give an instance or two of what we mean. Those who on
pure cosmopolite principles, or on the ground of abstract humanity, affect an extraordinary regard for the Turks and Tar-
tars, have been accused of neglecting their duties to their
friends and next-door neighbours. Well, then, what is the
state of the question here? One human being is, no doubt, as
much worth in himself, independently of the circumstances of
time or place, as another; but he is not of so much value to us
and our affections. Could our imagination take wing (with
our speculative faculties) to the other side of the globe or to
the ends of the universe, could our eyes behold whatever our
reason teaches us to be possible, could our hands reach as far
as our thoughts and wishes, we might then busy ourselves to
advantage with the Hottentots, or hold intimate converse with
the inhabitants of the Moon; but being as we are, our feelings
evaporate in so large a space—we must draw the circle of our
affections and duties somewhat closer—the heart hovers and
fixes near home. It is true, the bands of private, or of local
and natural affection, are often, nay in general, too tightly
strained, so as frequently to do harm instead of good: but the
present question is whether we can, with safety and effect, be
wholly emancipated from them? Whether we should shake
them off at pleasure and without mercy, as the only bar to the
triumph of truth and justice? Or whether benevolence, constructed upon a logical scale, would not be merely *nominal*,
whether duty, raised to too lofty a pitch of refinement, might
not sink into callous indifference or hollow selfishness? Again,
is it not to exact too high a strain from humanity, to ask us to
qualify the degree of abhorrence we feel against a murderer
by taking into our cool consideration the pleasure he may
have in committing the deed, and in the prospect of gratifying
his avarice or his revenge? We are hardly so formed as to
sympathise at the same moment with the assassin and his
victim. The degree of pleasure the former may feel, instead
of extenuating, aggravates his guilt, and shows the depth of
his malignity. Now the mind revolts against this by mere
natural antipathy, if it is itself well-disposed; or the slow
process of reason would afford but a feeble resistance to violence and wrong. The will, which is necessary to give consistency and promptness to our good intentions, cannot extend

so much candour and courtesy to the antagonist principle of evil: virtue, to be sincere and practical, cannot be divested entirely of the blindness and impetuosity of passion! It has been made a plea (half jest, half earnest) for the horrors of war, that they promote trade and manufactures. It has been said, as a set-off for the atrocities practised upon the negro slaves in the West Indies, that without their blood and sweat, so many millions of people could not have sugar to sweeten their tea. Fires and murders have been argued to be beneficial, as they serve to fill the newspapers, and for a subject to talk of—this is a sort of sophistry that it might be difficult to disprove on the bare scheme of contingent utility; but on the ground that we have stated, it must pass for mere irony. What the proportion between the good and the evil will really be found in any of the supposed cases, may be a question to the understanding; but to the imagination and the heart, that is, to the natural feelings of mankind, it admits of none!

Mr. Bentham, in adjusting the provisions of a penal code, lays too little stress on the co-operation of the natural prejudices of mankind, and the habitual feelings of that class of persons for whom they are more particularly designed. Legislators (we mean writers on legislation) are philosophers, and governed by their reason: criminals, for whose control laws are made, are a set of desperadoes, governed only by their passions. What wonder that so little progress has been made towards a mutual understanding between the two parties! They are quite a different species, and speak a different language, and are sadly at a loss for a common interpreter between them. Perhaps the Ordinary of Newgate[18] bids as fair for this office as anyone. What should Mr. Bentham, sitting at ease in his arm-chair, composing his mind before he begins to write by a prelude on the organ, and looking out at a beautiful prospect when he is at a loss for an idea, know of the principles of action of rogues, outlaws, and vagabonds? No more than Montaigne of the motions of his cat![19] If sanguine and tender-hearted philanthropists have set on foot an inquiry into the barbarity and the defects of penal laws, the practical improvements have been mostly suggested by reformed cutthroats, turnkeys, and thief-takers. What even can the Honourable House, who when the Speaker has pronounced the well-known, wished-for sounds, 'That this house do now adjourn,' retire, after voting a royal crusade or a loan of millions, to lie on down, and feed on plate in spacious palaces, know of what passes in the hearts of wretches in garrets and nightcellars, petty pilferers and marauders, who cut throats and pick pockets with their own hands? The thing is impossible. The laws of the country are, therefore, ineffectual and abor-

tive, because they are made by the rich for the poor, by the
wise for the ignorant, by the respectable and exalted in station for the very scum and refuse of the community. If Newgate would resolve itself into a committee of the whole Press-
yard[20] with Jack Ketch[21] at its head, aided by confidential
persons from the county prisons or the Hulks[22] and would
make a clear breast, some *data* might be found out to proceed
upon; but as it is, the *criminal mind* of the country is a book
sealed, no one has been able to penetrate to the inside! Mr.
Bentham, in his attempts to revise and amend our criminal
jurisprudence, proceeds entirely on his favourite principle of
Utility. Convince highwaymen and housebreakers that it will
be for their interest to reform, and they will reform and lead
honest lives; according to Mr. Bentham. He says, 'All men act
from calculation, even madmen reason.' And, in our opinion,
he might as well carry this maxim to Bedlam or St. Luke's,
and apply it to the inhabitants, as think to coerce or overawe
the inmates of a gaol, or those whose practices make them
candidates for that distinction, by the mere dry, detailed convictions of the understanding. Criminals are not to be influenced by reason; for it is of the very essence of crime to disregard consequences both to ourselves and others. You may
as well preach philosophy to a drunken man, or to the dead,
as to those who are under the instigation of any mischievous
passion. A man is a drunkard, and you tell him he ought to be
sober; he is debauched, and you ask him to reform; he is idle,
and you recommend industry to him as his wisest course; he
gambles, and you remind him that he may be ruined by this
foible; he has lost his character, and you advise him to get
into some reputable service or lucrative situation; vice becomes a habit with him, and you request him to rouse himself
and shake it off; he is starving, and you warn him if he breaks
the law, he will be hanged. None of this reasoning reaches the
mark it aims at. The culprit, who violates and suffers the
vengeance of the laws, is not the dupe of ignorance, but the
slave of passion, the victim of habit or necessity. To argue
with strong passion, with inveterate habit, with desperate
circumstances, is to talk to the winds. Clownish ignorance
may indeed be dispelled, and taught better; but it is seldom
that a criminal is not aware of the consequences of his act, or
has not made up his mind to the alternative. They are, in
general, *too knowing by half.* You tell a person of this stamp
what is his interest; he says he does not care about his interest, or the world and he differ on that particular. But there is
one point on which he must agree with them, namely, what
*they* think of his conduct, and that is the only hold you have
of him. A man may be callous and indifferent to what hap-

pens to himself; but he is never indifferent to public opinion,
or proof against open scorn and infamy. Shame, then, not
fear, is the sheet-anchor of the law. He who is not afraid of
being pointed at as a *thief*, will not mind a month's hard
labour. He who is prepared to take the life of another, is already reckless of his own. But everyone makes a sorry figure
in the pillory; and the being launched from the New Drop[23]
lowers a man in his own opinion. The lawless and violent
spirit, who is hurried by head-strong self-will to break the
laws, does not like to have the ground of pride and obstinacy
struck from under his feet. This is what gives the *swells* of the
metropolis such a dread of the *tread-mill*—it makes them ridiculous. It must be confessed, that this very circumstance renders the reform of criminals nearly hopeless. It is the apprehension of being stigmatized by public opinion, the fear of
what will be thought and said of them, that deters men from
the violation of the laws, while their character remains un-
impeachable; but honour once lost, all is lost. The man can
never be himself again! A citizen is like a soldier, a part of a
machine, who submits to certain hardships, privations, and
dangers, not for his own ease, pleasure, profit, or even conscience—but *for shame*. What is it that keeps the machine
together in either case? Not punishment or discipline, but
sympathy. The soldier mounts the breach or stands in the
trenches, the peasant hedges and ditches, or the mechanic
plies his ceaseless task, because the one will not be called a
*coward*, the other a *rogue*: but let the one turn deserter and
the other vagabond, and there is an end of him. The grinding
law of necessity, which is no other than a name, a breath,
loses its force; he is no longer sustained by the good opinion
of others, and he drops out of his place in society, a useless
clog! Mr. Bentham takes a culprit, and puts him into what he
calls a *Panopticon*,[24] that is, a sort of circular prison, with
open cells, like a glass bee-hive. He sits in the middle, and
sees all the other does. He gives him work to do, and lectures
him if he does not do it. He takes liquor from him, and society
and liberty; but he feeds and clothes him, and keeps him out
of mischief; and when he has convinced him, by force and
reason together, that this life is for his good, he turns him out
upon the world a reformed man, and as confident of the success of his handy-work, as the shoemaker of that which he has
just taken off the last, or the Parisian barber in Sterne,[25] of
the buckle of his wig. 'Dip it in the ocean,' said the per-
ruquier, 'and it will stand!' But we doubt the durability of our
projector's patchwork. Will our convert to the great principle
of Utility work when he is from under Mr. Bentham's eye,

because he was forced to work when under it? Will he keep sober, because he has been kept from liquor so long? Will he not return to loose company, because he has had the pleasure of sitting vis-à-vis with a philosopher of late? Will he not steal, now that his hands are untied? Will he not take the road, now that it is free to him? Will he not call his benefactor all the names he can set his tongue to, the moment his back is turned? All this is more than to be feared. The charm of criminal life, like that of savage life, consists in liberty, in hardship, in danger, and in the contempt of death, in one word, in extraordinary excitement; and he who has tasted of it, will no more return to regular habits of life, than a man will take to water after drinking brandy, or than a wild beast will give over hunting its prey. Miracles never cease, to be sure; but they are not to be had wholesale, or *to order*. Mr. Owen,²⁶ who is another of those proprietors and patentees of reform, has lately got an American savage with him, whom he carries about in great triumph and complacency, as an antithesis to his *New View of Society*,²⁷ and as winding up his reasoning to what it mainly wanted, an epigrammatic point. Does the benevolent visionary of the Lanark cotton-mills really think this *natural man* will act as a foil to his *artificial man*? Does he for a moment imagine that his *Address to the higher and middle classes*,²⁸ with all its advantages of fiction, makes anything like so interesting a romance as Hunter's *Captivity among the North American Indians*?²⁹ Has he anything to show, in all the apparatus of New Lanark and its desolate monotony, to excite the thrill of imagination like the blankets made of wreaths of snow under which the wild wood-rovers bury themselves for weeks in winter? Or the skin of a leopard, which our hardy adventurer slew, and which served him for great-coat and bedding? Or the rattle-snake that he found by his side as a bedfellow? Or his rolling himself into a ball to escape from him? Or his suddenly placing himself against a tree to avoid being trampled to death by the herd of wild buffaloes, that came rushing on like the sound of thunder? Or his account of the huge spiders that prey on blue-bottles and gilded flies in green pathless forests; or of the great Pacific Ocean, that the natives look upon as the gulf that parts time from eternity, and that is to waft them to the spirits of their fathers? After all this, Mr. Hunter must find Mr. Owen and his parallelograms trite and flat, and will, we suspect, take an opportunity to escape from them!

Mr. Bentham's method of reasoning, though comprehensive and exact, labours under the defect of most systems—it is too *topical*. It includes everything; but it includes everything alike. It is rather like an inventory, than a valuation of different arguments. Every possible suggestion finds a place, so that the mind is distracted as much as enlightened by this perplexing accuracy. The exceptions seem as important as the rule. By attending to the minute, we overlook the great; and in summing up an account, it will not do merely to insist on the number of items without considering their amount. Our author's page presents a very nicely dove-tailed mosaic pavement of legal commonplaces. We slip and slide over its even surface without being arrested anywhere. Or his view of the human mind resembles a map, rather than a picture: the outline, the disposition is correct, but it wants colouring and relief. There is a technicality of manner, which renders his writings of more value to the professional inquirer than to the general reader. Again, his style is unpopular, not to say unintelligible. He writes a language of his own, that *darkens knowledge*. His works have been translated into French—they ought to be translated into English. People wonder that Mr. Bentham has not been prosecuted for the boldness and severity of some of his invectives. He might wrap up high treason in one of his inextricable periods, and it would never find its way into Westminster-Hall. He is a kind of Manuscript author —he writes a cypher-hand, which the vulgar have no key to. The construction of his sentences is a curious frame-work with pegs and hooks to hang his thoughts upon, for his own use and guidance, but almost out of the reach of everybody else. It is a barbarous philosophical jargon, with all the repetitions, parentheses, formalities, uncouth nomenclature and verbiage of law-Latin; and what makes it worse, it is not mere verbiage, but has a great deal of acuteness and meaning in it, which you would be glad to pick out if you could. In short, Mr. Bentham writes as if he was allowed but a single sentence to express his whole view of a subject in, and as if, should he omit a single circumstance or step of the argument, it would be lost to the world for ever, like an estate by a flaw in the title-deeds. This is over-rating the importance of our own discoveries, and mistaking the nature and object of language altogether. Mr. Bentham has *acquired* this disability—it is not natural to him. His admirable little work *On Usury*,[30] published forty years ago, is clear, easy, and vigorous. But Mr. Bentham has shut himself up since then 'in nook monastic,' conversing only with followers of his own, or with 'men of Ind,' and has endeavoured to overlay his natural humour, sense, spirit, and style, with the dust and cobwebs of an obscure solitude. The best of it is, he thinks his present mode of expressing himself perfect, and that whatever may be objected to his law or logic, no one can find the least fault with the purity, simplicity, and perspicuity of his style.

Mr. Bentham, in private life, is an amiable and exemplary character. He is a little romantic, or so; and has dissipated part of a handsome fortune in practical speculations. He lends an ear to plausible projectors, and, if he cannot prove them to be wrong in their premises or their conclusions, thinks himself bound *in reason* to stake his money on the venture. Strict logicians are licenced visionaries. Mr. Bentham is half-brother to the late Mr. Speaker Abbott*[31]—*Proh pudor!*[32] He was educated at Eton, and still takes our novices to task about a passage in Homer, or a metre in Virgil. He was afterwards at the University,[33] and he has described the scruples of an ingenuous youthful mind about subscribing the articles, in a passage in his *Church-of-Englandism*,[34] which smacks of truth and honour both, and does one good to read it in an age, when to be honest' (or not to laugh at the very idea of honesty) is to be one man picked out of ten thousand!' Mr. Bentham relieves his mind sometimes, after the fatigue of study, by playing on a fine old organ, and has a relish for Hogarth's prints. He turns wooden utensils in a lathe for exercise, and fancies he can turn men in the same manner. He has no great fondness for poetry, and can hardly extract a moral out of Shakespeare. His house is warmed and lighted by steam. He is one of those who prefer the artificial to the natural in most things, and think the mind of man omnipotent. He has a great contempt for out-of-door prospects, for green fields and trees, and is for referring everything to Utility. There is a little narrowness in this; for if all the sources of satisfaction are taken away, what is to become of utility itself? It is, indeed, the great fault of this able and extraordinary man, that he has concentrated his faculties and feelings too entirely on one subject and pursuit, and has not 'looked enough abroad into universality.'†

* Now Lord Colchester. [w. h.]
† Lord Bacon's *Advancement of Learning*. [w. h.]

# Mr. Coleridge*

THE present is an age of talkers, and not of doers; and the reason is, that the world is growing old. We are so far advanced in the Arts and Sciences, that we live in retrospect, and doat on past achievements. The accumulation of knowledge has been so great, that we are lost in wonder at the height it has reached, instead of attempting to climb or add to it; while the variety of objects distracts and dazzles the looker-on. What *niche* remains unoccupied? What path untried? What is the use of doing anything, unless we could do better than all those who have gone before us? What hope is there of this? We are like those who have been to see some noble monument of art, who are content to admire without thinking of rivalling it; or like guests after a feast, who praise the hospitality of the donor 'and thank the bounteous Pan'— perhaps carrying away some trifling fragments; or like the spectators of a mighty battle, who still hear its sound afar off, and the clashing of armour and the neighing of the war-horse and the shout of victory is in their ears, like the rushing of innumerable waters!

Mr. Coleridge has 'a mind reflecting ages past';[1] his voice is like the echo of the congregated roar of the 'dark rearward and abyss' of thought. He who has seen a mouldering tower by the side of a chrystal lake, hid by the mist, but glittering in the wave below, may conceive the dim, gleaming, uncertain intelligence of his eye: he who has marked the evening clouds uprolled (a world of vapours), has seen the picture of his mind, unearthly, unsubstantial, with gorgeous tints and ever-varying forms—

> That which was now a horse, even with a thought
> The rack dislimns, and makes it indistinct
> As water is in water.[2]

* [Of these selections from *The Spirit of the Age* (1825), the pieces on Coleridge and Wordsworth had not previously been published by Hazlitt.]

Our author's mind is (as he himself might express it) *tangential*. There is no subject on which he has not touched, none on which he has rested. With an understanding fertile, subtle, expansive, 'quick, forgetive, apprehensive,' beyond all living precedent, few traces of it will perhaps remain. He lends himself to all impressions alike; he gives up his mind and liberty of thought to none. He is a general lover of art and science, and wedded to no one in particular. He pursues knowledge as a mistress, with outstretched hands and winged speed; but as he is about to embrace her, his Daphne turns—alas! not to a laurel! Hardly a speculation has been left on record from the earliest time, but it is loosely folded up in Mr. Coleridge's memory, like a rich, but somewhat tattered piece of tapestry: we might add (with more seeming than real extravagance), that scarce a thought can pass through the mind of man, but its sound has at some time or other passed over his head with rustling pinions. On whatever question or author you speak, he is prepared to take up the theme with advantage—from Peter Abelard down to Thomas Moore, from the subtlest metaphysics to the politics of the *Courier*. There is no man of genius in whose praise he descants, but the critic seems to stand above the author, and 'what in him is weak, to strengthen, what is low, to raise and support':[3] nor is there any work of genius that does not come out of his hands like an illuminated Missal, sparkling even in its defects. If Mr. Coleridge had not been the most impressive talker of his age, he would probably have been the finest writer; but he lays down his pen to make sure of an auditor, and mortgages the admiration of posterity for the stare of an idler. If he had not been a poet, he would have been a powerful logician; if he had not dipped his wing in the Unitarian controversy, he might have soared to the very summit of fancy. But in writing verse, he is trying to subject the Muse to *transcendental* theories: in his abstract reasoning, he misses his way by strewing it with flowers. All that he has done of moment, he had done twenty years ago: since then, he may be said to have lived on the sound of his own voice. Mr. Coleridge is too rich in intellectual wealth, to need to task himself to any drudgery: he has only to draw the sliders of his imagination, and a thousand subjects expand before him, startling him with their brilliancy, or losing themselves in endless obscurity—

> And by the force of blear illusion,
> They draw him on to his confusion.[4]

What is the little he could add to the stock, compared with the countless stores that lie about him, that he should stoop to pick up a name, or to polish an idle fancy? He walks abroad in the majesty of an universal understanding, eyeing the 'rich strond,' or golden sky above him, and 'goes sounding on his way,' in eloquent accents, uncompelled and free!

Persons of the greatest capacity are often those, who for this reason do the least; for surveying themselves from the highest point of view, amidst the infinite variety of the universe, their own share in it seems trifling, and scarce worth a thought, and they prefer the contemplation of all that is, or has been, or can be, to the making a coil about doing what, when done, is no better than vanity. It is hard to concentrate all our attention and efforts on one pursuit, except from ignorance of others; and without this concentration of our faculties, no great progress can be made in any one thing. It is not merely that the mind is not capable of the effort; it does not think the effort worth making. Action is one; but thought is manifold. He whose restless eye glances through the wide compass of nature and art, will not consent to have 'his own nothings monstered':[5] but he must do this, before he can give his whole soul to them. The mind, after 'letting contemplation have its fill,' or

> Sailing with supreme dominion
> Through the azure deep of air,[6]

sinks down on the ground, breathless, exhausted, powerless, inactive; or if it must have some vent to its feelings, seeks the most easy and obvious; is soothed by friendly flattery, lulled by the murmur of immediate applause, thinks as it were aloud, and babbles in its dreams! A scholar (so to speak) is a more disinterested and abstracted character than a mere author. The first looks at the numberless volumes of a library, and says, 'All these are mine': the other points to a single volume (perhaps it may be an immortal one) and says, 'My name is written on the back of it.' This is a puny and groveling ambition, beneath the lofty amplitude of Mr. Coleridge's mind. No, he revolves in his wayward soul, or utters to the passing wind, or discourses to his own shadow, things mightier and more various!—Let us draw the curtain, and unlock the shrine.

Learning rocked him in his cradle, and while yet a child,

> He lisped in numbers, for the numbers came.[7]

At sixteen he wrote his *Ode on Chatterton,* and he still reverts to that period with delight, not so much as it relates to himself (for that string of his own early promise of fame rather jars than otherwise) but as exemplifying the youth of a poet. Mr. Coleridge talks of himself, without being an egotist, for in him the individual is always merged in the abstract and general. He distinguished himself at school and at the University by his knowledge of the classics, and gained several prizes for Greek epigrams. How many men are there (great scholars, celebrated names in literature) who having done the same thing in their youth, have no other idea all the rest of their lives but of this achievement, of a fellowship and dinner, and who, installed in academic honours, would look down on our author as a mere strolling bard! At Christ's Hospital, where he was brought up, he was the idol of those among his school-fellows, who mingled with their bookish studies the music of thought and of humanity; and he was usually attended round the cloisters by a group of these (inspiring and inspired) whose hearts, even then, burnt within them as he talked, and where the sounds yet linger to mock ELIA on his way, still turning pensive to the past![8] One of the finest and rarest parts of Mr. Coleridge's conversation, is when he expatiates on the Greek tragedians (not that he is not well acquainted, when he pleases, with the epic poets, or the philosophers, or orators, or historians of antiquity)—on the subtle reasonings and melting pathos of Euripides, on the harmonious gracefulness of Sophocles, tuning his love-laboured song, like sweetest warblings from a sacred grove; on the high-wrought trumpet-tongued eloquence of Æschylus, whose Prometheus, above all, is like an Ode to Fate, and a pleading with Providence, his thoughts being let loose as his body is chained on his solitary rock, and his afflicted will (the emblem of mortality)

Struggling in vain with ruthless destiny.[9]

As the impassioned critic speaks and rises in his theme, you would think you heard the voice of the Man hated by the Gods, contending with the wild winds as they roar, and his eye glitters with the spirit of Antiquity!

Next, he was engaged with Hartley's[10] tribes of mind, 'etherial braid, thought-woven'—and he busied himself for a year or two with vibrations and vibratiuncles and the great law of association that binds all things in its mystic chain, and the doctrine of Necessity (the mild teacher of Charity) and the Millennium, anticipative of a life to come—and he plunged deep into the controversy on Matter and Spirit, and, as an escape from Dr. Priestley's Materialism, where he felt himself imprisoned by the logician's spell, like Ariel in the cloven pine-tree, he became suddenly enamoured of Bishop Berkeley's fairy-world,* and used in all companies to build the universe, like a brave poetical fiction, of fine words—and he was deep-read in Malebranche,[12] and in Cudworth's Intellectual System[13] (a huge pile of learning, unwieldy, enormous) and in Lord Brook's hieroglyphic theories,[14] and in Bishop Butler's Sermons,[15] and in the Duchess of Newcastle's fantastic folios,[16] and in Clarke and South and Tillotson,[17] and all the fine thinkers and masculine reasoners of that age—and Leibnitz's *Pre-Established Harmony*[18] reared its arch above his head, like the rainbow in the cloud, covenanting with the hopes of man—and then he fell plump, ten thousand fathoms down (but his wings saved him harmless) into the *hortus siccus*[19] of Dissent, where he pared religion down to the standard of reason and stripped faith of mystery, and preached Christ crucified and the Unity of the Godhead, and so dwelt for a while in the spirit with John Huss and Jerome of Prague and Socinus and old John Zisca,[20] and ran through Neal's History of the Puritans,[21] and Calamy's Non-Conformists' Memorial,[22] having like thoughts and passions with them—but then Spinoza became his God, and he took up the vast chain of being in his hand, and the round world became the centre and the soul of all things in some shadowy sense, forlorn of meaning, and around him he beheld the living traces and the sky-pointing proportions of the mighty Pan—but poetry redeemed him from this spectral philosophy, and he bathed his heart in beauty, and gazed at the golden light of heaven, and drank of the spirit of the universe, and wandered at eve by fairy-stream or fountain,

> —When he saw nought but beauty,
> When he heard the voice of that Almighty One
> In every breeze that blew, or wave that murmured—[23]

and wedded with truth in Plato's shade, and in the writings of Proclus and Plotinus saw the ideas of things in the eternal mind, and unfolded all mysteries with the Schoolmen and fathomed the depths of Duns Scotus and Thomas Aquinas, and entered the third heaven with Jacob Behmen,[24] and walked hand in hand with Swedenborg through the pavilions

---

* Mr. Coleridge named his eldest son (the writer of some beautiful Sonnets) after Hartley, and the second after Berkeley. The third was called Derwent, after the river of that name. Nothing can be more characteristic of his mind than this circumstance. All his ideas indeed are like a river, flowing on for ever, and still murmuring as it flows, discharging its waters and still replenished—

> And so by many winding nooks it strays,
> With willing sport to the wild ocean.[11] [W. H.]

of the New Jerusalem, and sung his faith in the promise and in the word in his *Religious Musings*—and lowering himself from that dizzy height, poised himself on Milton's wings, and spread out his thoughts in charity with the glad prose of Jeremy Taylor, and wept over Bowles's Sonnets, and studied Cowper's blank verse, and betook himself to Thomson's Castle of Indolence, and sported with the wits of Charles the Second's days and of Queen Anne, and relished Swift's style and that of the John Bull (Arbuthnot's we mean, not Mr. Croker's), and dallied with the British Essayists and Novelists, and knew all qualities of more modern writers with a learned spirit, Johnson, and Goldsmith, and Junius, and Burke, and Godwin, and the Sorrows of Werter, and Jean Jacques Rousseau, and Voltaire, and Marivaux, and Crebillon, and thousands more—now 'laughed with Rabelais in his easy chair' or pointed to Hogarth, or afterwards dwelt on Claude's classic scenes, or spoke with rapture of Raphael, and compared the women at Rome to figures that had walked out of his pictures, or visited the Oratory of Pisa, and described the works of Giotto and Ghirlandaio and Massacco, and gave the moral of the picture of the Triumph of Death, where the beggars and the wretched invoke his dreadful dart, but the rich and mighty of the earth quail and shrink before it; and in that land of siren sights and sounds, saw a dance of peasant girls, and was charmed with lutes and gondolas—or wandered into Germany and lost himself in the labyrinths of the Hartz Forest and of the Kantean philosophy, and amongst the cabalistic names of Fichte and Schelling and Lessing, and God knows who—this was long after, but all the former while, he had nerved his heart and filled his eyes with tears, as he hailed the rising orb of liberty, since quenched in darkness and in blood, and had kindled his affections at the blaze of the French Revolution, and sang for joy when the towers of the Bastille and the proud places of the insolent and the oppressor fell, and would have floated his bark, freighted with fondest fancies, across the Atlantic wave with Southey and others to seek for peace and freedom—

In Philarmonia's undivided dale![25]

Alas! 'Frailty, thy name is *Genius!*'—What is become of all this mighty heap of hope, of thought, of learning, and humanity? It has ended in swallowing doses of oblivion and in writing paragraphs in the *Courier.*—Such, and so little is the mind of man!

It was not to be supposed that Mr. Coleridge could keep on at the rate he set off; he could not realize all he knew or

thought, and less could not fix his desultory ambition; other
stimulants supplied the place, and kept up the intoxicating
dream, the fever and the madness of his early impressions.
Liberty (the philosopher's and the poet's bride) had fallen a
victim, meanwhile, to the murderous practices of the hag,
Legitimacy.[26] Proscribed by court-hirelings, too romantic for
the herd of vulgar politicians, our enthusiast stood at bay,
and at last turned on the pivot of a subtle casuistry to the
*unclean side:* but his discursive reason would not let him
trammel himself into a poet-laureate or stamp-distributor,[27]
and he stopped, ere he had quite passed that well-known
'bourne from whence no traveller returns'—and so has sunk
into torpid, uneasy repose, tantalized by useless resources,
haunted by vain imaginings, his lips idly moving, but his heart
for ever still, or, as the shattered chords vibrate of themselves,
making melancholy music to the ear of memory! Such is the
fate of genius in an age, when in the unequal contest with
sovereign wrong, every man is ground to powder who is not
either a born slave, or who does not willingly and at once offer
up the yearnings of humanity and the dictates of reason as a
welcome sacrifice to besotted prejudice and loathsome power.

Of all Mr. Coleridge's productions, the *Ancient Mariner* is
the only one that we could with confidence put into any person's hands, on whom we wished to impress a favourable idea
of his extraordinary powers. Let whatever other objections be
made to it, it is unquestionably a work of genius—of wild,
irregular, overwhelming imagination, and has that rich, varied
movement in the verse, which gives a distant idea of the lofty
or changeful tones of Mr. Coleridge's voice. In the *Christabel,*
there is one splendid passage on divided friendship. The
*Translation of Schiller's Wallenstein* is also a masterly production in its kind, faithful and spirited. Among his smaller pieces
there are occasional bursts of pathos and fancy, equal to what
we might expect from him; but these form the exception, and
not the rule. Such, for instance, is his affecting Sonnet to the
author of the *Robbers.*

> Schiller! that hour I would have wish'd to die,
>    If through the shudd'ring midnight I had sent
>    From the dark dungeon of the tower time-rent,
> That fearful voice, a famish'd father's cry—
> That in no after-moment aught less vast
>    Might stamp me mortal! A triumphant shout
>    Black horror scream'd, and all her goblin rout
> From the more with'ring scene diminish'd pass'd.
> Ah! Bard tremendous in sublimity!
>    Could I behold thee in thy loftier mood,
>    Wand'ring at eve, with finely frenzied eye,

> Beneath some vast old tempest-swinging wood!
> Awhile, with mute awe gazing, I would brood,
> Then weep aloud in a wild ecstasy.

His Tragedy, entitled *Remorse*, is full of beautiful and striking passages, but it does not place the author in the first rank of dramatic writers. But if Mr. Coleridge's works do not place him in that rank, they injure instead of conveying a just idea of the man, for he himself is certainly in the first class of general intellect.

If our author's poetry is inferior to his conversation, his prose is utterly abortive. Hardly a gleam is to be found in it of the brilliancy and richness of those stores of thought and language that he pours out incessantly, when they are lost like drops of water in the ground. The principal work, in which he has attempted to embody his general views of things, is the FRIEND,[28] of which, though it contains some noble passages and fine trains of thought, prolixity and obscurity are the most frequent characteristics.

No two persons can be conceived more opposite in character or genius than the subject of the present and of the preceding sketch. Mr. Godwin, with less natural capacity, and with fewer acquired advantages, by concentrating his mind on some given object, and doing what he had to do with all his might, has accomplished much, and will leave more than one monument of a powerful intellect behind him; Mr. Coleridge, by dissipating his, and dallying with every subject by turns, has done little or nothing to justify to the world or to posterity, the high opinion which all who have ever heard him converse, or known him intimately, with one accord entertain of him. Mr. Godwin's faculties have kept at home, and plied their task in the workshop of the brain, diligently and effectually: Mr. Coleridge's have gossiped away their time, and gadded about from house to house, as if life's business were to melt the hours in listless talk. Mr. Godwin is intent on a subject, only as it concerns himself and his reputation; he works it out as a matter of duty, and discards from his mind whatever does not forward his main objects as impertinent and vain. Mr. Coleridge, on the other hand, delights in nothing but episodes and digressions, neglects whatever he undertakes to perform, and can act only on spontaneous impulses, without object or method. 'He cannot be constrained by mastery.' While he should be occupied with a given pursuit, he is thinking of a thousand other things; a thousand tastes, a thousand objects tempt him, and distract his mind, which keeps open house, and entertains all comers; and after being fatigued and amused with morning calls from idle visi-

tors, finds the day consumed and its business unconcluded.
Mr. Godwin, on the contrary, is somewhat exclusive and un-
social in his habits of mind, entertains no company but what
he gives his whole time and attention to, and wisely writes
over the doors of his understanding, his fancy, and his senses
—'No admittance except on business.' He has none of that
fastidious refinement and false delicacy, which might lead
him to balance between the endless variety of modern attainments. He does not throw away his life (nor a single half-hour
of it) in adjusting the claims of different accomplishments,
and in choosing between them or making himself master of
them all. He sets about his task (whatever it may be) and
goes through it with spirit and fortitude. He has the happiness
to think an author the greatest character in the world, and
himself the greatest author in it. Mr. Coleridge, in writing an
harmonious stanza, would stop to consider whether there was
not more grace and beauty in a *Pas de trois*,[29] and would not
proceed till he had resolved this question by a chain of metaphysical reasoning without end. Not so Mr. Godwin. That is
best to him, which he can do best. He does not waste himself
in vain aspirations and effeminate sympathies. He is blind,
deaf, insensible to all but the trump of Fame. Plays, operas,
painting, music, ball-rooms, wealth, fashion, titles, lords,
ladies, touch him not—all these are no more to him than to the
magician in his cell, and he writes on to the end of the chapter, through good report and evil report. *Pingo in eternita-
tem*[30] is his motto. He neither envies nor admires what others
are, but is contented to be what he is, and strives to do the
utmost he can. Mr. Coleridge has flirted with the Muses as
with a set of mistresses: Mr. Godwin has been married twice,
to Reason and to Fancy, and has to boast no short-lived
progeny by each. So to speak, he has *valves* belonging to his
mind, to regulate the quantity of gas admitted into it, so that
like the bare, unsightly, but well-compacted steam-vessel,[31]
it cuts its liquid way, and arrives at its promised end: while
Mr. Coleridge's bark, 'taught with the little nautilus to sail,'[32]
the sport of every breath, dancing to every wave,

Youth at its prow, and Pleasure at its helm,[33]

flutters its gaudy pennons in the air, glitters in the sun, but
we wait in vain to hear of its arrival in the destined harbour.
Mr. Godwin, with less variety and vividness, with less subtlety and susceptibility both of thought and feeling, has had
firmer nerves, a more determined purpose, a more comprehensive grasp of his subject, and the results are as we find
them. Each has met with his reward: for justice has, after all,

been done to the pretensions of each; and we must, in all cases, use means to ends!

It was a misfortune to any man of talent to be born in the latter end of the last century. Genius stopped the way of Legitimacy, and therefore it was to be abated, crushed, or set aside as a nuisance. The spirit of the monarchy was at variance with the spirit of the age. The flame of liberty, the light of intellect, was to be extinguished with the sword—or with slander, whose edge is sharper than the sword. The war between power and reason was carried on by the first of these abroad—by the last at home. No quarter was given (then or now) by the Government-critics, the authorised censors of the press, to those who followed the dictates of independence, who listened to the voice of the tempter, Fancy. Instead of gathering fruits and flowers, immortal fruits and amaranthine flowers, they soon found themselves beset not only by a host of prejudices, but assailed with all the engines of power, by nicknames, by lies, by all the arts of malice, interest and hypocrisy, without the possibility of their defending themselves 'from the pelting of the pitiless storm,' that poured down upon them from the strongholds of corruption and authority. The philosophers, the dry abstract reasoners, submitted to this reverse pretty well, and armed themselves with patience 'as with triple steel' to bear discomfiture, persecution, and disgrace. But the poets, the creatures of sympathy, could not stand the frowns both of king and people. They did not like to be shut out when places and pensions, when the critic's praises, and the laurel-wreath were about to be distributed. They did not stomach being *sent to Coventry*, and Mr. Coleridge sounded a retreat for them by the help of casuistry, and a musical voice.—'His words were hollow, but they pleased the ear'[34] of his friends of the Lake School, who turned back disgusted and panic-struck from the dry desert of unpopularity, like Hassan the camel driver,

> And curs'd the hour, and curs'd the luckless day,
> When first from Shiraz' walls they bent their way.[35]

They are safely inclosed there, but Mr. Coleridge did not enter with them; pitching his tent upon the barren waste without, and having no abiding place nor city of refuge!

# Rev. Mr. Irving*

THIS GENTLEMAN has gained an almost unprecedented, and not an altogether unmerited popularity as a preacher.[1] As he is, perhaps, though a burning and a shining light, not 'one of the fixed,' we shall take this opportunity of discussing his merits, while he is at his meridian height; and in doing so, shall 'nothing extenuate, nor set down aught in malice.'

Few circumstances show the prevailing and preposterous rage for novelty in a more striking point of view, than the success of Mr. Irving's oratory. People go to hear him in crowds, and come away with a mixture of delight and astonishment—they go again to see if the effect will continue, and send others to try to find out the mystery—and in the noisy conflict between extravagant encomiums and splenetic objections, the true secret escapes observation, which is, that the whole thing is, nearly from beginning to end, a *transposition of ideas*. If the subject of these remarks had come out as a player, with all his advantages of figure, voice, and action, we think he would have failed; if, as a preacher, he had kept within the strict bounds of pulpit-oratory, he would scarcely have been much distinguished among his Calvinistic brethren: as a mere author, he would have excited attention rather by his quaintness and affectation of an obsolete style and mode of thinking, than by anything else. But he has contrived to jumble these several characters together in an unheard-of and unwarranted manner, and the fascination is altogether irresistible. Our Caledonian divine is equally an anomaly in religion, in literature, in personal appearance, and in public speaking. To hear a person spout Shakespeare on the stage is nothing—the charm is nearly worn out—but to hear anyone spout Shakespeare (and that not in a sneaking under-tone, but at the top of his voice, and with the full breadth of his chest) from a Calvinistic pulpit, is new and wonderful. The *Fancy* have lately lost something of their gloss in public estimation, and after the last fight, few would go far to see a Neat

* [*New Monthly Magazine*, Feb. 1824.]

or a Spring set-to[2]—but to see a man who is able to enter the ring with either of them, or brandish a quarter-staff with Friar Tuck,[3] or a broad-sword with Shaw the Life-guard's man,[4] stand up in a strait-laced old-fashioned pulpit, and bandy dialectics with modern philosophers, or give a *cross-buttock*[5] to a cabinet minister, there is something in a sight like this also, that is a cure for sore eyes. It is as if Crib or Molyneux[6] had turned Methodist parson, or as if a Patagonian savage were to come forward as the patron-saint of Evangelical religion. Again, the doctrine of eternal punishment was one of the staple arguments with which, everlastingly drawled out, the old school of Presbyterian divines used to keep their audiences awake, or lull them to sleep; but to which people of taste and fashion paid little attention, as inelegant and barbarous, till Mr. Irving, with his cast-iron features and sledge-hammer blows, puffing like a grim Vulcan, set to work to forge more classic thunderbolts, and kindle the expiring flames anew with the very sweepings of sceptical and infidel libraries, so as to excite a pleasing horror in the female part of his congregation. In short, our popular declaimer has, contrary to the Scripture-caution, put new wine into old bottles, or new cloth on old garments. He has, with an unlimited and daring licence, mixed the sacred and the profane together, the carnal and the spiritual man, the petulance of the bar with the dogmatism of the pulpit, the theatrical and theological, the modern and the obsolete—what wonder that this splendid piece of patchwork, splendid by contradiction and contrast, has delighted some and confounded others? The more serious part of his congregation indeed complain, though not bitterly, that their pastor has converted their meeting-house into a play-house: but when a lady of quality, introducing herself and her three daughters to the preacher, assures him that they have been to all the most fashionable places of resort, the opera, the theatre, assemblies, Miss Macauley's readings,[7] and Exeter-Change,[8] and have been equally entertained nowhere else, we apprehend that no remonstrances of a committee of ruling-elders will be able to bring him to his senses again, or make him forego such sweet, but ill-assorted praise. What we mean to insist upon is, that Mr. Irving owes his triumphant success, not to any one quality for which he has been extolled, but to a combination of qualities, the more striking in their immediate effect, in proportion as they are unlooked-for and heterogeneous, like the violent opposition of light and shade in a picture. We shall endeavour to explain this view of the subject more at large.

Mr. Irving, then, is no common or mean man. He has four

or five qualities, possessed in a moderate or in a paramount degree, which, added or multiplied together, fill up the important space he occupies in the public eye. Mr. Irving's intellect itself is of a superior order; he has undoubtedly both talents and acquirements beyond the ordinary run of every-day preachers. These alone, however, we hold, would not account for a twentieth part of the effect he has produced: they would have lifted him perhaps out of the mire and slough of sordid obscurity, but would never have launched him into the ocean-stream of popularity, in which he 'lies floating many a rood'[9]—but to these he adds uncommon height, a graceful figure and action, a clear and powerful voice, a striking, if not a fine face, a bold and fiery spirit, and a most portentous obliquity of vision, which throw him to an immeasurable distance beyond all competition, and effectually relieve whatever there might be of commonplace or bombast in his style of composition. Put the case that Mr. Irving had been five feet high—Would he ever have been heard of, or, as he does now, have 'bestode the world like a Colossus?' No, the thing speaks for itself. He would in vain have lifted his Lilliputian arm to Heaven, people would have laughed at his monkey-tricks. Again, had he been as tall as he is, but had wanted other recommendations, he would have been nothing.

> The player's province they but vainly try,
> Who want these powers, deportment, voice, and eye.[10]

Conceive a rough, ugly, shock-headed Scotchman, standing up in the Caledonian Chapel, and dealing 'damnation round the land' in a broad northern dialect, and with a harsh, screaking voice, what ear polite, what smile serene would have hailed the barbarous prodigy, or not consigned him to utter neglect and derision? But the Rev. Edward Irving, with all his native wildness, 'hath a smooth aspect framed to make women' saints;[11] his very unusual size and height are carried off and moulded into elegance by the most admirable symmetry of form and ease of gesture; his sable locks, his clear iron-grey complexion, and firm-set features, turn the raw, uncouth Scotchman into the likeness of a noble Italian picture; and even his distortion of sight only redeems the otherwise 'faultless monster' within the bounds of humanity, and, when admiration is exhausted and curiosity ceases, excites a new interest by leading to the idle question whether it is an advantage to the preacher or not. Farther, give him all his actual and remarkable advantages of body and mind, let him be as tall, as straight, as dark and clear of skin, as much at his ease, as silver-tongued, as eloquent and as argumentative as he is, yet with all these, and without a little charlatanry to set them off he had been nothing. He might, keeping within the rigid line of his duty and professed calling, have preached on for ever; he might have divided the old-fashioned doctrines of election, grace, reprobation, predestination, into his sixteenth, seventeenth, and eighteenth heads, and his *lastly* have been looked for as a 'consummation devoutly to be wished'; he might have defied the devil and all his works, and by the help of a loud voice and strong-set person—

A lusty man to ben an Abbot able—[12]

have increased his own congregation, and been quoted among the godly as a powerful preacher of the word; but in addition to this, he went out of his way to attack Jeremy Bentham, and the town was up in arms. The thing was new. He thus wiped the stain of musty ignorance and formal bigotry out of his style. Mr. Irving must have something superior in him, to look over the shining close-packed heads of his congregation to have a hit at the *Great Jurisconsult* in his study. He next, ere the report of the former blow had subsided, made a lunge at Mr. Brougham,[13] and glanced an eye at Mr. Canning[14]; *mystified* Mr. Coleridge, and *stultified* Lord Liverpool[15] in his place—in the Gallery. It was rare sport to see him, 'like an eagle in a dovecote, flutter the Volscians in Corioli.'[16] He has found out the secret of attracting by repelling. Those whom he is likely to attack are curious to hear what he says of them: they go again, to show that they do not mind it. It is no less interesting to the bystanders, who like to witness this sort of *onslaught*—like a charge of cavalry, the shock, and the resistance. Mr. Irving has, in fact, without leave asked or a licence granted, converted the Caledonian Chapel into a Westminster Forum or Debating Society, with the sanctity of religion added to it. Our spirited polemic is not contented to defend the citadel of orthodoxy against all impugners, and shut himself up in texts of Scripture and huge volumes of the Commentators as an impregnable fortress; he merely makes use of the strong-hold of religion as a resting-place, from which he sallies forth, armed with modern topics and with penal fire, like Achilles of old rushing from the Grecian tents, against the adversaries of God and man. Peter Aretine[17] is said to have laid the Princes of Europe under contribution by penning satires against them: so Mr. Irving keeps the public in awe by insulting all their favourite idols. He does not spare their politicians, their rulers, their moralists, their poets, their players, their critics, their reviewers, their magazine-writers; he levels their resorts of business, their places of amusement, at a blow—their cities, churches, palaces, ranks and professions, refinements, and elegances—and leaves nothing standing but himself, a mighty landmark in a degenerate age, overlooking the wide havoc he has made! He makes war upon all arts and sciences, upon the faculties and nature of man, on his vices and his virtues, on all existing institutions, and all possible improvements, that nothing may be left but the Kirk of Scotland, and that he may be the head of it. He literally sends a challenge to all London in the name of the KING OF HEAVEN, to evacuate its streets, to disperse its population, to lay aside its employments, to burn its wealth, to renounce its vanities and pomp; and for what?—that he may enter in as the *King of Glory;* or after enforcing his threat with the battering-ram of logic, the grape-shot of rhetoric, and the cross-fire of his double vision, reduce the British metropolis to a Scottish heath, with a few miserable hovels upon it, where they may worship God according to *the root of the matter,* and where an old man with a blue bonnet, a fair-haired girl, and a little child would form the flower of his flock! Such is the pretension and the boast of this new Peter the Hermit,[18] who would get rid of all we have done in the way of improvement on a state of barbarous ignorance, or still more barbarous prejudice, in order to begin again on a *tabula rasa*[19] of Calvinism, and have a world of his own making. It is not very surprising that when nearly the whole mass and texture of civil society is indicted as a nuisance, and threatened to be pulled down as a rotten building ready to fall on the heads of the inhabitants, that all classes of people run to hear the crash, and to see the engines and levers at work which are to effect this laudable purpose. What else can be the meaning of our preacher's taking upon himself to denounce the sentiments of the most serious professors in great cities, as vitiated and stark-naught, of relegating religion to his native glens, and pretending that the hymn of praise or the sigh of contrition cannot ascend acceptably to the throne of grace from the crowded street as well as from the barren rock or silent valley? Why put this affront upon his hearers? Why belie his own aspirations?

God made the country, and man made the town.[20]

So says the poet; does Mr. Irving say so? If he does, and finds the air of the city death to his piety, why does he not return home again? But if he can breathe it with impunity, and still retain the fervour of his early enthusiasm, and the simplicity and purity of the faith that was once delivered to the saints, why not extend the benefit of his own experience to others, instead of taunting them with a vapid pastoral theory? Or, if our popular and eloquent divine finds a change in himself, that flattery prevents the growth of grace, that he is becoming the God of his own idolatry by being that of others, that the glittering of coronet-coaches rolling down Holborn-Hill to Hatton Garden, that titled beauty, that the parliamentary complexion of his audience, the compliments of poets, and the stare of peers discompose his wandering thoughts a little; and yet that he cannot give up these strong temptations tugging at his heart; why not extend more charity to others, and show more candour in speaking of himself? There is either a good deal of bigoted intolerance with a deplorable want of self-knowledge in all this; or at least an equal degree of cant and quackery. [. . .]

# Sir Walter Scott[*]

SIR WALTER SCOTT is undoubtedly the most popular writer of the age—the 'lord of the ascendant' for the time being. He is just half what the human intellect is capable of being: if you take the universe, and divide it into two parts, he knows all that it *has been;* all that it *is to be* is nothing to him. His is a mind brooding over antiquity—scorning 'the present ignorant time.' He is 'laudator temporis acti'—a *'prophesier* of things past.' The old world is to him a crowded map; the new one a dull, hateful blank. He dotes on all well-authenticated superstitions; he shudders at the shadow of innovation. His retentiveness of memory, his accumulated weight of interested prejudice or romantic association have overlaid his other faculties. The cells of his memory are vast, various, full even to bursting with life and motion; his speculative understanding is empty, flaccid, poor, and dead. His mind receives and treasures up everything brought to it by tradition or custom— it does not project itself beyond this into the world unknown, but mechanically shrinks back as from the edge of a precipice. The land of pure reason is to his apprehension like *Van Dieman's Land*[1]—barren, miserable, distant, a place of exile, the dreary abode of savages, convicts, and adventurers. Sir Walter would make a bad hand of a description of the *Millennium,* unless he could lay the scene in Scotland five hundred years ago, and then he would want facts and worm-eaten parchments to support his drooping style. Our historical novelist firmly thinks that nothing *is* but what *has been*—that the moral world stands still, as the material one was supposed to do of old—and that we can never get beyond the point where we actually are without utter destruction, though everything changes and will change from what it was three hundred years ago to what it is now—from what it is now to all that the bigoted admirer of the good old times most dreads and hates!

It is long since we read, and long since we thought of our author's poetry. It would probably have gone out of date with

* [*New Monthly Magazine,* April 1824.]

the immediate occasion, even if he himself had not contrived to banish it from our recollection. It is not to be denied that it had great merit, both of an obvious and intrinsic kind. It abounded in vivid descriptions, in spirited action, in smooth and flowing versification. But it wanted *character*. It was 'poetry of no mark or likelihood.' It slid out of the mind as soon as read, like a river; and would have been forgotten, but that the public curiosity was fed with ever new supplies from the same teeming liquid source. It is not every man that can write six quarto volumes in verse, that are caught up with avidity, even by fastidious judges. But what a difference between *their* popularity and that of the Scotch Novels! It is true, the public read and admired the *Lay of the Last Minstrel, Marmion*,[2] and so on, and each individual was contented to read and admire because the public did so: but with regard to the prose-works of the same (supposed) author, it is quite *another-guess*[3] sort of thing. Here everyone stands forward to applaud on his own ground, would be thought to go before the public opinion, is eager to extol his favourite characters louder, to understand them better than everybody else, and has his own scale of comparative excellence for each work, supported by nothing but his own enthusiastic and fearless convictions. It must be amusing to the Author of Waverley to hear his readers and admirers (and are not these the same thing?*) quarrelling which of his novels is the best, opposing character to character, quoting passage against passage, striving to surpass each other in the extravagance of their encomiums, and yet unable to settle the precedence, or to do the author's writings justice—so various, so equal, so transcendant are their merits! His volumes of poetry were received as fashionable and well-dressed acquaintances: we are ready to tear the others in pieces as old friends. There was something meretricious in Sir Walter's ballad-rhymes; and like those who keep opera *figurantes*,[5] we were willing to have our admiration shared, and our taste confirmed by the town: but the Novels are like the betrothed of our hearts, bone of our bone, and flesh of our flesh, and we are jealous that anyone should be as much delighted or as thoroughly acquainted with their beauties as ourselves. For which of his poetical

---

* No! For we met with a young lady who kept a circulating library and a milliner's shop, in a watering-place in the country, who, when we inquired for the Scotch Novels, spoke indifferently about them, said they were 'so dry she could hardly get through them,' and recommended us to read *Agnes*.[4] We never thought of it before; but we would venture to lay a wager that there are many other young ladies in the same situation, and who think *Old Mortality* 'dry.' [w. h.]

heroines would the reader break a lance so soon as for Jeanie Deans? What *Lady of the Lake* can compare with the beautiful Rebecca? We believe the late Mr. John Scott[6] went to his death-bed (though a painful and premature one) with some degree of satisfaction, inasmuch as he had penned the most elaborate panegyric on the "Scotch Novels" that had as yet appeared!—The "Epics" are not poems, so much as metrical romances. There is a glittering veil of verse thrown over the features of nature and of old romance. The deep incisions into character are 'skinned and filmed over'—the details are lost or shaped into flimsy and insipid decorum; and the truth of feeling and of circumstance is translated into a tinkling sound, a tinsel *commonplace*. It must be owned, there is a power in true poetry that lifts the mind from the ground of reality to a higher sphere, that penetrates the inert, scattered, incoherent materials presented to it, and by a force and inspiration of its own, melts and moulds them into sublimity and beauty. But Sir Walter (we contend, under correction) has not this creative impulse, this plastic power, this capacity of reacting on his first impressions. He is a learned, a literal, a *matter-of-fact* expounder of truth or fable:* he does not soar above and look down upon his subject, imparting his own lofty views and feelings to his descriptions of nature—he relies upon it, is raised by it, is one with it, or he is nothing. A poet is essentially a *maker;* that is, he must atone for what he loses in individuality and local resemblance by the energies and resources of his own mind. The writer of whom we speak is deficient in these last. He has either not the faculty or not the will to impregnate his subject by an effort of pure invention. The execution also is much upon a par with the more ephemeral effusions of the press. It is light, agreeable, effeminate, diffuse. Sir Walter's Muse is a *Modern Antique*. The smooth, glossy texture of his verse contrasts happily with the quaint, uncouth, rugged materials of which it is composed; and takes away any appearance of heaviness or harshness from the body of local traditions and obsolete costume. We see grim knights and iron armour; but then they are woven in silk with a careless, delicate hand, and have the softness of flowers. The poet's figures might be compared to old tapestries copied on the finest velvet: they are not like Raphael's Cartoons, but they are very like Mr. Westall's drawings,[7] which accompany, and are intended to illustrate them. This facility and grace of execution is the more remarkable, as a story goes that not long before the appearance of the *Lay of the Last Minstrel* Sir Walter (then Mr.) Scott, having, in the company of a friend,

---

* Just as Cobbett is a matter-of-fact reasoner. [W. H.]

to cross the Firth of Forth in a ferry-boat, they proposed to beguile the time by writing a number of verses on a given subject, and that at the end of an hour's hard study, they found they had produced only six lines between them. 'It is plain,' said the unconscious author to his fellow-labourer, 'that you and I need never think of getting our living by writing poetry!' In a year or so after this, he set to work, and poured out quarto upon quarto, as if they had been drops of water. As to the rest, and compared with true and great poets, our Scottish Minstrel is but 'a metre ballad-monger.' We would rather have written one song of Burns, or a single passage in Lord Byron's *Heaven and Earth,* or one of Words-worth's 'fancies and good-nights,' than all his epics. What is he to Spenser, over whose immortal, ever-amiable verse beauty hovers and trembles, and who has shed the purple light of Fancy, from his ambrosial wings, over all nature? What is there of the might of Milton, whose head is canopied in the blue serene, and who takes us to sit with him there? What is there (in his ambling rhymes) of the deep pathos of Chaucer? Or of the o'er-informing power of Shakespeare, whose eye, watching alike the minutest traces of characters and the strong-est movements of passion, 'glances from heaven to earth, from earth to heaven,' and with the lambent flame of genius, play-ing round each object, lights up the universe in a robe of its own radiance? Sir Walter has no voluntary power of combi-nation: all his associations (as we said before) are those of habit or of tradition. He is a mere narrative and descriptive poet, garrulous of the old time. The definition of his poetry is a pleasing superficiality.

Not so of his NOVELS AND ROMANCES. There we turn over a new leaf—another and the same—the same in matter, but in form, in power how different! The author of *Waverley* has got rid of the tagging of rhymes, the eking out of syllables, the supplying of epithets, the colours of style, the grouping of his characters, and the regular march of events, and comes to the point at once, and strikes at the heart of his subject, without dismay and without disguise. His poetry was a lady's waiting-maid, dressed out in cast-off finery: his prose is a beautiful, rustic nymph, that, like Dorothea in *Don Quixote,* when she is surprised with dishevelled tresses bathing her naked feet in the brook, looks round her, abashed at the admiration her charms have excited! The grand secret of the author's success in these latter productions is that he has completely got rid of the trammels of authorship; and torn off at one rent (as Lord Peter got rid of so many yards of lace in the *Tale of a Tub*) all the ornaments of fine writing and worn-out sentimentality. All is fresh, as from the hand of nature: by going a century or two back and laying the scene in a remote and uncultivated district, all becomes new and startling in the present advanced period.—Highland manners, characters, scenery, superstitions, Northern dialect and costume, the wars, the religion, and politics of the sixteenth and seventeenth centuries, give a charming and wholesome relief to the fastidious refinement and 'over-laboured lassitude' of modern readers, like the effect of plunging a nervous valetudinarian into a cold-bath. The Scotch Novels, for this reason, are not so much admired in Scotland as in England. The contrast, the transition is less striking. From the top of the Calton Hill, the inhabitants of 'Auld Reekie'[8] can descry, or fancy they descry the peaks of Ben Lomond and the waving outline of Rob Roy's country: we who live at the southern extremity of the island can only catch a glimpse of the billowy scene in the descriptions of the Author of Waverley. The mountain air is most bracing to our languid nerves, and it is brought us in ship-loads from the neighbourhood of Abbot's-Ford. There is another circumstance to be taken into the account. In Edinburgh there is a little opposition and something of the spirit of cabal between the partisans of works proceeding from Mr. Constable's and Mr. Blackwood's shops. Mr. Constable gives the highest prices; but being the Whig bookseller, it is grudged that he should do so. An attempt is therefore made to transfer a certain share of popularity to the second-rate Scotch novels, 'the embryo fry, the little airy[9] of *ricketty* children,' issuing through Mr. Blackwood's shop-door. This operates a diversion, which does not affect us here. The Author of Waverley wears the palm of legendary lore alone. Sir Walter may, indeed, surfeit us: his imitators make us sick! It may be asked, it has been asked, 'Have we no materials for romance in England? Must we look to Scotland for a supply of whatever is original and striking in this kind?' And we answer—'Yes!' Every foot of soil is with us worked up: nearly every movement of the social machine is calculable. We have no room left for violent catastrophes; for grotesque quaintnesses; for wizard spells. The last skirts of ignorance and barbarism are seen hovering (in Sir Walter's pages) over the Border. We have, it is true, gipsies in this country as well as at the Cairn of Derncleugh[10]: but they live under clipped hedges, and repose in camp-beds, and do not perch on crags, like eagles, or take shelter, like sea-mews, in basaltic subterranean caverns. We have heaths with rude heaps of stones upon them: but no existing superstition converts them into the Geese of

Micklestane-Moor, or sees a Black Dwarf groping among them. We have sects in religion: but the only thing sublime or ridiculous in that way is Mr. Irving, the Caledonian preacher, who 'comes like a satyr staring from the woods, and yet speaks like an orator!'[11] We had a Parson Adams not quite a hundred years ago—a Sir Roger de Coverley rather more than a hundred! Even Sir Walter is ordinarily obliged to pitch his angle (strong as the hook is) a hundred miles to the North of the 'Modern Athens' or a century back. His last work,* indeed, is mystical, is romantic in nothing but the title-page. Instead of 'a holy-water sprinkle dipped in dew,'[12] he has given us a fashionable watering-place—and we see what he has made of it. He must not come down from his fastnesses in traditional barbarism and native rusticity; the level, the lit-tleness, the frippery of modern civilization will undo him as it has undone us!

Sir Walter has found out (oh, rare discovery) that facts are better than fiction; that there is no romance like the ro-mance of real life; and that if we can arrive at what men feel, do, and say in striking and singular situations, the result will be 'more lively, audible, and full of vent,' than the fine-spun cobwebs of the brain. With reverence be it spoken, he is like the man who having to imitate the squeaking of a pig upon the stage, brought the animal under his coat with him. Our author has conjured up the actual people he has to deal with, or as much as he could get of them, in 'their habits as they lived.' He has ransacked old chronicles, and poured the contents upon his page; he has squeezed out musty records; he has consulted wayfaring pilgrims, bed-rid sibyls; he has invoked the spirits of the air; he has conversed with the living and the dead, and let them tell their story their own way; and by borrowing of others, has enriched his own genius with everlasting variety, truth, and freedom. He has taken his ma-terials from the original, authentic sources, in large concrete masses, and not tampered with or too much frittered them away. He is only the amanuensis of truth and history. It is impossible to say how fine his writings in consequence are, unless we could describe how fine nature is. All that portion of the history of his country that he has touched upon (wide as the scope is), the manners, the personages, the events, the scenery, lives over again in his volumes. Nothing is wanting —the illusion is complete. There is a hurtling in the air, a trampling of feet upon the ground, as these perfect repre-sentations of human character or fanciful belief come throng-ing back upon our imaginations. We will merely recall a few

* *St. Ronan's Well.* [w. h.]

of the subjects of his pencil to the reader's recollection; for nothing we could add, by way of note or commendation, could make the impression more vivid.

There is (first and foremost, because the earliest of our acquaintance) the Baron of Bradwardine, stately, kind-hearted, whimsical, pedantic; and Flora MacIvor (whom even *we* forgive for her Jacobitism) the fierce Vich Ian Vohr, and Evan Dhu, constant in death, and Davie Gellatly roasting his eggs or turning his rhymes with restless volubility, and the two staghounds that met Waverley, as fine as ever Titian painted, or Paul Veronese: then there is old Balfour of Burley, brandishing his sword and his Bible with fire-eyed fury, trying a fall with the insolent, gigantic Bothwell at the 'Change-house, and vanquishing him at the noble battle of Loudon-hill; there is Bothwell himself, drawn to the life, proud, cruel, selfish, profligate, but with the love-letters of the gentle Alice (written thirty years before), and his verses to her memory, found in his pocket after his death: in the same volume of *Old Mortality* is that lone figure, like a figure in Scripture, of the woman sitting on the stone at the turning to the mountain, to warn Burley that there is a lion in his path; and the fawning Claverhouse, beautiful as a panther, smooth-looking, blood-spotted; and the fanatics, Macbriar and Mucklewrath, crazed with zeal and sufferings; and the inflexible Morton, and the faithful Edith, who refused to 'give her hand to another while her heart was with her lover in the deep and dead sea.' And in *The Heart of Mid-Lothian* we have Effie Deans (that sweet, faded flower) and Jeanie, her more than sister, and old David Deans, the patriarch of St Leonard's Crags, and Butler, and Dumbiedikes, eloquent in his silence, and Mr. Bartoline Saddletree and his prudent helpmate, and Porteous swinging in the wind, and Madge Wildfire, full of finery and madness, and her ghastly mother.—Again, there is Meg Merrilies, standing on her rock, stretched on her bier with 'her head to the east,' and Dirk Hatterick (equal to Shakespeare's Master Barnardine), and Glossin, the soul of an attorney, and Dandy Dinmont, with his terrier-pack and his pony Dumple, and the fiery Colonel Mannering, and the modish old counsellor Pleydell, and Dominie Sampson,* and Rob Roy (like the eagle in his eyry), and Baillie Nicol Jarvie, and the inimitable Major Galbraith, and Rashleigh Osbaldistone, and Die Vernon, the best of secret-keepers; and in the *Antiquary*, the ingenious and abstruse Mr. Jonathan

---

* Perhaps the finest scene in all these novels, is that where the Dominie meets his pupil, Miss Lucy, the morning after her brother's arrival. [W. H.]

Oldbuck, and the old beadsman Edie Ochiltree, and that preternatural figure of old Edith Elspeith,[13] a living shadow, in whom the lamp of life had been long extinguished, had it not been fed by remorse and 'thick-coming' recollections; and that striking picture of the effects of feudal tyranny and fiendish pride, the unhappy Earl of Glenallan; and the Black Dwarf, and his friend Habby of the Heughfoot (the cheerful hunter), and his cousin Grace Armstrong, fresh and laughing like the morning; and the *Children of the Mist,* and the baying of the blood-hound that tracks their steps at a distance (the hollow echoes are in our ears now), and Amy and her hapless love, and the villain Varney, and the deep voice of George of Douglas—and the immoveable Balafre, and Master Oliver the Barber in *Quentin Durward*—and the quaint humour of *The Fortunes of Nigel,* and the comic spirit of *Peveril of the Peak*—and the fine old English romance of *Ivanhoe.* What a list of names! What a host of associations! What a thing is human life! What a power is that of genius! What a world of thought and feeling is thus rescued from oblivion! How many hours of heartfelt satisfaction has our author given to the gay and thoughtless! How many sad hearts has he soothed in pain and solitude! It is no wonder that the public repay with lengthened applause and gratitude the pleasure they receive. He writes as fast as they can read, and he does not write himself down. He is always in the public eye, and we do not tire of him. His worst is better than any other person's best. His *backgrounds* (and his later works are little else but backgrounds capitally made out) are more attractive than the principal figures and most complicated actions of other writers. His works (taken together) are almost like a new edition of human nature. This is indeed to be an author!

The political bearing of the Scotch Novels has been a considerable recommendation to them. They are a relief to the mind, rarefied as it has been with modern philosophy, and heated with ultra-radicalism. At a time also, when we bid fair to revive the principles of the Stuarts, it is interesting to bring us acquainted with their persons and misfortunes. The candour of Sir Walter's historic pen levels our bristling prejudices on this score, and sees fair play between Roundheads and Cavaliers, between Protestant and Papist. He is a writer reconciling all the diversities of human nature to the reader. He does not enter into the distinctions of hostile sects or parties, but treats of the strength or the infirmity of the human mind, of the virtues or vices of the human breast, as they are to be found blended in the whole race of mankind. Nothing

can show more handsomely or be more gallantly executed.
There was a talk at one time that our author was about to take
Guy Faux[14] for the subject of one of his novels, in order to
put a more liberal and humane construction on the Gunpowder Plot than our 'No Popery' prejudices have hitherto
permitted. Sir Walter is a professed *clarifier* of the age from
the vulgar and still lurking old-English antipathy to Popery
and Slavery. Through some odd process of *servile* logic, it
should seem, that in restoring the claims of the Stuarts by
the courtesy of romance, the House of Brunswick are more
firmly seated in point of fact, and the Bourbons, by collateral
reasoning, become legitimate! In any other point of view, we
cannot possibly conceive how Sir Walter imagines 'he has
done something to revive the declining spirit of loyalty' by
these novels. His loyalty is founded on *would-be* treason: he
props the actual throne by the shadow of rebellion. Does he
really think of making us enamoured of the 'good old times'
by the faithful and harrowing portraits he has drawn of
them? Would he carry us back to the early stages of barbarism, of clanship, of the feudal system as 'a consummation devoutly to be wished?' Is he infatuated enough, or does he so
dote and drivel over his own slothful and self-willed prejudices, as to believe that he will make a single convert to
the beauty of Legitimacy, that is, of lawless power and savage
bigotry, when he himself is obliged to apologise for the horrors he describes, and even render his descriptions credible to
the modern reader by referring to the authentic history of
these delectable times?* He is indeed so besotted as to the

---

\* [*Ivanhoe*, ch. 23] And here we cannot but think it necessary to
offer some better proof than the incidents of an idle tale, to vindicate the melancholy representation of manners which has been just
laid before the reader. It is grievous to think that those valiant
Barons, to whose stand against the crown the liberties of England
were indebted for their existence, should themselves have been
such dreadful oppressors, and capable of excesses, contrary not only
to the laws of England, but to those of nature and humanity. But
alas! we have only to extract from the industrious Henry one of
those numerous passages which he has collected from contemporary
historians, to prove that fiction itself can hardly reach the dark
reality of the horrors of the period.

The description given by the author of the Saxon Chronicle of the
cruelties exercised in the reign of King Stephen by the great barons
and lords of castles, who were all Normans, affords a strong proof of
the excesses of which they were capable when their passions were
inflamed. 'They grievously oppressed the poor people by building
castles; and when they were built, they filled them with wicked
men or rather devils, who seized both men and women who they

moral of his own story, that he has even the blindness to go out of his way to have a fling at *flints* and *dungs* (the contemptible ingredients, as he would have us believe, of a modern rabble) at the very time when he is describing a mob of the twelfth century[15]—a mob (one should think) after the writer's own heart, without one particle of modern philosophy or revolutionary politics in their composition, who were to a man, to a hair, just what priests, and kings, and nobles *let* them be, and who were collected to witness (a spectacle proper to the times) the burning of the lovely Rebecca at a stake for a sorceress, because she was a Jewess, beautiful and innocent, and the consequent victim of insane bigotry and unbridled profligacy. And it is at this moment (when the heart is kindled and bursting with indignation at the revolting abuses of self-constituted power) that Sir Walter *stops the press* to have a sneer at the people, and to put a spoke (as he thinks) in the wheel of upstart innovation! This is what he calls 'backing his friends'—it is thus he administers charms and philtres to our love of Legitimacy, makes us conceive a horror of all reform, civil, political, or religious, and would fain put down the *Spirit of the Age*. The Author of Waverley might just as well get up and make a speech at a dinner at Edinburgh, abusing Mr. MacAdam[16] for his improvements in the roads, on the ground that they were nearly *impassable* in many places 'sixty years since';[17] or object to Mr. Peel's *Police-Bill*,[18] by insisting that Hounslow-Heath was formerly a scene of greater interest and terror to highwaymen and travellers, and cut a greater figure in the Newgate Calendar than it does at present.—Oh! Wickliff, Luther, Hampden, Sidney, Somers, mistaken Whigs, and thoughtless Reformers in religion and politics, and all ye, whether poets or philosophers, heroes or sages, inventors of arts or sciences, patriots, benefactors of the human race, enlighteners and civilisers of the world, who have (so far) reduced opinion to reason, and power to law, who are the cause that we no longer burn witches and heretics at slow fires, that the thumb-screws are no longer applied by ghastly, smiling judges, to extort confession of imputed crimes from sufferers for conscience sake;

---

imagined had any money, threw them into prison, and put them to more cruel tortures than the martyrs ever endured. They suffocated some in mud, and suspended others by the feet, or the head, or the thumbs, kindling fires below them. They squeezed the heads of some with knotted cords till they pierced their brains, while they threw others into dungeons swarming with serpents, snakes, and toads.' But it would be cruel to put the reader to the pain of perusing the remainder of the description. (*Henry's Hist.* edit. 1805, vol. vii, p. 346.) [w. h.]

that men are no longer strung up like acorns on trees without judge or jury, or hunted like wild beasts through thickets and glens, who have abated the cruelty of priests, the pride of nobles, the divinity of kings in former times; to whom we owe it, that we no longer wear round our necks the collar of Gurth the swineherd, and of Wamba the jester; that the castles of great lords are no longer the dens of banditti, from whence they issue with fire and sword, to lay waste the land; that we no longer expire in loathsome dungeons without knowing the cause, or have our right hands struck off for raising them in self-defence against wanton insult; that we can sleep without fear of being burnt in our beds, or travel without making our wills; that no Amy Robsarts are thrown down trap-doors by Richard Varneys with impunity; that no Red Reiver of Westburn-Flat sets fire to peaceful cottages; that no Claverhouse signs cold-blooded death-warrants in sport; that we have no Tristan the Hermit, or Petit-André, crawling near us, like spiders, and making our flesh creep, and our hearts sicken within us at every moment of our lives—ye who have produced this change in the face of nature and society, return to earth once more, and beg pardon of Sir Walter and his patrons, who sigh at not being able to undo all that you have done! Leaving this question, there are two other remarks which we wished to make on the Novels. The one was, to express our admiration of the good-nature of the mottos, in which the author has taken occasion to remember and quote almost every living author (whether illustrious or obscure) but himself[19]—an indirect argument in favour of the general opinion as to the source from which they spring—and the other was, to hint our astonishment at the innumerable and incessant instances of bad and slovenly English in them, more, we believe, than in any other works now printed. We should think the writer could not possibly read the manuscript after he has once written it, or overlook the press.

If there were a writer, who

> born for the universe, narrow'd his mind,
> And to party gave up what was meant for mankind—[20]

who, from the height of his genius looking abroad into nature, and scanning the recesses of the human heart, 'winked and shut his apprehension up' to every thought or purpose that tended to the future good of mankind—who, raised by affluence, the reward of successful industry, and by the voice of fame above the want of any but the most honourable patronage, stooped to the unworthy arts of adulation, and abetted the views of the great with the pettifogging feelings of the meanest dependant on office—who, having secured the admiration of the public (with the probable reversion of immortality), showed no respect for himself, for that genius that had raised him to distinction, for that nature which he trampled under foot—who, amiable, frank, friendly, manly in private life, was seized with the dotage of age and the fury of a woman, the instant politics were concerned—who reserved all his candour and comprehensiveness of view for history, and vented his littleness, pique, resentment, bigotry, and intolerance on his contemporaries—who took the wrong side, and defended it by unfair means—who, the moment his own interest or the prejudices of others interfered, seemed to forget all that was due to the pride of intellect, to the sense of manhood—who, praised, admired by men of all parties alike, repaid the public liberality by striking a secret and envenomed blow at the reputation of everyone who was not the ready tool of power—who strewed the slime of rankling malice and mercenary scorn over the bud and promise of genius, because it was not fostered in the hot-bed of corruption, or warped by the trammels of servility—who supported the worst abuses of authority in the worst spirit— who joined a gang of desperadoes to spread calumny, contempt, infamy, wherever they were merited by honesty or talent on a different side—who officiously undertook to decide public questions by private insinuations, to prop the throne by nicknames, and the altar by lies—who being (by common consent) the finest, the most humane and accomplished writer of his age, associated himself with and encouraged the lowest panders of a venal press; deluging, nauseating the public mind with the offal and garbage of Billingsgate abuse and vulgar *slang;* showing no remorse, no relenting or compassion towards the victims of this nefarious and organized system of party-proscription, carried on under the mask of literary criticism and fair discussion, insulting the misfortunes of some, and trampling on the early grave of others—

> Who would not grieve if such a man there be?
> Who would not weep if Atticus were he?[21]

But we believe there is no other age or country of the world (but ours) in which such genius could have been so degraded!

# Mr. Wordsworth*

MR. WORDSWORTH'S genius is a pure emanation of the Spirit of the Age. Had he lived in any other period of the world, he would never have been heard of. As it is, he has some difficulty to contend with the hebetude of his intellect, and the meanness of his subject. With him 'lowliness is young ambition's ladder': but he finds it a toil to climb in this way the steep of Fame. His homely Muse can hardly raise her wing from the ground, nor spread her hidden glories to the sun. He has 'no figures nor no fantasies, which busy *passion* draws in the brains of men:'[1] neither the gorgeous machinery of mythologic lore, nor the splendid colours of poetic diction. His style is vernacular: he delivers household truths. He sees nothing loftier than human hopes; nothing deeper than the human heart. This he probes, this he tampers with, this he poises, with all its incalculable weight of thought and feeling, in his hands; and at the same time calms the throbbing pulses of his own heart, by keeping his eye ever fixed on the face of nature. If he can make the life-blood flow from the wounded breast, this is the living colouring with which he paints his verse: if he can assuage the pain or close up the wound with the balm of solitary musing, or the healing power of plants and herbs and 'skyey influences,' this is the sole triumph of his art. He takes the simplest elements of nature and of the human mind, the mere abstract conditions inseparable from our being, and tries to compound a new system of poetry from them; and has perhaps succeeded as well as anyone could. 'Nihil humani a me alienum puto'[2] is the motto of his works. He thinks nothing low or indifferent of which this can be affirmed; everything that professes to be more than this, that is not an absolute essence of truth and feeling, he holds to be vitiated, false, and spurious. In a word, his poetry is founded on setting up an opposition (and pushing it to the utmost length) between the natural and the arti-

* [See source note to "Mr. Coleridge," p. 305.]

ficial; between the spirit of humanity, and the spirit of fashion and of the world!

It is one of the innovations of the time. It partakes of, and is carried along with, the revolutionary movement of our age: the political changes of the day were the model on which he formed and conducted his poetical experiments. His Muse (it cannot be denied, and without this we cannot explain its character at all) is a levelling one. It proceeds on a principle of equality, and strives to reduce all things to the same standard. It is distinguished by a proud humility. It relies upon its own resources, and disdains external show and relief. It takes the commonest events and objects, as a test to prove that nature is always interesting from its inherent truth and beauty, without any of the ornaments of dress or pomp of circumstances to set it off. Hence the unaccountable mixture of seeming simplicity and real abstruseness in the *Lyrical Ballads*. Fools have laughed at, wise men scarcely understand them. He takes a subject or a story merely as pegs or loops to hang thought and feeling on; the incidents are trifling, in proportion to his contempt for imposing appearances; the reflections are profound, according to the gravity and the aspiring pretensions of his mind.

His popular, inartificial style gets rid (at a blow) of all the trappings of verse, of all the high places of poetry: 'the cloud-capt towers, the solemn temples, the gorgeous palaces,' are swept to the ground, and 'like the baseless fabric of a vision, leave not a wreck behind.'[3] All the traditions of learning, all the superstitions of age, are obliterated and effaced. We begin *de novo*, on a *tabula rasa*[4] of poetry. The purple pall, the nodding plume of tragedy are exploded as mere pantomime and trick, to return to the simplicity of truth and nature. Kings, queens, priests, nobles, the altar and the throne, the distinctions of rank, birth, wealth, power, 'the judge's robe, the marshal's truncheon, the ceremony that to great ones 'longs,'[5] are not to be found here. The author tramples on the pride of art with greater pride. The Ode and Epode, the Strophe and the Antistrophe, he laughs to scorn. The harp of Homer, the trump of Pindar and of Alcæus are still. The decencies of costume, the decorations of vanity are stripped off without mercy as barbarous, idle, and Gothic. The jewels in the crisped hair, the diadem on the polished brow are thought meretricious, theatrical, vulgar; and nothing contents his fastidious taste beyond a simple garland of flowers. Neither does he avail himself of the advantages which nature or accident holds out to him. He chooses to have his subject a foil to his invention, to owe nothing but to himself. He gathers manna in the wilderness, he strikes the barren rock for the gushing moisture.

He elevates the mean by the strength of his own aspirations;
he clothes the naked with beauty and grandeur from the stores
of his own recollections. No cypress grove loads his verse with
funeral pomp: but his imagination lends 'a sense of joy

> To the bare trees and mountains bare,
> And grass in the green field.'[6]

No storm, no shipwreck startles us by its horrors: but the rainbow lifts its head in the cloud, and the breeze sighs through
the withered fern. No sad vicissitude of fate, no overwhelming
catastrophe in nature deforms his page: but the dew-drop
glitters on the bending flower, the tear collects in the glistening
eye.

> Beneath the hills, along the flowery vales,
> The generations are prepared; the pangs,
> The internal pangs are ready; the dread strife
> Of poor humanity's afflicted will,
> Struggling in vain with ruthless destiny.[7]

As the lark ascends from its low bed on fluttering wing, and
salutes the morning skies; so Mr. Wordsworth's unpretending
Muse, in russet guise, scales the summits of reflection, while
it makes the round earth its footstool, and its home!

Possibly a good deal of this may be regarded as the effect
of disappointed views and an inverted ambition. Prevented
by native pride and indolence from climbing the ascent of
learning or greatness, taught by political opinions to say to the
vain pomp and glory of the world, 'I hate ye,' seeing the path
of classical and artificial poetry blocked up by the cumbrous
ornaments of style and turgid *commonplaces*, so that nothing
more could be achieved in that direction but by the most
ridiculous bombast or the tamest servility; he has turned back
partly from the bias of his mind, partly perhaps from a judi-
cious policy—has struck into the sequestered vale of humble
life, sought out the Muse among sheep-cotes and hamlets and
the peasant's mountain-haunts, has discarded all the tinsel
pageantry of verse, and endeavoured (not in vain) to aggran-
dise the trivial and add the charm of novelty to the familiar.
No one has shown the same imagination in raising trifles into
importance: no one has displayed the same pathos in treating
of the simplest feelings of the heart. Reserved, yet haughty,
having no unruly or violent passions (or those passions having
been early suppressed), Mr. Wordsworth has passed his life
in solitary musing, or in daily converse with the face of nature.
He exemplifies in an eminent degree the power of *association*;

for his poetry has no other source or character. He has dwelt among pastoral scenes, till each object has become connected with a thousand feelings, a link in the chain of thought, a fibre of his own heart. Everyone is by habit and familiarity strongly attached to the place of his birth, or to objects that recall the most pleasing and eventful circumstances of his life. But to the author of the *Lyrical Ballads*, nature is a kind of home; and he may be said to take a personal interest in the universe. There is no image so insignificant that it has not in some mood or other found the way into his heart: no sound that does not awaken the memory of other years.

> To him the meanest flower that blows can give
> Thoughts that do often lie too deep for tears.[8]

The daisy looks up to him with sparkling eye as an old acquaintance: the cuckoo haunts him with sounds of early youth not to be expressed: a linnet's nest startles him with boyish delight: an old withered thorn is weighed down with a heap of recollections: a grey cloak, seen on some wild moor, torn by the wind, or drenched in the rain, afterwards becomes an object of imagination to him: even the lichens on the rock have a life and being in his thoughts. He has described all these objects in a way and with an intensity of feeling that no one else had done before him, and has given a new view or aspect of nature. He is in this sense the most original poet now living, and the one whose writings could the least be spared: for they have no substitute elsewhere. The vulgar do not read them, the learned, who see all things through books, do not understand them, the great despise, the fashionable may ridicule them: but the author has created himself an interest in the heart of the retired and lonely student of nature, which can never die. Persons of this class will still continue to feel what he has felt: he has expressed what they might in vain wish to express, except with glistening eye and faltering tongue! There is a lofty philosophic tone, a thoughtful humanity, infused into his pastoral vein. Remote from the passions and events of the great world, he has communicated interest and dignity to the primal movements of the heart of man, and ingrafted his own conscious reflections on the casual thoughts of hinds and shepherds. Nursed amidst the grandeur of mountain scenery, he has stooped to have a nearer view of the daisy under his feet, or plucked a branch of white-thorn from the spray: but in describing it, his mind seems imbued with the majesty and solemnity of the objects around him— the tall rock lifts its head in the erectness of his spirit; the cataract roars in the sound of his verse; and in its dim and

mysterious meaning, the mists seem to gather in the hollows
of Helvellyn, and the forked Skiddaw hovers in the distance.
There is little mention of mountainous scenery in Mr. Wordsworth's poetry; but by internal evidence one might be almost
sure that it was written in a mountainous country, from its
bareness, its simplicity, its loftiness and its depth!

His later philosophic productions have a somewhat different
character. They are a departure from, a dereliction of his first
principles. They are classical and courtly. They are polished
in style, without being gaudy; dignified in subject, without
affectation. They seem to have been composed not in a cottage
at Grasmere, but among the half-inspired groves and stately
recollections of Cole-Orton.[9] We might allude in particular,
for examples of what we mean, to the lines on a Picture
by Claude Lorraine, and to the exquisite poem, entitled
*Laodamia*. The last of these breathes the pure spirit of the
finest fragments of antiquity—the sweetness, the gravity, the
strength, the beauty and the languor of death—

Calm contemplation and majestic pains.[10]

Its glossy brilliancy arises from the perfection of the finishing,
like that of careful sculpture, not from gaudy colouring—the
texture of the thoughts has the smoothness and solidity of
marble. It is a poem that might be read aloud in Elysium,
and the spirits of departed heroes and sages would gather
round to listen to it! Mr. Wordsworth's philosophic poetry,
with a less glowing aspect and less tumult in the veins than
Lord Byron's on similar occasions, bends a calmer and keener
eye on mortality; the impression, if less vivid, is more pleasing
and permanent; and we confess it (perhaps it is a want of
taste and proper feeling) that there are lines and poems of our
author's, that we think of ten times for once that we recur
to any of Lord Byron's. Or if there are any of the latter's writings, that we can dwell upon in the same way, that is, as
lasting and heart-felt sentiments, it is when laying aside his
usual pomp and pretension, he descends with Mr. Wordsworth
to the common ground of a disinterested humanity. It may be
considered as characteristic of our poet's writings, that they
either make no impression on the mind at all, seem mere
*nonsense-verses*, or that they leave a mark behind them that
never wears out. They either

Fall blunted from the indurated breast[11]

without any perceptible result, or they absorb it like a passion.
To one class of readers he appears sublime, to another (and

we fear the largest) ridiculous. He has probably realised Milton's wish—'and fit audience found, though few'; but we suspect he is not reconciled to the alternative. There are delightful passages in the *Excursion*, both of natural description and of inspired reflection (passages of the latter kind that in the sound of the thoughts and of the swelling language resemble heavenly symphonies, mournful *requiems* over the grave of human hopes); but we must add, in justice and in sincerity, that we think it impossible that this work should ever become popular, even in the same degree as the *Lyrical Ballads*. It affects a system without having any intelligible clue to one; and instead of unfolding a principle in various and striking lights, repeats the same conclusions till they become flat and insipid. Mr. Wordsworth's mind is obtuse, except as it is the organ and the receptacle of accumulated feelings: it is not analytic, but synthetic; it is reflecting, rather than theoretical. The *Excursion*, we believe, fell still-born from the press. There was something abortive, and clumsy, and ill-judged in the attempt. It was long and laboured. The personages, for the most part, were low, the fare rustic: the plan raised expectations which were not fulfilled, and the effect was like being ushered into a stately hall and invited to sit down to a splendid banquet in the company of clowns, and with nothing but successive courses of apple-dumplings served up. It was not even *toujours perdrix!*[12]

Mr. Wordsworth, in his person, is above the middle size, with marked features, and an air somewhat stately and Quixotic. He reminds one of some of Holbein's heads, grave, saturnine, with a slight indication of sly humour, kept under by the manners of the age or by the pretensions of the person. He has a peculiar sweetness in his smile, and great depth and manliness and a rugged harmony, in the tones of his voice. His manner of reading his own poetry is particularly imposing; and in his favourite passages his eye beams with preternatural lustre, and the meaning labours slowly up from his swelling breast. No one who has seen him at these moments could go away with an impression that he was a 'man of no mark or likelihood.' Perhaps the comment of his face and voice is necessary to convey a full idea of his poetry. His language may not be intelligible, but his manner is not to be mistaken. It is clear that he is either mad or inspired. In company, even in a *tête-à-tête*, Mr. Wordsworth is often silent, indolent, and reserved. If he is become verbose and oracular of late years, he was not so in his better days. He threw out a bold or an indifferent remark without either effort or pretension, and relapsed into musing again. He shone most (because he seemed most roused and animated) in reciting his own poetry, or in talking about it. He sometimes gave striking views of his feelings and trains of association in composing certain passages; or if one did not always understand his distinctions, still there was no want of interest—there was a latent meaning worth inquiring into, like a vein of ore that one cannot exactly hit upon at the moment, but of which there are sure indications. His standard of poetry is high and severe, almost to exclusiveness. He admits of nothing below, scarcely of anything above himself. It is fine to hear him talk of the way in which certain subjects should have been treated by eminent poets, according to his notions of the art. Thus he finds fault with Dryden's description of Bacchus in the *Alexander's Feast*, as if he were a mere good-looking youth, or boon companion—

> Flushed with a purple grace,
> He shows his honest face—

instead of representing the God returning from the conquest of India, crowned with vine-leaves, and drawn by panthers, and followed by troops of satyrs, of wild men and animals that he had tamed. You would think, in hearing him speak on this subject, that you saw Titian's picture of the meeting of Bacchus and Ariadne—so classic were his conceptions, so glowing his style. Milton is his great idol, and he sometimes dares to compare himself with him. His Sonnets, indeed, have something of the same high-raised tone and prophetic spirit. Chaucer is another prime favorite of his, and he has been at the pains to modernize some of the Canterbury Tales. Those persons who look upon Mr. Wordsworth as a merely puerile writer, must be rather at a loss to account for his strong predilection for such geniuses as Dante and Michael Angelo. We do not think our author has any very cordial sympathy with Shakespeare. How should he? Shakespeare was the least of an egotist of anybody in the world. He does not much relish the variety and scope of dramatic composition. 'He hates those interlocutions between Lucius and Caius.'[13] Yet Mr. Wordsworth himself wrote a tragedy when he was young; and we have heard the following energetic lines quoted from it, as put into the mouth of a person smit with remorse for some rash crime:

> Action is momentary,
> The motion of a muscle this way or that;
> Suffering is long, obscure, and infinite![14]

Perhaps for want of light and shade, and the unshackled spirit
of the drama, this performance was never brought forward.
Our critic has a great dislike to Gray, and a fondness for
Thomson and Collins. It is mortifying to hear him speak of
Pope and Dryden, whom, because they have been supposed
to have all the possible excellences of poetry, he will allow to
have none. Nothing, however, can be fairer, or more amusing,
than the way in which he sometimes exposes the unmeaning
verbiage of modern poetry. Thus, in the beginning of Dr.
Johnson's *Vanity of Human Wishes*—

> Let observation with extensive view
> Survey mankind from China to Peru—

he says there is a total want of imagination accompanying
the words, the same idea is repeated three times under the
disguise of a different phraseology: it comes to this—'let *observation*, with extensive *observation*, *observe* mankind'; or take
away the first line, and the second,

> Survey mankind from China to Peru,

literally conveys the whole. Mr. Wordsworth is, we must say,
a perfect Drawcansir[15] as to prose writers. He complains of
the dry reasoners and matter-of-fact people for their want
of *passion;* and he is jealous of the rhetorical declaimers and
rhapsodists as trenching on the province of poetry. He condemns all French writers (as well of poetry as prose) in the
lump. His list in this way is indeed small. He approves of
Walton's Angler, Paley,[16] and some other writers of an inoffen-
sive modesty of pretension. He also likes books of voyages
and travels, and Robinson Crusoe. In art, he greatly esteems
Bewick's woodcuts, and Waterloo's sylvan etchings.[17] But he
sometimes takes a higher tone, and gives his mind fair play.
We have known him enlarge with a noble intelligence and
enthusiasm on Nicolas Poussin's fine landscape-compositions,
pointing out the unity of design that pervades them, the super-
intending mind, the imaginative principle that brings all to
bear on the same end; and declaring he would not give a rush
for any landscape that did not express the time of day, the
climate, the period of the world it was meant to illustrate, or
had not this character of *wholeness* in it. His eye also does
justice to Rembrandt's fine and masterly effects. In the way
in which that artist works something out of nothing, and
transforms the stump of a tree, a common figure into an *ideal*
object, by the gorgeous light and shade thrown upon it, he
perceives an analogy to his own mode of investing the minute

details of nature with an atmosphere of sentiment; and in pronouncing Rembrandt to be a man of genius, feels that he strengthens his own claim to the title. It has been said of Mr. Wordsworth,[18] that 'he hates conchology, that he hates the Venus of Medicis.' But these, we hope, are mere epigrams and *jeux-d' esprit,* as far from truth as they are free from malice; a sort of running satire or critical clenches—

> Where one for sense and one for rhyme
> Is quite sufficient at one time.[19]

We think, however, that if Mr. Wordsworth had been a more liberal and candid critic, he would have been a more sterling writer. If a greater number of sources of pleasure had been open to him, he would have communicated pleasure to the world more frequently. Had he been less fastidious in pronouncing sentence on the works of others, his own would have been received more favourably, and treated more leniently. The current of his feelings is deep, but narrow; the range of his understanding is lofty and aspiring rather than discursive. The force, the originality, the absolute truth and identity with which he feels some things, makes him indifferent to so many others. The simplicity and enthusiasm of his feelings, with respect to nature, renders him bigoted and intolerant in his judgments of men and things. But it happens to him, as to others, that his strength lies in his weakness; and perhaps we have no right to complain. We might get rid of the cynic and the egotist, and find in his stead a commonplace man. We should 'take the good the Gods provide us': a fine and original vein of poetry is not one of their most contemptible gifts, and the rest is scarcely worth thinking of, except as it may be a mortification to those who expect perfection from human nature; or who have been idle enough at some period of their lives, to deify men of genius as possessing claims above it. But this is a chord that jars, and we shall not dwell upon it.

Lord Byron we have called, according to the old proverb, 'the spoiled child of fortune': Mr. Wordsworth might plead, in mitigation of some peculiarities, that he is 'the spoiled child of disappointment.' We are convinced, if he had been early a popular poet, he would have borne his honours meekly, and would have been a person of great *bonhomie* and frankness of disposition. But the sense of injustice and of undeserved ridicule sours the temper and narrows the views. To have produced works of genius, and to find them neglected or treated with scorn, is one of the heaviest trials of human patience. We exaggerate our own merits when they are denied by others, and are apt to grudge and cavil at every particle of praise bestowed on those to whom we feel a conscious superiority. In mere self-defence we turn against the world, when it turns against us; brood over the undeserved slights we receive; and thus the genial current of the soul is stopped, or vents itself in effusions of petulance and self-conceit. Mr. Wordsworth has thought too much of contemporary critics and criticism; and less than he ought of the award of posterity, and of the opinion, we do not say of private friends, but of those who were made so by their admiration of his genius. He did not court popularity by a conformity to established models, and he ought not to have been surprised that his originality was not understood as a matter of course. He has *gnawed too much on the bridle;* and has often thrown out crusts to the critics, in mere defiance or as a point of honour when he was challenged, which otherwise his own good sense would have withheld. We suspect that Mr. Wordsworth's feelings are a little morbid in this respect, or that he resents censure more than he is gratified by praise. Otherwise, the tide has turned much in his favour of late years—he has a large body of determined partisans—and is at present sufficiently in request with the public to save or relieve him from the last necessity to which a man of genius can be reduced—that of becoming the God of his own idolatry!

# Mr. Crabbe*

[ . . . ] MR. CRABBE presents an entire contrast to Mr. Campbell.[1] The one is the most ambitious and aspiring of living poets, the other the most humble and prosaic. If the poetry of the one is like the arch of the rainbow, spanning and adorning the earth, that of the other is like a dull, leaden cloud hanging over it. Mr. Crabbe's style might be cited as an answer to Audrey's question—'Is poetry a true thing?'[2] There are here no ornaments, no flights of fancy, no illusions of sentiment, no tinsel of words. His song is one sad reality, one unraised, unvaried note of unavailing woe. Literal fidelity serves him in the place of invention; he assumes importance by a number of petty details; he rivets attention by being tedious. He not only deals in incessant matters of fact, but in matters of fact of the most familiar, the least animating, and the most unpleasant kind; but he relies for the effect of novelty on the microscopic minuteness with which he dissects the most trivial objects—and for the interest he excites, on the unshrinking determination with which he handles the most painful. His poetry has an official and professional air. He is called in to cases of difficult births, of fractured limbs, or breaches of the peace; and makes out a parochial list of accidents and offences. He takes the most trite, the most gross and obvious and revolting part of nature, for the subject of his elaborate descriptions; but it is Nature still, and Nature is a great and mighty Goddess! It is well for the Reverend Author that it is so. Individuality is, in his theory, the only definition of poetry. Whatever *is*, he hitches into rhyme. Whoever makes an exact image of anything on the earth, however deformed or insignificant, according to him, must succeed—and he himself has succeeded. Mr. Crabbe is one of the most popular and admired of our living authors. That he is so, can be accounted for on no other principle than the strong ties that bind us to the world about us,

* [From "Mr. Campbell and Mr. Crabbe." Hazlitt's piece on Crabbe first appeared, in more expansive form, in *The London Magazine*, May 1821.]

and our involuntary yearnings after whatever in any manner powerfully and directly reminds us of it. His Muse is not one of the *Daughters of Memory*, but the old toothless, mumbling, dame herself, doling out the gossip and scandal of the neighbourhood, recounting *totidem verbis et literis*,[3] what happens in every place of the kingdom every hour in the year, and fastening always on the worst as the most palatable morsels. But she is a circumstantial old lady, communicative, scrupulous, leaving nothing to the imagination, harping on the smallest grievances, a village oracle and critic, most veritable, most identical, bringing us acquainted with persons and things just as they chanced to exist, and giving us a local interest in all she knows and tells. Mr. Crabbe's Helicon is choked up with weeds and corruption; it reflects no light from heaven, it emits no cheerful sound: no flowers of love, of hope, or joy spring up near it, or they bloom only to wither in a moment. Our poet's verse does not put a spirit of youth in everything, but a spirit of fear, despondency, and decay: it is not an electric spark to kindle or expand, but acts like the torpedo's touch to deaden or contract. It lends no dazzling tints to fancy, it aids no soothing feelings in the heart, it gladdens no prospect, it stirs no wish; in its view the current of life runs slow, dull, cold, dispirited, half under ground, muddy, and clogged with all creeping things. The world is one vast infirmary; the hill of Parnassus is a penitentiary, of which our author is the overseer: to read him is a penance, yet we read on! Mr. Crabbe, it must be confessed, is a repulsive writer. He contrives to 'turn diseases to commodities,' and makes a virtue of necessity. He puts us out of conceit with this world, which perhaps a severe divine should do; yet does not, as a charitable divine ought, point to another. His morbid feelings droop and cling to the earth, grovel where they should soar; and throw a dead weight on every aspiration of the soul after the good or beautiful. By degrees we submit, and are reconciled to our fate, like patients to the physician, or prisoners in the condemned cell. We can only explain this by saying, as we said before, that Mr. Crabbe gives us one part of nature, the mean, the little, the disgusting, the distressing; that he does this thoroughly and like a master, and we forgive all the rest.

Mr. Crabbe's first poems were published so long ago as the year 1782, and received the approbation of Dr. Johnson only a little before he died.[4] This was a testimony from an enemy; for Dr. Johnson was not an admirer of the simple in style or minute in description. Still he was an acute, strong-minded man, and could see truth when it was presented to him, even through the mist of his prejudices and his foibles. There was something in Mr. Crabbe's intricate points that did not, after all, so ill accord with the Doctor's purblind vision; and he knew quite enough of the petty ills of life to judge of the merit of our poet's descriptions, though he himself chose to slur them over in high-sounding dogmas or general invectives. Mr. Crabbe's earliest poem of *The Village* was recommended to the notice of Dr. Johnson by Sir Joshua Reynolds; and we cannot help thinking that a taste for that sort of poetry, which leans for support on the truth and fidelity of its imitations of nature, began to display itself much about that time, and, in a good measure, in consequence of the direction of the public taste to the subject of painting. Book-learning, the accumulation of wordy commonplaces, the gaudy pretensions of poetical fiction, had enfeebled and perverted our eye for nature. The study of the fine arts, which came into fashion about forty years ago, and was then first considered as a polite accomplishment, would tend imperceptibly to restore it. Painting is essentially an imitative art; it cannot subsist for a moment on empty generalities: the critic, therefore, who had been used to this sort of substantial entertainment, would be disposed to read poetry with the eye of a connoisseur, would be little captivated with smooth, polished, unmeaning periods, and would turn with double eagerness and relish to the force and precision of individual details, transferred, as it were, to the page from the canvas. Thus an admirer of Teniers or Hobbema might think little of the pastoral sketches of Pope or Goldsmith; even Thomson describes not so much the naked object as what he sees in his mind's eye, surrounded and glowing with the mild, bland, genial vapours of his brain—but the adept in Dutch interiors, hovels, and pig-styes must find in Mr. Crabbe a man after his own heart. He is the very thing itself; he paints in words, instead of colours: there is no other difference. As Mr. Crabbe is not a painter, only because he does not use a brush and colours, so he is for the most part a poet, only because he writes in lines of ten syllables. All the rest might be found in a newspaper, an old magazine, or a county-register. Our author is himself a little jealous of the prudish fidelity of his homely Muse, and tries to justify himself by precedents. He brings as a parallel instance of merely literal description, Pope's lines on the gay Duke of Buckingham, beginning 'In the worst inn's worst room see Villiers lies!'[5] But surely nothing can be more dissimilar. Pope describes what is striking, Crabbe would have described merely what was there. The objects in Pope stand out to the fancy from the mixture of the mean with the gaudy, from the contrast of the scene and the character. There is an appeal to the imagination; you see what is passing in a poetical point of view. In Crabbe there is no foil, no contrast, no impulse given to the mind. It is all on a level and of a piece. In fact, there is so little connection between the subject-matter of Mr. Crabbe's lines and the ornament of rhyme which is tacked to them, that many of his verses read like serious burlesque, and the parodies which have been made upon them are hardly so quaint as the originals.

Mr. Crabbe's great fault is certainly that he is a sickly, a querulous, a uniformly dissatisfied poet. He sings the country; and he sings it in a pitiful tone. He chooses this subject only to take the charm out of it, and to dispel the illusion, the glory, and the dream, which had hovered over it in golden verse from Theocritus to Cowper. He sets out with professing to overturn the theory which had hallowed a shepherd's life, and made the names of grove and valley music to our ears, in order to give us truth in its stead; but why not lay aside the fool's cap and bells at once? Why not insist on the unwelcome reality in plain prose? If our author is a poet, why trouble himself with statistics? If he is a statistic writer, why set his ill news to harsh and grating verse? The philosopher in painting the dark side of human nature may have reason on his side, and a moral lesson or remedy in view. The tragic poet, who shows the sad vicissitudes of things and the disappointments of the passions, at least strengthens our yearnings after imaginary good, and lends wings to our desires, by which we, 'at one bound, high overleap all bound' of actual suffering. But Mr. Crabbe does neither. He gives us discoloured paintings of life; helpless, repining, unprofitable, unedifying distress. He is not a philosopher, but a sophist, a misanthrope in verse; a *namby-pamby* Mandeville, a Malthus turned metrical romancer.[6] He professes historical fidelity; but his vein is not dramatic; nor does he give us the *pros* and *cons* of that versatile gipsy, Nature. He does not indulge his fancy or sympathise with us, or tell us how the poor feel; but how he should feel in their situation, which we do not want to know. He does not weave the web of their lives of a mingled yarn, good and ill together, but clothes them all in the same dingy linsey-woolsey, or tinges them with a green and yellow melancholy. He blocks out all possibility of good, cancels the hope, or even the wish for it as a weakness; checkmates Tityrus and Virgil at the game of pastoral cross-purposes, disables all his adversary's white pieces, and leaves none but black ones on the board. The situation of a country clergyman is not necessarily favourable to the cultivation of the Muse. He is set down, perhaps, as he thinks, in a small curacy for life, and he takes his revenge by imprisoning the reader's imagination in luckless verse. Shut out from social converse, from learned colleges and halls, where he passed his youth, he has no cordial fellow-feeling with the unlettered manners of *The Village* or *The Borough;* and he describes his neighbours as more uncomfortable and discontented than himself. All this while he dedicates successive volumes to rising generations of noble patrons; and while he desolates a line of coast with sterile, blighting lines, the only leaf of his books where honour, beauty, worth, or pleasure bloom, is that inscribed to the Rutland family![7] We might adduce instances of what we have said from every page of his works: let one suffice—

> Thus by himself compelled to live each day,
> To wait for certain hours the tide's delay;
> At the same times the same dull views to see,
> The bounding marsh-bank and the blighted tree;
> The water only when the tides were high,
> When low, the mud half-covered and half-dry;
> The sun-burnt tar that blisters on the planks,
> And bank-side stakes in their uneven ranks;
> Heaps of entangled weeds that slowly float,
> As the tide rolls by the impeded boat.
> When tides were neap, and in the sultry day,
> Through the tall bounding mud-banks made their way,
> Which on each side rose swelling, and below
> The dark warm flood ran silently and slow;
> There anchoring, Peter chose from man to hide,
> There hang his head, and view the lazy tide
> In its hot slimy channel slowly glide;
> Where the small eels, that left the deeper way
> For the warm shore, within the shallows play;
> Where gaping muscles, left upon the mud,
> Slope their slow passage to the fall'n flood:
> Here dull and hopeless he'd lie down and trace
> How side-long crabs had crawled their crooked race;
> Or sadly listen to the tuneless cry
> Of fishing gull or clanging golden-eye;
> What time the sea-birds to the marsh would come,
> And the loud bittern, from the bull-rush home,
> Gave from the salt-ditch-side the bellowing boom:
> He nursed the feelings these dull scenes produce
> And loved to stop beside the opening sluice;
> Where the small stream, confined in narrow bound,
> Ran with a dull, unvaried, saddening sound;
> Where all, presented to the eye or ear,
> Oppressed the soul with misery, grief, and fear.[8]

This is an exact *facsimile* of some of the most unlovely parts of the creation. Indeed the whole of Mr. Crabbe's *The Borough,* from which the above passage is taken, is done so to the life, that it seems almost like some sea-monster, crawled out of the neighbouring slime, and harbouring a breed of strange vermin, with a strong local scent of tar and bulge-water. Mr. Crabbe's *Tales*[9] are more readable than his *Poems;* but in proportion as the interest increases, they become more oppressive. They turn, one and all, upon the same sort of teazing, helpless, mechanical, unimaginative distress—and though it is not easy to lay them down, you never wish to take them up again. Still in this way, they are highly finished, striking, and original portraits, worked out with an eye to nature, and an intimate knowledge of the small and intricate folds of the human heart. Some of the best are the "Confi-dant," the story of "Silly Shore," the "Young Poet," the "Painter." The episode of "Phœbe Dawson" in *The Village*[10] is one of the most tender and pensive; and the character of the methodist parson who persecutes the sailor's widow with his godly, selfish love is one of the most profound. In a word, if Mr. Crabbe's writings do not add greatly to the store of entertaining and delightful fiction, yet they will remain, 'as a thorn in the side of poetry,' perhaps for a century to come!

# V

---

*FINAL YEARS*

*From*

# Notes of a Journey Through France and Italy

CHAPTER I*

THE RULE for travelling abroad is to take our common sense with us, and leave our prejudices behind us. The object of travelling is to see and learn; but such is our impatience of ignorance, or the jealousy of our self-love, that we generally set up a certain preconception beforehand (in self-defence, or as a barrier against the lessons of experience) and are surprised at or quarrel with all that does not conform to it. Let us think what we please of what we really find, but prejudge nothing. The English, in particular, carry out their own defects as a standard for general imitation; and think the virtues of others (that are not *their* vices) good for nothing. Thus they find fault with the gaiety of the French as impertinence, with their politeness as grimace. This repulsive system of carping and contradiction can extract neither use nor meaning from anything, and only tends to make those who give way to it uncomfortable and ridiculous. On the contrary, we should be as seldom shocked or annoyed as possible (it is our vanity or ignorance that is mortified much oftener than our reason!), and contrive to see the favourable side of things. This will turn both to profit and pleasure. The intellectual, like the physical, is best kept up by an exchange of commodities, instead of an ill-natured and idle search after grievances. The first thing an Englishman does on going abroad is to find fault with what is French, because it is not English. If he is determined to confine all excellence to his own country, he had better stay at home.

On arriving at Brighton (in full season), a lad offered

* [First published in *The Morning Chronicle*, Sept. 14, 1824.]

to conduct us to an inn. 'Did he think there was room?' He was sure of it. 'Did he belong to the inn?' No, he was from London. In fact, he was a young gentleman from town, who had been stopping some time at the White-Horse Hotel, and who wished to employ his spare time (when he was not riding out on a blood-horse) in serving the house, and relieving the perplexities of his fellow-travellers. No one but a Londoner would volunteer his assistance in this way. Amiable land of *Cockayne*, happy in itself, and in making others happy! Blest exuberance of self-satisfaction, that overflows upon others! Delightful impertinence, that is forward to oblige them!

There is something in being near the sea, like the confines of eternity. It is a new element, a pure abstraction. The mind loves to hover on that which is endless, and forever the same. People wonder at a steam-boat, the invention of man, managed by man, that makes its liquid path like an iron railway through the sea—I wonder at the sea itself, that vast Leviathan, rolled round the earth, smiling in its sleep, waked into fury, fathomless, boundless, a huge world of water-drops—Whence is it, whither goes it, is it of eternity or of nothing? Strange, ponderous riddle, that we can neither penetrate nor grasp in our comprehension, ebbing and flowing like human life, and swallowing it up in thy remorseless womb—what art thou? What is there in common between thy life and ours, who gaze at thee? Blind, deaf and old, thou seest not, hearest not, understandest not; neither do we understand, who behold and listen to thee! Great as thou art, unconscious of thy greatness, unwieldy, enormous, preposterous twin-birth of matter, rest in thy dark, unfathomed cave of mystery, mocking human pride and weakness. Still is it given to the mind of man to wonder at thee, to confess its ignorance, and to stand in awe of thy stupendous might and majesty, and of its own being, that can question thine! But a truce with reflections.

The Pavilion at Brighton is like a collection of stone pumpkins and pepper-boxes. It seems as if the genius of architecture had at once the dropsy and the *megrims*. Anything more fantastical, with a greater dearth of invention, was never seen. The King's stud (if they were horses of taste) would petition against so irrational a lodging.

Brighton stands facing the sea, on the bare cliffs, with glazed windows to reflect the glaring sun, and black pitchy bricks shining like the scales of fishes. The town is however gay with the influx of London visitors—happy as the conscious abode of its sovereign! Everything here appears in motion—coming or going. People at a watering-place may be compared to the flies of a summer; or to fashionable dresses, or suits of clothes walking about the streets. The only idea you gain is, of finery and motion. The road between London and Brighton presents some very charming scenery; Reigate is a prettier English country-town than is to be found anywhere—out of England! As we entered Brighton in the evening, a Frenchman was playing and singing to a guitar. It was a relief to the conversation in the coach, which had been chiefly supported in a nasal tone by a disciple of Mrs. Fry[1] and amanuensis of philanthropy in general. As we heard the lively musician warble, we forgot the land of Sunday-schools and spinning-jennies. The genius of the South had come out to meet us.

We left Brighton in the steam-packet, and soon saw the shores of Albion recede from us. *Out of sight, out of mind.* How poor a geographer is the human mind! How small a space does the imagination take in at once! In travelling, our ideas change like the scenes of a pantomime, displacing each other as completely and rapidly. Long before we touched on French ground, the English coast was lost in distance, and nothing remained of it but a dim mist; it hardly seemed 'in a great pool a swan's nest.'[2] So shall its glory vanish like a vapour, its liberty like a dream!

We had a fine passage in the steam-boat (Sept. 1, 1824). Not a cloud, scarce a breath of air; a moon, and then starlight, till the dawn, with rosy fingers, ushered us into Dieppe. Our fellow-passengers were pleasant and unobtrusive, an English party of the better sort: a Member of Parliament, delighted to escape from 'late hours and bad company;' an English General, proud of his bad French; a Captain in the Navy, glad to enter a French harbour peaceably; a Country Squire, extending his inquiries beyond his paternal acres; the younger sons of wealthy citizens, refined through the strainers of a University-education and finishing off with foreign travel; a young Lawyer, quoting Peregrine Pickle, and divided between his last circuit and projected tour. There was also a young Dutchman, looking mild through his mustachios, and a new-married couple (a French Jew and Jewess) who grew uxorious from the effects of sea-sickness, and took refuge from the qualms of the disorder in paroxysms of tenderness. We had some difficulty in getting into the harbour, and had to wait till morning for the tide. I grew very tired, and laid the blame on the time lost in getting some restive horses on board, but found that if we had set out two hours sooner, we should only have had to wait two hours longer. The doctrine of *Optimism* is a very good and often a very true one in travelling. In advancing up the steps to give the officers our passport, I was prevented by a young man and woman, who said they were before me, and on making a second attempt, an elderly gentleman and lady set up the same claim, because they stood *behind* me. It seemed that a servant was waiting with passports for four. Persons in a certain class of life are so full of their own business and importance, that they imagine everyone else must be aware of it. I hope this is the last specimen I shall for some time meet with of city-manners. After a formal custom-house search, we procured admittance at Pratt's Hotel, where they said they had reserved a bed for a Lady. France is a country where they give *honneur aux Dames*.[3] The window looked out on the bridge and on the river, which reflected the shipping and the houses; and we should have thought ourselves luckily off, but that the bed, which occupied a niche in the sitting-room, had that kind of odour which could not be mistaken for otto of roses.

**Dieppe.**—This town presents a very agreeable and romantic appearance to strangers. It is cut up into a number of distinct divisions by canals, drawbridges, and bastions, as if to intercept the progress of an enemy. The best houses, too, are shut up in close courts and high walls on the same principle, that is, to stand a further siege in the good old times. There are rows of lime-trees on the quay, and some of the narrow streets running from it look like wells. This town is a picture to look at; it is a pity that it is not a nosegay, and that the passenger who ventures to explore its nooks and alleys is driven back again by 'a compound of villainous smells,' which seem to grow out of the ground. In walking the streets, one must take one's nose with one, and that sense is apt to be offended in France as well as in Scotland. Is it hence called in French the *organ of sense?* The houses and the dresses are equally old-fashioned. In France one lives in the imagination of the past; in England everything is new and on an improved plan. Such is the progress of mechanical invention! In Dieppe there is one huge, mis-shapen, but venerable-looking Gothic Church (a theological fixture) instead of twenty new-fangled erections, Egyptian, Greek or Coptic. The head-dresses of the women are much the same as those which the *Spectator* laughed out of countenance a hundred years ago in England, with high plaited crowns, and lappets hanging down over the shoulders. The shape and colours of the bodice and petticoat are what we see in Dutch pictures; the faces of the common people we are familiarized with in Mieris and Jan Steen. They are full and fair like the Germans, and have not the *minced* and peaked character we attribute to the French. They are not handsome, but good-natured, expressive, placid. They retain the look of peasants more than the town's-people with us, whether from living more in the open air, or from greater health and temperance, I cannot say. What I like in their expression (so far) is not the vivacity, but the goodness, the simplicity, the thoughtful resignation. The French are full of gesticulation when they speak; they have at other times an equal appearance of repose and content. You see the figure of a girl sitting in the sun, so still that her dress seems like streaks of red and black chalk against the wall; a soldier reading; a group of old women (with skins as tough, yellow, and wrinkled as those of a tortoise) chatting in a corner and laughing till their sides are ready to split; or a string of children tugging a fishing-boat out of the harbour as evening goes down, and making the air ring with their songs and shouts of merriment (a sight to make Mr. Malthus shudder!). Life here glows, or spins carelessly round on its soft axle. The same animal spirits that supply a fund of cheerful thoughts, break out into all the extravagance of mirth and social glee. The air is a cordial to them, and they drink drams of sunshine. My particular liking to the French is, however, confined to their natural and unsophisticated character. The good spirits 'with which they are clothed and fed,' and which eke out the deficiencies of fortune or good government, are perhaps too much for them, when joined with external advantages, or artificial pretensions. Their vivacity becomes insolence in office; their success, presumption; their gentility, affectation and grimace. But the national physiognomy (taken at large) is the reflection of good temper and humanity. One thing is evident, and decisive in their favour—they do not insult or point at strangers, but smile on them good-humouredly, and answer them civilly.

> Gay, sprightly land of mirth and social ease,
> Pleas'd with thyself, whom all the world can please![4]

Nothing shows the contented soul within, so much as our not seeking for amusement in the mortifications of others: we only envy their advantages, or sneer at their defects, when we are conscious of wanting something ourselves. The customs and employments of the people here have a more primitive and picturesque appearance than in England. Is it that with us everything is made domestic and commodious, instead of being practised in the open air, and subject to the casualties of the elements? For instance, you see the women washing clothes in the river, with their red petticoats and bare feet, instead of standing over a washing-tub. Human life with us is framed and set in comforts: but it wants the vivid colouring, the glowing expression that we meet elsewhere. After all, is not the romantic effect produced partly owing to the novelty of the scene; or do we not attribute to a superiority in others what is merely a greater liveliness of impression in ourselves, arising from curiosity and contrast? If this were all, foreigners ought to be as much delighted with us, but they are not. A man and woman came and sung 'God save the King,' before the windows of the Hotel, as if the French had so much loyalty at present that they can spare us some of it. What an opinion must they have formed of the absurd nationality of the English, to suppose that we can expect them to feel this sort of mock-sentiment towards our King! What English ballad-singer would dream of flattering the French visitors by a song in praise of Louis *le Desiré*⁵ before a Brighton or a Dover Hotel?

As the door opened just now, I saw the lad or *garçon*, who waits on us, going upstairs with a looking-glass, and admiring himself in it. If he is pleased with himself, he is no less satisfied with us, and with everything else.


## CHAPTER XIX*

'As London is to the meanest country town, so is Rome to every other city in the world.'

So said an old friend of mine, and I believed him till I saw it. This is not the Rome I expected to see. No one from being in it would know he was in the place that had been twice mistress of the world. I do not understand how Nicolas Poussin could tell, taking up a handful of earth, that it was 'a part of the ETERNAL CITY.' In Oxford an air of learning breathes from the very walls: halls and colleges meet your eye in every direction; you cannot for a moment forget where you are. In London there is a look of wealth and populousness which is to be found nowhere else. In Rome you are for the most part lost in a mass of tawdry, fulsome *common-places*. It is not the contrast of pig-styes and palaces that I complain of, the distinction between the old and new; what I object to is the want of any such striking contrast, but an almost uninterrupted succession of narrow, vulgar-looking streets, where the smell of garlic prevails over the odour of antiquity, with the dingy, melancholy flat fronts of modern-built houses, that seem in search of an owner. A dunghill, an outhouse, the weeds growing under an imperial arch offend me not; but what has a green-grocer's stall, a stupid English china warehouse, a putrid *trattoria*,¹ a barber's sign, an old clothes or old picture shop or a Gothic palace, with two or three lacqueys in modern liveries lounging at the gate, to do with ancient Rome? No! this is not the wall that Romulus leaped over:

* [*The Morning Chronicle*, Aug. 12, 1825.]

this is not the Capitol where Julius Cæsar fell: instead of
standing on seven hills, it is situated in a low valley: the
golden Tiber is a muddy stream: St. Peter's is not equal to
St. Paul's: the Vatican falls short of the Louvre, as it was in
my time; but I thought that here were works immoveable,
immortal, inimitable on earth, and lifting the soul half way
to heaven. I find them not, or only what I had seen before in
different ways: the Stanzas of Raphael[2] are faded, or no better
than the prints; and the mind of Michael Angelo's figures, of
which no traces are to be found in the copies, is equally absent
from the walls of the Sistine Chapel. Rome is great only in
ruins: the Coliseum, the Pantheon, the Arch of Constantine
fully answered my expectations; and an air breathes round her
stately avenues, serene, blissful, like the mingled breath of
spring and winter, betwixt life and death, betwixt hope and
despair. The country about Rome is cheerless and barren.
There is little verdure, nor are any trees planted, on account
of their bad effects on the air. Happy climate! in which shade
and sunshine are alike fatal. The Jews (I may add while I
think of it) are shut up here in a quarter by themselves. I see
no reason for it. It is a distinction not worth the making. There
was a talk (it being *Anno Santo*[3]) of shutting them up for the
whole of the present year. A soldier stands at the gate, to tell
you that this is the Jews' quarter, and to take anything you
choose to give him for this piece of Christian information. A
Catholic church stands outside their prison, with a Crucifixion
painted on it as a frontispiece, where they are obliged to hear
a sermon in behalf of the truth of the Christian religion every
Good Friday. On the same day they used to make them run
races in the Corso, for the amusement of the rabble (high
and low)—now they are compelled to provide horses for the
same purpose. Owing to the politeness of the age, they no
longer burn them as of yore, and that is something. Religious
zeal, like all other things, grows old and feeble. They treat
the Jews in this manner at Rome (as a local courtesy to St.
Peter), and yet they compliment *us* on our increasing liberality
to the Irish Catholics. The Protestant chapel here stands outside the walls, while there is a British monument[4] to the
memory of the Stuarts, inside of St. Peter's; the tombs in the
English burying-ground were destroyed and defaced not long
ago; yet this did not prevent the Prince Regent from exchanging portraits with the Pope and his Ministers!—'Oh! liberalism—lovely liberalism!' as Mr. Blackwood would say.

From the window of the house where I lodge, I have a view
of the whole city at once: nay, I can see St. Peter's as I lie in
bed of a morning. The town is an immense mass of solid stone-
buildings, streets, palaces, and churches; but it has not the

beauty of the environs of Florence, nor the splendid background of Turin, nor does it present any highly picturesque or commanding points of view like Edinburgh. The pleasantest walks I know are round the Via Sistina, and along the Via di Quattro-Fontane—they overlook Rome from the North-East on to the churches of Santa Maria Maggiore, and of St. John Lateran, towards the gate leading to Naples. As we loitered on, our attention was caught by an open greensward to the left, with foot-paths, and a ruined wall and gardens on each side. A carriage stood in the road just by, and a gentleman and lady, with a little child, had got out of it to walk. A soldier and a girl were seen talking together further on, and a herd of cattle were feeding at their leisure on the yielding turf. The day was close and dry—not a breath stirred. All was calm and silent. It had been cold when we set out, but here the air was soft—of an Elysian temperature, as if the winds did not dare to visit the sanctuaries of the dead too roughly. The daisy sprung beneath our feet—the fruit-trees blossomed within the nodding arches. On one side were seen the hills of Albano, on the other the Claudian gate; and close by was Nero's Golden House, where there were seventy thousand statues and pillars, of marble and of silver, and where senates kneeled, and myriads shouted in honour of a frail mortal, as of a God. Come here, oh man! and worship thine own spirit, that can hoard up, as in a shrine, the treasures of two thousand years, and can create out of the memory of fallen splendours and departed grandeur a solitude deeper than that of desert wildernesses, and pour from the out-goings of thine own thoughts a thunder louder than that of maddening multitudes! No place was ever so still as this; for none was ever the scene of such pomp and triumph! Not far from this are the Baths of Titus; the grass and the poppy (the flower of oblivion) grow over them, and in the vaults below they show you (by the help of a torch) paintings on the ceiling eighteen hundred years old, birds, and animals, a figure of a slave, a nymph and a huntsman, fresh and elegantly foreshortened, and also the place where the Laocoon was discovered[5]. A few paces off is the Coliseum, or Amphitheatre of Titus, the noblest ruin in Rome. It is circular, built of red stone and brick, with arched windows, and the gillyflower and fennel growing on its walls to the very top: one side is nearly perfect. As you pass under it, it seems to raise itself above you, and mingle with the sky in its majestic simplicity, as if earth were a thing too gross for it; it stands almost unconscious of decay, and may still stand for ages—though Mr. Hobhouse has written Annotations upon it![6] There is a hypocritical inscription on it, to say that it has been kept in repair by the Popes, in order to preserve the memory of the martyrs that suffered here in cruel combats with wild beasts. As I have alluded to this subject, I will add that I think the finest stanza in Lord Byron is that where he describes the "Dying Gladiator," who falls and does not hear the shout of barbarous triumph echoing from these very walls:

> He hears it not; his thoughts are far away,
> Where his rude hut beside the Danube lay;
> There are his young barbarians, all at play,
> They and their Dacian mother; he their sire
> Is doom'd to make a Roman holiday.
> When will ye rise, ye Goths? awake and glut your ire!
>
> *Childe Harold* [IV, cxli]

The temple of Vesta is on the Tiber. It is not unlike an hour-glass—or a toad-stool; it is small, but exceedingly beautiful, and has a look of great antiquity. The Pantheon is also as fine as possible. It has the most perfect unity of effect. It was hardly a proper receptacle for the Gods of the Heathens, for it has a simplicity and grandeur like the vaulted cope of Heaven. Compared with these admired remains of former times I must say that the more modern churches and palaces in Rome are poor, flashy, up-start looking things. Even the dome of St. Peter's is for the most part hid by the front, and the Vatican has no business by its side. The sculptures there are also indifferent, and the mosaics, except two—the Transfiguration and St. Jerome, ill chosen. I was lucky enough to see the Pope here on Easter Sunday. He seems a harmless, infirm, fretful old man. I confess I should feel little ambition to be at the head of a procession, at which the ignorant stare, the better informed smile. I was also lucky enough to see St. Peter's illuminated to the very top (a project of Michael Angelo's) in the evening. It was finest at first, as the kindled lights blended with the fading twilight. It seemed doubtful whether it were an artificial illumination, the work of carpenters and torch-bearers, or the reflection of an invisible sun. One half of the cross shone with the richest gold, and rows of lamps gave light as from a sky. At length a shower of fairy lights burst out at a signal in all directions, and covered the whole building. It looked better at a distance than when we went nearer it. It continued blazing all night. What an effect it must have upon the country round! Now and then a life or so is lost in lighting up the huge fabric, but what is this to the glory of the church and the salvation of souls, to which it no doubt tends? I can easily conceive some of the wild groups that I saw in the streets the following day to have been led by delight and wonder from their mountain-haunts, or even from the bandits' cave, to worship at this new starry glory, rising from the earth. The whole of the immense space before St. Peter's was in the afternoon crowded with people to see the Pope give his benediction. The rich dresses of the country people, the strong features and orderly behaviour of all, gave this assemblage a decided superiority over anything of the kind I had seen in England. I did not hear the *Miserere* which is chanted by the Priests and sung by a single voice (I understand like an angel's) in a dim religious light in the Sistine Chapel; nor did I see the exhibition of the relics, at which I was told all the beauty of Rome was present. It is something even to miss such things. After all, St. Peter's does not seem to me the chief boast or most imposing display of the Catholic religion. Old Melrose Abbey, battered to pieces and in ruins, as it is, impresses me much more than the collective pride and pomp of Michael Angelo's great work. Popery is here at home, and may strut and swell and deck itself out as it pleases, on the spot and for the occasion. It is the pageant of an hour. But to stretch out its arm fifteen hundred miles, to create a voice in the wilderness, to have left its monuments standing by the Teviot-side, or to send the midnight hymn through the shades of Vallombrosa, or to make it echo among Alpine solitudes, that is faith, and that is power. The rest is a puppet-show! I am no admirer of Pontificals, but I am a slave to the picturesque. The Priests talking together in St. Peter's, or the common people kneeling at the altars, make groups that shame all art. The inhabitants of the city have something French about them—something of the cook's and the milliner's shop—something pert, gross, and cunning; but the Roman peasants redeem the credit of their golden sky. The young women that come here from Gensano and Albano, and that are known by their scarlet bodices and white head-dresses and handsome good-humoured faces, are the finest specimens I have ever seen of human nature. They are like creatures that have breathed the air of Heaven, till the sun has ripened them into perfect beauty, health, and goodness. They are universally admired in Rome. The English women that you see, though pretty, are pieces of dough to them. Little troops and whole families, men, women, and children, from the Campagna and neighbouring districts of Rome, throng the streets during Easter and Lent, who come to visit the shrine of some favourite Saint, repeating their *Aves* aloud, and telling their beads with all the earnestness imaginable. Popery is no farce to them. They surely think St. Peter's is the way to Heaven. You even see priests counting their beads, and looking grave. If they can contrive to get possession of this world for themselves, and give the laity the reversion of the next, were it only in imagination, something is to be said for the exchange.

I only hate half-way houses in religion or politics, that take from us all the benefits of ignorance and superstition, and give us none of the advantages of liberty or philosophy in return. Thus I hate Princes who usurp the thrones of others, and would almost give them back, sooner than allow the rights of the people. Once more, how does that monument to the Stuarts happen to be stuck up in the side-aisle of St. Peter's? I would ask the person who placed it there, how many Georges there have been since James III? His ancestor makes but an ambiguous figure beside the posthumous group—

So sit two Kings of Brentford on one throne![7]

The only thing unpleasant in the motley assemblage of persons at Rome, is the number of pilgrims with their greasy oil-skin cloaks. They are a dirty, disgusting set, with a look of sturdy hypocrisy about them. The Pope (*pro forma*)[8] washes their feet; the Nuns, when they come, have even a less delicate office to perform. Religion, in the depth of its humility, ought not to forget decorum. But I am a traveller, and not a reformer. [. . .]

# Of Persons One Would
# Wish To Have Seen *

*Come like shadows—so depart.*[1]

L[AMB] IT WAS, I think, who suggested this subject, as well as the defence of Guy Faux,[2] which I urged him to execute. As, however, he would undertake neither, I suppose I must do both—a task for which he would have been much fitter, no less from the temerity than the felicity of his pen—

> Never so sure our rapture to create
> As when it touch'd the brink of all we hate.[3]

Compared with him I shall, I fear, make but a commonplace piece of business of it; but I should be loth the idea was entirely lost, and besides I may avail myself of some hints of his in the progress of it. I am sometimes, I suspect, a better reporter of the ideas of other people than expounder of my own. I pursue the one too far into paradox or mysticism; the others I am not bound to follow farther than I like, or than seems fair and reasonable.

On the question being started, A[yrton][4] said, 'I suppose the two first persons you would choose to see would be the two greatest names in English literature, Sir Isaac Newton and Mr. Locke?' In this A[yrton], as usual, reckoned without his host. Everyone burst out a laughing at the expression of L[amb]'s face, in which impatience was restrained by courtesy. 'Yes, the greatest names,' he stammered out hastily, 'but they were not persons—not persons.'—'Not persons?' said A[yrton], looking wise and foolish at the same time, afraid his triumph might be premature. 'That is,' rejoined L[amb], 'not characters, you know. By Mr. Locke and Sir Isaac New-

* [*New Monthly Magazine*, Jan. 1826. The speaker's names were established by Howe; but Hazlitt dramatizes—he may fuse one character with another or transpose a point of view (see correspondence in the *Times Literary Supplement*, Feb. 27 to June 12, 1953).]

:on, you mean the *Essay on the Human Understanding*, and
:he *Principia*, which we have to this day. Beyond their con-
:ents there is nothing personally interesting in the men. But
what we want to see anyone *bodily* for, is when there is some-
:hing peculiar, striking in the individuals, more than we can
earn from their writings, and yet are curious to know. I dare
say Locke and Newton were very like Kneller's portraits of
:hem. But who could paint Shakespeare?'—'Ay,' retorted
A[yrton], 'there it is; then I suppose you would prefer seeing
him and Milton instead?'—'No,' said L[amb], 'neither. I have
seen so much of Shakespeare on the stage and on book-stalls,
n frontispieces and on mantle-pieces, that I am quite tired of
:he everlasting repetition: and as to Milton's face, the impressions that have come down to us of it I do not like; it is too
starched and puritanical; and I should be afraid of losing
some of the manna of his poetry in the leaven of his countenance and the precisian's band and gown.'—'I shall guess no
more,' said A[yrton]. 'Who is it, then, you would like to see
"in his habit as he lived,"[5] if you had your choice of the whole
range of English literature?' L[amb] then named Sir Thomas
Browne and Fulke Greville, the friend of Sir Philip Sidney,
as the two worthies whom he should feel the greatest pleasure
:o encounter on the floor of his apartment in their night-gown
and slippers, and to exchange friendly greeting with them.
At this A[yrton] laughed outright, and conceived L[amb] was
esting with him; but as no one followed his example, he
:hought there might be something in it, and waited for an
explanation in a state of whimsical suspense. L[amb] then
(as well as I can remember a conversation that passed twenty
years ago—how time slips!) went on as follows. 'The reason
why I pitch upon these two authors is, that their writings are
riddles, and they themselves the most mysterious of personages. They resemble the soothsayers of old, who dealt in dark
hints and doubtful oracles; and I should like to ask them the
meaning of what no mortal but themselves, I should suppose,
can fathom. There is Dr. Johnson, I have no curiosity, no
strange uncertainty about him: he and Boswell together have
pretty well let me into the secret of what passed through his
mind. He and other writers like him are sufficiently explicit:
my friends, whose repose I should be tempted to disturb
(were it in my power) are implicit, inextricable, inscrutable.

> And call up him who left half-told
> The story of Cambuscan bold.[6]

When I look at that obscure but gorgeous prose-composition
(the *Urn-burial*) I seem to myself to look into a deep abyss,

at the bottom of which are hid pearls and rich treasure; or it is
like a stately labyrinth of doubt and withering speculation,
and I would invoke the spirit of the author to lead me through
it. Besides, who would not be curious to see the lineaments
of a man who, having himself been twice married, wished
that mankind were propagated like trees![7] As to Fulke Greville, he is like nothing but one of his own "Prologues spoken
by the ghost of an old king of Ormus," a truly formidable
and inviting personage: his style is apocalyptical, cabalistical,
a knot worthy of such an apparition to untie; and for the
unravelling a passage or two, I would stand the brunt of an
encounter with so portentous a commentator!'—'I am afraid
in that case,' said A[yrton], 'that if the mystery were once
cleared up, the merit might be lost;'—and turning to me,
whispered a friendly apprehension, that while L[amb] continued to admire these old crabbed authors, he would never
become a popular writer. Dr. Donne was mentioned as a
writer of the same period, with a very interesting countenance,
whose history was singular, and whose meaning was often
quite as *uncomeatable*, without a personal citation from the
dead, as that of any of his contemporaries. The volume was
produced; and while someone was expatiating on the exquisite
simplicity and beauty of the portrait prefixed to the old edition, A[yrton] got hold of the poetry, and exclaiming 'What
have we here?' read the following:

> Here lies a She-Sun and a He-Moon there,
> She gives the best light to his sphere,
> Or each is both and all, and so
> They unto one another nothing owe.[8]

There was no resisting this, till L[amb], seizing the volume,
turned to the beautiful 'Lines to his Mistress,' dissuading her
from accompanying him abroad, and read them with suffused
features and a faltering tongue.

> By our first strange and fatal interview,
> By all desires which thereof did ensue,
> By our long starving hopes, by that remorse
> Which my words' masculine persuasive force
> Begot in thee, and by the memory
> Of hurts, which spies and rivals threaten'd me,
> I calmly beg. But by thy father's wrath,
> By all pains which want and divorcement hath,
> I conjure thee; and all the oaths which I
> And thou have sworn to seal joint constancy
> Here I unswear, and overswear them thus,

Thou shalt not love by ways so dangerous.
Temper, oh fair Love! love's impetuous rage,
Be my true mistress still, not my feign'd Page;
I'll go, and, by thy kind leave, leave behind
Thee, only worthy to nurse in my mind
Thirst to come back; oh, if thou die before,
My soul from other lands to thee shall soar.
Thy (else Almighty) beauty cannot move
Rage from the seas, nor thy love teach them love,
Nor tame wild Boreas' harshness; thou has read
How roughly he in pieces shiver'd
Fair Orithea, whom he swore he lov'd.
Fall ill or good, 'tis madness to have prov'd
Dangers unurg'd: Feed on this flattery,
That absent lovers one with th' other be.
Dissemble nothing, not a boy; nor change
Thy boy's habit, nor mind; be not strange
To thyself only. All will spy in thy face
A blushing, womanly, discovering grace.
Richly cloth'd apes are called apes, and as soon
Eclips'd as bright we call the moon the moon.
Men of France, changeable cameleons,
Spittles of diseases, shops of fashions,
Love's fuellers, and the rightest company
Of players, which upon the world's stage be,
Will quickly know thee. . . .⁹ O stay here! for thee
England is only a worthy gallery,
To walk in expectation; till from thence
Our greatest King call thee to his presence.
When I am gone, dream me some happiness,
Nor let thy looks our long hid love confess,
Nor praise, nor dispraise me; nor bless, nor curse
Openly love's force, nor in bed fright thy nurse
With midnight startings, crying out, Oh, oh,
Nurse, oh, my love is slain, I saw him go
O'er the white Alps alone; I saw him, I,
Assail'd, fight, taken, stabb'd, bleed, fall, and die.
Augur me better chance, except dread Jove
Think it enough for me to have had thy love.

Someone then inquired of L[amb] if we could not see from
the window the Temple-walk in which Chaucer used to take
his exercise; and on his name being put to the vote, I was
pleased to find that there was a general sensation in his favour
in all but A[yrton], who said something about the ruggedness
of the metre, and even objected to the quaintness of the
orthography. I was vexed at this superficial gloss, pertina-
ciously reducing everything to its own trite level, and asked
'if he did not think it would be worth while to scan the eye
that had first greeted the Muse in that dim twilight and early

dawn of English literature; to see the head, round which the visions of fancy must have played like gleams of inspiration or a sudden glory; to watch those lips that "lisped in numbers, for the numbers came"[10]—as by a miracle, or as if the dumb should speak? Nor was it alone that he had been the first to tune his native tongue (however imperfectly to modern ears); but he was himself a noble, manly character, standing before his age and striving to advance it; a pleasant humourist withal, who has not only handed down to us the living manners of his time, but had, no doubt, store of curious and quaint devices, and would make as hearty a companion as Mine Host of Tabard. His interview with Petrarch is fraught with interest. Yet I would rather have seen Chaucer in company with the author of the *Decameron*,[11] and have heard them exchange their best stories together, the "Squire's Tale" against the "Story of the Falcon," the "Wife of Bath's Prologue" against the "Adventures of Friar Albert." How fine to see the high mysterious brow which learning then wore, relieved by the gay, familiar tone of men of the world, and by the courtesies of genius. Surely, the thoughts and feelings which passed through the minds of these great revivers of learning, these Cadmuses[12] who sowed the teeth of letters, must have stamped an expression on their features, as different from the moderns as their books, and well worth the perusal. Dante,' I continued, 'is as interesting a person as his own Ugolino,[13] one whose lineaments curiosity would as eagerly devour in order to penetrate his spirit, and the only one of the Italian poets I should care much to see. There is a fine portrait of Ariosto by no less a hand than Titian's; light, Moorish, spirited, but not answering our idea. The same artist's large colossal profile of Peter Aretine is the only likeness of the kind that has the effect of conversing with "the mighty dead," and this is truly spectral, ghastly, necromantic.' L[amb] put it to me if I should like to see Spenser as well as Chaucer; and I answered without hesitation, 'No'; for that his beauties were ideal, visionary, not palpable or personal, and therefore connected with less curiosity about the man. His poetry was the essence of romance, a very halo round the bright orb of fancy; and the bringing in the individual might dissolve the charm. No tones of voice could come up to the mellifluous cadence of his verse; no form but of a winged angel could vie with the airy shapes he has described. He was (to our apprehensions) rather "a creature of the element, that lived in the rainbow and played in the plighted clouds,"[14] than an ordinary mortal. Or if he did appear, I should wish it to be as a mere

vision, like one of his own pageants, and that he should pass
by unquestioned like a dream or sound—

> *That* was Arion crown'd:
> So went he playing on the wat'ry plain![15]

Captain B.[16] muttered something about Columbus, and
M. C.[17] hinted at the Wandering Jew; but the last was set
aside as spurious, and the first made over to the New World.

'I should like,' said Miss L[amb], 'to have seen Pope talking
with Patty Blount;[18] and I *have* seen Goldsmith.' Everyone
turned round to look at Miss L[amb], as if by so doing they
too could get a sight of Goldsmith.

'Where,' asked a harsh croaking voice,[19] 'was Dr. Johnson
in the years 1745–6? He did not write anything that we know
of, nor is there any account of him in Boswell during those
two years.[20] Was he in Scotland with the Pretender? He seems
to have passed through the scenes in the Highlands in company with Boswell many years after "with lack-lustre eye,"
yet as if they were familiar to him, or associated in his mind
with interests that he durst not explain. If so, it would be an
additional reason for my liking him; and I would give something to have seen him seated in the tent with the youthful
Majesty of Britain, and penning the Proclamation to all true
subjects and adherents of the legitimate Government.'

'I thought,' said A[yrton], turning short round upon L[amb],
'that you of the Lake School did not like Pope?'—'Not like
Pope! My dear sir, you must be under a mistake—I can read
him over and over for ever!'—'Why certainly, the "Essay on
Man" must be allowed to be a masterpiece.'—'It may be so,
but I seldom look into it.'—'Oh! then it's his Satires you admire?'—'No, not his Satires, but his friendly Epistles and his
compliments.'—'Compliments! I did not know he ever made
any.'—'The finest,' said L[amb], 'that were ever paid by the
wit of man. Each of them is worth an estate for life—nay,
is an immortality. There is that superb one to Lord Cornbury:

> Despise low joys, low gains;
> Disdain whatever Cornbury disdains;
> Be virtuous, and be happy for your pains.[21]

'Was there ever more artful insinuation of idolatrous praise?
And then that noble apotheosis of his friend Lord Mansfield
(however little deserved), when, speaking of the House of
Lords, he adds—

> Conspicuous scene! another yet is nigh,
> (More silent far) where kings and poets lie;
> Where Murray (long enough his country's pride)
> Shall be no more than Tully or than Hyde![22]

'And with what a fine turn of indignant flattery he addresses
Lord Bolingbroke—

> Why rail they then, if but one wreath of mine,
> Oh! all accomplish'd St. John, deck thy shrine?[23]

'Or turn,' continued L[amb], with a slight hectic on his
cheek and his eye glistening, 'to his list of early friends:

> But why then publish? Granville the polite,
> And knowing Walsh, would tell me I could write;
> Well-natured Garth inflamed with early praise,
> And Congreve loved and Swift endured my lays:
> The courtly Talbot, Somers, Sheffield read,
> Ev'n mitred Rochester would nod the head;
> And St. John's self (great Dryden's friend before)
> Received with open arms one poet more.
> Happy my studies, if by these approved!
> Happier their author, if by these beloved!
> From these the world will judge of men and books,
> Not from the Burnets, Oldmixons, and Cooks.'[24]

Here his voice totally failed him, and throwing down the
book, he said, 'Do you think I would not wish to have been
friends with such a man as this?'

'What say you to Dryden?'—'He rather made a show of
himself, and courted popularity in that lowest temple of Fame,
a coffee-house, so as in some measure to vulgarise one's idea
of him. Pope, on the contrary, reached the very *beau ideal*[25]
of what a poet's life should be; and his fame while living
seemed to be an emanation from that which was to circle his
name after death. He was so far enviable (and one would feel
proud to have witnessed the rare spectacle in him) that he
was almost the only poet and man of genius who met with
his reward on this side of the tomb, who realised in friends,
fortune, the esteem of the world, the most sanguine hopes of
a youthful ambition, and who found that sort of patronage
from the great during his lifetime which they would be
thought anxious to bestow upon him after his death. Read
Gay's verses to him on his supposed return from Greece, after
his translation of Homer was finished, and say if you would
not gladly join the bright procession that welcomed him home,
or see it once more land at Whitehall-stairs.'—'Still,' said Miss
L[amb], 'I would rather have seen him talking with Patty

Blount, or riding by in a coronet-coach with Lady Mary Wortley Montagu!'

P[hillips],[26] who was deep in a game of piquet at the other end of the room, whispered to M. C. to ask if Junius would not be a fit person to invoke from the dead. 'Yes,' said L[amb], 'provided he would agree to lay aside his mask.'

We were now at a stand for a short time, when Fielding was mentioned as a candidate: only one, however, seconded the proposition. 'Richardson?'—'By all means, but only to look at him through the glass-door of his back-shop, hard at work upon one of his novels (the most extraordinary contrast that ever was presented between an author and his works), but not to let him come behind his counter lest he should want you to turn customer, nor to go upstairs with him, lest he should offer to read the first manuscript of Sir Charles Grandison, which was originally written in eight and twenty volumes octavo, or get out the letters of his female correspondents, to prove that Joseph Andrews was low.'

There was but one statesman in the whole of English history that anyone expressed the least desire to see—Oliver Cromwell, with his fine, frank, rough, pimply face, and wily policy; and one enthusiast, John Bunyan, the immortal author of the *Pilgrim's Progress*. It seemed that if he came into the room, dreams would follow him, and that each person would nod under his golden cloud, 'nigh-sphered in Heaven,' a canopy as strange and stately as any in Homer.

Of all persons near our own time, Garrick's name was received with the greatest enthusiasm, who was proposed by J[ohn] L[amb]. He presently superseded both Hogarth and Handel, who had been talked of, but then it was on condition that he should act in tragedy and comedy, in the play and the farce, Lear and Wildair and Abel Drugger.[27] What a *sight for sore eyes* that would be! Who would not part with a year's income at least, almost with a year of his natural life, to be present at it? Besides, as he could not act alone, and recitations are unsatisfactory things, what a troop he must bring with him—the silver-tongued Barry, and Quin, and Shuter and Weston, and Mrs. Clive and Mrs. Pritchard, of whom I have heard my father speak as so great a favourite when he was young! This would indeed be a revival of the dead, the restoring of art; and so much the more desirable, as such is the lurking scepticism mingled with our overstrained admiration of past excellence, that though we have the speeches of Burke, the portraits of Reynolds, the writings of Goldsmith, and the conversation of Johnson, to show what people could do at that period, and to confirm the universal testimony to the merits of Garrick; yet, as it was before our time, we have our

misgivings, as if he was probably after all little better than
a Bartlemy-fair actor, dressed out to play Macbeth in a scarlet
coat and laced cocked-hat. For one, I should like to have seen
and heard with my own eyes and ears. Certainly, by all accounts, if anyone was ever moved by the true histrionic
*æstus*,[28] it was Garrick. When he followed the Ghost in
*Hamlet*, he did not drop the sword, as most actors do behind
the scenes, but kept the point raised the whole way round,
so fully was he possessed with the idea, or so anxious not to
lose sight of his part for a moment. Once at a splendid dinner-
party at Lord ———'s, they suddenly missed Garrick, and could
not imagine what was become of him, till they were drawn
to the window by the convulsive screams and peals of laughter
of a young negro boy, who was rolling on the ground in an
ecstasy of delight to see Garrick mimicking a turkey-cock in
the court-yard, with his coat-tail stuck out behind, and in a
seeming flutter of feathered rage and pride. Of our party only
two persons present had seen the British Roscius,[29] and they
seemed as willing as the rest to renew their acquaintance with
their old favourite.

We were interrupted in the hey-day and mid-career of this
fanciful speculation, by a grumbler in a corner, who declared
it was a shame to make all this rout about a mere player and
farce-writer, to the neglect and exclusion of the fine old dramatists, the contemporaries and rivals of Shakespeare. L[amb]
said he had anticipated this objection when he had named
the author of Mustapha and Alaham; and out of caprice
insisted upon keeping him to represent the set, in preference
to the wild hair-brained enthusiast Kit Marlowe; to the sexton
of St. Ann's, Webster, with his melancholy yew-trees and
death's-heads; to Dekker, who was but a garrulous proser;
to the voluminous Heywood; and even to Beaumont and
Fletcher, whom we might offend by complimenting the wrong
author on their joint productions. Lord Brook, on the contrary, stood quite by himself, or in Cowley's words, was 'a
vast species alone.' Someone hinted at the circumstance of his
being a lord, which rather startled L[amb], but he said a *ghost*
would perhaps dispense with strict etiquette, on being regularly addressed by his title. Ben Jonson divided our suffrages
pretty equally. Some were afraid he would begin to traduce
Shakespeare, who was not present to defend himself. 'If he
grows disagreeable,' it was whispered aloud, 'there is H[azlitt]
can match him.' At length, his romantic visit to Drummond
of Hawthornden was mentioned, and turned the scale in his
favour.

L[amb] inquired if there was anyone that was hanged that

I would choose to mention? And I answered, Eugene Aram.[*][30] The name of the 'Admirable Crichton'[31] was suddenly started as a splendid example of *waste* talents, so different from the generality of his countrymen. This choice was mightily approved by a North-Briton present, who declared himself descended from that prodigy of learning and accomplishment, and said he had family-plate in his possession as vouchers for the fact, with the initials A. C.—*Admirable Crichton!* R[ickman][32] laughed or rather roared as heartily at this as I should think he has done for many years.

The last-named Mitre-courtier[†] then wished to know whether there were any metaphysicians to whom one might be tempted to apply the wizard spell? I replied, there were only six in modern times deserving the name—Hobbes, Berkeley, Butler, Hartley, Hume, Leibnitz; and perhaps Jonathan Edwards,[33] a Massachusets man.[‡] As to the French, who talked fluently of having *created* this science, there was not a title in any of their writings, that was not to be found literally in the authors I had mentioned. (Horne Tooke, who might have a claim to come in under the head of Grammar, was still living.[34]) None of these names seemed to excite much interest, and I did not plead for the re-appearance of those who might be thought best fitted by the abstracted nature of their studies for their present spiritual and disembodied state, and who, even while on this living stage, were nearly divested of common flesh and blood. As A[yrton] with an uneasy fidgetty face was about to put some question about Mr. Locke and Dugald Stewart, he was prevented by M. C. who observed, 'If C[oleridge] was here, he would undoubtedly be for having up those profound and redoubted scholiasts, Thomas Aquinas and Duns Scotus.' I said this might be fair enough in him who had read or fancied he had read the original works, but I did not see how we could have any right to call up these

[*] See Newgate Calendar for 1758. [w. h.]

[†] L[amb] at this time occupied chambers in Mitre-court, Fleet Street. [w. h.]

[‡] Lord Bacon is not included in this list, nor do I know where he should come in. It is not easy to make room for him and his reputation together. This great and celebrated man in some of his works recommends it to pour a bottle of claret into the ground of a morning, and to stand over it, inhaling the perfumes. So he sometimes enriched the dry and barren soil of speculation with the fine aromatic spirit of his genius. His *Essays* and his *Advancement of Learning* are works of vast depth and scope of observation. The last, though it contains no positive discoveries, is a noble chart of the human intellect, and a guide to all future inquiries. [w. h.]

authors to give an account of themselves in person, till we had looked into their writings.

By this time it should seem that some rumour of our whimsical deliberation had got wind, and had disturbed the *irritabile genus*[35] in their shadowy abodes, for we received messages from several candidates that we had just been thinking of. Gray declined our invitation, though he had not yet been asked: Gay offered to come and bring in his hand the Duchess of Bolton, the original Polly:[36] Steele and Addison left their cards as Captain Sentry and Sir Roger de Coverley: Swift came in and sat down without speaking a word, and quitted the room as abruptly: Otway and Chatterton were seen lingering on the opposite side of the Styx, but could not muster enough between them to pay Charon his fare: Thomson fell asleep in the boat, and was rowed back again—and Burns sent a low fellow, one John Barleycorn, an old companion of his who had conducted him to the other world, to say that he had during his lifetime been drawn out of his retirement as a show, only to be made an exciseman of, and that he would rather remain where he was. He desired, however, to shake hands by his representative—the hand, thus held out, was in a burning fever, and shook prodigiously.

The room was hung round with several portraits of eminent painters. While we were debating whether we should demand speech with these masters of mute eloquence, whose features were so familiar to us, it seemed that all at once they glided from their frames, and seated themselves at some little distance from us. There was Leonardo with his majestic beard and watchful eye, having a bust of Archimedes before him; next him was Raphael's graceful head turned round to the Fornarina,[37] and on his other side was Lucretia Borgia, with calm, golden locks; Michael Angelo had placed the model of St. Peter's on the table before him; Correggio had an angel at his side; Titian was seated with his Mistress between himself and Giorgione; Guido was accompanied by his own Aurora, who took a dice-box from him; Claude held a mirror in his hand; Rubens patted a beautiful panther (led in by a satyr) on the head; Vandyke appeared as his own Paris, and Rembrandt was hid under furs, gold chains and jewels, which Sir Joshua eyed closely, holding his hand so as to shade his forehead. Not a word was spoken; and as we rose to do them homage, they still presented the same surface to the view. Not being *bona-fide* representations of living people, we got rid of the splendid apparitions by signs and dumb show. As soon as they had melted into thin air, there was a loud noise at the outer door, and we found it was Giotto, Cimabue, and Ghirlandaio, who had been raised from the dead by their earnest desire to see their illustrious successors—

> Whose names on earth
> In Fame's eternal records live for aye!

Finding them gone, they had no ambition to be seen after them, and mournfully withdrew. 'Egad!' said L[amb], 'those are the very fellows I should like to have had some talk with, to know how they could see to paint when all was dark around them?'

'But shall we have nothing to say,' interrogated G[eorge] D[yer],[38] 'to the Legend of Good Women?'—'Name, name, Mr. D[yer],' cried R[ickman] in a boisterous tone of friendly exultation, 'name as many as you please, without reserve or fear of molestation!' D[yer] was perplexed between so many amiable recollections, that the name of the lady of his choice expired in a pensive whiff of his pipe; and L[amb] impatiently declared for the Duchess of Newcastle. [39] Mrs. Hutchinson[40] was no sooner mentioned, than she carried the day from the Duchess. We were the less solicitous on this subject of filling up the posthumous lists of Good Women, as there was already one in the room as good, as sensible, and in all respects as exemplary, as the best of them could be for their lives! 'I should like vastly to have seen Ninon de l'Enclos,'[41] said that incomparable person; and this immediately put us in mind that we had neglected to pay honour due to our friends on the other side of the Channel: Voltaire, the patriarch of levity, and Rousseau, the father of sentiment, Montaigne and Rabelais (great in wisdom and in wit), Molière and that illustrious group that are collected round him (in the print of that subject) to hear him read his comedy of the Tartuffe at the house of Ninon; Racine, La Fontaine, Rochefoucault, St. Evremont, etc.

'There is one person,' said a shrill, querulous voice,[42] 'I would rather see than all these—Don Quixote!'

'Come, come!' said R[ickman]; 'I thought we should have no heroes, real or fabulous. What say you, Mr. L[amb]? Are you for eking out your shadowy list with such names as Alexander, Julius Cæsar, Tamerlane, or Ghengis Khan?'—'Excuse me,' said L[amb], 'on the subject of characters in active life, plotters and disturbers of the world, I have a crotchet of my own, which I beg leave to reserve.'—'No, no! come, out with your worthies!'—'What do you think of Guy Faux and Judas Iscariot?' R[ickman] turned an eye upon him like a wild Indian, but cordial and full of smothered glee. 'Your most exquisite reason!' was echoed on all sides; and A[yrton] thought that L[amb] had now fairly entangled himself. 'Why, I cannot but think,' retorted he of the wistful countenance, 'that Guy Faux, that poor fluttering annual scare-crow of straw and rags, is an ill-used gentleman. I would give something to see him sitting pale and emaciated, surrounded by his matches and his barrels of gunpowder, and expecting the moment that was to transport him to Paradise for his heroic self-devotion; but if I say any more, there is that fellow H[azlitt] will make something of it. And as to Judas Iscariot, my reason is different. I would fain see the face of him, who, having dipped his hand in the same dish with the Son of Man, could afterwards betray him. I have no conception of such a thing; nor have I ever seen any picture (not even Leonardo's very fine one) that gave me the last idea of it.'— 'You have said enough, Mr. L[amb], to justify your choice.'

'Oh! ever right, Menenius,—ever right!'[43]

'There is only one person I can ever think of after this,' continued R[ickman]; but without mentioning a name that once put on a semblance of mortality. 'If Shakespeare was to come into the room, we should all rise up to meet him; but if that person was to come into it, we should all fall down and try to kiss the hem of his garment!'

As a lady present seemed now to get uneasy at the turn the conversation had taken, we rose up to go. The morning broke with that dim, dubious light by which Giotto, Cimabue, and Ghirlandaio must have seen to paint their earliest works; and we parted to meet again and renew similar topics at night, the next night, and the night after that, till that night overspread Europe which saw no dawn. The same event, in truth, broke up our little Congress that broke up the great one.[44] But that was to meet again: our deliberations have never been resumed.

*From*

# The New School
# of Reform *

---

R. What is it you so particularly object to this school? Is there anything so very obnoxious in the doctrine of Utility, which they profess? Or in the design to bring about the greatest possible good by the most efficacious and disinterested means?

S. Disinterested enough, indeed: since their plan seems to be to sacrifice every individual comfort for the good of the whole. Can they find out no better way of making human life run smooth and pleasant, than by drying up the brain and curdling the blood? I do not want society to resemble a *Living Skeleton*, whatever these 'Job's Comforters' may do. They are like the fox in the fable—they have no feeling themselves, and would persuade others to do without it. Take away the *dulce* of the poet, and I do not see what is to become of the *utile*.[1] It is the common error of the human mind, of forgetting the end in the means.

R. I see you are at your *Sentimentalities*[2] again. Pray, tell me, is it not their having applied this epithet to some of your favourite speculations, that has excited this sudden burst of spleen against them?

S. At least I cannot retort this phrase on those printed *circulars* which they throw down areas and fasten under knockers. But pass on for that. Answer me then, what is there agreeable or ornamental in human life that they do not explode with fanatic rage? What is there sordid and cynical that they do not eagerly catch at? What is there that delights others that does not disgust them. What that disgusts others with which they are not delighted? I cannot think that this is owing to

---

* [*Plain Speaker;* written Feb. 1826.]

375

philosophy, but to a sinister bias of mind; inasmuch as a marked deficiency of temper is a more obvious way of accounting for certain things than an entire superiority of understanding. The Ascetics of old thought they were doing God good service by tormenting themselves and denying others the most innocent amusements. Who doubts now that in this (armed as they were with texts and authorities and awful denunciations) they were really actuated by a morose and envious disposition, that had no capacity for enjoyment itself or felt a malicious repugnance to the idea of it in anyone else? What in them took the garb of religion, with us puts on the semblance of philosophy; and instead of dooming the heedless and refractory to hell-fire or the terrors of purgatory, our modern polemics set their disciples in the stocks of Utility, or throw all the elegant arts and amiable impulses of humanity into the Limbo of Political Economy.

R. I cannot conceive what possible connection there can be between the weak and mischievous enthusiasts you speak of, and the most enlightened reasoners of the nineteenth century. They would laugh at such a comparison.

S. Self-knowledge is the last thing which I should lay to the charge of *soi-disant* philosophers; but a man may be a bigot without a particle of religion, a monk or an Inquisitor in a plain coat and professing the most liberal opinions.

R. You still deal, as usual, in idle sarcasms and flimsy generalities. Will you descend to particulars, and state facts before you draw inferences from them?

S. In the first place then, they are mostly Scotchmen—lineal descendants of the Covenanters and Cameronians, and inspired with the true John Knox zeal for mutilating and defacing the carved work of the sanctuary——

R. Hold, hold—this is vulgar prejudice and personality——

S. But it's the fact, and I thought you called for facts. Do you imagine if I hear a fellow in Scotland abusing the Author of Waverley, who has five hundred hearts beating in his bosom, because there is no Religion in his works, and a fellow in Westminster doing the same thing because there is no Political Economy in them, that anything will prevent me from supposing that this is virtually the same Scotch pedlar with his pack of Utility at his back, whether he deals in tape and stays or in drawling compilations of history and reviews?

R. I did not know you had such an affection for Sir Walter——

S. I said the *Author of Waverley*. Not to like him would be not to love myself or human nature, of which he has given so many interesting specimens: though for the sake of that same human nature, I have no liking to Sir Walter. Those 'few and recent writers,' on the contrary, who by their own account 'have discovered the true principles of the greatest happiness to the greatest numbers,'[3] are easily reconciled to the Tory and the bigot, because they here feel a certain superiority over him; but they cannot forgive the great historian of life and manners, because he has enlarged our sympathy with human happiness beyond their pragmatical limits. They are not even 'good haters': for they hate not what degrades and afflicts, but what consoles and elevates the mind. Their plan is to *block out* human happiness wherever they see a practicable opening to it.

R. But perhaps their notions of happiness differ from yours. They think it should be regulated by the doctrine of Utility. Whatever is incompatible with this, they regard as spurious and false, and scorn all base compromises and temporary palliatives.

S. Yes; just as the religious fanatic thinks there is no salvation out of the pale of his own communion, and damns without scruple every appearance of virtue and piety beyond it. Poor David Deans![4] how would he have been surprised to see all his follies—his 'right-hand defections and his left-hand compliances,' and his contempt for human learning, blossom again in a knot of sophists and professed *illuminés!*[5] Such persons are not to be treated as philosophers and metaphysicians, but as conceited sectaries and ignorant mechanics. In neither case is the intolerant and proscribing spirit a deduction of pure reason, indifferent to consequences, but the dictate of presumption, prejudice, and spiritual pride, or a strong desire in the ELECT to narrow the privilege of salvation to as small a circle as possible, and in 'a few and recent writers' to have the whole field of happiness and argument to themselves. The enthusiasts of old did all they could to strike the present existence from under our feet to give us another—to annihilate our natural affections and worldly vanities, so as to conform us to the likeness of God: the modern sciolists offer us Utopia in lieu of our actual enjoyments; for warm flesh and blood would give us a head of clay and a heart of steel, and conform us to their own likeness—'a consummation not very devoutly to be wished!' Where is the use of getting rid of the trammels of superstition and slavery, if we are immediately to be handed over to these new ferrets and inspectors of a *Police-Philosophy;* who pay domiciliary visits to the human mind, catechise an expression, impale a sentiment, put every enjoyment to the rack, leave you not a moment's ease or respite, and imprison all the faculties in a round of cant-phrases—the Shibboleth of a party? They are far from indulging or even tolerating the strain of exulting enthusiasm expressed by Spenser:

What more felicity can fall to creature
Than to enjoy delight with liberty,
And to be lord of all the works of nature?
To reign in the air from earth to highest sky,
To feed on flowers and weeds of glorious feature,
To taste whatever thing doth please the eye?
Who rests not pleased with such happiness,
Well worthy he to taste of wretchedness![6]

Without air or light, they grope their way underground, till
they are made 'fierce with dark keeping':* their attention, confined to the same dry, hard, mechanical subjects, which they
have not the power nor the will to exchange for others, frets
and corrodes; and soured and disappointed, they wreak their
spite and mortification on all around them.

R. I cannot but think your imagination runs away with your
candour. Surely the writers you are so ready to inveigh against
labour hard to correct errors and reform grievances.

S. Yes; because the one affords exercise for their vanity, and
the other for their spleen. They are attracted by the odour of
abuses, and regale on fancied imperfections. But do you suppose they like anything else better than they do the Government? Are they on any better terms with their own families
or friends? Do they not make the lives of everyone they come
near a torment to them, with their pedantic notions and
captious egotism? Do they not quarrel with their neighbours,
placard their opponents, supplant those on their own side of
the question? Are they not equally at war with the rich and
the poor? And having failed (for the present) in their project
of *cashiering kings*, do they not give scope to their troublesome, overbearing humour, by taking upon them to *snub* and
lecture the poor *gratis*? Do they not wish to extend 'the greatest happiness to the greatest numbers,' by putting a stop to
population[8]—to relieve distress by withholding charity, to
remedy disease by shutting up hospitals? Is it not a part of
their favourite scheme, their nostrum, their panacea, to prevent the miseries and casualties of human life by extinguishing
it in the birth? Do they not exult in the thought (and revile
others who do not agree to it) of plucking the crutch from
the cripple, and tearing off the bandages from the agonized
limb? Is it thus they would gain converts, or make an effectual
stand against acknowledged abuses, by holding up a picture
of the opposite side, the most sordid, squalid, harsh, and repulsive, that narrow reasoning, a want of imagination, and a
profusion of bile can make it? There is not enough of evil
already in the world, but we must harden our feelings against

---

* Lord Bacon, in speaking of the *Schoolmen*.[7] [w. h.]

the miseries that daily, hourly, present themselves to our
notice and set our faces against everything that promises to
afford anyone the least gratification or pleasure. This is their
*idea of a perfect commonwealth:* where each member performs his part in the machine, taking care of himself, and no
more concerned about his neighbours, than the iron and wood-
work, the pegs and nails in a spinning-jenny. Good screw!
good wedge! good ten-penny nail! Are they really in earnest,
or are they bribed, partly by their interests, partly by the unfortunate bias of their minds, to play the game into the adversary's hands? It looks like it; and the Government give them
'good *œillades*'9—Mr. Blackwood pats them on the back—Mr.
Canning[10] grants an interview and plays the amiable.—Mr.
Hobhouse keeps the peace. One of them has a place at the
India-House[11]: but then nothing is said against the India-
House, though the poor and pious Old Lady sweats and almost swoons at the conversations which her walls are doomed
to hear, but of which she is ashamed to complain. One triumph of the *School* is to throw Old Ladies into hysterics!*
The obvious (I should still hope not the intentional) effect of
the *Westminster*[13] tactics is to put every volunteer on the same
side *hors de combat*,[14] who is not a zealot of the strictest sect
of those they call Political Economists; to come behind you
with dastard, cold-blooded malice, and trip up the heels of
those stragglers whom their friends and patrons in the *Quarterly* have left still standing; to strip the cause of Reform (out
of seeming affection to it) of everything like a *misalliance*
with elegance, taste, decency, common sense, or polite literature (as their fellow labourers in the same vineyard had
previously endeavoured to do out of acknowledged hatred)—
to disgust the friends of humanity, to cheer its enemies; and
for the sake of indulging their unbridled dogmatism, envy and
uncharitableness, to leave nothing intermediate between the
Ultra-Toryism of the courtly scribes and their own Ultra-
Radicalism—between the extremes of practical wrong and impracticable right. Their, *our* antagonists will be very well
satisfied with this division of the spoil: give them the earth,
and anyone who chooses may take possession of the moon for
them!

R. You allude to their attacks on the *Edinburgh Review?*

* This is not confined to the *Westminster.* A certain *Talking
Potatoe*[12] (who is now one of the props of Church and State), when
he first came to this country, used to frighten some respectable old
gentlewomen, who invited him to supper, by asking for a slice of
the 'leg of the Saviour,' meaning a leg of Lamb; or a bit of 'the
Holy Ghost pie,' meaning a pigeon-pie on the table. Ill-nature and
impertinence are the same in all schools. [w. H.]

S. And to their articles on Scott's Novels, on Hospitals,[15] on National Distress, on Moore's *Life of Sheridan,* and on every subject of taste, feeling, or common humanity. Sheridan, in particular, is termed 'an unsuccessful adventurer.' How gently this Jacobin jargon will fall on ears polite! This is what they call attacking principles and sparing persons: they spare the persons indeed of men in power (who have places to give away), and attack the characters of the dead or the unsuccessful with impunity! [. . .]

# On the Feeling
# of Immortality in
# Youth *

> *Life is a pure flame, and we live by an invisible sun within us.* —SIR THOMAS BROWNE.

NO YOUNG MAN believes he shall ever die. It was a saying of my brother's, and a fine one. There is a feeling of Eternity in youth, which makes us amends for everything. To be young is to be as one of the Immortal Gods. One half of time indeed is flown—the other half remains in store for us with all its countless treasures; for there is no line drawn, and we see no limit to our hopes and wishes. We make the coming age our own.

The vast, the unbounded prospect lies before us.[1]

Death, old age, are words without a meaning, that pass by us like the idle air which we regard not. Others may have undergone, or may still be liable to them—we 'bear a charmed life,'[2] which laughs to scorn all such sickly fancies. As in setting out on a delightful journey, we strain our eager gaze forward——

Bidding the lovely scenes at distance hail,—[3]

and see no end to the landscape, new objects presenting themselves as we advance; so, in the commencement of life, we set no bounds to our inclinations, nor to the unrestricted opportunities of gratifying them. We have as yet found no obstacle, no disposition to flag; and it seems that we can go on so for ever. We look round in a new world, full of life, and motion, and ceaseless progress; and feel in ourselves all the vigour and

* [*Monthly Magazine*, March 1827.]

spirit to keep pace with it, and do not foresee from any present symptoms how we shall be left behind in the natural course of things, decline into old age, and drop into the grave. It is the simplicity, and as it were *abstractedness* of our feelings in youth, that (so to speak) identifies us with nature, and (our experience being slight and our passions strong) deludes us into a belief of being immortal like it. Our short-lived connection with existence, we fondly flatter ourselves, is an indissoluble and lasting union—a honeymoon that knows neither coldness, jar, nor separation. As infants smile and sleep, we are rocked in the cradle of our wayward fancies, and lulled into security by the roar of the universe around us—we quaff the cup of life with eager haste without draining it, instead of which it only overflows the more—objects press around us, filling the mind with their magnitude and with the throng of desires that wait upon them, so that we have no room for the thoughts of death. From that plenitude of our being, we cannot change all at once to dust and ashes, we cannot imagine 'this sensible, warm motion, to become a kneaded clod'[4]— we are too much dazzled by the brightness of the waking dream around us to look into the darkness of the tomb. We no more see our end than our beginning: the one is lost in oblivion and vacancy, as the other is hid from us by the crowd and hurry of approaching events. Or the grim shadow is seen lingering in the horizon, which we are doomed never to overtake, or whose last, faint, glimmering outline touches upon Heaven and translates us to the skies! Nor would the hold that life has taken of us permit us to detach our thoughts from present objects and pursuits, even if we would. What is there more opposed to health, than sickness; to strength and beauty, than decay and dissolution; to the active search of knowledge than mere oblivion? Or is there none of the usual advantage to bar the approach of Death, and mock his idle threats; Hope supplies their place, and draws a veil over the abrupt termination of all our cherished schemes. While the spirit of youth remains unimpaired, ere the 'wine of life is drank up,' we are like people intoxicated or in a fever, who are hurried away by the violence of their own sensations: it is only as present objects begin to pall upon the sense, as we have been disappointed in our favourite pursuits, cut off from our closest ties, that passion loosens its hold upon the breast, that we by degrees become weaned from the world, and allow ourselves to contemplate, 'as in a glass, darkly,' the possibility of parting with it for good. The example of others, the voice of experience, has no effect upon us whatever. Casualties we must avoid: the slow and deliberate advances of age we can play at *hide-and-seek* with. We think ourselves too lusty and too nimble for that blear-eyed decrepit old gentleman to catch us. Like the foolish fat scullion, in Sterne, when she hears that Master Bobby is dead, our only reflection is—'So am not I!'[5] The idea of death, instead of staggering our confidence, rather seems to strengthen and enhance our possession and our enjoyment of life. Others may fall around us like leaves, or be mowed down like flowers by the scythe of Time: these are but tropes and figures to the unreflecting ears and overweening presumption of youth. It is not till we see the flowers of Love, Hope, and Joy, withering around us, and our own pleasures cut up by the roots, that we bring the moral home to ourselves, that we abate something of the wanton extravagance of our pretensions, or that the emptiness and dreariness of the prospect before us reconciles us to the stillness of the grave!

> Life! thou strange thing, that hast a power to feel
> Thou art, and to perceive that others are.*

Well might the poet begin his indignant invective against an art, whose professed object is its destruction, with this animated apostrophe to life. Life is indeed a strange gift, and its privileges are most miraculous. Nor is it singular that when the splendid boon is first granted us, our gratitude, our admiration, and our delight should prevent us from reflecting on our own nothingness, or from thinking it will ever be recalled. Our first and strongest impressions are taken from the mighty scene that is opened to us, and we very innocently transfer its durability as well as magnificence to ourselves. So newly found, we cannot make up our minds to parting with it yet and at least put off that consideration to an indefinite term. Like a clown at a fair, we are full of amazement and rapture, and have no thoughts of going home, or that it will soon be night. We know our existence only from external objects, and we measure it by them. We can never be satisfied with gazing; and nature will still want us to look on and applaud. Otherwise, the sumptuous entertainment, 'the feast of reason and the flow of soul,'[7] to which we were invited, seems little better than a mockery and a cruel insult. We do not go from a play till the scene is ended, and the lights are ready to be extinguished. But the fair face of things still shines on; shall we be called away, before the curtain falls, or ere we have scarce had a glimpse of what is going on? Like children, our step-mother Nature holds us up to see the raree-show of the universe; and then, as if life were a burthen to support, lets

* Fawcett's[6] *Art of War*, a poem, 1794. [w. h.]

us instantly down again. Yet in that short interval, what 'brave sublunary things' does not the spectacle unfold; like a bubble at one minute reflecting the universe, and the next, shook to air!—To see the golden sun and the azure sky, the outstretched ocean, to walk upon the green earth, and to be lord of a thousand creatures, to look down giddy precipices or over distant flowery vales, to see the world spread out under one's finger in a map, to bring the stars near, to view the smallest insects in a microscope, to read history, and witness the revolutions of empires and the succession of generations, to hear of the glory of Sidon and Tyre, of Babylon and Susa, as of a faded pageant, and to say all these were, and are now nothing, to think that we exist in such a point of time, and in such a corner of space, to be at once spectators and a part of the moving scene, to watch the return of the seasons, of spring and autumn, to hear

> The stockdove plain amid the forest deep,
> That drowsy rustles to the sighing gale,[8]

to traverse desert wildernesses, to listen to the midnight choir, to visit lighted halls, or plunge into the dungeon's gloom, or sit in crowded theatres and see life itself mocked, to feel heat and cold, pleasure and pain, right and wrong, truth and falsehood, to study the works of art and refine the sense of beauty to agony, to worship fame and to dream of immortality, to read Shakespeare and belong to the same species as Sir Isaac Newton,* to be and to do all this, and then in a moment to be

---

* Lady Wortley Montague[9] says, in one of her letters,[10] that 'she would much rather be a rich *effendi*,[11] with all his ignorance, than Sir Isaac Newton, with all his knowledge.' This was not perhaps an impolitic choice, as she had a better chance of becoming one than the other, there being many rich effendis to one Sir Isaac Newton. The wish was not a very intellectual one. The same petulance of rank and sex breaks out everywhere in these *Letters*. She is constantly reducing the poets or philosophers who have the misfortune of her acquaintance, to the figure they might make at her Ladyship's levee or toilette, not considering that the public mind does not sympathise with this process of a fastidious imagination. In the same spirit, she declares of Pope and Swift, that 'had it not been for the *good-nature* of mankind, these two superior beings were entitled, by their birth and hereditary fortune, to be only a couple of link-boys.'[12] *Gulliver's Travels,* and the *Rape of the Lock,* go for nothing in this critical estimate, and the world raised the authors to the rank of superior beings, in spite of their disadvantages of birth and fortune, *out of pure good-nature!* So, again, she says of Richardson, that he had never got beyond the servants' hall, and was utterly unfit to describe the manners of people of quality; till in the capri-

nothing; to have it all snatched from one like a juggler's ball
or a phantasmagoria; there is something revolting and incredible to sense in the transition, and no wonder that, aided

cious workings of her vanity, she persuades herself that Clarissa is
very like what she was at her age, and that Sir Thomas and Lady
Grandison strongly resembled what she had heard of her mother
and remembered of her father. It is one of the beauties and advantages of literature, that it is the means of abstracting the mind from
the narrowness of local and personal prejudices, and of enabling us
to judge of truth and excellence by their inherent merits alone. Woe
be to the pen that would undo this fine illusion (the only reality),
and teach us to regulate our notions of genius and virtue by the
circumstances in which they happen to be placed! You would not
expect a person whom you saw in a servants' hall, or behind a
counter, to write *Clarissa;* but after he had written the work, to
*pre-judge* it from the situation of the writer, is an unpardonable
piece of injustice and folly. His merit could only be the greater
from the contrast. If literature is an elegant accomplishment, which
none but persons of birth and fashion should be allowed to excel in,
or to exercise with advantage to the public, let them by all means
take upon them the task of enlightening and refining mankind: if
they decline this responsibility as too heavy for their shoulders, let
those who do the drudgery in their stead, however inadequately,
for want of their polite example, receive the meed that is their due,
and not be treated as low pretenders who have encroached on the
province of their betters. Suppose Richardson to have been acquainted with the great man's steward, or valet, instead of the
great man himself, I will venture to say that there was more difference between him who lived in an *ideal world,* and had the genius
and felicity to open that world to others, and his friend the steward,
than between the lacquey and the mere lord, or between those who
lived in different rooms of the same house, who dined on the same
luxuries at different tables, who rode outside or inside of the same
coach, and were proud of wearing or of bestowing the same tawdry
livery. If the lord is distinguished from his valet by anything else,
it is by education and talent, which he has in common with our
author. But if the latter shows these in the highest degree, it is
asked what are his pretensions? Not birth or fortune, for neither
of these would enable him to write a *Clarissa.* One man is born with
a title and estate, another with genius. That is sufficient; and we
have no right to question the genius for want of the *gentility,* unless
the former ran in families, or could be bequeathed with a fortune,
which is not the case. Were it so, the flowers of literature, like
jewels and embroidery, would be confined to the fashionable circles;
and there would be no pretenders to taste or elegance but those
whose names were found in the court list. No one objects to
Claude's Landscapes as the work of a pastrycook, or withholds from
Raphael the epithet of *divine,* because his parents were not rich.
This impertinence is confined to men of letters; the evidence of the
senses baffles the envy and foppery of mankind. No quarter ought
to be given to this *aristocratic* tone of criticism whenever it appears.

by youth and warm blood, and the flush of enthusiasm, the
mind contrives for a long time to reject it with disdain and
loathing as a monstrous and improbable fiction, like a monkey
on a house-top, that is loath, amidst its fine discoveries and
specious antics, to be tumbled headlong into the street, and
crushed to atoms, the sport and laughter of the multitude!

The change, from the commencement to the close of life
appears like a fable, after it has taken place; how should we
treat it otherwise than as a chimera before it has come to
pass? There are some things that happened so long ago, places
or persons we have formerly seen, of which such dim traces
remain, we hardly know whether it was sleeping or waking
they occurred; they are like dreams within the dream of life,
a mist, a film before the eye of memory, which, as we try to
recall them more distinctly, elude our notice altogether. It is
but natural that the lone interval that we thus look back upon
should have appeared long and endless in prospect. There are
others so distinct and fresh, they seem but of yesterday—their
very vividness might be deemed a pledge of their perma-
nence. Then, however far back our impressions may go, we
find others still older (for our years are multiplied in youth);
descriptions of scenes that we had read, and people before our
time, Priam and the Trojan war; and even then, Nestor was
old and dwelt delighted on his youth, and spoke of the race

---

People of quality are not contented with carrying all the external
advantages for their own share, but would persuade you that all
the intellectual ones are packed up in the same bundle. Lord Byron
was a later instance of this double and unwarrantable style of pretension—*monstrum ingens, biforme*.[13] He could not endure a lord
who was not a wit, nor a poet who was not a lord. Nobody but
himself answered to his own standard of perfection. Mr. Moore
carries a proxy in his pocket from some noble persons to estimate
literary merit by the same rule. Lady Mary calls Fielding names,
but she afterwards makes atonement by doing justice to his frank
free, hearty nature, where she says 'his spirits gave him raptures
with his cook-maid, and cheerfulness when he was starving in a
garret, and his happy constitution made him forget everything when
he was placed before a venison-pasty or over a flask of cham-
pagne.'[14] She does not want shrewdness and spirit when her petulance and conceit do not get the better of her, and she has done
ample and merited execution on Lord Bolingbroke. She is, however,
very angry at the freedoms taken with the Great; *smells a rat* in
this indiscriminate scribbling, and the familiarity of writers with
the reading public; and inspired by her Turkish costume, foretells
a French or English revolution as the consequence of transferring
the patronage of letters from the *quality* to the mob, and of supposing that ordinary writers or readers can have any notions in
common with their superiors.

of heroes that were no more—what wonder that, seeing this long line of being pictured in our minds, and reviving as it were in us, we should give ourselves involuntary credit for an indeterminate period of existence? In the Cathedral at Peterborough there is a monument to Mary, Queen of Scots, at which I used to gaze when a boy, while the events of the period, all that had happened since, passed in review before me. If all this mass of feeling and imagination could be crowded into a moment's compass, what might not the whole of life be supposed to contain? We are heirs of the past; we count upon the future as our natural reversion. Besides, there are some of our early impressions so exquisitely tempered, it appears that they must always last—nothing can add to or take away from their sweetness and purity—the first breath of spring, the hyacinth dipped in the dew, the mild lustre of the evening-star, the rainbow after a storm—while we have the full enjoyment of these, we must be young; and what can ever alter us in this respect? Truth, friendship, love, books, are also proof against the canker of time; and while we live, but for them, we can never grow old. We take out a new lease of existence from the objects on which we set our affections, and become abstracted, impassive, immortal in them. We cannot conceive how certain sentiments should ever decay or grow cold in our breasts; and, consequently, to maintain them in their first youthful glow and vigour, the flame of life must continue to burn as bright as ever, or rather, they are the fuel that feed the sacred lamp, that kindle 'the purple light of love,' and spread a golden cloud around our heads! Again, we not only flourish and survive in our affections (in which we will not listen to the possibility of a change, any more than we foresee the wrinkles on the brow of a mistress), but we have a farther guarantee against the thoughts of death in our favourite studies and pursuits, and in their continual advance. Art we know is long; life, we feel, should be so too. We see no end of the difficulties we have to encounter: perfection is slow of attainment, and we must have time to accomplish it in. Rubens complained that when he had just learnt his art, he was snatched away from it: we trust we shall be more fortunate! A wrinkle in an old head takes whole days to finish it properly: but to catch 'the Raphael grace, the Guido air,' no limit should be put to our endeavours. What a prospect for the future! What a task we have entered upon! and shall we be arrested in the middle of it? We do not reckon our time thus employed lost, or our pains thrown away, or our progress slow—we do not droop or grow tired, but 'gain new vigour at our endless task'[15]; and shall Time grudge us the opportunity to finish what we have auspiciously begun, and have formed a sort of compact with nature to achieve? The fame of the great names we look up to is also imperishable; and shall not we, who contemplate it with such intense yearnings, imbibe a portion of ethereal fire, the *divinæ particula auræ*, which nothing can extinguish? I remember to have looked at a print of Rembrandt for hours together, without being conscious of the flight of time, trying to resolve it into its component parts, to connect its strong and sharp gradations, to learn the secret of its reflected lights, and found neither satiety nor pause in the prosecution of my studies. The print over which I was poring would last long enough; why should the idea in my mind, which was finer, more impalpable, perish before it? At this, I redoubled the ardour of my pursuit, and by the very subtlety and refinement of my inquiries, seemed to bespeak for them an exemption from corruption and the rude grasp of Death.*

Objects, on our first acquaintance with them, have that singleness and integrity of impression that it seems as if nothing could destroy or obliterate them, so firmly are they stamped and rivetted on the brain. We repose on them with a sort of voluptuous indolence, in full faith and boundless confidence. We are absorbed in the present moment, or return to the same point—idling away a great deal of time in youth, thinking we have enough and to spare. There is often a local feeling in the air, which is as fixed as if it were of marble; we loiter in dim cloisters, losing ourselves in thought and in their glimmering arches; a winding road before us seems as long as the journey of life, and as full of events. Time and experience dissipate this illusion; and by reducing them to detail, circumscribe the limits of our expectations. It is only as the pageant of life passes by and the masques turn their backs upon us, that we see through the deception, or believe that the train will have an end. In many cases, the slow progress and monotonous texture of our lives, before we mingle with the world and are embroiled in its affairs, has a tendency to aid the same feeling. We have a difficulty, when left to ourselves, and without the resource of books or some more lively pursuit, to 'beguile the slow and creeping hours of time,' and argue that if it moves on always at this tedious snail's-pace, it can never come to an end. We are willing to skip over certain portions of it that separate us from favourite objects, that irritate ourselves at the unnecessary delay. The young are prodigal of life from a superabundance of it; the old are tenacious

---

* Is it not this that frequently keeps artists alive so long, *viz*, the constant occupation of their minds with vivid images, with little of the *wear-and-tear* of the body? [w. h.]

on the same score, because they have little left, and cannot
enjoy even what remains of it.

For my part, I set out in life with the French Revolution,
and that event had considerable influence on my early feelings, as on those of others. Youth was then doubly such. It was
the dawn of a new era, a new impulse had been given to
men's minds, and the sun of Liberty rose upon the sun of Life
in the same day, and both were proud to run their race together. Little did I dream, while my first hopes and wishes
went hand in hand with those of the human race, that long
before my eyes should close, that dawn would be overcast, and
set once more in the night of depotism—'total eclipse!'[16]
Happy that I did not. I felt for years, and during the best part
of my existence, *heart-whole* in that cause, and triumphed in
the triumphs over the enemies of man! At that time, while the
fairest aspirations of the human mind seemed about to be
realised, ere the image of man was defaced and his breast
mangled in scorn, philosophy took a higher, poetry could
afford a deeper range. At that time to read the *Robbers* was
indeed delicious, and to hear

> From the dungeon of the tower time-rent,
> That fearful voice, a famish'd father's cry,[17]

could be borne only amidst the fulness of hope, the crash of
the fall of the strongholds of power, and the exulting sounds
of the march of human freedom. What feelings the death-
scene in *Don Carlos*[18] sent into the soul! In that headlong
career of lofty enthusiasm, and the joyous opening of the prospects of the world and our own, the thought of death crossing
it, smote doubly cold upon the mind; there was a stifling sense
of oppression and confinement, an impatience of our present
knowledge, a desire to grasp the whole of our existence in one
strong embrace, to sound the mystery of life and death, and
in order to put an end to the agony of doubt and dread, to
burst through our prison-house, and confront the King of
Terrors in his grisly palace! . . . As I was writing out this
passage, my miniature-picture when a child lay on the mantle-
piece, and I took it out of the case to look at it. I could perceive few traces of myself in it; but there was the same placid
brow, the dimpled mouth, the same timid, inquisitive glance
as ever. But its careless smile did not seem to reproach me
with having become a recreant to the sentiments that were
then sown in my mind, or with having written a sentence that
could call up a blush in this image of ingenuous youth!

'That time is past with all its giddy raptures.'[19] Since the
future was barred to my progress, I have turned for consola-

tion to the past, gathering up the fragments of my early recollections, and putting them into a form that might live. It is thus, that when we find our personal and substantial identity vanishing from us, we strive to gain a reflected and substituted one in our thoughts: we do not like to perish wholly, and wish to bequeath our names at least to posterity. As long as we can keep alive our cherished thoughts and nearest interests in the minds of others, we do not appear to have retired altogether from the stage, we still occupy a place in the estimation of mankind, exercise a powerful influence over them, and it is only our bodies that are trampled into dust or dispersed to air. Our darling speculations still find favour and encouragement, and we make as good a figure in the eyes of our descendants, nay, perhaps, a better than we did in our life-time. This is one point gained; the demands of our self-love are so far satisfied. Besides, if by the proofs of intellectual superiority we survive ourselves in this world, by exemplary virtue or unblemished faith, we are taught to ensure an interest in another and a higher state of being, and to anticipate at the same time the applauses of men and angels.

> Even from the tomb the voice of nature cries;
> Even in our ashes live their wonted fires.[20]

As we advance in life, we acquire a keener sense of the value of time. Nothing else, indeed, seems of any consequence; and we become misers in this respect. We try to arrest its few last tottering steps, and to make it linger on the brink of the grave. We can never leave off wondering how that which has ever been should cease to be, and would still live on, that we may wonder at our own shadow, and when 'all the life of life is flown,' dwell on the retrospect of the past. This is accompanied by a mechanical tenaciousness of whatever we possess, by a distrust and a sense of fallacious hollowness in all we see. Instead of the full, pulpy feeling of youth, everything is flat and insipid. The world is a painted witch, that puts us off with false shows and tempting appearances. The ease, the jocund gaiety, the unsuspecting security of youth are fled: nor can we, without flying in the face of common sense,

> From the last dregs of life, hope to receive
> What its first sprightly runnings could not give.[21]

If we can slip out of the world without notice or mischance, can tamper with bodily infirmity, and frame our minds to the becoming composure of *still-life*, before we sink into total insensibility, it is as much as we ought to expect. We do not in the regular course of nature die all at once: we have mould-ered away gradually long before; faculty after faculty, attach-ment after attachment, we are torn from ourselves piecemeal while living; year after year takes something from us; and death only consigns the last remnant of what we were to the grave. The revulsion is not so great, and a quiet *euthanasia* is a winding-up of the plot, that is not out of reason or nature.

That we should thus in a manner outlive ourselves, and dwindle imperceptibly into nothing, is not surprising, when even in our prime the strongest impressions leave so little traces of themselves behind, and the last object is driven out by the succeeding one. How little effect is produced on us at any time by the books we have read, the scenes we have witnessed, the sufferings we have gone through! Think only of the variety of feelings we experience in reading an inter-esting romance, or being present at a fine play—what beauty, what sublimity, what soothing, what heart-rending emotions! You would suppose these would last for ever, or at least sub-due the mind to a correspondent tone and harmony—while we turn over the page, while the scene is passing before us, it seems as if nothing could ever after shake our resolution, that 'treason domestic, foreign levy, nothing could touch us far-ther!'²² The first splash of mud we get, on entering the street, the first pettifogging shop-keeper that cheats us out of two-pence, and the whole vanishes clean out of our remembrance, and we become the idle prey of the most petty and annoying circumstances. The mind soars by an effort to the grand and lofty: it is at home in the grovelling, the disagreeable, and the little. This happens in the height and hey-day of our existence, when novelty gives a stronger impulse to the blood and takes a faster hold of the brain (I have known the impres-sion on coming out of a gallery of pictures then last half a day),—as we grow old, we become more feeble and querulous, every object 'reverbs its own hollowness,' and both worlds are not enough to satisfy the peevish importunity and extravagant presumption of our desires! There are a few superior, happy beings, who are born with a temper exempt from every trifling annoyance. This spirit sits serene and smiling as in its native skies, and a divine harmony (whether heard or not) plays around them. This is to be at peace. Without this, it is in vain to fly into deserts, or to build a hermitage on the top of rocks, if regret and ill-humour follow us there: and with this, it is needless to make the experiment. The only true retirement is that of the heart; the only true leisure is the repose of the passions. To such persons it makes little difference whether they are young or old; and they die as they have lived, with graceful resignation.

# On a Sun-Dial *

---

*To carve out dials quaintly, point by point.*
SHAKESPEARE.[1]

*Horas non numero nisi serenas*—is the motto of a sun-dial nea[r]
Venice. There is a softness and a harmony in the words and i[n]
the thought unparalleled. Of all conceits it is surely the mos[t]
classical. 'I count only the hours that are serene.' What a blan[d]
and care-dispelling feeling! How the shadows seem to fade o[n]
the dial-plate as the sky lours, and time presents only a blan[k]
unless as its progress is marked by what is joyous, and all tha[t]
is not happy sinks into oblivion! What a fine lesson is conveye[d]
to the mind—to take no note of time but by its benefits, t[o]
watch only for the smiles and neglect the frowns of fate, t[o]
compose our lives of bright and gentle moments, turning al[-]
ways to the sunny side of things, and letting the rest slip from
our imaginations, unheeded or forgotten! How different from
the common art of self-tormenting! For myself, as I rode along
the Brenta, while the sun shone hot upon its sluggish, slim[y]
waves, my sensations were far from comfortable; but the
reading this inscription on the side of a glaring wall in a[n]
instant restored me to myself; and still, whenever I think of o[r]
repeat it, it has the power of wafting me into the region o[f]
pure and blissful abstraction. I cannot help fancying it to b[e]
a legend of Popish superstition. Some monk of the dark age[s]
must have invented and bequeathed it to us, who, loitering i[n]
trim gardens and watching the silent march of time, as hi[s]
fruits ripened in the sun or his flowers scented the balmy air,
felt a mild languor pervade his senses, and having little to do o[r]
to care for, determined (in imitation of his sun-dial) to efface
that little from his thoughts or draw a veil over it, making o[f]
his life one long dream of quiet! *Horas non numero nisi sere-*
*nas*—he might repeat, when the heavens were overcast and
the gathering storm scattered the falling leaves, and turn
to his books and wrap himself in his golden studies! Out

* [*New Monthly Magazine*, Oct. 1827.]

of some such mood of mind, indolent, elegant, thoughtful this exquisite device (speaking volumes) must have
originated.

Of the several modes of counting time, that by the sun-dial
is perhaps the most apposite and striking, if not the most con-
venient or comprehensive. It does not obtrude its observations,
though it 'morals on the time,'[2] and, by its stationary character, forms a contrast to the most fleeting of all essences. It
stands *sub dio*—under the marble air, and there is some connexion between the image of infinity and eternity. I should
also like to have a sun-flower growing near it with bees fluttering round.* It should be of iron to denote duration, and have
a dull, leaden look. I hate a sun-dial made of wood, which is
rather calculated to show the variations of the seasons, than
the progress of time, slow, silent, imperceptible, chequered
with light and shade. If our hours were all serene, we might
probably take almost as little note of them, as the dial does of
those that are clouded. It is the shadow thrown across, that
gives us warning of their flight. Otherwise, our impressions
would take the same undistinguishable hue; we should scarce
be conscious of our existence. Those who have had none of
the cares of this life to harass and disturb them, have been
obliged to have recourse to the hopes and fears of the next to
enliven the prospect before them. Most of the methods for
measuring the lapse of time have, I believe, been the contrivance of monks and religious recluses, who, finding time
hang heavy on their hands, were at some pains to see how they
got rid of it. The hour-glass is, I suspect, an older invention;
and it is certainly the most defective of all. Its creeping sands
are not indeed an unapt emblem of the minute, countless portions of our existence; and the manner in which they gradually
slide through the hollow glass and diminish in number till not
a single one is left, also illustrates the way in which our years
slip from us by stealth: but as a mechanical invention, it is
rather a hindrance than a help, for it requires to have the
time, of which it pretends to count the precious moments,
taken up in attention to itself, and in seeing that when one
end of the glass is empty, we turn it round, in order that it
may go on again, or else all our labour is lost, and we must
wait for some other mode of ascertaining the time before we
can recover our reckoning and proceed as before. The philosopher in his cell, the cottager at her spinning-wheel must,
however, find an invaluable acquisition in this 'companion of

* Is this a verbal fallacy? Or in the close, retired, sheltered scene
which I have imagined to myself, is not the sun-flower a natural
accompaniment of the sun-dial? [w. h.]

the lonely hour,' as it has been called,* which not only serves
to tell how the time goes, but to fill up its vacancies. What a
treasure must not the little box seem to hold, as if it were
a sacred deposit of the very grains and fleeting sands of life!
What a business, in lieu of other more important avocations,
to see it out to the last sand, and then to renew the process
again on the instant, that there may not be the least flaw or
error in the account! What a strong sense must be brought
home to the mind of the value and irrecoverable nature of the
time that is fled; what a thrilling, incessant consciousness of
the slippery tenure by which we hold what remains of it! Our
very existence must seem crumbling to atoms, and running
down (without a miraculous reprieve) to the last fragment.
'Dust to dust and ashes to ashes' is a text that might be fairly
inscribed on an hour-glass: it is ordinarily associated with the
scythe of Time and a Death's-head, as a *Memento morti;* and
has, no doubt, furnished many a tacit hint to the apprehensive
and visionary enthusiast in favour of a resurrection to another
life!

The French give a different turn to things, less *sombre* and
less edifying. A common and also a very pleasing ornament to
a clock, in Paris, is a figure of Time seated in a boat which
Cupid is rowing along, with the motto, *L'Amour fait passer le
Temps*³—which the wits again have travestied into *Le Temps
fait passer L'Amour*. All this is ingenious and well; but it wants
sentiment. I like a people who have something that they love
and something that they hate, and with whom everything is
not alike a matter of indifference or *pour passer le temps*. The
French attach no importance to anything, except for the moment; they are only thinking how they shall get rid of one
sensation for another; all their ideas are *in transitu*. Everything is detached, nothing is accumulated. It would be a million of years before a Frenchman would think of the *Horas
non numero nisi serenas*. Its impassioned repose and *ideal*
voluptuousness are as far from their breasts as the poetry of
that line in Shakespeare—'How sweet the moonlight sleeps
upon that bank!'⁴ They never arrive at the classical—or the
romantic. They blow the bubbles of vanity, fashion, and
pleasure; but they do not expand their perceptions into refinement, or strengthen them into solidity. Where there is
nothing fine in the groundwork of the imagination, nothing
fine in the superstructure can be produced. They are light,
airy, fanciful (to give them their due)—but when they attempt
to be serious (beyond mere good sense) they are either dull

---

\* Once more, companion of the lonely hour,
   I'll turn thee up again.
         Bloomfield's *Poems—The Widow to her Hour-glass*. [w. h.]

or extravagant. When the volatile salt has flown off, nothing but a *caput mortuum*[5] remains. They have infinite crotchets and caprices with their clocks and watches, which seem made for anything but to tell the hour—gold-repeaters, watches with metal covers, clocks with hands to count the seconds. There is no escaping from quackery and impertinence, even in our attempts to calculate the waste of time. The years gallop fast enough for me, without remarking every moment as it flies; and farther, I must say I dislike a watch (whether of French or English manufacture) that comes to me like a footpad with its face muffled, and does not present its clear, open aspect like a friend, and point with its finger to the time of day. All this opening and shutting of dull, heavy cases (under pretence that the glass-lid is liable to be broken, or lets in the dust or air and obstructs the movement of the watch) is not to husband time but to give trouble. It is mere pomposity and self-importance, like consulting a mysterious oracle that one carries about with one in one's pocket, instead of asking a common question of an acquaintance or companion. There are two clocks which strike the hour in the room where I am. This I do not like. In the first place, I do not want to be reminded twice how the time goes (it is like the second tap of a saucy servant at your door when perhaps you have no wish to get up): in the next place, it is starting a difference of opinion on the subject, and I am averse to every appearance of wrangling and disputation. Time moves on the same, whatever disparity there may be in our mode of keeping count of it, like true fame in spite of the cavils and contradictions of the critics. I am no friend to repeating watches. The only pleasant association I have with them is the account given by Rousseau of some French lady, who sat up reading the *New Heloise* when it first came out, and ordering her maid to sound the repeater, found it was too late to go to bed, and continued reading on till morning.[6] Yet how different is the interest excited by this story from the account which Rousseau somewhere else gives of his sitting up with his father reading romances, when a boy, till they were startled by the swallows twittering in their nests at daybreak, and the father cried out, half angry and ashamed—'Allons, mon fils; je suis plus enfant que toi!'[7] In general, I have heard repeating watches sounded in stage-coaches at night, when some fellow-traveller suddenly awaking and wondering what was the hour, another has very deliberately taken out his watch, and pressing the spring, it has counted out the time; each petty stroke acting like a sharp puncture on the ear, and informing me of the dreary hours I had already passed, and of the more dreary ones I had to wait till morning.

The great advantage, it is true, which clocks have over

watches and other dumb reckoners of time is, that for the most part they strike the hour—that they are as it were the mouth-pieces of time; that they not only point it to the eye, but impress it on the ear; that they 'lend it both an understanding and a tongue.' Time thus speaks to us in an audible and warning voice. Objects of sight are easily distinguished by the sense, and suggest useful reflections to the mind; sounds, from their intermittent nature, and perhaps other causes, appeal more to the imagination, and strike upon the heart. But to do this, they must be unexpected and involuntary—there must be no trick in the case—they should not be squeezed out with a finger and a thumb; there should be nothing optional, personal in their occurrence; they should be like stern, inflexible monitors, that nothing can prevent from discharging their duty. Surely, if there is anything with which we should not mix up our vanity and self-consequence, it is with Time, the most independent of all things. All the sublimity, all the superstition that hang upon this palpable mode of announcing its flight, are chiefly attached to this circumstance. Time would lose its abstracted character, if we kept it like a curiosity or a jack-in-a-box: its prophetic warnings would have no effect, if it obviously spoke only at our prompting, like a paltry ventriloquism. The clock that tells the coming, dreaded hour—the castle bell, that 'with its brazen throat and iron tongue, sounds one unto the drowsy ear of night'[8]—the curfew, 'swinging slow with sullen roar'[9] o'er wizard stream or fountain, are like a voice from other worlds, big with unknown events. The last sound, which is still kept up as an old custom in many parts of England, is a great favourite with me. I used to hear it when a boy. It tells a tale of other times. The days that are past, the generations that are gone, the tangled forest glades and hamlets brown of my native country, the woodsman's art, the Norman warrior armed for the battle or in his festive hall, the conqueror's iron rule and peasant's lamp extinguished, all start up at the clamorous peal, and fill my mind with fear and wonder. I confess, nothing at present interests me but what has been—the recollection of the impressions of my early life, or events long past, of which only the dim traces remain in a smouldering ruin or half-obsolete custom. That *things should be that are now no more*, creates in my mind the most unfeigned astonishment. I cannot solve the mystery of the past, nor exhaust my pleasure in it. The years, the generations to come, are nothing to me. We care no more about the world in the year 2300 than we do about one of the planets. Even George IV is better than the Earl of Windsor. We might as well make a voyage to the moon as think of stealing a march upon Time with impunity.

*De non apparentibus et non existentibus eadem est ratio.*[10]
Those who are to come after us and push us from the stage
seem like upstarts and pretenders, that may be said to exist
*in vacuo,*[11] we know not upon what, except as they are blown
up with vain and self conceit by their patrons among the
moderns. But the ancients are true and *bona-fide* people, to
whom we are bound by aggregate knowledge and filial ties,
and in whom seen by the mellow light of history we feel our
own existence doubled and our pride consoled, as we ruminate
on the vestiges of the past. The public in general, however, do
not carry this speculative indifference about the future to
what is to happen to themselves, or to the part they are to act
in the busy scene. For my own part, I do; and the only wish
I can form, or that ever prompts the passing sigh, would be to
live some of my years over again—they would be those in
which I enjoyed and suffered most!

The ticking of a clock in the night has nothing very interesting nor very alarming in it, though superstition has magni-
fied it into an omen. In a state of vigilance or debility, it preys
upon the spirits like the persecution of a teasing pertinacious
insect; and haunting the imagination after it has ceased in
reality, is converted into the death-watch. Time is rendered
vast by contemplating its minute portions thus repeatedly and
painfully urged upon our attention, as the ocean in its immensity is composed of water-drops. A clock striking with a
clear and silver sound is a great relief in such circumstances,
breaks the spell, and resembles a sylph-like and friendly spirit
in the room. Foreigners, with all their tricks and contrivances
upon clocks and time-pieces, are strangers to the sound of
village-bells, though perhaps a people that can dance may
dispense with them. They impart a pensive, wayward pleasure
to the mind, and are a kind of chronology of happy events,
often serious in the retrospect—births, marriages, and so
forth. Coleridge calls them 'the poor man's only music.'[12] A
village spire in England peeping from its cluster of trees is
always associated in imagination with this cheerful accompaniment, and may be expected to pour its joyous tidings on
the gale. In Catholic countries, you are stunned with the everlasting tolling of bells to prayers or for the dead. In the Apen-
nines, and other wild and mountainous districts of Italy, the
little chapel-bell with its simple tinkling sound has a romantic
and charming effect. The Monks in former times appear to
have taken a pride in the construction of bells as well as
churches; and some of those of the great cathedrals abroad
(as at Cologne and Rouen) may be fairly said to be hoarse
with counting the flight of ages. The chimes in Holland are a
nuisance. They dance in the hours and the quarters. They

leave no respite to the imagination. Before one set has done ringing in your ears, another begins. You do not know whether the hours move or stand still, go backwards or forwards, so fantastical and perplexing are their accompaniments. Time is a more staid personage, and not so full of gambols. It puts you in mind of a tune with variations, or of an embroidered dress. Surely, nothing is more simple than time. His march is straightforward; but we should have leisure allowed us to look back upon the distance we have come, and not be counting his steps every moment. Time in Holland is a foolish old fellow with all the antics of a youth, who 'goes to church in a coranto, and lights his pipe in a cinque-pace.'[13] The chimes with us, on the contrary, as they come in every three or four hours, are like stages in the journey of the day. They give a fillip to the lazy, creeping hours, and relieve the lassitude of country-places. At noon, their desultory, trivial song is diffused through the hamlet with the odour of rashes of bacon; at the close of day they send the toil-worn sleepers to their beds. Their discontinuance would be a great loss to the thinking or unthinking public. Mr. Wordsworth has painted their effect on the mind when he makes his friend Matthew, in a fit of inspired dotage,

> Sing those witty rhymes
> About the crazy old church-clock
> And the bewilder'd chimes.[14]

The tolling of the bells for deaths and executions is a fearful summons, though, as it announces, not the advance of time but the approach of fate, it happily makes no part of our subject. Otherwise, the 'sound of the bell' for Macheath's execution in the *Beggar's Opera*, or for that of the Conspirators in *Venice Preserved*, with the roll of the drum at a soldier's funeral, and a digression to that of my Uncle Toby, as it is so finely described by Sterne, would furnish ample topics to descant upon. If I were a moralist, I might disapprove the ringing in the new and ringing out the old year.

> Why dance ye, mortals, o'er the grave of Time?

St. Paul's bell tolls only for the death of our English kings, or a distinguished personage or two, with long intervals between.*

Those who have no artificial means of ascertaining the

---

* Rousseau has admirably described the effect of bells on the imagination in a passage in the *Confessions*, beginning '*Le son des cloches m'a toujours singulièrement affecté*'[15] etc. [w. h.]

progress of time, are in general the most acute in discerning its immediate signs, and are most retentive of individual dates. The mechanical aids to knowledge are not sharpeners of the wits. The understanding of a savage is a kind of natural almanac, and more true in its prognostication of the future. In his mind's eye he sees what has happened or what is likely to happen to him, 'as in a map the voyager his course.'[16] Those who read the times and seasons in the aspect of the heavens and the configurations of the stars, who count by moons and know when the sun rises and sets, are by no means ignorant of their own affairs or of the common concatenation of events. People in such situations have not their faculties distracted by any multiplicity of inquiries beyond what befalls themselves, and the outward appearances that mark the change. There is, therefore, a simplicity and clearness in the knowledge they possess, which often puzzles the more learned. I am sometimes surprised at a shepherd-boy by the roadside who sees nothing but the earth and sky, asking me the time of day—he ought to know so much better than anyone how far the sun is above the horizon. I suppose he wants to ask a question of a passenger, or to see if he has a watch. Robinson Crusoe lost his reckoning in the monotony of his life and that bewildering dream of solitude, and was fain to have recourse to the notches in a piece of wood. What a diary was his! And how time must have spread its circuit round him, vast and pathless as the ocean!

For myself, I have never had a watch nor any other mode of keeping time in my possession, nor ever wish to learn how time goes. It is a sign I have had little to do, few avocations, few engagements. When I am in a town, I can hear the clock; and when I am in the country, I can listen to the silence. What I like best is to lie whole mornings on a sunny bank on Salisbury Plain, without any object before me, neither knowing nor caring how time passes, and thus 'with light-winged toys of feathered Idleness' to melt down hours to moments. Perhaps some such thoughts as I have here set down float before me like motes before my half-shut eyes, or some vivid image of the past by forcible contrast rushes by me—'Diana and her fawn, and all the glories of the antique world;' then I start away to prevent the iron from entering my soul, and let fall some tears into that stream of time which separates me farther and farther from all I once loved! At length I rouse myself from my reverie, and home to dinner, proud of killing time with thought, nay even without thinking. Somewhat of this idle humour I inherit from my father, though he had not the same freedom from *ennui,* for he was not a metaphysician; and there were stops and vacant intervals in his being which he did not know how to fill up. He used in these cases, and as an obvious resource, carefully to wind up his watch at night, and 'with lack-lustre eye' more than once in the course of the day look to see what o'clock it was. Yet he had nothing else in his character in common with the elder Mr. Shandy. Were I to attempt a sketch of him, for my own or the reader's satisfaction, it would be after the following manner:——but now I recollect, I have done something of the kind once before, and were I to resume the subject here, some bat or owl of a critic, with spectacled gravity, might swear I had stolen the whole of this Essay from myself—or (what is worse) from him! So I had better let it go as it is.

# A Farewell
# to Essay-Writing*†

*This life is best, if quiet life is best!*[1]

FOOD, warmth, sleep, and a book; these are all I at present ask
—the *ultima thule*[2] of my wandering desires. Do you not then
wish for

> A friend in your retreat,
> Whom you may whisper, solitude is sweet?[3]

Expected, well enough—gone, still better. Such attractions are
strengthened by distance. Nor a mistress? 'Beautiful mask! I
know thee!' When I can judge of the heart from the face, of
the thoughts from the lips, I may again trust myself. Instead
of these, give me the robin red-breast, pecking the crumbs at
the door, or warbling on the leafless spray, the same glancing
form that has followed me wherever I have been, and 'done
its spiriting gently'[4]; or the rich notes of the thrush that startle
the ear of winter, and seem to have drunk up the full draught
of joy from the very sense of contrast. To these I adhere and
am faithful, for they are true to me; and, dear in themselves,
are dearer for the sake of what is departed, leading me back
(by the hand) to that dreaming world, in the innocence of
which they sat and made sweet music, waking the promise of
future years, and answered by the eager throbbings of my
own breast. But now 'the credulous hope of mutual minds is
o'er,'[5] and I turn back from the world that has deceived me,
to nature that lent it a false beauty, and that keeps up the
illusion of the past. As I quaff my libations of tea in a morning, I love to watch the clouds sailing from the west, and
fancy that 'the spring comes slowly up this way.'[6] In this
hope, while 'fields are dank and ways are mire,'[7] I follow the

* Written at Winterslow Hut, February 20, 1828. [W. H.]
† [*London Weekly Review*, March 29, 1828.]

same direction to a neighbouring wood, where, having gained the dry, level greensward, I can see my way for a mile before me, closed in on each side by copse-wood, and ending in a point of light more or less brilliant, as the day is bright or cloudy. What a walk is this to me! I have no need of book or companion—the days, the hours, the thoughts of my youth are at my side, and blend with the air that fans my cheek. Here I can saunter for hours, bending my eye forward, stopping and turning to look back, thinking to strike off into some less trodden path, yet hesitating to quit the one I am in, afraid to snap the brittle threads of memory. I remark the shining trunks and slender branches of the birch trees, waving in the idle breeze; or a pheasant springs up on whirring wing; or I recall the spot where I once found a wood-pigeon at the foot of a tree, weltering in its gore, and think how many seasons have flown since 'it left its little life in air.' Dates, names, faces come back—to what purpose? Or why think of them now? Or rather, why not think of them oftener? We walk through life, as through a narrow path, with a thin curtain drawn around it; behind are ranged rich portraits, airy harps are strung— yet we will not stretch forth our hands and lift aside the veil, to catch glimpses of the one, or sweep the chords of the other. As in a theatre, when the old-fashioned green curtain drew up, groups of figures, fantastic dresses, laughing faces, rich banquets, stately columns, gleaming vistas appeared beyond; so we have only at any time to 'peep through the blanket of the past,'[8] to possess ourselves at once of all that has regaled our senses, that is stored up in our memory, that has struck our fancy, that has pierced our hearts—yet to all this we are indifferent, insensible, and seem intent only on the present vexation, the future disappointment. If there is a Titian hanging up in the room with me, I scarcely regard it: how then should I be expected to strain the mental eye so far, or to throw down, by the magic spells of the will, the stone-walls that enclose it in the Louvre? There is one head there of which I have often thought, when looking at it, that nothing should ever disturb me again, and I would become the character it represents—such perfect calmness and self-possession reigns in it! Why do I not hang an image of this in some dusky corner of my brain, and turn an eye upon it ever and anon, as I have need of some such talisman to calm my troubled thoughts? The attempt is fruitless, if not natural; or, like that of the French, to hang garlands on the grave, and to conjure back the dead by miniature pictures of them while living! It is only some actual coincidence, or local association that tends, without violence, to 'open all the cells where memory slept.'[9] I can easily, by stooping over the long-sprent[10] grass and clay-cold clod, recall the tufts of primroses, or purple hyacinths, that formerly grew on the same spot, and cover the bushes with leaves and singing-birds, as they were eighteen summers ago; or prolonging my walk and hearing the sighing gale rustle through a tall, strait wood at the end of it, can fancy that I distinguish the cry of hounds, and the fatal group issuing from it, as in the tale of Theodore and Honoria.[11] A moaning gust of wind aids the belief; I look once more to see whether the trees before me answer to the idea of the horror-stricken grove, and an air-built city towers over their grey tops.

> Of all the cities in Romanian lands,
> The chief and most renown'd Ravenna stands.[12]

I return home resolved to read the entire poem through, and, after dinner, drawing my chair to the fire, and holding a small print close to my eyes, launch into the full tide of Dryden's couplets (a stream of sound), comparing his didactic and descriptive pomp with the simple pathos and picturesque truth of Boccaccio's story, and tasting with a pleasure, which none but an habitual reader can feel, some quaint examples of pronunciation in this accomplished versifier.

> Which when Honoria view'd,
> The fresh *impulse* her former fright renew'd.   [ll. 342–3]

> And made th' *insult*, which in his grief appears,
> The means to mourn thee with my pious tears.
>                    *Sigismunda and Guiscardo.* [668–69]

These trifling instances of the wavering and unsettled state of the language give double effect to the firm and stately march of the verse, and make me dwell with a sort of tender interest on the difficulties and doubts of an earlier period of literature. They pronounced words then in a manner which we should laugh at now; and they wrote verse in a manner which we can do anything but laugh at. The pride of a new acquisition seems to give fresh confidence to it; to impel the rolling syllables through the moulds provided for them, and to overflow the envious bounds of rhyme into time-honoured triplets. I am much pleased with Leigh Hunt's mention[13] of Moore's involuntary admiration of Dryden's free, unshackled verse, and of his repeating *con amore*, and with an Irish spirit and accent, the fine lines—

> Let honour and preferment go for gold,
> But glorious beauty isn't to be sold.[14]

What sometimes surprises me in looking back to the past, is, with the exception already stated, to find myself so little changed in the time. The same images and trains of thought stick by me: I have the same tastes, likings, sentiments, and wishes that I had then. One great ground of confidence and support has, indeed, been struck from under my feet; but I have made it up to myself by proportionable pertinacity of opinion. The success of the great cause, to which I had vowed myself, was to me more than all the world: I had a strength in its strength, a resource which I knew not of, till it failed me for the second time.

> Fall'n was Glenartny's stately tree!
> Oh! ne'er to see Lord Ronald more![15]

It was not till I saw the axe laid to the root, that I found the full extent of what I had to lose and suffer. But my conviction of the right was only established by the triumph of the wrong; and my earliest hopes will be my last regrets. One source of this unbendingness (which some may call obstinacy) is that, though living much alone, I have never worshipped the Echo. I see plainly enough that black is not white, that the grass is green, that kings are not their subjects; and, in such self-evident cases, do not think it necessary to collate my opinions with the received prejudices. In subtler questions, and matters that admit of doubt, as I do not impose my opinion on others without a reason, so I will not give up mine to them without a better reason; and a person calling me names, or giving himself airs of authority, does not convince me of his having taken more pains to find out the truth than I have, but the contrary. Mr. Gifford once said, that 'while I was sitting over my gin and tobacco-pipes, I fancied myself a Leibnitz.'[16] He did not so much as know that I had ever read a metaphysical book— was I therefore, out of complaisance or deference to him, to forget whether I had or not? I am rather disappointed, both on my own account and his, that Mr. Hunt has missed the opportunity[17] of explaining the character of a friend, as clearly as he might have done. He is puzzled to reconcile the shyness of my pretensions with the inveteracy and sturdiness of my principles. I should have thought they were nearly the same thing. Both from disposition and habit, I can *assume* nothing in word, look, or manner. I cannot steal a march upon public opinion in any way. My standing upright, speaking loud, entering a room gracefully proves nothing; therefore I neglect these ordinary means of recommending myself to the good graces and admiration of strangers (and, as it appears, even of philosophers and friends). Why? Because I have other resources, or, at least, am absorbed in other studies and pursuits. Suppose this absorption to be extreme, and even morbid, that I have brooded over an idea till it has become a kind of substance in my brain, that I have reasons for a thing which I have found out with much labour and pains, and to which I can scarcely do justice without the utmost violence of exertion (and that only to a few persons)—is this a reason for my playing off my out-of-the-way notions in all companies, wearing a prim and self-complacent air, as if I were 'the admired of all observers'? or is it not rather an argument (together with a want of animal spirits) why I should retire into myself, and perhaps acquire a nervous and uneasy look, from a consciousness of the disproportion between the interest and conviction I feel on certain subjects, and my ability to communicate what weighs upon my own mind to others? If my ideas, which I do not avouch, but suppose, lie below the surface, why am I to be always attempting to dazzle superficial people with them, or smiling, delighted, at my own want of success?

What I have here stated is only the excess of the common and well-known English and scholastic character. I am neither a buffoon, a fop, nor a Frenchman, which Mr. Hunt would have me to be. He finds it odd that I am a close reasoner and a loose dresser. I have been (among other follies) a hard liver as well as a hard thinker; and the consequences of that will not allow me to dress as I please. People in real life are not like players on a stage, who put on a certain look or *costume*, merely for effect. I am aware, indeed, that the gay and airy pen of the author does not seriously probe the errors or misfortunes of his friends—he only glances at their seeming peculiarities, so as to make them odd and ridiculous; for which forbearance few of them will thank him. Why does he assert that I was vain of my hair when it was black, and am equally vain of it now it is grey, when this is true in neither case? This transposition of motives makes me almost doubt whether Lord Byron was thinking so much of the rings on his fingers as his biographer was. These sort of criticisms should be left to women. I am made to wear a little hat, stuck on the top of my head the wrong way. Nay, I commonly wear a large slouching hat over my eyebrows; and if ever I had another, I must have twisted it about in any shape to get rid of the annoyance. This probably tickled Mr. Hunt's fancy, and retains possession of it, to the exclusion of the obvious truism, that I naturally wear 'a melancholy hat.'[18]

I am charged with using strange gestures and contortions of features in argument, in order to 'look energetic.' One would rather suppose that the heat of the argument produced the extravagance of the gestures, as I am said to be calm at other times. It is like saying that a man in a passion clenches his teeth, not because he is, but in order to seem, angry. Why should everything be construed into air and affectation? With Hamlet, I may say, 'I know not *seems.*'

Again, my old friend and pleasant 'Companion' remarks it, as an anomaly in my character, that I crawl about the Fives-Court like a cripple till I get the racket in my hand, when I start up as if I was possessed with a devil. I have then a motive for exertion; I lie by for difficulties and extreme cases. *Aut Cæsar aut nullus.*[19] I have no notion of doing nothing with an air of importance, nor should I ever take a liking to the game of battledoor and shuttlecock. I have only seen by accident a page of the unpublished Manuscript relating to the present subject, which I dare say is, on the whole, friendly and just, and which has been suppressed as being too favourable, considering certain prejudices against me.

In matters of taste and feeling, one proof that my conclusions have not been quite shallow or hasty, is the circumstance of their having been lasting. I have the same favourite books, pictures, passages that I ever had: I may therefore presume that they will last me my life—nay, I may indulge a hope that my thoughts will survive me. This continuity of impression is the only thing on which I pride myself. Even L[amb], whose relish of certain things is as keen and earnest as possible, takes a surfeit of admiration, and I should be afraid to ask about his select authors or particular friends, after a lapse of ten years. As to myself, anyone knows where to have me. What I have once made up my mind to, I abide by to the end of the chapter. One cause of my independence of opinion is, I believe, the liberty I give to others, or the very diffidence and distrust of making converts. I should be an excellent man on a jury: I might say little, but should starve 'the other eleven obstinate fellows' out. I remember Mr. Godwin writing to Mr. Wordsworth, that 'his [Godwin's] tragedy of Antonio could not fail of success.' It was damned past all redemption.[20] I said to Mr. Wordsworth that I thought this a natural consequence; for how could anyone have a dramatic turn of mind who judged entirely of others from himself? Mr. Godwin might be convinced of the excellence of his work; but how could he know that others would be convinced of it, unless by supposing that they were as wise as himself, and as infallible critics of dramatic poetry—so many Aristotles sitting in judgment on Euripides! This shows why pride is connected with shyness and reserve; for the really proud have not so high an opinion of the generality as to suppose that they can understand them, or that there is any common measure be-

tween them. So Dryden exclaims of his opponents with bitter
disdain—

> Nor can I think what thoughts they can conceive.[21]

I have not sought to make partisans, still less did I dream of
making enemies; and have therefore kept my opinions myself,
whether they were currently adopted or not. To get others to
come into our ways of thinking, we must go over to theirs; and
it is necessary to follow, in order to lead. At the time I lived
here formerly, I had no suspicion that I should ever become
a voluminous writer; yet I had just the same confidence in my
feelings before I had ventured to air them in public as I have
now. Neither the outcry *for* or *against* moves me a jot: I do not
say that the one is not more agreeable than the other.

Not far from the spot where I write, I first read Chaucer's
*Flower and Leaf*,[22] and was charmed with that young beauty,
shrouded in her bower, and listening with ever-fresh delight
to the repeated song of the nightingale close by her—the impression of the scene, the vernal landscape, the cool of the
morning, the gushing notes of the songstress,

> And ayen, methought she sung close by mine ear,[23]

is as vivid as if it had been of yesterday; and nothing can
persuade me that that is not a fine poem. I do not find this
impression conveyed in Dryden's version, and therefore
nothing can persuade me that that is as fine. I used to walk
out at this time with Mr. and Miss L[amb] of an evening, to
look at the Claude Lorraine skies over our heads, melting from
azure into purple and gold, and to gather mushrooms, that
sprung up at our feet, to throw into our hashed mutton at
supper. I was at that time an enthusiastic admirer of Claude,
and could dwell for ever on one or two of the finest prints
from him hung round my little room; the fleecy flocks, the
bending trees, the winding streams, the groves, the nodding
temples, the air-wove hills, and distant sunny vales; and tried
to translate them into their lovely living hues. People then
told me that Wilson was much superior to Claude. I did not
believe them. Their pictures have since been seen together at
the British Institution, and all the world have come into my
opinion. I have not, on that account, given it up. I will not
compare our hashed mutton with Amelia's;[24] but it put us in
mind of it, and led to a discussion, sharply seasoned and well
sustained, till midnight, the result of which appeared some
years after in the *Edinburgh Review*.[25] Have I a better opinion
of those criticisms on that account, or should I therefore main-

tain them with greater vehemence and tenaciousness? Oh no!
Both rather with less, now that they are before the public,
and it is for them to make their election.

It is in looking back to such scenes that I draw my best
consolation for the future. Later impressions come and go,
and serve to fill up the intervals; but these are my standing
resource, my true classics. If I have had few real pleasures or
advantages, my ideas, from their sinewy texture, have been to
me in the nature of realities; and if I should not be able to
add to the stock, I can live by husbanding the interest. As to
my speculations, there is little to admire in them but my admiration of others; and whether they have an echo in time to
come or not, I have learned to set a grateful value on the past,
and am content to wind up the account of what is personal
only to myself and the immediate circle of objects in which
I have moved, with an act of easy oblivion,

And curtain close such scene from every future view.[26]

# The Life
# of Napoleon Buonaparte*

## PREFACE

OF MY OBJECT in writing the LIFE here offered to the public, and of the general tone that pervades it, it may be proper that I should render some account in order to prevent mistakes and false applications. It is true, I admired the man; but what chiefly attached me to him, was his being, as he had been long ago designated, 'the child and champion of the Revolution.' Of this character he could not divest himself, even though he wished it. He was nothing, he could be nothing but what he owed to himself and to his triumphs over those who claimed mankind as their inheritance by a divine right; and as long as he was *a thorn in the side of kings* and kept them at bay, his cause rose out of the ruins and defeat of their pride and hopes of revenge. He stood (and he alone stood) between them and their natural prey. He kept off that last indignity and wrong offered to a whole people (and through them to the rest of the world) of being handed over, like a herd of cattle, to a particular family,[1] and chained to the foot of a legitimate throne. This was the chief point at issue—this was the great question, compared with which all others were tame and insignificant—Whether mankind were, from the beginning to the end of time, born slaves or not? As long as he remained, his acts, his very existence gave a proud and full answer to this question. As long as he interposed a barrier, a gauntlet, and an arm of steel between us and them who alone could set up the plea of old, indefeasible right over us, no increase of power could be too great that tended to shatter this claim to pieces: even his abuse of power and aping the style and title

---

* Vols. I and II published in 1828: III and IV in 1830. Hazlitt's Preface, written in Paris in 1827, first appeared as Chapter 31, the opening chapter of Vol. III; restored as Preface in Howe's edition: see Howe's *Life of Hazlitt*.

of the imaginary Gods of the earth only laughed their pretensions the more to scorn. He did many things wrong and foolish; but they were individual acts, and recoiled upon the head of the doer. They stood upon the ground of their own merits, and could not urge in their vindication 'the right divine of kings to govern wrong;'[2] they were not precedents; they were not exempt from public censure or opinion; they were not softened by prescription, nor screened by prejudice, nor sanctioned by superstition, nor rendered formidable by a principle that imposed them as sacred obligations on all future generations: either they were state-necessities extorted by the circumstances of the time, or violent acts of the will, that carried their own condemnation in their bosom. Whatever fault might be found with them, they did not proceed upon the avowed principle, that 'millions were made for one,' but one for millions; and as long as this distinction was kept in view, liberty was saved, and the Revolution was untouched; for it was to establish it that the Revolution was commenced, and to overturn it that the enemies of liberty waded through seas of blood, and at last succeeded. It is the practice of the partisans of the old school to cry *Vive le Roi, quand même!*[3] Why do not the people learn to imitate the example? Till they do, they will be sure to be foiled in the end by their adversaries, since half-measures and principles can never prevail against whole ones. In fact, Buonaparte was not strictly a free agent. He could hardly do otherwise than he did, ambition apart, and merely to preserve himself and the country he ruled. France was in a state of siege; a citadel in which Freedom had hoisted the flag of revolt against the threat of hereditary servitude; and that in the midst of distraction and convulsions consequent on the sentence of ban and anathema passed upon it by the rest of Europe for having engaged in this noble struggle, required a military dictator to repress internal treachery and headstrong factions, and repel external force. Who then shall blame Buonaparte for having taken the reins of government and held them with a tight hand? The English, who having set the example of liberty to the world, did all they could to stifle it? Or the Continental Sovereigns, who were only acquainted with its principles by their fear and hatred of them? Or the Emigrants, traitors to the name of men as well as Frenchmen? Or the Jacobins, who made the tree of liberty spout nothing but blood? Or its *paper* advocates, who reduce it to a harmless theory? Or its true friends, who would sacrifice all for its sake? The last, who alone have the right to call him to a severe account, will not; for they know that, being but a handful or scattered, they had not the power to effect themselves what they might have recommended to him;

and that there was but one alternative between him and that slavery, which kills both the bodies and the souls of men! There were two other feelings that influenced me on this subject; a love of glory, when it did not interfere with other things, and the wish to see personal merit prevail over external rank and circumstance. I felt pride (not envy) to think that there was one reputation in modern times equal to the ancients, and at seeing one man greater than the throne he sat upon.

## NAPOLEON AND THE LOUVRE*

[ . . . ] On entering the States of Parma, Napoleon at the passage of the Trebbia received envoys from the Prince, suing for peace and his protection. This was granted on condition that the Duke paid two millions in French money, furnished the stores of the army with a quantity of hay and wheat, and supplied 1600 horses for the artillery and cavalry. It was on this occasion also that Napoleon exacted a contribution of works of art to be sent to the Museum at Paris, being the first instance of the kind that occurs in modern history. Parma furnished twenty pictures chosen by the French commissioners, among others the famous St. Jerome of Correggio. The Duke offered £80,000 to be allowed to keep this picture; the opinion of the army-agents was decidedly in favour of acceptance of the money. The General-in-Chief said, there would very soon be an end of the two millions of francs; while the possession of such a masterpiece by the city of Paris would remain a proud distinction to that capital, and would produce other *chefs-d'œuvre* of the same kind. Vain hope! Not a ray of the sentiment or beauty contained in this picture dawned upon a French canvas during the twenty years it remained there, nor ever would to the end of time. A collection of works of art is a noble ornament to a city, and attracts strangers; but works of genius do not beget other works of genius, however they may inspire a taste for them and furnish objects for curiosity and admiration. Correggio, it is said, the author of this inimitable performance, scarcely ever saw a picture. Parma, where his works had been treasured up and regarded with idolatry for nearly three hundred years, had produced no other painter like him. A false inference has been drawn from works of science to works of art, as if there could be a perpetual addition and progression both in one and the other: but science advances because it never loses any of its former results, which are definable and mechanical; whereas art is wholly

* [From Ch. IX, "Campaign in Italy."]

conversant with undefinable and evanescent beauties and can
never get beyond the point to which individual nature and
genius have carried it. The accumulation of models and the
multiplication of schools, after the first rudiments are conquered and the language is as it were learnt, only create indolence, distraction, pedantry, and mediocrity. No age or nation
can ever ape another. The Greek sculptors copied Greek
forms; the Italian painters embodied the sentiments of the
Roman Catholic religion. How is it possible to arrive at the
same excellence without seeing the one or feeling the other?
From the time that men begin to borrow from others instead
of themselves and to study rules instead of nature, the progress
of art ceases. In Italy there has not been a painter worthy of
the name for the last hundred and fifty years! It was not amiss,
in one point of view, that the triumphs of human genius
should be collected together in the Louvre as trophies of
human liberty; or to deck out the stern, gaunt form of the
Republic which was declared incapable of maintaining the
relations of peace and amity with the richest spoils of war:
otherwise these works would make most impression and are
most likely to give a noble and enthusiastic impulse to the
mind in the places which gave them birth and in connexion
with the history and circumstances of those who produced
them—torn from these, they lose half their interest and vital
principle. Besides, the French see nothing but what is French.
Barbarism and rusticity may perhaps be instructed, but false
refinement is incorrigible. They have no turn for the fine arts,
music, poetry, painting. They have indeed caricatured and
ill-coloured the Greek statues, as they have paraphrased the
Greek drama; but that is all. This people are 'born to converse,
to write, and live with ease,' but they are qualified for nothing
that requires the mind to make an arduous effort to soar beyond its ordinary flight. Buonaparte could do and did a great
deal for France; but he could not *unmake* the character of the
people. Give them David's pictures, and they are satisfied;
and no other country will ever quarrel with them for the possession of the prize!*—Still, justice should be done to the taste

* This celebrated artist, looking at some fine Caraccis no longer
in the Louvre, said to a friend who was with him, 'Don't you remember the time when we were sufficiently absurd to admire those
daubs?' His own works now fill up the vacancy. The entrance of
the Apollo, the Dying Gladiator, and other great works from Rome,
at the end of the year, was celebrated by a procession of the two
Councils, the Artists, by bands of music, and appropriate inscriptions, by the rehearsing of a long dithyrambic poem and the chaunting of Horace's *Carmen Seculare*,[1] through the streets of Paris:
so oddly do they mix up new and old! Is not this *mélange* to be
accounted for from the spirit of the Catholic Religion? [w. н.]

and judgment with which the selection was made, which was no less striking than the universality of the sources from whence it was drawn. As a gallery, the Louvre was unrivalled: even the Vatican shrinks before it. Not a first-rate picture is to be met with on the Continent, but it found its way to the Louvre. Among other claims to our gratitude and wonder, it shortened the road to Italy; and it was 'a journey like the path to heaven,' to visit it for the first time. You walked for a quarter of a mile through works of fine art; the very floors echoed the sounds of immortality. The effect was not broken and frittered by being divided and taken piecemeal, but the whole was collected, heaped, massed together to a gorgeous height, so that the blow stunned you, and could never be forgotten. This was what the art could do, and all other pretensions seemed to sink before it. School called unto school; one great name answered to another, swelling the chorus of universal praise. Instead of robbery and sacrilege, it was the crowning and consecration of art; there was a dream and a glory, like the coming of the Millennium. These works, instead of being taken from their respective countries, were given to the world, and to the mind and heart of man, from whence they sprung. The shades of those who wrought these miracles might here look down pleased and satisfied to see the pure homage paid to them, not out of courtesy or as a condescension of greatness, but as due to them of right as the 'salt of the earth.' The load that killed Correggio here first fell off, and Raphael might smile at having missed a Cardinal's hat. Art, no longer a bondswoman, was seated on a throne, and her sons were kings. The spirit of man walked erect, and found its true level in the triumph of real over factitious claims. Whoever felt the sense of beauty or the yearning after excellence haunt his breast, was amply avenged on the injustice of fortune, and might boldly answer those who asked what there was but birth and title in the world that was not base and sordid—'Look around! These are my inheritance; this is the class to which I belong!' He who had the hope, nay, but the earnest wish to achieve anything like the immortal works before him, rose in imagination and in the scale of true desert above principalities and powers. All that it had entered into his mind to conceive, his thought in tangled forests, his vision of the night, was here perfected and accomplished, was acknowledged for the fair and good, honoured with the epithet of *divine*, spoke an intelligible language, thundered over Europe, and received the bended knee of the universe. Those masterpieces were the true handwriting on the wall, which told the great and mighty of the earth that their empire was passed away—that empire of arrogance and frivolity which assumed all superiority to itself, and scoffed at everything that could give a title to it. They might be considered as naturalized and at home in this their adopted country, which set an exclusive value on what could contribute to the public ornament or the public use, and had disallowed all claims to distinction that could insult over or interfere with those of truth, nature, and genius. The Louvre was therefore 'a great moral lesson;' a school and discipline of humanity! Buonaparte has explained his views on this point in a letter publicly addressed to Oriani, the celebrated mathematician, where he assures him that all men of genius, all who had distinguished themselves in the republic of letters, were to be accounted natives of France, whatever might be the actual place of their birth. 'Hitherto,' he says, 'the learned in Italy did not enjoy the consideration to which they were entitled—they lived retired in their laboratories and libraries, too happy if they could escape the notice, and consequently the persecution of kings and priests. It is now no longer thus—there is no longer religious inquisition nor despotic power. Thought is free in Italy. I invite the literary and scientific persons to consult together, and propose to me their ideas on the subject of giving new life and vigour to the fine arts and sciences. All who desire to visit France will be received with distinction by the Government. The people of France have more pride in enrolling among their citizens a skilful mathematician, a painter of reputation, a distinguished man in any class of letters, than in adding to their territories a large and wealthy city.' This is the true spirit of Jacobinism; and not the turning the Tuileries into a potato-garden.—Once more, as to the charge of plunder and robbery, all the collections in Europe answer it, for they are composed of works by the same masters. If these works were heirlooms, and sacred to the soil where they grew, they could not be removed. What is subject of barter and sale in time of peace, may be reckoned among the spoils of war. The Cartoons, the Elgin Marbles answer it. That these pictures were received in lieu of other contributions is proved by this, that £80,000 were offered for the restoration of the St. Jerome, and refused. If the army-agents had had their way, we should have heard nothing about the robbery, because we ourselves should have liked to have pocketed the same sum. We who transfer whole people and bombard peaceful towns, talk at our ease about rapine and sacrilege committed on statues and pictures, because they offer no temptation to our cupidity. [. . .]

# Byron and Wordsworth*

I AM much surprised at Lord Byron's haste to return a volume of Spenser, which was lent him by Mr. Hunt,[1] and at his apparent indifference to the progress and (if he pleased) *advancement* of poetry up to the present day. Did he really think that all genius was concentred in his own time, or in his own bosom? With his pride of ancestry, had he no curiosity to explore the heraldry of intellect? or did he regard the Muse as an upstart—a mere modern *blue-stocking* and fine lady? I am afraid that high birth and station, instead of being (as Mr. Burke predicates), 'a cure for a narrow and selfish mind,' only make a man more full of himself, and, instead of enlarging and refining his views, impatient of any but the most inordinate and immediate stimulus. I do not recollect, in all Lord Byron's writings, a single recurrence to a feeling or object that had ever excited an interest before; there is no display of natural affection—no twining of the heart round any object: all is the restless and disjointed effect of first impressions, of novelty, contrast, surprise, grotesque costume, or sullen grandeur. *His* beauties are the *houris*[2] of Paradise, the favourites of a seraglio, the changing visions of a feverish dream. His poetry, it is true, is stately and dazzling, arched like a rainbow, of bright and lovely hues, painted on the cloud of his own gloomy temper—perhaps to disappear as soon! It is easy to account for the antipathy between him and Mr. Wordsworth. Mr. Wordsworth's poetical mistress is a Pamela; Lord Byron's an Eastern princess or a Moorish maid. It is the extrinsic, the uncommon that captivates him, and all the rest he holds in sovereign contempt. There is the obvious result of pampered luxury and high-born sentiments. The mind, like the palace in which it has been brought up, admits none but new and costly furniture. From a scorn of homely simplicity, and a surfeit of the artificial, it has but one resource left in exotic manners and preternatural effect. So we see in novels, written by ladies of quality, all the marvellous allurements of

* [*London Weekly Review*, April 5, 1828.]

a fairy tale, jewels, quarries of diamonds, giants, magicians, condors and ogres.* The author of the *Lyrical Ballads* describes the lichen on the rock, the withered fern, with some peculiar feeling that he has about them: the author of *Childe Harold* describes the stately cypress, or the fallen column, with the feeling that every schoolboy has about them. The world is a grown schoolboy, and relishes the latter most. When Rousseau called out—'*Ah! voilà de la pervenche!*'⁴ in a transport of joy at sight of the periwinkle, because he had first seen this little blue flower in company with Madame Warens thirty years before, I cannot help thinking, that any astonishment expressed at the sight of a palm-tree, or even of Pompey's Pillar,⁵ is vulgar compared to this! Lord Byron, when he does not saunter down Bond-street, goes into the East: when he is not occupied with the passing topic, he goes back two thousand years, at one poetic, gigantic stride! But instead of the sweeping mutations of empire, and the vast lapses of duration, shrunk up into an antithesis, commend me to the 'slow and creeping foot of time,' in the commencement of *Ivanhoe*, where the jester and the swine-herd watch the sun going down behind the low-stunted trees of the forest, and their loitering and impatience make the summer's day seem so long, that we wonder how we have ever got to the end of the six hundred years that have passed since! That where the face of nature has changed, time should have rolled on its course, is but a common-place discovery; but that where all seems the same (the long rank grass, and the stunted oaks, and the innocent pastoral landscape), all should have changed—this is to me the burthen and the mystery. The ruined pile is a memento and a monument to him that reared it—oblivion has here done but half its work; but what yearnings, what vain conflicts with its fate come over the soul in the other case, which makes man seem like a grasshopper—an insect of the hour, and all that he is, or that others have been —nothing!

* See *Ada Reis.*³ [w. h.]

# *From*

# Conversations
# of James Northcote

## CONVERSATION THE SEVENTEENTH*

**N.** That is your diffidence, which I can't help thinking you carry too far. For anyone of real strength, you are the humblest person I ever knew.

**H.** It is owing to pride.

**N.** You deny you have invention too. But it is want of practice. Your ideas run on before your executive power. It is a common case. There was Ramsay,[1] of whom Sir Joshua used to say that he was the most sensible among all the painters of his time; but he has left little to show it. His manner was dry and timid. He stopped short in the middle of his work, because he knew exactly how much it wanted. Now and then we find hints and sketches which show what he might have been, if his hand had been equal to his conceptions. I have seen a picture of his of the Queen, soon after she was married—a profile, and slightly done; but it was a paragon of elegance. She had a fan in her hand: Lord! how she held that fan! It was weak in execution and ordinary in features—all I can say of it is, that it was the farthest possible removed from everything like vulgarity. A professor might despise it; but in the mental part, I have never seen anything of Vandyke's equal to it. I could have looked at it forever. I showed it to J——n; and he, I believe, came into my opinion of it. I don't know where it is now; but I saw in it enough to convince me that Sir Joshua was right in what he said of Ramsay's great superiority. His own picture of the King, which is at the Academy, is a finer composition and shows greater boldness and mastery of hand; but I should find it difficult to produce anything of Sir Joshua's that conveys an idea of more grace and delicacy than the one I have mentioned. Reynolds would have finished it

* [*The Atlas*, April 19 and 26, 1829.]

better: the other was afraid of spoiling what he had done, and so left it a mere outline. He was frightened before he was hurt.

H. Taste and even genius is but a misfortune, without a correspondent degree of manual dexterity or power of language to make it manifest.

N. W[ilkie] was here the other day. I believe you met him going out. He came, he said, to ask me about the famous people of the last age, Johnson, Burke, etc. (as I was almost the only person left who remembered them), and was curious to know what figure Sir Walter Scott would have made among them.

H. That is so like a North-Briton—'to make assurance doubly sure,' and to procure a signature to an acknowledged reputation as if it were a receipt for the delivery of a bale of goods.

N. I told him it was not for me to pronounce upon such men as Sir Walter Scott: they came before another tribunal. They were of that height that they were seen by all the world, and must stand or fall by the verdict of posterity. It signified little what any individual thought in such cases, it being equally an impertinence to set one's self against or to add one's testimony to the public voice; but as far as I could judge, I told him, that Sir Walter would have stood his ground in any company: neither Burke nor Johnson nor any of their admirers would have been disposed or able to set aside his pretensions. These men were not looked upon in their day as they are at present: Johnson had his *Lexiphanes*,[2] and Goldsmith was laughed at—their merits were to the full as much called in question, nay, more so, than those of the Author of Waverley have ever been, who has been singularly fortunate in himself or in lighting upon a barren age: but because their names have since become established, and as it were sacred, we think they were always so; and W[ilkie] wanted me, as a competent witness and as having seen both parties, to affix the same seal to his countryman's reputation, which it is not in the power of the whole of the present generation to do, much less of any single person in it. No, we must wait for this! Time alone can give the final stamp: no living reputation can ever be of the same value or quality as posthumous fame. We must throw lofty objects to a distance in order to judge of them: if we are standing close under the Monument, it looks higher than St. Paul's. Posterity has this advantage over us—not that they are really wiser, but they see the proportions better from being placed further off. For instance, I liked Sir Walter, because he had an easy, unaffected manner, and was ready to converse on all subjects alike.[3]

He was not like your friends, the L[ake] poets, who talk about nothing but their own poetry. If, on the contrary, he had been stiff and pedantic, I should, perhaps, have been inclined to think less highly of the author from not liking the man; so that we can never judge fairly of men's abilities till we are no longer liable to come in contact with their persons. Friends are as little to be trusted as enemies: favour or prejudice makes the votes in either case more or less suspected; though 'the vital signs that a name shall live' are in some instances so strong, that we can hardly refuse to put faith in them, and I think this is one. I was much pleased with Sir Walter, and I believe he expressed a favourable opinion of me. I said to him, 'I admire the way in which you begin your novels. You set out so abruptly, that you quite surprise me. I can't at all tell what's coming.'—'No!' says Sir Walter, 'nor I neither.' I then told him, that when I first read *Waverley*, I said it was no novel: nobody could invent like that. Either he had heard the story related by one of the surviving parties, or he had found the materials in a manuscript concealed in some old chest: to which he replied, 'You're not so far out of the way in thinking so.' You don't know him, do you? He'd be a pattern to you. Oh! he has a very fine manner. You would learn to rub off some of your asperities. But you admire him, I believe.

H. Yes; on this side of idolatry and Toryism.

N. That is your prejudice.

H. Nay, it rather shows my liberality, if I am a devoted enthusiast, notwithstanding. There are two things I admire in Sir Walter, his capacity and his simplicity; which indeed I am apt to think are much the same. The more ideas a man has of other things, the less he is taken up with the idea of himself. Everyone gives the same account of the author of *Waverley* in this respect. When he was in Paris, and went to Galignani's, he sat down in an outer room to look at some book he wanted to see: none of the clerks had the least suspicion who it was: when it was found out, the place was in a commotion. Cooper, the American, was in Paris at the same time: his looks and manners seemed to announce a much greater man. He strutted through the streets with a very consequential air; and in company held up his head, screwed up his features, and placed himself on a sort of pedestal to be observed and admired, as if he never relaxed in the assumption nor wished it to be forgotten by others, that he was the American Sir Walter Scott. The real one never troubled himself about the matter. Why should he? He might safely leave that question to others. Indeed, by what I am told, he carries his indifference too far: it amounts to an implied contempt for the public and *misprision*

*of treason* against the commonwealth of letters. He thinks
nothing of his works, although 'all Europe rings with them
from side to side.'—If so, he has been severely punished for
his infirmity.[4]

N. Though you do not know Sir Walter Scott, I think I
have heard you say you have seen him.

H. Yes, he put me in mind of Cobbett, with his florid face
and scarlet gown, which were just like the other's red face
and scarlet waistcoat. The one is like an English farmer, the
other like a Scotch *laird*. Both are large, robust men, with
great strength and composure of features; but I saw nothing
of the *ideal* character in the romance-writer, any more than I
looked for it in the politician.

N. Indeed! But you have a vast opinion of Cobbett too,
haven't you? Oh! he's a giant! He has such prodigious
strength; he tears up a subject by the roots. Did you ever
read his Grammar?[5] Or see his attack on Mrs ——?[6] It was like
a hawk pouncing on a wren. I should be terribly afraid to get
into his hands. And then his homely, familiar way of writing
—it is not from necessity or vulgarity, but to show his contempt for aristocratic pride and arrogance. He only has a
kitchen-garden; he could have a flower-garden too if he chose.
Peter Pindar[7] said his style was like the Horse-Guards, only
one story above the ground, while Junius's had all the airy
elegance of Whitehall: but he could raise his style just as high
as he pleased; though he does not want to sacrifice strength
to elegance. He knows better what he is about.

H. I don't think he'll set up for a fine gentleman in a hurry,
though he has for a Member of Parliament; and I fancy he
would make no better figure in the one than the other. He appeared to me, when I once saw him, exactly what I expected:
in Sir Walter I looked in vain for a million of fine things! I
could only explain it to myself in this way, that there was a
degree of capacity in that huge double forehead of his, that
superseded all effort, made everything come intuitively and almost mechanically, as if it were merely transcribing what was
already written, and by the very facility with which the highest beauty and excellence was produced, left few traces of it
in the expression of the countenance, and hardly any sense of
it in the mind of the author. Expression only comes into the
face as we are at a loss for words, or have a difficulty in bringing forward our ideas; but we may repeat the finest things by
rote without any change of look or manner. It is only when
the powers are tasked, when the moulds of thought are full,
that the effect or the *wear-and-tear* of the mind appears on
the surface. So, in general, writers of the greatest imagination
and range of ideas, and who might be said to have all nature

obedient to their call, seem to have been most careless of
their fame and regardless of their works. They treat their
productions not as children, but as 'bastards of their art;'
whereas those who are more confined in their scope of intellect and wedded to some one theory or predominant fancy,
have been found to feel a proportionable fondness for the offspring of their brain, and have thus excited a deeper interest
in it in the minds of others. We set a value on things as they
have cost us dear: the very limitation of our faculties or exclusiveness of our feelings compels us to concentrate all our
enthusiasm on a favourite subject; and strange as it may
sound, in order to inspire a perfect sympathy in others or to
form a school, men must themselves be *egotists!* Milton has
had fewer readers and admirers, but I suspect more devoted
and bigotted ones, than ever Shakespeare had: Sir Walter
Scott has attracted more universal attention than any writer
of our time, but you may speak against him with less danger
of making personal enemies than if you attack Lord Byron.
Even Wordsworth has half a dozen followers, who set him up
above everybody else from a *common idiosyncrasy* of feeling
and the singleness of the elements of which his excellence is
composed. Before we can take an author entirely to our bosoms, he must be another self; and he cannot be this, if he is
'not one, but all mankind's epitome.'[8] It was this which gave
such an effect to Rousseau's writings, that he stamped his own
character and the image of his self-love on the public mind—
*there* it is, and there it will remain in spite of everything. Had
he possessed more comprehension of thought or feeling, it
would have only have diverted him from his object. But it was
the excess of his egotism and his utter blindness to everything else, that found a corresponding sympathy in the conscious feelings of every human breast, and shattered to pieces
the pride of rank and circumstance by the pride of internal
worth or upstart pretention. When Rousseau stood behind the
chair of the master of the *château* of ——,[9] and smiled to hear
the company dispute about the meaning of the motto of the
arms of the family, which he alone knew, and stumbled as he
handed the glass of wine to his young mistress, and fancied
she coloured at being waited upon by so learned a young footman—then was first kindled that spark which can never be
quenched, then was formed the germ of that strong conviction
of the disparity between the badge on his shoulder and the
aspirations of his soul—the determination, in short, that external situation and advantages are but the mask, and that the
mind is the man—armed with which, impenetrable, incorrigible, he went forth conquering and to conquer, and over-
threw the monarchy of France and the hierarchies of the

earth. Till then, birth and wealth and power were all in all, though but the frame-work or crust that envelopes the man; and what there was in the man himself was never asked, or was scorned and forgot. And while all was dark and grovelling within, while knowledge either did not exist or was confined to a few, while material power and advantages were everything, this was naturally to be expected. But with the increase and diffusion of knowledge, this state of things must sooner or later cease; and Rousseau was the first who held the torch (lighted at the never-dying fire in his own bosom) to the hidden chambers of the mind of man—like another Prometheus, breathed into his nostrils the breath of a new and intellectual life, enraging the Gods of the earth, and made him feel what is due to himself and his fellows. Before, physical force was everything: henceforward, mind, thought, feeling was a new element—a fourth estate in society. What! shall a man have read Dante and Ariosto, and be none the better for it? Shall he be still judged of only by his coat, the number of his servants in livery, the house over his head? While poverty meant ignorance, that was necessarily the case: but the world of books overturns the world of things, and establishes a new balance of power and scale of estimation. Shall we think only rank and pedigree divine, when we have music, poetry, and painting within us? Tut! we have read *Old Mortality;* and shall it be asked whether we have done so in a garret or a palace, in a carriage or on foot? Or knowing them, shall we not revere the mighty heirs of fame, and respect ourselves for knowing and honouring them? This is the true march of intellect, and not the erection of *Mechanics' Institutions,*[10] or the printing of *twopenny trash,*[11] according to my notion of the matter, though I have nothing to say against them neither.

N. I thought you never would have done; however, you have come to the ground at last. After this rhapsody, I must inform you that Rousseau is a character more detestable to me than I have power of language to express: an aristocrat filled with all their worst vices, pride, ambition, conceit and gross affectation: and though endowed with some ability, yet not sufficient ever to make him know right from wrong: witness his novel of *Eloisa.* His name brings to my mind all the gloomy horrors of a mob-government, which attempted from their ignorance to banish truth and justice from the world. I see you place Sir Walter above Lord Byron. The question is not which keeps longest on the wing, but which soars highest: and I cannot help thinking there are essences in Lord Byron that are not to be surpassed. He is on a par with Dryden. All the other modern poets appear to me vulgar in the compar-

ison. As a lady who comes here said, there is such an air of
nobility in what he writes. Then there is such a power in the
style, expressions almost like Shakespeare—'And looked round
on them with their *wolfish* eyes.'

H. The expression is in Shakespeare, somewhere in *Lear*.

N. The line I repeated is in *Don Juan*.[12] I do not mean to
vindicate the immorality or misanthropy in that poem—perhaps his lameness was to blame for this defect—but surely no
one can deny the force, the spirit of it; and there is such a
fund of drollery mixed up with the serious part. Nobody
understood the tragi-comedy of poetry so well. People find
fault with this mixture in general, because it is not well managed; there is a comic story and a tragic story going on at
the same time, without their having anything to do with one
another. But in Lord Byron they are brought together, just
as they are in nature. In like manner, if you go to an execution at the very moment when the criminal is going to be
turned off, and all eyes are fixed upon him, an old apple-
woman and her stall are overturned, and all the spectators
fall a-laughing. In real life the most ludicrous incidents
border on the most affecting and shocking. How fine that is
of the cask of butter in the storm![13] Some critics have objected
to it as turning the whole into burlesque; on the contrary, it
is that which stamps the character of the scene more than anything else. What did the people in the boat care about the
rainbow, which he has described in such vivid colours; or
even about their fellow-passengers who were thrown over-
board, when they only wanted to eat them? No, it was the
loss of the firkin of butter that affected them more than all the
rest; and it is the mention of this circumstance that adds a
hardened levity and a sort of ghastly horror to the scene. It
shows the master-hand—there is such a boldness and sagacity
and superiority to ordinary rules in it! I agree, however, in
your admiration of the Waverley Novels: they are very fine.
As I told the author, he and Cervantes have raised the idea
of human nature, not as Richardson has attempted, by affectation and a false varnish, but by bringing out what there is
really fine in it under a cloud of disadvantages. Have you
seen the last?[14]

H. No.

N. There is a character of a common smith or armourer in
it, which, in spite of a number of weaknesses and in the most
ludicrous situations, is made quite heroical by the tenderness and humanity it displays. It is his best, but I had not
read it when I saw him. No; all that can be said against Sir
Walter is, that he never made a *whole*. There is an infinite
number of delightful incidents and characters, but they are

disjointed and scattered. This is one of Fielding's merits: his novels are regular compositions, with what the ancients called a *beginning*, a *middle*, and an *end*: every circumstance is foreseen and provided for, and the conclusion of the story turns round as it were to meet the beginning. *Gil Blas* is very clever, but it is only a succession of chapters. *Tom Jones* is a masterpiece, as far as regards the conduct of the fable.

H. Do you know the reason? Fielding had a hooked nose, the long chin. It is that introverted physiognomy that binds and concentrates.

N. But Sir Walter has not a hooked nose, but one that denotes kindness and ingenuity. Mrs. Abington[15] had the pug-nose, who was the perfection of comic archness and vivacity: a hooked nose is my aversion.

## CONVERSATION THE SEVENTEENTH[*]

N. I sometimes get into scrapes that way by contradicting people before I have well considered the subject, and I often wonder how I get out of them so well as I do. I remember once meeting with Sir——, who was talking about Milton; and as I have a natural aversion to a coxcomb, I differed from what he said, without being at all prepared with any arguments in support of my opinion.

H. But you had time enough to think of them afterwards.

N. I got through with it somehow or other. It is the very risk you run in such cases that puts you on the alert and gives you spirit to extricate yourself from it. If you had full leisure to deliberate and to make out your defence beforehand, you perhaps could not do it so well as on the spur of the occasion. The surprise and flutter of the animal spirits gives the alarm to any little wit we possess, and puts it into a state of immediate requisition.

H. Besides, it is always easiest to defend a paradox or an opinion you don't care seriously about. I would sooner (as a matter of choice) take the wrong side than the right in any argument. If you have a thorough conviction on any point and good grounds for it, you have studied it long, and the real reasons have sunk into the mind; so that what you can recall of them at a sudden *pinch*, seems unsatisfactory and disproportionate to the confidence of your belief and to the magisterial tone you are disposed to assume. Even truth is a matter of habit and professorship. Reason and knowledge, when at their height, return into a kind of instinct. We understand the grammar of a foreign language best, though we do not speak

* [*The Atlas*, May 1829.]

it so well. But if you take up an opinion at a venture, then you lay hold of whatever excuse comes within your reach, instead of searching about for and bewildering yourself with the true reasons; and the odds are that the arguments thus got up are as good as those opposed to them. In fact, the more sophistical and superficial an objection to a received or well-considered opinion is, the more we are staggered and teased by it; and the next thing is to lose our temper, when we become an easy prey to a cool and disingenuous adversary. I would much rather (as the safest side) insist on Milton's pedantry than on his sublimity, supposing I were not in the company of very good judges. A single stiff or obscure line would outweigh a whole book of solemn grandeur in the mere flippant encounter of the wits, and, in general, the truth and justice of the cause you espouse is rather an encumbrance than an assistance; or it is like heavy armour which few have strength to wield. Anything short of complete triumph on the right side is defeat: any hole picked or flaw detected in an argument which we are holding earnestly and conscientiously, is sufficient to raise the laugh against us. This is the greatest advantage which folly and knavery have. We are not satisfied to be right, unless we can prove others to be quite wrong; and as all the world would be thought to have some reason on their side, they are glad of any loop-hole or pretext to escape from the dogmatism and tyranny we would set up over them. Absolute submission requires absolute proofs. Without some such drawback, the world might become too wise and too good, at least according to every man's private prescription. In this sense *ridicule is the test of truth;* that is, the levity and indifference on one side balances the formality and presumption on the other. [. . .]

# The Spirit
# of Philosophy*

THE SPIRIT of philosophy consists in having the power to think, and patience to wait for the result. I do not mean to recommend an entire suspension of opinion as a matter of belief or feeling (that would be nearly impossible, and might be dangerous), what I mean, is, that one is to wait for the *proofs* till they come, however slowly or painfully; and not take up out of indolence, prejudice, or vanity with anything short of a clear and satisfactory account, as a rational and philosophical solution. We may indulge our fancy or prejudices to a certain extent, so long as we do not mistake *prejudices* for *reasoning*. We must keep the understanding free; the judgment must be unbiassed. If we endeavour to shut out and suppress all natural feeling and inclination to one side of a question rather than another, this will be more likely to warp and precipitate our judgment, and make us impose false and premature arguments upon ourselves as the true, in order to get rid of so uneasy and artificial a state. But with a reasonable latitude allowed to our general notions and conjectures as to where the truth is to be found, we shall wait with more resolution and calmness for the dogmatical and formal issues of our inquiries. We may fancy, as mere common mortals, that a thing is so; but as philosophers, we are bound to show that it is so; and we should take care how we set up a pretence of being able to do this, either in our own minds, or as a law to others, before we are quite sure of our ground. A man may indulge in a lax and loose belief of anything as a matter of ease and convenience to himself; but when he comes forward to assign the *why* and *how*, he becomes a dictator to others, and is inexcusable if he does not scrupulously discard all sinister influences of habit, authority, interest, and let reason alone usurp the empire of his breast. People in general suppose they have a right to have an opinion on all subjects, and that

* [*The Amulet*, an annual for 1836.]

they are bound, and are able to prove satisfactorily, that they are in the right; because they have never thought about the question at all, it appears to them self-evident. It is no wonder, therefore, that with such universal and cheap pretensions to infallibility, they are impatient of having any doubt or objection thrown in their way, or of the smallest trouble or serious expense of mental labour in removing it. They very easily satisfy their own minds with some form of words, and are equally ready to convince others by menaces or blows, who do not come into their *commonplace* conclusions, and blindly go all lengths with them. Many persons are willing to suspend their decision, and nearly indifferent what side they shall take; but no one having adopted an opinion is willing to allow he has done so without good reason, and is angry with anyone who does not assent to his all-sufficiency in this respect. We find indeed that the most blind and bigoted belief is the most dogmatical; and that those ages and nations which are the most ignorant, are the most intolerant of a shadow of difference from their grossest creeds (for having no evidence to adduce in their favour, they cannot afford to have them called in question), and are the most bent on writing the proofs of their faith in the blood of their enemies. Heresy is, then, chiefly a statutable crime; and antipathies of opinion amount to antipathies of kind. A philosopher should take warning, and avoid this vulgar error. He should have firmness and candour to say, 'I think a thing is so, but I do not know why; I will not rest till I have found out the cause (if possible); but till I have, I will not deceive you, or amuse myself with a foolish and idle theory.' To encourage this tone of feeling, and to show that there is nothing degrading to the most acute, in waiting for an answer to the question, 'What is truth?' it may suffice to observe, that instead of that encyclopedia of wit and wisdom, which every sciolist would hang about his neck, and universal upstart pretension to be thoroughly informed *de omni scibile et quibusdam aliis*,[1] it is as much as anyone can hope to do, to discover a single truth in the course of a long and studious life; and often instead of taking for his motto, 'I will lead you into all knowledge,' he should be contented to say, 'I will show you a mystery.' The more we are convinced of the value of the prize, the less we shall be tempted to lay rash and violent hands on it; and the more apt to console ourselves for the slowness of our progress and our frequent failures, by the hope of ultimate success.

When we place our pride in the difficulty and nobleness of the pursuit rather than our own proficiency in it, we may, without a blush, confess that we know little or nothing; but 'if reasons were as plenty as blackberries,' we ought, then, to be able to 'give every man a reason upon compulsion.'[2] I conceive that the mind, in the search after knowledge, very much resembles the truffle-hunter: the dog finds out, and is led to the spot where the object of his pursuit lies by the smell, but it is by his teeth and claws that he is able to remove the rubbish that hides it. So there is a certain air of truth which hovers over particular conclusions, and directs our attention towards them, but it is only the acuteness and strength of the reasoning faculty that digs down to the roots of things. In this way common sense or a certain tact may be said to be the foundation of truest philosophy; for there is always a certain number of facts with a general impression from them treasured up in the memory, which it is the business of the understanding to examine, and not to cavil at or contradict. This is one of the general errors of philosophy and sources of sophistry, that persons of more pretension than sincerity try to take an advantage of you, by denying the facts which are notorious to common observation, or for which an appeal may be had to their own consciousness, solely on the plea that you cannot explain them; whereas if the real phenomena are so (which is the first question), it is their business to account for them as much as yours, and not to make your deficiency in logic a ground of triumph equally over you and truth. Here, indeed, there is a kind of dilemma; for unless you are impressed with a belief of a certain thing, how are you to submit to the drudgery of finding out a reason for it? And on the other hand, if we take a thing for granted before we know, and are able to prove it to a demonstration, are we not in danger of giving a wrong bias to the mind, and bestowing vast pains and exhausting all our ingenuity to prop up a prejudice, instead of establishing a truth? The only preventive to this, is a strong love of truth, and openness to conviction; for, inquiring into the grounds and principles of certain facts, the facts themselves are brought again and again under review; and if they appear to be ill-supported or overpowered by a number of contrary facts, it is, then, high time to retreat from an untenable position, before it crumbles under our feet. The worst is, where interest and authority interfere to patch up a ricketty conclusion, and the mind is made the advocate and slave of established creeds and systems. Perhaps nine-tenths of the exertions of the human intellect have been directed (if we may judge from the contents of learned libraries) to prove the truth of doctrines, of which each individual neither believed nor understood a tittle, except from hearsay, and on the authority of others. Even vanity and the affectation of novelty, owes its force as an engine of sophistry and paradox, to the detection of the weakness and fallacy of so many prevailing and inveterate prejudices. Hence as one party are inclined to believe that everything is entitled to their assent that is old, there are others, who, in the spirit of contradiction, and in their contempt for antiquated absurdity, are fully satisfied that everything that is new-fangled, and of recent date, must be true. Where neither of these biasses exists, and where the mind judges for itself, and from an undistorted, though vague induction of particulars, there is little apprehension that the inquirer should persist in an error of presumption, after there is sufficient evidence to the contrary; and as long as he does not see ground to change his original impression, he may persist in endeavouring to find out the positive proof, without fear of losing his labour. There is no reason to despair because the required solution does not come in a day; it is well if it comes 'with healing on its wings'[3] at the end of years. It is not too long to stay, nor too much to expect, if we have but the right clue to it. This is everything. If we keep the object we have in view always in mind, and are on the alert to make use of every observation or suggestion of our own thoughts that can illustrate it, then we may (not presumptuously, but with calm and confident breast) promise ourselves a successful result. But the better-grounded our hopes are, the more deep and unwearied our aspirations, the less we shall be disposed to anticipate the lucky minute—with the greater fortitude, and mixture of pride and humility, shall we gird ourselves up to our allotted task—and the more firmly shall we reject every specious appearance and idle shadow that would impose itself on us, for the very substance of truth. The love of truth, like charity, when it is sincere, 'hopeth all things, trieth all things, endureth all things.'[4] There should be no desire for immediate applause, no inclination to gloss over shallow sophistry with the colours of style; a passion for truth, an interest in it that nothing can bribe or divert, a power of brooding over and deriving a supreme consolation from it, must be the basis of all true philosophy. There must be no flirting with mere popularity, no willingness to dazzle others and blind ourselves by a *leurre de dupe*,[5] no eagerness to pluck the fruit of knowledge while yet green and unripe, no soothing flattery of friends, no angry collision with antagonists; but we must be contented to commune with ourselves and our own hearts, and nourish the appetite and the faith, in truth, in silence, and in lone obscurity, till a light breaks in upon us like a light from heaven; and the shape we have so long wooed, stands suddenly revealed in all its brightness to our longing sight. There is no art or method of invention to 'constrain' the truth, or force it to appear by certain cabalistic words or formal arrangements; it comes when least expected, like a thief in the night; it is given to our vows and prayers, to our thoughts ever intent on the unperverted impressions of things, and their workings in the mind, so as to bring out the causes by the continual weighing and scanning of numberless effects—not to a trick, or a *fiat* of the will, or a pragmatical conceit of ourselves. All great truths (with the previous disposition of mind we have described) are owing, not to system, but to accident; the condition of all discovery is to be involuntary (for what follows mechanically is not in the nature of a discovery). This is the fault of Lord Bacon's *Novum Organon,* who, after exploding the subtle distinctions and logomachies of the schoolmen, and referring everything to experiment, sets up a scheme of invention of his own, and seems to think that ingenuity can lay a trap for truth, and hedge it in with an alternate series of affirmations and negations. This might be feasible, if the facts were (as he supposes) all known and limited in number; but the phenomena are infinite, obscure, and intricately inwoven together, so that it is only by being always alive to their tacit and varying influences, that we can hope to seize on the power that guides and binds them together, by seeing it manifested in some strong aspect or more remarkable instance of the kind. Suppose, for example, there is a contradiction involved in the notion of personal identity; so long as I confine my idea of the subject to the present state, this contradiction may not be so glaringly brought out, as that I should discover it; but let me transfer the notion to a future state of existence where this identity has been interrupted, and I have to begin *de novo;*[6] and the incompatibility all at once becomes obvious—it stares me in the face; but I could not foresee that I should make such a discovery from this new comparison (or *invent* the example for that purpose), till I had actually and unexpectedly made it. But by turning over a subject long and late, these prizes in the wheel turn up oftener; and our incessant vigilance and search, do not go unrewarded. The finding out a *reason* is like finding out a *word;* it does not come at the moment we want it, but of its own accord afterwards, from the effort we have previously made, and our having set our minds upon it, which puts the desired train of association in motion. We know when we have got the right *word;* if we take up with a wrong one, it is wilfully, and because we prefer sloth to sterling pains, the evasion of a difficulty to a triumph over it; and so it may be said with respect to the search after truth. The temper and spirit of a true and improved method of philosophising, have been agreeably de-

scribed by a philosophical poet of the present day, and I shall
relieve the dryness of this description by quoting the lines:

> The eye—it cannot choose but see,
>     We cannot bid the ear be still;
> Our bodies feel where'er they be,
>     Against or with our will.
>
> Nor less I dream that there are powers,
>     Which of themselves our minds impress:
> That we can feed this mind of ours,
>     In a wise passiveness.
>
> Think you, mid all this mighty sum
>     Of things for ever speaking,
> That nothing of itself will come,
>     But we must still be seeking?
>
> One impulse from a vernal wood
>     May teach you more of man—
> Of moral evil and of good,
>     Than all the sages can.
>
> Sweet is the lore which Nature brings:
>     Our meddling intellect
> Misshapes the beauteous forms of things,
>     —We murder to dissect.
>
> Enough of science and of art!
>     Close up these barren leaves;
> Come forth, and bring with you a heart
>     That watches and receives.*

True philosophy is softened by feeling, and owes allegiance
to nature. Passion, it is true, may run away with reason; but
when the question is the nature and government of the passions, how understand without entering into them? The blind
might as well discourse of colours! This is the flagrant error,
the crying sin of a set of philosophers in our time, who, referring all things to utility, and a hard calculation of consequences, make clownish war upon all the pleasures and amen-
ities of life, and leave not a single item in their account of
good for the sum total to be composed of. They would reduce
men to mere machines of iron or of wood; and in their reasoning on the nature of society, suppose that this transformation
is not only eligible, but has already taken place. Like the 'O
Lord, Sir!' in Shakespeare, their favourite phrase, 'the calcula-

* Wordsworth's *Lyrical Ballads*. [W. H.]

tion of consequences,' answers all questions, and solves all difficulties. Courage is with them 'a calculation of consequences'—cowardice is so too; so that, by their account, courage is cowardice. Madmen, they say, reason. But at this rate, the world might be a greater Bedlam than it is, and yet they would persuade you that the patients are strict logicians. It is easy to repeat a set of cant phrases by rote, and call it philosophy, while the science of man is not advanced a single jot, but is rather obfuscated and obscured by an arrangement of 'tall, opaque words,' that pretend to explain everything, and in reality mean nothing. The schoolmen were famous for these verbal fallacies; the moderns (without sufficient reason), affect to be free from them, and to appeal in all cases to experiment and ocular proof. They lay their hands upon some fact or object of sense, and think they have discovered a truth. Thus a bump on the head is an organ or faculty of the soul, and the brain is the mind itself. We can indeed feel the bump on the head or dissect the brain, but we know no more of the mind than we did before. Modern metaphysics is (as it has been defined by some of its self-satisfied professors), *'the art of naming'*; that is, it is calling one thing by the name of another, and arises from a want of the true spirit of philosophy, or from an impatience of inquiring into the real causes of things, and a determination to substitute a positive and tangible idea for an obscure and remote one, whether right or wrong. The exchange from *names* to *things* as symbols and exponents of general truths, is not always, therefore, an improvement. The nose on a man's face is a fact, a positive image; but am I, therefore, at liberty to assert (as a cover for my own ignorance, or a bribe to the indolence and credulity of others), that wit or memory is nothing but the nose on a man's face? This would be a strange perversion of the experimental philosophy; and yet it is one that is often made with great parade and formality. Another rule in philosophising is not merely to persevere with the strictest watchfulness and self-denial till we arrive at the goal, but to know where to stop. A man, by great labour and sagacity, finds out one truth; but from the importunate craving of the mind to know all, he would fain persuade himself that this one truth includes all others. Such has been the error of almost all systems and system-makers, who lose the advantage of the conquests they have achieved by pushing them too far, and aiming at universal empire—

> Vaulting ambition that o'erleaps itself,
> And falls on t'other side![7]

Thus the doctrine of the *association of ideas* was a great discovery in intellectual science, and an admirable clue to the development of an infinite variety of phenomena; but when it is made to explain everything, and set up as the sole and primary principle of thought and action (which is impossible by the very terms), it becomes merely a confusion of ideas, and a handle for quackery and paradox.

# The Letter-Bell*

COMPLAINTS are frequently made of the vanity and shortness of human life, when, if we examine its smallest details, they present a world by themselves. The most trifling objects, retraced with the eye of memory, assume the vividness, the delicacy and importance of insects seen through a magnifying glass. There is no end of the brilliancy or the variety. The habitual feeling of the love of life may be compared to 'one entire and perfect chrysolite,' which, if analysed, breaks into a thousand shining fragments. Ask the sum-total of the value of human life, and we are puzzled with the length of the account and the multiplicity of items in it: take any one of them apart, and it is wonderful what matter for reflection will be found in it! As I write this, the *Letter-Bell* passes: it has a lively, pleasant sound with it, and not only fills the street with its importunate clamour, but rings clear through the length of many half-forgotten years. It strikes upon the ear, it vibrates to the brain, it wakes me from the dream of time, it flings me back upon my first entrance into life, the period of my first coming up to town, when all around was strange, uncertain, adverse—a hubbub of confused noises, a chaos of shifting objects—and when this sound alone, startling me with the recollection of a letter I had to send to the friends I had lately left, brought me as it were to myself, made me feel that I had links still connecting me with the universe, and gave me hope and patience to persevere. At that loud-tinkling, interrupted sound (now and then), the long line of blue hills near the place where I was brought up waves in the horizon, a golden sunset hovers over them, the dwarf-oaks rustle their red leaves in the evening-breeze, and the road from [Wem] to [Shrewsbury], by which I first set out on my journey through life, stares me in the face as plain, but from time and change not less visionary and mysterious, than the pictures in the *Pilgrim's Progress*. I should notice, that at this time the light of the French Revolution circled my head like a glory, though dab-

* [*Monthly Magazine*, March 1831, "by the late William Hazlitt."]

bled with drops of crimson gore: I walked comfortable and
cheerful by its side—

> And by the vision splendid
> Was on my way attended.[1]

It rose then in the east: it has again risen in the west.[2] Two
suns in one day, two triumphs of liberty in one age, is a miracle which I hope the Laureate[3] will hail in appropriate verse.
Or may not Mr. Wordsworth give a different turn to the fine
passage, beginning

> What though the radiance which was once so bright,
> Be now for ever vanished from my sight;
> Though nothing can bring back the hour
> Of glory in the grass, of splendour in the flower?[4]

For is it not brought back, 'like morn risen on mid-*night*';[5] and
may he not yet greet the yellow light shining on the evening
bank with eyes of youth, of genius, and freedom, as of yore?
No, never! But what would not these persons give for the
unbroken integrity of their early opinions—for one unshackled,
uncontaminated strain—one *Io pæan*[6] to Liberty—one burst
of indignation against tyrants and sycophants, who subject
other countries to slavery by force, and prepare their own for it
by servile sophistry, as we see the huge serpent lick over its
trembling, helpless victim with its slime and poison, before
it devours it! On every stanza so penned should be written the
word RECREANT! Every taunt, every reproach, every note of
exultation at restored light and freedom, would recall to them
how their hearts failed them in the Valley of the Shadow of
Death. And what shall we say to *him*—the sleep-walker, the
dreamer, the sophist, the word-hunter, the craver after sympathy, but still vulnerable to truth, accessible to opinion, because not sordid or mechanical? The Bourbons being no
longer tied about his neck, he may perhaps recover his
original liberty of speculating; so that we may apply to him
the lines of his own *Ancient Mariner*—

> And from his neck so free
> The Albatross fell off, and sank
> Like lead into the sea.

This is the reason I can write an article on the *Letter-Bell*, and
other such subjects; I have never given the lie to my own soul.
If I have felt any impression once, I feel it more strongly a
second time; and I have no wish to revile or discard my best
thoughts. There is at least a thorough *keeping* in what I write

—not a line that betrays a principle or disguises a feeling. If
my wealth is small, it all goes to enrich the same heap; and
trifles in this way accumulate to a tolerable sum. Or if the
Letter-Bell does not lead me a dance into the country, it fixes
me in the thick of my town recollections, I know not how long
ago. It was a kind of alarm to break off from my work when
there happened to be company to dinner or when I was going
to the play. *That* was going to the play, indeed, when I went
twice a year, and had not been more than half a dozen times
in my life. Even the idea that anyone else in the house was
going, was a sort of reflected enjoyment, and conjured up a
lively anticipation of the scene. I remember a Miss D——, a
maiden lady from Wales (who in her youth was to have been
married to an earl), tantalised me greatly in this way, by
talking all day of going to see Mrs. Siddons' 'airs and graces'
at night in some favourite part; and when the Letter-Bell
announced that the time was approaching, and its last receding sound lingered on the ear, or was lost in silence, how
anxious and uneasy I became, lest she and her companion
should not be in time to get good places—lest the curtain
should draw up before they arrived—and lest I should lose one
line or look in the intelligent report which I should hear the
next morning! The punctuating of time at that early period—
everything that gives it an articulate voice—seems of the utmost consequence; for we do not know what scenes in the
*ideal* world may run out of them: a world of interest may
hang upon every instant, and we can hardly sustain the
weight of future years which are contained in embryo in the
most minute and inconsiderable passing events. How often
have I put off writing a letter till it was too late! How often
had to run after the postman with it—now missing, now recovering the sound of his bell—breathless, angry with myself
—then hearing the welcome sound come full round a corner—
and seeing the scarlet costume which set all my fears and self-
reproaches at rest! I do not recollect having ever repented
giving a letter to the postman, or wishing to retrieve it after
he had once deposited it in his bag. What I have once set
my hand to, I take the consequences of, and have been always
pretty much of the same humour in this respect. I am not like
the person who, having sent off a letter to his mistress, who
resided a hundred and twenty miles in the country, and dis-
approving, on second thoughts, of some expressions contained
in it, took a postchaise and four to follow and intercept it the
next morning. At other times, I have sat and watched the de-
caying embers in a little *back* painting-room (just as the
wintry day declined) and brooded over the half-finished copy
of a Rembrandt, or a landscape by Vangoyen, placing it

where it might catch a dim gleam of light from the fire;
while the Letter-Bell was the only sound that drew my
thoughts to the world without, and reminded me that I had a
task to perform in it. As to that landscape, methinks I see it
now—

> The slow canal, the yellow-blossomed vale,
> The willow-tufted bank, the gliding sail.[7]

There was a windmill, too, with a poor low clay-built cottage
beside it: how delighted I was when I had made the tremulous, undulating reflection in the water, and saw the dull canvas become a lucid mirror of the commonest features of
nature! Certainly, painting gives one a strong interest in nature and humanity (it is not the *dandy-school* of morals or
sentiment)—

> While with an eye made quiet by the power
> Of harmony and the deep power of joy,
> We see into the life of things.[8]

Perhaps there is no part of a painter's life (if we must tell 'the
secrets of the prison-house') in which he has more enjoyment
of himself and his art, than that in which after his work is
over, and with furtive, sidelong glances at what he has done,
he is employed in washing his brushes and cleaning his pallet
for the day. Afterwards, when he gets a servant in livery to
do this for him, he may have other and more ostensible
sources of satisfaction—greater splendour, wealth, or fame; but
he will not be so wholly in his art, nor will his art have such a
hold on him as when he was too poor to transfer its meanest
drudgery to others—too humble to despise aught that had to
do with the object of his glory and his pride, with that on
which all his projects of ambition or pleasure were founded.
'Entire affection scorneth nicer hands.'[9] When the professor
is above this mechanical part of his business, it may have
become a *stalking-horse* to other worldly schemes, but is no
longer his *hobby-horse* and the delight of his inmost thoughts—

> His shame in crowds, his solitary pride![10]

I used sometimes to hurry through this part of my occupation,
while the Letter-Bell (which was my dinner-bell) summoned
me to the fraternal board, where youth and hope

> Made good digestion wait on appetite
> And health on both—[11]

or oftener I put it off till after dinner, that I might loiter longer and with more luxurious indolence over it, and connect it with the thoughts of my next day's labours.

The dustman's-bell, with its heavy, monotonous noise, and the brisk, lively tinkle of the muffin-bell, have something in them, but not much. They will bear dilating upon with the utmost licence of inventive prose. All things are not alike *conductors* to the imagination. A learned Scotch professor found fault with an ingenious friend and arch-critic for cultivating a rookery on his grounds: the professor declared 'he would as soon think of encouraging a *froggery*.' This was barbarous as it was senseless. Strange, that a country that has produced the Scotch novels and *Gertrude of Wyoming*[12] should want sentiment!

The postman's double knock at the door the next morning is 'more germain to the matter.' How that knock often goes to the heart! We distinguish to a nicety the arrival of the Twopenny or the General Post. The summons of the latter is louder and heavier, as bringing news from a greater distance, and as, the longer it has been delayed, fraught with a deeper interest. We catch the sound of what is to be paid—eight-pence, nine-pence, a shilling—and our hopes generally rise with the postage. How we are provoked at the delay in getting change—at the servant who does not hear the door! Then if the postman passes, and we do not hear the expected knock, what a pang is there! It is like the silence of death—of hope! We think he does it on purpose, and enjoys all the misery of our suspense. I have sometimes walked out to see the Mail-Coach pass, by which I had sent a letter, or to meet it when I expected one. I never see a Mail-Coach, for this reason, but I look at it as the bearer of glad tidings—the messenger of fate. I have reason to say so. The finest sight in the metropolis is that of the Mail-Coaches setting off from Piccadilly. The horses paw the ground, and are impatient to be gone, as if conscious of the precious burden they convey. There is a peculiar secrecy and despatch, significant and full of meaning, in all the proceedings concerning them. Even the outside passengers have an erect and supercilious air, as if proof against the accidents of the journey. In fact, it seems indifferent whether they are to encounter the summer's heat or winter's cold, since they are borne on through the air in a winged chariot. The Mail-Carts drive up; the transfer of packages is made; and, at a signal given, they start off, bearing the irrevocable scrolls that give wings to thought, and that bind or sever hearts for ever. How we hate the Putney and Brentford stages that draw up in a line after they are gone! Some persons think the sublimest object in nature is a ship launched

on the bottom of the ocean: but give me, for my private satisfaction, the Mail-Coaches that pour down Piccadilly of an
evening, tear up the pavement, and devour the way before
them to the Land's-End![13]

In Cowper's time, Mail-Coaches were hardly set up; but he
has beautifully described the coming in of the Post-Boy:

> Hark! 'tis the twanging horn o'er yonder bridge,
> That with its wearisome but needful length
> Bestrides the wintry flood, in which the moon
> Sees her unwrinkled face reflected bright:—
> He comes, the herald of a noisy world,
> With spattered boots, strapped waist, and frozen locks;
> News from all nations lumbering at his back.
> True to his charge, the close-packed load behind,
> Yet careless what he brings, his one concern
> Is to conduct it to the destined inn;
> And having dropped the expected bag, pass on.
> He whistles as he goes, light-hearted wretch!
> Cold and yet cheerful; messenger of grief
> Perhaps to thousands, and of joy to some;
> To him indifferent whether grief or joy.
> Houses in ashes and the fall of stocks,
> Births, deaths, and marriages, epistles wet
> With tears that trickled down the writer's cheeks
> Fast as the periods from his fluent quill,
> Or charged with amorous sighs of absent swains
> Or nymphs responsive, equally affect
> His horse and him, unconscious of them all.[14]

And yet, notwithstanding this, and so many other passages
that seem like the very marrow of our being, Lord Byron
denies that Cowper was a poet!—The Mail-Coach is an improvement on the Post-Boy; but I fear it will hardly bear so
poetical a description. The picturesque and dramatic do not
keep pace with the useful and mechanical. The telegraphs[15]
that lately communicated the intelligence of the new revolution to all France within a few hours, are a wonderful contrivance; but they are less striking and appalling than the
beacon-fires (mentioned by Æschylus), which, lighted from
hill-top to hill-top, announced the taking of Troy, and the return of Agamemnon.

# Notes

## i *LITERATURE AND POLITICS*

### Observations on Mr. Wordsworth's Poem *The Excursion*

1 *Genesis* I: 2; *Paradise Lost* I, 21–2.
2 Gray to Horace Walpole; *Correspondence* (ed. Toynbee & Whibley) I, 47.
3 Wordsworth's phrase apparently; see Hazlitt's *Political Essays:* "he hates Shakespeare, or what he calls 'those interlocutions between Lucius and Caius,' because he would have all the talk to himself . . ." (*Complete Works*, vol. 7, p. 144).
4 Goldsmith, *Deserted Village*, 136.
5 Milton, *L'Allegro*, 138.
6 Wycherley, *Love in a Wood*, III, i.
7 *Excursion* II, 484.
8 A meditating man is deplorable.
9 Wordsworth has "mild."
10 Wordsworth, *Intimations of Immortality*, 175.
11 By Southey and Wordsworth respectively.
12 *Paradise Lost* III, 550.
13 *Lycidas*, 161.
14 subdivision of a county.
15 Andrew Bell (1753–1832), Joseph Lancaster (1770–1838), rival educational reformers.
16 Mateo Aleman, 1599.
17 Dedicatory Sonnet to the Earl of Lonsdale.

### A Modern Tory Delineated

1 1814.
2 Edward Jenner (1749–1823), discoverer of vaccination.
3 as a warning.
4 Napoleon.
5 The Prince Regent's.
6 At Nîmes, 1815, after the restoration of Louis XVIII.
7 The House of Commons.

## Coriolanus

1 *Macbeth,* I, vi, 6–8.
2 *Coriolanus,* II, i, 150.
3               But Thy most dreaded instrument,
              In working out a pure intent,
              Is Man—arrayed for mutual slaughter,
              —Yea, Carnage is thy daughter!
                      Wordsworth, "Ode, 1815" [on Waterloo].
This quatrain (eventually toned down in 1845) "perhaps more than any had given offence to Wordsworth's friends and foes alike" (de Selincourt).
4 III, i, 80f.

# ii *THE LECTURER*

## On Poetry in General

1 Dedication (1625), Bacon's *Essays.* "I doe now publish my *Essayes* . . . it seems, they come home, to Mens Businesse, and Bosomes."
2 *Romeo and Juliet,* I, i, 150–1.
3 *King Lear,* II, iv, 266.
4 *Midsummer Night's Dream,* V, i, 4–18.
5 *The Republic* X.
6 *Hamlet,* III, iv, 138–9.
7 *Advancement of Learning* II, iv, 2.
8 *Macbeth,* II, i, 44.
9 *Midsummer Night's Dream,* V, i, 19–22.
10 *Cymbeline,* II, ii, 19–21.
11 *King Lear,* IV, vii, 70.
12 *Othello,* IV, ii, 58–61.
13 18th-century dramatists.
14 *On the Sublime and Beautiful* I, 15.
15 *Merchant of Venice,* IV, i, 51–2.
16 *Dunciad* I, 89–90.
17 "Ode to Fear" 10, 14–15.
18 I, iv, 259–61.
19 *Hamlet,* III, ii, 20 (to the Players).
20 Gray, *Correspondence* (ed. Toynbee & Whibley) I, 47.
21 Thomas Chalmers, D.D., *A Series of Discourses on the Christian Revelation, viewed in connection with Modern Astronomy* (1817).
22 At the Dulwich Gallery; in fact, by Aert de Gelder (1645–1727).
23 *Macbeth,* V, v, 11–13.
24 Perhaps by Purcell; for D'Avenant's production, 1672.
25 *The Times,* Dec. 10, 1817, quoting New York papers, Oct. 27: "the piece . . . militates against . . . morality, literary taste, and instruction blended with innocent amusement."
26 Dodsley's *Collection of Poems.*

27  *Julius Caesar*, II, i, 63–9.
28  Now in the Victoria & Albert Museum, London.
29  i.e., the Elgin marbles in the British Museum.
30  *Paradise Lost* III, 37–8.
31  *Love's Labour's Lost*, V, ii, 917.
32  Milton, *L'Allegro*, 144.
33  *Love's Labour's Lost*, IV, ii, 117.
34  Gray, "Progress of Poesy," 116–7.
35  1705; on Marlborough's victory of Blenheim.
36  By Joseph Warton, in *An Essay on the Genius and Writings of Pope*.
37  Milton, *L'Allegro*, 137.
38  Spenser, *Ruines of Time*, 431.
39  By Sophocles.
40  *Twelfth Night*, II, iv, 20–1.
41  "a dead head"; from Alchemy: the worthless residue from which gold emerged.
42  *Timon of Athens*, I, i, 23–7.
43  The much-admired mock translations (1762-63) by James Macpherson, attributed to the Gaelic poet Ossian.
44  *1 Henry IV*, IV, i, 98–104.
45  *Psalms*, 139, 9f.
46  Abandon hope, ye that enter here; *Inferno* III, 9.
47  *Inferno* XI, 8.
48  *Inferno* XXXIII.
49  See following piece.
50  Colma's Lament, in the *Songs of Selma*.

## Sir Joshua Reynolds

1  The Roman sculpture.
2  In *The History of English Poetry*, 1781.
3  In "Speech on the Nabob of Arcot's Debts."

## Milton

1   *Paradise Lost* III, 35–36.
2   *PL* VII, 27.
3   *PL* XI, 324–5.
4   From the Preface to Book II of *The Reason of Church Government*.
5   *Faerie Queene* I, v, i.
6   *Hamlet*, V, i, 277.
7   Compositions "formed by joining scraps from other authors" (Johnson's *Dictionary*).
8   *PL* I, 204.
9   *Comus*, 556.
10  On a colossal statue, which gave out music when struck by the rising sun.
11  *L'Allegro*, 138–40.
12  i.e., the plot or story.
13  *Imitations of Horace*, 1st Epis., 2nd Bk, 102.

14   l.109 should read "And what is else not to be overcome?"
     Masson notes that Todd (1801) and later 18th-century editors
     "print this not as an interrogation, but as a clause in continu-
     ation of the four preceding", a reading which he rightly calls
     "languid."

15   *PL* II, 147–50.

16   *PL* I, 157–8.

17   *PL* I, 225–6.

18   *Defensio pro Populo Anglicano* (1651), a reply to a defense of
     Charles I by Claudius Salmasius of Leyden.

19   *PL* I, 46.

20   *PL* II, 547–50.

21   Dr. Stoddart, Hazlitt's brother-in-law, editor of *The Times*.

22   Napoleon.

23   *The Tempest*, II, i, 141f.

24   *The Excursion* VI, 554–7.

25   *PL* VII, 103: "unapparent," i.e., invisible.

26   Cowper, *Truth*, 327.

27   *St. Matthew* VI: 28–9.

28   Wordsworth, *Tintern Abbey*, 38–41.

29   *PL* I, 620.

# On the Periodical Essayists

1    Pope, *Essay on Man* II, 2.

2    Bacon, *Essays*, Dedication.

3    Juvenal, *Satire* I, 85–6. The motto of *The Tatler:* Everything
     men do is the motley subject of our paper.

4    *Hamlet*, III, ii, 24.

5    *Henry V*, I, i, 51–2.

6    *All's Well That Ends Well*, IV, iii, 67.

7    Horace, *Epistles*, I, 2, ll. 3–4: It shows us what is fair, what is
     foul, what is profitable, what not, more fully and better than a
     Chryssipus or a Crantor [who were exceptionally voluminous
     writers].

8    Michel de Montaigne (1533–92): *Essais*, 1580–88.

9    *Tristram Shandy*, III, 12.

10   *Imitations of Horace*, Sat. I, 51–2.

11   ethics by observation.

12   *Moral Essays* I, 87–8; Charron, friend of Montaigne, wrote
     *De la Sagesse* (On Wisdom).

13   Confound those who have said our best things before us.

14   Lucretius, *De Rerum Natura* II, 753–4.

15   Shaftesbury (1671–1713); *The Moralists, a philosophical rhap-
     sody*, 1709; *Characteristics*, 1711.

16   easy, unconstrained.

17   Judge of morals and manners.

18   *Macbeth*, III, i, 129.

19   Tuesday, April 12, 1709, to Jan. 2, 1711.

20   i.e., Steele; the name was adopted from Swift.

21   *Tatler*, No. 107.

22   No. 132.

23   No. 86.
24   Nos. 155, 160.
25   No. 238. The poem is Swift's.
26   Charles Lillie, shopkeeper of snuff, perfumes, etc.
27   Thomas Betterton (d.1710), a notable Hamlet and Brutus.
28   *The Spectator* appeared March 1, 1711, to Dec. 6, 1712; and
     June to Dec. 1714.
29   Dryden, *Aurengzebe*, IV, i.
30   *The Spectator,* No. 2.
31   No. 113.
32   Nos. 115, 116.
33   No. 122.
34   No. 122.
35   No. 130.
36   No. 117.
37   No. 109.
38   No. 106.
39   No. 112.
40   No. 108, etc.
41   No. 2, etc.
42   *The Tatler,* No. 250. The rest of the set, Nos. 253, 256, 259,
     262, 265, is the joint production of Addison and Steele.
43   Nos. 153, 157.
44   No. 95.
45   No. 151.
46   No. 104.
47   No. 94.
48   No. 82.
49   No. 172.
50   No. 117.
51   Bernard Mandeville (1670–1733); see Johnson's "Life of Addi-
     son."
52   No. 226.
53   *Lectures on Painting delivered at the Royal Academy,* 1820.
54   March to October 1713; Steele and Addison were the major
     contributors.
55   March 1750–March 1752.
56   will-o'-the-wisp.
57   *Paradise Lost* IV, 345–7.
58   Boswell, *Life of Johnson* (ed. Hill), II, 231.
59   Cowper, *The Task* IV, 119.
60   Boswell, I, 228–31.
61   Burns, "Auld Rob Morris," 2.
62   Boswell, II, 260.
63   II, 450.
64   I, 250–1.
65   II, 362.
66   I, 201.
67   II, 120.
68   IV, 321–2: Talfourd describes this point in the Lecture—"at
     which a titter arose from some, who were struck by the picture
     as ludicrous, and a murmur from others, who deemed the allu-

sion unfit for ears polite: he paused for an instant, and then added, in his sturdiest and most impressive manner, 'an act which realises the parable of the Good Samaritan'; at which his moral and his delicate hearers shrunk, rebuked, into deep silence." *Final Memorials of Lamb,* 1850, p.314.

69   Gray, *Elegy*, Epitaph.
70   1752–54.
71   1753–56; 1754–56.
72   Actually, in *The World*, No. 176.
73   Republished 1762, 2 vols.
74   *Merchant of Venice*, II, ix, 37–9.
75   By Lord Lyttleton, 1735.
76   literary censorship.
77   *The Citizen of the World*, Letter X.
78   *The Mirror*, Edinburgh, January 1779 to May 1780; *The Lounger*, February 1785 to January 1786. Henry Mackenzie (1745–1831) was chief contributor.
79   *The Mirror*, Nos. 42–44.
80   *Tristram Shandy*, VI, 6f.
81   Mackenzie, 1773.
82   1777.
83   1798, by Charles Lamb.
84   1771.

# On the English Novelists

1   April 1742.
2   1727–60.
3   *Joseph Andrews* III, 1.
4   John Eachard (d.1697).
5   a party of four.
6   Pope, *Essay on Man* IV, 3–4.
7   Part I, 1605; Part II, 1615.
8   By Mateo Aleman, 1599; translated by James Mabbe, 1623.
9   1553.
10   *The Rogue*, Mabbe's title.
11   By Alain-René Le Sage (1668–1747); 4 vols., 1715–35.
12   1748.
13   inside and out.
14   By Sheridan, 1775.
15   Boswell, *Life of Johnson* (ed. Hill), II, 174.
16   Wordsworth, "Personal Talk."
17   Boswell, *Life of Johnson* (ed. Hill), II, 222.
18   such a good unassuming little man.
19   1688 and 1714.
20   George III, reigned 1760–1820.

# On the Works of Hogarth

1   Lamb, "On the Genius and Character of Hogarth," 1811.
2   Pope, *Rape of the Lock* IV, 123–4.
3   *Othello* I, iii, 391–2.

4  Burke, *Reflections on the French Revolution.*
5  barrier.
6  Fielding compares Bridget Allworthy: *Tom Jones* I, xi.
7  See *Paradise Lost* I, 795–7.
8  with a deep, sudden plunge.
9  Perhaps Sir George Beaumont (1753–1827), painter, art patron, friend of Wordsworth.
10 David Wilkie (1785–1841), born Fife, Scotland.
11 David Teniers, the younger (1610–90), born Antwerp.
12 John Liston: "the only person on the stage with whom I have ever had any personal intercourse . . ." [Preface, *A View of the English Stage*]. "Mr. Liston has more comic humour, more power of farce, and a more genial and happy vein of folly, than any other actor we remember. His farce is not caricature: his drollery oozes out of his features, and trickles down his face: his voice is a pitch-pipe for laughter . . ." [*The Drama: No. I*, in *The London Magazine*, 1820].
13 "Evening" in *The Four Times of the Day*, 1738.
14 Paulson (*Hogarth's Graphic Works*, 1965) identifies this figure as a sow-gelder.
15 Reputedly based on a cousin of Dr. Johnson: Boswell, *Life of Johnson* (ed. Hill), I, 49.
16 Pope, *Essay on Man*, I, 200.
17 Rudolph Ackermann (1764–1834), fine art publisher, lithographer. His *Repository of Arts, Literature, Fashions, Manufactures, etc.* appeared regularly 1809–28.
18 See the Bedlam scene, "The Rake's Progress" Pl. 8; her name is carved on the bannisters.
19 A Wordsworthian phrase; see "Stray Pleasures."
20 *Romans* XII:2.
21 *Midsummer Night's Dream*, V, i, 14–17.
22 Scott, *Guy Mannering*, Ch. 55.
23 One of the Cartoons.
24 *2 Corinthians* V:1.
25 Thomson, *The Seasons*, "Summer," 1347.
26 Wordsworth, Sonnet, "The world is too much with us."
27 Wordsworthian echo: *Tintern Abbey*, 109–10.
28 Milton, *Comus*, 251.

## The Age of Elizabeth: A General View

1  *Paradise Lost* II, 1034.
2  *Cymbeline*, III, iv, 138–9.
3  *Paradise Lost* IV, 266.
4  *Hamlet*, I, v, 166–7.
5  Pope, *Imitations of Horace*, "To Augustus," 70.
6  *Paradise Lost* I, 779.
7  Sonnet 24.
8  *Paradise Lost* I, 590.
9  Sonnet, "London, 1802."
10 *Paradise Lost* II, 692.
11 1682.

12  *L'Allegro*, 132.
13  *Habakkuk* II:2.
14  *St. John* XIV:27 and XV:12.
15  *St. John* XIX:26–27.
16  1 *Corinthians* I:23.
17  Unidentified.
18  *Hamlet*, III, iii, 71 (Claudius praying).
19  *The Honest Whore*, Pt. 1., V, ii.
20  connoisseurship.
21  *Paradise Lost* III, 568–70.
22  *Faerie Queene* II, introduction.
23  *Hamlet*, III, iv, 138–9.
24  *Midsummer Night's Dream*, I, i, 134.
25  Burke, *Reflections on the French Revolution*.
26  Killed at Battle of Zutphen, 1586.
27  Executed, 1547.
28  "The Session of the Poets."
29  Keats, "Sleep and Poetry," 237.
30  *Canterbury Tales*, Prologue, 345.
31  *The Honest Whore*, Pt. 1, V, ii.
32  By Middleton.
33  *Othello*, II, i, 125f.
34  Ovid, *Metamorphoses* II, 5: The workmanship outshone the material.
35  Lyly, *Midas*, IV, i.


# iii  ESSAYIST AND CRITIC

## The Manager

1  *Daniel* II:31f.
2  Fairy-tale character who also had an inexhaustible purse.
3  drinkable gold.
4  *The Tempest*, V, i, 50.
5  Pope, *Moral Essays* III, 305–6.

## On the Pleasure of Painting

1  Cowper, *The Task* III, 227–8.
2  rich spoils; highest achievement.
3  Goethe, *The Sorrows of Young Werther*, Bk. I, Letter May 26.
4  Sir Edward Dyer (d.1607).
5  Bacon, *Advancement of Learning* I, viii, 3.
6  Dryden, *Satires of Persius*, II, 133.
7  Cf. "Prose-Style of Poets": Burke's style "savours of the texture of what he describes, and his pen slides or drags over the ground of his subject like the painter's pencil."
8  Richard Wilson (1714–82).
9  Claude Lorrain, settled in Rome, 1627; died there 1682.
10  Italian = bright-dark.
11  1 *Corinthians* XIII:12.

12  Wordsworth, *Tintern Abbey*, 49.
13  17th-century Dutch painters.
14  *Paradise Lost* V, 435–6.
15  John Opie (1761–1807), portrait and history painter.
    Henry Fuseli (1741–1825), born Switzerland: "The Night-
    mare" (1782); professor of painting at Royal Academy (1799).
    James Northcote (1746–1831), portrait painter.
16  Jonathan Richardson (1665–1745): *Essays*, 1715 and 1719.
17  Donne, *Second Anniversary* 245–6.
18  1705–74; Hazlitt abridged his 7-vol. *The Light of Nature
    Pursued*.
19  *2 Henry IV*, IV, iv, 92.
20  December 2, 1805.

## The Indian Jugglers

1   John Wolcot (1738–1819), physician and satirist.
2   Hazlitt speaks from experience; see Howe, *Life*, pp.61–2.
3   *The Deserted Village*, 211–12.
4   Hindu idol, dragged in procession.
5   e.g., Hayman, Highmore, Hoppner, Hudson.
6   Gray, *Correspondence* I, 47.
7   Pope, *Essay on Man*, I, 218.
8   Leigh Hunt.
9   melodious trifles.
10  An illiterate arithmetical genius, d. 1772.
11  A contrivance of John Napier (1550–1617) inventor of loga-
    rithms.
12  d. 1793.
13  By Hazlitt.
14  Fives; played in a walled court, the ball struck with the hand.
15  Horace, *Odes* III, 40.
16  ace: i.e., any one point.
17  See Boswell, *Life of Johnson* (ed. Hill), I, 414.
18  Here lies . . .; Wordsworth, "Ellen Irwin."

## On Antiquity

1   Song by Lady Ann Barnard (1750–1825), taken to be a "relic."
2   Confound those who have said our good things before us.
3   15th-century prose romance.
4   By Richard Johnson, 1596–97.
5   *Tempest*, I, ii, 50.
6   Used by Shakespeare; John Stow (d.1605), editor of Holinshed.
7   *Faerie Queene* II, ix, 56.
8   Cimabue, d. 1302; Giotto, d. 1336; Ghirlandaio, 1449–94.
9   Bk. II, Cto. x.
10  *Alaham*, actually.
11  III, 1461–2.
12  An ancient Greek.
13  A travel book (1611) by Thomas Coryate.

14  An encyclopaedia (1662) of English local history etc.
15  Thomas Warton (1728–90): Hazlitt admired his Sonnets.
16  Hazlitt reviewed Mrs. Siddons's Lady Macbeth in 1817: "It is nearly twenty years since we first saw her in this character, and certainly the impression which we have still left on our minds from that first exhibition, is stronger than the one we received the other evening. The sublimity of Mrs. Siddons's acting is such, that the first impulse which it gives to the mind can never wear out . . . The impression is stamped there for ever, and any after-experiments and critical enquiries only serve to fritter away and tamper with the sacredness of the early recollection."
17  literally and verbatim.
18  Hazlitt appends the whole exchange between Rosalind and Orlando: *As You Like It*, III, ii, 290–310.
19  Hazlitt appends a long passage (from Vol. 30) referring to "the dark and sceptical spirit prevalent through the works" of Lord Byron, and contrasting "the comparative disregard and indifference" with which Greek and Roman authors "contemplated those subjects of darkness and mystery which afford at some period or other of his life, so much disquiet—we had almost said so much agony, to the mind of every reflecting modern."

## On a Landscape of Nicolas Poussin

1  Shown in 1821 at the annual exhibition of Old Masters, British Institution, London; now in Metropolitan Museum of Art, New York.
2  *Paradise Lost* VII, 373–4.
3  *Othello*, III, iii, 432; Hazlitt and Lamb were the first to adopt this phrase into general usage.
4  *Isaiah* XL: 15.
5  *Midsummer Night's Dream*, V, i, 16–17.
6  By Mrs. Graham (1820).
7  Benjamin West (1738–1820), born Pennsylvania, succeeded Reynolds as President of the Royal Academy in 1792.
8  "The Plague at Ashdod," in the Louvre.
9  Or "Winter," Louvre.
10  "Cephalus and Aurora," National Gallery, London.
11  *Faerie Queene* I, vi, 14.
12  I too have lived in Arcady! Both Hazlitt's quotation and general description are poetic rather than precise; see E. Panofsky, *Meaning in the Visual Arts* (1955), "*Et in Arcadia Ego*: Poussin and the Elegiac Tradition."
13  Milton, *Lycidas*, 136.
14  *Hamlet*, I, v, 103–4 (Hazlitt's parenthesis).
15  Milton, *Comus*, 263.
16  Milton, Sonnet XVII, to Lawrence.
17  *Faerie Queene* III, vi, 31, 32.
18  The paintings were restored to Italy on Napoleon's fall; Napoleon had died on May 5, 1821.

## On Going a Journey

1  Bloomfield, *The Farmer's Boy*, "Spring," 31.
2  A smack at the Picturesque.
3  Cowper, *Retirement*, 741–2.
4  *Comus*, 378–80.
5  Beaumont and Fletcher, *Philaster*, V, v.
6  The house in Somerset where Wordsworth stayed, 1797–98. Coleridge lived in the neighbouring village of Nether Stowey.
7  Fletcher, I, v.
8  Cowper, *The Task* IV, 39–40.
9  *Aeneid* VI, 258: Away, away, unhallowed ones.
10  makes no mischief.
11  *Othello*, I, ii, 26–7.
12  Dryden, *To my Honour'd Kinsman*, 18; for "name" read "wife." This and the preceding quotation both refer to the ties of marriage; at the time of writing Hazlitt was living apart from his wife.
13  Simon Gribelin published the Raphael Cartoons 1707.
14  Rousseau, *La Nouvelle Héloïse* IV, xvii.
15  "Ode to the Departing Year," VII.
16  Coleridge, *Wallenstein*, V, i, 68.
17  See Wordsworth, *Tintern Abbey*, 55–6.
18  *Tintern Abbey*, 61.
19  Etherege, *The Man of Mode*, V, ii: Harriet to Dorimant.
20  *Paradise Lost* III, 550.
21  From a popular song in which William Roscoe, Liverpool businessman, voluminous writer, and patron of Hazlitt as a painter, saluted the French Revolution.
22  Boswell, *Life of Johnson* (ed. Hill), III, 352.

## The Fight

1  the patrons, fanciers, of boxing.
2  poor-quality gin.
3  Joseph Parkes (1796–1865), lawyer, frequenter of Jeremy Bentham.
4  each other's self.
5  P. G. Patmore.
6  *Muiopotmos*, St. 27.
7  Keeper of the Castle tavern, Holborn; younger brother of the famous prizefighter, James (Jim) Belcher.
8  *Julius Caesar*, IV, iii, 284.
9  *The Indian Emperor*, IV, iii.
10  John Thurtell (1794–1824), organizer of sporting events; shortly after, a murderer.
11  Tom Hickman, of London.
12  producing merriment, cheering.
13  Bill Richmond, the Negro boxing master; Hazlitt seems to have taken lessons from him.
14  *Macbeth*, III, iv, 38–9.
15  *Henry V*, IV, i, 272–3.

16  drug from crabapple; poison from wolf's-bane (Shakespeare).
17  of a fine day.
18  Cowper's John Gilpin.
19  Charles Matthews, actor.
20  *Canterbury Tales,* Prologue 167.
21  his stick.
22  ill-smelling, unkempt.
23  In *Henry IV,* Pt. 1.
24  Cobbett's weekly paper.
25  Tom Cribb beat Belcher in 1807 and 1809.
26  John Gully (1783–1863), former boxer, later a racing book-maker.
27  Henry Pearce (1777–1809).
28  *Julius Caesar,* II, i, 63–5.
29  heavy traveling coat.
30  a line drawn across the ring.
31  *Paradise Lost* II, 714–16.
32  John ("Gentleman") Jackson, the well-known fighter; retired 1803.
33  Jack Scroggins, prizefighter.
34  "Ballad of Chevy-Chase," St. 50.
35  Begone, profane ones.
36  knowledgeable sporting followers.
37  Rousseau's famous romance.
38  Conqueror of Scroggins.
39  Actually in 1741.

## On the Prose-Style of Poets

1  Hazlitt writes in a theater criticism of 1816: "There is a tone of recitation in this actor's delivery, perhaps not ill suited to the whining sentimentality of the parts he has to play, but which is very tiresome to the ear. We might say to him as Caesar did to someone, Do you read or sing? If you sing, you sing very ill."
2  John Horne Tooke (1736–1812), politician and philologist; elected Member of Parliament for Old Sarum, 1801.
3  Wordsworth, "A Poet's Epitaph."
4  Liberal politician; d. 1806.
5  a break in the text.
6  = against the grain; Horace, *Ars Poetica,* 385.
7  at his pleasure.
8  A diamond-like quartz.
9  Wordsworth, "Personal Talk."
10  Shakespeare, *Sonnets,* cvi.
11  Published 1796; addressed to his friend Earl Fitzwilliam, a reply "on the attacks made upon Mr. Burke and his pension, in the House of Lords, by the Duke of Bedford and the Earl of Lauderdale . . ."
12  *Aeneid* IX, 448-9: as long as the house of Aeneas shall dwell on the Capitol's unshaken rock, and the Father of Rome hold sovereign sway [Loeb translation].

13  while the pleasure lasts.
14  Ode, "On a Distant Prospect of Eton College."
15  "Speech on the Nabob of Arcot's Debts," Feb. 28, 1785.
16  *A Letter to a Noble Lord.*
17  *Paradise Lost* I, 200–2.
18  *Job* XLI, 1–2.
19  *The Sheffield Iris*, begun by James Montgomery in 1794.
20  Castlereagh committed suicide August 12, 1822.
21  See Pope's "self-praise," *Epistle to Dr. Arbuthnot*, 340–1, "That not in Fancy's Maze he wandered long, / But stooped to Truth, and moralized his song."
22  *Love's Labour's Lost*, V, ii, 917.
23  His early revolutionary drama (1794), published to his embarrassment in 1817.
24  Leigh Hunt, *The Story of Rimini*, 1816.
25  Ran from October 1819 to March 1821.
26  Author of *Holy Living and Holy Dying*, 1650–51; chaplain to Charles I.

# My First Acquaintance with Poets

1  *Paradise Lost* II, 964–5.
2  *Coriolanus*, V, vi, 115–6.
3  Gray, "The Bard," 28.
4  Pope, "Ode on St. Cecilia's Day," 90–1.
5  Rousseau, *La Nouvelle Héloise*, VI, 7: St. Preux to Julie, a telescoped quotation. There are impressions which neither time nor circumstances can efface. Though I should live whole centuries, the sweet time of my youth can never be born again, nor can it ever wear away in my memory.
6  *St. John* VI:15.
7  *Comus*, 556.
8  *St. Matthew* III:3–4.
9  Pope, *Epistle to Robert, Earl of Oxford*, 1.
10  Divine Right.
11  *Lycidas*, 106.
12  Thomson, *Castle of Indolence* II, xxxiii.
13  1759–97; wife of Godwin, mother of Mary Shelley, author of *Vindication of the Rights of Women* (1792). James Mackintosh (1765–1832); his "Rights of the French" (1791) was an answer to Burke's *Reflections on the French Revolution*.
14  Second son (1771–1805) of the potter.
15  Thomas Holcroft (1745–1809), author, friend of Paine and Godwin. Hazlitt edited and completed his *Memoirs;* published 1816.
16  The River Dee in Cheshire.
17  A romance by La Calprenède.
18  Apella the Jew can believe it! (not me); Horace, *Satires*, I, v, 100.
19  Boswell, *Life of Johnson* (ed. Hill), I, 471.
20  It eventually appeared as *An Essay on the Principles of Human Action*, 1805.

21  William Paley (1743–1805); *Evidences of Christianity*, 1794.
22  *Paradise Lost* VIII, 648–50.
23  *Biographia Literaria*, Ch. 10.
24  Byron's, just published, in *The Liberal*, No. 1.
25  Charles Murray, solicitor to the Constitutional Association, founded 1821, with offices at New Bridge St., "to support the laws for suppressing seditious publications, and for defending the country from the fatal influence of disloyalty and sedition."
26  By Bernardin de St. Pierre (1788).
27  By Fanny Burney (1796).
28  Wordsworth in fact rented the house for one year at £23. His previous residence, Racedown, had been freely lent him by the Pinneys of Bristol.
29  Ben Jonson, "To Sir Robert Wroth."
30  i.e., Wordsworth's "The Idiot Boy"; this, with the other poems named, was published in *Lyrical Ballads*, September 1798.
31  Pope, *Essay on Man* I, 293.
32  Thomson, *Seasons*, "Spring," 18.
33  *Paradise Lost* II, 559–60.
34  Sir Francis Chantrey (1781–1841).
35  Benjamin R. Haydon (1786–1846); see his *Autobiography* I, 260: "I now [1817] put Hazlitt's head into my picture looking at Christ as an investigator. It had a good effect. I then put in Keats in the background, and resolved to introduce Wordsworth bowing in reverence and awe. Wordsworth was highly pleased. . . ." The painting was exhibited in 1820.
36  *ad captandum vulgus* = aimed to appeal to popular taste.
37  Composed 1798, published 1819.
38  A hot sweetened mixture of beer and spirits.
39  At the banquet given by the Magistrates of Edinburgh to George IV in August, 1822.
40  *The Wanderings of Cain*.
41  Solomon Gessner, *Tod Abels* (1758).
42  William Godwin's first novel (1794).
43  *Ancient Mariner*, 227.
44  "Remarks on the Systems of Hartley and Helvetius," added to his *Essay on Human Action*.
45  Produced 1813.
46  Unidentified.
47  Wordsworth, "Hart-leap Well," 95–6.

## On Londoners and Country People

1  A dark room, into which views of the world outside are projected through a lens.
2  i.e., keeps to the nongutter side of the pavement in passing.
3  Anterooms of a theater.
4  A tout for shop, auction, etc.
5  A dealer in the cheapest clothes.
6  Objects turned on a lathe.

7   Richard Whittington (d.1423), three times Lord Mayor of London.
8   Thomas Pennant, *Some Account of London*, 1790.
9   Built, 1612, by Sir Baptist Hicks. Milestones on the Great North Road were measured from it.
10  Operatic tenors.
11  Jack Randall, pugilist.
12  Author of *A Discourse of Freethinking* (1713).
13  i.e., Hazlitt's review of *The Excursion*.
14  Sheridan, *The Duenna*, III, v.
15  *2 Henry IV*, III, ii.

# Whether Genius Is Conscious of Its Powers?

1   *Julius Caesar*, I, ii, 52–3.
2   *Paradise Lost* V, 272.
3   The workmanship overwhelmed the material.
4   *Timon of Athens*, I, i, 23–7.
5   against the grain.
6   Now attributed to Aert de Gelder (Dulwich Gallery).
7   Lamb, "Lines on the celebrated Picture by Lionardo da Vinci, called the Virgin of the Rocks", 1805.
8   Gray, *Correspondence* I, 47.
9   Sir Edward Dyer.
10  For his *Lectures on the English Comic Writers* IV, "On Wycherley, Congreve, etc."
11  In Dekker's *Honest Whore: Lectures on the Age of Elizabeth* III.
12  William Gifford (1756–1826) first editor of *The Quarterly Review* and one of Hazlitt's malicious attackers.
13  i.e., Napoleon.
14  *Revelation* XIII:15.
15  William Jerdan (1782–1869), a Tory arbiter of the influential *Literary Gazette*. Hazlitt's collection of aphorisms, *Characteristics*, appeared in 1823.
16  treason.
17  Leigh Hunt (1784–1859), friend of Keats, Shelley, Byron.
18  *Lycidas*, 132–3.
19  William Blackwood (1776–1834), Edinburgh publisher of the magazine. John Wilson Croker (1780–1857), Tory politician, Secretary to the Admiralty, contributor to *The Quarterly*. Thomas Moore (1779–1852), the Irish poet and musician.
20  *All's Well That Ends Well*, I, i, 79–81.
21  *Romeo and Juliet*, II, ii, 21–2.
22  Cowper, *The Task* V, 901.
23  Juvenal, *Satires* VII, 154: second helping of cabbage; the line refers to the "fatal" effect on schoolmasters of hearing pupils repeat recitations.
24  Titian was working on this.
25  Pseudonymous author of a series of brilliant political attacks, 1769–71.

## The Dulwich Gallery

1  Shakespeare, Sonnet 73.
2  Edward Alleyn (1566–1626), actor, founder of the College.
3  Latin grammar.
4  *Twelfth Night*, II, iv, 112.
5  Roman historian, frequent textbook.
6  A kind of marbles.
7  Landscape painter to George III; died 1811.
8  Picture dealer (d.1807), house in Pall Mall.
9  *Il Penseroso*, 160.
10  Albert Cuyp (1620–91).
11  Middleton, *Women Beware Women*, III, i.
12  *Macbeth*, II, i, 44–5.

## The Marquis of Stafford's Gallery

1  *Advancement of Learning* I, viii, 6.
2  In the Uffizi, Florence.
3  From the Parthenon; collected by Earl of Elgin, sold to British
   Government; in British Museum 1816.
4  In the Vatican.
5  David Wilkie (1785–1841).
6  John Hoole (1727–1803), translator of Tasso's *Jerusalem Delivered* (1763) and Ariosto's *Orlando Furioso* (1783).
7  *Julius Caesar*, IV, iii, 22.
8  At present in the National Gallery of Scotland.

# iv *THE SPIRIT OF THE AGE*

## (selections)
## Jeremy Bentham

1  *St. Matthew*, XIII:57.
2  "Bentham had many disciples among the patriots of South
   America, and in 1808 thought seriously of going to Mexico"
   (Waller & Glover).
3  Alexander I, Czar of Russia.
4  John Cam Hobhouse, Member of Parliament for Westminster,
   returned 1820.
5  John Rolle, "sat for the great maritime county of Devonshire"
   (Waller & Glover).
6  Pope, *Eloisa to Abelard*, 58: "And waft a sigh from Indus to
   the Pole."
7  M.P. for Westminster, died 1819.
8  i.e., the records of burial and baptism kept by the parishes of
   London.
9  Towns sending representatives to Parliament, but "owned" by
   private interests; not open to public competition.
10  Placed by Hazlitt himself: "In the spring of 1811 my father
   removed to London, and tenanted of Mr. Bentham the house

in York Street, Westminster, once honoured in the occupation of Milton, a circumstance which is commemorated on a small tablet, in the yard at the back of the house, placed there by my father in his veneration for the Poet and the Patriot" [Hazlitt's son, *Literary Remains,* 1836]. Hazlitt rented the house until 1819.

11  To apply the reformer Joseph Lancaster's principles to the education of the middle classes. It came to nothing. Chrestomathic = devoted to learning useful matters.

12  Benjamin Franklin (1706–90) the celebrated American scientist and statesman.

13  1749–1806; liberal politician.

14  *Paradise Lost* III, 602–3.

15  "a dead head"; from alchemy; what is left after the gold has been made.

16  last, most remote concern of the philosophers.

17  *Aeneid* I, 203. It will some day be a joy to recall.

18  The chaplain of Newgate prison.

19  *Essays,* II, xii.

20  From which prisoners of old Newgate set out for execution.

21  Died 1686; notorious public hangman and executioner.

22  Introduced on the Thames, 1776.

23  "A contrivance for executing felons at Newgate" (*New English Dictionary,* Oxford).

24  A scheme published in 1791; it came to nothing.

25  *A Sentimental Journey.*

26  Robert Owen (1771–1858), socialist and businessman; developed mills at New Lanark on the Clyde (from 1800 onwards) on philanthropic principles.

27  A pamphlet describing his principles.

28  Coleridge's second *Lay Sermon* (1817) was "addressed to the higher and middle classes."

29  J. Dunn Hunter, *Memoirs of a Captivity amongst the Indians of North America, from Childhood to the Age of Nineteen,* 1824.

30  *A Defence of Usury,* 1787.

31  Charles Abbot, Speaker of the House of Commons, 1802–17.

32  For shame!

33  At Queen's College, Oxford, 1760–66.

34  Published 1818.

## Mr. Coleridge

1  From commendatory verses on Shakespeare, in the Second Folio.

2  *Anthony and Cleopatra,* IV, xiv, 9–11.

3  *Paradise Lost* I, 22–3.

4  *Macbeth,* III, v, 28–9: "blear illusion," *Comus,* 155.

5  *Coriolanus,* II, ii, 75.

6  Gray, "Progress of Poesy," 115–6.

7  Pope, *Epistle to Arbuthnot,* 128.

8  See Lamb, *Essays of Elia,* "Christ's Hospital 35 Years Ago."

9   Wordsworth, *Excursion* VI, 557.
10  David Hartley (1705–57), author of *Observations on Man* (1749).
11  *Two Gentlemen of Verona*, II, vii, 31–2.
12  1638–1715.
13  1678.
14  Fulke Greville, Lord Brooke (1554–1628).
15  Joseph Butler (1692–1752).
16  Margaret Cavendish (1624–74).
17  Three late 17th-century–early 18th-century divines.
18  "Leibnitz [in opposition to Locke] contended that there was a germ or principle of truth, a pre-established harmony between its innate faculties and its acquired ideas, implied in the essence of the mind itself." Hazlitt, *Lectures on English Philosophy*, "On Locke's 'Essay on the Human Understanding'."
19  dry garden (plants dried and arranged in a book).
20  15th-century Bohemian protestant martyrs; Socinus, 16th-century Italian theologian.
21  1732–8.
22  Edmund Calamy (1671–1732), *Account of the Ministers, Lecturers, Masters and Fellows of Colleges and Schoolmasters who were Ejected or Silenced after the Restoration in 1660*.
23  Coleridge, *Remorse*, IV, ii, 101–3.
24  Jacob Boehme (1575–1624), the mystic.
25  See Coleridge's *Monody on the Death of Chatterton* (later version), 151.
26  The Divine Right of the Bourbons.
27  A glance at Southey and Wordsworth respectively.
28  *A Series of Essays to Aid in the Formation of Fixed Principles, in Politics, Morals, and Religion, with Literary Amusements Interspersed*, 2nd edn., 1818.
29  Dance for three.
30  I paint for all time.
31  The first British seagoing steamship sailed in 1815, Liverpool–Glasgow.
32  Pope, *Essay on Man* III, 177.
33  Gray, *The Bard* II, 2.
34  See *Paradise Lost* II, 112–7.
35  Collins, *Oriental Eclogues* II.

# Rev. Mr. Irving

1   Edward Irving (1792-1834) came from Glasgow to London in 1822 as minister of the Caledonian Asylum Chapel, Hatton Garden.
2   Bill Neate (see "The Fight") lost to Tom Spring in May 1823 after eight rounds and thirty-seven minutes.
3   The fat priest in the legend of Robin Hood.
4   Pugilist, killed at Waterloo.
5   A throw in wrestling.
6   Tom Cribb, Tom Molineaux, pugilists.
7   "Elizabeth Wright Macauley (1785–1837), poetess, actress,

public reader, pamphleteer and preacher, appeared at Covent Garden in 1819 in the roles of Mary Stuart and Jane Shore, but did not satisfy the managers, and was dismissed. After that, she gave public readings and became a woman with a grievance" [Waller & Glover].

8 "The upper rooms . . . were let for various purposes, among others . . . a menagerie" [Waller & Glover].

9 *Paradise Lost* I, 196.

10 Robert Lloyd, "The Actor" (1760).

11 "framed to make women false": *Othello*, I, iii, 391–2.

12 *Canterbury Tales*, Prologue, 167.

13 Liberal politician, a founder of *The Edinburgh Review*.

14 Politician and author, founder of *The Anti-Jacobin*.

15 Prime Minister.

16 *Coriolanus*, V, vi, 115–6.

17 Pietro Aretino (1492–1557).

18 Peter of Amiens (c.1050–1115), soldier, Crusader, and monk.

19 clear slate.

20 Cowper, *The Task* I, 749.


# Sir Walter Scott

1 Tasmania.

2 1805, 1808.

3 of a different kind.

4 *Agnes, or the Triumph of Principle*, 1822.

5 ballet dancers.

6 No relation; editor of *The London Magazine*; died after a duel, 1821.

7 Richard Westall illustrated *Marmion* and *The Lord of the Isles*.

8 Edinburgh, or "the Modern Athens."

9 i.e., eyrie (as in *Hamlet*, II, ii, 334).

10 In *Guy Mannering*.

11 Earl of Roscommon, translation of Horace, *Art of Poetry*, 281–2.

12 *Faerie Queene* III, xii, 13.

13 Hazlitt means Elspeth Mucklebackit.

14 The most famous member of the Roman Catholic conspiracy to blow up the Houses of Parliament in 1605.

15 Hazlitt refers to *Ivanhoe*, beginning of Ch. 43: "But the earnest desire to look on blood and death is not peculiar to those dark ages. . . . Even in our own days, when morals are better understood, an execution, a bruising match, a riot, or a meeting of radical reformers, collects at considerable hazard to themselves, immense crowds of spectators, otherwise little interested, except to see how matters are to be conducted, or whether the heroes of the day are, in the heroic language of insurgent tailors, flints or dunghills."

16 John Loudon McAdam (1756–1836), inventor of "tarmac."

17 *'Tis sixty years since*, the second title of *Waverley*.

18  The Metropolitan Police were eventually established by Robert
    Peel in 1829.
19  Those marked "Old Play" etc. are by Scott himself. He did
    not publicly admit authorship until 1827.
20  Goldsmith, *Retaliation*, 31–2; of Burke.
21  Pope, *Epistle to Dr. Arbuthnot*, 213–4. Hazlitt here regards
    Scott as a founder of the *Quarterly*, an associate of *Black-
    wood's*, and a recent subsidizer of the *Beacon*, a scurrilous
    anti-Radical paper.

## Mr. Wordsworth

1   *Julius Caesar*, II, i, 231–2.
2   I hold that nothing human is foreign to me.
3   *Tempest*, IV, i, 151–6.
4   anew, on a clean slate.
5   *Measure for Measure*, II, ii, 59–61.
6   Wordsworth, "To my Sister."
7   *Excursion* VI.
8   *Ode, Intimations of Immortality*.
9   The seat of Sir George Beaumont.
10  *Laodamia*, 72.
11  Goldsmith, *The Traveller*, 232.
12  nothing but partridge.
13  See note to *Excursion* review.
14  *The Borderers*, written 1795–6, published 1842; see ll. 1539–
    43.
15  One who slays "both friend and foe"; Duke of Buckingham,
    *The Rehearsal*, V, i.
16  William Paley (1743–1805), author of *Evidences of Christian-
    ity* (1794).
17  Thomas Bewick (1753–1828); Antoine Waterloo, C17.
18  By Hazlitt himself; in one of his "Illustrations of the Times
    Newspaper," and in his Lecture "On the Living Poets."
19  Butler, *Hudibras* II, 29–30.

## Mr. Crabbe

1   Thomas Campbell (1777–1844), author of *The Pleasures of
    Hope* (1799), *Gertrude of Wyoming* (1809), "Hohenlinden,"
    etc.
2   *As You Like It*, III, iii, 15.
3   literally and verbatim.
4   Crabbe's first poem was "Inebriety" (1775); Johnson approved
    *The Village* (1783); see Boswell, *Life of Johnson* (ed. Hill),
    IV, 175.
5   *Moral Essays* III, 299.
6   Bernard Mandeville (1670–1733), of *The Fable of the Bees;*
    Thomas Malthus (1766–1834), of *An Essay on the Principle
    of Population*.

7  Crabbe was chaplain to the Fourth Duke of Rutland; *The Borough* is dedicated to the Fifth.
8  *The Borough*, Letter XXII, "Peter Grimes."
9  i.e., from *The Parish Register* (1807) onwards.
10 Actually, *Parish Register* II.

# v  FINAL YEARS

## Notes of a Journey through France and Italy: Ch. I

1  Elizabeth Fry (1780–1845), Quaker and prison reformer.
2  *Cymbeline*, III, iv, 138.
3  respect to the ladies.
4  Goldsmith, *The Traveller*, 41–2.
5  Louis XVIII, the Desired.

## Notes of a Journey . . . Ch. XIX (*in part*)

1  eating-house.
2  In the Vatican.
3  Holy Year.
4  By Canova, 1819.
5  In the 16th century.
6  Byron's friend produced *Historical Illustrations of the Fourth Canto of 'Childe Harold'* in 1818.
7  Cowper, *The Task* I, 78; alludes to the Duke of Buckingham's farce *The Rehearsal,* in which the two rival kings are reconciled.
8  for form's sake.

## Of Persons One Would Wish to Have Seen

1  *Macbeth*, IV, i, 111.
2  Of the Gunpowder Plot, 1605.
3  Pope, *Moral Essays* II, 51–2.
4  William Ayrton (1777–1858), music critic.
5  *Hamlet*, III, iv, 135.
6  *Il Penseroso*, 109–10.
7  *Religio Medici* II, ix; written 1635. Browne married once, in 1641, and produced 12 children.
8  "Epithalamion on the Lady Elizabeth and Count Palatine," 85–8.
9  Hazlitt (or Lamb) omits, in deference to the ladies, the short passage about "th' indifferent Italian . . . well content to think thee Page" and the "spungy hydroptique Dutch."
10 Pope, *Epistle to Arbuthnot*, 128.
11 Boccaccio.
12 Cadmus, traditionally introducer of letters to Greece.
13 *Inferno* XXXIII.
14 *Comus*, 299–301.
15 *Faerie Queene* IV, xi, 23.

16 Capt. James Burney, brother of Fanny.
17 Unidentified.
18 Martha Blount, to whom Pope dedicated "Of the Characters of Women."
19 Unidentified.
20 See Boswell, *Life of Johnson* (ed. Hill), I, 176 & n.
21 *Imitations of Horace*, "Epistle to Murray," 60–2.
22 *Ibid.*, 50–3.
23 *Epilogue to the Satires* II, 138–9.
24 *Epistle to Arbuthnot*, 135–46.
25 highest excellence.
26 Edward Phillips, parliamentary secretary.
27 Farquhar, *Sir Harry Wildair*, and Jonson, *The Alchemist*.
28 fire.
29 Famous Roman actor.
30 Hanged for murder.
31 James Crichton (1560–85), educated at St. Andrews; Catholic, linguist, swordsman, served in French army. His title originated in Sir Thomas Urquhart's account of him, 1652.
32 John Rickman (1771–1840), census taker.
33 1703–58; philosopher, preacher, missionary.
34 Died 1809.
35 irritable race [of authors]; Horace.
36 In *The Beggar's Opera;* Lavinia Fenton married the Third Duke in 1751.
37 "The Bakeress," by Raphael, Rome.
38 School-usher and poet; an absent-minded eccentric. See Lamb's *Essays of Elia*, "Amicus Redivivus."
39 Margaret Cavendish (1624–74).
40 Lucy, b. 1620; wrote a life of her husband, Colonel Hutchinson, published 1806.
41 A 17th-century beauty.
42 Hazlitt's.
43 *Coriolanus*, II, i, 182–3.
44 Napoleon's return from Elba, 1815, which broke up the Congress of Vienna.

## The New School of Reform (*in part*)

1 the beautiful; the useful, respectively.
2 J. S. Mill in the *Edinburgh Review* (April 1824), instancing Hazlitt, considered "declamation and sentimentality" a current fault in English writing even more than French.
3 "That action is best which promises the greatest happiness to the greatest numbers." Hutcheson, *Inquiry into the Original of our Ideas of Beauty and Virtue* (1720). Bentham adopted the phrase.
4 The Cameronian in Scott's *Heart of Mid-Lothian*.
5 persons claiming special enlightenment.
6 *Muiopotmos*, 209f.
7 *Advancement of Learning* I, iv, 7.
8 "Malthus's population principle was quite as much a banner,

and point of union among us, as any opinion specially belonging to Bentham. This great doctrine, originally brought forward as an argument against the indefinite improvability of human affairs, we took up with ardent zeal in the contrary sense, as indicating the sole means of realizing that improvability by securing full employment at high wages to the whole labouring population through a voluntary restriction of the increase of their numbers." J. S. Mill, *Autobiography*, Ch. iv.

9  flirtatious winks.

10 George Canning (1770–1827), contributor to *The Anti-Jacobin*, appointed Foreign Secretary, 1822.

11 James Mill, father of J. S., appointed Assistant-Examiner of Indian Correspondence in 1819.

12 J. W. Croker.

13 *The Westminster Review*, a quarterly financed and founded by Bentham in 1824.

14 out of the fight.

15 The article "Charitable Institutions," July 1824, advocated the closing of dispensaries and foundling and lying-in hospitals in the name of "the principle of population."

## On the Feeling of Immortality in Youth

1  Addison, *Cato*, V, i.

2  *Macbeth*, V, viii, 12.

3  Collins, "The Passions," 32.

4  *Measure for Measure*, III, i, 121–2.

5  *Tristram Shandy* V, vii.

6  Joseph Fawcett (d.1804), Unitarian minister, poet, an early friend of Hazlitt.

7  Pope, *Imitations of Horace*, Satire I, 128.

8  Thomson, *Castle of Indolence* I, st. 4.

9  Mary Wortley Montagu (1689–1762), wife of an ambassador to Constantinople; introduced smallpox inoculation to England.

10 I, 415 (ed. Halsband).

11 Turkish bureaucrat.

12 III, 57 (ed. Halsband): link-boy = torch-carrier for lighting people along streets.

13 a huge two-shaped monster; *Aeneid* III, 658, adapted.

14 *Letters* III, 87.

15 Cowper, *Charity*, 104.

16 *Samson Agonistes*, 81.

17 Coleridge, Sonnet "To the Author of 'The Robbers'" (Schiller).

18 Schiller's drama (1787).

19 Wordsworth, *Tintern Abbey*, 83–5.

20 Gray, *Elegy*, 91–2.

21 Dryden, *Aurengzebe*, IV, i.

22 *Macbeth*, III, ii, 25–6.

## On a Sun-Dial

1 *3 Henry VI*, II, v, 24.
2 *As You Like It*, II, vii, 29.
3 Love makes Time pass.
4 *Merchant of Venice*, V, i, 54.
5 dead head (Alchemy): i.e., a worthless residue.
6 *Confessions* II, xi.
7 "Come, my son; I am more of a child than you!" *Confessions* I, i.
8 *King John*, III, iii, 38–9.
9 *Il Penseroso*, 76.
10 The invisible and the nonexistent are to be accounted the same.
11 in vacancy.
12 "Frost at Midnight," 29.
13 *Twelfth Night*, I, iii, 120 (approximately); *Coranto, cinque-pace*, kinds of dance.
14 "The Fountain," 13–15 (approximately).
15 The sound of bells has always particularly affected me.
16 Cowper, *The Task* VI, 17.

## A Farewell to Essay-Writing

1 *Cymbeline*, III, iii, 29–30.
2 farthest region.
3 Cowper, *Retirement*, 741–2.
4 *The Tempest*, I, ii, 298.
5 Byron, *Don Juan*, I, ccxvi.
6 Coleridge, *Christabel*, 22.
7 Milton, Sonnet XVII, to Lawrence.
8 *Macbeth*, I, v, 50.
9 Cowper, *The Task* VI, 11–12.
10 sprinkled with dew.
11 By Dryden.
12 "Theodore and Honoria," 1–2.
13 Hunt, *Lord Byron and some of his Contemporaries*, p. 168; published January 1828.
14 "Epilogue to Lee's *Mithridates*."
15 Scott, *Glenfinlas*.
16 *The Quarterly Review*, July 1819.
17 In his *Lord Byron;* he suppressed his chapter on Hazlitt.
18 Suckling, "A Session of the Poets."
19 Either Caesar or nothing.
20 December 13, 1800, at Drury Lane.
21 *The Hind and the Panther* I, 315.
22 Not by Chaucer; mid-15th century.
23 Stanza 15.
24 Fielding, *Amelia* X, v.

25 February, 1815: "Standard Novels and Romances."
26 Collins, "On the Poetical Character," 76.

## Preface to *The Life of Napoleon Buonaparte*

1 The Bourbons.
2 Pope, *Dunciad* IV, 188.
3 Long live the King, even so!

## Napoleon and the Louvre

1 Centenary Song: an invocation to the gods to pour blessings on the state, commanded by Augustus for the games of 17 B.C.

## Byron and Wordsworth

1 See Leigh Hunt, *Lord Byron and his Contemporaries*, 45–6.
2 Mohammedan nymphs.
3 By Lady Caroline Lamb (1823).
4 *Confessions* I, vi.
5 Column erected at Alexandria, A.D. 302, to the Emperor Diocletian.

## Conversations of James Northcote: Conversation 16

1 Allan Ramsay (1713–84), portrait painter, son of the poet.
2 A parody of his style (1767).
3 He sat to Northcote in 1828.
4 His publisher Constable failed in 1826, with Scott liable for about £130,000.
5 Published 1818.
6 Perhaps Hannah More.
7 John Wolcot (1738–1819).
8 Dryden, *Absalom and Achitophel* I, 546.
9 Gouvon: *Confessions* I, iii.
10 The London Mechanics' Institution, "for the diffusion and advancement of human knowledge," was formed in 1823. It built its own lecture-hall.
11 Cobbett's name for his *Register*.
12 "The longings of the cannibal arise/ (Although they spoke not) in their wolfish eyes." *Don Juan* II, 72. ". . . thy wolfish visage." *King Lear*, I, iv, 308.
13 *Don Juan* II, 46.
14 *The Fair Maid of Perth* (1828).
15 Frances Abington (1737–1815); retired from stage, 1790. "I would rather have seen Mrs. Abington's Millamant, than any Rosalind that appeared on the stage." *Lectures on the Comic Writers* IV.

## The Spirit of Philosophy

1   about everything knowable and certain other things besides.
2   *2 Henry IV*, II, iv, 268–70.
3   *Malachi* IV:2.
4   *1 Corinthians* XIII:7.
5   trap for the gullible.
6   anew.
7   *Macbeth*, I, vii, 27–8.

## The Letter-Bell

1   Wordsworth, *Intimations of Immortality*, 74–5.
2   The Revolution of July 1830; Charles X abdicated, ending the Bourbon regime in France.
3   Southey.
4   *Intimations of Immortality*, 176–9.
5   *Paradise Lost* V, 310–11.
6   song of praise.
7   Goldsmith, *The Traveller*, 293–4.
8   Wordsworth, *Tintern Abbey*, 47–9.
9   *Faerie Queene* I, viii, 40.
10  Goldsmith, *The Deserted Village*, 412.
11  *Macbeth*, III, iv, 38–9.
12  Thomas Campbell's poem.
13  The southernmost point of England.
14  *The Task* IV, 1–22.
15  A semaphore system of posts with moveable arms, invented by Chappe in France, 1793; superseded by electric telegraph in the 1840s.

# Textual Note

THE TEXT is based on the *Complete Works* edited by P. P. Howe, giving Hazlitt's latest versions. Spelling and punctuation have been slightly modified, e.g., "anyone" for "any one," "show" for "shew." Waller and Glover, and Howe, have tracked down the vast majority of Hazlitt's quotations. I have given references to many of these: though generally used as familiar items of equipment rather than with careful point, they are often illuminating—and they convey something of the pattern of Hazlitt's reading. The quotations are, of course, as Hazlitt made them—nearly always from memory. The arrangement of pieces, with a few minor exceptions, is chronological. Nearly all pieces are given in full; omissions are indicated by [. . .]. Source notes give, where applicable, book publication and the periodical in which a piece first appeared.

# Selected Bibliography

## HAZLITT'S PRINCIPAL WORKS

*An Essay on the Principles of Human Action*   1805
*Free Thoughts on Public Affairs*   1806
*An Abridgement of The Light of Nature Pursued, by Abraham Tucker*   1807
*The Eloquence of the British Senate*   1807
*A Reply to the Essay on Population, by the Rev. T. R. Malthus*   1807
*A New and Improved Grammar of the English Tongue*   1810
*Memoirs of the Late Thomas Holcroft*   1816
*The Round Table*   1817
*Characters of Shakespear's Plays*   1817
*A View of the English Stage*   1818
*Lectures on the English Poets*   1818
*A Letter to William Gifford, Esq.*   1819
*Lectures on the English Comic Writers*   1819
*Political Essays, with Sketches of Public Characters*   1819
*Lectures chiefly on the Dramatic Literature of the Age of Elizabeth*   1820
*Table-Talk*   1821–22
*Liber Amoris: or the New Pygmalion*   1823
*Characteristics: in the Manner of Rochefoucault's Maxims*   1823
*Sketches of the Principal Picture-Galleries in England*   1824
*The Spirit of the Age: or Contemporary Portraits*   1825
*The Plain Speaker: Opinions on Books, Men, and Things*   1826
*Notes of a Journey through France and Italy*   1826
*The Life of Napoleon Buonaparte*   1828–30
*Conversations of James Northcote, Esq., R.A.*   1830

*Collected Works*, ed. A. R. Waller and A. Glover (13 vols.) 1902–06

*Complete Works*, ed. P. P. Howe (21 vols.)    1930–34: an expanded reissue of Waller and Glover.

## BIOGRAPHY AND CRITICISM
## (Including Books Containing Chapters or Passages on Hazlitt)

Albrecht, W. P., *Hazlitt and the Creative Imagination*, Lawrence, Kansas, 1965

Baker, Herschel, *William Hazlitt*, Cambridge, Mass., 1962

Haydon, Benjamin R., *Autobiography and Memoirs*, Intr. by Aldous Huxley, London, 2 vols., 1926

Hazlitt, W. C., *Memoirs of William Hazlitt*, 2 vols., London, 1867

————, *Four Generations of a Literary Family*, 2 vols., London, 1897.

Howe, P. P., *Life of William Hazlitt*, London, 1922, revised 1928, Intr. by F. Swinnerton, 1947

Jack, Ian, *English Literature 1815–1832* (Oxford History), 1963: includes bibliography

————, *Keats and the Mirror of Art*, London, 1967

Maclean, Catherine M., *Born under Saturn*, London, 1943

Patmore, P. G., *My Friends and Acquaintance*, 3 vols., London, 1854

Patterson, C. I., "Hazlitt as a Critic of Prose Fiction," *P.M.L.A.* 68, 1953

Procter, Bryan W., *The Literary Recollections of Barry Cornwall* (ed. R. W. Armour), Boston, 1936

Robinson, H. Crabb, *On Books and their Writers* (ed. E. J. Morley), 3 vols., London, 1938

Saintsbury, George, *History of Criticism*, 3 vols., Edinburgh and London, 1904

Schneider, Elisabeth, *The Aesthetics of William Hazlitt*, Philadelphia, 1933, 1952

————, *The English Romantic Poets and Essayists: a Review of Research and Criticism* (ed. Houtchens), New York, 1957

Talfourd, Thomas Noon, *Final Memorials of Charles Lamb*, 2 vols., London, 1848, 1 vol., 1850

Thompson, E. P., *The Making of the English Working Class*, London, 1963

Thorpe, C. D., "Keats and Hazlitt," *P.M.L.A.* 62, 1947

Wellek, René, *History of Modern Criticism, 1750–1950*, 4 vols., London, 1955

Wilcox, S. C., *Hazlitt in the Workshop: the Manuscript of "The Fight,"* Baltimore, 1943

Woolf, Virginia, *The Common Reader II*, London, 1932

# The SIGNET Classic Shakespeare

☐ **ALL'S WELL THAT ENDS WELL, Sylvan Barnet,** ed., Tufts University. (#CD296—50¢)
☐ **ANTONY AND CLEOPATRA, Barbara Everett,** ed., Cambridge University. (#CT392—75¢)
☐ **AS YOU LIKE IT, Albert Gliman,** ed., Boston University. (#CT520—75¢)
☐ **THE COMEDY OF ERRORS, Harry Levin,** Harvard. (#CD326—50¢)
☐ **CORIOLANUS, Reuben Brower,** ed., Harvard. (#CD328—50¢)
☐ **CYMBELINE, Richard Hosley,** ed., University of Arizona. (#CT394—75¢)
☐ **HAMLET, Edward Hubler,** ed., Princeton University. (#CT528—75¢)
☐ **HENRY IV, Part II, Norman H. Holland,** ed., M.I.T. (#CT539—75¢)
☐ **HENRY V, John Russell Brown,** ed., University of Birmingham. (#CD327—50¢)
☐ **HENRY VI, Part I, Lawrence V. Ryan,** ed., Stanford. (#CD333—50¢)
☐ **HENRY VI, Part II, Arthur Freeman,** ed., Boston. (#CD336—50¢)
☐ **HENRY VI, Part III, Milton Crane,** ed., George Washington University. (#CT383—75¢)
☐ **HENRY VIII, Samuel Schoenbaum,** ed., Northwestern University. (#CT374—75¢)
☐ **JULIUS CAESAR, William and Barbara Rosen,** eds., University of Connecticut. (#CT529—75¢)
☐ **KING JOHN, William H. Matchett,** ed., University of Washington. (#CD330—50¢)
☐ **KING LEAR, Russel Fraser,** ed., Princeton University. (#CD160—50¢)
☐ **LOVE'S LABOR LOST, John Arthos,** ed., University of Michigan. (#CD306—50¢)

---

**THE NEW AMERICAN LIBRARY, INC.**
P.O. Box 999, Bergenfield, New Jersey 07621

Please send me the SIGNET CLASSIC BOOKS I have checked above. I am enclosing $_____(check or money order — no currency or C.O.D.'s). Please include the list price plus 15¢ a copy to cover mailing costs.

Name_____

Address_____

City_____State_____Zip Code_____
Allow at least 3 weeks for delivery

## SIGNET CLASSICS by British Authors

- ☐ **ANIMAL FARM by George Orwell.** Introduction by C. M. Woodhouse. (#CT304—75¢)
- ☐ **BURMESE DAYS by George Orwell.** Afterword by Richard Rees. (#CT478—75¢)
- ☐ **ADAM BEDE by George Eliot.** Foreword by F. R. Leavis. (#CQ483—95¢)
- ☐ **ADVENTURES IN THE SKIN TRADE by Dylan Thomas.** Afterword by Vernon Watkins. (#CQ516—95¢)
- ☐ **ALICE'S ADVENTURES IN WONDERLAND AND THROUGH THE LOOKING GLASS by Lewis Carroll.** Foreword by Horace Gregory. Tenniel Illustrations. (#CP530—60¢)
- ☐ **ALMAYER'S FOLLY AND OTHER STORIES by Joseph Conrad.** Afterword by Jocelyn Baines. (CP#258—60¢)
- ☐ **ANGLO-SAXON ATTITUDES by Angus Wilson.** Foreword by Frank Kermode. (#CT151—75¢)
- ☐ **THE AUTOBIOGRAPHY OF JOHN STUART MILL.** Foreword by Asa Briggs. (#CT269—75¢)
- ☐ **BARCHESTER TOWERS by Anthony Trollope.** Afterword by Robert W. Daniel. (#CQ524—95¢)
- ☐ **BLEAK HOUSE by Charles Dickens.** Afterword by Geoffrey Tillotson. (#CY410—$1.25)
- ☐ **EREWHON by Samuel Butler.** Afterword by Kingsley Amis. (#CT513—75¢)
- ☐ **FAR FROM THE MADDING CROWD by Thomas Hardy.** Afterword by James Wright. Wessex edition. (#CQ572—95¢)
- ☐ **GULLIVER'S TRAVELS by Jonathan Swift.** Foreword by Marcus Cunliffe. Illustrated. (#CD14—50¢)
- ☐ **HARD TIMES by Charles Dickens.** Afterword by Charles Shapiro. (#CQ514—95¢)

□ **PRIDE AND PREJUDICE by Jane Austen.** Afterword by Joann Morse. (#CD82—50¢)

□ **QUENTIN DURWARD by Sir Walter Scott.** Afterword by Denis W. Brogan. (#CT181—75¢)

□ **RETURN OF THE NATIVE by Thomas Hardy.** Afterword by Horace Gregory. (#CP439—60¢)

□ **ROBINSON CRUSOE by Daniel Defoe.** Afterword by Harvey Swados. (#CP542—60¢)

□ **RODERICK RANDOM by Tobias Smollett.** Afterword by John Barth. (#CT255—75¢)

□ **SENSE AND SENSIBILITY by Jane Austen.** Afterword by Caroline G. Mercer. (#CP533—60¢)

□ **A SENTIMENTAL JOURNEY AND THE JOURNAL TO ELIZA by Laurence Sterne.** Afterword by Monroe Engel. (#CP254—60¢)

□ **SILAS MARNER by George Eliot.** Afterword by Walter Allen. (#CD21—50¢)

□ **A TALE OF TWO CITIES by Charles Dickens.** Afterword by Edgar Johnson. (#CP416—60¢)

□ **TONO-BUNGAY by H. G. Wells.** Foreword by Harry T. Moore. (#CQ474—95¢)

□ **THE VICAR OF WAKEFIELD by Oliver Goldsmith.** Afterword by J. H. Plumb. (#CP428—60¢)

□ **THE WAY OF ALL FLESH by Samuel Butler.** Afterword by J. Sherwood Weber. (#CP402—60¢)

□ **WUTHERING HEIGHTS by Emily Brontë.** Foreword by Geoffrey Moore. (#CD10—50¢)

---

**THE NEW AMERICAN LIBRARY, INC.**
P.O. Box 999, Bergenfield, New Jersey 07621

Please send me the SIGNET CLASSIC BOOKS I have checked above. I am enclosing $_____(check or money order — no currency or C.O.D.'s). Please include the list price plus 15¢ a copy to cover mailing costs.

Name_____

Address_____

City_____State_____Zip Code_____
Allow at least 3 weeks for delivery

## The SIGNET CLASSIC Poetry Series

- ☐ **THE SELECTED POETRY OF BROWNING.** Edited by George Ridenour. (#CQ313—95¢)
- ☐ **THE SELECTED POETRY OF BYRON.** Edited by W. H. Auden. (#CQ346—95¢)
- ☐ **THE SELECTED POETRY OF DONNE.** Edited by Marius Bewley. (#CQ343—95¢)
- ☐ **THE SELECTED POETRY OF DRYDEN.** Edited by John Arthos. (#CW496—$1.50)
- ☐ **THE SELECTED POETRY OF GEORGE HERBERT.** Edited by Joseph H. Summers. (#CY366—$1.25)
- ☐ **THE SELECTED POETRY OF KEATS.** Edited by Paul de Man. (#CQ325—95¢)
- ☐ **THE SELECTED POETRY OF MARVELL.** Edited by Frank Kermode. (#CQ363—95¢)
- ☐ **THE COMPLETE POETRY AND SELECTED CRITICISM OF EDGAR ALLAN POE.** Edited by Allen Tate. (#CY384—$1.25)
- ☐ **THE SELECTED POETRY OF POPE.** Edited by Martin Price. (#CY495—$1.25)
- ☐ **THE SELECTED POETRY AND PROSE OF SIDNEY.** Edited by David Kalstone. (#CY498—$1.25)
- ☐ **THE SELECTED POETRY OF SHELLY.** Edited by Harold Bloom. (#CQ342—95¢)
- ☐ **THE SELECTED POETRY OF SPENCER.** Edited by A. C. Hamilton. (#CY350—$1.25)
- ☐ **THE SELECTED POETRY AND PROSE OF WORDSWORTH.** Edited by G. H. Hartman. (#CY506—$1.25)

---